RAGING BATTLE

Across a landscape consumed by the scorching emotions of Civil War, comes an epic tale of love and capture, desire and hate, of a woman who burned with her entire being for one man—and was stirred to the depths of her soul by another.

BLAZING PASSION

When war erupted, lovely, golden-haired Kitty Wright was a woman too rebellious to stay at home. But in the fury of battle, she was ripped from her homeland and spirited north, where her loyalty to the South was challenged by her growing passion for a dashing Yankee cavalryman.

REBELLIOUS LOVE!

She was engaged to a charming Southern aristocrat, but after a savage wilderness ordeal with a contingent of Union soldiers, she no longer knew the truth of her heart. For even in the arms of her fiancé, her woman's heart cried out the name of the man who had enslaved her— the one man she could leave, but never forget.

Other Avon Books by
Patricia Hagan

LOVE AND GLORY
PASSION'S FURY
THE RAGING HEARTS
SOULS AFLAME

PATRICIA HAGAN

AVON
PUBLISHERS OF BARD, CAMELOT, DISCUS AND FLARE BOOKS

LOVE AND WAR is an original publication of Avon Books. This work has never before appeared in book form.

AVON BOOKS
A division of
The Hearst Corporation
959 Eighth Avenue
New York, New York 10019

First Avon Printing, July, 1978

AVON TRADEMARK REG. U.S. PAT. OFF. AND IN
OTHER COUNTRIES, MARCA REGISTRADA,
HECHO EN U.S.A.

Printed in the U.S.A.

WFH 10 9 8 7 6

❧ Chapter One ❧

THE sky was gray and overcast. Kitty Wright sat in the rocking chair in the main room of the old wooden farmhouse, staring through the window at the stark, brown field beyond. The tatting her mother insisted she labor over lay neglected in her lap. She longed to be outside, anywhere but there in that cold, dreary room, alone with her thoughts.

A sudden, sharp rapping on the door intruded upon her dreamy state. Laying aside the lace-weaving, she moved swiftly across the thin plank floor to yank the door open eagerly.

The crisp, early November air swirled her muslin skirt about her legs as she stared into the anxious face of the old black man, Jacob. Twisting a ragged straw hat in trembling hands, he bowed his graying head slightly and said, "Miss Kitty, you better find your pappy. I heard ol' Betsy wailin', and I peeked in the barn, and she looks 'bout ready to drop that calf. I don't know nothin' 'bout birthin' no calf, and Fanny, she out helpin' with Nora Brown's sick young'uns. . . ."

Kitty nodded, frowning. That calf was important, because it meant meat on the table one day, something they seldom had. In fact, her father was out hunting right then, because a neighbor had stopped by to report wild turkeys feeding near the river. She had even begged to go along, but her mother had reacted angrily, saying it wasn't fitting for a young lady to take up arms and hunt like a man.

Lena Wright had ranted and raged until John Wright told Kitty they would go together another time. Since she was old enough to tag along behind him, Kitty had loved to go into the woods with her father, but she didn't pursue the argument any further that day. She and her father both knew only too well that Lena would make their lives miserable for days on end if she were opposed. It was easier to give in.

Kitty motioned to Jacob, "You go to the barn and stay with Betsy. Let me get my shawl, and I'll be right there."

"Oh, no, you won't," the sharp voice made Kitty snap her head around to find her mother standing just behind her, face pinched with anger. "I'm not going to have you out there groveling in blood and straw like a common farmhand. . . ."

This time, Kitty was determined not to give in to her. She brushed past, moving toward the little lean-to kitchen her father had built onto the house. Lena insisted on attempting to pattern her life-style after the rich plantation owners as nearly as possible, refusing to accept the fact that they were but poor dirt farmers. A separate room for cooking had been something she had nagged about until she got it.

"Katherine," her mother was right behind her. "Do you hear me, girl? Let Jacob see to that old cow. How do you think it would look to our neighbors? You groveling like a slave. . . ."

Kitty pulled a worn woolen shawl around her shoulders, then turned to give her mother a defiant look. "I can deliver that calf as well, or better, than any farmhand or slave, Mother, and we can't afford to lose that calf. Betsy is old and might not make it through the birth. Then what would we do for milk and butter this winter? Poppa will be home soon, but I've got to do whatever I can till he gets here."

"Jacob can do what has to be done." She followed her to the door, stepping back as the sudden blast of cold wind engulfed her. Kitty ran on down the rickety steps into the dirt yard.

"You let Jacob do it, I say!" Lena screamed.

Kitty turned long enough to shout back, "Jacob doesn't

2

have to do anything he doesn't want to do, Mother. He isn't a slave, anymore. He stays because he's our friend!"

Jolted by bitter memories, Lena's face twisted into an ugly grimace as she raised a fist in the air and shrieked, "He was a slave, till your father got those damned foolish Federalist notions, and now you see how the land starves for want of hands to work it . . . how you allow yourself to become a common peasant girl with calloused hands and sun-parched skin."

Kitty ran on across the yard, eager to escape the shrieking tirade. Reaching the barn, she yanked open the heavy door and stepped inside to find Jacob there, kneeling beside the cow. He moved aside to let her stoop down beside him.

"It's going to be okay, girl," Kitty patted the animal on her flanks.

"She's hurtin' something fierce. I can feel her belly knottin' up and lettin' go, but nothin' happens that I can see."

The cow was still standing, tied inside a stall, and Kitty said she needed to be moved into the main part of the barn so she wouldn't be so restrained. Jacob did as she instructed, then she told him to stand by while she went after lard.

He blinked at her in wonder. "Lard?"

"I may have to pull that calf out," she snapped. "Haven't you ever heard about using lard in a difficult birth, Jacob, as many babies as Fanny has brought into the world?"

His thick lips spread into a wide grin, showing yellowed, chipped teeth. "Yassum, I knowed about it, all right, but I didn't think you did."

"You're as bad as Mother. Just because most of the young girls about are so silly and empty-headed that they faint at the thought of giving birth doesn't mean that I should, too. I'm *me*, Jacob, not a twin to every spineless female about!"

Silently she scolded herself for snapping at him. It wasn't his fault that he questioned her rebellion against the established role of womanhood, a young lady's "place," as Lena called it. Everyone about raised eyebrows over her behavior, even her father and old Doc Musgrave, the two

3

people who seemed to understand her—and humor her—even if they did, at times, look upon her in complete bewilderment—and amusement.

Lena was standing inside the kitchen door, waiting to start a fresh onslaught of criticism, but Kitty ignored her as she hurried into the pantry to fill a bucket with soft lard.

"Just what do you plan to do with that? Katherine, I don't know what's to become of you. You're going to wind up a spinster, that's what. Look at you! Eighteen years old and no young man courting. What man wants a wife who acts like a man instead of a lady? I'm going to insist that your father send you to the Goldsboro Female College. Maybe they can teach you what I haven't been able to.

"Oh, Katherine . . ." she followed her once again to the door. "I've wanted much better for you than what life has given to *me*. Why won't you listen to me?"

Kitty hurried from the house, anxious to escape the familiar harangue that she knew by heart. There was no money for the fancy finishing school, so there was no need to worry about that threat. Poppa wouldn't hear of it, anyway. He understood her and knew how she felt about life. They spent much time talking together, whenever she could get out of the house and away from Lena, who insisted that she spend so many hours each day tatting or sewing or doing other things Kitty considered boring and a waste of time. Why should she have to do those things just because she was a girl? She was still an individual, wasn't she? She had a right to live her own life the way she wanted, didn't she? At least Poppa understood, and she loved him all the more for it. Life would have been completely unbearable if it weren't for the times they were able to slip away together to hunt and fish.

Of course, Lena Wright blamed her husband for the way their daughter had turned out, saying because she couldn't give him a son, he, in turn, tried to make their daughter into a son, and she intended to fight him with every breath in her body.

Kitty was used to hearing the threats that she would surely wind up a spinster, and this never failed to make her bristle angrily. What difference did it make, anyway, if she couldn't marry for love? She despised the way the young girls around primed themselves for marriage as though it were their sole purpose in having been born a female—to be some man's wife and have a baby every year and sit around and tat or sew and try to look pretty. Why, the rich women with slaves even had wet nurses for their babies—black women with milk in their breasts, who suckled their mistresses' babies—so their mistresses' breasts would not sag.

Ridiculous, Kitty thought, and she wanted no part of it.

Besides, she thought with a sudden flutter, there was only one man in all of Wayne County that she even wanted to come calling, and that was Nathan Collins. She didn't dare let her mother know she felt that way, either, or she would stop at nothing to promote the union, which would be quite embarrassing. Nathan was the son of the county's richest plantation owner, and every young girl of age chased after him. There were even rumors that certain married women took a fancy to him also. Kitty saw him in church on Sundays, and once in a while at a rare community social, but more often than not that snobby Nancy Warren was wrapped around him.

Shoving aside thoughts of Nathan, she quickened her steps at the sound of Jacob's anxious calling. "Miss Kitty, it's gonna be all right. The calf is comin'. I can see it now."

She hurried to examine the cow, then rocked back on her heels and shook her head. "That's a hoof coming, Jacob. That's not the right way for a calf to be born."

Betsy gave a mournful cry, her body shuddering in pain.

"No wonder it's such a hard birth." Kitty began rolling up her sleeves. "I'm going to have to turn that calf. . . ."

Suddenly the barn door squeaked behind them, but Kitty didn't bother to turn around. Her father wouldn't be home for some time yet, so it could only be Lena, coming in to continue her nagging. Kitty knew she wouldn't stay long, though, once she saw all the blood.

Lena took one look at the sight before her and covered her face with her handkerchief as she swayed and reached out for a nearby supporting post to steady her. "Come out of here at once, Katherine," she commanded, gagging as she turned her face away. "I demand that you leave this minute."

"Go back to the house, Mother," Kitty snapped. "I've

5

got work to do, and it has to be done quickly, or we'll lose both Betsy and her calf."

"But you have a caller," Lena sounded desperate, pleading. "And it won't do for him to find you here. It's Nathan Collins, Katherine. Now please come out of here. This might be your big chance to mix and mingle with the right people in this county."

Kitty didn't speak.

"Katherine, don't you see? I've wanted this for you all your life. This is your chance. He's waiting for you in the house now. Please . . . please come with me."

At the sound of Nathan's name, Kitty felt another flutter, and an unfamiliar warmth rippled through her body. But she was not about to walk out now and leave Jacob to do something she knew she could do better. "Just tell him I'm busy. I'm sorry, but please . . . just go and leave us alone."

The door squeaked again, and Kitty's attention was back on Betsy as she smeared lard up and down her arms, unaware that anyone else had entered the barn until she heard a shocked voice say, "Katherine Wright, whatever are you doing?"

Whipping her head about, she was only vaguely aware of her mother's stricken face as she realized Nathan Collins was standing there, breathtakingly handsome in a tweed riding habit, leather crop held in gloved hands, soft, sand-colored curls tumbling down upon his forehead. His brows were knit together quizzically, the play of a smile on his lips.

For a moment, Kitty just stared at him. Oh, why did he have to come out here and find her like this, down on her knees in the straw in a blood-stained dress with lard smeared up and down her arms?

Betsy bellowed mournfully, and there was no time to dwell on the predicament. "I have to deliver this calf, Nathan. She's having a hard time, and we can't afford to lose her or her calf."

Clearing his throat self-consciously, he said, "Well, I suppose the gentlemanly thing for me to do would be to assist you, Katherine, but I'm afraid I've never done this sort of thing before."

She managed a laugh. "Well, I have. I've helped Poppa

with the farm animals since I was a child." She waited for the cow's contraction to subside, then slipped greased hands inside the birth canal, explaining that it was necessary to work fast between contractions, adding, "He's trying to come out turned the wrong way."

Lena took a peek, gasped, then turned away again. "I don't think you should be here, Katherine," she said feebly.

"Why not, Mother?" she couldn't miss the opportunity to goad her a bit. She gave her long reddish blond braids a toss back from her perspiring face and said, "To hear you talk, women are fit for nothing except what this old cow is doing right now—having a baby!"

"Oh, Katherine!" Lena gasped again. "To speak of such a thing in front of Nathan . . ."

Jacob and Kitty looked at each other and exchanged grins as Lena hurried from the barn.

Nathan's presence was forgotten for the moment as Kitty worked her hands in and out between Betsy's contractions, turning the calf gently into a position for birth and finally easing it downward. The process was slow and tedious, and Kitty felt as though she were walking on eggs—each step had to be made carefully, lest something break.

"You should be a doctor, Miss Kitty," Jacob whispered reverently, his eyes looking upon her with respect. "I seen men before that couldn't do what you're doin'!"

"When it depends on food in your stomach, Jacob, you work that much harder. Besides, I've watched Poppa, and I've slipped off with Doc Musgrave on a few occasions."

Nathan watched in silent amazement. Katherine Wright was easily the most beautiful young woman in all of Wayne County. Men talked about her silken golden hair, and her eyes so blue they were almost purple. Violet, someone once called them, violet eyes that danced with the fire of the devil in hell when she was riled.

His eyes moved slowly over her body, which was also graciously endowed with the physical attributes of feminine beauty, with voluptuous breasts straining against the confines of her dress. Her waist was so tiny that she had no need for featherbone corsets that other less fortunate young women so tightly laced themselves into.

Nathan thought how beautiful she was, even at such a moment. And even though his parents, particularly his father, were adamantly opposed to his courting the daughter of a Federalist sympathizer, Nathan's eyes reflected his desire for her. He had laid awake many nights with the image of her in his mind, wanting to taste the sweetness of her lips and hold her body close, wrapping himself in her warmth.

Kitty had been on her knees, and suddenly she fell back on her bottom with an undignified plop, as the calf slid from its mother. They all laughed with relief as the wet, slick animal fought to stand on his wobbly legs, his mother already beginning to nuzzle him lovingly.

Jacob was jumping up and down, crying, "I can't wait to tell your pappy, missy. He's gonna be real proud of what you done. I'm gonna go find Fanny and tell her right now." And he ran from the barn excitedly.

Suddenly, Kitty was all too aware of her appearance—bloody, lard-smeared arms, stained dress, perspiration dripping down her face. She knew she smelled terribly, too. With embarrassment, she looked at Nathan, "I'm sorry. I'm a sight, I know. But this had to be done. . . ."

"I understand," he nodded and smiled slightly, and she thought how lovely were the crinkles in the corners of his eyes. "I heard that your father freed his slaves last year, Katherine, and I don't imagine it's easy running this farm without any."

"Oh, we never had all that many," she said quickly, wiping her hands on a nearby rag. "Poppa never believed in owning slaves. The only reason we ever had any at all was because of my mother. To her, slaves are a status symbol. Poppa finally freed what we had, but Jacob and Fanny stayed on, because they love Poppa so."

Leaning against a post, he watched as she rinsed her face and arms in a pail of clean water. "I remember when we used to go to the settlement school," he said thoughtfully. "James Freeman came to school one day with a little slave boy totin' his books for him. The slave boy dropped the books in a mud puddle, and James thought he did it on purpose, so he took the bookstrap and started beating him with it. You jumped on James and shoved him down in the puddle. You really gave him a beating. I never saw a girl fight like that before. You punched him right in the face with your fists."

Kitty felt her face grow hot. "It wasn't very ladylike of me to fight like that. Mom gave me one of the worst whippings of my life when she found out, but I couldn't stand back and watch James beat that boy like he was a mongrel dog."

"I've never forgotten that day," Nathan smiled.

"Slavery gets me all fired up," she retorted.

"You might feel differently if your father had a large plantation and needed a lot of slaves to run it. I've heard when he did have slaves, he actually paid them for working."

Their eyes met and held, and, for a moment, Kitty was able to shove aside her feelings for Nathan as she said vehemently, "I would never hold to putting a man in chains or thinking it's right to own his soul, Nathan. I think it's wrong to buy and sell human beings as though they're no more than animals. On this subject, you and I and everyone else in Wayne County . . . in the whole South, it seems, differ in our opinions."

He gave her a mock salute, and his eyes crinkled once again at the corners. "It's refreshing to find a young woman with an opinion. Maybe that's why I like you so much . . . because you're so different from the girls I'm usually around."

"Well, if that's meant to be a compliment, thank you."

"I came here to invite you to a party," he went on, "but I'm afraid when you hear the reason for the party you'll refuse my invitation."

"I'm curious about the party, Nathan," Kitty said, "and I'd like to hear about it."

He took a deep breath, then said, "You know who Weldon Edwards is?"

"Who doesn't? He's a Radical. I know who he is and why he comes to this part of the state. Poppa talks to me about politics, and he says that Weldon Edwards is trying to round up support for the secessionist meeting planned in Raleigh."

"My father is honored to have him as a guest, and he's planned a barbecue in his honor on Sunday, the eleventh. I'd like for you to come as my guest."

"Me sit down to a table to eat with a Radical?" she cried, then she realized that he was looking at her with amusement, and that was annoying. She hated the way men felt women should not know, or care, anything about politics, much less dare to voice an opinion.

And now he stared at her as though she were an amusing child, and she stamped her foot and glared up at him, eyes stormy. "Don't look at me like that. I'm not trying to be funny, Nathan. I know what I'm talking about. That man wants war. . . ."

He raised an eyebrow. "I guess you'll tell me next that you know enough about the subject that you don't feel secession—or war—is wise for North Carolina."

She nodded firmly, eyes still fiery.

Shaking his head, Nathan sighed and reached out to touch her shoulder, but she stepped back. "Katherine, secession, like war, is imminent. It's merely a matter of time. Whether you like it or not, you've got to be loyal to your state—and to the South."

"I have no sympathy for the Radicals and all those who want war," she stormed. "And neither does my father."

"But he would be loyal to his state, Katherine, and whatever position his state voted to take if war does come." This time he reached out to touch her cheek, and she did not pull away. "Those of us who stand together won't have any sympathy for those who stand apart. But do you and I have to quarrel? If you only knew how long I've wanted to call on you, but you never gave me any inclination that I might have a chance. I've heard about how you turn away every man who comes to your door."

Through lowered lashes, she looked at him teasingly. "Then why do you come now to invite me to a party for a man who supports something I stand against?"

"Because I've waited too long already," his voice was firm, and his arms encircled her waist. "Besides, last Sunday in church I happened to catch you looking at me, and there was a little sparkle of interest in those lovely eyes of yours, so I dared to hope maybe I'd have a chance. Now will you go to the party with me? We won't have to worry about Weldon Edwards. We can be together."

A wave of dizziness washed over her. No one had ever made her feel this way—all quivery inside as though everything within would explode and burst any second. Confused, not knowing what to say, she turned to gaze out the barn window at the stark, naked fields beyond. To her father, this land was beautiful, and she shared his affection, because it was theirs. But to someone like Nathan, whose family owned hundreds and hundreds of acres of farmland, tended by a hundred or more slaves, this was poverty—a squalid dirt farm. Why, then, when they obviously lived in two different worlds, was he asking her to attend an important party at his family's home?

And then she remembered Nancy Warren, his constant companion at every social occasion. Snapping her head back to stare at him, she bluntly asked, "What about Nancy Warren? Did she go away to visit someone and leave you without someone to escort to the party?"

"Now why do you have to be so stubborn?" His hands moved to clamp firmly on her shoulders, shaking her gently. "Can't you get it through your head that you're the girl I've yearned for all these years? I just never thought I'd have a chance with you, Katherine. Believe me, there's no one else I'd rather be with than you."

She pulled away from him and walked slowly to the barn window. He followed and stood beside her. A few chickens pecked about in the yard, cackling softly to each other. "What about your family?" she asked. "Would they approve of your courting me, Nathan?"

Quickly he reached to spin her around, their faces so close she could feel the warmth of his breath upon her cheeks. "You're so beautiful. . . . I've dreamed of this moment . . ."

And then his lips came down, slowly, gently, at first, as she stiffened, then yielded, and the kiss became demanding as he tightened his arm about her to draw her body closer. For long, seemingly endless moments, they clung together. Kitty began to tremble with longing for more. There had been stolen kisses in corncribs or haystacks with boys when she was but a child, but never had there been a kiss like this, with fire and passion, a kiss that brought every fiber of her being alive and tingling with emotions she never dreamed existed with such force.

Someone giggled. They pulled away instantly. Kitty turned just in time to see one of Jacob's little boys scrambling down the rope that hung from the hayloft opening, escaping to the ground below, outside the barn.

Once again they were alone. He reached for her, but she held back, whispering nervously, "We shouldn't . . ."

"Oh, yes, we should," he pulled her against his chest. "I've wanted this for a long, long time, Katherine, and don't lie to me and say you haven't wanted it, too. I've seen you looking at me from across a room. Say you'll come to the party with me. Don't keep us apart when we feel this way about each other."

"I'll talk to Poppa about it," she said finally.

"You don't have to tell him that Mr. Edwards will be there."

"He probably already knows about it. Poppa hears all the gossip and talk."

"Would he forbid you to come?"

She shook her head. "He lets me make my own decisions."

He sighed with relief, then said, respectfully, "You and your father are very close, aren't you?"

"Yes. I love Poppa very much, Nathan. My mother and I, well," she bit her lip, then went on, "we don't agree on many things, and we quarrel a lot. She blames it on Poppa, saying he's raised me as though I were the son he always wanted but never had. But that isn't true. I just happen to believe that I have the right to speak my own mind and live my own life according to my will . . . and no one else's."

His sparkling eyes reflected the pleasure he felt over hearing a young lady speak in such a manner. "I've never known anyone like you, Katherine Wright. You really are a free spirit, aren't you? Maybe that's why I find you so fascinating, because you're such a challenge. I think I'd like to be the man to tame that spirit of yours."

"You think it can be tamed?" she challenged him.

"I think I've wanted to since that day you sat on James Freeman in the mud puddle."

Her hand flew to her mouth in astonishment. "Did I really *sit* on him, Nathan? Oh, I don't remember doing that. I just remember Momma whipping me for it."

"Yes, you sat on him," he assured her, laughing, "and I'll never forget the sight. The other girls were horrified, and I think they and a lot of the boys have been scared of you ever since."

The smile faded from her lips, but Nathan did not notice, nor did he know that he had just triggered painful memories. The other girls had avoided her for as long as she could remember; but she had tried not to let it bother her. There had been plenty to do to keep her busy on the farm, but still it hurt to hear of a birthday party or a summer afternoon tea she was not invited to.

Nathan was prodding her once again. "Will you come to the party, Katherine?"

She almost said yes, because she wanted to go with all her heart, but then she remembered that she had nothing to wear. "Nathan, I don't even own a ball gown. We're poor people, and there's no money for such things. I'm very flattered that you invited me, and I'd be honored to go with you, but I don't have a proper dress to wear." The muslin dress she had on and another for Sunday were the only two dresses she owned. Her other clothes consisted of old pants and shirts of her father's that she cut down to fit.

"I'm sorry," she blinked back tears. "I really am."

"It doesn't matter. I know it matters to girls, though. Look, my sister, Adelia, is away in school, and she has ball gowns in her wardrobe that have never been worn. I could slip one out to you, and no one would ever know."

She was flattered by his thoughtfulness but knew how hurt her father would be if he found out she borrowed a dress to wear. And she knew, but did not want to say, that her mother would find a way, if one were possible, to get a dress for her to wear to the party. If anyone could work a miracle at that point, it would be Lena Wright, who would be very anxious to have her daughter attend a party at the Collins plantation.

"Could you ride by in a few days, Nathan? I will give you my answer then."

He kissed her again, rekindling the flames, his hand sliding around her waist, aching to touch the tempting swell of her breast, but not daring just yet. This time, there was no giggling, snooping child to make them draw apart, only the furious beating of two flaming hearts, pounding in unison, stirred and driven by the passion swelling between them.

Reluctantly, he drew away. "I'll come by, Katherine, and I'll be praying that you'll tell me you'll go to the party with me."

Shyly, she held his hand as they left the barn and walked to his waiting horse. Mounting, he spurred the animal into a trot, turning to wave before disappearing in a swirl of dust.

Turning toward the house, Kitty hugged herself with delight, finally breaking into a run, her skirt swirling about her ankles. Nathan Collins had kissed her, had invited her to a party, asked if he could court her, and he had kissed her again.

At that moment, Kitty Wright felt that life was wonderful, that she was the happiest she had ever been in all of her seventeen years . . . that chilly day in early November, eighteen hundred and sixty.

❧ Chapter Two ❧

"WHY do you keep staring out that window?" Lena noticed that Kitty was keeping a vigil. "And why won't you tell me about Nathan's visit? You two stayed in that barn such a long time it didn't look proper."

Kitty decided it was best to keep silent. She didn't want to talk about the invitation to the party until she had a chance to talk to her father about it, because if he strongly objected to her going to a party in honor of Weldon Edwards—well, she just wouldn't go, and there was no need to give Lena more reason to nag.

She was silently praying that he wouldn't object. Just the thought of being with Nathan, being close to him, dancing with him, was enough to make her blush. But she knew only too well how John Wright felt about the secessionist movement, and he might ask her not to go to the party. If he did . . . but she didn't want to think about that. He just had to say it was all right. He just *had* to.

The tall, gangly man with stooped shoulders stepped out of the woods and into a bare field that bordered the farmhouse. He carried the flintlock musket that had belonged to his grandfather, and he wore a ragged wool jacket, faded overalls, and the old straw hat he had woven himself. At his side, the old hound "Killer" loped along lazily. The dog was harmless and it was a known fact that he was no

15

more a hunter than his owner was a rich plantation owner. But the two were inseparable, and sometimes Kitty thought they could even communicate with each other.

His bearded face looked weary, even from a distance, and Kitty warmed with affection at the sight of his lanky body plodding through the knee-high weeds. They had always been closer than most fathers and daughters, and this had come about because Lena had always been on the sickly side, spending days and weeks in bed, complaining with first one ailment, then another. As a child, Kitty's playing had made her nervous, and since Lena objected to her playing with the children of the few slaves on the farm, she was only too glad for John to take their daughter with him. It was many years later that she realized Kitty was hunting and riding and fishing like a man, and she was upset over the discovery.

Accused of trying to make a son out of his daughter, John laughingly spoofed at Lena's scorn. That was when she began to spend time with Kitty for the first time in her life, insisting that she learn the socially acceptable talents for a young lady of the day—sewing, tatting, recitation—all of which Kitty detested and rebelled against.

A closeness had developed between John Wright and his daughter that could not easily be dissolved. To pacify his wife, John urged Kitty to allow herself to be taught feminine "qualities," and Kitty gave in, all the while yearning to be with her father instead. She loved the farm, loved working with the animals and being outdoors in the fresh air and sunshine. The sewing, tatting, weaving, and sitting with hands folded primly in her lap while her mother read poetry—these were the times she hated, loathed, and despised.

And as she watched the approach of her father, Kitty wondered anxiously how he was going to react to Nathan's declaration of his intentions to become a suitor. She'd heard him speak often of Nathan's father, Aaron Collins, and how he owned many slaves and allowed his overseer, Luke Tate, to treat them mercilessly. She feared that he was not going to approve, and he would be completely opposed to her being in the company of a man like Weldon Edwards who was fighting for the secession of North Carolina.

John was halfway across the field when Jacob came out of the barn, waving excitedly. He turned in that direction, and Kitty ached to join them, but apprehension over the discussion that was to come held her back. He wouldn't forbid her to go. That was not his way. He would tell her the decision was hers. But, loving him as she did, respecting him as she did—all it would take for her to abandon thoughts of the party would be to see a flash of anger, or hurt, in his eyes. The question of Nathan was another matter, and this made her feel a bit guilty, for the way she felt about Nathan . . . well, that was something altogether different. New emotions were rippling through her body now.

Lena had gone into the bedroom and returned to dip a cloth once more into the bucket of water that sat on the table. Wringing it, she pressed it to her forehead, sighing, "If I could only get rid of this wretched headache. I've had it ever since that horribly embarrassing scene in the barn. You and that cow!" She shuddered.

"Have you seen your father? I intend to talk to him about the way you acted in front of Nathan this afternoon." She stared at Kitty scornfully. "The very idea! I hope he gives you the sound thrashing you deserve, young lady."

Sinking down on the bench that ran alongside the long, wooden table, Lena continued her angry glare. Kitty's thoughts drifted as she tried to blot out the sounds of the nagging. Her father had made that table when he was but a young man, filled with visions of one day seating his many children along each side, himself at the head.

Her eyes moved about the room. A crude wooden box sat beside the fireplace, where a pot boiled with the night's stew of fish and potatoes and fresh eggs. The kitchen floor was clay. John never got around to putting in planks. With a chopping block to one side, a few wooden shelves, the room was dismal and bleak.

Suddenly Lena pounded both her fists on the table. Kitty jumped, startled.

"Are you going to tell me why Nathan came here? When you ignore me, Katherine, you make this pain in my head worse. Why won't you tell me? You're acting very strangely. . . ."

17

Kitty continued to stare out the window in the direction of the barn, where her father had disappeared with Jacob.

"Katherine!" the voice rose hysterically. "Why do you treat me this way? Why do you hate me so? Why do you try to shut me out of your life? I love you. You're my only child. I only want you to be happy. Dear God, what have I ever done to deserve such scorn and disrespect from my own flesh and blood? Will you just tell me what I ever did to you for you to treat me this way?"

Kitty knew only too well what was coming if she didn't tell her mother what she wanted to know. She would start to cry, and then she might have one of her screaming tantrums, and all of them would be in for a miserable evening. It could go on for days.

Sighing, she turned and looked at the red-faced woman. "He invited me to a party next Sunday afternoon, Mother," she said quietly, feeling disgust, mingled with pity, over the way her mother instantly calmed herself.

Lena's face spread into one huge grin. Her face was thin and gaunt, made even more so by her hair being pulled back from her face and wrapped in a bun at her neck. Her eyes were sharp—narrow, but she was not an unattractive woman. If she didn't cry so much, Kitty thought suddenly, perhaps there would not be so many wrinkles. Like now, when she was smiling, Kitty mused, she was almost pretty, and the wrinkles did not matter so much.

"Oh, Katherine, this is wonderful. Nathan comes from a fine family. Aaron Collins is one of the richest men in the state. This must mean he wants to court you. Think how wonderful that would be! Oh, I hope you didn't scare him off by letting him see you wallowing beneath that cow in all that blood and straw and dirt."

She was like a delighted child, Kitty thought, watching her pat her hands together gleefully.

"Maybe you didn't run him off, after all. He did ask you to go to the party with him *after* he saw you with that old cow. You'll just have to put your best foot forward at that party and make him glad he invited you, let him know you appreciate the chance to show him you aren't some white trash farmhand."

"I have to talk to Poppa first."

"What do you want to talk to him about?" Her eyes widened with surprise. "I should think you would realize by now that you've spent far too much time talking and listening to him instead of me. What does he have to do with any of this?"

Kitty realized she could not tell the complete truth, because if her father did object once he knew who the party was being given for, and she decided not to go, then it would only make her mother angry, and she would place the blame on John. No, she thought, it's best to leave out the name of the guest of honor.

"I don't have a dress to wear to a party."

"Is that all that's bothering you?" Lena leaped to her feet, grabbing her hand and pulling her toward the bedroom. "There's something in my trunk that I've saved all these years, if the moths haven't ruined it. A few repairs will put it in good shape, though."

Lena dropped her hand once they were inside the bedroom, then she hurried to a far corner where, beneath a pile of homemade quilts, the trunk was concealed. She fumbled with the top, and it finally opened with a reluctant squeak.

Lena knelt on the floor as she began pulling items from the trunk, lovingly fondling each item. "This was my hope chest. My mother and my grandmother helped me with it. I had fine linens and quilts and tapestries, and they never knew I would never need these things on a poor dirt farm." There was sadness mixed with bitterness in her tone.

Feeling the need to defend her father, Kitty spoke up quickly. "You loved him when you married him, didn't you, Mother? He's done his best . . ."

"That's what he'd have you to believe," Lena scoffed, frowning. She smoothed out a piece of delicate tatted lace. "We could've had a rich plantation if he'd bought more slaves, and bred them, and raised them to be a powerful workforce like Aaron Collins had the good sense to do. But no, he felt it was good enough as long as he could feed his family. 'Fine things and rich living isn't important enough to beat a man over' he'd say. Well, you see what it got him, don't you? Smell the fish cooking? Fish stew every night for a week now. I imagine the food is much better over at the Collins plantation."

When she was like this, there was no reasoning with her, Kitty thought. It would be wasted breath to try and convince her that John Wright had done the best he could for his family, without going against the principles of life he believed in.

"Ahhh, here it is," Lena pulled out a faded red velvet gown, smoothing out the tiny rows of bows and lace that were crushed and wrinkled. "We can pound it smooth with the pressing stone, and it will do just fine."

Trying to hide her disappointment, Kitty moved forward for a closer look at the gown. Maybe it wasn't all that bad. It was too large, though, because she was a lot smaller than her mother had been even years ago. The velvet was hopelessly flat and crushed. There was nothing to do, she decided, but admit that the dress was all wrong. "Maybe we can make something from the petticoats." She lifted the skirt and looked at the red taffeta underslips hopefully.

"You can't make a ball gown out of petticoats, child," came Lena's shocked reaction. Whoever heard of such a thing?"

"I can if I want to go badly enough. Maybe I can salvage some of these ribbons, too. And there's a piece of nice lace. Maybe I can make do. . . ." her voice trailed off dully. It was hopeless, but she didn't want her mother to realize that fact just yet. When she was all worked up, as she was at the moment, it was best to try and let her down gently.

"Slippers!" Lena cried, extracting a pair of molded ankle-high shoes with pointed toes and tiny buttons up the sides. "I wore these on my wedding day but haven't had an occasion to have them on since. Try them on and see if they fit."

Obediently, Kitty slipped one on her foot. It slipped and slid on her heel when she tried to walk around the room. "We can pad the toes with something," Lena said quickly, ". . . and where they're molded, I can scrub them. They'll do nicely."

"Well, what's going on in here?"

They turned at the sound of John's happily booming voice. Without waiting for a reply to his greeting, he was across the room in two quick steps to wrap his arms around Kitty and cry, "Kitty, baby, you did it. Jacob told me how you pulled ol' Betsy and her calf through, and I'm real

20

proud of you. I couldn't have done a better job, and I doubt Doc Musgrave could have, either."

Before she could speak, Lena slammed the trunk lid and got to her feet. "It was disgusting! It was absolutely sickening for her to be groveling in the straw, reaching inside a cow's . . . Disgusting!"

"Well, would you have had the cow and the calf both die?" John looked at her in wonder. "Be thankful Kitty had the good sense to think otherwise. We'll have meat on our table next year . . . something we won't have this winter—you can be sure of that. I didn't find a single turkey today."

"Oh, Poppa, I'm sorry," Kitty hugged him. "I'll go out with you tomorrow, and maybe between the two of us, we can scare them up. We'll ask Jacob to go along, too."

"You'll be working on your dress for the party," Lena sniffed.

John scratched at his beard. "What party? Jacob said the Collins lad was by here today. Does he have anything to do with this talk of a party?"

She hadn't wanted him to hear it this way, but it was too late. Lena was only too eager to tell about Nathan's visit to invite Kitty to a party at the Collins plantation on Sunday.

John kept scratching at his beard, something he did when he was trying to sort things out in his mind. He pursed his lips, a sign that he was trying to find the right words to *say* what he finally had sorted out.

He went into the kitchen, with Kitty scurrying behind him. "Poppa, what do you think?" she asked anxiously. "Do you approve of Nathan?"

He sat down in his chair at the head of the table, then drew her down to sit on his knee as he'd done when she was a child. "Kitty, you know I've raised you to make your own decisions, and this may well be the first really important one you've been faced with."

"Nathan is a gentleman," she reminded him. "He has a good name."

Nodding in agreement, he said, "I'm sure you're right on both counts, honey, but you have to realize we're living in troubled times. Nathan Collins and his family want slavery. I don't. They want North Carolina to secede from the union. I don't. They want war. I don't. They're willing to have that war and maybe get killed just so they can preserve the so-called right to own another human being."

He paused to take a deep breath and look directly into her eyes. "God never meant for a man to be bought and sold like an animal, Kitty. I'm a peaceful, God-fearing man. I've freed what slaves I had, and I try to mind my own business and stay out of all this talk of war. I'm mightily afraid, though, if war comes, as it surely will, none of us will be able to stay out of it.

"What I'm trying to say is that I have all ideas that Aaron Collins won't take kindly to his son courting my daughter, and you should realize that before you set foot in his house on his son's arm. I'm not going to ask you not to go, but I want you to think about what you might be letting yourself in for. I'm afraid I have a lot of enemies now. But you have to make up your own mind about the way you feel."

Lena had been silently dipping up the fish stew into wooden bowls. As she placed them on the table, she grinned, "Praise be, John. For once, you're staying out of the child's life. If you'll keep that up, maybe she'll be lucky enough to land Nathan for a husband, and then some of the miserable years I've spent with you will seem almost worthwhile."

Years of living with her nagging had taught John that she only got worse if she thought her needling irritated him. Turning his head slightly so he wouldn't even have to look at her, he turned his full attention upon the daughter he loved so much that it helped make up for some of his own misery in the life he'd shared with Lena.

"Weldon Edwards is going to be at that party. You know who he is?"

Kitty nodded, slipping from his lap to take a seat on the bench. "He's a Radical, and he wants war."

"Right. He's here to round up support for a secession meeting planned in Raleigh, and he's also soliciting funds from wealthy slaveowners like Aaron Collins to help finance the cause and get an army ready."

"I don't care about that or the talk of war, Poppa, because I want to go to the party and just have a good time."

Lena dramatically pretended to drop her spoon. "Praise

be to hear you say so, Katherine. Maybe the good Lord has heard my prayers, after all. You just go on to that party and keep your mouth shut about your father's traitorous political views. You believe every word he says as though it were God's own gospel. But you keep your mouth shut, and you just might snare Nathan Collins for a husband and find yourself living in that mansion of theirs, with slaves to wait on you hand and foot, and you'll never have to worry about a thing for the rest of your life."

John slowly shook his head from side to side, a sad expression on his face. It became increasingly difficult to remember any love he might have once had for his wife. More and more, he was called upon to stretch the recesses of his mind to attempt to remember a good reason for ever having married her in the first place. Beauty? Yes, that was what had attracted him. Lena had once been beautiful. Not nearly so lovely as Kitty, but, back then, Lena had been the prettiest girl around. And sweet, too. She never nagged or complained, hanging onto his every word as she vowed that all she wanted from life was to be his wife and follow him to the end of the world, if need be.

"Your mother makes it sound so simple," he said finally, eyes grim above his wrinkled, sun-parched face. "Life isn't all that easy, honey, and I hope you never get the idea that it is."

"Let's don't talk about it anymore." Kitty felt uneasy as the tension in the room mounted. "I'll go to the party and have a good time and won't worry about political issues."

"You should never concern yourself with political issues," her mother said sharply.

John stiffened. Over and over again, he'd told himself never to drag out philosophies and ideals and display them for all to see and make light of. He would do well to keep his feelings and opinions locked safely inside. But more and more lately, with the countryside alive with all the talk of secession and war, it was becoming harder and harder to keep silent.

"Politics affects women's lives, too," he said stiffly. "Why shouldn't a woman be aware of the world about her? It's refreshing to talk to a female who knows about something besides havin' babies and cooking."

Lena's eyes blazed. "If I had a servant to do all my work for me, maybe I'd have time to 'concern' myself with other things. I'd sit on a porch swing and fan myself and spend my days reading poetry and approving menus and giving orders on how I want my house run. I'd have a baby every year like you'd have me do, because I'd have a wet nurse to take care of it.

"But I don't have the time to learn about anything else, because all I do is work my fingers to the bone around here. A poor provider you've been, John Wright. I've had to grovel for every bite I've ever put in my mouth since I married you!"

Their eyes met and held angrily. John brushed at the tip of his nose with the back of his hand, then tucked both hands into his pockets, as though he were afraid of what might happen if he didn't confine them.

"And you've been a damned poor wife, Lena," his voice came out hoarse and rasping. "I know you hurt a lot when Kitty was born, but all women hurt when they have babies. But you thought you were something special, and you didn't like the pain, so ever since then, you've used every excuse you could find to turn me away from you. But you and I both know it's because you're not woman enough to try to have another baby!

"Say it!" his voice rose. "Why don't you tell the truth for once in your life instead of needling and nagging and lying about *me*?"

Out came his right hand, and he balled it into a fist and brought it crashing down on the table, angry with himself for letting her rile him so. Each time she would start one of her attacks, he would promise himself not to let her make him lose his temper again . . . and each time he lost all control of his senses. He had never hit her. She had not quite driven him to that point, and he prayed she never would, but his hands trembled with the desire to strike her.

Lena's eyes were darting with anger as her tongue pushed against her teeth nervously, anxious to attack. Her body twitched with excitement.

"How dare you talk to me this way in front of Katherine?" the words came out in a rush. "I wasn't afraid to have another baby, you old fool. It was the thoughts of your touching me that made me sick. You're lazy, John

Wright . . . lazy and shiftless, and a nigger-lover to boot! You're no good, and all our neighbors are calling you 'white trash' because of your fool Federalist notions. The truth is—you don't want war because you're too big a coward to fight!"

Kitty's eyes were on her father, frightened at the way the color was rising in his cheeks above his beard.

Suddenly, swiftly, he reached down and snatched up the bowl of fish stew sitting in front of him, and, with one swift motion, sent it hurtling through the air to crash and splatter against the far wall of the kitchen. Jumping up, his chair falling with a dull plop onto the clay floor, he towered over Lena, his body almost convulsing in anger.

"You get out of my sight, woman, or I'll give you the beating you're begging for. Don't say another word to me, or so help me, I think I'll kill you!"

Face pinched, knowing she had pushed him as far as she dared, Lena swished from the kitchen and disappeared into the bedroom, slamming the door behind her.

John picked up his chair and slumped down into it, hand over his chest. Kitty started to get something to clean up the mess from the thrown stew, but she turned to him anxiously instead. "Are you all right? You look funny. . . ." and then her voice broke. "Oh, Poppa, I hate it when you two fight like that!"

"I know, I know," he waved a hand in the air for silence, not wanting to hear any admonishment. "It scares me the way she can make me so angry. She makes me lose almost all control, and one day, she'll bring out the worst. . . ." He shuddered.

Kitty went about cleaning up the mess from the wall and the floor as John sat in silence. When she finished, he stood up once again and held out his hand to her. "Let's go out to the barn and take another look at Betsy and the new calf."

They walked side by side, hand in hand, across the bare ground. Next spring they would plant potatoes and beans and corn in the clearings beyond, and Kitty would be right beside her father, helping him furrow rows and little trenches where the seeds would be sown.

It was a much different scene from the farm of Aaron Collins, with his maybe four hundred acres, abundant with plantings of corn, tobacco, and cotton. Aaron Collins had the slaves necessary to work such vast holdings, and the threat of slavery being abolished caused him, and others like him, much apprehension and worry.

John paused to stare out at the clearing, now raw and stubbled with broken, dying, cornstalks. "I believe those Scuppernong vines are going to have a good harvest next year, Kitty. You know what that means? I might just have a money-making crop besides the money I'll get from the beehives." He sighed. "If war doesn't come . . ." his voice trailed off, evidence of his depression and concern over the clouds that were gathering in the South.

Kitty didn't want to talk about war. She chose instead to pursue the subject of the grapes. "I hope they do better than those vines you planted a few years ago. We hardly got enough from them to have fruit for cobblers."

"Well, I went to Raleigh about this variety, because I'd read in one of those agricultural newspapers about how the Scuppernong will grow in this soil, 'cause it's sandy. I talked to one of those agricultural men, and he told me all about setting them out . . . what to do for them and all. And it looks as though I just might have something."

"I hope so." She squeezed his hand as he continued to gaze thoughtfully across the empty fields.

"Tobacco's going to be king one day," he said. "No matter what them agricultural fellows say about abandoning it for a less demanding crop. Sure, it exhausts the soil. And I've read about how a planter should move his crop around each year from one acre to another, but how can you do that when you don't have that much land to start with? Maybe some farmers will have to give it up, but it's still going to be king. Remember that, because all of this will be yours one day. You learn what you can, and you turn this land into tobacco land. There's still plenty of ground where you see all that timber over yonder. I'm not as poor as your mother thinks. As long as a man's got land, he's never poor."

He paused, as though lost in thought, then took a deep breath and went on. "Sure, I had to sell off some land now and then, and I hated having to do it, but I've hung on. I'd rather have my land than all the gold on earth, because you know it's going to be there tomorrow. With money, you never know.

"Don't ever sell this land, Kitty, girl," he said, almost fiercely. "I'd rather see you starve to death, I think, than sell the Wright land."

"I won't, Poppa," she said firmly, "but if war comes . . ."

"If war comes, we'll lose everything." He ground out the words. "Men who want war are fools. I say free the slaves and let all men live free. Let those with large plantations hire their labor or dig the soil themselves. War will destroy us. Civil war can be glorious news to none but demons or mindless fools . . . or maddened men. And I, for one, will never take up arms to defend slavery!"

They walked on slowly toward the barn, each in private thought. Kitty pushed thoughts of war from her mind, and she thought instead of the magnificent Collins mansion, with its avenue of tall cedars leading the way from the main road around a circular drive. There was wisteria in the spring, glorious lavender blossoms splashing down over the verandas, bright and cheery against the white-washed brick of the two-story columnar house. And the lawn was green and rolling. It was beautiful. She'd been there several times, riding in the wagon beside her father as he delivered honey from his beehives to the Collins family.

Turning her head slightly, she looked back at the delapidated little house that was her home. Three rooms and the added-on kitchen. But she was grateful for whatever was given to her. She'd never coveted the riches and wealth of others. Sure, there had been times in the past, when she attended the one-room schoolhouse in the settlement, when classmates had snubbed her and the other poor children. But she had held her head up proudly, remembering her father's declaration that "a man's true wealth is valued by the purity of his soul," and she liked to think *her* soul *was* pure, therefore making her extremely wealthy.

"I had a dream once," her father was saying, a faraway look in his eyes. "I guess you could even call it an illusion, maybe, but either way, I was going to take this land that's been in the Wright family for two generations . . . and I was going to make it into one of the finest plantations in all of North Carolina. But to do that, I had to have slaves, and I didn't believe in it then, just as I don't believe in slavery now. So most of the land stands in uncleared timber."

He stopped walking again, turning to put his hands on Kitty's shoulders as he gazed down into her eyes. "I guess what I want now is to one day see you do to this land what I couldn't."

His hands dropped away, his shoulders slumping as he began shuffling along. "An old man's dream, I guess. War will come, and the land will be lost along with every Southerner's dream. But I don't guess I'll ever stop dreaming. A man shouldn't ever part with his dreams or illusions, 'cause when they're gone, well . . . he might still exist . . . but he will have ceased to live."

"I'll share your dream, Poppa," she blinked back the tears. "Together, we can make it come true."

"Another thing, Kitty," he said thoughtfully. "Don't be mad with your mother. She's not the girl I married. Just pity her, as I do, and try to love her in spite of the way she is. I know it's hard, but I guess it's what God wants us to do, 'cause when He gets tired of the way she acts, He'll just deal with her directly. It's not up to me to beat her in the ground the way I'd like to sometimes. . . ."

She laughed, because his eyes were twinkling and he was no longer angry. The tension had passed.

Reaching the barn, John paused. "I'm going to take you into town tomorrow and buy you the prettiest hoop dress we can find. I've got some money put back from selling honey, and I want you to walk into Aaron Collins's house looking so pretty that every man there will turn his head to look at you!"

Laughing, he reached out to tug one of her long braids. "That is, you'll be pretty if I can get you to stop braiding your hair like an Indian and fix yourself up a bit." Then, his voice gruff with emotion, he added, "I just want the best for you, girl."

Tears stinging her eyes, she threw herself against his chest, burrowing her face in his old woolen jacket, overcome with the deep love she felt for her father. How could her mother treat him the way she did? He was a wonderful man. Maybe he wasn't rich and never would be, but he was good and kind and loving. "You're the most wonderful man I know," she murmured.

Pleased, he patted her gently, then moved to open the door to the barn and reach for the lantern hanging just to the left inside. When it was lit, they moved on inside the sourish-smelling barn.

"You did a fine job, Kitty," John said as they stood together looking at Betsy peacefully munching hay as her newborn calf nuzzled beneath her.

Once again, Kitty was blinking away the tears that stung her eyes. It had been a wonderful day, even if it had ended with her mother and father fighting again. Her father was proud of her, and Nathan Collins had kissed her and declared he wanted to come courting. Despite the war clouds that hung heavy over their world that November day in 1860, Kitty Wright was happy.

❧ Chapter Three ❧

THE wind was cold, whipping about with the force of a giant, invisible sword, cutting, slashing. Along the roadside the blackberry brambles and plum bushes concealed the water-filled gulches that bordered flat, swampy lowlands spreading into the winter-dead forest beyond.

The wagon carrying John Wright and his daughter, Kitty, toward Goldsboro, moved through the flat countryside to a slightly higher region, past Waylon Sutton's cotton field. The pickers had not left much. The broken, decaying stalks held little evidence of the white cotton balls that had once dazzled the field like tiny fists of puffy clouds sprinkled among a sea of green.

There were few houses along the way. The finer homes, even the small clapboard houses like the one they lived in, were all set back from the main road, nestled at the edge of woodlands. Only the terribly delapidated were located closer, those occupied mostly by slave families.

Just before reaching the bridge that would take them across the Neuse River, there was a deep, swampy area, with rotting trees upon the ground, and thick underwood. Just a little farther an old cabin came into view. It was constructed of logs, one or two of them rotting and falling out of rank on the front side, which gave the whole structure a dangerous lean to one corner. The yard was littered with trash and weeds and decaying stumps, and hogs rooted about in the dirt.

As the wagon moved closer, a young boy in his early teens came running from around the back of the house, waving. His hair was a fiery shade of red and hung shaggily about his bright, freckled face. He wore no shirt beneath his faded, patched overalls, and his feet were bare despite the coldness of the day.

"Miss Kitty!" he called excitedly, running toward them, his face spread in a wide grin. "Please wait up. . . ."

"I hope we don't run into his pappy," John mumbled as he pulled up on the reins of the old mule.

Kitty ignored his remark as she called, "Andy Shaw, how good to see you. You surely do look better than the last time I saw you." Her eyes went to his bare feet reproachfully. "But you're going to be back in bed, if you don't stop running around in this weather with no shoes on!"

"Ain't got none," he said simply, obviously not making excuses for his family being so poor that there was no money for such luxuries. Nodding politely to John, he turned to Kitty once again and said, "I've been meanin' to get down and see you and say thanks for making me well, but since I been back on my feet, Pa's kept me busy choppin' wood for winter."

"I'd say you've had a good rest, Andy. That spell of yours had you laid up for almost a week, before your momma ever came and got me. And I'll just bet you were a few more days getting over it once you started taking that tonic I fixed up for you."

He dug into the dirt road with his bare toe, hands jammed down into his pockets as he grinned slowly. "I reckon I was at that, but I sure felt poorly till you came along. . . ."

The front door to the house squeaked open, and a thin woman stepped out on the porch and waved, her coarse muslin dress whipping about her in the wind. The curious faces of smaller children appeared at the glassless windows to peer out.

"God bless you, Kitty," Ruth Shaw called. "I sure appreciate what you did for my boy."

"Glad I could help you," Kitty called back. Then she spotted Orville Shaw emerging from the woods. Nudging John, she whispered, "There's Orville Shaw. Let's leave."

John popped the reins over the mule's rump to start him lumbering along as they waved goodbye to Andy and his mother. John had no intention of getting involved in a conversation with Orville Shaw, who sought constantly to draw him into a heated discussion about slavery and war. And Orville could get downright mean when he wanted to.

Orville quickened his step, cutting across the field to walk straight down the middle of the road toward them. "You hold up there, John Wright," he yelled, waving his arms above his head. "I aim to have some words with you!"

With him walking directly toward them, there was nothing to do but stop. As Orville came closer, it was obvious that he was already mad, his brows knit, lips pursed angrily.

"You come by here to charge me for what your girl did to my boy?" he roared. "I never asked her to come, and she ain't no doctor no how. She ain't got no business mixin' up them potions of hers and peddlin' 'em. You're just wastin' your time if you think I'm gonna pay her anything!"

John whispered to Kitty, "You didn't say anything to me about treating that Shaw boy. What in thunderation did you give him?"

"His mother came to get me," she answered quickly, also whispering as Orville came closer. "She knew I wouldn't charge her anything, and they didn't have money to pay Doc Musgrave. Andy had chills and fever, so I made a tonic from some wild cherry bark and a dogwood tree, like Doc taught me."

He let out his breath in an exasperated sigh. "If your momma finds out you've been traipsin' after Doc again, Kitty, she's going to have another one of her fits. I don't mind. You know that. But your momma says it isn't proper for a young lady to be trying to do a man's work—like doctoring."

"It's proper if it's what I want to do," she fired back at him, suddenly rebellious. She loved medicine. She loved treating and caring for sick people. It didn't matter that it was considered unladylike. She would like nothing better than to be a doctor—a dream she shared only with Doc Musgrave, who seemed to understand.

Orville reached the wagon, face tight with anger. "Don't think you're gonna get any money out of me, John Wright. That girl of yours ain't no doctor, and she had no business comin' here. I didn't even know she was comin' till the old lady told me she'd done been and gone. I don't owe you nothin'—now git!"

"I don't expect money from you, Mister Shaw," Kitty defended herself. "I only came to help Andy, because he was sick."

"You ain't no doctor," he shook his fist at her, "and I don't owe you a damn thing!"

"Just hold it, Shaw," John stood up and glared down from the wagon. "Don't you talk to my daughter like that, or I'll take the whip to you, for sure."

Orville spat tobacco juice in the direction of the wagon, and it hit the side with a splat, dribbling downward as he wiped at his brown-stained mouth with the back of his hand. His voice came out threatening, "I don't want no damn nigger-lover comin' on my property, you hear? Not even passin' through. You ain't one of us, John Wright, and I don't want you or any of your kin comin' around here. Now git!"

Kitty saw her father's hands tightening on the whip, knuckles turning white. "Poppa, let's go," she touched his arm. "Don't fight with him, please."

John snapped the reins, and the mule pulled the wagon forward. Behind them, Orville shouted curses upon them.

They rode along for a while without speaking, but then Kitty broke the silence. "It's getting worse, isn't it?"

"What?"

"People being mad because of the way you feel about things."

"Silence gives consent. I don't want anyone to think I'm in favor of slavery or the war, so when they ask me, I tell them how I feel."

"Do you really think there will be a war?"

He nodded, feeling sad as he admitted, "If Lincoln was elected president yesterday, Kitty, I'm afraid that war is not far off. That's another reason I wanted to come to Goldsboro today—to hear the news."

"And you think the South will go to war because Lincoln wants to free the slaves?" She was not really sure just why there was even talk of war, except that it had something to do with the slavery issue.

"It isn't all a matter of slavery," he answered. "The North and South are just different from each other, and I guess both sides want different things from the government. Slavery just happens to be the one issue on which both sides hotly disagree, and there doesn't seem to be any chance now for any kind of a compromise."

"If you're going to be in the company of Weldon Edwards," he continued, "you need to know a little something about what's got everyone so fired up these days. Both sides just keep getting hotter and hotter and madder and madder. The Fugitive Slave Act has the South all fired up, because runaway slaves can get help from the North now, and the South can't do anything about it. Then there's that book that Stowe woman wrote . . . *Uncle Tom's House.* . . ."

"Cabin," Kitty corrected him. She had read the book, and it had angered her, too, because she felt it unfair to judge the whole South by a single book.

"It brought a whole wave of folks hating slavery, and it made a lot of the people around here mad. They said the book caused more trouble." He shook his head slowly. "Yes, it looks as though we are going to have a war, and it will mean death and suffering on both sides, and I wish to God everyone would realize that and find a peaceable way to settle things."

She sighed. "I guess our neighbors are afraid you wouldn't fight with them because you don't sympathize with them."

She thought about Nathan. What would happen if war did come? He would surely fight, and what would become of this new feeling that was developing between them? Surely, he felt it, too. She wondered if he worried about going off to war and leaving her behind now when things were so wonderful. Maybe it was just men-talk, and the war wouldn't really come. . . .

Suddenly she realized John was staring straight ahead and had not spoken a word since her last comment about him fighting. "Poppa, you *would* fight with the South, wouldn't you? I mean, we have our home, our land . . . so

much to defend. You wouldn't fight for the North. . . ."
That was too incredible an idea to fully comprehend.

Never altering his gaze, he moved to pat her hands,
which were folded in her lap. "I'm for staying out of war,
girl. If it comes, who's to say what I'll do? When that time
comes, I'll just search my heart and find the answer there."

War! Why did there have to be talk of war? For the
past year, her world had revolved around slipping away
from her mother to follow Doc Musgrave, because she
loved helping the sick. She had been so preoccupied with
the problem of making a decision whether to study medicine, when it was unheard of for a woman to do so, that
she had not really concerned herself with other matters.
Then, in the past twenty-four hours, Nathan Collins had
awakened a sleeping giant within her—that giant emotion
of womanhood that now made everything in her life so
confusing. Her mind ordered her to follow one course—her
heart, another. And something else was telling her that war
was going to have an effect on both directions of her life.

Each lost in thought, they rode on into Goldsboro without further conversation. Kitty liked the town—the way the
railroad tracks ran right down the middle of a crossroads,
north and south, with the station house built right in the
middle, extending from one side of the main street to the
other. The trains passed through the middle of the building,
and she hoped she would get to see one of the wood-
burning engines chug through while they were in town.

John pulled the wagon up in front of the Griswold Hotel
and tied the mule securely to a hitching post. Kitty stared
thoughtfully at the huge building. She'd heard it had as
many as seventy-six rooms. Feeling a wave of jealousy, she
remembered overhearing Nancy Warren at church last
summer, bragging about the military ball she had attended
there with Nathan in July.

It was close to two o'clock. Her father helped her down
from the wagon, then pressed some money in her hand and
said, "I'll meet you here when you're through with your
buying, and we'll go have some supper at the hotel."

The hotel—where Nancy had danced in Nathan's arms
in the ballroom. No matter. She had been in his arms yesterday. She would be in them again tomorrow.

She hurried across the street to a dress shop near the hotel, determined to buy the prettiest dress in town.

Time was forgotten as she tried on over a dozen dresses, unable to decide which would make her the most irresistible. There was a pink organdy, but that made her look little-girlish. Then there was a green silk with puffed sleeves and a princess lace collar—but that looked too old and matronly.

The shopkeeper looked annoyed, but Kitty ignored her. The dress had to be just right.

She tried on a yellow barred muslin with large, wide insets of lace around the hem. "Oh, it makes me look so young," she said woefully, twirling about in front of the full-length mirror.

"Too young . . . too old," the shopkeeper pursed her lips, patting the bun at the nape of her neck in a gesture of agitation. "Just what kind of effect are you trying to achieve, young lady? Maybe I could help you if you'd tell me. And where do you plan to wear the dress? It must be something terribly special."

"Oh, it is," Kitty replied, feeling the sudden need to share her excitement and happiness. "Nathan Collins has invited me to a party this Sunday afternoon, and I want something very special to wear."

Her voice trailed off as she caught the look on the shopkeeper's face by her mirrored reflection. Whirling about, she asked, "Did I say something wrong?"

Her face was turning into mottled shades of red, lips starting to quiver. "I had heard that Nathan had invited someone else to the party. Nancy Warren happens to be my niece, and I know how hurt she is by his rudeness."

"They were almost betrothed. . . ." she went on, stepping back as though she couldn't bear to be any closer to her, eyes accusing.

Kitty, like her father, could only be pushed so far, and she never allowed herself to be backed up at all when she was completely innocent. "I didn't ask Nathan, *he* asked me," she said curtly. "If your niece is heartbroken, then maybe she saw more in her relationship with him than actually existed. He certainly didn't act as if he were doing something he shouldn't when he invited me to go with him."

They glared at each other. "Now, are you going to show me some more dresses, or would you rather I take my business elsewhere?" Kitty demanded.

In silent anger, Nancy Warren's aunt moved about the shop gathering up the ugliest dresses she could find. One was even a black bombazine, and Kitty bit her tongue to keep from saying cattily that Nancy should wear such a garment since she seemed to be in need of a mourning dress.

Afterward, she told herself if she had not been so annoyed, she never would have chosen such a provocative dress. But when she tried it on, twisting about in front of the mirror, the reflection on the other woman's face told her quite plainly that here was the dress that would make everyone at the party turn their heads in her direction. The menfolk would envy Nathan and the women would be seething with jealousy. Nathan, himself, would be wild with desire for her—she was positive.

The dress was made of bright, blood-red taffeta, and against her creamy white skin and golden-blond hair, the effect was stunning. Her violet eyes seemed to attract the crimson and dance with secret fires. The décolletage was daringly low, and her large, firm breasts were pushed high by the stays—a slight hint of her rosy pink nipples showing provocatively.

This was the dress!

She also bought lace pantalets, a linen corset cover, and four billowing lace and linen petticoats. Sullen-faced, the shopkeeper bundled the items and pushed them across the counter.

As Kitty left the store, the sun was starting to go down, and she realized that she had been gone longer than planned. Hurrying to the wagon, she saw eight or nine men surrounding her father, and she hesitated. Why, she wondered in dismay, couldn't these people just leave her father alone?

Kitty had worked herself into anger by the time she reached the wagon. A few of the men glanced in her direction, but it was obvious they had been drinking, and the presence of a lady had no effect upon the situation at hand. John was standing near the hitching post, trying to be heard above the hooting, as he attempted to explain his stand.

"I don't claim to be a Federalist, and I'm certainly no Yankee. I was born right here in Wayne County just as all of you were. I'm only trying to tell you that war will not be easily won. A lot of good men will be killed—a lot of land lost and destroyed. And for what?"

He was almost pleading, gesturing helplessly as he said, "If the South loses, what will happen? Have you thought of that possibility?"

Kitty had placed her packages in the wagon bed and hoisted herself up to the wooden bench. Appraising the situation, she counted nine men surrounding her father, and none of them shared his views. She knew one of them— Aaron Collins' overseer, Luke Tate, a known troublemaker who loved to fight, and who once beat a slave to death with a whip.

John Wright had stretched his tall, lanky frame to his full six feet of height, and he was waving his long, thin arms back and forth over his head, pleading once again to be heard. "North Carolina can remain neutral, don't you see? We can stay out of the war. How many of you own slaves, anyway? Luke, you're just an overseer. . . ."

"You let your slaves go, didn't you, Wright?" Luke cried, to the delight of those around him, who were cheering him on. "You set them free, didn't you? I'll bet you even help runaways through the underground, don't you? I'll bet you're even a spy for the Federals. . . ."

"Now wait a minute, Luke," John forced a laugh, trying to quell the rising emotions. "You're carrying this too far now. You came up to me while I was standing here minding my own business and started this whole thing. Now you call me a spy! I think it's time we ended this conversation. I just hate to see all of you listen to the 'fire-eaters' who're going to bring war and bloodshed to the South. . . ."

"*You* wait a minute," Luke snarled, lips curling. "I ain't got no use for them what don't stick up for their neighbors, and this is what I think of you. . . ."

And he spat in John's face contemptuously.

A shocked hush fell over the crowd as the brown, tobacco-stained spittle ran slowly down John's cheek. Kitty threw her hands to her mouth to stifle a scream.

The two men glared at each other, John's fists clenching and unclenching at his sides as he fought for control, his body shuddering. Then, very swiftly, he snatched a handkerchief from the pocket of his overalls, and wiped the spit from his face with a quick swipe.

Luke had mistaken the movement, and, thinking John was reaching for a weapon, had brought out his knife with a quick jerk. The steel gleamed ominously in the fading sunlight.

"Come on, Luke, he ain't got no knife," someone yelled.

It happened quickly. Luke brought his knee up to smash into John's crotch. John fell, and Luke kicked him viciously in the stomach as he writhed painfully in the dirt, clutching himself with both hands.

He brought his leg back again, ready to kick at the face this time, but Kitty had come out of her shocked stupor and reached down to snatch up her father's flintlock musket that was lying at her feet. She screamed at Luke just as his broganed foot went smashing into the side of John's head.

"She's got a gun!" one of the men shouted, and everyone scattered as Luke turned toward Kitty. He was still holding his knife, and he lurched toward her just as she pointed the musket and fired.

His body seemed to leap backward into the crowd that was fighting each other to run for cover. They stopped, eyes fixed on Luke as he sank to the ground. Suddenly, he was no longer a part of them . . . or they, a part of him. They wanted no part of the fight, or the girl with the gun that she obviously knew how to use.

Kitty quickly reached for the powder flask to fill the primer pan and reload, but a big, beefy hand closed over her arm as a gruff voice said, "I'll take over now, Miss Kitty."

She looked into the grim eyes of the sheriff.

John moaned, struggling to get up, and someone reached to help her down as she moved quickly to get to him.

"I'm all right, just bruised a bit," he said to her. His eyes went anxiously to where Luke Tate lay on his side, blood oozing from the hole in his right shoulder. Luke clutched at it with his left hand, blood trickling between his fingers as he groaned in pain.

Footsteps were running toward them. Kitty saw a man with a black bag, gratefully recognizing Doc Musgrave. He rushed over to John, who waved him toward Luke. "He's hit, Doc. I'll be okay."

Some of the men helped the doctor take Luke away to his office, and a few stood about watching Kitty help her father to the wagon. "I want you to let Doc check you over," she said anxiously.

"No, I just want to go home and get out of this mess. I think half the town is drunk."

She helped him up to the seat, then untied the mule and climbed up herself. Her father slumped next to her as she snapped the reins and started them rolling down the street. A few people watched as they passed, and Kitty recognized the storekeeper where she had bought her dress, glaring at her.

Kitty's mind was in a whirl. She had shot a man! She had actually pointed a gun at a human being and fired! It all seemed unreal now. When she had fired, it hadn't mattered whether she killed Luke or not. Fortunately for him, the ball went in his shoulder, and he had his life, and she didn't have to have his death on her conscience.

"Well, you did it, girl," her father spoke finally when they were outside of town and headed down the road for home. "You shot a man."

He sounded reproachful, and she shot a quick glance at him. "I had no choice, Poppa. He had a knife."

"I know, I know," he sounded very old . . . very tired. "I guess trouble was bound to come. I appreciate what you did for me, Kitty, but I wished it hadn't happened. Nothin' good ever comes from fighting."

"Poppa, you *never* fight," she said bluntly, unable to keep silent about it any longer. "Jacob tells me how the men goad you, but you just walk away. If you'd get mad just one time and break a few skulls open . . ."

He laughed. "Now that's a fine way for a young lady to be talking. What would your momma say if she heard you?"

They looked at each other, realization washing over them simultaneously. Lena Wright was going to have the biggest fit of her whole life when she heard that Kitty had shot a man.

40

"Let her!" Kitty burst out, and they both laughed at their exchange of silent thoughts.

Then the humor passed, and Kitty pursued the subject. "Poppa, why don't you fight?"

Sighing, he rubbed at his bloodied cheek. "There's a lot about your old poppa you don't know, girl," he said quietly. "Maybe it's time you knew, so you won't think I'm a coward."

And he told her—about another argument, but that time he had been younger, and he had left home to make his own way. He had wanted to be free and explore life before settling down on the family land to farm for the rest of his life.

John wound up in the mountains of North Carolina, and he got to drinking with another man one night. They got into an argument and went at each other with knives. When it was over, the stranger lay dead in a pool of thickening blood, and John realized he didn't even know his name.

Kitty shuddered, but he didn't notice.

"I couldn't even remember what in thunderation we were arguing about—what was so important that I got riled to the point of slashing that man's throat from ear to ear! We had camped out in the woods, and nobody knew it happened, so I just buried him in an unmarked grave and got out of there and came home. For a while, I drank myself into a stupor, trying to forget, but then I realized I was killing myself. So I settled down, married your ma, and tried to put it out of my mind.

"But it comes back," he passed a hand over his eyes, as though trying to wipe away the pain and torture of his sin. "Every time I find myself getting riled to fight, I close my eyes and see that dead stranger's eyes staring up at me, his throat gaped open with white bone showing. . . ."

"Poppa, stop!" She fought the impulse to retch.

He shook himself and came back to the present. Reaching over to touch her arm, his voice was gentle. "I'm sorry, Kitty. I didn't mean to upset you, child. I just thought you should know why I don't want to get in a fight. I can't have you thinking me a coward, especially now, with things like they are."

"Maybe the war won't come," she said, childlike, as

though wishing might make it come true. "Maybe the war won't come, and everyone can go on living like they have been, and there won't be any bloodshed."

He didn't speak. She turned to look at him and saw his brow furrow, his eyes shadowed with fear.

"Poppa, what is it?" she asked in alarm. "You *are* hurt, aren't you?"

She started to pull up on the reins, but he motioned her to keep going. "I'm all right," his voice was tight. "It just sounds very sad to hear you wishing for things that just aren't going to happen, Kitty. War *is* coming."

Forcing a smile, she said, "Maybe not, Poppa. Maybe it's all just talk. Maybe . . ."

"Shut up!"

He ground out the words so forcefully that Kitty yanked on the reins, stopping the old mule as she turned to stare at him incredulously. Never had her father spoken so sharply to her.

"Stop living in your dream world, Kitty," he said through gritted teeth, eyes squeezed shut, fists clenched in his lap. "You've heard me talk about the situation. I told you what was going on. Don't pretend you don't know all the signs point to war. You're not like the other women about, who refuse to face up to reality."

He opened his eyes, and Kitty saw tears glimmering in them. "When the war comes, girl, I want you to be ready. I want you to be able to look after yourself if anything happens to me. . . ."

Kitty was bewildered. What had come over her father for him to sound so . . . so *desperate!*

He seemed to realize that she just didn't understand.

His voice was low with dread. "Lincoln was elected president yesterday, Kitty. I heard the news today. I don't believe anything can stop the South from seceding from the Union now and heading straight into war . . . and *hell.*"

❧ Chapter Four ❧

WHEN Nathan came by to find out whether or not Kitty would go to the party with him, he made it a point to speak to John Wright and apologize for the incident in town with his father's overseer. John had gruffly told him to forget about it—the matter was closed.

"I can't believe you actually shot him," he had said to Kitty, his gaze upon her a mixture of surprise and respect. "Most young ladies would have fainted."

"I'm not 'most young ladies,'" she had smiled demurely, teasingly, no longer embarrassed over the incident despite her mother's continued nagging over such a "scandal."

Voice husky, he had whispered, "How well I know, Kitty," eyes moving over her caressingly. Kitty had embraced that moment for the remaining, seemingly endless, days until the party.

When the day finally arrived, she sat beside Nathan in the carriage, well aware that her dress had achieved the effect she was seeking. "God, you're beautiful, Kitty," he whispered, slipping an arm about her shoulders as he signaled to the driver to be on his way. "I'll be the envy of every man at the party."

She felt suddenly warm, but then heard the echo of her mother's predictions about the Collins family's reaction to what had happened in town, and said, "Nathan, did your parents have anything to say about your taking me to the party after they heard about the shooting?"

She saw a muscle tighten in his jaw, and a shadow passed across his eyes momentarily. His smile, she thought, was forced. "We talked about it, Kitty, and for a while, I have to be honest with you, they were upset. But then I told them about my conversation with someone who witnessed the whole thing, and their attitude changed. We all regret that it happened, and Daddy had a lot to say to Luke about it."

"I'm going to feel that everybody is whispering about me," she said dejectedly, the happy glow she'd felt suddenly disappearing. "I wish it hadn't happened, but Luke brought it on, and I did what I had to do."

"I'm sure of that," he assured her. "Everyone is tense these days. People say things in the heat of the moment, then regret it later. Don't you worry about anything—just have a good time, and let me show you off to everyone."

In her usually blunt way, Kitty asked, "Is Nancy going to be there?"

"I'm afraid so," he said, remembering the scene with his mother. "She's my second cousin, you know, and the whole family is gathering to honor Mr. Edwards. But don't you worry about Nancy. That relationship has been forced upon me by my mother, and I'm not going to be pushed into anything. I think everyone knows that by now. I've got my eyes on you, Kitty, and don't forget it."

He leaned closer, cupping her face in his hand as his lips touched hers. Kitty's partially exposed breasts were pushed against his ruffled shirt, and she felt his body shuddering as he pulled away and said gruffly, "I've got to control myself better than that, or I'll make a fool out of myself."

For a moment, she didn't know what he meant, but then it dawned on her, and, without thinking of what she was doing, her eyes went to his tight fawn trousers. "Oh," she gasped, instantly embarrassed that she had looked, turning her face away.

"It's all right, Kitty," Nathan laughed, drawing her close to him once again. "I'm only human, you know, and that dress you're wearing is enough to make any man wild with desire."

She chewed her lower lip nervously, not knowing what to say. He turned her face with his fingertips, forcing her to look at him. "Don't be embarrassed. You want me, too, don't you? I can feel it, Kitty, and I think we've both felt it for a long time but neither of us did anything about it."

"I would never . . ." she gasped, and he quickly interrupted, "I know you wouldn't, and I would never ask you to, but I am going to ask you to marry me, Kitty, and soon. I love you, you know . . ."

No, she hadn't known, and as his lips came down on hers once again, her hand slipped behind his head to pull him even closer. He was the one man she could love, and maybe she already loved him. Her heart was pounding furiously, alive and happy with the emotions of joy surging through her.

When he did ask, she wondered wildly, what would her answer be? The talk of war—it made everything erratic in people's lives now. But surely, there would be a way for the two of them to share a love.

The carriage hit a bump in the road, and they sprang apart. "We're almost there," Nathan said, pulling away to straighten his coat and fluff out the ruffles of his linen shirt. Kitty pushed at her hair, piled high in curls on top of her head and trailing down her back onto bare shoulders. She knew it wasn't necessary to pinch her cheeks to make them rosy. Her insides were on fire, and she could feel the flame that crept into her face.

The house came into view. Beautiful. The perfect symmetry of tall white columns, wide verandas. The most beautiful house she had ever seen.

The yard was filled with people, and she could see the women in their finest hoop dresses, bright colors contrasting against the men resplendent in short coats and fawn and gray trousers. The shrieks and laughter of children playing on the wide, sprawling lawn reached her ears, and she smiled. It was going to be a grand party, and she shivered with anticipation.

Beneath the grove of pecan trees, where the branches were not quite stripped of leaves and would offer some shade, long trestled picnic tables, covered with fine linen cloths, had been placed. The setting was far enough away from the long barbecue pits to avoid the smoke from the red embers with the meat turning on spits above, juices dripping down to hiss upon the coals.

The smell of crisp fresh pork tickled her nostrils deliciously, mingled with the succulent odors of barbecue sauce and Brunswick stew bubbling in huge, iron washpots. She could see black house servants bustling about the tables with bowls of rich roasted yams and crisp, chopped cabbage.

Their carriage moved around the tree-lined curving driveway, which was filled with saddle horses and carriages. Their driver brought them to a stop directly at the front steps. Nathan moved to get out so that he could help her descend, and Kitty checked the bodice of her dress one last time before making her appearance. She had pulled up the tight stretch of taffeta so that the pinkness of her nipples did not show—still, the dip was perhaps an inch lower than the other young ladies' dresses that she had seen, and if she happened to lean over, her breasts would be exposed. But no matter, she thought defiantly, everyone would be talking about her, anyway, after that horrible scene in town.

Nathan reached for her through the open carriage door, his hands fastening about her tiny waist. As he lifted her up, his lips were close enough to whisper, "God, you're so beautiful, Kitty . . ."

Once again the warmth of pleasure pounded into her face, and a shiver of happiness spread through her body. But the glow was quickly dimmed once her feet touched the ground, and she realized that everyone milling about had turned to stare—and not with the admiration and envy she had hoped for. The men looked at her with curious eyes, and the women were obviously hostile. A few of them busily whispered back and forth behind their nervously fluttering fans, as they glared at her.

Chin jutting high, Kitty lifted her skirts as Nathan took her arm, and started up the steps. She was not going to let them bother her. This day belonged to Nathan, and no one else mattered.

And then she found herself staring up into the angry eyes of Nathan's mother, Lavinia Collins. Her gaze took in the low bodice disapprovingly, and her lips tightened even more on her pinched face. She was a short woman, rather dumpy, Kitty thought. Her dress was brown taffeta, stiff and high-collared with a trim of fine lace. Her hair was pulled back into a tight bun at the nape of her neck. She had probably once been a pretty woman, but now she looked unpleasant and . . . Kitty searched for the right word . . . *sour*. That was it.

She was standing beside Aaron Collins, and it was impossible to tell how he reacted to her presence. Known for his charm, Aaron would never be so ill-mannered as to make a guest feel uncomfortable in his home. Bowing graciously, he kissed the hand Kitty extended to him as Nathan made the introductions.

"I've heard so much about you from my son, Kitty," he said quietly. "I feel as though I should know you, since I've been seeing you with your father delivering honey ever since you were a child."

Kitty thought he resembled Nathan, except that his hair was salt and pepper gray, and he was taller, heavier, but still a fine figure of a man with deep-set eyes that crinkled at the corners when he smiled.

"Welcome to Collins Manor," Aaron bowed again slightly.

Lavinia Collins did not speak, merely nodding her head curtly as the two of them passed. "She's mad because you asked me here, isn't she?" Kitty whispered to Nathan as they moved on up the steps.

"Don't pay any mind to her. If Mother doesn't get her way about everything, she can be rather unpleasant. Daddy warned her about being polite, but I guess she didn't trust herself and chose to keep silent instead."

"Then she *is* mad with you for bringing me here," Kitty whispered again, this time with an urgency.

"I think Nancy must've had one of her tantrums and gone crying to Mother when she found out I had no intention of bringing her here today. I told you, Kitty, I'm not going to be pushed into anything, and those two started talking marriage once the war talk got stronger. If I marry anybody, it's going to be you." He squeezed her arm, smiling down at her, and she thought she would melt under his gaze.

They reached the top of the stairs and the sun-splashed veranda where several of Nathan's young friends surged upon them. They exchanged greetings, and then someone blurted out: "Did you shoot to kill Tate, Kitty, or did you mean to only wound him?"

"He's still alive, isn't he?" her voice came out sharper than she intended, and an awkward silence followed. She did not want to spend the afternoon reliving something she would rather forget.

"It's over with now," Nathan spoke firmly. "Let's just forget about it."

"I agree."

Kitty turned to find herself looking into the sad eyes of David Stoner, and she suddenly felt uncomfortable. Was it a year ago that he had proposed to her? She couldn't remember. She had liked David a lot—and still did. He was a handsome young man, with reddish brown hair and deep green eyes, a firmness to his face that gave him character and an air of wisdom in spite of his youth. But she didn't love him, and she had told him so. With tears in his eyes, he had sworn to her that he could never love another the way he did her. Ever since, when they met, he looked at her with the same expression of sadness.

He looked from her to Nathan and nodded. It was more than a greeting, Kitty knew. He was acknowledging their relationship, painful though it was.

"Ahh, here's our guest of honor," the tension of the moment was dispelled as Nathan turned to greet the short, plump man with the sharp, piercing eyes and rather long, hooked nose. "May I present Weldon Edwards from Warrenton."

He kissed Kitty's hand. She thought his manner pleasant. He didn't look like someone hysterically screaming for war and bloodshed.

Attention turned from Kitty to the noted lawyer, as someone asked, "Mr. Edwards, I'm as anxious to get the war started and over with as anyone else. How long do you think it will be before we start fighting?"

". . . now that Lincoln's been elected President," another added excitedly.

Weldon Edwards thought a moment, then said, "I think the election of Lincoln to the Presidency will trigger the secession of the states of the lower South, but unless we can get North Carolina's secession movement to grow rapidly, I think the General Assembly, and Governor Ellis, will continue the 'wait and see' attitude.

"I'm leaving this afternoon for a secession meeting in Cleveland County," he told the hovering group. And next week, we meet in Wilmington. We must try to call a state-wide convention of the people to determine a policy for the state—and that policy must be secession, even if it means war."

Kitty could contain herself no longer. "War, sir? What if secession does bring war, as it surely will. Are these young men here to die for your cause?"

"It's our cause, too," Daniel Roberts, the youngest of the group spoke up, striking his fist in the air. "Yes, I'll die for North Carolina. . . ."

Nathan gripped her arm so tightly that she winced with pain as he steered her away from the group and toward the front doors of the house. "Please, Kitty," he whispered anxiously. "It's just not proper for women to get involved in political discussions."

"I'm not talking about politics," she jerked out of his grasp and faced him defiantly, not caring who heard. "I'm talking about war—death, bloodshed! And it's my right to be concerned, too. Being a woman has nothing to do with it. I can get killed by the Yankees as quickly as a man."

"You aren't going to get killed. The war won't last over a few months, and we'll never let them get this far. Now please, Kitty, people are staring. . . ."

She allowed him to steer her into the entrance foyer, and for the moment, she was so impressed with the opulence of the house that she forgot about the talk of war.

The floors gleamed—the mahogany hand-polished to a high sheen. The walls were covered in soft gold velvet, and high above, a crystal chandelier danced in its cluster of diamond-studded prisms. On either side of the foyer, the carpeted stairway curved upward to the next floor, its railings and bannisters entwined with early branches of holly for decoration. Several vases of bright yellow marigolds filled the room with fragrance.

No one was about, and Nathan pressed his lips to her forehead as his fingertips caressed her bare shoulders.

"Now you go upstairs to freshen, and I'll get a plate of barbecue for you. We'll eat on the back lawn, away from the others."

"Are you trying to keep me away from everyone because I'm so awful?" she snapped.

"Oh, Kitty, don't be this way," he frowned, sighing with exasperation. "I just don't want any trouble. I want the two of us to be happy and enjoy ourselves, not get into heated debates about war. Isn't it enough that everyone is whispering about the fact that you shot my father's overseer?"

"Then why didn't you just leave me at home if you're so ashamed of me, Nathan? It isn't my fault that you hire an overseer who wanders about half the time drunk and sparking for a fight. I . . . I wish I'd killed him," she spat out the words furiously, "and I wish I'd stayed home and not come to your party!"

"Kitty . . ."

She hoisted her skirts and ran up the steps, taking them two at a time, not caring how unladylike it might look.

"Kitty, won't you please listen?" Nathan pleaded from below. "I didn't mean to make you mad. . . ."

She didn't know which direction to turn. Somewhere, she knew, a room would have been designated for female guests to freshen themselves. But which one?

"Are you looking for something, Kitty?"

At the sound of the voice, she whipped her head about to see Nancy Warren standing in the doorway of a nearby room. She was wearing a powdery blue hoop dress, the bodice low but filled in with delicate lace. The sleeves were puffed, and she wore a velvet ribbon around her neck. Her dark brown hair was curled in ringlets about her face.

Nancy would be pretty, Kitty thought fleetingly, if she did not have such a pinched, disapproving, and superior look to her face. Her lips curved upward, brown eyes flashing with malice. "Well, don't just stand there gawking. You must hurry and get back downstairs before someone snatches Nathan away from you." She laughed—an ugly sound. "Wouldn't that be terrible, after the way you threw yourself at him to get him to bring you here today? But why should you worry? As coarse and rough as you are,

Kitty, dear, all you have to do is shoot the girl who dares, right?"

Kitty started to reply. All the angry words were dancing on her tongue, waiting to be unleashed. Instead, she laughed. Nancy blinked, bewildered by Kitty's reaction.

"Oh, Nancy, why don't you give up?" She shook her head from side to side, still laughing. "You really aren't worth me worrying about, you know. I'll admit that you used to really get under my skin. I'd run home from school and throw myself across my bed and cry for hours, because of something you'd said, making fun of me or my family. But now, all of a sudden, I find it doesn't matter. Instead of being mad or hurt with you, I think I honestly feel sorry for you—because I've got the one thing you want— and can't have."

Kitty had walked slowly across the room to where the curving pine washstand stood beside a window. She lifted the blue porcelain pitcher and poured water into the matching bowl. Then she dipped one hand and began to pat her face, trying to cool her flushed skin.

"If you're talking about having *Nathan*, Kitty Wright," Nancy spluttered, eyes narrowed to angry slits as she stood just behind her, "You haven't got him, and you'll *never* get him. His parents would disown him before they let him marry the likes of trash like you. . . ."

"Who are you calling trash, Nancy?" Kitty whipped around, still holding the pitcher.

Pressing, because she had obviously found a vulnerable spot in Kitty's cool veneer, Nancy smirked. "Everybody in Wayne County knows your family is white trash. They say your daddy is a negro-lover, that he helps runaway slaves get to the underground. They say your mother is crazy. They say your daddy is too sorry and lazy to work the land he owns, and that's why you're dirt poor. And you dare to think you're good enough for Nathan. . . ."

She didn't plan to do it, but when Kitty heard Nancy's tirade against her father, it was too much. Slowly, deliberately—almost under its own will, her arm raised and the pitcher of water tipped, splashing down on Nancy's head.

"What are you doing?" she screamed, covering her head

with both hands and backing away. But it was too late. Her carefully curler-ironed tresses hung sopping wet around her face—the bodice and sleeves of her dress limp and splotched.

Calmly, Kitty returned the pitcher to the washstand. "Think again before you go calling someone white trash, Nancy," she said, walking toward the door.

Nancy was sobbing and shrieking, and the sound brought several other young girls running into the room. "Look what she did! Look what that trash did!" Nancy was yelping.

Stomping down the steps one at a time, Kitty scolded herself for having come in the first place. She didn't belong here. What was so important about social acceptance, anyway? She'd have much preferred to go riding or hunting, and if Nathan loved her, he would just have to understand.

A group of women stood inside the door, exchanging glances as they looked from Kitty to the direction of the sobbing and screaming. Casting a contemptuous glance in their direction, Kitty walked by them, head high. They looked like a clump of fat hens, clucking and chattering. What did they know about straddling a saddle, galloping in the song of the wind with hair blowing wildly about their faces instead of tiptoeing gracefully along in their stiff crinolines and ruffles? They would never thrill to the sound of "Killer" baying excitedly as he picked up the scent of a 'coon, leading the way for the final triumphant moment. And let them scream and faint at the sight of blood. They didn't know the goodness that spread within when a little black boy cut his finger and smiled at you with eternal devotion because you cleaned it and bandaged it and then kissed it to make it well.

She had more than any of those sour-faced women would ever have—and what they thought of her did not matter.

She burst onto the veranda breathlessly, gulping in the fresh air. They were still there—Weldon Edwards and David Stoner and Nathan, and the others, heatedly talking about the war.

"We can beat them in a month—"

"One Southerner can beat twenty Yankees—"

"—teach them a lesson they won't forget!"

"Peacefully? Abe Lincoln don't know the meanin' of the word. He'll never let any state secede from the union peacefully. We'll go to war, sir."

War, secession, fighting, Lincoln—words Kitty was sick of hearing. "Gentlemen, you are all fools!" she exploded as heads turned, mouths dropped open in shock. "You condemn my father for not joining in your enthusiasm for war, but have any of you ever stopped to listen to the wisdom of his words? He says there's not a factory to build cannons that lies below the Mason-Dixon Line. And what about the cotton factories? With the exception of North Carolina, there aren't many others, and we can't supply the whole South if war comes."

They continued to stare at her silently, a few of them coughing nervously as they darted sidelong glances at Nathan, who was shuffling uncomfortably. Then he started toward her, but she stepped back, holding up her hands to hold him away, not about to be led off once again like a naughty child.

"The Yankees will blockade our harbors quickly, and then where will we be? Could you get cotton out to sell overseas? The Yankees have the factories and the money. The South has nothing but a bunch of patriotic-minded fools who think there is glory in war!"

"Kitty, that's enough!" Nathan's voice was harsh, rasping, as he grabbed her outstretched arms and shoved them down to her sides, gripping and giving her a shake. He whispered, "Let me take you home. Obviously, you don't feel well. . . ."

Jerking away from him, she cried, "I feel very well. I refuse to let you people make me sick!"

"Nathan. . . ." Lavinia Collins ran onto the veranda, her face white with shock, her personal maid beside her, fluttering nervously in fear that her mistress would faint. "Nathan, do you know what this . . . this creature has done? She's poured water on little Nancy Warren!"

A round of laughter went up from the young men, and one of them called out, "Nancy should be glad Kitty didn't have a gun, or she'd be nursing a wound like your overseer."

Nathan's hands fell away from his grip on her arms. It was too much. "Oh, Kitty . . ." he moaned, shaking his head.

She knew she had shamed him and, turning, she ran toward the end of the veranda and the side steps. "Wait, I'll get the carriage . . ." Nathan called.

"No . . . I don't need you . . ." Kitty cried, hoisting her skirts once again to run down the steps. "I don't need anyone. . . ."

Across the lawn she ran, her carefully coiffured hair falling down around her face. She headed straight for the woods. It was a good two miles or more to her house through the woods and swamps, but she had hunted these parts for years and knew her way. The walk would be good for her, she decided, slowing down as she made her way through the thicket. She needed the time to sort out everything that had happened, before she faced her mother.

The scream halted Kitty's steps. Here, the woods were thick, with brambles and thickets of overgrowth. Her dress was being snagged and torn, but she'd been too angry to care.

"Master, don't . . . please don't, the baby . . ."

Turning toward the direction of the pleading cries, Kitty saw a clearing she hadn't realized was about. Moving closer, she realized she was right next to the slave compound for the Collins plantation. There were perhaps a dozen or more wooden shacks lined up in a circle around a clearing. The porches of the houses were clustered with frightened, wide-eyed slaves. Small children clutched their mothers' legs, peering out from behind at the scene taking place in the middle of the clearing.

A young black girl, swollen with child, lay writhing in the dirt at the feet of a white man who held a whip in his left hand—his right arm was wrapped in a sling.

Luke Tate!

"Don't beat me, please. You'll kill my baby . . ."

"I'll kill you, you black wench. I'll teach you to steal . . ." He reached down with his left hand, still holding the whip, and with a quick yank, ripped her thin cotton dress from her body. She groveled naked at his feet, trying to wrap her arms around her bulging, unprotected stomach—and her unborn child.

54

The Collins mansion stood on a hill above the clearing, barely visible from the distance. A young black man came running from that direction, waving his arms frantically. "Don't you hit her, Tate. You hit me instead. . . ." He reached the clearing, face churning with fear and anger, chest heaving with exhaustion from the run. "I give her that meat. You cut off her food to punish her las' week, and she an' that baby were starvin'. I had to feed her, don't you see? If you beat anybody, beat me."

Luke Tate turned. "I'll beat the both of you," he screamed, bringing the whip down with a crackling whistle through the air. The lash cut across the black man's face, laying open the flesh. Covering his face with both hands and shrieking in pain, he slumped forward in the dirt.

The black woman cried, struggled to her feet to reach the young man, but Luke's whip slashed again—this time across her back. She was no match for the cutting leather, and she crumpled under the first blow—the blood already flowing from the slice that laid open her skin.

Luke raised his arm again, but Kitty had managed to make her way out of the brambles by then and was running toward him, crying, "Stop! Stop that, you dirty bastard, Luke Tate!"

He turned as she threw herself upon him, raking his face with her clawing hands, kicking at him, pummelling him with her fists in a rage of fury.

For a moment, she'd caught him unaware, but he quickly recovered to fling her away effortlessly, throwing back his head to laugh and sneer at her. "You shoulda killed me when you had the chance, you little spitfire, because you're going to get the beating you deserve. . . ."

He raised the whip high above his head once again, and Kitty threw up her arms to protect herself as best she could. Closing her eyes in anticipation of the cutting slice that would be crashing down upon her—she blinked them open again at the sound of his laughter—and saw that he was flinging the whip aside.

"Naw, it'd be a shame to mess up anything that looks like you do." He leaned over, and she could smell the red-eye on his breath. Scooping her up as she hit at him uselessly, he roared, "A good fuckin' is what you need to calm you down, and I'm the man whut can give it to you. . . ."

55

He started off with her slung over his shoulders, in the direction of one of the slave cabins. "Get the hell outta there!" he roared, and slaves scattered, emptying the shack.

Stepping inside, he set her down and hooked the fingers of his left hand into her bodice and ripped it down, her breasts spilling out. "God. . . ." he breathed, as she staggered backward, trying to cover herself.

"Don't you touch me!" she cried hoarsely, darting her eyes about for any kind of a weapon. "Nathan will kill you for this. . . ."

"I'm willin' to take that chance . . ." He licked his puffy lips as he fumbled with his pants. "You just lay down on that cot yonder and it'll be good for both of us. You need this, Kitty . . . you need tamin' . . ."

"Not by you, Tate!"

They looked to the doorway where Nathan Collins stood, fists clenched, legs apart, eyes boiling with the fury of his anger. In one of his clenched fists, he held the bullwhip Tate had discarded, and without warning, he brought it slashing down across the overseer's shocked face.

Tate fell to his knees as Nathan hit him again, and the sound of the leather slicing into flesh and muscle made bile rise in Kitty's throat. She stumbled away from the shack and out into the cool November air, retching against the hands she pressed to her lips.

The sounds of the whip-stopped. She could hear Tate moaning. "You get off this land by sundown," Nathan yelled. "If I ever lay eyes on you again, I'll kill you. I swear it!"

She shook herself back to reality, moving quickly from the porch across the clearing to where a crowd was gathering around the pregnant woman. They parted respectfully as she shoved her way through.

"Move this woman into a cabin so I can examine her," Kitty ordered, then she turned to the boy, whose face was streaming with blood. Reaching down, she ripped one of her petticoats to make a wad of bandage to press against the cut. "Someone see to him. You've tended whip cuts before."

"Please take care of Jenny," the boy whimpered as she moved away. "Don't let nothin' happen to our baby. . . ."

Nathan ran up just as Kitty was about to enter the slave

cabin where Jenny had been taken. "I've sent for the carriage. I'm taking you home. I'm sorry all this has happened, Kitty, but it's best you leave now."

An agonized snarl made both of them jerk around to see Luke Tate staggering into the clearing. His face was covered in blood, and his shirt hung in bloodied shreds of cotton. Pointing a finger at them, he cried, "I'll get you both for this . . . you're a dead man, Nathan Collins, and I'll make you beg for mercy, Kitty Wright. . . ."

He stumbled toward the woods, and Nathan ignored his outburst, more concerned at the moment with taking Kitty home and getting her out of the terrible situation. "Come on now," he grasped her waist. "I'm so sorry, Kitty. I want to get you out of this . . ."

"No!" Jerking away she moved on toward the cabin door. "I've got to see to Jenny."

The woman was lying on a filthy mattress stuffed with corn shucks, writhing and moaning, hands clutching her stomach. An old black woman was bent over between her legs. Straightening, she said to Kitty, "It ain't her time yet, missy, but she's a'birthin'. . . ."

"Kitty, listen to me." Nathan stepped inside the slave shack, then, realizing several women were milling about as Kitty bent to examine the girl in labor, he raised his voice to snap, "Get out of here! All of you!"

The women scurried, bumping into each other as they each rushed to follow their master's orders. Then Nathan was across the dirt floor in two great steps to clamp his hands down on Kitty's shoulders, yanking her up and whirling her about to face him.

"You listen to me, Kitty," he hissed, eyes blazing with fury. "You've got to get out of here. This is an embarrassing situation for you to be in. In case you've forgotten, I'm in love with you. My parents are going to be very upset about all this, and your staying isn't going to help matters. . . ."

"Nathan, you're in my way," she said softly.

He stood back as Kitty shouted for the other women to get busy with boiling water and clean rags. "Well," she jerked her head up to see him still standing there, gawking. "This is no place for a man. Get out of here, will you?"

He stumbled backward, turned, and then bolted through the door.

Fortunately, the baby came easily, but it was tiny—about two months early, Kitty figured, as she held him in her arms and sponged away the blood and mucus. Wrapping him in a blanket someone handed her, she instructed them on how to care for him, keeping him warm by snuggling him close for their body heat.

"And don't let her try to nurse him," Kitty nodded to the young mother who was panting with exhaustion. "One of you with milk in your breasts can take care of him until she gets her strength back." She instructed them to get in touch with Doc Musgrave right away if Jenny developed fever or any sign of complications.

"No white doctor comin' here," an old gray-haired woman said tonelessly. "If she get sick, we take care of her."

"Doctor Musgrave will come here if you ask him to," Kitty snapped. "And if he's busy, I'll come and do what I can. Do you understand?"

The women nodded.

Kitty sighed and gathered the remnants of her dress about her and stepped out onto the front porch. A small cluster of white men sitting atop their horses was directly in front of the cabin.

One of them was Aaron Collins, and as she stepped onto the porch, he dismounted and walked toward her. Kitty noticed that Nathan, standing nearby, hung back.

"Miss Kitty, I'd like to have a few words with you," Aaron motioned for her to walk with him out of hearing range of the others. Wearily, she fell in step beside him, apprehensive of what was to come because of the grim, set lines of his face, the cold anger mirrored in his eyes.

"I'm shocked by what has happened here today," he said tightly, popping his riding crop against the smooth leather of his boot as they walked.

"On top of everything that happened at the party," he sighed, "you embarrass my son and my family further by remaining to deliver a . . . a slave baby."

Kitty could take no more. She stopped walking, turned to face him, and, not caring who heard, cried, "Mister Collins! Lest you forget, *I'm* the one who was insulted here today. Yes, I delivered that little baby. He's a human being, and I always help human beings when I have the opportunity—which is more than I can say for you. I'm shocked at *you*, Mister Collins, and if it takes going to war to free these people from the likes of you, then maybe I'm all for it!"

They stood there, glaring at each other, both afraid to say more.

Nathan, unable to stay out of the situation any longer, hurried to where they stood. He took Kitty's arm, "Come on, I'm taking you home."

"Yes, I think that's a good idea," Aaron Collins' blazing eyes did not waver from the young girl who returned his fury. "Take her home . . . get her off of Collins land . . . and do not bring her back here again."

"Father. . . ."

"I mean it, son. And further, I forbid you to call on this girl. She's not our kind."

"Thank God for that," Kitty whirled about and walked toward the waiting carriage, head held high.

❧ Chapter Five ❧

KITTY's escapades at the Collins party spread throughout the county like dandelions in a March wind.
John Wright laughed and said Aaron Collins got what he
deserved. Lena Wright was so upset she went to bed for
three days with a sick headache.

Kitty, herself, was a mixture of emotions. All things considered, she regretted only that she had obviously lost
Nathan. It had been three weeks since the party. November had turned to December, and the war clouds grew
darker and thicker. The air that hung over the countryside
was tense and strained. Everywhere, people talked of war.
Kitty could think only of Nathan, and the love she felt for
him. Now she realized that the emotion had smoldered
within her for years, and once it erupted, instead of something wonderful happening—the fire was choked out before
it had a chance to burn brightly.

She tried to stay busy around the farm. Winter was just
a few weeks away. In fact, any morning they could wake
up to sleet. Once in a while they even had a light snowfall.

The day Nathan came, Kitty had decided to get away
for a while with her thoughts, and she had saddled one of
their few horses and gone riding in the woods.

The oak trees were bare except for scattered clumps of
mistletoe high in their tops, but the pine trees were thick
and green with needles, the air fresh and sweet with their

fragrance. She rode along a gurgling creek, thrilling at the sight of a doe pausing to drink, then sprinting through the woods as her nostrils picked up a human scent.

Squirrels and chipmunks danced along the ground, gathering the last of the pecans for winter hoarding. A cardinal sang to her from a nearby branch. She looked at his bright red feathers and closed her eyes and made a wish. Her father said wishes made on redbirds usually came true.

"Kitty. . . ." her eyes flashed open at the sound.

He was just a few yards away from her, still hidden by the thick underbrush, sitting atop his horse.

Wishes on redbirds *did* come true, she thought with a rush of joy. "Oh, Nathan. . . ." his name escaped her lips as they both sprang from their horses at the same time, running across the brush with arms outstretched.

They came together, entwined, lips meeting for quick, anxious kisses—and then one so deep it took their breath away. Gasping, they drew apart. "I've been riding in these woods every day for weeks, waiting for a chance to speak to you," he said excitedly. "I thought you'd never show up, Kitty."

"I thought you never wanted to see me again."

He took her hand and sat down on the mossy velvet carpet beneath a huge old pine tree, pulling her down beside him. His arm slipped around her shoulders as he pulled her closer. "I had to see you, Kitty. I love you. I can't let you go."

Her heart was pounding. "But your father forbid you to see me, Nathan."

"I'll have to be honest and say that your name brings instant wrath when mentioned around our house. Mother is especially mad about the whole situation. She's moved Nancy in with us, determined to get us married before I get a chance to become involved with you. What they don't know is that I'm already very much involved."

"But your father won't let you call on me. . . ."

"Then we'll meet here, in the woods," he kissed the tip of her nose. "I'm not going to let anything stop me from loving you, Kitty, and if you love me, you'll be willing to slip out and be with me."

She thought a moment. Her father had said he thought

it had all happened for the best, that a union between her and Nathan Collins just wasn't meant to be. He further said that he disapproved but hadn't said so before, because he wanted her to make her own decisions. If she were to slip out to meet Nathan, it would be best to keep it a secret from everyone, including her poppa.

And then she remembered the clouds above. "Nathan, how long before we go to war? And what happens to us then?"

"War will come soon," he sighed, gazing toward the brook with worried eyes. "And you and I will be married before I go off to fight."

"Married?" she blinked at him.

He kissed her briefly, then smiled, "I'm not about to go off to war without a wife waiting for me. Already we're forming a company, calling ourselves the 'Wayne Volunteers.' We've got twenty-two men, with more expected to join up as the war comes closer. My father's going to pay for our uniforms—soon as we get the orders and know what they'll look like—he's having them made at a factory in Wilmington."

"Hey . . ." he snapped his fingers with enthusiasm, "Kitty, would you make our battle flag?"

"Battle flag?" she echoed blankly.

"Sure. Every company has to take a flag into battle. It's important. And when our company leaves for the war, Father says we'll have a big ceremony in Goldsboro, with bands and speeches, and everything. And you can present us with the flag.

"That's a good idea," he went on, more to himself than to her. "It will be the perfect way to let everyone know about us. You present the flag to me, because I've been chosen as our company sergeant. Of course, when we join up with the army to be established, I'm hoping to move right on up in rank."

He sounded proud, and Kitty felt it was justified. She always thrilled to his quiet, commanding good looks—the firm line of his jaw. But he was a man whose every fiber bowed to the dominance of his father, although every young man about was raised to be similarly obedient and respectful.

"I'll make your battle flag, Nathan," she murmured,

trembling with the love she felt for him and his nearness. She could feel the heat of his body against her skin, rising in unison with her own. "I love you, Nathan. . . ."

"And will you marry me before I go away?" he looked deep into her eyes, as though trying to reach the inner depths of her soul. "Will you be my wife?"

Marriage. The thought overwhelmed her. What would she do while he was gone? Only last week she had gone with Doc Musgrave to make his rounds, and they had stopped his carriage beneath a pecan grove to talk about the war. He had told her that he planned to work with Dr. Charles E. Johnson, who was expected to be named Surgeon General of the North Carolina troops. Johnson planned to locate a hospital in Goldsboro. Doc wanted her to help him as a nurse.

She told this to Nathan, who reacted as she feared he would. "A nurse? Oh, Kitty, I'd much rather you stay home with the other womenfolk. There will be plenty for you to do, I'm sure. The war shouldn't last long, but I don't want my wife going off to work in a hospital. That's not for ladies."

"Not for ladies," she echoed with bitterness. "How I hate those words, Nathan. Why should the fact that I'm a woman keep me from doing something I want to do? Doc has taught me so much about medicine. If I can help our men, I want to."

"We'll talk about that later, Kitty. If we get married, I'll want you to stay at home with the other women. It wouldn't be proper for you to do otherwise. And besides, once we *are* married, knowing my family, they'll try to make the best of the situation and accept you—if you'll let them."

He kissed her again, then said he had to go home. There was work to be done. He left her after they set a meeting date for the next afternoon.

And after he had gone, she sat there sorting out her thoughts. Doc Musgrave would need her. The Southern soldiers would need her. Nathan would have to understand this. When war came she would do her share . . . her part. If he couldn't understand that, then it would be best if they did not marry until after the war was over.

But she would make the battle flag for the Wayne Volunteers. She would do it secretly, and when the presentation was made at the ceremonies in Goldsboro, everyone would know that Nathan had spoken for her—that they were betrothed.

It was getting late, and Kitty brought herself out of her daydreaming to mount her horse and head back to the farm. It was chilly, and she was glad she'd slipped on an old woolen jacket of her father's. Smiling, she thought of the way Nathan had looked at her as he surveyed her clothing—the jacket, an old faded shirt, and a pair of her father's trousers with a rope belt to take up the slack. With her hair in long braids she did not make a very feminine picture, she knew, but Nathan must still find her attractive. He had just asked her to marry him, hadn't he?

As she rode out of the woods and into the rutted clearing of the field that led up to the farmhouse, Kitty could see several men on horses standing behind the barn. They formed a semicircle around her father. Digging her heels into the horse's flanks, she galloped across the field. If Nathan's father had discovered their meeting and was arguing with John about it, she needed to be there to tell them he had known nothing about it.

As she rode closer, she spotted the white stallion of Nathan's father, Aaron Collins. Orville Shaw was with him, and David Stoner, and two other men she recognized—William Brundy and Paul Creech.

They looked at her critically as she approached, except for David. David always warmed at the sight of Kitty, and now he smiled and nodded politely. Her father gave her a look that plainly said he'd rather she keep moving, but she ignored him, reining up her horse a few feet behind the others but close enough that she could hear the conversation.

"I'm stayin' out of the war if it comes," John Wright was saying, leaning on a pitchfork. "So you're wasting your time asking me to join up."

Aaron Collins had been staring contemptuously at Kitty, who easily returned his gaze. He turned back to John. "We'll consider any man who doesn't join us a traitor."

"Oh, be reasonable, Aaron," John snorted. "Everyone knows that North Carolina is divided on the war issue. There's just as many folks that don't want war as there are those who do. Just because you're a big landowner and you've got a lot of money, you think you can bully people into thinkin' like you do. You oughta know by now that you can't bully me."

Orville Shaw spat a wad of tobacco juice that landed with a splat near John's feet. John shot him a hate-filled look as Orville snarled, "Why don't you just get the hell out of this county and move on North to join the goddamned Yankees, Wright? We're gonna feel mighty nervous havin' a traitor around when the balls start flyin'. I don't mind dyin' for the cause, mind you, but I don't want to go out with a *traitor's* ball in my back." He spat again.

"That's enough out of you, Orville," John shook the pitchfork at him. "I said I was stayin' out of the fightin'. None of you need worry about me bein' a traitor. I just plan to stay out of all of it."

"And what about her?" Orville nodded toward Kitty, who had moved a little closer. "I reckon we're supposed to trust her, too, when the slaves are all but prayin' to her these days, since she saved that slave girl of Aaron's from a beatin' she deserved."

"Leave her out of it, Orville," David Stoner commanded in a tone that made everyone turn to look at him.

Orville's lips curled. "Naw, hell, I ain't leavin' her out of it. She's the reason my cousin, Luke, had to run away. Luke was only doin' his job, and she . . ."

"Orville, I said to leave her out of it!"

"I think we've wasted enough time here." Aaron straightened in his saddle, spurred his horse to take a few steps backward. "You think about what we said, Wright. When the war comes and North Carolina secedes and calls for troops—whichever comes first—we'll be expecting you to join up with us."

"You can 'expect' all you want to, Aaron," John yelled as they rode away. "I won't be forced into going against my principles, and my principles are dead set against this damned war!"

His last words were buried by the sound of the thundering hooves as they rode away.

Kitty slid down from the saddle. "What was all that about?"

"Oh, you heard enough to know they want me to join

that company they're forming. To hell with them. Aaron Collins doesn't like anyone that doesn't bend to his will. It's not that they want me to join that bad—he's just trying to prove a point."

He hoisted the pitchfork over his shoulder and started walking toward the barn. "I'm staying out of the war. I'm staying right here to tend my land, and they can do whatever they want. I'm having no part of it."

Kitty stared at the cloud of dust flying upward from the disappearing horses. Then she looked at her father as he walked away, shoulders slumped.

Could any of them, she thought painfully, not take a part if war came? She feared not. The war was going to affect all their lives. There would be no escape.

She could only pray that it would be over soon.

❧ Chapter Six ❧

THE icy winter rains came, and many afternoons Kitty was forced to sit in the drab living room of the farmhouse, staring morosely out the window, unable to meet Nathan in the woods. She had spent the time knitting Nathan a pair of socks for a Christmas gift. Usually, Lena slept in the afternoons, but on the occasions when she took her place in another rocking chair to whine and complain about her sad lot in life, Kitty would pull a shawl about her shoulders and make a dash for the privacy of the hayloft, where she would continue her knitting by the glow of a lantern.

It was five days before Christmas. The socks were almost finished. Kitty huddled in the cold barn hooking the yarn around the clicking needles, her thoughts on Nathan, wishing they were together. It grew harder and harder to control the heated emotions that sought to consume them each time they met. She thought of the previous afternoon, a Wednesday. It had been bitterly cold, and they'd huddled together beneath a blanket Nathan had brought along. Carried along by the tide that swept over them, he had lifted the skirt she was wearing, tugging at her pantalets. She felt the bulge of his manhood against her thigh as his lips had traced a path of fire down her neck, closer and closer to her breasts.

67

Only at the last moment had she mustered the self-control to push him away. Nathan had apologized, ". . . only for attempting to force myself on you, Kitty. I'll never apologize for wanting you so badly."

Her cheeks grew warm with the memory. She wanted him as much as he wanted her, but they had to wait for marriage. To do otherwise was unthinkable.

The barn door suddenly opened with a swoosh, banging against the wall outside with a loud crash. Kitty dropped her knitting, startled, reaching to blow out the lantern's flame.

"Kitty, girl, you in there?" John Wright stood in the doorway, the gathering twilight forming against his silhouette. "I know you're in here. . . ."

"Poppa?" Kitty scrambled through the hay in the loft, alarmed because her father sounded excited—and disturbed. "What's the matter? How did you know I'd sneaked out here?"

"There's a lot going on that I know about," he said gruffly. "But that's not what I've come to tell you."

She climbed quickly down the ladder, and then they stood facing each other, Kitty searching his face for some sign of what had disturbed him so. He took a deep breath and said, "I've just come from Goldsboro. I just got the news. South Carolina has seceded from the Union."

Kitty swayed momentarily. It was the beginning. Which state would be next? North Carolina? She asked her father, and he shook his head, slinging his arm across her shoulders as they stepped out into the wind and began walking toward the house.

"People in town were all excited, most of 'em. There's still plenty of folks who don't want war. I guess it's up to the legislators and the General Assembly to decide what we do next. Let's pray they've got the good sense to stay out of it."

When they reached the house, the kitchen was warm, and Lena had a pot of fish stew bubbling over the fire. "Well, what's wrong now?" she greeted them. "You both look as though Judgment Day is here and your names aren't in the Lamb's book."

"Might as well be." John slumped into a chair. "South Carolina has seceded from the Union. It's the beginning."

"Praise God!" she whooped with joy, then pointed her wooden cooking spoon at her husband, juice trickling down onto the clay floor. "If you're smart, John Wright, you'll get yourself over to Aaron Collins and tell him you're ready to join that company they're forming. They need all the men they can get, and they won't take kindly to your not going along with them."

Kitty looked at her father. He was scratching at his beard, which meant he was thinking deeply about something.

"Well, why are you sitting there?" Lena shook the spoon again. "It's bad enough that Katherine's unforgivable behavior at Aaron's party made her lose the best prospect for a husband she's ever had, without you bringing more shame on this house. You get yourself right on over there."

"I don't want to hear no more about it," he said in a fierce tone, glaring at his wife beneath bushy brows. "It's my decision, and I go along with my principles. I want no part of this fool war."

Sometimes, Lena either got so mad she couldn't speak, or she knew she'd driven John as far as she could for the time being. Either way, she lapsed into silence, for which Kitty was grateful as they started eating the greasy stew.

The winds howled, and they huddled silently near the fire, each of them lost in thought as the twilight turned to night.

Suddenly, there was the sound of horses thundering towards the house, and they sprang to their feet simultaneously, exchanging puzzled glances. John reached above the fireplace, and, taking musket in hand, walked to the door and opened it.

Kitty and her mother hovered behind him, gasping at the sight of Aaron Collins, David Stoner, Orville Shaw— and about ten others. Kitty's heart skipped as she saw Nathan on the edge of the group.

"Wright, this is your last chance," Aaron boomed as his great horse pawed and danced upon the ground. "We're taking our company to Wilmington. We've received word that the citizens there are going to capture Fort Caswell and Fort Johnston before the Yankees move in. Either you go with us . . . join us now . . . or face the consequences of your traitorous action."

Lena tugged at his sleeves and whispered, "Go with them, John, please. . . ."

He shrugged her off and said, "Hush, woman. Stay out of my business." To Aaron and the others he said, "I'll not be threatened. . . ."

"You goddamned coward," Orville Shaw shouted. "We oughta tar and feather you right here and now afore you join up with them Yankees!"

A ripple went through the crowd. Kitty stared straight at Nathan, begging him to do something, anything, to stop this madness. He glanced away, unable to take a stand against his own father in favor of hers, and he could not bear the way she was looking at him.

John slowly, but deliberately, lowered his musket to point in their direction. A few immediately backed their horses away, but Aaron and Orville stood their ground.

"Get off my property, you fire-eaters, or I'll blow you off! Go to war if that's what you're so damned eager to do, but leave peace-lovin' folks alone."

Wheeling horses about, they turned and charged into the night—except Nathan, who stood back. Kitty pushed past her parents and ran across the yard to cling to his legs and cry tearfully, "Nathan, why? Why do they insist on persecuting my father?"

"They fear he's a traitor, Kitty, I'm sorry," he looked down at her sadly. "Talk to him. See if you can change his mind, and remember, I can do nothing for him. But one thing I will do . . ." he spoke through gritted teeth. "I'll have no part in bullying him anymore. You can be sure that whatever happens, I have no part in it."

"If that's supposed to make me feel better . . ." she said bitterly.

"Kitty, I can't change their minds about your pa. I can't do it. Don't ask me to try. It's only asking for trouble. Now you talk to him. All they want is for him to join them. He's a fine, able-bodied man."

"That's not it and you know it," she said angrily. "Your father doesn't like anyone bucking his power—that's the problem! Poppa will stand up to him till the day he dies, and you can tell him that."

She started to turn, but he leaned down and grabbed

her arm, yanking her back toward him. John had been watching from the door, unable to hear their conversation, but he saw Nathan snatching at his daughter, and he yelled, "You get your hands off of her, Collins, or I'll put a ball in you . . ."

"Poppa, it's okay," Kitty called quickly, then turned to face Nathan. "You'd better go now. . . ." Anger was coursing through her veins, replacing the love she had felt moments before.

"All right," he released her. "Maybe my father is right. Maybe you are just like your stubborn old poppa. Maybe I'd best just let Nancy Warren make that battle flag for our company."

"That's fine with me, Nathan. I might have known you have no more honor than your father!"

She ran toward the house, and Nathan, suddenly contrite, slid quickly from his saddle to go after her. "Kitty, wait. I didn't mean it . . ."

She had reached the porch and darted past her father, who blocked the doorway. Nathan slid to a stop before him.

"Now that's about as far as you're going, Collins. You just get your tail off my porch and off my property. We've had a gut full of you and your daddy tonight. Now git!"

He gave the muzzle a shove, and Nathan sucked in his stomach and stepped back. He had no choice but to turn and go, misery washing over him.

"Now what was going on between you and Nathan?" Lena screeched as Kitty burst into tears.

"Leave her be." John replaced his musket in the rack above the kitchen fireplace. "A girl has some right to privacy, woman."

Lena turned, remembering what had started the whole turmoil of the evening. "Why didn't you go with those men? What's wrong with you, John?"

He sat down and slowly lit his corncob pipe, taking deep draws as the smoke curled around his face. Kitty had stopped crying and sat watching him. Finally, he said to the anxiously waiting women, "I heard about what they planned to do when I was in town. I overheard Orville Shaw talking about how they'd gotten wind that some men

71

in Wilmington wanted to take over those two forts near the mouth of the Cape Fear River, before the Yankees declared them Federal Forts. I'm not about to get involved in such madness."

Lena shrieked. "You're the one who's mad, John Wright. My God, I think you're a coward! I think you hide behind your so-called principles because deep down, you're scared to death of fighting! If I were a man, I'd take up arms to show my neighbors I intend to stick up for my state."

He got to his feet, held out a hand to Kitty, which she took. They started toward the door.

"Where do you think you're going, damn you! I'm not through talking to you, yet, you old fool."

"Well, I'm through listening," he said soberly, as they stepped onto the porch, the door slamming behind them.

It was cold. Kitty pulled her shawl tightly about her, grateful they were heading quickly for the barn. Once inside, it was a bit warmer. John lit a lantern, and they sat down on two kegs. "I had to get out of there," he said quietly. "Sometimes that woman nags me till I start seeing red things floating before my eyes, and it gets hard to breathe."

Kitty didn't know what to say. She understood how he felt, because Lena's nagging got to her, too, but she hated to speak out against her.

"You been slipping off to see Nathan Collins, haven't you?"

The question took her by surprise. She stuttered, "Why . . . why do you ask me that?"

He snorted. "I'm not the fool your mother thinks I am. I know what goes on around here."

"Are you mad about it?" She glanced at him from the corner of her eye, trying to read the expression on his face.

"No. I just hope you know what you're doing, Kitty. It's easy for a young girl with an anxious heart to be blinded to a lot of things. You probably find him handsome—exciting, and I know at your age your blood can run pretty hot."

She felt her face growing warm. It was very intimate talk that her father was dishing out. She didn't want him to think badly of her, so she blurted, "Poppa, we haven't done anything wrong. We'd never do *that*."

"His daddy forbid him to see you, girl. Where's your pride? Why'd you lower yourself to sneak off in the woods like an animal? What kind of man is he that he won't stand up to his daddy if he really loves you? Have you thought about that? Have you?"

She nodded, suddenly ashamed. "Yes, and I guess I just love him so much that I was willing to sneak to be with him. He's asked me to marry him. He had asked me to make the battle flag for his company. He was going to marry me before he went off to fight when war came. Now all that's changed." She dug in the dirt with her heels.

"No, he was running after you to straighten things out when I made him git. He'll be back."

". . . and you don't want me to see him anymore, do you, Poppa?" she raised tear-filled eyes to meet his sad gaze. "You don't like Nathan, and you don't want me to marry him, do you?"

He withdrew his pipe stem from his lips and looked at her incredulously. "Now, Kitty, you know I'm not going to tell you what to do with your life. You've got your own decisions to make. I'm just telling you what I think. When you get to be as old as I am, you'll learn to judge people by little things they say and do . . . or things they *don't* say and *don't* do. Personally, I think Nathan Collins hasn't got the guts to stand up to his father, and I think you're foolish to slip around to meet him. If he loved you the way you want him to, he'd stand up to Aaron and face him like a man."

He drew on his pipe once again. Kitty pulled her knees up against her chest.

"You aren't going to fight with the Wayne Volunteers, are you?" she asked quietly, wanting to talk about something else.

"No, I'm not. I don't aim to be pushed into doing anything I don't want to do, particularly something I don't believe in. I'm staying out of this war."

Kitty's mind was in a whirl. She loved Nathan, and she was sure that he loved her. But what Poppa said made sense. Nathan should stand up to his father. He was a grown man. It was an insult for him to expect her to sneak and meet him. She wasn't guilty of anything. What had she done except stand up for something she believed in?

If Aaron condemned her for that and felt it made her unworthy of his son, then damn him.

And if Nathan didn't love her enough to stand up to his brutish, powerful father—then damn him, too.

But the thought made her blink back tears.

Damn *me*, she thought. I love him.

❧ Chapter Seven ❧

CHRISTMAS came and went. It was a bleak time, with the talk of war gloomily overshadowing any attempt at holiday festivities. Kitty did not hear from Nathan, nor did she go to their meeting place in the woods on the chance that he might be waiting for her there. She needed time to think, to sort out the turmoil bubbling within her.

On New Year's eve, 1861, the citizens of Wilmington, North Carolina, worried over the war threats, wired the Governor of the state, John W. Ellis, to request permission to seize Forts Caswell and Johnston, located near the mouth of the Cape Fear River. John Wright brought this news from town, as well as the information that Aaron Collins and his men were down in Wilmington, waiting for the Governor's permission and threatening to help seize the important installations even if it did not come. Governor Ellis refused the request on the grounds that he had no authority to grant it, and the word from Wilmington was that the people were not about to be discouraged. They felt the seizure of the forts was important to their city's welfare and safety.

John brought home a newspaper that had a story in it about a man named W. W. Ashe heading up a commission that had visited the governor personally in Raleigh, begging for permission to take over the forts. Again, he had refused.

A few days into the new year, Aaron Collins and his band of men came home, only to rush back to Wilmington when word arrived that a United States Revenue Cutter with fifty men and eight guns was on its way to Fort Caswell. The next day, the forts were seized. When Governor Ellis learned of the action, he demanded the immediate evacuation of the forts, condemning the action as being taken without authority of law.

"I reckon Aaron will stay home and mind his own business for a while," John said, thumping a copy of the *Goldsboro Weekly Telegraph* that he was reading by firelight. Kitty sat nearby, listening intently. He said, "The Governor got in touch with President Buchanan and told him the whole story, and the President has sent word back through his Secretary of War, Joseph Hilt, that he has no intentions of garrisoning the forts in North Carolina. I reckon Aaron and his blood-thirsty bunch will have to wait a while longer before they have their precious war."

Lena put her sewing down and sighed dramatically. "John, why do you criticize Aaron and the other men who only want to protect our people? Just because you're a coward, you don't have the right to condemn those who have some guts. You just lack courage."

"Courage?" he threw back his head, laughing loudly. "The real test of courage, woman, is to live—not die. Believe me, it takes more courage for me to live standing up to what I believe in than it would for me to take up arms and fall in behind Aaron Collins as he goes searching for blood.

"Besides," he went on, "why do you think Aaron refuses to join with the Goldsboro militia group—the one they call 'The Goldsboro Rifles' that Dr. Craton organized? Because Aaron is blood-thirsty and ruthless and wants to run things his way, that's why."

"He's always been so charming, how can you say that?"

He snorted. "That was an act. Aaron Collins has always been ruthless."

"What do you think, Katherine?" Lena looked at Kitty. "After all, he's the one who forbid his son to court you, thanks to your unforgivable behavior at his party."

"I'd rather not talk about that."

"I can see why you wouldn't," she sniffed. "You're as big a disgrace as your father."

"Now if you want to call someone gutless," John folded the newspaper, "put the name on Nathan Collins. He's too weak to stand up to his father and court the girl he professes to love."

"Poppa, please," Kitty stood up, not wanting to discuss such things. "Let's not talk about this anymore."

"Nathan is respecting his father's wishes," Lena snapped, "and I can't say as I blame him, even if I would've liked to see Katherine marry up with someone from such a fine family. I can see why Aaron wouldn't want him courting Katherine after the way she behaved. . . ."

John and Kitty were no longer listening to her. The sound of hurried footsteps across the creaky wooden front porch had made John step to the mantel and reach up to get his musket.

There was a quick pounding on the door. "See who it is," John ordered Kitty in a whispered voice. "Then step back." He leveled the musket.

Kitty opened the door to find Jacob standing there with wide, frightened eyes, twisting his old straw hat in trembling fingers. Nodding to her, then to Lena, he looked past them to where John was lowering his gun. "Mastah, you better come . . ."

Without question, John left the room and returned quickly with his coat. Taking up his gun once again, he started to follow the old man. Kitty asked them where they were going, but her father refused to answer her questions as he followed Jacob off the porch and around the side of the house.

The door closed, and Lena took up her sewing again. "Oh, let them go. Who cares what they do? I stopped caring long ago."

There had been other nights when Jacob came for John unexpectedly late at night. Sometimes, Kitty suspected from the sounds that awakened her that John slipped out after everyone was supposed to be asleep. But something about this night, the frightened look in Jacob's eyes, alarmed her.

Kitty walked toward her room. "I think I'll go to bed.

I'm very tired tonight." She closed the door and in the darkness stripped off her muslin dress and changed quickly into overalls and an old shirt. Then, slipping on a warm jacket, she moved quietly to the window. Would it open without squeaking? She was in luck. It slid open, and the blast of cold January air made her shiver. Stepping over the sill and onto the ground below, she closed the window behind her.

She ran through the inky black night toward the rear of the house. The barn loomed darkly in the distance. If her father were there with Jacob, they had not lit a lantern.

She moved closer, then something caught her eye, off in the distance, toward the woods beyond the barn, where the trees and uncleared foliage ran thickly through a swamp. She had been there but once or twice, due to the danger of quicksand and moccasins. But now she could see a bobbing light disappearing into the denseness. Why did Jacob take John there at this time of night? Her skin was prickling apprehensively as she turned in that direction.

She ran, stumbling several times over mounds of dirt or roots, trying to keep up before the light disappeared altogether. She hated being so sneaky, but with so much turmoil going on in their lives, she felt a driving need to follow her father and find out what was going on. Despite the closeness they had always felt, there had been times when she had the feeling she did not know everything about her father's life. This proved that her feelings were correct.

She reached the swampland, groping slowly in the darkness that engulfed her. Once her foot slipped into something cold and mushy, and she stifled a scream. Jacob and John's movement had slowed, as they, too, worked their way through the intricate surroundings.

She heard the sound of voices and slowed apprehensively. She was still too far away to make out what they were saying, but she could hear a woman's voice, then the soft mewing sound of a baby crying. She had to get closer. A few more steps, very quietly, very slowly.

". . . you gave me no warning, Willie," that was John speaking, sounding upset. "No arrangements have been made. . . ."

"You've helped others that ran away with no warnin' . . . Mistah Wright, you gotta help Jenny and me. Mastah Collins, he going to take me to the block tomorrow and sell me, and I want to be with Jenny and our baby. We'll never see each other agin. Taint fair . . . taint right. We going to run away even if you don't help us. . . ."

"Now hold on." Her father's voice again. "I didn't say I wouldn't help you, did I? Just give me time to think a minute. If I can get you to Raleigh, there are people there who will take over and get you North, but how much time do we have? Jacob, how long have they been hiding here? Has anyone had time to miss them yet?"

"Nawsuh. Willie, he come to my cabin, and I went and fetched you. They ain't been gone too long."

The baby started to cry again. Kitty had quietly moved closer, and in the dim glow of the lantern she could see Jenny, the slave-girl whose baby she had delivered, pulling out a brown-skinned breast, pressing her nipple against the baby's eagerly waiting lips. He began to suck, and the crying stopped.

So it was true, Kitty thought feverishly. The accusations about her father were true. He *did* help runaway slaves. He *was* connected with the underground. But didn't he know how dangerous this was, she thought with gritted teeth and clenched fists. If Aaron and his men ever found out for sure, especially now, with the war hanging over them, men distraught and anxious . . .

"All right," John was saying. "I'll do everything I can. This swamp runs clear to the Neuse River, about ten miles or so, and I keep a flatboat hidden there. Jacob and I will take you there, and then I'll let Jacob take you on to Raleigh. You'll have to travel at night and hide out during the day. Jacob knows who to find once you get to Raleigh. You'll be safe once you get there, if we're lucky."

"Oh, bless you, bless you. . . ." Jenny cried. "Willie and me, we love each other. . . ."

"Now there's no time for thanks," John said gruffly. "Jacob, go back to your cabin and get a sack of corn dodgers and a water pouch. Jenny's nursin' that baby and she'll need to keep her strength up. It'll take you two or three nights to make Raleigh."

Jacob began moving through the brush, passing within only a few feet of where Kitty pressed herself against a tree trunk.

"As soon as he gets back, you can be on your way."

Kitty wondered what she should do. Her father would be angry because she was spying on him, so she couldn't step out and let herself be seen. If she tried to go back to the house now, she might be heard. There was nothing to do but wait in the murky darkness for them to leave, then find her way back.

Suddenly, a dog started barking. Killer! John had brought his old hound with him, and Kitty panicked as she realized he had picked up her scent and was alerting them to her presence. But no, she realized with fright, the barking was fierce, angry—certainly not the way the old dog would bark at *her*.

"Get down," she heard her father command just as footsteps and horses began crashing through the brush.

Every nerve in her body screamed with terror at the first sight of the torches being suddenly fired up against the black sky. She could see the white-hooded men on foot—on their horses, carrying their torches and clubs and guns, as they formed an inescapable circle around her father and the two slaves.

The Vigilantes! Dear God, no, the terrifying, feared-by-all Vigilantes had found them!

Frozen in terror, Kitty heard a man's booming voice, "Well, we finally caught you in the act, you traitorous son of a bitch. All this time, we've never been able to catch you. . . ."

John fired—and Kitty opened her mouth to scream just as a sweaty palm was mashed over her face. Twisting with her free hands, she fought to see what was happening, her blood flowing so rapidly through her body that she became dizzy. The old gun had misfired. Hooded men were grappling with her father, forcing him to the ground.

Kitty watched in horror, still fighting the hand that held her silent, as the baby was snatched from Jenny's arms. Willie started fighting but crumpled to the ground as a club came crashing down over his head. Jenny fought to get to her baby, as she, too, was felled by a swift blow from another club.

"Get them on those mules and take them back," someone was yelling. "Tie the baby on top of them. That trouble-makin' slave will be sold tomorrow, for sure, and we'll take the baby away from that woman to teach her a lesson. . . ."

Kitty twisted around, eyes bulging with shock as she realized it was Jacob holding her, tears streaming down his face in the flickering fire from the torches that reached the spot where they hid in the thick bushes. "We can't help him now," he whispered. "They'd hurt us, too. We can't do nothin' but hide here and pray they don't see us."

Killer had tried to defend his master but was struck with a club and lay somewhere still and quiet. There was no sound from John, either, as the men hoisted him atop another mule and began moving through the night, disappearing into the swamps.

Kitty was no match for the old negro's strength as he held her fiercely against his chest. She had to help her father. They would kill him now, for sure! And what about Jenny's baby? What would they do with him? They had to go for help! They couldn't stand by and let this horrible thing happen.

After what seemed an eternity, Kitty was released, and she whirled on Jacob screaming, "How could you, you old fool? How could you stand here and not help him after the kind of a friend he's been to you and your people? Are you crazy? Don't you know those murdering cutthroats will kill him? They caught him helping runaway slaves, for God's sake. You know they're going to kill him!"

"They'd kill us, too, missy. I'd have gone to help him if I hadn't seen you hidin' here after I sensed somebody was around and came back to warn Mistah John. But I had to keep you still. Those men would do somethin' terrible to a white woman interferin' in their business. Your daddy would've wanted me to keep you out of this. Now I gotta fetch Killer and see if he's dead, and I gotta get back and find help for your daddy, and you have, too."

Kitty waited in a frenzy, alternately cursing and sobbing, as Jacob went after Killer. He brought him back in his arms, limp, but still breathing. Then she followed him as he made his way expertly out of the swamp, knowing the way even in the pitch darkness. Once they reached the cleared land, she began running, stumbling, falling, picking herself up again.

She got to the barn and quickly lit the lantern just inside the door, then hurried to a stall and led out her father's horse. He was faster than her own, and she had to ride quickly. Jacob came in carrying Killer just as she finished saddling the horse and was mounting him.

"You stay here, Jacob," Kitty said, able to take command of the situation at last. "No need for them to come after you, too."

". . . but where you goin', Miss Kitty?" he looked up at her with frightened, tear-filled eyes.

"I'll find Doc Musgrave. He'll help me find others that will help."

She galloped out of the barn and down the path that led around the house and to the road beyond. The cold January wind sliced into her as her hair whipped in a frenzy about her face, but she was oblivious to anything but the driving need to find help for her father. The Vigilantes were vicious. They were evil, blood-thirsty men who could kill if the notion struck them. Everyone feared their wrath!

The three miles to Doc Musgrave's small house seemed endless. Kitty thundered the horse into the yard with such a commotion that Doc heard her and was emerging from the front door, lantern in hand, by the time she dismounted.

He stood there, nightshirt flapping around his ankles, eyes growing wider with each word that tumbled from her quivering lips. He ran trembling fingers through thin graying hair, pulled at his pointed mustache and beard as the gravity of the situation soaked into his sleepy state. Old, but alert, he nodded with squinting gray eyes and disappeared inside the house to return a moment later fully clothed, black leather bag in hand.

"They may have taken him to the slave cemetery down by the bend in the creek," he said, as she allowed him to mount the horse, then pulled her up behind him on the horse's rump. "We've found a few of their victims there."

But he was turning the horse in the opposite direction, and she tugged at his shoulder and yelled, "You're going the wrong way. The cemetery is back toward my house. . . ."

"We'll need help," he yelled, spurring the horse into a gallop. "In case they're not through with him. I'm going after David Stoner and his father."

"But David rides with Aaron Collins," she cried into the wind. "And a lot of people think Aaron is the leader of the Vigilantes. Poppa has said so."

"David would have no part in the Vigilantes, you can be sure of that."

The horse stumbled in the darkness, and for a moment, it looked as though both of them would go spilling onto the road. Regaining his footing, the horse slowed his pace, and Doc let him, fearing to go any faster lest he stumble in a rut and break a leg.

"Whoah. . . ." Doc pulled up on the reins, and just as Kitty was about to ask him why he was stopping, she heard the sound of hoofbeats coming toward them. "Who is it?" Doc shouted into the night.

"Allen Stoner and son David," the voice came back and Kitty breathed a sigh of relief. They rushed forward, horses pawing and prancing in the road. "We were coming after you, Doc. David just told me he couldn't keep quiet any longer. He knew the Vigilantes were going after John Wright tonight. They set up a trap to catch him helping some runaway slaves."

"Then it *was* a trap!" Kitty cried, and the two men saw her on the horse behind Doc for the first time.

"Kitty, I'm so sorry," David spoke anxiously, moving closer to her. "I couldn't say anything, no matter how bad I wanted to. The word is that they knew if that slave, Willie, was threatened with being sold, he'd take that girl who had his baby and high-tail it for whoever it is around here who helps the runaways get to the underground in Raleigh. Everyone figured it was your daddy."

"It was," she said miserably, wishing her father had stayed out of the whole mess. "I saw them come take him away in the swamps. I would've killed them with my bare hands if I could, but Jacob stopped me, made us hide. I came for help. . . ."

"Jacob was wise to hold you back," Allen Stoner said

tightly. "Now let's ride to that cemetery and see if we can put a stop to this madness."

They turned the horses, running as fast as they dared through the night. They reached the creek, following its edge as they made their way around dark, shapeless blobs of overgrowth, forced to move agonizingly slow.

"We have no light," Doc said in frustration. "How can we search for him if we can't see a hand in front of our faces?"

"If we wait till morning, he might be beyond help," Allen Stoner said quietly.

"If we just had a torch. . . ."

"Shhh! I hear something."

They reined the horses to a stop. And then they all heard it. A low, moaning sound—a sound filled with pain that wrenched Kitty to the very depths of her soul. She almost knocked Doc from the saddle as she swung her leg over to leap to the ground, falling to her knees as she landed in a pock hole.

"Up there," someone shouted. "Oh, God, get him down quick!"

The men were running toward the moaning, gasping shroud of black that seemed to hang suspended in the air. There was the sound of a knife sawing into rope—a crumpling body falling into waiting arms—sudden gurgles rushing in fresh air in great gulps.

"Is he alive?"

"Yes, he's alive. Can't you hear him struggling to breathe?"

"But he's barely alive."

"Doc, do something. . . ."

Kitty had bitten her lower lip until her mouth filled with the saltiness of her own blood. Forcing wooden legs to move forward, she could see their shadowy hulks bending over her father's body.

". . . got to get him back to the house where I can see to tend to him," Doc was saying. "Easy now . . . get him on the horse. Somebody get a blanket to wrap him in. The dirty cowards beat him naked."

With each movement of the horse, John moaned. The sound got weaker and weaker as they moved as fast as they dared. Kitty sat behind David on his horse, arms about his waist to hang on, her head pressed against his back as she sobbed softly . . . and prayed.

Doc's wife, Kate, was waiting. Many lanterns were glowing softly as the men carried John in and placed him on the wooden table Doc used in the front room he called an office.

Kitty took one look at the bloodied, shriveled flesh and stumbled outside, vomiting. David went with her, holding her on her feet as her sagging knees threatened to buckle any moment.

John was beaten from head to toe, his body stripped of all his clothing. The lashes of the whips and knotted ropes had dug into the flesh again and again, leaving it in strips, threads of muscle hanging from gaping wounds, blood and matter oozing forth among the shreds of skin. Even his genitals had been the target of many blows—swollen and blackened and bloodied with the Vigilantes' abuse.

"He's in bad shape, Kitty, real bad," Doc told her in a sad voice when she returned to the room. "He's lost a lot of blood, and being exposed like that with so many open wounds might give him the fever. I've got my special ointment, and I'll put as much of that on him as I can tonight, and we'll just have to wait till morning and see what happens.

"I'm sorry. . . ." he added quietly.

Someone had pressed whiskey to John's lips, and after a few sips, he had mercifully sunk into unconsciousness. Doc was then able to apply more ointment. "He couldn't stand for me to touch him if he was awake. Goddamn them, they tried to kill him!"

"No, I don't think so," David said, still holding onto Kitty. "They'd have gone ahead and hanged him if they meant to kill him. They left him barely alive, for an example to anyone else who thinks about helping runaway slaves—and who goes against the way they think."

Doc had to agree. "Yes, I hear slaves rebelling is getting to be a problem, with the war talk. They made an example all right . . . an example of the kinds of no-good sons of bitches that they really are."

Kitty remembered something and twisted away from David, turning her wrath upon him. "You *knew*, David. You knew they planned to do this to my daddy, and you waited too late to do anything to help him. You're just as bad as they are!"

"No, Kitty, I only heard the rumors," his face grew pale. "I got worried and told Daddy, and he said we should check on it."

He held out a hand to her, but she slapped it away, then reached to send a stinging palm across his face. "You're as guilty as they are. And I'll bet Nathan knew, too."

"No, Nathan didn't know. . . ." They all turned astonished faces to the open doorway where Nathan stood, eyes angry, lips set grimly. "I didn't know a damn thing till the noise from the slaves screaming woke up everybody in the house."

He walked slowly into the room, toward the table where John lay unconscious. He muttered an oath under his breath, running nervous fingers through his sandy blond curls. Turning toward Kitty, a stricken look on his face, he gestured helplessly, "By the time I got dressed and ran to the slave cabins, the Vigilantes had already killed Willie —hanged him. They beat Jenny so bad they say she won't live. Nobody knows what they did with her baby."

Kitty swayed, and David took her back into his arms. Nathan saw it and frowned.

"I heard the slaves whispering about the white man that was supposed to have been hanged for helping Jenny and Willie," he continued, "and I figured out what was going on. I started for John's house and passed here and noticed all the lights and horses. . . ."

He crossed to where Kitty and David stood, unable to control himself any longer. Yanking her from David's arms he wrapped his own about her and said, "Kitty, darling, I'm sorry. I didn't know. You've got to believe me. If I had known, I would've warned your daddy. But no one told me, 'cause they knew I'd tell."

John stirred, moaned softly, and they all turned to stare at him. He opened his eyes slowly, then closed them, and Kitty screamed. "It's all right," Doc said quickly, stepping forward to fasten his fingers around John's wrist to feel for a pulse. "He isn't dead. He just passed out again. That's good. Let him sleep. He won't hurt that way."

Doc turned worried eyes upon Kitty. "He's hurt bad,

honey. He may not live. Somebody's got to tell your mother."

"I . . . I'll go," she said after a moment of silence, her body shaking. "It's best that I be the one to do it."

Nathan spoke up quickly. "I'll go with you. My horse is right outside. We'll go to your house and bring your mother back in your daddy's wagon."

✺ Chapter Eight ✺

KITTY had been too distraught on the ride home to talk. She had clung to Nathan's back and wept silently as the horse trotted through the night along the rutted dirt road.

Lena had reacted when told about John's beating in the way that Kitty had expected. She went into hysterics, and Nathan had to carry her out to the wagon once he had it hitched to a team of mules. Kitty felt scornful of her behavior, knowing it was only an act for Nathan's benefit. She didn't love her father. How could she, the way she treated him?

When they had arrived at Doc's, Lena had scrambled down from the wagon, not waiting for Nathan to help her, and she ran into the house screaming at the top of her lungs. Doc, in a show of strength despite his wiry size, met her at the door and pushed her back onto the porch, gruffly ordering her to calm down or he would not let her enter. Subdued, finally, Lena allowed Kate Musgrave to lead her back to the kitchen for a cup of warm broth before letting her see John.

The night wore on, and as an orange sun rose against the watermelon sky that heralded a new day, Doc told Kitty he was going to need more laudanum to still John's pain as he was starting to awaken. "I've done what I can with the salve, but his whole body is just one big mass of wounded flesh. I'll need some opium for the laudanum."

Kitty nodded and got to her feet. She had been sitting at the fireplace hearth, Nathan hovering anxiously nearby. "Where are you going?" he asked as she started for the door.

"To pick some poppies from the shed where Doc grows them for his opium," she answered dully. "In winter, he has to grow the flowers indoors or the cold will kill them."

"You know how to make opium?" he asked incredulously.

"Of course, she does," Doc snapped. He snorted before returning to where John had been put to bed on a soft, goose-feather mattress.

Nathan followed Kitty to the back of Doc's house, where she crossed the dirt yard to an old wooden shed. Stepping inside, they could see rows of poppies in the early morning sunlight that filtered through an open window, giving them warmth.

Kitty took the handle of a woven straw basket that hung on a nail near the door, then knelt among the poppies. "You have to pick the heads, just after they've ripened," she explained.

"How'd you learn to do that?" Nathan wanted to know.

"Oh, Doc taught me when I was real little. He taught me all about making medicine from plants. I know how to make quinine from the dogwood tree."

"Quinine from dogwood trees?" he asked, amazed. "I never knew that. Do you use the flower? They only bloom at Easter. . . ."

"No, not the flower. We use the berries that come in the fall. We make enough quinine then and hope it will last for a year. Doc says the bark has alkaloid—which has something called 'cinchona and Peruvian bark' in it.

"Did you know that the cordial you take for dysentery is made from blackberry roots?" she asked as she searched the poppies for ripe bulbs, anxious to talk about something to take her mind off her father for a little while. "And you can also make it from ripe persimmons, but we don't have many of those around here. Doc also taught me how to make an extract from the barks of the wild cherry, dogwood, poplar, and wahoo trees, that you can use for chills. Then for coughs, we make a syrup from the leaves and roots of the mullein plant and globe flower. Castor oil, of course, comes from the castor bean."

"And you know how to do all this?" he was unable to keep the shock and amazement from his voice.

"What's so strange about that?"

"Well, most young ladies . . ."

"Most young ladies make me sick," she snapped. "I told you before, Nathan, I love medicine. I love helping sick people. You find that shocking, but I don't. Women have the right to do what they want with their lives, just as men do."

He shook his head in wonder. "I . . . I guess you have a point, Kitty."

She stood up, the necessary supply of poppy heads in her basket. "I know I do. My father agrees with me," and she began to blink back tears as she thought of the condition he was in.

Hurrying back to the house, she sat down at the kitchen table with Kate to extract the opium from the poppies. Nathan watched as they used a large-sized sewing needle to pierce the bulbs, catching the opium gum in a cup.

They finished their chore and Doc came in to finish making the laudanum. "Go sit by your father," he told Kitty. "If he wakes up, I want you to get your mother out of there. No telling what she's liable to do—probably start lambasting him for helping those runaways."

Nathan went with her, and she was grateful for his presence—and his strength when she needed it. They stared down at John's body, covered in deep cuts surrounded by purple and blackened trenches of torn flesh. There was one deep cut that looked as though the very tip of the whip had slashed right into his eye, and the eyelid was puffed out in a fleshy, swollen bag of broken blood vessels and bruised skin.

"He's going to lose the sight in the eye," Kitty said with painful resignation. "He's going to be blind in that left eye."

"Maybe not," Nathan said, patting her shoulder to give her comfort. "Maybe when the swelling goes down, it will

be all right. He is going to have some bad scars, though."
He shook his head as his eyes swept over the mutilated
body.

Kitty's head snapped up at the sound of approaching
horses. "Someone's coming. . . ." She started to get up, but
Nathan pushed her back down.

"I'll see who it is." He crossed to a window and peered
out, then, giving her an anxious look said, "Kitty, it's my
father."

She leaped to her feet, face flooding with the redness
of anger. "How dare he come here? Everyone knows he's
one of them . . . probably the leader."

"No, you don't know that's true," he said quickly. "That's
only a rumor, Kitty. No one knows who the Vigilantes are.
I don't believe he'd be here if he were a part of this, and,
besides, he was asleep at home last night, just as I was."

She could hear voices through the closed slat door—the
solicitous tone of Aaron Collins—the gushing voice of her
mother who had a special voice she used around those she
considered "society folk."

Kitty opened the door and stepped out, lips set in a
tight line. Aaron turned and bowed slightly, resplendent in
a fashionable black coat, his pleated shirt topped by the
widest and most elegant of black cravats. He wore mustard-
colored trousers, and his boots were polished to a glossy
sheen. He looked at her with eyes that reminded her of
Nathan, his salt and pepper hair curling about his ears
the way Nathan's did. But there the resemblance of father
and son ended. She prayed that the man she loved could
never be as ruthless as his father.

"Miss Kitty, I came here to tell you how it grieved me
to hear of the unfortunate beating your father suffered at
the hands of the Vigilantes. All of the county is upset that
such a thing has happened. Is there anything I can do to
help?"

"Oh, that's kind of you. . . ." Lena gushed.

Kitty cut her off by snapping, "Do you really expect me
to believe you are grieved, Aaron Collins, when it was
your slaves my father was helping to escape?"

"Surely you don't think *I* had anything to do with this?"

"I only know my father might die because of those murdering bastards," she cried angrily. "And I know everyone says you are the leader of the Vigilantes. How can you have the gall to come here and pretend sympathy?" She was shaking in her wrath, and Nathan stepped forward to clamp steadying hands on her shoulders.

"Believe me," Aaron spoke quietly. "I was home in my bed asleep when the screaming of the slaves woke me up. By the time Nathan and I got to the cabins, Willie was dead, and the girl called Jenny terribly beaten." His voice lowered as he added, "She died this morning. They haven't found the baby."

Kitty gasped, turning her face away as she blinked furiously to keep the tears back. She would not let them see her cry.

"I would suggest," she said, mustering composure as she turned back to face him, "that you send your men out to search for the Vigilantes and see that they are charged with murder, since you pretend to be so concerned by all that has happened."

"My men are already out asking questions," Aaron assured her. "It was not anyone's place to pursue the runaways but mine, since they belonged to me. And it was certainly not their place to kill them."

Through the partially closed door, the sound of John's anguished moaning reached them. "I must go to my father," Kitty said. "Excuse me." And she turned and went back into the bedroom, closing the door tightly behind her.

Doc was already there, ready with the laudanum he hoped would ease the pain. He lifted John's head with one hand, spooning in the thick liquid with the other. John swallowed, and Doc lowered his head back to the pillow.

"Poppa, can you hear me?" Kitty asked anxiously. "You're here at Doc's, and we're going to take care of you. You're going to be all right."

". . . tried to kill me. . . ." he whispered so low they had to bend their heads to hear the words being forced through swollen, purple lips. ". . . passed out, and they kept . . . beating me. . . ."

"John, you need to rest," Doc spoke firmly. "You need to build up your strength. You're hurt bad. . . ."

". . . goin' to kill them. . . ." he whispered. "So help me, God. . . . I'll get them."

"Poppa, hush now," Kitty cried, her heart constricting with pain.

Doc forced down another spoonful of laudanum. ". . . my dog . . ." John moaned then, remembering. ". . . . Killer."

"He's going to be all right," Kitty told him, remembering Jacob telling them about the old hound when they had returned to get Lena. "Jacob says he'll be fine."

He closed his eyes, sighed, and grew very still. She looked at Doc anxiously, who nodded, "He's just asleep. The laudanum should knock him out for several hours, and he needs his rest. That's what's going to save him, honey—rest and getting his strength back so those wounds will heal. We'll keep watch to make sure if infection does set in, we're ready. Now why don't you let Nathan take you home so you can get some sleep? You've been up all night, and you're starting to show signs of wear. It won't do your daddy any good if you collapse. And I'd like to get your mother out of here, too. She's no good to anybody with that constant harping of hers."

Kitty nodded. She had no intentions of going home to stay, however. But she would take Lena there and leave her.

Returning to the hallway, she saw her mother on the porch bidding goodbye to Aaron Collins. She came inside as Nathan hung back to speak privately to his father. Kitty wondered what that was all about. Then Lena was standing in front of her, eyes shining as she said, "He had nothing to do with all this, Katherine, and he's so upset by it that he wants to make up for the way he's been feeling toward you. He says he'll have no objections in the future to Nathan courting you."

"Oh, Mother, you didn't say anything to him about that!" Kitty was mortified.

"I certainly did," Lena was belligerent. "I have a right as your mother to be concerned about your future. I still have hopes that you and Nathan will get married, and when that happens, you'll thank me for everything I've done."

"I'll thank you to stay out of my life and let me run it." Suddenly she felt very weary and tired. "Look, we're going home now. Doc has given Poppa something to make him sleep for a long time. There's no point in you being here to get in the way. People will be coming soon for Doc's regular office hours, anyway, so we need to get home and see to things there."

Lena's lips tightened. "Folks will wonder why I'm not at my husband's side. . . ."

"They'll know you need your rest, too, besides, some of your neighbors might be calling on you once they hear what's happened."

Her mother's eyes glittered with excitement. "That's true. I'll need to have some pie and coffee to serve them, and I'd better get home and get to baking."

Kitty shook her head and sighed. Only her mother would turn such a happening into a social gathering. They moved onto the porch, and she told Nathan they were ready to go home. "As soon as I get Mother settled, I'll ride back with you so I can look after Poppa. Kate will be needed to help Doc with his patients when they start coming in."

Her mother hurried inside, and Nathan and Kitty ran to the barn to check on Killer's condition. The old dog lay in a corner on a pile of straw, Jacob sitting beside him looking sad and dejected. "He going to be all right," Jacob told them. ". . . got a bad place on his head that'll take some time to heal, but he gonna live. You tell Mastah John that. He'll want to know about his dog. . . ."

Kitty told him that John had already awakened and asked about him, and Jacob nodded quietly and said, "I'm gonna keep on prayin', Miss Kitty. Your pappy's too fine a man to die. We need him. . . ."

"Yes, Jacob, we do need him, and God isn't going to let him die." Blinking back tears, she let Nathan lead her from the barn to where his stallion was waiting.

He mounted the horse, then pulled her up behind him. "I really should change clothes," she said dully, "but I want to get back to Poppa."

"You're fine as you are," he assured her, starting the horse off in a gentle gait. "I'll come back this afternoon and get some fresh clothes for you. That way you won't have to be around your mother anymore today."

"That will be a relief," she almost laughed.

It was a clear, beautiful day, despite the chill of the air. A thin coating of frost covered the fields, and patches of ice could be seen in the water that ran in the ditches alongside the road. Kitty shivered as the wind rushed at them, cutting into her. Nathan felt her chill and spurred the horse into a faster gait.

Ahead, the path that led alongside the creek and into the negro cemetery loomed up at them. Impulsively, Kitty squeezed Nathan and cried, "Nathan, turn down that path. Let's go back to the cemetery, and maybe we'll find something that will tell us who was in on it."

"Now, Kitty, there's no need . . ."

"Please! If you don't, I'll jump off this horse and go on foot."

Knowing she meant it, he reined the horse to turn into the brush-shrouded path. Low-hanging branches slapped at them, and they were forced to move slowly along a path that was used only rarely by slaves burying their dead—and they usually made the journey on foot, carrying the wooden box that served as a coffin upon their shoulders.

The trip into the woods had probably been even more difficult last night, Kitty thought, but she hadn't noticed—intent on finding her father.

They moved along the creek, where the brush was trampled by the hooves of many horses. "See!" Kitty pointed excitedly. "We didn't notice in the dark last night how the weeds are all trampled. The Vigilantes rode in here."

"They probably came down the creek," Nathan commented. "It would've been easier riding at night than through the woods. The creek runs all the way from the woods in back of your place, remember?"

She nodded.

They came to the cemetery. Kitty felt her spine tingle as she looked at the sight before her—crude, rotting, makeshift crosses that the slaves used to mark the graves of their dead. In several places the ground was sunken and caved-in where the crosses stood, evidence of the fulfillment of the Good Book's proclamation of "ashes to ashes . . . dust to dust." Wincing, she saw splinters of wood sticking up out of one of the gaping holes—and a glimmer of white bone.

"Don't they ever come here and fill these graves in?" she whispered, not really knowing why she felt it necessary to lower her voice.

"Periodically," Nathan answered drily, himself moved by the awesome sight. "They don't dig the graves very deep to start with, and sometimes if they're real poor, they don't even put the body in a coffin—just wrap it in a shroud. Let a hard, soaking rain come along, and it doesn't take long for the body to rot and the ground to cave in. They'll be coming here in a day or two to bury Willie and Jenny, and they'll see what shape the place is in and do something about it."

Ahead of them loomed the massive oak tree, and from one of its lower branches swung the remnants of the rope where John had been found swinging, half-dead. Kitty stared at it, transfixed as thoughts of the horrors that had taken place here moved through her mind.

Nathan reined his horse to a halt, got down, then turned to help Kitty dismount. She walked to the spot and swallowed hard, swaying momentarily as she pointed to the ground nearby. "Blood," she said in a choked voice, "and there . . ." She pointed to the tree trunk, where bits of flesh and dried clots of blood clung to the rough bark. "They tied him there to beat him before they hung him."

Nathan was beside her to hold her and give her strength, but she pushed him away, eyes intent upon the ground, around the tree, searching for any kind of a clue to the identity of the Vigilantes.

But she found nothing.

"Kitty, you didn't expect to find anything, did you?" Nathan asked her worriedly. She looked so strange, walking about, a wild look in her eyes. "What did you think they'd leave behind? A glove? A spur?"

"I was only hoping to find something that would tell us who they are." She felt defeated. Sighing, she turned to where Nathan's horse waited, pawing the ground impatiently. "We might as well be on our way. If Poppa wakes up, I want to be with him."

He helped her mount, then turned the stallion toward the path that led alongside the gurgling creek. Kitty slumped against him, eyes half-closed as she looked down at the swirling, curving patterns in the ice that lined the bank.

Suddenly she sat straight up. Could it be? No. . . . No,

they wouldn't . . . they couldn't . . . not even the lowest form of animal could do such a thing.

She screamed, the sound ripping from the very depths of her soul, the stillness of the winter morning exploding as her shrieks filled the quiet air. Nathan, stunned, jerked the reins so hard that the great animal beneath him reared up on his hind legs, forelegs pawing the air above him in fright.

Losing her grip on Nathan's waist, Kitty went sliding over the horse's rump to land on the ground, quickly twisting sideways to escape the dancing hooves as Nathan fought to bring the horse under control.

"Kitty, for God's sake, what's wrong?" he watched her crawling on her hands and knees toward the edge of the creek. His eyes followed her horror-stricken gaze.

There, in the creek, weighted down by a large rock, he could see something dark beneath the surface. Slowly the shape took form. The gurgling clear waters glistened over the shriveled brown skin, tiny arms and legs bobbing in the ripples.

It was Jenny's baby.

❧ Chapter Nine ❧

THE inevitability of war hung over the South like a giant, black thunder cloud, threatening a storm from the North at any time, but no one was quite sure just when the cloud would break upon the lands.

On January 9, 1861, Mississippi seceded from the Union, followed by Florida the next day. The secession of Alabama came on January 11th, and Georgia made her announcement on the 19th. Extreme pressure in the face of these events was put on the General Assembly of North Carolina to call a convention. The Conservatives, who opposed secession, diminished in number, and on January 29th, the Assembly adopted a bill directing the people of the state to vote on the question of calling a convention and to elect 120 delegates.

Both radicals and conservatives worked hard to gain control of the convention, set for the 28th day of February. To the surprise of many, the vote was a victory for the conservatives, and the proposal for a convention was defeated.

But neither side accepted the result as final. Everyone knew that North Carolina would soon have to make a definite decision on whether to join her sister states in secession—or to remain a part of the Federal Union. The vote not to call a convention merely prolonged that decision.

Winter dwindled into spring as April warmth came to kiss the frozen South awake.

Kitty sat on the back-porch steps, knees hugged against her chest as she stared toward the woodlands and the beauty of the dogwood trees bursting in glorious popcorn blossoms of beauty. Leaves were budding on the trees, and a warm gentle breeze blew against her face. Spring was upon them . . . planting time had arrived.

Turning her head slightly, she could see her father sitting motionless in a rocking chair. His face bore the flesh-gouged scars of the whip; his left eye was covered with a black cotton patch. The vision in that eye was lost forever. He was hunched over, bearded chin tucked against his chest, but she knew the rope burns were there around his neck, caused by the hanging. Beneath the clothes he wore she knew there were more scars that would always be there, but none as deep and penetrating as the one that seemed to have warped the very depths of his mind and soul.

He seldom spoke anymore. And he did nothing but shuffle from his bed to the table to the back porch, where he would sit the entire day staring out into nothingness, only to reverse the procedure when the sun went down, shuffling to the table—then to bed. One day blended into the next.

His spirit was gone, and Kitty was heartsick because she could not bring it back. It had taken long, agonizing weeks for him to recover from the sadistic beating he had suffered. And during those weeks he had said nothing, merely lying in bed and staring up at the ceiling, as though he had removed his consciousness from the present.

He no longer heard Lena's harping, and if he heard Kitty's gentle coaxing to get him to talk to her, he showed no sign. How could he shut her out, too, she thought painfully, when they had always been so close.

Doc said a beating such as John took does strange things to some men. Only time could heal those wounds deep inside, that can only be felt, and not seen. More and more Kitty worried that her father's wounds upon his soul and his mind would never heal.

"Poppa, it's time to start the planting," she said to him,

turning to see if he acknowledged her remark. He blinked his eyes and stared straight ahead.

"Poppa, we've got to plant our garden, or there won't be anything to eat. . . ."

Slowly, perhaps because the pain was so evident in his daughter's voice, he turned to look at her. His remaining eye was watery. His words came out a croaking whisper, "It doesn't matter anymore, girl."

She scrambled across the rough plank floor of the porch to wrap her arms around his knees and cry, "Oh, Poppa, it does matter. Life has to go on. What happened was terrible, I know, but we've got to go on. I'll help you with the planting. We'll start a new life. . . ."

"No," he shook his head from side to side. "I won't be here. It won't matter about me."

Kitty withdrew her arms and covered her face with trembling hands, tears springing to her eyes. He could not be reached. He was in another world, not this one, and it was impossible to communicate with him.

At the sound of a horse approaching, Kitty sat up straight, waiting anxiously, but John just stared straight ahead. If he heard the hoofbeats, he did not give evidence of the fact.

Nathan came around the corner of the house, grinning broadly and waving. Kitty's heart warmed as it always did when he appeared. "Come with me to Goldsboro," he cried jubilantly, "everyone is going to town to wait at the telegraph office for word on Fort Sumter."

She stared at him, puzzled. Since early dawn, she had noticed more activity than usual on the main dirt road in front of their house, but lost in thought about her father, she hadn't really wondered about the reasons for such unusual traveling by her neighbors.

"Haven't you heard, Kitty?" He sounded impatient. "Our forces are bombarding Fort Sumter in South Carolina."

"No," she shook her head slowly. She didn't know anything about it. This was the first time she had seen Nathan in over a week. It had been raining, and everyone had stayed indoors. On days when the sun shone he had been busy with the planting in the Collins fields.

He dismounted, and, still holding his horse's reins,

propped one foot on the bottom porch step. Leaning forward and looking at John, he nodded, "Good morning, sir."

John stared straight ahead and did not acknowledge his presence.

"Still the same, huh?" Nathan looked at Kitty. "Do you think he's ever going to come out of it?"

"Please, Nathan," she whispered anxiously, "Don't speak of him as though he's just a . . . a thing. He can still hear."

"I'm sorry."

"Now tell me about Fort Sumter. We don't get a paper now that Poppa doesn't go into town. Jacob never thinks to buy one, and we don't know what's going on unless someone drops by to tell us."

"Well, it seems that the Confederates in South Carolina felt that that United States flag flying over that Federal fort near the mouth of Charleston Harbor was just more than they could take. Now that they're no longer part of the union and consider themselves an independent state, they don't want a foreign flag, as they call it, flying in one of their harbors. They asked the Yankees to evacuate, but the commanding officer there, Major Anderson, I heard his name was, sent word that he was going to keep the flag flying and he'd never give up the fort. One of father's men came during the night to tell us that the Confederates were firing on the fort."

Nathan's handsome face was flushed with excitement, but Kitty felt a strange lump in the pit of her stomach—a feeling of foreboding that this latest development just might be the breaking point for the South.

"Come along," he urged her. "I'll help you saddle a horse. Let's go to town and wait with everyone to see what happens."

She chewed her lower lip as she shot an anxious glance at her father. His expression had not changed. It was as though he were dead. She shivered. Anything was better than spending another day sitting listlessly on the backsteps staring out at the empty, hungry fields.

"All right." She got to her feet, smoothed out the cotton trousers she wore. "Let me change into something suitable. I can't ride into town looking like this."

She hurried inside, past her mother, who started asking questions. "I haven't time to explain," she said, reaching for a soft blue muslin dress she had just finished sewing.

Kitty hurried back outside, Lena behind her, and Nathan began to lead his horse toward the barn, falling into step beside Kitty, who was anxious to get away from her mother.

Nathan saddled the horse that John once rode, and they hurried toward Goldsboro. "I wanted you with me today," Nathan called to her, grinning. "When a man hears good news, he likes to have the woman he loves at his side."

"And she likes to be at his side," Kitty called back as they galloped into the wind, faces flushed excitedly. "I do love you, Nathan."

The road was crowded with wagons and carriages moving toward town. And by the time they reached the main avenue through Goldsboro—Center Street—it was obvious that everyone in the county was there to crowd around the telegraph office to hear the latest word from South Carolina.

Men jostled and tipped their jugs of whiskey and called happily to each other. Women stood in the crowd with their children beside them, heads bonneted in the bright April sunshine. A band was set up near the train station playing the new song everyone was so emotionally charged by, the tune called "Dixie."

It was a festive, happy occasion. A celebration, Kitty thought as she marveled at the excited milling people. She couldn't remember ever having seen so many people gathered at one time in revelry. Caught up in the tide of joy, she sought Nathan's hand, and he squeezed strong fingers about hers, leaning to kiss the tip of her nose.

Kitty noticed that some of the people, however, wore expressions of deep concern and sadness, obviously not sharing in the revelry. The conservatives, she decided. The ones, like her father, who thought war was for fools. If he were here today, John would be standing with them, she knew.

They passed the midway point on Center Street where the slave market, called Washington Tower, stood. Kitty saw that no auction was being held that day. She wondered where Nathan was leading her, for he seemed to have some goal in mind as they waded through the endless sea of bustling people.

Stepping up on the boardwalk, Nathan shoved her through one final throng and into the open door of Gidden's Jewelry store. "What are we here for?" she asked, as he looked down at her, grinning.

A clerk came forward, and Nathan waved an arm ceremoniously. "I want a wedding ring," he said happily. "And I want my bride to pick it out herself."

"Oh, Nathan," she cried, swaying, trying to grasp what was happening. "It . . . it's too soon."

"No, it isn't too soon," he put his arms about her and kissed her soundly, then stood back rocking on his heels and grinning like a small boy. "I love you, and I want to marry you as soon as possible, and today is the day we get your ring."

"Kitty, I thought I saw you come in here," Doc Musgrave boomed as he stepped inside the jewelry store. "I need to talk to you. Been meaning to come by and check on your pa, but it seems like with the change in season, everybody in the countryside has come down with the croup. I've been up night and day."

"You should have let me go with you to help," she said quickly.

"No, I figure you're needed with your pa," he had removed his old cotton hat, and his face took on an expression of sadness. "If he ever comes out of it, it'll be because of you, not your ma. I think her nagging just sends him further and further away from the world around him. Is he any better at all?"

She hated to tell him that he wasn't. "He did speak this morning when I told him we had to plant the garden or we wouldn't have anything to eat. He said it didn't matter, because he wouldn't be here, anyway."

Doc pursed his lips beneath his bushy gray mustache. "Beat the spirit right out of that man, they did. John Wright was one of the most courageous men I knew. Never afraid to speak his mind if he believed in something. . . ."

Nathan shifted his weight from one foot to another impatiently as he said, "Doc, if you don't mind, we've got some business to take care of in here, and it's rather important."

"Well, I won't keep you," he flicked his eyes over Nathan, registering his dislike for the young man. "I've got important business, too, with Kitty, but it won't take long."

He stepped between the two of them, turning his back on Nathan. "Kitty, this bombardment on Fort Sumter may bring war that much closer, especially if the Confederates are able to take the fort. The word from Raleigh is that secession is inevitable. I've been in touch with Dr. Charles Johnson, who's expected to be named Surgeon General of the state, and as I told you once before, he wants to establish a hospital here in Goldsboro. There's going to be a nursing service, and I'd like to be able to count on you to work with us."

"No!" Nathan shouldered his way into the conversation, eyes blazing. "Kitty is going to marry me, and I'm not going off to war and have my wife working in some hospital with a lot of blood and gore . . . and dying." He dropped his voice for an instant. "No, she'll stay home where she belongs, like the other women. You forget about her working in any hospital!"

Something flashed deep within her as Kitty stood watching the way Nathan's nostrils flared when he was angry. She wondered, as she fought the turmoil churning within her, why Doc Musgrave was smiling. Perhaps he knew that she would never have such an order bestowed upon her by any man—not even the man she professed to love.

Did she want to marry Nathan? She was sure she loved him. But marriage? Sitting at home and making quilts while he marched off to war in glory? There was no glory in war. Poppa had said so. Maybe his spirit was dead now, but once it had lived, and it lived on in her. A woman had a right to pursue her own happiness in life, he had once told her. Why should she sit at home and do what other women did? Why did she have to copy someone else when she had a brain of her own? A will of her own? Nathan was seeking to destroy that will—just as the Vigilantes had destroyed her father's spirit.

It came to her then, that the spirit can be crushed by someone in other ways besides the use of force. If Nathan really loved her, why wouldn't he allow her to do whatever made her happy? She loved medicine. She loved helping sick people. And if war came, everything humanly possible must be done to help the wounded. There would be far too many women who would scream at the sight of blood and refuse to go near an injured soldier. Those who could bear it, especially those who had the training Kitty had, would be committing a mortal sin to refuse to do everything in their power to help those who needed them.

Both men were looking at her—Nathan with angry impatience, Doc with that funny little smile on his lips.

"Well, tell him, Kitty," Nathan said finally.

"I will help you, Dr. Musgrave," her chin jutting upward, the way it did whenever she meant to have her way. "You let me know when you need me, and you can count on me to be there."

"Good girl," he hugged her briefly, then turned to leave.

Screams and cheers arose from outside in the streets. Guns were being fired from pistols and rifles, and the band struck up the surging melody of "Dixie." It was as though everyone had suddenly gone mad—delirious with joy.

The clerk rushed by Kitty and Nathan as they stood staring silently at each other, their faces showing both anger and determination. Neither was about to bend to the will of the other.

"They just got word! They just heard from Charleston!" The clerk was dancing in circles and waving his arms in the air, almost hysterical. "The Confederates ran them out. The Yankees gave up! Fort Sumter surrendered!"

Outside, the sounds of merriment grew louder as the people began dancing in the streets and guns exploded repeatedly. Men sailed their hats in the air, whooping and shouting, and the band kept playing "Dixie" over and over again. The whistle of a train at the depot began to scream blast after blast to finish splitting the air about them.

"I think," Nathan spoke finally, each word carefully delivered, "that we no longer belong here, Kitty. Shall we step outside and join the others?"

❧ Chapter Ten ❧

WITH John Wright no longer in touch with reality, Kitty had to depend on passersby to tell her the latest developments in the impending war. Two weeks had passed since Nathan brought her home from town, both of them too angry to even say goodbye, and she had not seen nor heard from him since.

It doesn't matter, she told herself as she bent over the rows of freshly turned earth to drop in the seeds for the beans. *Nathan doesn't really love me, or he'd accept me for the way I am. He'd understand why I can't sit back on my bottom and tat and sew and pretend I'm ladylike and refined.*

"I'm me!" she said out loud, and Jacob, a few yards ahead digging at the ground with a hoe, turned to look at her in surprise.

"You say somethin' to me, Miss Kitty?"

It was hot. She wiped at the perspiration on her face with the back of her hand, straightening a moment to stretch weary, tight muscles in her aching back. "No, Jacob. I'm just talking to myself. All this work in the hot sun is making me tetched, I guess. Don't pay any mind to me."

". . . a lotta work for nothin', if you ask me," he mumbled, chopping into the ground with almost a vengeance. "We ain't doin' nothin' but plantin' beans for the Yankees!"

Kitty had to laugh, in spite of her weariness. Jacob's lower lip was jutting out in a pout, and she knew he really believed in what he was saying. "Oh, Jacob, you mustn't think like that. Everyone says that when the war comes it will be over quickly. The Yankees won't come this far south. They'll be whipped soundly way up north somewhere. I doubt that we'll hear even a gun fire."

"No, that ain't so," he turned quickly, waving the hoe in the air excitedly. "Your pappy an' me, we talked a lot before he got sick, and he used to tell me how the Southern folks was gonna get fooled if they thought war wouldn't spread over all the land, and ever'body'd be hurt by it!"

She stared toward the back porch where her father sat, his dog at his feet, looking out across the field at nothing in particular. The shell of a man now. As empty as a hound-sucked egg, she thought bitterly.

"There's the doc," Jacob pointed with the hoe, and Kitty looked up to see Doc Musgrave riding toward them. Was he going to ask her to go with him to see a patient, she wondered, hoping that he wasn't. The planting just had to get done, and Lena would certainly never set foot in a field to do any work. She seldom did anything these days, anyway, except sip from the jug she kept hidden that she thought Kitty didn't know anything about.

The doctor greeted them, swinging off his horse. "I came by to tell you the latest developments. I didn't know whether or not you had heard about President Lincoln issuing a call to the governor for troops from North Carolina."

"Oh, my God, no." Her hand flew to her throat, and she swayed, caught herself, and stared at him incredulously. "You mean Lincoln actually asked for us to send troops to help the Yankees?"

Nodding solemnly, he went on, "The Governor wired him back and told him he'd get no troops from North Carolina. Lincoln had asked for two regiments—and he also called for troops from all over—75,000 men in all, they say. Says he's going to put down what he calls the 'Southern insurrection.'" He snorted contemptuously.

"Then what happened?" Kitty sensed this was only the beginning of Doc's news.

"Well, on the same day Lincoln called for troops, Governor Ellis ordered men into Forts Caswell, Johnston, and Macon. The news I hear is that he's also sending troops into that arsenal down at Fayetteville *and* to the United States Mint up at Charlotte."

"It sounds bad, doesn't it?"

"If you don't want war, it does, but I, for one, am ready, so we can get it over with and go back to peaceful living, if that's possible, anymore."

"Doc, just how long do you think it's going to be before we go to war?"

"Honey, you might as well say we're at war already. Fort Sumter's been taken. All over the country, young men are rushing to take sides. Virginia pulled out about ten days ago. . . ."

"Oh, no," she shook her head, then decided there was no point in wishing anymore that a miracle would happen and there would be no war. Whatever happened next, at least the years of drift and indecision would be over. "I wish you had come by and told me about all this sooner, Doc. I've just been so busy with the planting that I haven't had time to ride into town, and no one stops by much, the way Poppa is and all," her voice trailed away, eyes once more staring toward the silent creature on the porch.

Jacob, having picked up a little bit of war gossip, dropped his hoe and went running as fast as his aging legs would carry him, off to find Fanny and spread the news.

"Do you think he'll ever get any better?" Kitty asked, still staring at her father.

He followed her gaze. "Who can say, honey? Doctors treat the body, not the spirit. We only see the physical injuries, not the ones that scar the mind and wrench the soul. Only John, those Vigilantes, and God, Himself, know what agony your daddy suffered that night."

Blinking back the tears that seemed to spring so easily since that last day with Nathan, she asked, "Have you seen Nathan, Doc? Has he joined up?"

"He's training with the Wayne Volunteers. They're getting ready to go like everyone else. Aaron Collins bought all of them brand-new Enfield muskets. They say that gun is accurate as far away as eight hundred yards, and some say it'll shoot even farther. Real fancy, they are. Even have bayonets. It's a breech-loader, weighs about nine pounds. He bought them all fancy uniforms, too, and boots."

He saw that she wasn't interested in all the little details. "It's Nathan himself you want to hear about, isn't it?" he asked sympathetically. She only nodded, and he sighed. "Well, he's brooding. I've heard several speak about the way he's acting. He loves you, Kitty. I brought both of you into the world and watched you grow up and I reckon I knew you two were in love before you did. But you're stubborn, and so is he when it comes to his notions about how a woman is supposed to be. And until the two of you can make some changes, you're never going to get together."

"Well, there's no need in even worrying about that now, is there?" She tried to smile, but she couldn't fool Doc. "I guess the best thing to do is get on with the war."

"Have you told Lena about your joining up with me at the hospital?"

"No, and I won't till the last possible moment. She doesn't like being around Poppa at all now. She says he's spooky, and he makes her nervous. But she'll have to look after him when I go. I hate leaving him in her hands, the way she is, drinking more and more every day when she thinks no one knows, but it's what he would want. He'd want me to do what I thought was right . . . to do my part."

They looked at each other. Kitty shrugged. "Just let me know when I'm needed. I'll be ready."

❧ Chapter Eleven ❧

IT was a Monday, May 20th, 1861. Kitty had just finished scrubbing the week's wash and spreading the garments along the fence to dry in the mid-afternoon sunshine.

She paused to look out at the woods, where the last of the flowering crabtrees were bursting their buds and rioting in color from soft white to delicate, deepest pink. In the pine straw beneath the tall trees, the sunshine made dancing patterns. She took a deep breath, filling herself with the sweet fragrance of the wild honeysuckle. It was a glorious day, and she wished she could capture it and keep it inside of her for always and always.

She thought of Nathan, the love she felt for him. Why did life have to be so complicated. If the war had not come, they would have married, and she would have given up her dreams of being anything but his wife. This, she was sure of.

She had that sick feeling again, the one that lurched in the pit of her stomach and bubbled up to lodge and choke in her throat whenever she thought about the possibility of Nathan getting killed. She would never know the joy of lying in his arms each night, thrilling to his lovemaking, knowing the fulfillment of bearing his child. Why, oh, why, had she been so foolish, she cursed herself. What was more

important—being the wife of the man she loved or traips-
ing off to some hospital to help wounded soldiers?

Instantly she was contrite. She could not turn her back
on her countrymen, and Nathan was wrong to expect her
to do so merely because he had been raised to place a
woman upon a pedestal and keep her there. She hadn't
asked to be put there, nor would she allow herself to be.
There had to be a distinct, individual place for her in the
world, despite the way tradition ruled that a woman was
born into one particular little niche, and she was to keep
herself there in silence, thinking of no other life. She would
have no part of it—even if it meant she had lost Nathan
forever! She was being foolish to have any regrets.

She felt somewhat better after moments of wrestling
with her churning emotions. As she turned to walk toward
the back porch where her father sat staring, as usual, into
nothingness, she recognized the great black stallion that
belonged to Nathan.

Don't run, she told her shaking legs. Don't you dare run
and make a fool of me. Walk slowly as though it doesn't
matter whether you ever see him again or not.

And her legs obeyed. Slowly she had walked to the
porch, and by the time she got there, Nathan had dismounted and stood waiting. There was no mistaking the
way his eyes were shining at the sight of her. She only
hoped that she was controlling herself better, hiding her
eagerness. He wanted her to be like other women, didn't
he? Well, she could be coy and pretend indifference.

"Hello Nathan." She sat down on the steps primly.
"What brings you out here?"

He took a deep breath, then jerked his head suddenly
toward John as he whispered, "Can he hear me?"

"He isn't deaf," she snapped.

"I didn't mean that," he apologized. "I mean . . . does
he know what people say around him? I don't want to
upset him."

She glanced at her father. His right eye, his only remaining eye, was expressionless, glassy in its detachment
from the world around him. "He hasn't spoken in weeks.
I doubt he would understand anything you say, Nathan.
Go ahead. Why are you here?"

"Kitty . . ." he faltered.

She could tell he was very excited about something, and his dawdling in sharing the news with her was becoming frustrating. "Nathan! Will you just tell me what you've come to say, please? I'm very busy."

"Kitty, I've just come from town. The telegraph office just got the message." His eyes were glowing, his voice quivering, his whole body shaking with eagerness. "Kitty, today North Carolina seceded from the union. We're going to war!"

Once he began talking, there was no stopping him. He exulted over the war preparations made thus far. He told her that a bill had been passed authorizing the counties of North Carolina to make subscriptions for the purpose of arming and equipping volunteers, and that Governor Ellis announced he wanted ten regiments of State troops and fifty thousand volunteers. The State troops would serve for as long as the war lasted, which everyone said wouldn't be but for a few months anyway, and the volunteers were to serve for a year.

"They've even passed a five-million-dollar bond issue to meet expenses," he gushed on. "Isn't it wonderful, Kitty? The people were so divided on the war issue, but now that we've seceded, the whole state is rallying behind the cause. We're united."

A chair creaked. They turned to see John getting to his feet very slowly. The expression on his face did not change. Shuffling along, he moved across the porch and into the house.

"That's strange," Kitty said, watching him disappear through the doorway. "He never budges from that chair until time to eat, and it's several hours till supper."

"Kitty, I can't wait for you to see our troop. Father had our uniforms specially made. Ride with me now to the house. There's going to be a big party tonight, and we're going to march and show off our uniforms and Enfield muskets."

She raised an eyebrow. "Why do you want me to come, Nathan? I think we had an understanding at the jewelry store a few weeks ago, didn't we? An agreement, silently, that we just aren't meant for each other? We each want something different out of life."

He reached out for her, and she did not pull away. "I want you to listen to me, Kitty Wright. I happen to love you more than anything in the world, but I have certain beliefs just as you do. We're both stubborn. But we also love each other. Right now, there's a war to be fought—and won, and when it's over, we can settle our own personal war between us. Are you willing?"

With a singing heart, she nodded happily. It wasn't over for them! He loved her as she loved him, and that's the way it was, and together they'd work out their problems. It was wonderful, and she threw herself against him to kiss him deeply . . . deliciously.

He pulled away, touching his teeth to his lower lip thoughtfully.

"What is it?" she asked fearfully. He looked so worried, his eyes shadowy.

"Kitty, I want to marry you before I leave, but . . ."

"I know," she nodded. "You don't want me to be a nurse, but Nathan, it's my war, too, and I have to do my part."

"No, no, it isn't that anymore," he waved his hand, dismissing that particular fear for her. "Do you remember my telling you about a man named Jefferson Davis being inaugurated in February as Provisional President of the Confederate States of America in a place called Montgomery, Alabama?"

She nodded. What did that have to do with their getting married if he no longer minded her being a nurse?

"The capital is being moved to Richmond, Virginia, and troops are being sent there to defend it. That's very close to Washington, so it's important to get as many men there as possible—as quickly as they can get there."

She was bewildered. "I don't understand . . ."

"Kitty, the Wayne Volunteers are being sent to Virginia just as soon as we can get our gear together and move out. We plan to leave this Sunday by train from Goldsboro. There's no time for us to be married, not the way I want us to be."

She understood.

"You'll be home soon," she hoped the smile that she forced upon her face was convincing. "I'll be planning a wedding. You can count on it."

He moved to kiss her again, but the sound of the back

door opening made them spring apart. John was shuffling out, but instead of returning to his chair, he was moving down the steps very slowly.

And he was carrying a knapsack—and his old musket.

Kitty sprang away from Nathan's arms which were still around her. "Poppa, where are you going with that gun?" she started after him, with Nathan right behind her.

"Katherine, where's your father going?" Lena stepped out of the house, swaying against the porch railing.

"Mother, go back inside." Kitty hated for Nathan to see her mother this way. She'd obviously been drinking the whole day. "I'll handle this."

"The old fool . . ." her voice slurred. "He needs to be put away someplace, so's he won't hurt himself . . . or hurt other people. He has no business with that gun. Nathan! You go take that gun away from that old fool before he shoots somebody. I mean it."

"Mother, please. . . ." Kitty was forced to stop her pursuit of her father and turn back to the house. She hoped Nathan would keep on going, but he went along with her. Stepping onto the porch, she put her hands on Lena's shoulders and pushed her toward the door, hissing softly, "You should be ashamed of yourself, out here drunk in front of Nathan this way."

"Who's drunk?" Lena roared indignantly, swaying once again. Kitty caught her and held her, or she would have fallen. "So I drink a little now and then? Is that a crime?

"The way I'm forced to live? Out here in the dirt . . . in poverty . . . hungry most of the time . . . living with an ungrateful daughter who's doomed to be an old maid 'cause her father raised her like she was a boy . . . living with a crazy old coot that sits and stares out of one eye all day. Gotta right to drink, I tell you. Don't tell me I can't drink."

Kitty looked at Nathan beseechingly. "Help me get her inside, please. I don't know where Poppa's going, but whatever is wrong, she'll only make it worse if he hears her screaming."

Nathan stepped forward, seizing Lena by the arms and shoving her into the house. She seemed to melt against him once she realized it was him ordering her about. She let him push her along all the way to the bedroom, and once there, she fell across the bed in a drunken stupor.

"I'm sorry you had to see that," Kitty said quietly as they looked down at the snoring woman. An empty jug lay on the pillow beside her.

"How long has this been going on?" he asked.

She shrugged. "I don't know, really. Maybe for years, and I never noticed till she started getting worse. Poppa being like he is just brought it all out, I guess. Both of them seemed to have just stopped caring what goes on."

"Let's go check on your father," Nathan said, taking her hand and leading her outside.

They were almost to the barn when the large door swung open and out rode John Wright. They stared in surprise as he rode right by them, one good eye staring straight ahead, shoulders no longer slumped as he sat straight up in the saddle. He wasn't ducking his chin to his chest, either. It was jutted up, that same way Kitty's did when she was determined to be stubborn about something, her mind made up.

His knapsack was tied to the saddle, as well as a water pouch, the musket tucked into a strap. Kitty stared in amazement at the old hound, Killer, trotting along beside the horse with more energy than she'd ever seen him display in his whole life, practically—and surely since he'd been hit over the head with the club. Why, at times, as he lay at her father's feet, she'd had to touch him to make sure he was still breathing—he had grown so still and lazy, never moving from John's feet.

"Poppa, where are you going? Poppa, come back here! You have no business out riding. You're still sick. Poppa!"

Panic was washing over her in giant waves. Ignoring Jacob, who was standing in the doorway of the barn calling to her, she lifted her skirts and ran along behind the horse, which was still walking. "Poppa, for God's sake, you come back here. Where do you think you're going?"

"Kitty!" It was Nathan, running to catch up with her, grabbing her arm, and she tried to snatch away but could not escape his grasp. "Kitty, I'll get my horse and go after him, but it won't do any good. Not now."

"Poppa, please. . . ." she was crying in fright. He couldn't take care of himself, not now.

"I'll go after him. Let me ride your horse. He'll listen to me. I know he will." She was babbling, near hysterics, and she turned to run back to where the horse was tied, but Jacob stood, blocking her path.

"It won't do no good, Miss Kitty. You can't stop him now. I 'spected this would happen, and they just ain't no stoppin' him now."

"He's right, Kitty."

She looked from Jacob to Nathan, then back to Jacob. "What are you talking about?" she screamed. "Where has he gone? What are the two of you trying to tell me?"

They had turned their heads, and she did likewise. John had reached the main road. The horse was starting to trot along briskly. Killer was keeping up. The dust was swirling about them as they became smaller and smaller. The road seemed to open to swallow them.

Kitty moaned, shaking her head from side to side as Nathan held her. What was happening? What did Nathan and Jacob know that she did not?

"Oh, Miss Kitty, can't you see?" There was awe in the old negro's voice and respect shining in watery, red-veined eyes. "He got his spirit back. Can't you see the way he holds his head? Like the old days—when he's got his mind made up about sumthin' . . . he's got it back, Miss Kitty. I knowed all along it was gonna happen this way."

"Jacob, please." She was losing her patience. "*What* are you talking about?"

His eyes widened, as though he couldn't believe she hadn't finally seen it all for herself, just as he did. "Why, Miss Kitty, your daddy done gone off to war. He gone off to join up with the Yankees . . . just like I always knowed he would!"

She stared at her father, almost out of sight. The spirit had returned. It had never really been destroyed . . . merely waiting for the time when it would be needed.

John Wright had answered the calling of his conscience.

"God speed." Kitty whispered through her tears. There was no stopping him now.

The man, his horse, and his dog disappeared from sight.

❧ Chapter Twelve ❧

THE day the Wayne Volunteers boarded the train for Virginia, the whole countryside turned out to see them off with celebration and pageantry. With colors flying, and the women waving handkerchiefs, the band played "Dixie" as the men marched proudly down Center Street on their way to the railroad cars that would take them to war.

Earlier, in a ceremony in front of the courthouse, Kitty had thrilled at the sight of Nathan in his Captain's uniform. He wore a cadet gray tunic and black facings and stand-up collar, dark blue trousers with black velvet stripes down the sides, trimmed in gold cording . . . a black cravat and highly polished ankle boots . . . white gloves and a sash of red silk net, his sword and scabbard strapped at his side.

She had presented the flag she had lovingly made for the Wayne Volunteers—a square of white silk on which she had embroidered a proud-looking eagle. Nathan had kissed her deeply, in front of everyone, and he made a speech about how he and his men would protect that flag, and defend it, or they would not return, choosing death in battle instead.

And then he, and his men, were gone. And Kitty was left behind with the others.

It was unbearable around the house with John gone and

Lena in a continuous drunken stupor. Kitty instructed Jacob to plant what he could to feed his family, asking him to look after Lena, and then she busied herself following Doc on his daily rounds and preparing to open the hospital in Goldsboro.

Word spread that while the men of North Carolina had turned out in great number to answer the Governor's call for troops, equipment was desperately in demand. The shortage was somewhat lessened when the state took over the Federal Arsenal at Fayetteville and 37,000 pieces of armament were seized. But many of these were muskets of the old flintlock type, dating back to the Revolutionary War, and were not of much use to the troops. The alarming news came back from the Virginia front that some companies were without any arms at all, while others could only arm themselves with pikes—wooden poles capped at one end with iron.

The picture for artillery was even darker. Doc told Kitty that in all of the state there were only four old smoothbore cannons, and these had been purchased from the military schools at Charlotte and Hillsboro—so many artillery companies, like the infantry units, had left for battle without proper equipment.

Word came that President Lincoln had proclaimed a blockade of the south, but Doc assured Kitty that there were already blockade-runners slipping through with ease to unload valuable cargoes at Wilmington.

Summer settled upon the South, hot and steaming. News arrived that in June, at a place called Big Bethel, near Yorktown, Virginia, a small Confederate force commanded by Colonel John B. Magruder soundly defeated a much larger Federal Army under General Benjamin F. Butler. Over half of Magruder's men belonged to D. H. Hill's First North Carolina Regiment, to which Nathan's Wayne Volunteers had been assigned. The battle was so well fought that the Confederate Congress and the North Carolina Convention publicly thanked their troops.

"I know we're going to win," Kitty exulted early one morning in mid-August as she worked with Doc in the building also occupied by the Goldsboro Female College that was being converted into a hospital. "The last letter

I had from Nathan was just filled with optimism for an early ending. We may never have to use these bandages." She laid a fresh pile of cotton wrapping on a table.

"I wish I could share his enthusiasm," Doc carefully measured opium into tiny containers.

"Nathan says if we'd seen that battle, we'd know that one Confederate soldier is equal to a half-dozen Yankees. He was so proud of his men."

"Has he heard anything of John?"

She lowered her eyes, a flash of hurt surging through her body. "No one's heard from Poppa since he left. For all we know, he may be dead. I pray not."

"We all do, girl." He touched her shoulder and was about to offer more words of consolation when thundering steps outside made them whip their heads around to stare anxiously at the door.

It was Ben Jamison from the telegraph office, face bright with excitement as he waved a slip of paper in the air. "You got a telegram from the Surgeon General in Raleigh, Doc. He wants you to move out!"

"Give me that!" Doc snatched the telegram from his hand irritably, knowing the loud-mouthed old busybody had probably stopped along Center and William Streets to tell everyone he saw what was in the message from Dr. Johnson.

Kitty waited anxiously as she saw the grim expression take over Doc's face as he read the hastily scrawled words. Finally, he lifted his eyes to meet hers, and his voice, when he spoke, was filled with dread. "The Yankees have attacked the fort at Hatteras Inlet. We've got a lot of wounded men, and Dr. Johnson has asked that I take some assistants and supplies and get there as soon as possible to help out."

"Trouble is . . ." he went on dully, "I don't have any assistants. I don't have much of anything at this point but a lot of promises to help out when the going gets rough."

"Well, the going *is* rough," Kitty cried. "Let's round up some help and load a wagon with supplies and start for the coast. It will take us over a day's ride, or better, to get there."

He raised an eyebrow. "You sure you want to go, Kitty?

We're heading into the battle, you know. Nathan might not take too kindly to me letting you go along."

"It's not what Nathan thinks that rules my life, Doc." Already she was starting to gather things that they would need. "I told you that you could always count on me, and you can. So stop thinking that I'm a woman and look on me as one of your assistants. Now let's get busy so we can be on our way."

"Kitty . . ." he gestured helplessly.

She turned and looked at him with her chin tilting upward in a stubborn set. "Doc, you asked me to help you, remember? Now you, above all other people, should know that I have no intentions of hiding inside this building throughout the war and spending my time cutting bandages or spooning out tonics to the sick townspeople."

"Kitty, you don't understand. Dr. Johnson has set up a field hospital as close to the Pamlico Sound as we can get, and the wounded are being brought out there. It's swampland and wilderness down there, unlike anything you've ever seen around here. It's going to be dangerous. We don't know how long the forts can hold up, because we have no way of knowing the number of ships the Yankees have sent down here. We might all be over-run and captured. I can't have your life endangered this way. Your father and Nathan would never forgive me."

"It's *my* life, Doc. Not Nathan's . . . not my father's. They didn't ask *my* permission to go off to war, did they? I can shoot as well as any man, and I don't scream or faint at the sight of blood. I'm able to help you as well, if not better, than any man you can find in this county."

Doc swore under his breath in exasperation, then wadded the sheet of paper into a tight ball and flung it across the room. "All right, damnit, let's get busy. This is what I get for taking on a bull-headed snip of a woman to start with."

Kitty gathered up the necessary supplies while Doc went in search of more assistants to accompany them. She packed instruments, ligatures, chloroform, morphine, tourniquets, bandages, lint, splints—and whiskey. She was just finishing when Doc returned with two men named Silas Canby and Paul Gray.

They were big, husky men, and Kitty knew them only as dirt farmers. "They were good enough to say they'd come," Doc explained. "They don't know much about medicine, but then we can't be choosy. We never figured on being called on to do anything like this so soon."

The two men shifted their weight uneasily, and Kitty, sensing that they didn't particularly care for Doc's apologies, quickly said, "They'll do fine, Doc. When a man is hurt, you get help from God, not past experience."

They smiled at her gratefully.

Once the wagon was loaded they started out, down the road east toward Kinston. Giant black thunderclouds were gathering on the horizon, warning of a dreaded summer storm. Lightning flashed across the sky now and then, followed by deep rumbles of thunder that shook the ground beneath them. The two horses pulling the wagon snorted and pawed the ground nervously, and Silas held the reins tightly, trying to keep the excited animals under control.

As light turned to darkness they reached Kinston and moved on toward the northeast and the little town of Washington, which they hoped to make before morning, but Doc surmised it would be closer to midday, as the rain had started to fall, and the road was soon muddy. The horses were having difficulty moving through the muck, and several times they were forced to get down out of the wagon and push it when a wheel was mired-in.

The blackness turned to dull gray as morning came with no evidence of a rising sun in the overcast sky. They were soaked to the skin, but still they pushed onward. At Washington they stopped at a depot for dry clothing, and the men stretched a tarpaulin across the top of the wagon. The supplies were already covered by canvas, but the new covering would afford them some protection from the relentlessly driving rain.

Having eaten, they plodded onward, into the marshy swamplands of Pamlico Sound. Kitty looked around her at the majestic trees with hanging moss that towered above the gloomy waters. Before them on the road a rank growth of juniper, nightshade, and all manner of climbing and creeping shrubs and vines seemed to choke their path and render it all but impenetrable. The land on either side was low and marshy, a bed of quicksand and morass with broken and tangled weeds and vines that twined about gnarled roots. The forest looked dreary and ominous.

Doc was right. It was unlike anything she had ever seen back in Wayne County. That country she knew. She had grown up in it. This was new and dangerous, and she shivered with the dampness and gloom of her surroundings.

Paul Gray was driving, and Kitty and Doc and Silas huddled together beneath the sagging tarpaulin. "Doc, how much farther before we reach the camp?" Silas asked wearily.

"I have to admit that I don't know," Doc answered quietly. "All I know is that we'll run into it somewhere along this road. That man back at the way-station said they'd had a report early this morning that some wounded soldiers were being brought across the sound from Fort Hatteras."

Kitty had noticed that Doc had been strangely quiet since leaving the way-station. Reaching to touch his huddled shoulders lightly, she asked, "Doc, what's wrong? Did you hear something back there that you haven't told us about?"

Sighing, he closed his eyes for a moment, then said, "No one likes to talk about defeat, Kitty. I heard at the station that Fort Clark ran out of ammunition yesterday and had to spike their guns and abandon the fort. They've withdrawn to Hatteras. The rough weather and high seas are all that's kept the Yankees from moving onto the beach at Hatteras."

A chill rippled up her spine. The Yankees might take Fort Hatteras and move into North Carolina inland from the sea. Doc's grim fear might become a reality—they might be captured . . . or killed.

He was watching her thoughtfully as he said, "I could send you back on one of the horses, Kitty . . ."

"No!" She all but screamed the word. "I'm not running, Doc. I intend to go where I'm needed, and I wish you'd just stop thinking of me as a woman."

"I delivered you, young lady, remember? I knew you were a girl before you did!"

She almost laughed, and she probably would have, because the peppery old doctor's eyes were twinkling with humor in spite of the tense mission—but just then Silas, who had been watching her quietly ever since they had left Goldsboro, blurted out, "You heard anything from your pappy since he high-tailed it to join them goddamn Yankees?"

Kitty caught her breath. "No, I haven't," she said evenly, meeting his defiant gaze. "I pray that he's well."

"Even if he's fightin' for the Yankees and shootin' at our men? Maybe even firin' balls at that soldier boyfriend of yours, Nathan Collins?"

"Silas. . . ." Doc nudged him with his foot. "Let's not talk about it. We've got other things on our mind right now."

"Oh, let him go on, Doc," Kitty was unable to keep the biting anger silent. "Maybe he's concerned because he knows who the cowards were that hid behind those masks the night the Vigilantes whipped my father and killed three people."

A slow smile spread across his face as Silas nodded. "I might. I say they all got what they deserved. No telling how many slaves your pappy helped get away. What I can't figure out is why you didn't go with him when he ran away. I reckon that fancy-pants rich boy, Nathan, has you right where he wants you."

"Now I'm not going to stand for this," Doc leaned forward and pointed a stubby finger at Silas. "I asked you to come along because there was no one else I could ask, but I'm not going to tolerate your badgering this young woman."

"Know what I heard?" Silas said to no one in particular. "I heard that Luke Tate is riding with the 'Buffaloes.'"

"And what, pray tell, is a 'Buffalo'?" Doc asked.

"Oh, some say they're Confederates—and some say they're really Union men. Nobody knows for sure. I guess they fight on whichever side is armed the heaviest."

Kitty gave an unladylike snort. "And you call my father a traitor? At least people know which side he's on."

"I think the Buffaloes are smart," Silas went on, almost reverently. He reached into his pocket and pulled out a plug of tobacco and bit off a chew, his eyes never leaving

Kitty's face. "They don't have to worry about getting their heads blown off if they don't go with a winner, now do they?"

Doc shook his head. "I don't understand you, Silas. I thought you were really concerned about the fighting on the coast. You said you wanted to come along and do your part. Now you're taking up for men who are obviously outlaws with no principles at all."

"And condemning my father," Kitty reminded him.

"Oh, I reckon I had my reasons for coming along," he was smiling again. He leaned over to spit out the back of the wagon before saying, "Luke's a distant cousin of mine. I don't like the way he got run off the Collins plantation because of *you*." He all but snarled at Kitty as his eyes narrowed maliciously.

Doc started to say something, but just then Paul Gray turned to yell, "Hey, I don't know where the hell you think we're going, Doc, but I'm lost. I can't see the road, and we just ain't gettin' nowhere."

"It was your idea to turn at that fork back there," Doc turned to Silas accusingly. "Suppose you tell us where we are since you claim to know this part of the country. We should have reached the camp an hour ago."

"And you would have," he laughed, "if you'd been goin' in the right direction, but you weren't."

"Just what the hell . . ."

Doc gasped into silence as Silas's smile disappeared as he brought out a pistol that had been concealed inside his jacket, and pointed it at them.

"Now you just sit quiet. Old Luke and his men should be along any minute now. Everything's worked out just fine so far, even the weather. He got that telegram to you, and I played the part of innocent country boy wanting to help the wounded soldiers and got invited along. And now Luke's got the supplies he needs for some of his men, and I've got a special surprise for him." He looked at Kitty and grinned meaningfully.

Realization of the hoax washed over Kitty, and anger overcame any fear she might have felt. For here they were, being held at gunpoint by a traitor, while somewhere nearby wounded Confederate soldiers needed their attention. Even if the telegram had been a trick, the battle raging on the nearby outer banks was a reality.

"You filthy scum!" She spat out the words furiously. "Some of our soldiers may die for lack of the supplies and attention we can give them, and you dared to condemn my father? Just how low do you crawl, Silas?"

"As low as I have to, so long as I don't love slaves like your pappy!" His eyes had narrowed. Gone was the pretense of friend and neighbor. "I rode with them Vigilantes, and I helped beat your daddy and kill them runaway slaves, and . . ."

That's all he had time to say when Kitty exploded. Here, before her was a man admitting that he had helped to nearly murder her father and had a hand in the killing of three people—she could control herself no longer. She lunged for him, oblivious to the gun, the shouts now sounding outside the wagon—nothing else mattered except the sudden unleashing of the animal called revenge that she had carried in her body ever since that dreadful, unforgettable night.

Unaware that the young girl possessed such fury, Silas was caught off guard. Doc leaped at the same moment, and the gun slipped from his hand as the two fell on top of him, both pummeling and hitting at the same time.

"What the hell? . . ." Paul turned to see the three of them thrashing against the sides of the wagon, knocking into the cartons of supplies.

The men who had ridden out of the swampland had encircled the wagon, and, hearing the commotion from within, several of them leaped from their horses to scurry inside. Kitty felt herself being dragged away, strong fingers twisting into her hair to yank her painfully back.

Suddenly, out of the corner of her eye, she saw Doc trying to scramble away, his arm reaching out, fingers closing around the gun that Silas had dropped.

Something exploded. He screamed and crumpled as Kitty fought for consciousness. Swaying against the one who held her, she struggled to get to Doc, her eyes bulging with terror at the sight of the blood seeping from beneath his body, his back torn open and gaping by the ball fired at such close range.

The man holding the smoking gun laughed . . . an ugly, taunting sound.

Kitty raised her eyes from Doc's body . . . to meet the triumphant gaze of Luke Tate.

❧ Chapter Thirteen ❧

LUKE had slung her up on the rump of his horse as casually as though she were just another saddlebag, carrying her to his camp deep in the swamp where there was a cave hidden in a steep dirt bank. She had begged to be allowed to dig a grave for the man she had loved almost as much as her own father, but her pleas had been answered by taunting laughter. She had hovered beside the body while they loaded the supplies onto their horses, then had to be dragged away.

She had been thrown to the ground beside a campfire, and the men shot anxious glances her way as they moved about to bring the supplies inside the cave. Kitty was terrified, but she told herself she could not let them know it. She had to be brave. Animals like these could never be allowed to think they had the upper hand. Over and over she told her screaming brain to stop her body from trembling, make her eyes glare with anger—not fear.

Suddenly, Luke Tate was squatting down in front of her, hands rubbing together in satisfaction between his hunched knees. "Well, well, Kitty, we meet again. I've waited for this time."

"Just as you waited for the time when you could beat my father and have plenty of help from your hooded friends?" She stared at him, unwaveringly defiant, proud of her control.

"Oh, I didn't get in on that," he grinned, showing his yellowed, chipped teeth in the glow from the firelight. "I got run off by that fancy-pants boyfriend of yours, remember? I've been waitin' for the chance to give him his, too, and it'll come. Wait long enough for something, and it comes to you, I always say."

His hand snaked out to clamp down on her left breast, squeezing painfully, and he laughed as she cried out and struggled to escape his grasp. "Stop struggling, and I'll stop squeezing. . . ." he taunted her.

She bit her lip and forced herself to be still, eyes glinting with hate and loathing.

"Now then . . ." he began to knead the flesh gently. "I've been waiting on you for quite a spell. It worked out just fine, too. I figured out a way to get the supplies and get you, too."

"And you killed Doc," she cried painfully, "and he was a good man—a *needed* man! You'll pay for it, Luke Tate—the same way you'll pay for what you had them do to my father."

Suddenly his face twisted evilly, and he reached to rip open his shirt, pulling the cloth down from one shoulder to expose the gouged pock-hole where the ball she had fired had ripped into the flesh. "And what about you paying for what you did to me, you little slut?" He sprang forward to twist the fingers of one hand into her hair, yanking her head back painfully as his other hand ripped her clothes to her waist.

He gasped as the perfectly formed mounds of flesh tumbled forward, and he quickly took one pink nipple between grimy nails to pinch, watching it turn to fiery red as it tightened against her will. Laughing, he leaned forward to duck his head and fasten his lips around it, and she jerked her head quickly to sink her teeth into his ear, biting down with all her strength.

"Goddamn you, bitch!" He yanked his head up, swinging his hand at the same time to strike her across her face, knocking her back onto the ground. He was up on his knees, blood trickling from his ear. Snatching at his trousers, he bellowed, "I'm going to teach you a lesson you won't forget, you little spitfire. I'm going to make you beg for mercy."

Her head still reeling from the blow, the sight of his bulging manhood, red and swollen, leaping from his trousers, gave her the strength she needed to bring one knee up and crashing into his testicles. With a howl of pain, he grabbed himself and rolled sideways, and Kitty was leaping to her feet, backing away from the men who were converging on her with angry faces.

"Get the bitch. . . ." Luke was moaning. "Get her and tie her down."

She had nowhere to go but backwards, and suddenly she felt the cold dirt wall of the cave pressing into her shoulders. Silas Canby was coming closer, and for the first time she recognized Orville Shaw. And they were laughing, taunting, hands snatching out to pinch at her breasts, her crotch . . .

"No, no. . . ." she began to swing at them, clawing, kicking. Where was a weapon? A club? Anything to defend herself. But there was nothing she could reach, and she was no match for the half-dozen men who quickly subdued her and pushed her to the floor, ripping the rest of her clothing from her body until she was completely naked.

Someone was hammering stakes into the ground. She felt her legs being spread apart . . . her arms pulled above her head and tied. Spread-eagled and naked—she was at their mercy.

"Hurry up, Luke . . ." someone said in a thick voice, heavy with desire. "Seein' her like that . . . God, what a body . . . I gotta have some, too."

"Did you ever see such big tits?" someone else chortled.

"Get back . . ." Luke was coming toward her. Through half-closed eyes, Kitty could see him approaching. He knelt between her spread knees, both hands clamping down on her breasts to twist viciously, painfully. "Nobody is gettin' her but me, understand? She's mine . . . all mine . . . and when I get through with her, there ain't gonna be enough left to spread around."

She felt a sharp, stabbing pain, and she screamed . . . screamed until her throat felt as though it were turning inside out. Jerking her head from side to side, the dirt floor clawed at her cheeks as she cried over and over as Luke plunged into her again and again. Her insides were burning, tearing, as he relentlessly pounded against her, grunting and moaning like a wild animal. She was dimly aware of something sticky running down her legs, realizing it was her own blood.

Finally, mercifully, he slumped against her as his body exploded within her. She felt herself drifting away into blackness, but he was shaking her, slapping her, ordering someone to throw cold water in her face. "Damn you, don't you pass out on me," he screamed. "I want you awake . . . I want you to feel every goddamned thing I do to you. I want you to hurt like I did when you put that ball in my shoulder. . . . I want you to hurt like I did when your boyfriend wrapped that bullwhip around my neck. . . . I want you to grovel and scream and beg. . . ."

He was entering her again, plunging, pushing, with knifelike jabs and jerks that shook her whole body. She could feel the flesh being torn against the ground as her back and hips were rocked to and fro. She could feel the skin splitting around her breasts and nipples as he bit and chewed against the tender flesh. On and on he went, and she prayed to sink into the blackness that sought to consume her . . . and each time she drifted away someone would sling a bucket of water into her face, bringing her back to face the stark, stabbing reality of the hell that Luke Tate was inflicting upon her body.

And finally, mercifully, she felt herself slipping once again . . . felt the sudden splash of water on her face . . . but even that could not bring her back as the inky black void opened up to claim her. She remembered thinking "this is what it's like to die."

Someone was holding a bitter liquid to her lips and commanding that she drink it or choke on it. Opening her eyes, she saw Luke bending over her. Beyond him, the sky was visible through the thick shroud of trees. The rain had ended. Where was she? Why was Luke Tate here? And where was Doc? They had to keep moving . . . get the supplies to the wounded . . .

Slowly, it came back to her, and she opened her mouth to scream with terror, and Luke tossed the burning whiskey inside her parted lips. Gagging, she spit it out, and he swore and wrapped strong fingers around her throat, snarling, "Drink it, damnit, or I'll drown you. You ain't gonna die on me, you hear?"

Blinking, she let the liquid trickle down her throat. It burned, but once it hit her stomach, it felt good, in spite of the stinging sensation. How long had it been since she had eaten? She couldn't remember.

Her body ached all over. Glancing down, she saw that someone had wrapped a blanket around her nakedness. Luke pulled her up to a sitting position and propped her against the wall of the cave. He yelled at someone to bring some food, and when it arrived, Kitty's stomach lurched at the sight and smell of the greasy-looking turtle stew.

"Well, I'm sorry you don't like our cooking," Luke laughed, forcing her to swallow the glob of stew he held in the scoop of his fingers. ". . . but we ain't had time to unpack your supplies and see what you brought us. Soon as you feel better, you can do the cooking for us."

The greasy concoction stuck in her swollen throat, and she gagged. Luke cursed, forcing more into her mouth. "Now eat, damn you! You're staying with us, and I don't want you all poor and sickly. We're going to be riding out of here in a few days, and you better be in good shape."

"Where . . . where are we going?" she asked, her head throbbing dizzily.

"Can't see where it's any of your business, but I guess it won't hurt for you to know that we're going to ride around and kill Yankees or Rebels, whichever gets in our way first. We're going to steal gold, food, anything we want, and when this war is over, we'll be the rich ones—not the poor dead heroes or slobbering leftovers with stumps where legs and arms used to be. Not us. . . ." He threw back his head and laughed, and Kitty stared at him contemptuously, realizing that she never thought she was capable of hating a human being as much as she hated Luke Tate. If she had her fingers around a knife or the trigger of a gun, she could easily kill him with no guilt or remorse whatsoever—and she silently cursed herself for not doing so when she had the chance.

He seemed to sense what she was thinking, and his face twisted into an ugly grimace. He threw the pan of foul-smelling stew to the floor of the cave, and it hit and splattered, as he reached to yank the blanket from her body, exposing her nakedness. "I think it's time to show you again who's boss. You want me to have the boys tie you up and watch again like they did last night, or you want to relax and enjoy the fun?"

Memories flooded back—Doc lying dead in a pool of blood—Luke raping her again and again. Give in to this blood-crazed, lust-filled creature? Never. She would sooner die. Her nails ached to rake the flesh from his face, gouge his eyeballs from their sockets. From deep within, she felt the trembling begin, but she sought to control the urge to fight, as another picture conjured painfully within her brain. Her father, sitting on the porch in his rocking chair, staring out into space, spirit broken, seemingly—but there all the same, smoldering, subconsciously waiting for the right time to come alive again. She saw the message in that flash of memory—the quick lesson that must be rapidly learned. Submission. If she answered the urgent cry smoldering within and fought back now, Luke would beat her, tie her, and rape her anyway. But if she submitted . . . if she pretended that he had broken her spirit . . . then she could wait for the right time and place and fight back . . . and perhaps win.

She did not move nor speak. Slowly, Luke grinned, fingers moving forward to pinch her nipples. She stiffened but did not cry out. He pushed her backward onto the ground, stretching out beside her. Closing her eyes, she felt him fumbling with his clothing once again. Gritting her teeth, she felt his lips move down her neck, to her breasts, then upward to fasten on her lips. She yielded but did not respond.

"I'll make you want me," he whispered as she fought the impulse to gag against his foul-smelling breath. "Sooner or later, you'll beg, but right now, you can pretend you don't like it."

Rough fingernails dug at the flesh between her legs as he forced them apart, plunging upward. Against her will, Nature's moisture spread downward. Chuckling to himself, Luke slid on top of her, entering her, but mercifully this time he did not rip into her as brutally as before.

She tasted blood as her teeth bit into her lower lip as she fought to hold back the screams that gurgled in her throat. It can't be happening, she thought wildly. None of this is real. It's a nightmare—a cruel, terrible nightmare.

She couldn't be here in the arms of this grunting animal, and Doc wasn't really dead back there on the side of a road waiting for wild animals to rip his body to shreds, and Poppa wasn't gone to God only knew where . . . and Nathan wasn't off fighting in the war, maybe dead, too. No, it couldn't be happening. It could not be real.

As bile rose in her throat, she shuddered, and Luke took the movement for her pleasure in spite of the fact that she was pretending not to respond. He moved faster, pounding into her.

And then, mercifully, she felt him slump against her—and for the moment, he was spent.

She turned her head to the cave wall and silently wept. It was real. It was not a tortured nightmare. She was here, naked beneath the sweating, stinking body of Luke Tate. Maybe it had always been this way. Perhaps none of the memories she held dear to her heart were real. There was no mossy bank beside a cool and rushing stream, where a bowing, graceful weeping tree held an embracing couple in the secret shroud of its leafy arms.

But it had to be true—she remembered every line of Nathan's dear face—his warm, soft eyes that could grow harsh with desire as his hands moved over her. "I want you, darling. . . ."—yes, she could even remember the words now. "I want you for always, for my wife, for the mother of my children, but right now, I want you for myself, because I never knew I could want a woman's body more. . . ."

And he had held back, because they both wanted everything about their love to be so perfect. But how could anything be perfect with war hanging over the country? She hadn't thought, deep down, that it would really come. She hadn't let herself believe that it would be quite so serious or tragic, or that so many lives would be affected. The North was a long way off. The Confederates would go North, Nathan had said, and whip the Yankees before they knew what hit them. And then he would come home —to her, to the beautiful life they would share.

She could remember the first afternoon that he had slipped her bodice down around her waist, cupping her breasts and marveling over their fullness and beauty. And he had touched gentle lips to each rosy nipple, both their bodies on fire, wanting consummation of their love. He had been lying halfway on top of her, his thighs touching hers, and she had felt his hardness pulsating against her skin. How hard it was to pull away. How painful and difficult to break apart and vow to wait for marriage.

And now there was nothing to wait for. Nothing was what they had then—and all that Kitty had at the moment. She had to withdraw from the present, move back into the past and the sweet, wonderful memories and make them come alive, make them meaningful. One day, Nathan would come for her, and he would take her home and make her his wife, and then all of this horror would really become a nightmare—with no meaning, no bearing on the life she would live.

For the present, she would have to endure. Wasn't that what Poppa had done all those weeks and months he had sat there listlessly in his rocking chair? Staring across the fields but seeing nothing. Now she understood. His present existence had been more than he could bear. The loss of vision in one eye, the cruel beating he had suffered at the hands of those vicious Vigilantes, seeing people he had sought to help murdered ruthlessly, and, finally, watching the world around him break into bits and pieces as the threat of war grew closer and finally descended upon them —like the changing of the seasons, knowing it is inevitable, but unable to pinpoint the exact time when one season becomes another, until it has.

And then Poppa's time had come. He could not stay and fight for something he did not believe in, so he left to go and defend his principles. But his spirit had been there all the while, smoldering, waiting to be unleashed. He had merely locked himself away from the painful reality of his present world to keep his sanity. This she could do also. She could take herself back to that mossy bank . . . to Nathan's strong, possessive arms, and by closing her eyes, could even remember the warmth of his lips over and over again. She would stay there, beside him, not here with this animal sweating in his stench across her naked body. She would return and remain there and nothing could bring her back to this world.

She would not allow it.

Luke Tate was up on his knees, fumbling with his pants. "Now get up and get some food a-cookin'," he ordered.

She moved woodenly, slowly, trying to concentrate upon Nathan—the day he told her he would rather die on the battlefield than come home and find her not waiting for him. "I love you that much, Kitty, my precious. I'd rather be in my grave if I can't spend my life with you beside me."

Yes, if she concentrated very hard, she could be right there with him, remembering each word . . . each touch . . . each caress.

She felt sticky, stubby fingers wrapping around her throat, halting her movement. "Let's get a few things straight, sugar. . . . I'm boss around here, and these men do what I tell them to do. Now you're my woman. I been hankering to have you with me ever since I left. I intend to make some money off this war, but it's hell not having a woman when I want one. You keep your mouth shut and don't try anything, and you'll do just fine, and I won't hurt you no more. You try anything—and I'll turn you over to my men, and when they finish with you, you'll wish you were dead. You hear me?"

She nodded. It was difficult to hear everything he said, exactly, because Nathan was talking to her just then, but she knew it was important to obey this man, to acknowledge him when he spoke to her. Fight back? Why, no, why should she? None of this was really happening. She wasn't here. She was at home, lying in Nathan's arms, laughing over a redbird that hopped on the grass outside the weeping willow's shroud, oblivious to their presence. She had never seen a redbird so close up . . . and Nathan was motioning for her to be very quiet, lest she frighten the bird away.

"Did you hear me, damn you?" Luke gave her a shake, and she choked and gagged. The bird flew away, frightened.

"Yes, I hear you," she whispered. "I'll do anything you say. Don't hurt me again, please. . . ."

He threw back his head and laughed. "I figured I could tame you, you little spitfire. All it took was a real man. . . ."

She stood there naked. Several of the others were also

watching, lust making their eyes water hungrily. Luke saw them watching, also, and he walked over to where some supplies were piled, rummaged around until he found what he was after, then returned and threw some clothing at her feet. "Put these on. Probably be too big, but that's okay. When we're riding, I want that long hair of yours tucked up into that hat, so's folks won't notice you're a woman."

She held the garments in her hand and stared at them— dark blue—a Yankee uniform—and blood-stained. Her eyes went to Luke questioningly. Shrugging, he said, "The blue-boys didn't want to give up their uniforms without a fight, so we had to cut their throats. Couldn't put a hole in 'em, could we?" He laughed. She still stared at him, and his eyes narrowed angrily as he snapped, "Come on, damnit, get into that uniform—unless you like standing around a campful of men stark naked."

She stepped into the uniform trousers, which were much too big. Luke had a belt, which he tightened until the waist of the trousers was snug about her slender lines. The shirt was big and bulky, and the bloodstains around the collar made the cotton cloth stiff and scratchy. She imagined she could even smell it. "I want to wash the blood out of the shirt," she said quietly, head bowed, not wanting to get Luke riled up.

"After we eat," he thundered. "Right now, you get over to that fire and rustle us up some decent food. You had flour and bacon in your wagon, and we unloaded it. Now get busy . . . and remember what I told you about my men."

Remember? Remember what? All she could remember was a young man's kisses and words of love. The ugly man ordering her around was only part of the nightmare, and when she awoke, he would be gone. She would not let him exist.

Kitty found the food supplies she and Doc had packed, and fried bacon and potatoes together into a mushy type of stew. The men devoured it eagerly, complimenting her on the pot of coffee she had brewed along with the stew over the open fire.

"How'd you manage to pick a gal who knows how to

cook on a campfire?" one of the men asked Luke with admiration.

Luke looked at Kitty, who was slowly spooning food into her silent lips, eyes staring straight ahead as though in a daze. "Dunno. But I'm glad I did. Her daddy freed his slaves. They were also a poor family. I reckon she had to know how to cook, but how she learned to do it so well over a campfire beats me."

He reached over and touched her shoulder with the tip of a greasy fork. "Hey, how'd you learn to cook on a campfire? Didn't your daddy have one of the cookstoves?"

She couldn't hear him. How could she hear him when he didn't really exist? She didn't want to tell him, anyway, not wanting to share the precious memories of the trips hunting with Poppa, camping in the woods, how he taught her the skills she knew. That was her memory—hers and hers alone—and she was not about to share such things with the terrifying character in a horrible nightmare.

When she did not respond Luke stretched out his left leg and kicked at her with his foot. "Hey, woman, I'm talkin' to you. You show me some respect."

She continued to stare straight ahead, slowly spooning the food into her mouth, chewing slowly.

"Goddamn you—I said answer me!" Luke threw his tin plate at her, the remainder of the stew splatting as it hit across her chest, knocking her own dish to her lap. She stared down at the mess silently.

Luke leaped to his feet, reaching to twist a handful of her long hair in his fingers and yank as she cried out in pain. "You're gonna learn to jump when I speak, unless you want me to beat that pretty face of yours to a bloody . . ."

"Luke, somebody's comin' . . ." someone cried. Luke released Kitty and reached for his Enfield. The men scattered for cover, and Luke jerked Kitty to her feet and gave her a shove in the direction of the cave, hissing at her to get down and keep quiet.

Kitty crouched inside the mouth of the cave, peering out as the sound of horses grew louder and closer. Then she saw them—about twelve Yankee soldiers in dark-blue uniforms, riding their mounts slowly into camp. One of them, wearing a slouch hat that almost covered his face, called out, "Hey, Luke, I gave the signal . . . don't shoot!"

Luke stepped out from behind the tree where he'd been hiding, his rifle pointed at the men. "Better learn to make a louder noise, Joe. That's a damn good way to get a ball between your eyes."

The men dismounted, moving anxiously toward the campfire and the simmering coffee. "It's over," the one called Joe was telling Luke. "We took the forts."

"It was quite a battle," one of the other men, an officer, spoke excitedly. "They say that Rebel Colonel Martin only had four hundred men or less."

Kitty listened painfully to each word as the Yankee soldiers recounted the battle that had led to victory on North Carolina's outer banks.

A Federal squadron consisting of seven warships mounting 149 guns had steamed out of Hampton Roads on August 26th. Accompanying the squadron was a fleet of transports that carried about 880 troops that belonged to the Ninth and Twentieth New York Volunteers. By the next afternoon they had arrived off Hatteras Inlet. The Confederates, under Colonel W. F. Martin, had less than four hundred men. The Yankees had been sent to clean up what they called the "Hatteras Hornet's Nest."

The Federals began their assault on the 28th with a heavy bombardment of Fort Clark. Colonel Max Weber took over three hundred men and two guns and landed up the beach. The surf was high, and they were afraid to try for more landings, but before noon, the Confederates at Fort Clark ran out of ammunition, so they spiked their guns and abandoned the fort and withdrew to Hatteras. Colonel Weber's men took the fort.

"We were afraid all night that the Confederates had us beaten," the Yankee officer said. "Two ships—'Harriet Lane' and the 'Pawnee'—were supposed to lay near the beach, but this storm we've had forced them to withdraw for fear of wrecking them on the coast. Weber's men were left at the mercy of the Rebels, and we all knew it. We figured we were beaten—and that during the night the Rebels would regroup and reinforce their forts and repair damages and take our soldiers prisoner and whip the hell out of us when the sun came up.

"Well, when the sun came up, we moved the ships into position and started shelling the fort. There wasn't a cloud in the sky and the sea was calm, and our flag was still waving over Fort Clark. We shelled the hell out of our guns and poured them on Fort Hatteras, and after three hours Commodore Barron surrendered the fort and over seven hundred men! Can you believe it?"

A round of triumphant cheers went up from the Yankees, as well as the Confederate traitors dressed in stolen uniforms. "Those stupid bastards had seven or eight hundred men, and they spent the night within six hundred yards of our troops—and we only had three or four hundred men—and they let us walk right in and take them. I think this war is going to be easier than we ever thought," the officer finished proudly.

Joe grinned at Luke. "I rode out there, just like you told me, and showed 'em where that farmer lived that had the horses they could confiscate. I told them we had supplies if they needed them."

"We don't need your supplies, presently," the officer interrupted, "and if you'll allow me to introduce myself—Lieutenant Herman Benyo of the Ninth New York Volunteers." He leaned forward to shake hands with Luke. "I wanted to come here when this . . . gentleman, told me about your band of men, how your company in Virginia sent you to scout for us when we made our landing. I wasn't aware that anyone was being sent, but we are very grateful since we don't know this land at all."

"Just tell us where you want to go," Luke smiled, and Kitty wondered how the Yankee officer could be so foolish as to think the ugly, snaggletoothed creature could be telling the truth. She was ashamed such a man was even from the South—how could the gentleman Yankee believe he was one of his kind, either?

"We were told to abandon the outer banks once we blocked the inlet, but General Butler has reassessed the situation and feels forced to disobey his instructions and will leave behind a force to hold the inlet." Lieutenant Benyo glanced about at Luke's men. "We plan to do some scouting on our own and report directly back to Colonel Hawkins at Fortress Monroe, so if you will be good enough to draw us some kind of map, showing us any nearby communities or the location of any Confederate troops—you can then be on your way back to your own troop. We hear the fighting is heavy in Virginia, and I'm sure you're needed there."

The Lieutenant seemed to be seeing the men for the first time, Kitty thought excitedly. Perhaps he realizes what they are—traitors to both sides—out to kill and rob and plunder, with allegiance to no one but Luke Tate.

She counted the Yankees—with the officer there were eleven of them. Her eyes darted back to Luke, and she could almost read his mind as he looked at the clean, unstained uniforms, the handsome leather saddles they had brought with them to use on the confiscated horses, the sword the Lieutenant carried—the new-looking guns the soldiers bore. Kitty had never seen such a model, and they looked expensive.

"We found a civilian a little ways back," the officer went on. "We found papers on him identifying him as a doctor. We were wondering why it was necessary to kill a doctor—they are desperately needed by both sides, you know."

"It was him or us." Luke's eyes had narrowed, his voice was low, even, no longer solicitous.

"Couldn't you take him prisoner? There were many of you—and obviously only one of him—it appears he was shot in the back."

"Don't tell me how to run my goddamn war!" Luke roared then, "Don't tell me what to do."

"How dare you speak to an officer that way," the Lieutenant whipped out his sword menacingly. "State your rank and your company commander's name. I intend to see that you're properly reprimanded, soldier, both for your disrespect and insubordination here—and your obvious misconduct previously in the unnecessary killing of a civilian. I'm taking you back to the fort to stand before Colonel Hawkins."

The soldiers had been milling about the campfire, eating the remains of the stew, drinking coffee and relaxing. They were caught off guard by the sudden stand their commanding officer had taken. But Luke's men had been waiting for just such a moment. As the soldiers realized what was happening and began to move toward their horses—and the rifles they had left there—Luke's men went into action.

Orville Shaw fired the first shot, hitting the Lieutenant, who clutched at his stomach and slumped to his knees. The others never made it to their horses—they were cut down by the rapid fire, and Kitty's screams could not be heard above those of the dying—and the thundering gunfire.

Covering her face, she turned away as Luke snatched the sword from the dying Lieutenant and plunged it into the back of his neck, blood gushing upward. "Kill them all!" she heard Luke shrieking. "Use your knives . . . don't waste your balls . . . slit their throats and finish it up."

The shrieks of death filled the air as knives sliced into flesh. Kitty forced herself to turn and watch. She had to become hardened to this, she realized. If she were to survive, if she were to nurture her smoldering spirit and be ready when the time came to fight for her own life, she had to learn not to weaken at the sight of blood and flesh being gouged and torn, and lives being hacked away into the dirt and muck of the earth below.

One last soldier remained, his arm dangling by a thread of flesh and muscle from the shoulder where a ball fired at close-range had ripped into it. "Don't . . ." he was on the ground, writhing in pain, holding up his remaining arm to fend off Luke, who was advancing toward him with the Lieutenant's bloodied sword. "Please, God, have mercy."

With one swift blow, Luke brought the sword down and around in a swishing arc, hacking into the pleading soldier's neck. Bile gushed into Kitty's throat and out past her lips, as the soldier's head jerked sideways like the trunk of an ax-hacked tree, blood spurting, white neck bone shining amidst the crimson flow.

Luke screamed triumphantly. "We got 'em all. Every last one of 'em. Look at these guns. I've heard about them —Sharps carbines . . . accurate to six hundred yards . . . it'll fire ten rounds a minute . . . and we got all of 'em."

"Hey, this one's got a gold watch," Orville Shaw cried excitedly, waving it in the air. "Look at this. Solid gold! Worth a couple of hundred dollars in Yankee gold, I'll bet."

Kitty saw another prying open the mouth of a dead soldier, peering inside—"A gold tooth!" he yelled. "Hey, check their teeth."

"Get anything you want," Luke roared. "That's what

we're here for. When this war is over, we'll be the winners,
'cause we'll be rich!"

Kitty vomited again, stumbling backward as she clutched
her stomach. It had to be a nightmare. Out there—those
dead, mutilated bodies—they couldn't be real. She could
even see one of Luke's men hacking at a dead soldier's
finger, because he could not remove the gold ring he wore.
Holding up the bloodied stub, he yelled happily and waved
it for all to see.

She backed into the cave wall, sliding downward. It
couldn't be real. If she allowed herself to believe it was
true and not a horrible illusion, she would lose all sanity.
She knew she would.

Time passed slowly. She crouched there in the dark,
damp cave for perhaps two hours, vomiting now and then,
swaying as she fought to remain conscious.

Suddenly she was aware that someone was walking in
the cave, coming toward her. Lifting fearful eyes, she saw
Luke, dressed in the dead Lieutenant's uniform, hat and
boots, his sword and scabbard now strapped to his side.
"Look at you . . ." He snorted disgustedly. "Puke all down
your shirt. Get down to that swamp and wash and clean
yourself up. Then get busy and help my men bury those
soldiers."

She obeyed, walking to the slimy swamp waters before
taking off the vomit-soaked clothing. Waist-deep in the
water, cringing as unseen creatures bumped against her
flesh, she hurriedly splashed her body, then emerged to the
muddy bank. Reaching for the fresh clothing Luke was
holding out to her, he snatched them away just as her
fingers touched the garments. He laughed, and his men
joined in to watch the taunting as Kitty begged.

And then Luke stopped laughing, his eyes becoming
glassy as mounting desire moved through him at the sight
of her naked, supple body kneeling before him. As easily
as though she were nothing more than a bag of flour, he
reached down and scooped her up, hoisting her over his
shoulder. Turning toward the cave, he stepped across the
mutilated bodies, moving between the men digging the
trench for a mass grave. They laughed, tossing obscene
remarks which Luke answered jovially.

Inside the cave he carried Kitty to the pallet where he

had ravished her only a few hours before. Laying her down, he began to remove his clothing, eyes raking over her.

"I'm gonna teach you some new tricks, you little spitfire," he said hoarsely, falling to his knees beside her. He placed his hand on the back of her neck, slowly pulling her face toward his loins as he whispered huskily, "I'm gonna teach you how to make it real good for a man."

Closing her eyes, she obediently parted trembling lips. It did not matter. She would not let it matter. None of it was real. The nightmare would continue until the day when she awakened to find Nathan and the comfort of his arms—the sweet solace of his love. Until then . . . let the horror and unreality continue.

She would not let the nightmare become a reality.

✥ Chapter Fourteen ✥

KITTY turned in her sleep, awaking suddenly as a pine needle prickled her skin. Even after six months she had not become accustomed to the pine-needle bed.

Wearily, she opened her eyes to the gray morning light that filtered through the cracks of the crude log cabin. The fire had long ago burned itself out. She could make out the lines of the sparse furniture—a table made from boards laid across upright barrels, the sawed logs they used for stools. On the far side, where Luke had made them sleep, the pallets of his men were empty.

Then she remembered. Early sounds. It had been dark outside when she heard them moving about, getting ready to go on another trip to raid and kill and loot. Thinking about it made her stomach lurch. Always they returned, triumphant over their success, boasting of the food and gold or money they were able to steal. And likely as not, they would have a fresh supply of whiskey, and Luke would get drunk and take her savagely to satiate his lust. But she had been lucky, she reminded herself. Luke was one to fall asleep easily, and she had been spared many nights when he fell across her snoring drunkenly before he was able to plunge into her.

Winter! Could any winter be as cold as the one they had spent along the border between the western mountain region of North Carolina and the southern line of West Virginia? It had begun to snow the early part of December, and for months the ground had been covered in the hollow where the cabin was built. The wind never stopped howling, and Kitty could not remember being warm for even a moment. The chill was constant.

Luke had moved his men into the region because he felt it was safer to plunder along the border, after Orville Shaw went out scouting and returned to report that the western counties of Virginia were against the war, and when Virginia left the Union, the westerners began to talk about seceding from Virginia. Luke felt they were safe as long as they knew when to disguise themselves as Confederates —and when to become Yankees.

Orville also brought back the news that the summer battle at Bull Run had awakened the North to the realization that the South was not going to be easily defeated. Word spread that President Lincoln had plucked the victorious George B. McClellan out of the western Virginia mountains to place him in command of the Army of the Potomac to build a real army with focus on organization, training, and discipline.

On the other side, Orville reported, the Confederate army was supposed to be building extensive lines of entrenchments around Manassas Junction, some twenty-five miles from Washington and the capital. Patrols were said to be heavy in the area, particularly along the Potomac River to blockade the water approach to Washington.

"This war's going to last forever," Luke had cried jubilantly when he heard the news. "And when it's over, we'll be the rich ones, no matter who wins."

Kitty hated him. She never knew she could hate and despise a human being as much as she did Luke Tate. Within weeks after her capture she had found it impossible to withdraw any longer and had been forced to admit that the nightmare was reality. If only she could get her hands on a knife or a gun, she knew she would kill him and every one of his men. But Luke sensed this and knew she was waiting for just such a chance. He made sure one did not come. Seldom was she left with her hands free—only when someone was around to make sure she did not seize an opportunity to grab a weapon. The rope-burned scars on her wrists were evidence of her restraint.

But one day, she promised herself with gritted teeth, she would have her chance. All she had to do was wait for it to come.

She was always glad to see Luke begin drinking with the others after supper, for usually he would wind up passed out, unable to assault her. It became increasingly difficult to lie still as his fingers probed and prodded, his slobbering, hungry lips devouring her breasts, sometimes moving down her stomach and below. Only his threat to turn her over to his men, should she resist, kept her from fighting back.

The winter was endless. Kitty did not speak unless spoken to. She cooked for them, stirring the flour and bacon into stew, wrapping meat, from the game they killed, around long sticks to roast in the fireplace. And when there was no more work to be done . . . when the wind and snow whipped about outside as the men drank and gambled in front of the fire . . . she would crawl into her corner bed of pine straw and turn her back to them—and close her eyes—and dream of Nathan.

Where was he? Had he gone home late in the summer as he had planned, expecting to find her waiting there to become his wife? Did he go in search of her when told she and Doc never returned from a mission to aid the wounded Confederates at the Outer Banks? Was he still alive?

And what about Poppa? And her mother? Were any of them alive? Was there any point, even, for her to go on living? Perhaps it would be best to rile Luke to the point of murdering her, ending this hellish existence.

But no—there was always the chance that they would all come out of this alive. Maybe Nathan was even now searching. She had to hang on—she had to.

Shivering, she knew she had to get up and start the fire. If Luke returned and the cabin was not warm, he would beat her. That was the only reason he had left her untied —so she could gather wood and start food cooking. Of course, he had made sure no weapons had been left lying around. He was so certain of what she would do should her hands wrap around a knife, that he would not even allow her to use a blade to cut up game. If the men were not in a good mood and didn't offer to cut it for her, she had to dig her nails into the flesh and rip it from the carcass in order to cook. The first time she had been forced to do so, they had stood around to watch and taunt, hoping, she knew, to see her gag or maybe even faint. But she had managed, even though it was an unpleasant experience.

There was no wood in the cabin. Struggling into worn Confederate trousers, she pulled on a jacket and headed outside for the woodpile. There were Yankee clothes in better condition, but somehow her flesh crawled when she wore the hated blue. The tales Luke and the others brought back about the war, the realization that it was war that got her into her present situation—all combined to make her despise the North for ever butting into her countrymen's business to start with, and her loathing included anything to do with the Yankees.

She wore an old pair of boots Luke had stripped off one of the Yankees he'd killed in the swamps last summer. For a long time, she wouldn't wear them, and he hadn't cared enough about her feet to order her to. But then when the cold came, and the snow, she had no choice if she didn't want her feet frostbitten. The shoes she'd worn when she and Doc left Goldsboro had long ago worn themselves thin and useless.

The sky was gray and thickly overcast, which meant more snow might come soon. In every direction, the whiteness of the ground cover was spread. Staring upward, she marveled at the height of the pine trees—some of them were maybe a hundred feet high. At the base of a few, there were green plumes struggling to burst upward through the snow. Here and there were a few sparse patches of dead brown grass and sassafras bushes and blackberry vines, which Nature first sends to hide the nakedness of the impoverished earth. Spring would soon come, but dear God, when? Once they were not so bogged down by the weather, perhaps Luke would want to start moving once again. The men seemed restless. If they were on the move, she would have a chance to escape. . . .

A grunting sound made her drop the logs she had lifted in her arms. Whipping about, she saw a wild hog—long, lanky, with a head shaped like a snake, his bony body covered with porcupine spriggles of hair. He dashed across her path, giving short, hasty grunts as he galloped, not looking either to the right or left. If only she had a gun, she thought desperately, there would be roast meat on the table tonight.

Suddenly the furious, awkward clopping of horses fighting their way through the frozen snow made her strain hopefully to see into the woodlands. Dear God, she prayed, let it be someone other than Luke and his men. Let a miracle happen . . . let there be Confederate soldiers, or Virginians, or Indians . . . *anyone* that might free her!

The hopeful pounding of her heart subsided with a sickening lurch as she recognized Luke's horse. There were others behind them, but she saw someone slumped in his saddle—coat splotched with blood, arm hanging limp. Someone sat behind him, holding him about the waist. And the others—where were they? She counted . . . three were missing . . . but before there was time to wonder further, Luke was upon her, sliding down off his horse to grab her arm and give her a shove toward the cabin.

"Get inside. Orville's shot. You've got to help him," his eyes were wide, angry. "Three of my men are dead, and goddamn it, I'm not losing another."

He shoved her along to the cabin while someone helped carry Orville inside. "Get him on a table," Luke ordered, then he saw the cold, blackened fireplace. "You lazy bitch!" He slapped her, sending her spinning against the wall. "You want him to die from the cold? Silas, get a fire going. Paul, get that bag from the Doc's wagon."

A pang of sorrow went up Kitty's spine as she saw Paul Gray bring in the familiar worn bag that had belonged to Doc Musgrave. She had not known they had taken it. He sat the bag down, and Luke cried, "Okay, get him on that table, and let's get busy."

Orville cried out in agony, and Paul Gray moved to lift a cup of whiskey to his lips. He gulped, coughed, then dropped his head back, eyes closing. For the moment, he was out of his misery.

Kitty stood there nervously chewing her lower lip, willing him to go on and die right then and there. She could feel Luke's eyes upon her, watching her, and finally, he exploded and reached to clutch her shoulders and shake her so hard she felt her teeth rattling in her mouth.

"Goddamn you, I know you can save him! I heard the talk around home . . . how you're as good a doctor as the Doc was himself. Now you do something for this man, or so help me, I'll kill you with my bare hands, Kitty Wright!"

Her eyes met his defiantly, and she choked out the words, not caring any longer whether she angered him or not. Let him kill her—she would not let him think she could perform miracles. "He's lost a lot of blood, and I'm no surgeon. The only way he's even got the slightest chance at all is to take that arm off!"

There were four other men in the room besides Luke and the unconscious Orville. No one moved or made a sound, each frozen where he stood, all eyes upon her.

After a strained moment, Luke ground out the words, "You saying you've got to cut his arm off?"

She felt sick. "I can't promise you that even amputation will save his life. Like I said, he's lost a lot of blood."

He stared at Orville thoughtfully, and Kitty took a chance and said in a rush, "Look, how much good will he be to you with just one arm? Or himself, for that matter? Why don't you just let him go on and die? Maybe he wouldn't want to live if he had the choice to make."

"That ain't your decision to make. Or mine. What we got to do is save him if we can. Now you get busy and do what you got to do!" He gave her a shove toward the table where Orville lay, the worn bag of Doc Musgrave's at his feet.

Kitty opened the bag and looked inside. It contained few instruments except a razor-sharp bowie knife, a half-broken probe, and a forceps for removing bullets, stained red by rust. There had been no war in Wayne County, and Doc seldom had to remove bullets or amputate limbs. He had delivered babies . . . did what he could for the fever and other ailments . . . treated some knife wounds now and then. The Surgeon General in Raleigh was to have sent new instruments to the hospital in Goldsboro, but when they had left for the Outer Banks, they had packed only what medicine and bandages they had. Doc had no shiny new instruments to take with him.

"Cut his shirt off," she said to no one in particular. There was a sound of cloth ripping and Orville stirring at the movement and moaning painfully.

Kitty stepped forward to explore the exposed wound. She had seen Doc treat this kind of injury before—the result of a drunken brawl that had ended in tragedy. Probing with her fingertips, she found that the bullet had entered the arm almost in the center of the elbow joint, smashing through. The bones of the elbow had splintered, and when she touched the drum-tight skin, it felt hot and lumpy. Doc had taught her how to feel along the muscles for a sign that inflammation was spreading, but she found no evidence of tell-tale swollen nodules in the armpit, which would mean a pus seepage from the wound into the body itself.

"Well, damnit, say something!" Luke cried angrily. "Can you fix him up without taking off his arm?"

"No," she answered quietly. She searched for the right words to tell them what it was going to be like to remove that arm, and how he might die anyway. What if they believed it was her way of taking out her revenge? If he died, they might blame her, think she purposely let him die. God, why did she have to be in a mess like this? Why couldn't Orville Shaw have just died with the others?

Luke reached over and picked up a nearby jug and lifted it to his lips, whiskey dribbling down his chest. "Get busy," he swiped at his mouth with the back of his hand. "Do what has to be done."

"It isn't going to be pleasant. You're going to have to tie him down, and he's going to scream, because it's going to hurt terribly. We don't have anything to give him but the whiskey, and I can't have him moving around."

"We'll hold him down. Don't you worry. You just get busy."

"Are you sure you can stand it?" she looked at each of them in turn. "Have any of you ever seen a man's arm cut off?"

"Have you ever cut a man's arm off?" Paul Gray snapped then, looking a bit pale.

She shook her head. "No. I helped Doc a couple of times, and I read the books he told me to. I think I can do it, but I'll need help. I don't want anyone fainting on me."

"Us . . . faint?" Luke snorted, took another swig from the jug. "You just do your part, and we'll do ours. Paul—get some rope, and let's tie him down."

"Are you sure you've got to take that arm off?" Silas Canby looked at her as he threw a log into the crackling fire.

She shrugged helplessly. "I can do an excision—remove the bone fragments and try to save the limb. It might take him months to get over it, though, and there's a chance the fever will set in. It's too soon to know, but I feel some pus forming around the wound."

"Luke, you said we'd move out when the spring thaw comes," Silas looked at the leader. "And we see signs the thaw might come soon. We can't stay behind because of Orville. Remember what we heard in that saloon before the fightin' started? The Yankees are close by—and I believe those were Yankees that fired on us at that house we was raidin' . . . couldn't see that good from where they were. We've got to be moving on. What if they track us? What if . . ."

"Shut up! Would you want someone to go off and leave you to die? Hell, no, you'd be screaming like a baby." Luke turned to Kitty. "Now you tell us what you want us to do, and we'll do it. And you do what you have to do. Just get on with it."

"I'll need some light. It's too dark in here. And I need plenty of bandages and lint. There were several boxes in Doc's wagon. Get them for me, please." She stared down at the sleeping man. The pain would be excruciating. He would never sleep through it at the start. Perhaps blessed oblivion would take over when it became unbearable. Doc had been using chloroform when necessary, but there was never much of it, and they'd had none when they set out for the Outer Banks.

Placing her hand on Orville's forehead, she noted that it was extremely hot. She hated him along with the others, having seen him plunder and kill innocent people. But now, at this moment, he was a human being, and there was something inborn, something she instinctively felt, that made her want to save him—enemy or not. If given the chance, she knew she could kill him herself. What, then, made the difference at this hour when she *did* have the opportunity to kill him and rid the earth of a useless creature? Doc would call it challenge—challenge, and desire to do battle with the clutching hands of death.

She placed a tourniquet on his arm, about four inches below the shoulder. Then she twisted the knot and anchored it tightly to hold back a hemorrhage. If possible, she would cut quickly and mercifully, in an effort to keep pain as low as possible. But there would be moments of excruciating agony when the blood vessels in the stump were clamped and tied off.

What was it Doc had told her? She fought to remember as she rinsed her hands in the water Silas had heated at her instruction. Let the tourniquet hold for a while, and the pressure will dull the nerves, maybe keep the patient from twitching in a movement that would be fatal as the knife cut down deep. He had also told her to be sure never to leave a tourniquet tied too long, for if the stump were deprived too long of blood, it would not heal properly.

"Get on with it," Luke snapped nervously, tipping the jug up for one last swallow. "He's starting to wake up."

"He'll wake up," she said. "Let's just pray he passes out again so deeply that he won't feel the pain, because I assure you there's going to be plenty of it, and there's nothing I can do about it. Just be ready with that jug, and maybe that will take some of the edge off."

Her fingers closed around the handle of the bowie knife. Suddenly, Luke's hand snaked out to close about hers. "Just don't get any funny ideas with that blade, you hear me?" he warned. "I'm going to watch every move you make, understand?"

Through gritted teeth, she ground out the words she had held back so long. "One day, I'll settle my debt to you, Luke Tate. First things first."

She yanked her hand away, and he did not try to continue his hold on her.

She had never done an amputation before . . . never seen one done without anesthesia. Now she prayed for the strength, the skill, to do what had to be done. She set the blade to the skin, outlining the contours of the flaps she would use. Doc had said to leave a long one at the back— a shorter one in the front. Closing her eyes momentarily, the gravelly voice of Doc came back to her.

"When you amputate, Kitty, it's important to make the posterior flap long, because the muscle has to cover the bone stump. Otherwise, the extremity is useless. . . ."

The blade bit into the flesh, bloodless now from the pressure of the tourniquet. She swept it up in a curving line, making real the contours of the flaps she had mentally outlined. Luke stood at her side, close enough to grab her if she turned on him or Orville. Paul Gray and Silas Canby stood at Orville's head, holding down his shoulders. Joe was holding the wounded man's legs.

She didn't dare look at Orville's face, as she prayed he would not awaken. Pushing the superficial tissues aside, the bulging red surface of the muscles beneath was exposed. She knew that the next slash of the knife was going to have to shear through muscle all the way to the bone, and it had to be at a slightly higher level, to make sure that the layers of tissue would fold and heal evenly across the cut end of the bone itself.

Again she brought the knife slicing down, and several large vessels could be seen gaping in the depths of the incision, a trickle of dark blood beginning to ooze upward. There was no time to worry about clamping.

She pressed the blade downward on the bone. Please, God, she whispered, give me the strength to break through the bone. She circled, leaving the white surface bare in the depths of the wound. "Give me linen," she whispered, licking dry, parched lips nervously. Someone handed her a strip, which she wrapped around the bone. Seizing the two ends, she pulled muscles and skin upward, exposing about two inches of bone.

"Cut it a few inches shorter than the other tissues or it will project and cause a painful stump. . . ." she repeated Doc's words out loud.

"There's an old surgical saw in the bottom of that case," she said to Luke, who was still hovering over her. "Get it for me, then do as I say." When she had the saw in her hand, she nodded to the linen thong she held and told Luke to take it, holding it in an even, upward pressure.

The act of sawing, Kitty knew, would be the most painful of all. Doc had told her how terribly it hurt when the steel cut through what he called the outer periosteum, and how it was sheer agony when it bit through into the sensitive marrow cavity. But it had to be done. Taking a deep breath, she mustered every bit of strength she possessed and bore down. The saw bit into the bone, the sharp teeth

—which were set precisely to cut the right depth, Doc had said—were making a harsh and muted noise in the gaping crimson cavity. The smell of bone dust permeated her nostrils, and for the first time she felt nauseous.

Suddenly the body twitched, jerked, and Orville Shaw's head slammed backward against the table as his lips parted to shriek forth the most God-awful sound Kitty had ever heard. Her fingers instinctively froze in their sawing motion, and she looked at him to see eyeballs rolling frantically in his head, then settling to stare straight upward before fluttering lids finally fell downward to cover the glare of agony.

He slumped. Kitty waited. She saw the rise and fall of his chest. He was still alive. She began the sawing motion again, and there was a splintering, cracking sound as the arm and elbow fell to the floor. The amputation was almost over.

Quickly, she moved to clamp off the major vessels, telling Luke how to hold the forceps for her, as she made the knots with the flax thread that was found in Doc's bag.

Luke followed orders, and they worked well together. Finally, Kitty was able to ease the tourniquet a bit. Then, when the vessels were all tied off securely, and the bleeding halted, she shaped the flaps, ligating the cut ends smoothly to bring the cut tissue together in a compact fold. She had seen Doc do this several times, and he had drawn her pictures and made her study them.

"A continuous fold, Kitty," Doc had said. ". . . without tension. You have to avoid tension, because it causes slough . . . and slough causes gangrene, as far as I'm concerned."

Suddenly, Kitty felt herself swaying. The tension and strain, the strength she'd had to muster to saw through the bone . . . the glimpse of the limb she'd just removed lying in a pool of blood on the dirt floor—it was all too much. "Someone else bandage, please. . . ."

Stepping backward, Luke slipped an arm around her waist and helped her to the pallet, where she slumped gratefully. "Rest a spell," he said gruffly. "Then get back over here. I want you to watch him every minute for a while, till he's over the worst of it."

Didn't he realize, she thought wearily, leaning against

the pine-needle bed and for the first time not feeling their prickle, that the worst of it could last for weeks?

She tried to sort her scrambling, exhausted thoughts . . . tried to piece together what had happened to them. They had obviously gone somewhere to a saloon—but where? Was there a settlement close by? They had come to this spot, where Luke decided to set up a camp, in the dead of night. She'd been unaware of her surroundings and not been anywhere since. But they had been gone how long? Several hours. They could not be far from a settlement, then, and Luke liked to brag that he could cover his tracks and hide better than any Indian.

Maybe they were followed, she thought with a sudden pang of hope. Maybe they would be captured. But there would be a fight. That was a certainty. Luke would never give himself up. He might even kill her rather than see her given freedom by his attackers.

The more she thought about it, the more she realized she had to be ready if an attack did come. It would be necessary to hide—but where? The cabin was one square room and very small with no windows—only the front door.

Suddenly, things looked more hopeless than ever, and she blinked back hot tears of frustration.

Luke kicked at her with his foot. "Get up and get some food going. If he wakes up, we want him to eat and get his strength back. We're going to move out of here first thing tomorrow."

"You can't do that!" she blinked at him incredulously. "You can't move him for more than a week. It will kill him."

"Not Orville. He's tough. He can take it. You just do as I tell you. Now get up and get busy. We're all hungry."

Instinctively, she moved first to check on her patient again, noticing out of the corner of her eye that the bag and instruments had been taken away. There was no opportunity now to slip the bowie knife beneath the bulky folds of her shirt to wait for the first chance to plunge it into Luke Tate's traitorous, murdering heart.

Orville was unconscious, and his breathing was labored, ragged. She lifted an eyelid and saw that his eyes were still rolled back into his head. His skin was pallid, felt hot and sticky. Checking the bandages on the stump, she was satisfied that the oozing of blood was minimal, with no cause for alarm. With proper treatment and rest, he just might pull through, she decided, but if he were moved, then he would probably die. But she wouldn't fret over that. Not now. She had done her job. If Luke insisted on moving him, and he died, then his blood would be on Luke's hands —not hers.

The water bucket was empty. Looking about, she saw that the others were settled in front of the fireplace, talking animatedly about the skirmish they'd been in earlier, the death of their friends. There was no need in asking, or expecting, anyone to fetch water from the stream below the cabin. She would have to do it herself.

She didn't remember taking off her coat when she'd come in before, but she pulled it back on, opening the door against the blast of cold wind. Snow was starting to fall once again. Ducking her head, she stepped outside, walking as briskly as possible without stumbling, down the rocky, slippery hillside to where the icy stream gurgled among snow-capped stones and rocks.

Placing the bucket sideways in the stream, she filled it with rushing water. When it was full, she straightened, pausing to gulp in the cold, crisp air. How easy it would be to just keep on walking down the hill, until she was able to break into a run and try to get away from the evil and horror that waited back there in that cabin. Was anyone nearby? Could she get to help? Or would Luke find her and shoot her in the back—or let her freeze to death .as she wandered about in the wilderness lost, not knowing which way to turn?

Looking back at the cabin and the gray wisp of smoke rising from the chimney, she made her decision. She would keep on walking, down the hill, moving as quickly as possible. If Luke came after her and caught her, she would say she was searching for special roots and herbs she needed to make proper medicine for Orville. And if she did get lost—or a wild animal attacked and killed her, then that would be her fate and there was no choice but to accept.

Enough is enough, she blinked back tears as they froze to her cheeks. *I can't take anymore. If I can't be free, then let me die,* she prayed.

A rabbit darted from a snow-crushed bush, bouncing across her path, fluffy tail flipping insolently as he disappeared. Somewhere, a bird called mournfully. There was no other sound except the gentle fluttering of the snow as it settled onto ice-crusted leaves. Cold. Oh, God, it was so terribly cold. But she forced herself to move onward, downward, slipping once to land on her bottom in the snow, only to scramble up again to keep moving as quickly as possible. There had to be help somewhere. There *had* to be.

She stumbled again, and this time, before she could scramble up, someone was rushing toward her from behind, fastening strong fingers about her throat to send her sprawling face-forward into the deepening snow.

"You think I didn't know what you were up to?" The familiar, snarling voice of Luke Tate burned into her ears. "You think I'm stupid enough to let you get away?"

Screaming, she rolled over on her back, swinging out at him with the pail she still held in one hand. It caught him on the forehead, gashing the skin. She swung again . . . this time his forearm flew up to ward off the blow. He caught her wrists; the bucket fell into the snow, and he positioned himself on top of her, spraddle-legged.

"You ever been had in the snow?" He laughed down at her, enjoying the struggles. "Hey, I'm glad to see you fighting for a change. I get goddamned tired of laying a damn stiff. . . ."

She tried to bring her knee up into his groin, but he only laughed louder, reaching quickly to pin both her arms over her head with one hand, while he ripped open her shirt with the other, lips moving to fasten on an exposed breast, teeth biting down until he tasted blood. Talking around her nipple, he said, mumbling, "You stop screaming, and I'll stop biting . . ."

The pain was excruciating as his teeth sank deeper into the tender flesh. Fighting within herself, she forced the screams to cease, lying still and quiet in the snow. He yanked at her trousers, pulling them down about her knees, pushing her legs apart.

She choked on the scream that bubbled upward as he plunged roughly inside her body. He seemed to delight in the knowledge that he could cause her intense pain when he wanted. Again and again he drove into her flesh, pumping, pushing, as he grunted and snorted. Like a wild hog . . . she thought wildly, painfully . . . like that snorting wild hog that ran across the path this morning . . . *anything*, she commanded herself, *think of anything to take me away from this horror . . . this pain . . . this degradation of my very soul. . . .*

At last, mercifully, Luke gave one final grunt as he fell against her, body heaving convulsively as he emptied himself within her. For a moment, he lay there breathing heavily. Then, getting to his feet and adjusting his trousers, he reached to lift her in his arms, her own trousers still down around her ankles, breasts jouncing exposed outside her open shirt as he headed toward the cabin.

"They're gonna enjoy this," he said, grinning down at her. "The boys need something to perk them up after today. And as soon as Orville's able, I'll see to it that he gets his share. I reckon I've been selfish with you, and it's time to share a good lay and teach you a lesson, to boot."

They were almost to the cabin when the first shot rang out. Instinctively, Luke dropped Kitty to the snow-covered ground and began running in a crouch toward the cabin. Kitty began to roll herself over and over as more shots rang out, trying to keep out of the line of fire.

Someone let out a blood-curdling scream, and she stopped rolling long enough to see one of Luke's men fall from the doorway of the cabin, blood gushing from his mouth. Horrified, she watched as Paul Gray leaped forward in a crouch, his carbine firing like the spit of a snake, but suddenly he screamed, clutched his stomach as a gush of blood and bowels burst forth, then he toppled head forward into the snow.

And then she saw them storming the cabin, rushing inside, heard the sound of more gunfire and screams. A cloud of gray smoke began to drift across the way toward her, as she tried to figure out just what was happening. Were they all dead? Were they now going to kill her, too? But if they were Confederates, then surely they would take care of her, see that she got home safely.

Yes, that was it! She straightened, smiling, relieved. They would only be after Luke and his men if they were Confederates. The nightmare was over. She was safe.

Someone was coming out of the cabin. He was walking toward her, down the hill. Then she saw the way he was looking at her, and, glancing downward, she groped to fix her trousers, tuck her breasts back into the torn shirt. "Thank God," she cried hoarsely, wondering suddenly why he wore no uniform. But he had to be on *our* side, she told her throbbing brain. "Thank God, you're here!"

His eyes lifted above her . . . beyond her . . . and as he said, "Sir, one got away . . . the one who was carrying this young woman," she turned to look behind her. Why hadn't she seen him before? He was right behind her—close enough to touch!

He was looking at the other man, not at her, as he said, "Are they all dead?"

"Yes, sir. There was one man that looked as though his arm had just been cut off, and we went ahead and shot him, too. But the one who was carrying her, he got away. Had a horse tied up around back. Guess he was afraid we'd follow them, and he was ready."

He was lowering his gaze to hers, and Kitty found herself staring into the coldest eyes she had ever seen. They were the color of steel—not blue, not black—but a sheen in between that would have been beautiful, save for the anger and disgust mirrored there. His hair was the color of the raven's wing, shining black, and he had a firm set to his jaw.

His eyes moved down, lingering on her heaving bosom. The smile he gave her was taunting, as though he knew she found him attractive. She cursed herself for the sudden flash of thought that asked what it would be like to feel those arrogantly smiling lips upon hers. His lips parted to show even, white teeth as he said, "Your lover got away, madam. I regret we must take you prisoner, as we don't kill women—unless forced to. I trust we'll have your co-operation to we can avoid any more unpleasantness."

"You don't understand." She spoke quickly, wanting to make him realize right away that she was not his prisoner —she had just been freed! "That man—Luke Tate—he's held me captive for the whole winter."

"Soldier, let's take this woman inside the cabin and persuade her to fix something to eat for us. Then we'll have to figure out what to do with her."

"No, you don't understand!" She threw herself at him then, beating at his chest with her fists. He wore a poncho, made of rubber cloth, and it was impossible to tell if he wore any kind of uniform beneath, but he was obviously a soldier, maybe even an officer. "I've been held prisoner. I want to go home, back to my people in North Carolina. I'm needed there, to work at the hospital. And there's my mother to care for, and my fiancé . . . he's an officer with the Wayne Volunteers . . . please, help me. . . ."

She was crying. Suddenly, it was all too much. He had to believe her. He had to. "Why won't you listen?" she cried.

He caught her wrists and held her away from him. "You're beautiful, you know that?" he whispered with that same taunting smile. "I can see why a man would hold you his prisoner if he couldn't keep you in his bed any other way."

She bristled with anger, indignant over the way those steel-blue eyes were raking over her body . . . the way his lips twisted into that arrogant, knowing grin that said he knew she wanted them to touch hers. It was ridiculous. The whole situation was absurd. After six months of hell, she was at last rescued—if only she could make this idiot realize that she had *been* rescued!

"I demand that you take me home, to my people in North Carolina."

The wind whipped about them, and she shivered. "Come along," he took her arm and steered her up the hill. "We're going inside and talk."

"But you have to listen to me. . . ." she cried as he yanked her along. "My name is Katherine Wright, and I'm from Wayne County in North Carolina. I was taken prisoner by the man who escaped, Luke Tate, after he ambushed Doctor Musgrave and me when we were answering a call to help our men at the Outer Banks last summer. . . ."

She stopped talking as they entered the cabin. The other men were dragging out the bodies. She winced when she saw the discarded arm of Orville Shaw being tossed unceremoniously into the fireplace. "It hardly seems like it was worth the effort to take it off and try to save him. . . ." she said tonelessly.

"What?" The steel-eyed man in the poncho whipped about to stare at her. "Are you saying *you* amputated that man's arm?"

"I certainly did! I told you that's why I'm anxious to go home. There's a Confederate hospital being set up in Goldsboro, and I'm supposed to be helping there. Doc Musgrave taught me a lot about doctoring, and I can help our people."

She noticed that the other men were exchanging amused glances. "I'd like to know what your men find so funny," she demanded.

"Miss Wright," he cleared his throat, grinning, one corner of his mouth tilting up when he smiled. "Are you aware that Luke Tate and his men have been plundering the countryside all winter, disguised both as Federal soldiers and Confederates, depending on which side was in the area to get the blame for their murdering and looting?"

"Yes, but there was nothing I could do about it. I told you. They held *me* prisoner."

"Today," he went on patiently, still smiling as though he knew a secret, "we managed to catch them in the act, and we killed three of their men before they got away. We trailed them here. Now I want to know—did you amputate that man's arm?"

She nodded.

"You did a good job, it seems."

"I told you——Doctor Musgrave trained me. That's why I'm needed at home, to help our people!"

One of the other men snickered, and he shot him a look that sent him into immediate silence. His eyes were over Kitty once again, as he said huskily, "You don't understand, Miss Wright. We were sent here to look for Luke Tate— find him and kill him. . . ."

She sighed with exasperation. "Well, that's fine. He got away, but I'm sure you can catch him. Just get me home. . . ."

He crossed the room, touched the coffeepot in the fireplace and found it warm. She watched with maddening impatience as he found a cup and poured the hot liquid into it. "There is only one slight problem for you," he said finally, his eyes melting into hers.

"Well, I won't *have* any problems if you'll escort me home." Her hands were on her hips indignantly, and she felt the flush of anger in her cheeks. Why did he keep looking at her that way, and why did she have to feel all warm inside when he did? He was arrogant and obviously a stubborn fool who delighted in tormenting women. His accent was not familiar. Perhaps he was a Virginian. Whichever, she was impatient. Stomping her foot, she cried, "Are you going to escort me home like a gentleman or do I strike out on foot?"

"You will do neither, young lady," he said, bowing with exaggerated flourish. "Allow me to introduce myself—Captain Travis Coltrane, and these are the men of my company. . . ."

"All right, so you have a rank!" She let her breath out in a rush. Would this madness never end? Freedom was so sweet, and the nightmare was over, if only this smiling stranger would stop being so mysterious.

He paused to take a long sip of his coffee, then set the cup down on the bloodied table where Orville Shaw's arm had been amputated. "Miss Wright," he said finally, "I don't think you understand. You see, I'm Captain Coltrane of the *Union* army . . . and you are now *my* prisoner."

❧ Chapter Fifteen ❧

TRAVIS knew that she only pretended to sleep. He sat with his back to the fire's warmth, watching the way the flickering light seemed to make the soft gold of her flowing hair dance with sparkles. She lay too stiff, too rigid, to be sleeping. He had ordered her to make her bed near him, so he could keep an eye on her, for the anger that crackled in those almost purple eyes told him she was not one to be easily subdued. After all, she was a Rebel, and she'd made it quite clear that her intention was to return to her family in North Carolina and work for the Southern cause. But he could not allow it. No. She was much too valuable a prisoner. General Grant had said that doctors and nurses were already scarce, and he, himself, had examined the wound on the dead man's arm from the amputation she had performed so skillfully. It was amazing, and he was not about to let her return to minister to the enemy.

In the soft glow of the flames he could make out the sleeping outlines of his men. They were exhausted from the day's battle and had scarcely done more than toss a few hungry gazes in the direction of their prisoner, except for one. Travis stared at the spot where Leon Brody lay flat on his back. For a long while after the others had fallen asleep, he had continued to dart furtive, longing glances in the direction of the young woman, and there was no mistaking his lust for her. Brody had quite a name where the women were concerned, and Travis had experienced a few run-ins with him during a couple of the raids they'd made. One particular scene had been rather ugly—he had threatened to kill the rebellious soldier when he found him raping a young black girl in the eastern part of Tennessee as they'd passed through.

Keeping Katherine Wright prisoner was going to take plenty of doing, he thought worriedly. She was beautiful. Long, silky hair that ached to be touched—eyes that could swallow a man in their dark fires and shadows. And he had seen her body. Oh, yes, he, like his men, had seen her large, firm breasts she tried to hide after the man called Luke Tate had dropped her into the snow. They poured from her torn shirt. And her skin. So soft, despite the hardships she had obviously endured through the winter. . . . Long, shapely, tapering legs with slender, delicate ankles . . . hips that were firm and tender to the touch.

Beautiful. God, she was beautiful. Even now he could feel the heat rising in his own body, the pressure of his swelling member as he thought of how it would be to lie down beside her, and hold her, and touch her, and enter the sweet, hungry flesh.

A smile tilted his lips to one side as he thought of the almost accusing way she had looked at him when he ordered her to move her bed closer to the fire so he could keep close watch on her. She had stood there, eyes blazing defiantly, lips set tightly, hands on her hips. "I suppose you plan to keep me for yourself the way Luke Tate did," she had cried. "And if I refuse to submit to your animal passion, you'll turn me over to your men to take their turns with me. . . ."

He had laughed at her. He had thrown back his head and laughed at her, and the effect had been devastating. Before anyone could make a move, she had whirled about to grab the first thing her fingers could fasten about—a tin cup half-filled with scalding coffee—sending the hot liquid splattering into his taunting face.

Any other woman, trapped by the impulse of her own hasty action, might have wilted beneath the burning, angry gaze he silently gave her as the coffee dripped slowly down his face and onto his dark blue shirt. But not this one. She clenched her fists and stood her ground, ready to defend herself if need be.

Again he laughed, and she blinked, surprised. First he had reacted to the idea of having sex with her as though he found it quite amusing. And then, after having hot coffee thrown in his face, he could still look at her and react with good humor.

"You flatter yourself," he said finally, lips smiling but eyes cold and hard. "You think I want to sow my seed in a Rebel garden? No, thanks, princess. I save myself for more valuable and choice property. You'll be safer lying near to me, as my men might not be quite as particular."

Gritting her teeth, she had flung herself upon her pallet. The hive would be warm, and the honey sweeter than the finest wine, but he had no intentions of getting stung by the angry queen bee. He knew his men raped whenever they had the chance, just as the Rebels ravished the Northern women. But he figured it only enhanced a woman's conceit to turn into a fawning, grunting animal in order to enter their orifices. And handing out compliments to boost a female ego was something he prided himself in never doing.

He forced himself to think of other things, like the war that was about to strike with full fury. General Ulysses S. Grant, himself, had sent him and his band of men to the western mountains of Virginia to rout the murdering group of raiders that reportedly had no mercy for either side. The whole countryside had heard of their brutal killings and raids, and General Grant wanted them out of the region when he left Cairo, Illinois, with 15,000 men early in February to attack the center of the 600-mile line of Confederate soldiers that were stationed between the Appalachian Mountains westward to the Mississippi River. It was a matter of honor, he said, to destroy the Rebel traitors who donned Union clothes to plunder and rob and murder innocent families. For the glory of the Union, they had to be destroyed.

And Luke Tate had escaped. That was unfortunate, Travis conceded, but his men were dead. It would take quite a while for him to round up a new band, and with the area crawling with soldiers from both sides, he would have difficulty—unless he was able to somehow get together the deserters, who, he felt, were unscrupulous enough to be glad to join a no-good scoundrel like Tate.

He had slept for short periods of time during the long night, the chill creeping through the crudely constructed cabin walls to penetrate the very marrow of his bones. The first streaks of morning light began to filter through. Soon it would be time to rouse the men and start the journey to rejoin General Grant. He was anxious to be back in the thick of battle with the Cavalry, charging the Rebel lines and smashing down those who fought to destroy the Union. Those who knew him accused him of loving war passionately, and perhaps they were right. He did not mind killing and destroying to defend something he believed in so strongly.

The last word that they'd been able to hear about the progress of General Grant was that he had been victorious at Fort Henry. A newspaper account told about how the Confederates had constructed twin forts in Tennessee just south of the Kentucky border to protect two important rivers—the Tennessee and the Cumberland. Fort Henry guarded the Tennessee; Fort Donelson stood menacingly on the banks of the Cumberland. On February 6th, while he had been searching the snowbound mountains of Virginia for the band of Rebel murderers that had both sides aching to see them destroyed, Grant had, with the aid of a Federal river fleet, battered Fort Henry into submission. And about ten days later, the word was that Grant had surrounded Fort Donelson and its reported 12,000 defenders. Travis had laughed with approval when he read the reply General Grant had given when the Confederate commander requested surrender terms. He had replied, "No terms but unconditional surrender," and now people were calling him "Unconditional Surrender" Grant.

Capture of the Henry and Donelson forts assured, Travis knew that the Union would have control of Kentucky and Tennessee and would open Mississippi and Alabama to Federal invasion. And, of course, the loss of the forts would be a severe blow to Southern morale. Now the Rebels knew that the Union army had the ability and the willingness to fight, by God!

And then, they had received more jubilant news. There

had been an important battle farther to the west for control of Arkansas and Missouri. During the first week in March, at a place called Pea Ridge in the state of Arkansas, a Confederate Army, said to be numbered around 16,000, attacked about 12,000 Federals fighting under the command of General Samuel R. Curtis. And what Travis and his men laughed about was the report that the Confederates were dressed in rags—few had on anything that even vaguely resembled a uniform. And they were armed with only shotguns and squirrel rifles. And they even had Indians fighting with them—about 3,500 or so, they'd heard—Indians that belonged to the Creek, Choctaw, Cherokee, Chickasaw, and Seminole tribes. And after only two days of heavy fighting, a counterattack by the Federals broke up the makeshift "army"—and with the defeat of Pea Ridge, the Confederates permanently lost Missouri and northern Arkansas.

Things were looking very good, and Travis wanted to get back to the war. He enjoyed raids and scouting, but after so many months of treking through the all but impassable mountains on his latest assignment, he was anxious to get back to civilization, even if it meant being in the middle of a boiling battle.

Now they had heard that Grant's army was near the Mississippi border, and he wanted to move as quickly as possible to get there. He and his men were qualified "Sharpshooters" of the Cavalry. They had been issued the best equipment and the finest horses. Their breech-loading Spencer repeating carbines were deadly, and the Rebels knew it. The ones they captured could not be used, because they lacked the special cartridges and, as yet, did not have the facilities or ample supply of metal for their manufacture. Travis knew his troop of men were valuable, and he was proud of this fact.

He had succeeded in pushing the thoughts of the young woman from his mind. Now she stirred, moaning in her sleep, turning her face toward the soft glow of the fire. She was beautiful, and he bit back the gasp that moved up his throat as he caught sight of one firm, milk-white breast tumbling from the loose-fitting shirt. He stared at it, licking his lips hungrily. Even in sleep, the nipple was taut, almost angry . . . defiant that he should be staring. And it seemed to be staring back—like an accusing red-pupiled eye. He felt the tautness in his loins as his lips twitched in a sucking motion—how he longed to clamp down on that glaring eye and feel the emotion ripple through the lovely young thing's body. But no, he checked himself. He had more self-control than that—even if it had been weeks since he had known the delight of emptying himself into a woman's belly.

Her eyes opened, very slowly, and he met her gaze, and she caught it and held his eyes for a moment, letting the half-taunting, half-defiant challenge leap into the tenseness between them.

Quickly, with the self-control of which he was so proud, Travis forced the moment to pass. Kitty saw that the predatory light she'd seen there only a few seconds ago vanished, to be replaced by indifference.

His eyes flicked down to her exposed breast, and he gave her an amused, half-mocking smile as he said, "I believe you lost something, princess. As I said before, some of my men aren't so particular about used goods, and they might see what you have to offer and take you up on it."

"Ohhhh!" She followed his gaze, realized her breast was exposed, and pushed herself back into the shirt so roughly that she accidentally pinched herself. "How dare you think I want you to touch me, you arrogant bastard. . . ."

He raised an eyebrow, still smiling. "The lady knows some dirty words. It seems your Rebel lover didn't mind the kind of language he used around women, and I thought all you Southern belles were supposed to be so ladylike and refined. Tsk! Tsk!" He shook his head from side to side, taunting her.

She pulled herself up to a sitting position on the pallet, tossing back her golden hair. With eyes blazing and lips trembling, she stared at him in fury. "Just why do you find me so despicable, Captain Coltrane? I've told you the truth about my capture, but yet you seem to take some sort of depraved pleasure in trying to torment me and shame me. I'd like to know why."

"Haven't you heard?" he chuckled. "We're at war, princess, and you happen to be the enemy."

"The enemy? I'm not at war with you, sir. I've been held prisoner and raped for over six months, and I'm anxious to go home and work to help the sick and wounded. Now why does that make me your enemy? Do I get a trial before you sentence me to be hanged?"

Now Travis saw the mocking light in her eyes, and instead of angry tantrums, she was giving him insolence and scorn. A nerve along his jawline tensed. "Why should I turn you loose to go home and help the ones who want to kill me and my kind? Oh, no, you're going to come with us and work with *our* sick and wounded. I'd be a fool to send you back to your people, and I don't like to be taken for a fool—especially by a *Southern* woman." His eyes twinkled, and he grinned as he saw that his remark had struck home, and she was again angry.

"You *are* a bastard! I'll not lift a finger to help a murdering Yankee. I hope all of you die and rot in hell—except for my father, who so foolishly went to fight with you."

He raised an eyebrow. "Your father joined the Union army?"

"His mind was never right after the Vigilantes nearly killed him when they caught him helping runaway slaves to the underground. He can't be blamed for his feelings. I just pray that he'll come to his senses and go back where he belongs."

"This war has turned brother against brother, Miss Wright, and father against son. And why? Because the South insists on making slaves out of human beings just because their skin happens to be black."

"I've never been in favor of forced slavery," she said, defending herself. "But I do uphold states rights. You and I will never agree, and I will never lift so much as a finger to help a dying Yankee. You understand *that* before you take me away from here. I'll *die* first!"

Her eyes had narrowed catlike, and she had spoken in a hissing sound, her whole body quivering with her wrath. It would take time to break her spirit, but Travis knew it would have to be done. Few women could withstand the horrors of wars. Most fainted at the sight of blood or the sound of a man screaming as his bones were hacked from his body. But not this one. No, she had courage, fortitude, and her services would be invaluable to the Union army. He had no intention of letting her go, nor would he turn such ripe, sweet flesh over to the lusts of his men if she refused to obey. No, there had to be another way, and he would find it. She would bend to his will. He made himself a promise to that effect—and he always kept his promises.

He got to his feet slowly. "I want you to fix some coffee and food for my men, and then we'll be on our way. You do as you're told, and you'll be safe as long as I'm alive. If anything happens to me, you'll be on your own, because these men seldom know their pleasure, and it's going to take some doing to keep them off of you as it is . . . ."

"Oh, how gallant!" She mocked him. "How wonderful you are. The brave Union Captain Travis Coltrane . . . ready to defend the honor of the flower of womanhood. I'm touched. Really I am." She scrambled to her feet to glare at him, lips curling back as though ready to strike and kill.

He stepped closer, and she moved backward with him walking slowly toward her, until there was no place to run. Her back was against the wall, and she continued to look at him with defiance, even though her body was shaking uncontrollably. Suddenly he reached out and grabbed her into his arms. It was a pure instinctive action—something he could no longer help. "I never said you were the flower of womanhood, princess, but let's find out. . . ."

He could smell the fragrance of the pine needles that clung to her hair, feel the teasing suppleness of her body. Anger, mixed with frustration, made him suddenly cruel. Wrapping his fingers in her hair to pull her head back, he covered her mouth with his hungrily. For a moment, she was rigid, not fighting back, but then her teeth clamped down viciously on his tongue which he had forced between her lips.

"You bitch!" He jerked back, tasting blood, and he brought his hand up to strike her, but the look she was giving him—the way she all but turned her cheek up to receive his blow, made him regain his control. She wanted him to hit her—wanted to put him on the same level as that murdering Luke Tate. Hell, she probably wanted him to rape her. She probably wanted it as much as he did— only she wanted to protect her so-called virtue and say she had been forced. Well, he had known plenty of women, and to his credit, not one of them had ever made him resort to taking what he wanted by force. Oh, no, he knew how to make a woman writhe and moan in his arms, begging him to take her over and over again. His back had been bloodied by frenzied, raking nails too many times by the throes of the ecstasy he produced in his women, for him to ever stoop to force.

Suddenly calm, he smiled that crooked, taunting smirk that Kitty already hated. "I'm afraid you failed the test, princess. Any flower of womanhood you might have possessed has long been plucked from the stem. Now get the hell over to that fire and get some food going for my men before I forget I'm a gentleman . . . and an officer . . . and give you the beating you deserve!"

She turned away, not knowing who she hated more at the moment—Captain Coltrane . . . or herself! Why did her knees feel so weak and watery, and why was her heart pounding? And what was the peculiar tremor she felt in her loins? Surely her own body would not betray her. Every time Luke Tate had ravished her, she had reacted with a wave of nausea and revulsion . . . never like this . . . so it could not be purely physical. She could not actually want that . . . that animal! She had never felt this way except when Nathan had held her and kissed her, and even then, it had been a controlled emotion, one that did not leave her trembling where she stood!

It was hatred! That's what it was. She had only thought she hated Luke Tate, but that feeling was nothing compared to the raw nerves that were making her whole being convulse in great waves of shuddering. Despicable! Travis Coltrane was a Yankee—a murdering, blood-thirsty Yankee who heaped war upon her people—no better than Luke Tate and the men he had killed yesterday.

She reached for the slab of bacon that hung on a rope by the fireplace, turning slightly to see where he had gone. Her eyes met his steely-blue gaze beneath lowered lashes. He stood with thumbs hooked in his belt, his feet spread apart. And he was smiling. That damned, insolent smile that made her livid with indignant rage.

He wanted her. She knew he did. Well, she could play his little game. He thought he was too good for the likes of a Southern woman who'd been raped by a low-life hoodlum. Now, if he insisted on holding her prisoner and taking her with him, she would make him pay—and pay dearly.

After all, she was a woman, she reminded herself, and men found her appealing and attractive. She would make the conceited, arrogant Yankee officer bend to her will, grovel with desire at her feet. And then she would laugh in his face.

Smiling, she turned and held out a hand to him. "If you trust me with a knife, sir, I'll slice this bacon to fry for your soldiers."

With a move so lightning quick she barely saw his arm move, he had whipped out a bowie knife and sent it slicing through the air to land with a sharp thud in the wall only inches from her head. Eyes mocking, lips taunting, he said, "I find nothing in you to fear, princess. When the day comes that I do . . . God pity me . . . and God help the Northern cause!"

Then start praying, you arrogant bastard, she thought silently, slicing at the greasy side of meat with a vengeance, attacking it with the sharp knife. *Get down on your knees and pray!*

❦ Chapter Sixteen ❧

THEY had not ridden far after leaving the area where
the cabin was situated before shots rang out from the
woods alongside the zigzagging road. "Take cover," Coltrane yelled, grabbing his rifle and leaping from his horse.
Kitty was on the horse directly behind him, and when he
turned to pull her from the saddle, he saw that she had
already dismounted and taken cover behind the trunk of a
large oak tree.

Kitty pressed herself against the rough bark, her heart
pounding furiously. She'd come too far to be killed now,
she thought in a frenzy, and she prayed that Coltrane and
his men would be shot, so she could be freed.

There were more shots zinging through the air, but she
was puzzled to notice that Coltrane's men were not all
firing. It didn't take long for her to realize why—suddenly
shouts came from the weeds and thickets beyond, and then
three of the Yankee soldiers were marching forward triumphantly, prodding two farmers with the ends of their
rifles.

"Goddamned settlers," one of the soldiers cursed, shoving the old man in front of him to the ground.

"Bishop, watch it!" Travis barked, stepping from his
cover. "These people don't know what's going on around
here. Hell, they've never been out of the mountains. . . ."

The old man was scrambling to his feet, dusting off his

173

clothes. There was no snow here, and the ground was dry. "Don't need to leave the mountains to know Yankees ain't got no business here. Now you git off my property."

Travis had walked up to him, and now he circled the two prisoners, eyeing them critically. "You two live close by?" He directed his questions to the younger man, who looked to be in his late twenties. He nodded an answer. "Then take us there."

"You ain't got no business . . ."

The soldier called Bishop rammed the butt of his carbine into the old man's stomach, and he clutched himself, moaning in pain, doubling over. This time Coltrane did not intervene.

"Just take us to your cabin. We want to see what you've got in the way of ammunition and food supplies. Then we'll be on our way. You've nothing to fear if you cooperate."

Kitty followed them doggedly, and they walked the horses through the thicket until they came to a clearing. A small, but neat-looking cabin sat beneath sprawling elms that were just beginning to bud to life. A lop-eared hound lying on the porch eyed them suspiciously but made no move.

"Is anyone inside?" Travis asked.

The younger one answered that they had families inside —three small children and their wives.

"Tell them to come out and throw down any guns they've got in there," he ordered.

The women appeared on the porch, looking frightened as they clung together with the children peering out wide-eyed from behind their long muslin skirts. One of the women was about the age of the old man, short and fat. The other was young and tidy, and she might have been pretty, had she not looked so worn-out and haggard from the hard life of a mountain woman.

Travis stood back with Kitty as his men made a thorough search of the house and reported back that the ammunition they'd found was not enough to worry about. There was a cow, some chickens, and the mule was skin and bones and looked diseased.

"Hell, run them chickens down," Bishop said, almost angrily, from where he sat on his horse. "We can eat them

for supper. I'm damn tired of that shit in our knapsacks.
And butcher that cow, too."

The young woman on the porch ran down the steps
toward them, waving her arms above her head as tears
streamed down her pale cheeks. "Please, God, don't kill
our cow and take our chickens. They're all we've got left
. . . we're starving. We barely made it through the winter,
and if you take all we have left, we'll starve before plantin'
time. Please. . . ."

She was yanking at Bishop's leg, pleading, and Kitty's
heart went out to her. Then she saw that Bishop was
bringing up his rifle butt, about to send it crashing down
into her face. Travis made a move, but Kitty was closer.
Throwing herself from her horse, she lunged for him, the
two of them falling from the horse's back and onto the
ground.

Stunned, Bishop quickly realized what had happened,
and he fastened his stubby fingers about her throat and
began shaking her and cursing. Travis stepped up and sent
his booted foot into his side with such force that he rolled
away, groaning painfully. He reached down to grab Kitty
by her shoulders and yank her to her feet.

"Are you all right?" he asked in a tone that Kitty thought
sounded as though he really didn't care one way or another.
She didn't answer him.

He gave her a shove toward the sobbing woman. "You
get inside and change clothes with her . . ."

"But this is the only dress I own," the other cried, backing away and wrapping her arms about herself. "I ain't
got nothin' else."

"You'll have the clothes this young lady is wearing.
Now do as I say or I'll have my men take your cow and
chickens." He gave Kitty a shove toward the woman's
retreating movements.

"Why are you doing this?" She flashed at him angrily.
"Why are you tormenting that poor woman? And you know
these clothes I've got on are more suitable for riding than
a dress!"

"I happen to like dresses, princess," he gave her that
mocking smile that set her teeth grinding. "Women belong
in dresses, not baggy trousers like a man. Now move."

"I'll wear what I damn well please!" She was so mad she was shaking, and she kept her fists clenched at her sides, afraid if she did what she was aching to do, a rifle butt would come crashing down on *her* head! "No man tells me how to dress. I've worn trousers all my life! I will not steal that woman's dress!"

With one quick movement he leaned over and gathered the front of her shirt in his hand, then ripped downward. Her naked breasts tumbled forth. The soldiers were watching, and a delighted gasp went up, as she threw her arms across her chest and backed away, humiliated and terrified of what was about to happen.

Pointing his finger at her, eyes blazing straight into hers menacingly, he said slowly and evenly, "Get yourself into that house and put on that woman's dress, or by God, you'll ride naked from here on!"

She had no choice but to clutch herself and run for the cabin as the men's laughter echoed in her ears. Tears stung her eyes, but she bit them back. Never would Travis Coltrane make her cry! Never! No matter what he did! No. If anyone cried, it would be him—when she plunged a knife into his back one day . . . or shot him . . . or something . . . but she would have her revenge! This, she swore.

The young woman held out her dress to Kitty, but she looked as though she pitied her, rather than being angry over having to give up her dress. "I don't really want it, you know," Kitty felt compelled to say. "And he tore the shirt I'm to give to you. I'm sorry."

"You a Yankee?" Curious eyes flicked over her.

Kitty bristled indignantly. "Certainly not. I'm their prisoner. I wish your menfolk had killed them so I could go free."

"Where you headin'?" Kitty thought she sounded positively wistful, and this was puzzling.

"I don't know. I heard them say something about joining General Grant. He's a Yankee. He's somewhere near the Mississippi border, wherever that is. I don't even know where we are. But if anyone comes by here asking questions, you tell them what I told you. You tell them Kitty Wright is being held a prisoner by them . . . I'm from Goldsboro, North Carolina, and I was kidnapped by a man named Luke Tate last summer. Now you remember this, because I have a Confederate fiancé that may be out searching for me."

She stopped talking and stared incredulously at the woman before her. She looked as though she were swaying. "Are . . . are you all right?"

"You're gonna think I'm crazy, Miss Wright, but it sounds so excitin'. I'm not but nineteen, and I've already had three babies and 'spectin' another. A baby a year for me, but you, you're beautiful, and that man out there . . . the one givin' orders. Gawd, he's handsome. I don't think I've ever seen a man that pretty."

Kitty shook herself. She, herself, had been raised on a farm, and there'd been times when socials and fun seemed like a distant thing. But never had she thought it would be exciting to be held prisoner by a band of men, no matter how good-looking one of them happened to be.

She struggled into the dress. It was tight, especially across the bosom. The other girl had smaller breasts, and this neckline was even lower than the one she'd worn to the Collins barbecue, which seemed a hundred years ago. "Why is it so low?" Kitty asked aloud.

"I told Tom that's what I wanted for Christmas—a real, honest-to-goodness, lady's dress like they say the women wear to parties in Nashville. And he went all the way to Nashville and bought it for me. Then I found out I was in the family way, so I wouldn't have been wearing it much longer, anyways," she finished lamely.

It was a cheap dress of poor quality, Kitty thought, but it had meant everything to the wistful-looking young woman in front of her. Impulsively, she reached out and hugged her. "I'm sorry, truly I am. Good luck to you, and I hope you don't have any more Yankees passing by."

"If I weren't gonna have a baby, maybe someone would up and carry me off," she called gaily, but Kitty was already out the door and walking toward the lean-to kitchen, with the girl running along beside her.

She glanced about the sparsely furnished room. "Where do you keep your knives?" This was her chance. Hide a knife in the folds of her skirt . . . wait until the right time and plunge it into Travis Coltrane's back and make her getaway. It was the only hope she had.

The girl looked at her with widening, frightened eyes.

"Don't just stand there," Kitty whispered frantically. "They'll come looking for me soon. Tell me where there's a knife."

He seemed to fill the doorway as he stepped forward, eyes mocking, lips taunting. "Now, princess, what would a lady, in an appealing dress like you're wearing, want with a nasty, dirty knife? It isn't feminine."

She picked up a piece of crockery sitting on the round wooden table and sent it sailing through the air to smash against the wall, just where his head had been before he ducked. He advanced toward her, and she reached for other dishes, throwing them. One hit and bounced off, breaking on the floor, and still he came. There were no more dishes . . . no place to run . . . and he towered over her, reaching out to wrap strong hands around her thin wrists, pressing them against her side as he pulled her body forward, her heaving breasts rubbing against the coarse woolen jacket he wore.

She could feel the heat of his breath on her face, see the way his nostrils flared as his eyes probed into hers.

And then his face was coming down, his lips bruising, crushing. Just as her knees turned to water, and the strange quivering in her loins began, he flung her away from him, so quickly, so forcefully, that she had to fight to regain her balance and not sprawl to the floor.

"Now get out there and get on that horse!" He spoke in the same harsh tone he used with his men. "And try to remember you're a lady, and you're a nurse for the Union army. Don't you Southern ladies have any breeding at all?"

The taunting smile was back, and she whirled to run from the lean-to kitchen, through the cabin, out the front door, and stumble across the yard. The tears were stinging, and she tasted blood as she bit down on her quivering lips to keep them back. He wasn't going to make her cry. Damn him! Damn him to hell! He would never make her cry! Damn him for keeping her prisoner and damn him for making her feel emotions that only Nathan had the right to create.

Her face was pressed into the horse's neck. Suddenly she felt hands wrapping around her bottom and swinging her upward and sideways, onto the saddle. Travis didn't smile as he said, "I've had about all I intend to take from you for one day, Kitty."

Doggedly, she dug her heels into the horse's flanks and followed the men deeper into the woods. She heard Travis saying something to someone about how they shouldn't have been traveling in the daylight hours. The snipers could have killed someone. She found herself wishing he'd been the one to get hit, as she glared at his back.

They reached the seclusion of a foliage-concealed ravine. The horses were led off to graze, and the others built a small campfire. Travis signaled to Kitty to prepare some sort of meal, which she silently did, aware that all eyes were upon her, watching every move she made.

Kitty hated the dress. What right did the conceited Yankee officer have to force her to wear it? The clothes she'd been forced to discard were far more comfortable. Right away, it was easy to see that Travis Coltrane was one of those pig-headed men who believed a woman belonged in skirts, sitting at home and sewing and weaving and having a baby every year. And such men infuriated her to no end! Nathan was a lot like that, causing much tension between them. But finally, when he had left for the war, it seemed that he had accepted her, reluctantly, for the person she was—not what social decorum proclaimed she should be.

Coltrane was telling everyone to lie down and try to take a nap; they would be moving out as soon as night fell. Kitty saw Leon Brody giving her a hungry look, but Travis saw it too, and motioned her to bring her saddle blanket to where he sat propped against the trunk of a large pine tree. Anything was better than the beady-eyed glare of that nasty-looking man, she decided. And, anyway, she wanted to work on her scheme to get around Travis's apparent dislike for her . . . catch him off guard . . . and only then could she hope to escape.

Lying down, she stared up at the azure sky. It was pretty here in the footlands of the Cumberland Mountains. The Shenandoah Valley, it was called. Way up high, a graceful eagle was soaring, swooping—free—the way she had once been . . . the way she could be again, if she was smart.

Propping her head on her hand, she looked at Travis,

who was chewing a blade of grass as he stared at her thoughtfully. "Would you mind telling me where we're going? I'm curious." She tried to sound pleasant, not hostile.

"To join Grant. Somewhere on the western bank of the Tennessee. The closer we get, the more Rebs are going to be crawling out of the ground, so we have to be careful."

He didn't sound quite so angry, so she pressed. "You know, you don't sound like a Yankee, but you have a different accent from what I'm used to hearing. Where are you from, Travis?"

He looked at her sharply, suspiciously. Then he seemed to relax as he quietly said, "Louisiana."

"Then why do you fight for the North?" She sat straight up, surprised.

"The same reason your father does," he said sharply. "Because I believe in something."

"Poppa had a personal grudge against his countrymen after they beat him and caused him to go blind in one eye. He didn't favor slavery, but he wouldn't have gone to war over it. He was a peace-loving man. Luke Tate spit in his face once when they were having a heated discussion over the prospects of war, and Poppa didn't lift a finger. He did reach for something to clean his face, though, and Luke thought he was reaching for a gun, so he pulled a knife on him."

"Then what happened?"

"I shot him," she said simply, wondering why his eyes were widening. ". . . with Poppa's musket that was in the wagon. I didn't try to kill him. Don't look so shocked. I only wounded him in the shoulder. We also had a nasty scene once when I tried to stop him from beating a slave girl who was in the family way. Poppa was trying to help her and her baby and the baby's father to escape when the Vigilantes caught them. They were all three murdered."

She waited for his reaction, but when it came, it was not as she had expected. "Do you shoot well?"

Indignantly, she replied, "Of couse I do. Poppa taught me all about guns and shooting. He used to take me hunting with him."

She stopped talking, watching as he reached to his side and brought his gun up to hand to her. "Have you ever

seen a gun like this?" She shook her head that she hadn't.
"It's a Spencer Repeating Carbine—a breech-loader—and
a damn fine weapon! Do you know how to load it?"

Again she shook her head, and he proceeded to show her
how to load and fire the gun. She listened attentively, then
burst out, "But why do you want me to know how to use
the gun? Aren't you afraid I'll shoot you?"

Shrugging, he smiled. "That's the chance I have to take.
You're valuable to us, Kitty. You know enough about treating wounds to work in a field hospital alongside a doctor.
But we're heading into a war, and there may come a time
when you have to defend yourself against the Rebels. I
want you to know how."

"I could never shoot at a Southerner!"

This time he threw his head back and laughed. "You
seem to forget that a Rebel is going to think you're a
Yankee, and he's going to be shooting at you, so you better
be able to shoot back unless your Southern pride means
more to you than your life. You may think you've known
violence, princess, being held prisoner by Luke Tate all
these months, but until you've been in a real battle, with
men dying all around you, legs and arms sprawled about
like wildflowers, you don't know what real violence is. But
you're going to know. I just hope you've got the guts to
take it."

"Is that why you put me in a dress?" Anger was bristling
uncontrollably within her. "You want me to look like a
woman, be humble and gracious, and yet you're sitting
here telling me that one day soon I might be fighting like
a man? It doesn't make sense."

"Oh, yes, it does. I'm hoping that Johnny Reb will spot
that dress and think twice before killing a woman."

So that was the reason for the dress—not his wanting to
put her in her "place." She felt a warmth spreading
through her bosom, but it was quickly replaced by a cold
chill when he snapped, "And also I figured if you had a
dress on, you might remember you're a woman and not
a man!"

She quickly turned her face away so he would not see
the anger that was surely written all over it. If she were
to gain his confidence and catch him off guard, then
temper tantrums had to be held back. Deciding to change

the subject, she asked, "Tell me what you did before the war, down in Louisiana."

"I was a fisherman on the bayou."

"Then what brought you into the war?"

Slowly, while she watched curiously, he pulled the poncho over his head, revealing the dark blue Yankee uniform shirt beneath. He unbuttoned it, then removed it. "Look at my skin."

She stared at the curly dark hairs on the solid, husky chest—eyes moving to the hard, firm muscles of his forearms. He had a beautiful body, and she cursed herself for thinking about such things. Trying to focus her attention solely on his skin, she said, "You have dark skin. You've been in the sun a lot."

The laugh he gave was bitter. "I'm a French creole, princess, and we're naturally dark-skinned people. Some of us are lighter than others, but my family happens to be darker than most."

"Well, what does that have to do with anything?" She didn't understand what he was getting at, and she noted that his eyes were clouding, as though something furious was smoldering from deep within.

"My sister was fourteen when she was kidnapped by slave traders," the words came chopping out. "Our parents were dead. I was trying to make a living from fishing, and I was away when they came for her. She was a beautiful girl—and even at the tender age of fourteen, men were wild for her. I didn't know *how* wild until I came home to find she'd been kidnapped. I searched for her, ready to kill someone. . . ."

His voice tapered off. He picked up a rock and threw it with vehemence. There was a moment of tense silence, and Kitty finally mustered the courage to ask, "And did you find her?"

"The goddamned bastards sold her into slavery. . . ." He turned to look at her with blazing eyes. "By the time I tracked her down and found her—she'd been raped by a hundred men. She had also killed herself!"

"Oh, dear God," she whispered, shocked, instinctively reaching out to touch his hand in sympathy.

Shrugging off her touch, he laughed bitterly. "So you

can see why I'm anxious to fight against slavery. Those bastards traded my sister off as being a slave!"

She didn't know what to say. Each man fights his own battles within his own soul—she'd heard her poppa say that often. Each man does what he has to do. Travis Coltrane had his reasons; her father had his . . . and she had hers.

After a few moments of awkwardness, he said gruffly, "Get some sleep, Kitty. We've got a rough night's ride ahead. And don't try to escape. I've got guards posted."

He still didn't trust her, but at least she'd made some progress. They could at least be civil to each other, and that was a start—and a start had to come from something. Lying down and pulling another blanket over her, she closed her eyes and was soon fast asleep—worn and weary from the long ride.

When Kitty again opened her eyes, it was pitch dark. For a moment, she groggily tried to get her wits together and figure out where she was and what was happening. Then she realized that Travis was shaking her, telling her to get up and get ready. They were moving out.

The movement through the woods, by night, was slow and dangerous. Travis admitted he was not sure where they would meet up with Grant. There was a chance they would encounter the Confederates first, and in all probability they would be outnumbered by the thousands.

It was almost April, and she was still freezing. It surprised her when Travis, riding beside her, noticed and took off his poncho to slip over her head. "Can't have you getting the fever and getting down," he said tartly. "We're going to need you when hell starts raining down on us from Rebel guns."

They moved very slowly, listening for the smallest of sounds. Suddenly, everyone was freezing, halting the horses. Travis reached out to catch the reins of the horse Kitty was riding, and he whispered for her to be quiet and not make a sound. "There's something ahead of us."

Without being ordered to do so, the two men at the head of the line dismounted and walked forward. Kitty tensed, fearful that at any moment there would be the sound of gunfire, and then all of them would be shot and killed.

But instead of gunfire, there came several shouts—excited, urging them to come quickly—and for God's sake, they screamed—bring the doctor lady.

Someone grabbed her from the saddle, and she knew it was not Travis. He was already charging forward. The soldier beside her pulled her along, and already, in the clearing up ahead, someone was trying to light a fire. There was the sound of moaning . . . agony . . . suffering . . . and then the fire was burning, and she could see, and the horror made her turn her face away for a moment.

There were maybe five or six bodies there—faces torn away, guts hanging from gaping wounds in the stomach. And then she was being dragged along to where a young soldier, perhaps seventeen or eighteen years of age, was propped against the stump of a tree. Right away, she could see that his left eye hung drooling from a bloody socket . . . and there was a gouging wound with flesh and matter oozing out. He was in some sort of stupor, moaning some, but not nearly as much as an alert soldier would cry out.

Kitty examined him quickly. There had been a good deal of bleeding. There was nothing she could do. It was obvious that the boy was almost dead, and she wondered how he could even be clinging to life at this point.

"I . . . want to talk to . . . officer. . . ." he gasped out the words, barely audible. Travis stepped forward, knelt, and identified himself as being in charge.

The boy was a Union soldier, and he was more concerned with the plight of his commander than he was his own life. "Get to Grant . . . quick . . . we know . . . tell him Rebels are coming to get him before he gets . . . help."

Travis turned to Kitty questioningly. She shook her head. The boy was almost gone. Her heart wrenched as he cried out in a sudden wave of agony, sliding sideways to the ground. She watched as the eyeball fell into the dirt, covering it with little flecks of sand . . . a strange, awesome sight in the flickering firelight.

"Are you sure?" Travis reached to give her a violent shake that made her head bob to and fro. "Goddamn you, Kitty, don't you lie to me. Can this boy be treated and recover?"

"No!" She all but yelled. "I'm sorry, but he's bleeding to death from that wound. He's almost dead now. . . ."

The soldier twisted in his agony, screamed, and then everyone watched in horror as he reached toward his face, clutching, guttural shrieks coming from his lips as he took hold of his eyeball and finished yanking it from the socket, flinging it out into the vast darkness.

She heard one of the men retching. A fresh gush of blood poured from somewhere inside the Yankee soldier's head. "I am sorry. . . ." Kitty whispered sincerely. There was just nothing she could do.

"We've got to get moving." A soldier named Sam Bucher spoke anxiously, glancing about at the bodies. "These boys were obviously sent out to get help. Grant must be in trouble, and we need to get to him before he gets pinned down."

"You can't leave him here!" Kitty cried in protest as they all began moving back from the dying soldier. "You can't leave him to just die alone. These mountains are full of wild animals! Do you want him left to be picked to pieces by wolves while he's still alive? God, have mercy. . . ."

A shot rang out. The boy's head snapped forward. His body was still—dead.

Raising eyes to see who had fired the shot to kill him, Kitty was not surprised to see Travis standing a few feet away, a smoking Spencer carbine held in his hand. "No," he said quietly, sternly. "We won't leave him here to die."

While she stood there blinking back tears, hating him for his brutality, Poppa's words seemed to whisper to her, "Sometimes it takes more courage to live than it does to die."

And slowly, Kitty realized that Travis had to shoot the boy. His leader was in trouble somewhere, and they had to get to him as quickly as possible. It had to be done.

Travis had the courage to live, Kitty thought, watching him walk toward his horse. She only prayed that when the time came—she would have that same quality.

⚝ Chapter Seventeen ⚝

TRAVIS had ordered Sam Bucher to ride ahead with all speed to try and locate General Grant's army. He didn't have many men with him, but by God, he told himself, they were well-trained Cavalrymen with the finest guns and horses. They were also sharpshooters and seldom missed their target, while among the ordinary infantrymen, the prediction was that it took a man's weight in lead to bring him down, due to the poor marksmanship of those shooting at him. Travis had to get to Grant before General Albert Sidney Johnston had a chance to regroup his forces and attack.

The President of the Confederacy, Jefferson Davis, had given Johnston over-all command in the West. Johnston was said to be perhaps the ablest of all the professional soldiers who had joined the South. He was a West Pointer of substantial reputation, and even after the beating he had taken at Fort Henry, Travis knew the man would lose no time in gathering new forces. They said he had retreated, but everyone said he would never give up completely.

It was a Sunday, April 6th, 1862, and even before Bucher came riding back with the news that Johnston apparently had mustered enough men and was attacking Grant at a place called Shiloh—the ground beneath them trembled with the distant sound of the cannons booming like the drums of hell.

Kitty tensed, her hands wrapping tighter around the reins. The sun was sinking—the end of another day. Would it also be the end of her life? She had only heard about the horrors of war, and now it looked as though with every step the horse took she came closer and closer to the actual horror. She lifted her eyes to Captain Coltrane, just ahead of her. He'd hardly spoken since shooting the young soldier. Was it possible that he actually cared that he had taken a human life? She doubted it. His kind—so arrogant and cocky—thought they could ride roughshod over everyone, even kill if anyone got in their way. No, he didn't care. All that mattered to him now, she thought, was that he hurry and get into the thick of the battle and cause more bloodshed, snuff out more young lives.

She heard Bucher excitedly, worriedly, telling Coltrane what he had found out. "I hid inside a hollow tree log till some of our soldiers came by. God, the Rebs are crawling around like ants out there. Hell, they're everywhere, Captain. . . ."

"Did you find out where General Grant is located?" Travis snapped impatiently.

"Yessir," he nodded. "He put his army on the western bank of that river they call the Tennessee at a place called Pittsburgh Landing, and from what those soldiers told me, most of the men in camp were near a country meetinghouse called Shiloh Church, about twenty miles from Corinth, and Johnston attacked at dawn this morning."

Travis cursed and slammed his fist into his palm. "I knew Johnston would figure that more of our troops were on the way. He wasn't taking any chances. He's smart, that one!" He looked at Bucher, who looked frightened. "And did our men say that Grant is winning?"

He swallowed hard, face turning a bit pale. "No, sir, he ain't winning. He's been pushed into the Tennessee River. If General Buell, they said, doesn't get here from Nashville with what they say is about 25,000 men, then the Rebs will kill every single one of our soldiers, including General Grant."

"All right," Travis cried, turning around to face the dozen or so men behind him, and Kitty, who stared wide-eyed and frightened. "We're going to make our way to our lines. We can cross the river a little ways down. The Rebs are everywhere, and we may not make it. We'll wait till it gets good and dark and move out, and I expect every single one of you to keep quiet and follow me and move as quickly as possible."

His eyes fell on Kitty, who quickly said, "Why don't you just let me go? I'll only be in your way now."

"You're going to be needed if General Grant's men are taking the beating we hear they are. You just keep your head down and keep quiet."

"I might faint," she taunted him. And he only laughed and shook his head, as though the thought of her being so feminine as to swoon was impossible to even consider. She felt herself bristling angrily, but there was no more time to ponder the situation. The men were reaching into their haversacks for hardtack, sipping water from their canteens—all of them silent, tense. The battle was not far away, and soon they would be in the thick of it. There was no need, or desire, to think of anything else at the moment.

As soon as Coltrane felt that it was dark enough, he gave the signal to move out. The ground was no longer trembling, but the air hung heavy with smoke, and as Coltrane signaled that the River was not far away, there was another odor that made their stomachs twitch with nausea. For some of them, the smell might be unfamiliar, but Kitty had stood with Doc in his office during amputations and operations too many times not to recognize the sweet, warm odor of *blood*.

The river looked like a giant black blob in the night, and it swirled around them like a huge cold fist as they moved their horses into the current. Travis rode beside Kitty, holding the reins of her horse, guiding him through the waters. She did not speak. To bring her countrymen's guns down on them now could kill her as easily as the Yankees she despised—particularly Captain Coltrane.

Bucher had ridden ahead to the spot where the soldiers said they would station someone to lead them to where they hoped to find Grant regrouping. There was the sound of an owl, which even Kitty recognized was faked, and then an answering sound as they stepped onto the muddy banks of the Tennessee River on the western side.

Silently, they moved into the thick woods, and they

hadn't gone far when a man up front, leading them, could be heard telling someone that General Buell's troops had been found marching this way by a scout. When the sun rose, the Rebels would have a surprise waiting for them.

She could hear the screams of agony from the wounded men, and Kitty tensed. Suddenly she realized she was right in the middle of Grant's forces, and hundreds and hundreds of soldiers lay dying in agony. In the flickering light of campfires, she could see the field surgeons at work, bones shimmering in the light as they were sawed from gouging wounds.

Her eyes darting about, horror-stricken at the gory sight, Kitty nearly fell from her horse when Coltrane gave her a gentle tug to pull her down. His arms about her, he righted her on her feet, then led her toward a tent.

"God, lady, help me, please . . ." someone cried. "Oh, God, let me die. . . . I ain't got no legs . . . I'm dyin' . . . please, somebody kill me. . . ."

"Do you think it will matter to you what uniform they wear?" Travis asked her sharply, steering her beside him. "When they scream like that, does it matter?"

"I . . . I guess not," she shook her head quickly. "They're human beings, and one of them could be my poppa. . . ." her voice cracked, and he squeezed her arm gently, as though he understood. But how could he, she thought? He wasn't capable of understanding another human being!

They stepped inside the tent, and the dark-haired, bearded man with the piercing eyes stopped pacing to stare at them quizzically.

"General Grant, sir," Coltrane saluted smartly. "I got here as fast as I could. . . ."

"But not before I've lost thousands of men today," the General snapped, then waved a hand in front of his face and said, shaking his head, "I'm sorry. I don't blame you, Captain. Your dozen or so men could have done precious little to stop what has happened here today." He walked over to a table where a bottle of whiskey sat, poured the amber liquid into two cups and handed one to Travis, and began sipping from the other himself.

"They didn't kill any Federals in bed, but they took us by surprise. We were able to rally quickly, and we've recovered somewhat since darkness fell, and with General Buell almost here, we'll be ready to counterattack first thing in the morning. . . ." His eyes rested on Kitty, as though seeing her for the first time. He raised an eyebrow and looked to Travis for an explanation.

"We found the men you sent us after," Travis explained quietly, respect in his voice. "Their leader, a man named Luke Tate, got away. We found this young woman in their company. She's a Southerner. . . ."

General Grant's look was such that Kitty cried indignantly, "How dare you look at me like that? I didn't go with them by choice! As I tried to tell this . . . this Captain of yours, I was kidnapped by Luke Tate and held prisoner. I asked him to let me return to my home in North Carolina, but he refused and dragged me into all of this!"

She stepped closer, and Travis moved forward, as though afraid she might attack the General. "You're obviously someone important, whoever you are," she said. "Will you let me go, or is it the way of Yankees to kidnap innocent women?"

"It would seem," said General Grant, scratching his beard, "that it is the way of your Southern gentlemen, if your story is true. But why did you bring her here?" He looked at Travis once again.

"One of the men we killed had just had his arm amputated, and expertly so. This young lady did the amputation."

"You?" The officer's eyes widened. "Extraordinary! You will be of much use to us. Later, when the battle is over, you will have to dine with me and tell me how you came to be so well trained."

He nodded to Travis. "Take her to the field hospital, and then report back here. I'm setting up heavy artillery near the river to stop the Confederates' advance."

Anxious to return to the leader he admired and respected and get on with the business of whipping the Confederates, Travis jerked Kitty roughly from the tent. It was not hard to find the way to the nearest hospital tent—all they had to do was follow the line of dead and dying along the path.

Kitty saw horrors she never knew existed—men with most of their faces shot away, some of them with gaping stomach wounds—intestines mingling with the blood and dirt on the ground beside them as they waited to die. One young soldier curled infantlike on a bloody blanket, his severed left leg held in his arms lovingly as he sobbed and slowly bled to death.

Inside a lantern-lit tent, Kitty swayed at the sight of the blood-slick table—the growing pile of arms and legs to one side. The surgeon, spattered with blood, looked up with annoyance. "Damnit, I don't like women around me. What the hell is she doing here?"

"She can do the job as well as you, Doc," Travis snapped. "Now give her a table and a knife and put her to work."

"I . . . I don't think I can. . . ." Kitty felt bile rising in her throat. A single operation on a single patient was one thing—wholesale severing of human limbs was something she had never experienced. "I don't think I can do it. Get me out of here, please. . . ."

The surgeon waved a bloody saw at them. "See what I mean? I can't have her around screaming and fainting. Now get her out of here."

"Listen to me," Travis gave her a shake so hard her head bobbed to and fro on her shoulders. "If it was your daddy laying out there dying, you'd want someone to help him, wouldn't you? Think about that—all these men, whether they're Federals or not—are loved by someone just like your daddy is loved by you—and the ones that love them would want you to help them. *Now are you going to help them?*"

She raised her head to look into those steely eyes. His nostrils flared angrily. She could not speak—could not move. The sound of another limb dropping to the bloody earth with a sickening thud made her shudder.

"I should have known," he sneered, his hands dropping away from her shoulders. "I should've known that for all your pretended toughness and guts, when it comes down to it, you're nothing but a simpering, helpless female like the rest of your kind. Get out of here. You make me sick. . . ."

He gave her a shove toward the tent exit, but she whirled around to knock his hand away. "Don't you dare touch me," her voice came out an ominous whisper. "And don't you talk to me that way! I'm every bit as good as a man when it comes down to a challenge."

"Then prove it!"

Their eyes met and held. The challenge had been made. Kitty, pushed by him, made her way to the surgeon. He heard her saying curtly, "I'm going to work with you. Now what do you want me to do?"

He stepped out of the tent, smiling to himself, as Kitty signaled to one of the soldiers to set up another table, bring in another patient.

Soon her arms were stained crimson to the elbow, her dress soaked with blood and perspiration as she worked over the wounded. As soon as one soldier was brought in and everything possible done to try and save him, he would be carried swiftly out and another brought in. There was one with his throat lacerated by a bullet that had crushed down the tissue that separated windpipe from esophagus, and Kitty worked swiftly to suture, praying the soldier would have the strength to somehow throw off the fever that was sure to come with such an injury.

There was another boy, perhaps only fifteen or sixteen, she guessed painfully, with a spurting artery—the hastily applied tourniquet on the battlefield had slipped during the trip to the hospital. He bled to death before Kitty could start to try and save his life.

God, she prayed silently, was this nightmare never going to end—this procession of mutilated, disfigured bodies, that came in one end of the tent and went out the other? A parade of the dying, she thought dizzily. God, let it end. Let it end before I go mad and run from this tent shrieking with insanity. *I don't think I can go on,* she cried silently, hands trembling as another wounded soldier was brought in.

On and on it went. Someone handed Kitty a cup of coffee once that she gulped down so quickly it burned her throat. Then there was a gulp of popskull—contraband liquor—and it seemed to peel the skin from her throat, but at least she was able to keep on her feet.

Outside, the artillery General Grant had set up along the river began to retch and rumble and explode their fury as dawn streaked the sky. Here and there she heard snatches of conversation among the soldiers who carried the wounded in and out of the tent. General Grant had his reinforcements. Buell had arrived. The Confederates were outnumbered. The Federals would win, they said. The Federals were using grapeshot—shells filled with balls the size of oranges, effective to seven hundred yards. And they were using Canister, a shell filled with lead balls about the size of plums, deadly for close action up to three hundred yards. And they had Napoleons—and they named another cannon—a Napoleon smoothbore howitzer, and it was powerful, they said. Rebels were dying by the hundreds!

Jubilant! They were jubilant because the Confederates were dying. Couldn't they see the dead all around them? Couldn't they see the suffering, the agony, on both sides? Was the death of the enemy so satisfying that it overshadowed the death of your own brother in uniform? None of it made any sense.

Before her, on the table, a soldier of eighteen or nineteen years of age lay writhing in the agony of having his lower jaw shot away. She began to wipe away the blood to see if anything could be done besides attempt to ease the boy's suffering while he awaited death. Outside the tent, someone screamed that the Confederates were retreating. Cheers and cries of joy went up from the hundreds and hundreds of wounded soldiers lying in the woods—those that were able to shout.

She felt like a traitor. Her countrymen were retreating, whipped, beaten, while she stood here fighting to save the enemy. What if Nathan were out there in the midst of the battle? What if he were already dead—or wounded. This soldier lying here struggling to even moan in agony might have been the one to kill the man she loved. And she was supposed to save him? Dear God, she could not. She could not lift one more finger to save the life of one more Yankee!

Chloroform. She would take the chloroform and pretend to put the soldier to sleep so she could work on his wound, only she would administer a fatal dose. Doc had taught her how to use chloroform, and she had also read the books in his small library. She would merely put the soldier out of his misery, and then, in the confusion, she would slip away—pretend to be sitting down for a rest—only she would move farther and farther away, all the way to the river, and perhaps she could follow the Confederate retreat and escape. Surely, no one would shoot a blood-stained woman!

Suddenly she was aware that someone was standing right behind her. Turning, she saw the haggard, drawn face of the doctor who had first been so opposed to having her work along with him. His eyes were misty, and his lips were quivering.

"It's . . . it's more than I can bear," he choked out the words. "All this killing . . ."

Kitty's frustration unleashed itself upon the first person who had spoken directly to her all night long and on into the day, except to discuss the business at hand. "It's what you Yankees want, isn't it?" she cried. "All the killing and blood and maiming and suffering? That's what you wanted all along when you tried to tell the South how to run her affairs. And now that war is here, and your own men are dying, you don't like it so well, do you? Well, I'm not helping another Yankee this day. . . ."

His eyes stared down at the soldier on the table, who was barely moaning now. Without shifting his gaze, he said, "I'm not a Yankee, miss. I'm a Southerner, like you, captured at Bull Run and forced to work as a doctor for the Federals. . . ."

She swayed, dizzy with disbelief and sudden fatigue that threatened to take her off her feet. "Then how do you do it? How do you stand here for hours and hours with only whiskey and coffee to keep you going—only to try to put Yankees back together again so they can go out and kill more of our countrymen?"

The boy on the table gave one final moan, gasped, and a rasping gurgle of blood oozed from the gaping wound onto his chest as his eyes rolled upward. He was dead.

The doctor reached over and touched the boy's forehead gently. "I told myself the day might come when someone I loved would come by my table . . . that I could help save him . . . but I couldn't do anything. . . ."

Kitty stared at the tears rolling down his cheeks as he smoothed back the blood-matted hair of the dead Yankee soldier. "He was my son. . . ." he choked out the words. "He wasn't a Yankee—he was my *son!*"

It was too much. Turning, she ran from the tent. In the confusion and shouting and the smoke from the guns, no one paid any attention to her. She fell, scrambled to her feet again, plunging into the woods deeper. Where was the river? She had no knowledge of where she was. Which way had the Yankees gone? Which way had the Confederates gone? She stumbled over a body, screamed at the sight of only half a body—the lower parts blown away. Whirling, she stumbled, fell across a wounded soldier who clawed out at her with a bloody hand, begging for help.

"No . . . no . . ." she cried, moving away, scrambling, clawing, running. It was too much—all of it—too much. . . .

She made her way through the brambles, felt her dress being torn to shreds, but still she kept moving. The uniforms on the bodies she passed looked different somehow, and through the hysterical fog that enveloped her consciousness, the realization came that these were Rebel soldiers. She was getting closer to the line of retreat. Escape was nearer now. If only she could keep running, she was bound to stumble upon some *live* Confederates who would help her. But dear God, she thought wildly, as the bodies seemed to be stacked on top of each other, were there any left alive? It was difficult to even take one step without her foot coming down on top of a dead soldier—and soon the ground was so strewn with bodies that she was walking on a carpet of death!

Soon it would be dark. She would be at the mercy of both sides, shooting carelessly at anything that moved in the dark. And with the daylight, with the Yankees obviously victorious, they would be out in number to round up any prisoners, and if she did not find the retreating Confederates before then—she would be recaptured.

She had to keep moving. Once her foot slipped down inside the gaping wound in the back of a long-dead body, and she felt bile once again gurgling from the pit of her stomach as the flesh and blood squeezed around her ankle. She was struggling to pull herself free when she heard the sound—weak, but yet strong enough to carry to her ears.

"Please . . . help me . . . please. . . ."

No, she thought in terror. *I can't help anyone now except myself. I have to keep going. I can't stop for anything!*

"Please . . . God . . . let it be so . . . *Miss Kitty.* . . ."

She froze. Her name. Someone had called her name! It wasn't so. She was dreaming. She was so tired, so bone-weary that she was having hallucinations. Doc had told her that happened to people sometimes, and it had to be happening to her. She had to get out of this sea of the dead before it drove her hopelessly insane.

"Miss . . . Kitty. . . ." There it was again. It had to be a nightmare. She jerked her foot free from the grizzle and muscle of the dead man's back, and, hoisting her ripped skirt high, began to move away.

"Help me . . . please. . . ."

She could not move. Something within compelled her to turn around, find out once and for all whether or not she was really hearing things that weren't really there. Her eyes moved slowly over the bodies strewn almost shoulder to shoulder along the ground.

"Miss Kitty . . . please. . . ."

And then she saw him—the soldier in bloody gray, stretching out a hand to her. Nathan? Could it be? Cautiously, afraid to even breathe, she moved closer. No, it was not Nathan—he was too young, too small.

And then she recognized him, and a scream erupted from her heart as she realized it was Andy Shaw reaching out to her!

Stooping quickly, she tried to hug him but saw through her tears that he was wounded and she did not want to touch him. A large splotch of red was on the front of his shirt. "A cavalryman got me—they got most of us right here in this clearing," he gasped out the words. "He stuck me with his sword. I think it's in my side . . . but it hurts all over."

Her fingers worked nervously to rip the shirt open. Using the hem of her skirt, she wiped the blood away gently. It was a sharp, piercing wound, in the side. With care, he could make it and live. If left here, he would die from the fever—if he didn't bleed to death.

"Can you move?"

"No," he whispered. "It hurts . . . to even talk. I . . . couldn't believe . . . I saw you. . . ."

"Thank God you did. I was running away from those damned Yankees to try and catch up with the retreating

Rebels. Maybe it's lucky I did stop, Andy, or I might not have found you."

"No . . . you've got to go on. . . ." He tried to raise his head but fell back weakly. "Catch up . . . escape. . . ."

"You lie still," she shushed him. "I won't leave you, Andy."

He closed his eyes, and she looked around frantically. There was no escape now, not if she stayed here. The Yankees would come through soon and find her. And she had to have help for Andy. How far away were the Confederates? How long before darkness fell?

Thundering horses suddenly came charging across the bodies as though they were only large clumps of earth to be trod upon. Yankees! They saw her and came toward her. "What in thunderation is a woman doing out here in the middle of this bloody mess?" the soldier in front cried.

It was no use. There was no escape now. She decided to tell the truth about how she came to be there. "Captain Coltrane brought me here night before last to help with the medical staff. I'm out here tending to the wounded."

The men exchanged confused glances. "I don't understand," the soldier who had spoken scratched at his beard. "You're a long way from the medical tents, and the only wounded soldiers out here are Rebs, and you sure don't want to waste your time on them. Come along now. We'll take you back with us. . . ."

He held out his hand to pull her up on the saddle behind him, but she did not move away from Andy.

"Come along now. I know war is hell, especially for pretty young ladies like you, but you have to put your loyalties in their proper place, and this is not the place for any kind of pity, believe me. They say we've lost over 10,000 men, so there's no time to cry over these dead bastards that did the killing!"

"I'm not leaving this boy . . . and he's just that—a boy, hardly past fourteen years of age." Kitty got to her feet slowly, the handgun she'd picked up at Andy's side carefully concealed in the folds of her skirt. "I'm taking him back to the field hospital. He's bleeding from a sword wound. He'll die without medical attention."

"You ain't taking that goddamn Reb anywhere. . . ."

Whipping the gun out, she pointed it at the soldier who

was doing the talking. "If your men shoot me, I'll get at least one shot into you before I die." Her voice was braver than she had dared hoped it would be. "I'm not about to leave this boy."

"You crazy?" the soldier's eyes bulged incredulously. "He's a Confederate! He was shootin' at our men, probably killed one or two. Now you put that gun away before someone gets hurt."

"Someone *is* hurt, and I intend to help him. Now are you going to help me take him back to the field hospital or do I have to carry him on my back?"

He got down off his horse and signaled to another soldier to help him with the wounded boy. Shaking his head, he grumbled, "That's the reason the battlefield is no place for a dang woman. They ain't got no sense."

Kitty could have told them just what Andy Shaw meant to her—but she didn't. The emotions churning within were hers and hers alone, not meant to be shared with outsiders. She'd known him all his life, tended to him when he was sick and Doc Musgrave wasn't around. In a way he was a symbol of the past that was very dear and precious, for she knew that life would never again be like the memories she held so fondly in her heart. There was no going back. Perhaps she would never see her home again, or her mother and father—or Nathan. She felt a stab of pain. Andy might have some news of Nathan—know something about his whereabouts; if he was still alive, if he had come back for her, then gone in search to find out why she had disappeared. Maybe he even knew something about Poppa. Had he come home? Had he been killed? Was he still in the war, fighting with the Yankees? Yes, Andy just might have some answers.

The soldiers lifted him onto a horse after Kitty made a compress from her torn skirt to press against the wound to help stifle the flow of blood. "You'll be all right, Andy," she smoothed back the unruly red hair, kissing his forehead. But he did not respond, mercifully unconscious and oblivious to the pain of his injury.

One of the soldiers held out his hand for her to ride behind him. She started forward—then stopped—heart constricting as a lump of terror knotted tightly in her throat.

There, in a puddle of blood and mud, in the spot where Andy had been lying—the flag lay, as though crumpled and defeated, never to fly so gloriously again.

The eagle was splattered with blood—the eagle of the flag of the Wayne Volunteers.

❧ Chapter Eighteen ❧

KITTY directed the soldiers to the hospital tent where she had been working. "It ain't gonna do you no good, lady," the one in charge told her as he helped lift the still unconscious body of Andy Shaw from the saddle. "With so many of our men wounded, they ain't gonna let you waste time on no Rebel soldier."

Just then the doctor who'd just lost his son stepped out of the tent and looked at them quizzically. "Doctor, this crazy woman insisted we bring in a wounded Reb," the soldier blared out indignantly. "Tell her there's no time to waste on a Rebel. She wouldn't listen to us. Pulled a gun, she did."

The doctor was tall and thin, with gaunt, hollow eyes beneath a thatch of thick, graying hair. His mustache and beard was matted with blood from the spatterings of the night before caused by so many amputations. He looked from Andy to Kitty, then spoke softly. "I was too busy to introduce myself properly last night, young lady. I'm Dr. Harold Davis, formerly a proud member of Company B, Fourth Regiment, Tennessee. Bring this boy in, and we'll see what can be done for him."

One of the soldiers in the back whispered, "That's that Rebel doctor they captured and put to work. What can you expect?"

Another said, "Yeah, what can you expect? They'll let our men suffer and die to save this damn Secesh."

Dr. Davis carried Andy in his arms to a wooden board placed on top of barrels that served as a table. It was slick with blood. Kitty silently reached for a bucket of water as she'd seen the helpers do during the endless hours of death and suffering, and she sloshed the water across the board, sending a murky liquid to the dirt floor to mingle with the stagnating, putrid puddles that had already formed there.

The doctor removed the compress, then used a wet cloth to sponge away the blood. Probing with his fingers as Andy moaned in his sleep, he said, "We're in luck. I don't think any vital organs have been severed or punctured. We'll suture and soak it in turpentine and keep a close watch. With God's blessing, he'll pull through."

Kitty sighed with relief, then set about to help with the suturing. When all had been done that could be, she supervised the moving of Andy to a spot outside the tent where she could check on him when there was time. As she tucked a dirty blanket under his chin, his eyes opened, blinked, and he tried to smile up at her.

"It *is* you. I thought I had died and gone to heaven . . . but it is you. . . ."

"I'm going to be nearby, Andy. You rest. You'll need your strength, but you're going to be fine."

He moved his lips to speak again, but the effort was too great, and he slipped away once more.

Straightening, she looked about her for the first time. As far as she could see in either direction, soldiers lay on the ground. Some in piles. These were the dead, to be buried as quickly as possible, because already the air was thick with the stench and the swarming of flies. Overhead, the vultures circled, waiting.

Some of them were hollow-eyed and sunken-cheeked, shot in every conceivable part of the body; some shrieking, calling upon their mothers; some laughing the hard, cackling laugh of one who suffers without hope. There were curses tossed to the winds, men writhing and groaning as other victims tossed against them in their agony. Nearby, one lay with his head blown open, and she felt sick as she saw his brain thumping in the cavity.

Dr. Davis called to her. "Kitty, I need you."

She turned and hurried toward the tent. It did not matter any longer that it was Yankee blood on her hands. Perhaps it never had, not when a human life was at stake. For somewhere, perhaps Poppa, or Nathan, were suffering and needing help, and she prayed that it would not matter to some doctor or nurse whether they were Yankee or Rebel.

Through the night they worked, and as often as possible, Kitty stepped outside to check on Andy. Once, she found him awake, and she brought hot coffee and hardtack and coaxed him to eat. By sunrise, her bones and muscles screaming with weariness, Dr. Davis told her to take a break or she would surely pass out. She went to a nearby campfire where some bacon stew was simmering, and, filling a cup, took it to Andy and woke him up to spoon down as much as he could swallow.

And then she slept, curled up beside him . . . a link with the life she had left behind.

"Miss Kitty. . . ."

Her eyes flashed open. Above, sunlight filtered down through a fig tree, and she blinked and fought to remember where she was. And why did she feel as though there had been no sleep, no rest? Dear God, never had there been such a feeling of weariness.

"Miss Kitty. . . ."

Turning her stiffened neck, it all came flooding back as Andy grinned, face bright with freckles. "Miss Kitty, are you all right? I feel so much better this morning, thanks to you."

Sitting up, she reached out to touch his forehead. It was warm, but there did not appear to be a fever. Checking his bandage, she was satisfied that the bleeding had stopped once the wound was sutured. Dr. Davis had been right. With the aid of turpentine to fight gangrene and fever, Andy had a good chance of surviving his wound. And he seemed so strong this morning. She checked herself as she looked upward. Already the sun was starting to sink in the west. Had she slept the whole day away?

"I'm going to get you something to eat." She started to get up but he said someone had been by with sorghum and hardtack, and he had eaten a bit.

"I can't get over seeing you way up here. How did you ever get to Tennessee, Kitty?" He looked so young lying there, but the sharp wisdom of the atrocities of war had given his youthful voice a tone of maturity, she realized.

"It isn't a pretty story, Andy. When Doc Musgrave and I left Goldsboro last August, it was a trap set by Luke Tate. Doc was killed."

He winced painfully. "I'm sorry. . . ." His voice broke, and he closed his eyes for a moment. Doc had brought him into the world.

"I was held a prisoner by Luke Tate until the Yankees came and killed everyone but Luke. He got away. They kept me with them because I know something about doctoring. I was running away myself when I found you, but I'm so glad I did.

"But tell me . . ." she said quickly, unable to contain herself any longer. "How is Momma? And did Poppa ever come back?"

He turned his eyes away, as though he hated to have to tell her he had no good news. "Your momma, well, she drinks a lot. I heard Ma talking about it with Preacher Brown one afternoon. Jacob's still there. He says he promised your pa he'd look after her, so he stays on and does what he can. Your pa, he never came back. Nobody's heard from him. 'Course I haven't been home since Christmas. I just couldn't take it anymore—all the news coming back about the fighting and all. I felt like I had to do my part, so Nathan, he came home for Christmas, and he said I could come back with him, and I did. Ma cried a lot, but she knew I had to do my part. . . ."

Kitty was no longer listening to what the boy was saying. Her heart was beating rapidly, and she felt herself swaying. Nathan. Oh, dear God, how she longed for the comfort and warmth of his arms. "Andy, was Nathan in the battle yesterday?"

Again there was that look in the boy's eyes, as though he did not want to answer her questions. "Nathan is a Major now. The Wayne Volunteers were assigned to the North Carolina State troops, you see, under Colonel George Anderson. They say he's a West Point graduate. Well . . ." He paused to take a breath, and Kitty knew she should not let him use his strength to talk so much, but she had to know if Nathan was all right. She had to have news of him.

"Colonel Anderson put the men through a lot of drill work and training, and he promoted Nathan to Major."

She nodded. "That's wonderful, but Andy, tell me, was he in the fighting yesterday? I'll have to go back and look . . ." She didn't finish the sentence. She did not want to put in words that she would have to go back and search the dead for Nathan's body. . . .

"No ma'am," he said finally. "Major Collins don't ride with his men anymore. He stays behind the line with his maps and charts and plans the artillery fire. Somebody has to do it, you know," he added defensively.

But Kitty did not notice. She was too relieved to hear that Nathan would have to be all right. But the fighting had spread for so many miles—and so many had been killed. Would she ever be able to find him?

"What's going to happen now? I mean, when I get well, will they send me to a prison? And what about you, Kitty? Are they going to keep you here and make you look after the Yankees? Nobody thought the war would last this long. I sure didn't. I thought I'd be home in time for spring planting."

Suddenly, she did not want to talk anymore, at least not about the future. They could not be sure that any of them had a future. Not now. Getting to her feet, she smoothed her torn, blood-stained dress. "Andy, I've got to go back and help Dr. Davis, but I'll keep a watch on you. The man who brought me here, Captain Coltrane . . . if he's still alive, he'll be back, and I'll talk to him and find out what's to become of you. If they send you to a prison, at least you'll be safe until the war is over."

"I'd rather fight," he said fiercely. "I'd rather fight and die on the battlefield than rot in some damned Yankee prison. . . ."

"Hush. Your ma wouldn't like for you to curse so. I know you're brave, Andy, and I'm proud of you, but war is no place for a boy as young as you. . . ."

"I've killed Yankees. Shot three yesterday, I did. I ain't afraid to fight, and I ain't afraid to die."

"I know. Now you rest."

She went back inside the tent. Dr. Davis was still at work, and she wondered how he could carry on. The line of wounded seemed endless. For every soldier that looked as though he might live, one would already be dead when brought in, or die on the table.

Dr. Davis told Kitty that she would have to continue to make decisions as to whether or not to amputate limbs. Arms sore and weakened, she could no longer use a saw to grind through bone, but there were strong-gutted assistants to do it for her. "Gangrene is what we're fighting here," he said. "These wounds from the minié balls are terrible. They shear and chop their way through muscle and tissue, and some of them hit with enough speed to split and shatter right into a bone. If you don't cut that bone off, gangrene will set in, and the patient will die. The balls leave jagged, ugly wounds, and in most cases, there is no alternative but to amputate." He gestured toward the steadily growing pile of arms and legs lying to one side.

"I don't feel qualified to make such a judgment," she said. "I'm not a doctor. It isn't right."

"We're short-handed. We have to do the best we can, and I've watched you, girl. You've got the gift. You'll do just fine."

Kitty went to work, hating every moment of it. Finally, the parade of death slowed, and just when she reached the point when she felt she could begin to minister to Andy and the others recuperating from their injuries, Captain Travis Coltrane returned.

He had been standing back, silently watching. Out of the flickering beam of the lantern overhead, Kitty had not seen him observing. How long had he been there? She did not know. A soldier had just died as she probed into the flesh of his chest for the bullet, and she lowered her face into blood-slick hands and wept.

Someone was fastening a strong hand around her wrist, pulling her toward him. Opening her eyes, she saw Travis standing there, tight-lipped and grim, steel-blue gaze burning into her face. Silently, he led her from the tent, away from the campfires and into the shadows.

"I hear you've done a remarkable job back there," he said finally, sitting down beneath a tree and pulling her down beside him. He pulled out a cigar and lit it with a burning twig he'd picked up as they passed a small fire.

She didn't speak.

"I also hear that you brought in a Rebel soldier and insisted on treating him."

"What should I have done?" She jerked around to glare at him in the darkness, hoping he could see her anger. "Leave him there to die, or shoot him the way you did one of your own?"

He ignored her anger. "You had a special reason for bringing him back. What was it?"

"I wish you'd been killed in the fighting," she ground out the words. There was something about this man that made her tremble and feel warm—and she didn't like the strange feeling, as though he had some secret power over her.

Even in the darkness she could tell that he was grinning at her in that cocky way with the side of his mouth tilted crookedly, mockingly. "Well, I wasn't. I killed a few of your people, though."

"They're your people, too. You're a traitor to your countrymen."

"Perhaps. Depends on how you look at it. If I don't think the way they do, why should I die for their convictions? But that's another story, princess, and that's not why I brought you out here. We'll have plenty of time later to talk about the war and why we're both in the middle of it, because we're going to spend a lot of time together."

She tensed. "If I have to be a prisoner, I want to stay with Dr. Davis."

"Sorry, but I've just finished a conference with General Grant, and I have another assignment, and I've asked for permission to take you with me, and the General granted it. He knows that I'll need some medical assistants with me, and the way I'll be traveling, a woman won't be so conspicuous."

"Conspicuous? What are you talking about, Coltrane?"

"General Grant wants me and my men to do what your friend, Tate, was doing, except for a different reason. I'm not after gold and plundering. I'll be after information, trying to find out what the enemy is going to be doing next. We don't want the Rebs to surprise us again if we can help it. So we're going to go out on our own, in civilian clothes, and we'll sit on both sides of the fence . . . whatever it takes to get the information we want."

"Spies. You're going to be spies!" she said accusingly.

He laughed. "You can call it that. Makes it sound more exciting, doesn't it? Actually, we'll be scouting and sending back messages about the Confederates' movements. Naturally, from time to time, we're bound to get in a skirmish, and we'll need medical aid. That's where you come in."

She started to get to her feet, but he grabbed her arm, yanking her back down roughly. "I'm not through talking to you yet, princess. There are a few things we need to have understood."

"I'm through talking to you, and you're wasting your breath, anyway. Helping save the lives of the soldiers wounded here was one thing, but riding with you and helping your men is another. I swear before God almighty that I'll never lift a finger to help any of you. So you might as well leave me behind with Dr. Davis to do what I can here. . . ."

"Oh, I think you *will* lift one of those pretty fingers, princess," he said with maddening taunt to his voice. "I think you will do just about anything you're told."

"You're mad!" Again she moved to get to her feet, and again he yanked her back down, rougher this time. He leaned forward, so close his breath was warm on her face.

"No, I'm not mad. You see, that Rebel soldier you saved is going to come along with us. And the first time you let one of my men suffer . . . the first time you refuse to help . . . that boy will die."

She knew he meant what he said. Once, she had planned to make him fall at her feet with desire. She had been willing to use every feminine trick available to make him want her so desperately that he would be caught off guard, and she could escape. Now it was clear that here was a man completely in control of himself at all times. Did he even have a weakness? She could not be sure.

And then she decided that he had to have a weakness. All men did, and perhaps, like most, Travis Coltrane's would be that of ego. She had to take a chance and try anything at this point.

Above, a silvery wisp of clouds parted to let the shimmer of the full moon gleam down and filter through the leaves. His face was clear now. She could make out every detail. He was handsome, ruggedly so. A quality of danger and intrigue that could turn the heads of most women. But Kitty considered herself different from most of her sex. Even though he did make her feel all warm and funny inside, she was not about to lose control of her senses.

"Why don't you just come right out and tell the truth? Why don't you just admit that the real reason you're taking me along is because you want me. . . ."

"*Want* you?" He raised an eyebrow, as though the thought of such a thing had never entered his mind. And this angered her even more.

"Yes!" She plunged on, fighting to keep calm and not to let him rile her or make her lose her composure. "Yes, you *want* me. You want me to ride with you so that you can rape me whenever you choose. You aren't fooling me, and you aren't fooling anyone else. You don't give a damn about having someone with some medical knowledge around in case it's needed. All you care about is satisfying your animal *lust*."

"And you think you could satisfy it?" He chuckled.

Kitty did lose control then, and she slapped him, taking him by surprise. Scrambling to her feet, she was about to run away, but his hand snaked out to wrap around her ankle, tripping her to fall upon the ground. Quickly, he was on top of her, rolling her onto her back, his body stretched out and pressing down against hers.

He held her by her wrists, his weight pinning her down. His lips were only inches from hers as he spoke in a harsh whisper. "You let me tell you something, you little spitfire, I don't rape women. I don't have to. And you know why? Because I make it so goddamned good to them that they try to rape me for *seconds*. And you know *how* I make it good to them? Well, I'm going to show you. . . ."

His lips came mashing down, and she tried to struggle and twist her head from side to side but there was no escaping. He stretched her arms together over her head, pinning them with one hand while his other moved down . . . slowly, tantalizingly to the bodice of her dress. Slipping inside, strong, firm fingers moved to manipulate the flesh, moving along to the nipple, which he slowly and expertly squeezed to erect tautness.

His tongue slipped inside her mouth as she struggled helplessly. His hands moved away, downward, reaching to shove her skirt upward to her waist. Beneath, she wore frayed, worn pantalets, and these he ripped away quickly with one jerk, exposing, making her naked, vulnerable to his touch.

Gently, he began to manipulate skilled fingertips between her thighs, which she was fighting to keep pressed tightly together. He had moved to one side, using his knee to probe between hers, forcing her legs apart. He knew just where to caress, where to touch that nucleus of nerves that would make her blood turn to thousands of needles of fire, coursing through her body.

Kitty was having spasms of unfamiliar joy that she could not control. She could feel her pelvic muscles tightening, contracting, insides straining to reach out and grab anything that would bring fulfillment to the strange, delicious hunger this man had been able to arouse within her.

She was forgetting to hate him, and the sounds of people not far away were being pushed into oblivion . . . voices, a horse neighing, a dying soldier somewhere screaming his last oath of defiance over being snatched to his grave. None of these things mattered any longer. They could not be heard. Not here, not now. She *wanted* him! She wanted him in a way she never thought she could want any man. The pulsating hardness against her thigh—this she wanted to plunge inward, upward, to pound again and again as hard as possible. Luke Tate had only aroused revulsion, disgust—never desire—never this wonderful feeling. Oh, sweet Jesus, never like this!

She was unable to control herself. As much as she tried to keep murmuring her hatred, she could not hold back the waves of frenzied, fevered longing that swept over her as the tide crashes along the shores. She had to have him— had to feel the sweet relief that would surely come!

He raised his lips slightly, fingers still caressing, breath hot upon her face. "Please . . ." she could hear a voice begging, realized feverishly the sound came from her own mouth. "Please . . . please . . . please . . ."

And then, a great shudder took hold. Kitty felt her insides exploding . . . as a giant wave of white-hot pleasure spread within the walls of her belly. Her teeth sank into her lower lip as she jerked her head backward into the ground, fighting to keep the screams silent. It was heaven . . . it was hell . . . it was fire and lightning and wind and rain and thunder and the wrath of God and the devil and gnashing teeth and trumpets blowing and drums beating. It was everything . . . and anything . . . and surely she was dying and would never see the light of another day. . . .

Slowly, his fingers slipped from their probe, and he released her wrists at the same time. Kitty lay gasping, spent, bewildered by the spasms that had exploded and left her weak. Rolling away, Travis moved to a sitting position, hands folded around his knees. And he was smiling. She could see him smiling in the moonlight and that was what brought her back to reality . . . that smirking, taunting smile.

Yanking down her dress and pushing her breasts back into the bodice, she sat up and turned her back on him, staring into the darkness, toward the camp, the fires, and that other world. "I hate you," she said between clenched teeth. "I hate you with every beat of my heart, Travis Coltrane."

"What a pity," he said, chuckling. "A moment ago you would have hated me more if I hadn't gone on and given you what every woman wants, although I could have done a much better job if you'd begged a little harder. I might have given you all of me, but then you would have screamed your pleasure and woke up the whole camp. Maybe one night will be your lucky night, and you'll have all of me. . . ."

Scrambling to her feet, she lifted her skirt and began to run, picking her way in the darkness. Angry with him, angry with herself, for the betrayal of her own body, she disappeared into the night, fighting to keep back the tears until she could be alone. Travis Coltrane would never see the day he witnessed bringing tears to her eyes!

He watched her go, a peculiar feeling moving through him. He prided himself in pleasuring women, that was true, but what made him goad this one, torture her, tease her into hating him? She was beautiful. Oh, Lord, she was beautiful. Never had he touched lips so sweet or skin so tender and soft. Never had his loins strained with agony to empty himself into any woman's body as he yearned for this one. Why, then, did he go out of his way to make her hate him? And why hadn't he gone ahead and jerked open his trousers and entered her and had his way with her? Was it because that was what she expected? And if so, what difference did it make? She was only a Southern girl, betrothed to a Southern soldier. She meant nothing to him, even if she was desirable and lovely. He could go ahead and make her beg him to take her, to ravish her, and afterward, forget her.

But it was more than that. Damn, there was something about her that made him want more than to just take her again and again and feel her nails rake the flesh of his back and scream his name in her passion as she begged for him to plunge harder and harder, again and again. Women wanted it as much as men did—this was something he firmly believed. They were just not allowed to *act* like it, not the ladies, anyway. The whores could writhe and groan and enjoy it, but not the ladies. And in spite of her spirit, Kitty *was* a lady.

Maybe it would have been different had they met under different circumstances. He might have courted her and made her fall in love with him. He'd never known a woman with so much spirit. Most were empty-headed giggling fools, with no thought, save snaring a husband. Not this one. She was independent, and he pitied any Federal soldier who came up against her if she had a weapon in her hands—any kind of weapon. He had seen her ride a horse as well as any man, and she could probably shoot a gun just as well, too. But he had stood there in the shadows in the tent and watched her cry because a soldier had died and there hadn't been anything she could do about it. She had wept and looked soft and tender and wonderful, and he had seen that despite the fire . . . the ice . . . the anger . . . there was a quality of warmth, softness, that shone through when her guard was down.

Damn, Kitty Wright was one hell of a woman. But he wasn't about to let her make a fool of him the way he'd seen other women do to other men . . . men like his father.

He felt a sickening lurch in the pit of his stomach as the painful memory washed over him. Would he ever forget? Would it ever stop haunting him?

He shook himself. No, he would not let Kitty get the best of him. He would drag her along, tie and gag her if need be, but she was going with him and his men. And if she gave him any trouble, he'd kill that freckle-faced Rebel soldier she seemed to think so damned much of—and if she ever got hold of a gun or a knife and came after him, well, he'd kill her, too. No matter how beautiful she was, or how desirable, she was still dangerous. He'd never turn his back on her.

And somewhere, along the way, she was going to beg him for everything he had to give—a promise he made to himself that would be kept. And that strange feeling twisting around inside him could go to hell. He cared nothing for her at all.

Only fools fall in love with women, he reasoned. Wise men use them, take their pleasures with them—then walk away to freedom and never look back.

And Travis Coltrane prided himself in being a very wise man.

❧ Chapter Nineteen ❧

WHEN the dust had finally settled after the battle of Shiloh, and the blood of 13,000 Federals and 10,000 Confederates had settled into the soil of Tennessee, Captain Travis Coltrane and twelve men, a woman nurse, and a Rebel prisoner not more than fourteen years of age, left General Grant's army and set out on their mission— scout the enemy, find their position, discover their movements and goals, and report back to Grant.

It was mid-May, 1862, and as Travis sat with his sergeant, Sam Bucher, he thought with discomfort that he'd never known such a hot night for so early in the summer. They had moved into Virginia, and he was sweltering. As he and Bucher discussed the latest war news, Travis had had to ask him twice to move farther back from the campfire. He'd felt a wave of nausea when Kitty handed him a plate of Drap Dumplin's with a tin of coffee.

"You don't like my cooking?" she had asked as though she really cared. Lately, the woman had been no trouble at all. She did as she was told, keeping out of the way and silent. The Rebel prisoner did likewise, obeying orders to do the dirty work that came along.

"There's nothing wrong with your cooking, Kitty," he had answered. "I just don't feel like eating—it's so blasted hot."

She had reached out to touch his forehead, but he jerked

away. Lately, she seemed to brush against him often, or was it his imagination? He didn't know. It was so hot—too hot to think about such things. He just didn't want anyone touching him.

"Are you sure you are feeling all right? It isn't that hot, Travis. And you don't look well. . . ."

"Leave me alone," he snapped, and she'd moved back, looking hurt. An act. The damned woman was incapable of feeling any kind of emotion for him. She only wanted to fool him into thinking she was humble. He'd never fall for that ploy. It had been tried too many times by too many other women.

"Coltrane, you listening to me?"

Jerking his head up, he saw that Sam was watching him intently. "I been talking to you for five minutes, but your eyes look plumb glassy. You ain't been hittin' the red-eye, have you?"

He shook his head, felt something crawling on his neck and slapped at it with his hand. Lice. Damn, they were everywhere. Once a week, he took a bath whenever a stream or river was available and no Rebs were around, but the varmints were always there waiting when he put his clothes back on. Kitty had seen him scratching and suggested he let her boil his uniform in harsh lye soap the next time he bathed. He'd asked her suggestively if she'd bathe with him, and she had actually smiled as though she just might.

Another act! He snorted.

"Travis, are you okay?"

"Yeah, yeah, I'm just tired. Aren't we all? I want this damned war to end. I want to go home. Back to Louisiana and the bayou, where it's quiet and peaceful. . . ."

"Well, that may be a long time off. I'm trying to tell you what I heard today when I went into town for supplies. Remember I told you that Lincoln's got McClellan's ass on the block, ready to kick it all the way to Mississippi. . . ."

Travis nodded. God, it was hot. And he felt so tired, dizzy, almost. The damned heat. How could anyone stand Virginia in the summer? It was unbearable.

"Lincoln never should have axed him as general-in-chief of all the armies," Sam was saying, "and just giving him command of the Army of the Potomac only last March. I don't give a damn what anybody says, George B. McClellan has no sympathy for the South, and he's no coward. Lincoln and that Secretary of War of his, Stanton, are just scared shitless that the Rebs will march on Washington. That's why George wound up with 90,000 men instead of the 130,000 he left with, when he started up the Peninsula. Hell, they took a whole army corps from his command and gave it to General McDowell—just to make sure they had plenty of soldiers around Washington. And now George is up against that Confederate Major General Magruder, and no telling how many men *he's* got."

Sam was smoking a cigar, and the smoke wafted to Travis's nostrils, and he felt a wave of nausea. "That's our job," he snapped, irritated with himself and taking it out on Sam. "Find out just how many men Magruder has and what George is up against. He's moving toward Yorktown. We're riding out tomorrow. . . ."

He swayed, caught himself. Sam leaned forward. "You're in no kind of shape to ride out of here, Coltrane. Why don't you let that nurse you dragged along take a look at you? She's been sneaking looks at you all evening, like she knows there's something ailing you. . . ."

Travis struggled to his feet. "I told you—there's nothing wrong with me. It's this damned Virginia heat. I can't stand it. I'm going down by the stream to sleep where it's cooler. Tell the men to be ready to ride about midnight. It'll be safer to scout around at night in case Magruder does have half the Confederate Army out there waiting for us."

He stumbled, righted himself, and moved as quickly as he could down the hill to where a stream offered some relief from the heat of the campsite. He didn't bother to lay down a blanket, just slumped to a bed of pine needles and closed his eyes.

Someone was shaking him. "Captain, sir, the men are ready."

He blinked his eyes, looked up to see Jim Dugan, a private from Texas staring down at him in the half-light of the moon. "Six men are saddled and ready to ride, sir," he said.

"All right." He moved to get to his feet but instead fell

backward. His head felt as though it were weighted down by a rock. His mouth felt dry and puffy.

"You all right, sir?"

"I wish everyone would quit worrying about me!" he cried.

Only sheer gut determination gave Travis the strength to make it up the hill to where his men were waiting. He caught sight of Kitty standing near the campfire, watching him curiously. Her dress was worn and tattered. He made a mental note to find her something decent to wear. She was too beautiful to be dressed in rags. Tomorrow. Tomorrow he would send one of his men into the nearest town and find her the prettiest dress anywhere. Beautiful. She was so damned beautiful, with her hair shining like golden red wine in the firelight.

What the hell was wrong with him? He was no lovesick boy. The girl meant nothing to him. Let her wear rags. What difference did it make? She was only along in case she was needed, and her cooking talents came in handy. And that youngster with her was good for dirty work. Convenient. That's all she was. And when he felt better, it would be time to once again take her in his arms and tease and torture her. This time she would beg . . . this time she would scream and beg him to take her. . . .

"Sir . . ." Someone held out a hand to him, holding his horse by the reins.

He slapped at the soldier's arm, shoving him back, grabbing at his horse's mane as he swung himself up into the saddle. "Since when do I need help getting on a horse?" he snapped irritably.

Something *was* wrong, but he forced himself to sit erect in the saddle. His head was swimming, and there was that wave of nausea again. He tasted bile rising in his throat. Now he was perspiring heavily, clothes soaked to the skin. *Stay awake,* he commanded himself. *For God's sake, stay awake!* What kind of officer was he if he let a little sickness put him flat on his back and keep him from his line of duty? He *had* to go on, *had* to take the men out. They looked up to him, respected him, and he knew it. And this was important. McClellan believed that Magruder was sitting out there with thousands of soldiers, just waiting for him. They had been seen, McClellan insisted. Travis said

Magruder was full of bullshit—he was tricky—known for being cunning and deceiving. But with President Lincoln and Secretary Stanton on his back, McClellan was being cautious. Too damned cautious. Already he had erected works facing the Yorktown lines, preparing to lay siege. Foolish, Travis thought, but he had to prove it. A waste of time. Magruder was merely stalling for time until more Confederates arrived to reinforce. Travis just felt this in his guts. But he had to prove it, and damnit, he wasn't even sure he could stay in the saddle, much less lead a patrol on a dangerous mission.

They had camped in a deep thicket, well hidden, they hoped. Travis took six men, left six with Kitty and Andy Shaw. They moved forward, going slowly, making their way through the thick undergrowth and through the forest. Sam Bucher led the way. He had been out earlier, when it was light, and he knew a good spot where they could wait for the sun to come up. It was a ridge, overlooking Magruder's lines.

It took almost two hours to reach the position, and as they arrived, Travis slid to the ground, felt his knees buckle and moved swiftly to clutch at the saddle to keep from falling. He hoped no one had seen. But of course they hadn't. It was dark. He felt relieved. He could not let them know how weak he really was.

"Nothing to do till morning," he said, trying not to sound so happy about it. He walked over and sat down beneath a sweet gum tree, leaned his head back, and promptly fell asleep.

Someone was shaking him anxiously. "Sir, sir, come look. Quickly. . . ."

He moved to leap quickly to his feet but his head was so heavy, legs so weak, that he pitched forward on his knees dizzily. It was daylight, past sunrise. How long? Why wasn't he awakened earlier? This was no time to sleep. He tried to stand up but could not. Looking around through glazed eyes, he realized that no one was watching him. They were all standing at the edge of a jutting ridge, looking down and shaking their heads in wonder.

"Look at that sonofabitch! Can you believe it. All he's been doing these past weeks is marching the same troops up and down that ridge so McClellan will see them and think he's got that many men. How many men did the Captain say General McClellan's got?"

"Around 90,000, I think."

"Well, I'll bet there ain't over 15,000 or so down there. Don't that beat all? McClellan could've taken them anytime he wanted to. Damndest thing I've ever seen. . . ."

"Captain." Someone was calling him, but he couldn't see who it was. Damnit, the sun was shining but all he could see was a bright, glaring haze that covered everything so that he could not distinguish faces, objects. And it was hot. Oh God, it was so hot. Had he been killed and gone to hell to burn? He'd always figured he'd wind up there, anyway. Why in thunder did Virginia have to be so hot? Why did the sun have to shine so brightly here?

"Captain, you were right. Magruder's been playing a trick. We've got to get word to McClellan."

"Damnit, Travis, you're sick. . . ." he heard Sam's voice somewhere through the haze. "Let's get him back to camp and let Kitty take a look at him."

"She'll kill me." The words came out hoarsely. "Give . . . her a chance . . . she'll kill me. . . ."

"I'll stay with you," Sam was promising. "Now come on, Travis, you never should have come out here, you stubborn bastard."

They were helping him into the saddle, and he was trying to push their hands away. He could make it back to camp. Kitty had poisoned him, that's what was wrong. She had slipped something into his food, and he was dying, and he wanted to last long enough to get back to camp and wrap his fingers around her neck and squeeze the life from her. That's what he was going to do. She wouldn't get away with it . . . he'd take her with him. . . .

He felt himself falling . . . down . . . down . . . down . . . and then there was nothing.

The words came to him through a deep, black void. Time stood still. He could hear but not speak. Slowly, the darkness tried to fade, and he could distinguish objects, shapes.

"He's trying to open his eyes. Praise God."

"Stand back, please. I've got to sponge his eyes with this." Kitty's voice. He could hear her speaking. Damn, was she in hell, too? Had he succeeded in murdering her and taking her with him? But no, it was cool here—cool and damp. He could feel it. But Lord, he was weak. He tried to lift his hand, to let them know he was all right, but he could not move a muscle.

"Stand back, I say. Honestly, Sam, after all these weeks, do you think I'm going to harm your precious Captain now?"

She knelt beside him, dipped a cloth in the vinegar and water solution and began to dab at his eyes. He jerked his head. "He moved. . . . Captain Coltrane?" she asked anxiously. "Can you hear me? Oh, thank God."

"Captain, you okay?" Sam Bucher's voice. Travis opened his eyes to see his longtime friend smiling down at him. "You're going to be okay. I told this girl if you died, I'd kill her and that Reb both, and I'd have done it," he added gruffly.

Kitty stared at Sam angrily. "Yes, you probably would have, even after I told you he had smallpox—and how many people live after they've had smallpox? The only reason he's not dead is because God doesn't want him, and the devil won't have him either. Now will you get the hell out of my way so I can put some of this in his eyes so he won't go blind?"

He smiled. He couldn't help himself. In spite of his weakness, he had to smile at Kitty cussing at old Sam that way. And it worked. Sam moved back out of her way. "Get him a cup of that wine cooling in the creek," she ordered. "And bring me another dose of that opiate I mixed up. He's still got a long way back."

"How . . . how long have I been out?" It surprised him that he even found the strength to speak.

She kept dabbing at his eyes.

"How . . . long?" he repeated.

"Three weeks."

"Three weeks?" He wanted to raise up but could not.

"Just be still. I've got to get this solution in your eyes. I wish you'd stayed unconscious. I don't think I can stand treating you awake."

Three weeks. What had happened during that time? Did they tell McClellan about Magruder's trickery? It was all coming back to him now—the sickness, the patrol, the discovery of Magruder's clever ploy. What had happened in the last three weeks?

He was in a tent. There was someone lying nearby. One of his men? He tried to turn his head but felt himself sinking. "Don't fight it, Captain," Kitty was saying. It surprised him to hear her sound so gentle. "Sleep. You need the sleep for your strength."

When he again opened his eyes, he found Sam Bucher sitting beside him on the ground. "Three weeks on a blanket on the cold hard ground ought to wake up any man," he quipped down at him. "How do you feel?"

"Weak."

"I imagine so. You had a rough time of it. For about three days there, Kitty said you could go any time. She stayed right with you, giving you some kind of stuff she mixed up out of herbs and roots. She sent one of the men into town for some medicine, too. We had to stay here. The woods are crawling with Rebs, especially after Johnston got his army to Magruder, finally." -

"Did you get word to McClellan that it was all a trick?"

He nodded, and Travis realized his vision was clearing up because he could see the lice crawling in Sam's dark beard. "Yep, we sure did, but McClellan already lost a month, and when he heard from us, he was going to open a big bombardment the next day, had his big guns in position and ready. And know what? Johnston evacuated Yorktown. Oh, they had a skirmish at Williamsburg, but the whole thing just made McClellan look worse to President Lincoln and Secretary Stanton."

"Hey . . . am I wearing you out?" Sam asked as Travis closed his eyes. "Kitty said you were to rest."

"Where is she?"

"Sleeping. It's nighttime now. You woke up around noon today and went back to sleep. It's my turn to sit up with you. She stayed with you day and night for the first three days, though. Said she'd never seen anybody stay unconscious so long. You really must've had quite a case. She said you stayed asleep 'cause you were too weak to be awake. I guess that makes sense."

Travis could turn his head finally. Someone was lying

nearby. "That's Vince Potter," Sam said quietly. "He just come down with it. Kitty says he probably won't make it. He was poorly to start with."

"Did anyone die?"

Sam looked away.

"I asked you, Sam, did anyone die?"

His voice broke. "Jim Dugan. And Lonnie Mack. They died the second week. Raney, he died a few days ago. Kitty says the worst of it may be over. You've got to get well, Travis. You've got to get well and get us out of here. I slipped into town the other day and all hell's breaking loose in the war now. We're needed bad. The rumor is that the Rebs will march on Washington, and everyone says if that happens, the war is lost."

"Bullshit."

"I thought I heard a familiar voice," Kitty stepped into the tent, her dress even more tattered and worn, if that was possible. Her hair hung loose and flowing around her face, and it gleamed golden in the firelight. Travis thought once again how damned beautiful she was—and those eyes —so blue they were purple. He'd never seen a woman with eyes such a strange color. And her lashes—as she leaned over him, he could see those long, dusty lashes. They sparkled with gold speckles, as though dusted with some magical powder. Strange—strange but lovely. He found himself wishing he had the strength to crush her in his arms and kiss her until she was breathless.

She told Sam to get some more wine, good for regaining strength, she said, and some of the boiled beef left from supper. He had to eat to get stronger, even if it meant forcing the food down.

He ate, and the food was good, and Sam said he'd get some rest if Kitty would stay up. She went to where Vince Potter lay in a stupor, tried to force some liquid down his throat but could not. Then she returned to sit by Travis.

"You know, the last thing I remember is thinking you had poisoned me, and that's why I was so sick. I was determined to get back to camp and kill you with my bare hands before I died."

She rubbed at her throat and laughed. "So that's why you tried to choke me so many times when I'd try to get you to keep wine and water going down your throat. Once you might have succeeded if Sam hadn't been close by to pry your fingers loose."

"I did that?"

She laughed. "You certainly did, and I didn't realize you hated me that much. All the men were talking about it, wondering why you insisted on keeping me around when you hated me enough to kill me. I wondered about it myself. And poor Andy, he's been worried to death you'd succeed and then your men would kill him."

He looked at her for a long time, and neither of them spoke, eyes holding in a steady gaze.

"I don't hate you, Kitty," he said finally. "I find you to be the most beautiful woman I've ever met. I just don't happen to trust women, and you are about the most deadly female I've ever run up against. I guess it was only natural for me to think you'd kill me the first chance you got, and now I find out I've got you to thank for saving my life."

"Well, Sam said if you died, he'd kill me and Andy." She fingered the hem of the frayed dress. Seeing so lovely a creature in such a horrible costume was like putting a wildflower in a field of weeds, he thought. Such a woman was not meant to wear rags.

"I doubt Sam could have killed you, Kitty. I think he only meant to frighten you, because he figured you'd be happy to see me dead and wouldn't do anything to try to get me over the pox. I'm grateful."

Outside, they could hear the night sounds—the crickets, a hooty owl mournfully calling from someplace not too far away. Inside the tent, the small fire burning at the entranceway crackled and sparkled, and they could hear the gasping, uneven breathing from where Vince Potter lay.

What was she thinking? He could not be sure. He was not even sure why he cared. She had saved his life, but only because she felt her own was threatened. Her actions had not been prompted because of any favor she felt toward him. So why did he feel a warmth in his chest at her nearness?

"Travis," she took a deep breath. "What do you intend to do with Andy and me? They say the war is going badly for the North. Why won't you let Andy and me go before we're killed?"

"No," he said sharply. "You're needed. I've told you that. Not many women are as skilled as you, and I can't send you home to use those skills on the enemy. Besides, didn't you tell me your father joined the North? Would you want him to suffer, perhaps die, because of lack of attention? Can you hate all the Federals when your own father wears our uniform and fights for our cause?"

"You forget that I'm engaged to a Confederate."

She looked away, and he reached out and touched her cheek, turning her face back to meet his gaze. "Do you love him so much?"

"I . . . I do love him," she said solemnly. "Nathan is a good man. We'll be very happy together once the war is over."

"Andy told me that Nathan didn't approve of your wanting to work in the hospital back in your hometown."

"You know his name?" She blinked incredulously. "You've talked to Andy about him—and *he* talked to *you?* Why? I don't understand. I . . . I'm not even sure I like it."

"Yes, we talked. Your fiancé's name is Nathan Collins and he fights with a group called the Wayne Volunteers. They were at Shiloh. Andy talked to me because he worries about you. I talked to him because I wanted to know if you were telling the truth about all that's happened to you."

Her eyes flashed defiantly. "And you believe me now?"

"Yes."

"And you still won't let me go?"

"No."

"Then I wish I'd let you die." She moved to get up, and he did not have the strength to stop her—but she paused, looked straight into his eyes and said, "Why do you hate women, Travis? Why do you take some sort of sick, perverted pleasure in seeing a woman suffer? Like that night you held me down and . . . and . . ."

"And gave you pleasure?" There was that crooked, insolent smile she hated.

She felt the color rising in her cheeks. "I can't help what my body does. But you took pleasure in making me want you, even though you wouldn't give yourself to me. I think that's sick. I want to know why you do these things —to women, to yourself."

He closed his eyes. He would not tell her. He had never told anyone but Sam Bucher, and then only because they were drunk one night, and the memories came flooding back to wrap around his throat and choke him into telling of his tortured past. He had loved his mother, respected her, as most young boys do. When his father was away in the bayou fishing for weeks at a time, he never thought much about his mother painting herself up to go into New Orleans because she said she was lonely. Even when she made him promise not to tell his father, he thought it was only a game.

But the game ended the night his father returned early because a storm was brewing out in the gulf, and even the waters of the bayou were starting to swell and churn. As the hurricane began to blow inland, twisting the trees to the ground, blowing houses into the wind, destroying, ravaging—Deke Coltrane had been battling a storm within himself as he set out for New Orleans to find his wife.

And he had found her—in the arms of another man. He had dragged her home as the hurricane screamed and ripped into the night, and as the wrath of nature destroyed the world around him, Deke Coltrane drank himself into a stupor and proceeded to destroy his wife—and himself.

Travis was twelve years old. His sister only two. He had hidden in the closet of the little wooden shack where they lived, the walls trembling in the forces of the storm. Petrified by what went on outside, and what was happening inside the shack, he held his sister in his arms throughout the night, unable to move as he heard his mother's screams again and again, the sounds of his father's fists pummeling into her flesh—beating her mercilessly.

When morning came, and the winds were calm, Travis had forced himself to step out of that closet, and he found himself in the pits of hell. His mother lay on the floor, a battered, bloody mass of what was once a beautiful woman. His father lay nearby, his throat cut with his own knife, by his own hand. Dead. Both of them dead.

Travis shielded his sister from the gory sight, and then

the men came looking for his father. They wanted to take him to jail for murdering the man he'd found with his wife. Only Deke Coltrane wasn't going anywhere except to a shallow hole in the ground.

Travis never forgot that night. He never would. He didn't even want to erase it from his memory. He wanted to remember it so he would learn by it. His father had loved his mother, trusted her, and that love had led him straight to hell, destroying three people in the process. Never be weak, he taught himself through those painful years of struggling to grow up, never be weak and love a woman.

But there had been women—oh, yes, at sixteen he foolishly thought he was in love with a young creole girl, and when he found out she was giving every boy around the one thing she said was his and his alone, he hated himself for being so stupid and blind as to think one woman in the whole world might exist that could be trusted.

So finally he had learned his lesson. Since then, he had made the women the ones to suffer. And he would never be weak again.

And then they came and took his sister away, and she had killed herself, and he had gone to join the war, wanting to strike out and kill. It didn't matter if he, himself, died. No, he had never been afraid of death—only of living. Perhaps that was why he was so valued by General Grant. He would charge into battle, slashing his sword, killing, showing no mercy. Three times he had leaped over gunners to have them disembowel his horse, and he'd fallen to the ground to face them in hand to hand combat. And never did he back away from fighting or possible death.

And now, before him, sat the most beautiful woman he had ever laid eyes on. She watched him intently with those gold-dusted eyelashes brushing gently against peach-colored cheeks, her lovely sunset hair falling softly about her face. His eyes moved to her breasts, firm, pointing. In spite of his weakness from his illness, he felt a tightening in his loins. He wanted her. He wanted her more than he'd ever wanted a woman in his life. He wanted to enter her and stay there until everything in him was drained into her. He wanted her beside him through the night, every night.

He wanted to kiss those pouting lips into submission. He wanted her to stand beside him as he let the whole world know that she belonged to him and him alone.

Fool! He let out his breath and forced his eyes away from her. *Fool! You're nothing but a fool! She's like all the rest. She's no different. She just happens to be the most beautiful. That's all.* It was the sickness, the weakness, that was making him lose his head. He had to get well, get his strength back, his control.

"I want to sleep now," he snapped. "Get over there and look after my soldier. He needs you more than I do."

Slowly, Kitty got to her feet, still staring at him, as though trying to see deep inside the facade of bitterness, to probe for the roots and foundation of that bitterness.

"I don't think, Travis Coltrane," Kitty whispered, "that you've ever needed anyone in your entire life."

✤ Chapter Twenty ✤

KITTY sat at the window, staring down at the street
below. It was late August, so hot in Richmond that
every stitch she wore was soaked with perspiration. The
room was stuffy, the air musty and close. How long had
she been a prisoner there? She had lost count of the days.
Or had it been weeks? Travis had deposited her there,
placed a guard outside the door. A tray of food was
brought to her twice a day, her chamber pot removed,
cleaned, returned. No one stayed long enough for conversation.

Straining her eyes against the glaring noonday sun, she
could see the street clock in front of the jewelry store. Back
in Goldsboro, there had been a similar clock in front of
Gidden's, but this was a larger store. Probably there were
thousands and thousands of dollars in merchandise on display in the big glass window. Her gaze moving over the
crowds in the streets, it was obvious that there were many
men about who could afford to shop at that store. She'd
heard some of the soldiers talking on the ride into town
about the huge amounts of money circulating thanks to
the army and the war and the trading in sugar, medicines,
coffee, and tea.

There were many blacks about, some free and others still
slaves. They were driving carriages or holding doors open,
sweeping sidewalks, stepping quickly out of the way to

allow white men to walk by freely, bowing to them curtly from their waists. Whenever a white woman passed, they glanced away quickly, the white men watching to make sure that they did.

Kitty had learned to identify many of the groups of soldiers by listening to their conversations as they passed beneath the windows. The Alabama soldiers wore blue. The soldiers from Georgia wore brown uniforms with full-skirted pants and green trim. The ones from Tennessee mostly wore coonskin caps, and the Texas soldiers wore cowboy hats. Some of the ones from Arkansas did, too. The Washington Artillery, from New Orleans, wore white gloves, and once she had seen a group that called themselves New Orleans Zouaves, dressed in baggy scarlet trousers, white gaiters, low-cut blue shirts, and their jackets were embroidered heavily and braided, each armed with a bowie knife held in a bright blue sash. Most of the other Confederates, like the ones from Florida and Mississippi and South Carolina, wore gray.

So many times Kitty had been tempted to call out that window to the soldiers and tell them she was being held prisoner by Yankee spies. But the last thing Travis had said to her was that if she wanted to see Andy Shaw alive again, she had better keep quiet. And she had. Because as Andy was led roughly away, down the hall to another room in the hotel, his eyes were wide and frightened. She couldn't risk endangering his life. No, there would be another way to escape, and she had to be patient.

The sound of the door being unlocked made her jump to her feet. She dared to hope it might be Travis at last, and she would know where they were going from here. But it wasn't Captain Coltrane. Instead, Sam Bucher came in with a tray and set it down on the table next to the bed. She looked at it and wrinkled her nose. "Rancid mutton . . . turnips . . . and dried-out corn bread! Sam, how much longer do you think I can live on this . . . this garbage?"

"Kitty, I'm sorry," he sounded as if he meant it. "The innkeeper runs a poor place, I know, but he minds his own business and doesn't ask a lot of questions about why we're here, and that's important."

"Not to me it isn't. I wish he would ask questions. I wish all those Confederate soldiers outside would ask questions. I wish they'd kill everyone of you and set me and Andy free. . . ."

He smiled down at her as she flopped down on the bed. "Come on now, Kitty, you don't mean that. You've grown kinda fond of us, as much as we've been through together."

She looked at him thoughtfully. Sam was peppery and gruff, but there was something about him that got to her. "Well, maybe if they'd kill your precious Captain and spare you. . . ."

"That's my girl!" He laughed and pulled up a chair and sat down. "Maybe in a day or two we can get out of here."

"How's Andy?"

"Fine. He just asked about you. He doesn't have a window in his room, so he's worse off than you are. Travis said we couldn't trust him not to panic and yell out, but you were smart enough to know we meant business when we said to keep quiet."

"But why are we here? And where has Travis gone? And why are all those Confederates coming and going day and night?"

"We're here because Travis and a few of the men are out getting information from drunken Rebs, and Richmond is a boiling pot of soldiers coming and going. And when soldiers come to town they drink . . . and when they drink, they talk. We're here to listen."

She picked at the turnips, tasted them, then shoved the plate away. Horrible. The food was horrible, and she just couldn't eat a bite. A fly settled down onto the green mass and promptly flew away. "See? Even the flies won't eat it."

"Maybe it won't be long, Kitty," Sam said sympathetically. "Believe me, I like the food you cook in camp a lot better. That cornbread looks like a pile of cow dung baked in the sun, don't it?"

She ignored his comment, thinking how crude Sam could be at times. Getting up and walking to the window, she stared down at the street once again. "I wish your Captain would come back."

"You miss him, don't you?"

"Miss him?" She whirled about to stare at him in wonder. "Sam, I hate him! He's holding me prisoner when I want to be home with my people—my mother! I . . . oh, no one knows how much I hate that man!"

He scratched at his beard, smiling. "Oh, I've seen the way you two look at each other when you think the other'n ain't watching. It's the war's got you at each other's throats. Any other time, I bet you'd fall in love."

"You're out of your mind!"

"Oh, I reckon I've been around a heap more than you and the Captain, and I see how foolish young folks can be." He got to his feet, picked up the tray. "Sure you don't want to eat anything? Supper ain't gonna be much better, I'm afraid."

She shook her head. He walked to the door, kicked it with his foot, and one of the men opened it and let him out. Then it closed, and she heard the sound of the key turning. Locked in again.

Dismally, she leaned her head against the window and stared down at the street. The crowds were thinning out due to the heat. There was nothing to look at anymore, so she went to the bed and laid down, thinking it was too hot to fall asleep.

Kitty opened her eyes. The room was dark. And it was cooler. For that much, she was grateful. Getting up, she hurried to the window to catch a breath of fresh air. Leaning out, she gulped, closed her eyes, felt the whisper of a breeze against her skin.

"Hello there!"

Kitty turned her head, startled. To the left, at the next window, a shadowed figure sat on the ledge. He wore a gray uniform, and her heart began to pound excitedly. A Confederate soldier! In the very next room! Did she dare tell him she was a prisoner? The sight of Andy's young, frightened face swam before her eyes.

"Hello. . . ." her voice came out a whisper.

"What's the matter?" the stranger asked. "Can't you talk to a lonely soldier? Do you have a jealous husband or something?" He laughed, but the laughter sounded forced, as though he genuinely hoped he was wrong, that she could offer him some companionship.

"I . . . I'm engaged," she blurted out, still in a half-whisper so the guard stationed outside the door would not hear her talking to someone.

"To a soldier?"

"Yes, a Confederate. . . ."

Again he laughed, but this time it sounded genuine. "Well, I should hope so. I can't picture a pretty girl like you getting mixed up with a dang Yankee. What's his outfit?"

"Wayne Volunteers. He's a Major, with a North Carolina Regiment. I don't know which one." Her heart was pounding excitedly. Did she dare to hope he might know Nathan —know something about him? "The last I heard, he fought at the Battle of Shiloh . . ."

"God, we lost a lot of men there—thousands. . . ." He swore under his breath. The light was dim from the lantern in his room. She could not make out all the details of his face, but he was young, bearded. That's about all she could tell of his features. "Haven't heard from him since? You sure he's all right? There's been a lot of fighting."

She wondered what to say next. How could she tell him she had no idea of what had been going on in the war? The only thing she knew was that the month was August, and they were in a town called Richmond, in the state of Virginia.

"I've been sick," she thought of the lie and told it quickly. "Smallpox. I'm . . . recuperating, here, away from people. I . . . I've lost touch."

"I guess you have," he let out his breath. "There's been a lot of smallpox. Lots have died with it. You were lucky. You sure picked a ratty place to hole up, though. . . ." He sounded curious, so she made a comment about not having much money for food and shelter, and that seemed to satisfy him.

He started talking about the war as Kitty listened intently, eager to hear anything he might tell her. In April, he said, it looked as though the Confederates were constantly on the defensive everywhere. New Orleans was lost, McClellan had been at the gates of Richmond, Halleck was storming in on Corinth. Missouri was gone, and it looked as though the whole Mississippi Valley would follow it. "But now it looks different," he said brightly. "It seems that victory for the South is not far away. McClellan got beat right in front of Richmond. And just a couple of weeks ago, Jackson advanced on Cedar Mountain and drove a detachment of General Pope's army into retreat. 'Course Jackson had to withdraw because Pope had some more men not far away, but the word is that General Lee is moving in a big army."

"I do hope it will all be over soon," Kitty said anxiously, glad to hear the good news. "I want to go home so badly."

"Well, you sound strong enough, if you'd quit that danged whispering," he teased her. "How about if I come over for a visit? I've been on the lines, and I'm mighty lonesome for the company of a pretty young thing like you. And that Major of yours wouldn't mind you keeping a poor Johnny Reb from spending a lonely night. . . ."

"All right," she said nervously. She had to take the chance. If she could talk to him, tell him the whole story, he would surely gather some soldiers and rescue both her and Andy. They could charge the hotel and rescue them before Sam and the others had a chance to kill them.

"But be careful," she rushed on. "There's a guard at my door."

"A guard?" He laughed and tilted the jug again. Then he lowered it and said, "You mean that Major put a guard at your door? Is he that afraid someone will take you away from him?"

"No, no, you don't understand," she cried, her brain screaming for the right words. Please, God, don't let him be so drunk he can't understand and grasp the situation. "I'm being held prisoner. That guard at the door is a *Yankee*, and they've got a fourteen-year-old Confederate held prisoner down the hall somewhere, and they've threatened to kill him if I ask for help. You're my only chance. You've got to be careful. . . ."

She heard the door opening softly, and she jumped away from the window. In the dim light, she could see the steel-blue eyes of Travis Coltrane gleaming angrily. "You talking to someone?" he asked sharply.

"No, no, of course not." She forced a smile as he set down the lantern he was carrying. "I was listening to the people on the street talking. It gets lonely in here, all by myself with no one to talk to. I . . . I just sit at the window all day and watch and listen. Ask Sam. He knows when he comes in here, I'm always at the window looking out. . . ."

She was talking nervously, and she knew it. He kept looking at her, eyes burning into hers, and finally she went over to the bed and sat down, folding her hands in her lap. "Well, you're back. That's good. I've missed you, Travis. I know we aren't exactly the best of friends, but we've been together so long now that I'm beginning to look forward to the times when we talk."

He forced his eyes to leave hers and walked to the door to tell the guard to find Sam Bucher and a bottle of whiskey. Then he started pacing up and down the room silently, ignoring her. Kitty knew he was worried about something, and she prayed he hadn't heard anything she said to the soldier—and she prayed that the soldier had been sober enough to understand what she was saying. Perhaps at this very moment he was out gathering Confederate soldiers to storm the hotel. . . .

Sam came in, nodded to her, then he and Travis sat down at the table in the far corner of the room, the bottle of whiskey Travis had ordered between them.

"It looks bad, Sam, damn bad," Travis said worriedly, his brow furrowed, lips tight and grim. "McClellan's now camped on the bank of the James River. He's still out there and strong enough to resume the offensive on short notice, but he needs those 50,000 men that are being held back because of Jackson's game in the Shenandoah Valley. This John Pope is moving down toward Richmond along the lines of the Orange and Alexandria Railroad, and there's just no way that Lee can fend off both Pope *and* McClellan. But Lee's smart, and I found out that he's got the notion that McClellan is going to be inactive for a while. I had a hunch about what he'd do, so I did some checking and found out I was right."

He paused, and Sam spoke up excitedly, "Go on, let's have it. What's Lee got up his sleeve?"

Kitty strained to hear every word. Somehow, she knew that this was the most important conversation she had overheard. What if they were, at this very moment, planning a move that might endanger Nathan's life? The thought made her spine tingle apprehensively. She had no way of knowing just where he was fighting with his men.

He took a deep breath, held it, then let it out at once. "Lee has sent Stonewall Jackson, with about 25,000 men, north to attack Pope."

Sam whistled between his teeth. "Goddamn, what do we do?"

"We round up the men and get ready to ride. Tell them to put on their Confederate uniforms so we can get through the lines, then we'll change clothes and head for *our* lines and get word to Pope. We can't let Jackson take him by surprise."

The chair scraped the floor noisily as Sam got to his feet. Without another word, he left the room. Kitty prayed fervently that the Confederate soldier would come soon. Now she had valuable information to give him, and there was even more reason to turn Travis over for what he was —a dangerous Yankee spy. He could not be allowed to leave Richmond with such information. She looked at him sitting there, sipping whiskey from the bottle. What if the soldier didn't come? What could she do then? She had to let their plans be known. But how? How could she get word to the Confederates?

She and Travis had not talked together for some time. In fact, he had hardly paid her any mind since that night he had rallied after being in a daze with the fever of smallpox. It was a surprise that he had even come into her room that night. His clothes were there, but she seldom saw him. He usually sent in Sam for what he needed, as though he didn't want to have to come in contact with her. Oh, thank God, she had heard that door open, or he might have slipped up behind to hear her telling that Confederate soldier how she was being held prisoner. Travis could be as quiet and slippery as the bobcats she and Poppa had hunted back home. But he hadn't heard, and now she wondered how to handle the situation. Could it be that she just might be able to reach him now, gain his trust? If so, she would stand a much better chance of catching him unawares than if she continued to be so resistant to his presence. A while back, before he'd come down with the illness, she had tried to subtly push herself at him, but he had not acknowledged her advances. Perhaps then he thought it was a trick. Now, since she had nursed him back to health and had done nothing to antagonize him lately, there just might be a chance.

She had to try, she thought feverishly. What was there to lose at this point? If the soldier from the next room had been too drunk to understand what she was saying, then she had to go ahead, on her own, push herself at Travis, then hopefully catch him off guard so she could tip his hand to the Confederates—even if it meant screaming to someone out the window!

Thoughts of her father crept painfully into her mind. What if he was fighting with this officer Pope or McClellan? What if she was, in fact, betraying him? It was a chance she had to take. Her freedom—maybe even her life, was at stake—as well as that of Andy Shaw. And there was Nathan to think about—Nathan and her countrymen —the Southerners. Poppa was only one man, a grown man, with a conscience and heart of his own. And he had made his decision just as she had to make hers, now. And Poppa would understand. She knew he would. He would know that she had to do what she thought was right. Wasn't that the code he, himself, had taught her to live by? Was there any other path for her to take except to Travis Coltrane's arms and make him think she wanted him desperately? Had yielded to his irresistible charms?

No, there was no other way. She had to do it. Slowly, she got up from the bed and moved across the floor to where he sat hunched over the table—and the bottle of whiskey which he continued to sip. She stood behind him, hardly daring to breathe as she fought to muster the courage for what must be done.

When he spoke, she jumped, startled. "Have you somehow come by a knife, princess? Are you waiting to plunge it into my back?" He sounded amused, not concerned about the possibility of death at her hands.

Not trusting herself to speak, she slid her hands up his back, caressing his shoulders, then moving to massage the muscles at the back of his neck. He did not move. She leaned forward, until her lips were almost touching his ear, forcing her voice not to quiver as she whispered, "It's been so long . . . here . . . in this room . . . alone without you, Travis. I've waited for this moment, this time."

She touched his ear, felt him quicken beneath her caress. "Hold me, love me . . . please," her voice was strong, husky.

Afraid she would lose her nerve if she did not keep moving, Kitty pushed herself around him, slid onto his lap, nervous, fluttering fingers working at the buttons of his shirt. His chest was strong, massive, covered with thick,

curling hair which she wrapped around her dancing fingertips. Pressing her lips against his, she felt the tickle of his
mustache, beard, her tongue darting into his mouth as he
quietly yielded to her.

Suddenly his fingers were snaking out to wrap into her
hair, pulling her head back. In the orange glow of the
lantern his eyes blazed like blue-red embers of coal. "So
the lady needs pleasuring," he smiled, half-taunting. "We
wave a flag of truce to give each other what we want, is
that it?"

"Yes." Her heart was pounding into her throat, blood
coursing through her veins. It *was* an act, she told herself.
She did not really want this horrible creature, but she had
to pretend, had to make him think that she was beside
herself with desire for him. Others died for the South,
would it be so great a sacrifice for her to offer the enemy
her body if it meant helping the cause? She could not
believe it was wrong. She could not even believe that
Nathan would frown upon it if he knew the cause was just
and worthy.

"Take me. . . ." She slid her hand down his bare chest
to his stomach, then lower, felt the bulging there that told
her he wanted her, was yielding to the bait.

The thin muslin dress tore easily beneath his snatching
hand, her breasts tumbling forth eagerly. He touched one
taut nipple between thumb and forefinger, squeezed as his
eyes searched hers for any sign of displeasure. Her eyelids
fluttered shut as she gasped deep in her throat, thrusting
her chest upwards to offer him even more of her bosom to
do with as he desired. He squeezed harder, and she
moaned out loud. "You like it, don't you, princess?" He
sounded angry. "You like to be hurt, don't you?"

She could only moan as her body began to betray her
with small flutters of involuntary pleasure beneath his hurting touch. With one quick movement he finished yanking
the dress downward, ripping the material until she was
completely naked there on his lap. His hands moved over
her roughly, squeezing, bruising, lips moving to kiss, bite,
probe, and torture.

Suddenly he was on his feet, lifting her in his arms to
carry her to the bed. Falling down beside her, he tugged
at his trousers until she felt the raw, hot flesh of his man-

hood pressing against her thigh. "Now. . . ." she moaned. "Oh, Travis, I love you . . . forgive me for all the unkind words I've spoken. I've loved you for so long . . . those horrible days and nights when I feared you'd die, I prayed for the time to come when I had the courage to tell you how much I do love you. . . ."

He continued to caress her, burning the skin everywhere he touched. He found that nucleus of sensation that made her arch her body, a giant roaring beginning deep within her brain, the recesses of all pretense being dissolved as wind against the sky. "Beg for it," he commanded harshly. "Beg, you vixen, and then beg some more . . . and I might pleasure you. . . ."

Had her body not been aflame with desire, had her senses not been parched beyond reason, perhaps she might have felt the smallest twinge of resentment at being forced to resort to begging that he take her. His lips danced along her body, making it quiver with tantalizing spasms of joy.

Moving on top of her, he roughly used one knee to spread her legs apart. She felt the tip of his throbbing member touch that pinnacle of sensation. Her whole body shuddered. It was warm, throbbing, aching to get inside of her, and she began to move her hips beneath him, urging him onward, into her.

He was no longer the enemy. He was no longer the arrogant, conceited Yankee officer that she had hated. He was a man, and she, a woman, and this was the way Nature meant for them to be together. It was not a part of a plan to catch him off guard, make him think she really and truly loved him so that he would think she had forgotten about her Confederate lover, the South, the war, all of it— this was another world, a reality that defied unreality, and yet none of it could actually be happening. This could not really be her—the Katherine Wright who once felt it only right to give her body inside the respectability of marriage —this was another woman, this she-devil who was thrusting hips so brazenly upward, vainly attempting to impale herself on the one above, who gave only so much, then withdrew to chuckle at the cries for more. Her nails dug into the flesh of his back as she screamed against his shoulder.

And at last, when she thought surely death would come

if he did not take her, there was the sweetness of pene-
tration. The waves crashed against the shore with all the
force and fury of the hurricane, and as the passion was
spent, Kitty felt herself floating out with the tide, as helpless and weak as a wounded gull upon the surface of the
now-calm waters.

"I do love you, Travis," she whispered against his
perspiration-slick chest when she was able to find her
voice. "I loved you a long time ago, but I was afraid
you wouldn't love me, too. War does strange things to
people. . . ."

"Yes, it does," he answered quietly, moving to his side
to cradle her against his chest, still holding her tightly in
his arms. "Kitty, I've waited for this moment so long."

A spark crackled within her. "Then you love me, too?
Oh, Travis, I never dared to hope that you might love me,
too, not after the way I've treated you, the way I talked
to you. . . ."

"And what about the man you want to marry? Have you
forgotten him so easily, Kitty?" Was he mocking her? She
could not tell. His voice sounded strange, as though he
were fencing with her. "And what about the Southern
cause? How do you feel about that, Kitty? Do you now
stand with the North? Do you turn your back on the
Confederates to stand beside me as my woman?"

"Oh, yes, of course, Travis." She admonished herself for
sounding too eager. Forcing herself to calm down, she said
carefully, "Travis, I do love you. I fought it, I'll admit, but
it happened, and nothing else matters now except that we
be together. Yes, I'll stand with you—and the North. God
as my witness, nothing matters but you."

She leaned forward, about to slip her hands around his
neck and draw his face close to hers, kiss those slightly
mocking lips as he gazed down at her. But he reached up
quickly to knock her hands away, as his eyes turned to
gleaming steel. "Oh, Kitty, did you think I was so stupid?"
His voice was laughing, but he continued to look at her
angrily, bitterly. "You're quite an actress, but fortunately
I've been around enough lying, cheating women that I'm
not easily fooled."

"Fooled? I don't understand. I told you . . ."

"I *know* what you told me," he snapped, shoving her

roughly back on the bed. "I also know what you told that soldier in the next room."

"I told him nothing. . . ." Her brain was spinning. He couldn't have heard. The door had opened, and he had been standing there, and she was not talking loud enough to be heard all the way across the room and through the closed door.

"Stop your lying! That soldier in the next room was a *Yankee* soldier, you little fool—a *Federal*—one of *our* men. I planted him there, to test your loyalty which I figured you would sooner or later pledge when you got hold of some information you thought was vital. And this is the first time I let you overhear something important. I wanted to test you, Kitty, because goddamn it, I was hoping you had changed. I guess I was hoping that you did care, just a little. You're a beautiful woman, a desirable woman, and I've wanted to take you in my arms and love you since the first time I laid eyes on you—but I knew, damn your soul, that you couldn't be trusted, but I had to prove it to myself—to Sam. He even thought you might've changed! I tried to tell him you hadn't, but he's more easily fooled than I am, much to your disadvantage."

Their eyes met and held, blazing defiantly. Kitty wanted to reach out and rake her nails into the flesh of his face as she had done to the skin on his back, but she checked herself. He was boiling inside, and in spite of her own anger, she knew he was capable in that moment of taking out his wrath physically. And she would be of no use to the Confederates, or to Nathan, if she were crippled or dead.

He got up and began putting on his clothes.

"What will you do with me now?" She spat out the words. "I suppose you've already murdered Andy. You probably cut his throat the first night you brought us here. Your kind . . ."

"My kind!" He whipped his head around, one leg in his trousers as he balanced nakedly. "What the hell do you know about my kind? What do you think you are? You just begged me to make love to you—and now you look at me like I'm dirt! I don't want to hear one more word out of you, Kitty. You keep your mouth shut and do as you're told, or so help me, I'll turn you over to the first marauding bunch of soldiers I run up with—and not give a damn what they do with you. It was one thing when you were honest about your dislike for me and your committed loyalty to the South—*that* I could understand, and even respect, because it was your right to believe in what you chose to believe in. But to do what you just did, throw yourself at me just to make me believe you loved me so I'd turn my back and let you stick a knife in it . . . *that*, I can't accept. You make me sick!"

"And you make me sick!" She screamed and leaped off the bed, running for the window, yelling as loud as she could, "Help! . . . Yankees! . . . help! . . ."

He dove for her, throwing his weight against her to send her slamming against the wall. Her head cracked against the mantle of the fireplace, and she crumpled silently to the floor.

He felt her wrist. She was still alive, only dazed by the blow. There was the sound of alarmed voices outside. "Hey, what the hell's going on up there?"

"Somebody say something about Yankees?"

"Get some soldiers up there. . . ."

Travis hurried to the window and peered out at the dozen or so faces peering up at him, angry and bewildered. He forced a laugh, "If you don't pleasure a lady these days the way she wants it, she figures it's a bigger insult to call you a Yankee than call you a son of a bitch!"

He was relieved to hear a round a good-natured laughter. The crowd broke up, moved away. Behind him, the door opened and Sam hurried in. "Oh, boy, was that close. I just knew we had a fight on our hands. . . ." His eyes went to Kitty, lying on the floor. He bent quickly, felt for her pulse as Travis watched silently. "She's all right. We might better have a doctor check her over, though . . ."

Travis walked over, lifted her in his arms, then placed her on the bed. He picked up the pitcher of water on the bedside table and threw it unceremoniously into her face. Kitty's eyes flashed open as she sat straight up, shaking her head furiously and gasping as the water dripped down her face. Sam stood back, chuckling.

"You get your clothes on, sweetheart," Travis said slowly and evenly, "because we're going to be riding out of here soon. Scream one more time, and so help me, God, the next one will come from that Rebel, Andy Shaw, because he's right down the hall waiting for you, and I'll kill him myself."

Dizzily, she got up from the bed and moved toward the pile of clothing Travis was pointing to. He watched her move, his thoughts whirling inside like a tornado—not knowing which way to go, but instinct saying motion must continue.

Kitty had only been pretending. She did not love him, perhaps had not even wanted him. And he hated himself for not being able to decide whether he was glad—or sorry.

❧ Chapter Twenty-one ❧

TRAVIS Coltrane had led his band of men out of Richmond in the protective cloak of night. His intentions had been to ride ahead and warn the Federals of Lee's plan, but they had not traveled far when they rode right into the Confederates' attack at Mechanicsville, northeast of Richmond. Travis lost three men getting to his own lines, where he found General FitzJohn Porter, who was ably counterattacking. Once again, Kitty was deposited at a field hospital where she was thrust into the middle of the blood, gore, and suffering.

"And what about Andy?" she had demanded of Travis when he turned her over to a Federal sergeant for close watch as she worked with the wounded.

Travis had looked from her to the mop-haired youngster, then met her eyes steadily as he smiled, "I think we'll just leave him here in your care, sweetheart. He can help with the sawing and burying."

His disappeared into the smoke and haze, the thunder of the big Napoleon guns roaring to swallow him in their wake. Kitty looked at Andy compassionately. "It's not going to be pleasant, Andy."

"War never is, I reckon." Suddenly he seemed much older than his fourteen years, Kitty realized. He sounded like an old, seasoned soldier as he said, "I went through a few skirmishes before Shiloh, Kitty, and I saw my friends and neighbors blown to bits. I held a few of them in my arms as they died. It'll be a bitter bite to swallow, helping Yankees, but I reckon we ain't got no choice."

The parade of death started. Kitty stood by assisting as a short, stocky Federal doctor decided what to cut and what to attempt to save. Soon the table—a board set up on barrels, was slick with blood. Andy quickly splashed water, then went back to digging the nearby trenches where the arms and legs would be buried.

Outside, all around, the guns belched death. The ground shook ominously. Daylight faded to darkness and the guns quieted, but the work inside the field tents went on. Wearily, Kitty was grateful when a soldier handed her a tin of coffee and told her to take a short nap. Andy was waiting nearby, and together they walked out into the warm summer night. The smell of gunpowder and blood touched their nostrils, and the sounds of the anguished and dying filled the air against the night stillness.

They found an empty spot, away from the rows and rows of bodies, beneath a birch tree. Sitting down with their coffee, Kitty looked about and shook her head worriedly. "Just think, Andy, my poppa might be out here somewhere, among all these wounded soldiers, and me not even know it. I feel like walking down the rows and searching for a man with a patch over his eye."

He followed her worried gaze. "Yep. He sure could be. The soldiers are spread out all over, fighting with any regiment that needs them. 'Course there's a lot of deserters, too. But somehow, once your father joined up, I can't see him running away."

"He'd never do that."

They sat in silence for a moment, and then Kitty was aware that someone was calling to her. "You get in here," the Yankee doctor said impatiently, pointing at her, "And you . . ." He looked at Andy. "Get your tail out there to where that soldier is waiting. They need you at one of the guns."

"Hell, no, I ain't shooting at the Rebels," Andy hooted, almost laughing at the absurdity of the order. "Those are my people out there, and I ain't about to go a-shootin' at them."

"You hear me, boy?" The doctor yelled, eyes blazing in his rage. "I said get your tail out there now."

Andy straightened, looking several inches taller all of a sudden, and in spite of the fear she felt for his refusal, Kitty was proud of him. "And *I* said," Andy bit out the words, "I ain't shootin' at my own men."

The doctor's hand lashed out, cracking him across the face. Andy stumbled backward, cursing, and Kitty saw the doctor reaching for a bloodied knife that lay on a nearby table. She jumped between them. "Don't you dare! Both of you, stop it."

Just then Sam Bucher strode up, holding his bloodied left hand with his right. He was sort of slumped over, as though in pain, but after quickly appraising the situation at hand, he stood up straight and ground out the words, "Just what the hell is going on here? Doctor, why are you chasing this prisoner with a goddamned knife?"

"I ordered him to get over to that Napoleon gun. They're short on men. Two just got hit and died. This young upstart refused."

"I ain't shootin' at the Confederates," Andy looked at Sam squarely. "You can go ahead and kill me right now, 'cause . . ."

To Kitty's surprise, and relief, Sam laughed. "Well, I guess you've got more spunk than most Rebs I've run up against, Andy. Tell you what. We need some help. How about if you just help bring the wounded in from the field? Will you do that so Coltrane won't have my head for not blowing your guts out this very minute?"

Andy smiled. "I'll help the wounded. If Kitty can do it, so can I."

"Thanks," she said to Sam when Andy had disappeared into the smoke and noise that was starting up again as the night faded. "Andy's a good boy, and he's got maybe too much spirit. Travis would probably have killed him on the spot."

She had taken him in the dimly lit tent, led him to a spot in the corner. Wincing at the sight of a nearby sawed-off, bloodied stump arm lying in wait for disposal, Sam held out his hand for her inspection. "Just barely nicked me. All I need is some bandaging."

"And some turpentine," she said crisply, reaching for water to wash the wound.

He made a face. "That stuff burns."

"Sam, nothing can hurt an old bear like you! I feel sorry for the Johnny Reb that tries."

They were a few yards away from the others, affording them some semblance of privacy in a night filled with hell. Kitty's touch was gentle, and Sam looked up at her gratefully. "You ain't all bad, Kitty. I swear you ain't. And I know I'm stickin' my neck out, but I was a-hoping that you and the Captain would start feeling a bit mellow toward one another."

"You're teasing me." She looked up from tending the wound to laugh at him. "I hate him, and he hates me. I don't think I've ever met a more despicable man in my whole life—so conceited, arrogant, ohhhh. . . ." Shaking her head, she could not go on. The list of names to call him was endless, and besides, Sam would only defend him.

"I've known him a hell of a long time, and he's had a lot of sorrow and grief, particularly where women is concerned. But you know what? I think in spite of all the words between you two, he thinks something of you. I've seen the way he looks at you when you think he ain't looking. And if any of the men, you know, get to drinking and get some high ideas and start talking about you like you was just a trollop, well, believe me, the Captain sets 'em straight and shuts 'em up. He don't allow nobody to talk about you with no disrespect."

"That's interesting," she said as though she didn't really think so. "Especially when he, himself, treats me like a trollop."

Sam looked away, embarrassed. "Well, I wouldn't know nothing about that, ma'am," he lied. He and the other men had overheard Travis's tirade in the hotel room that night and knew a little about the tenseness between them. "But he does care. I know he does. I'd like to see the two of you get together, 'specially after I seen the way you looked after him when he had smallpox. Now you can't tell me you didn't care whether he pulled through or not."

"Sam, when you love helping people as I do, when you've trotted along behind a doctor learning all you could

245

since you were knee-high to a hound dog, you don't even think about disliking the person you're treating when they need help. That's the way I felt about your Captain. He was just another solider, another sick man, and I did what I could because I've got this driving need in me to help the suffering. I don't care whether you believe me or not. I could never love, or even *like*, a man like Travis Coltrane, and aren't you forgetting I'm betrothed to a Confederate Major?"

"You don't even know if he's still alive, Kitty."

"Well, that's true," she admitted, "but I know I still love him, Sam, and that's what keeps me going . . . keeps me praying that he *is* alive, and that one day we'll be back together."

She finished bandaging his hand, and he held it up for inspection, then grinned at her, showing yellowed teeth beneath a bushy mustached mouth. "Thank you, Kitty. I say both men are lucky—your Rebel lover for having you love him—and the Captain for having you around. You're a danged beautiful woman, and even if you are a Reb at heart, I think I love you, too."

"Oh, Sam!" She reached out to ruffle his graying hair. She'd grown quite fond of the grizzly old soldier, who could be so mean and nasty one minute—and sweet and gentle the next. She sat down beside him, grateful for a moment away from the putrid smell of saws grinding into bones, the sight of bloodied stumps, and the wide-eyed, gaping faces of the soldiers that died on the slimy, bloodied operating tables. "What about you? What kind of life do you go back to when this war is over?"

"I'll go back to the bayou with Travis, I imagine. I got me a wife there, and three young'uns. I'll go back, I hope, to the quiet, sweet life on the water, where there's nobody to answer to but God."

"It's always puzzled me how you ever got yourself involved in this war. Travis told me about his sister being kidnapped into slavery, then killing herself, and I guess he feels he's got a grudge to settle. But how about you? Do you have any grudges that brought you out to face death every time you go into battle?"

"Well, I guess it's hard for you to understand, Kitty, but you see, I've known Travis since he was small. I was a good friend to his daddy. I saw all the suffering and hell he went through first-hand, and I felt like I owed it to his daddy, Deke Coltrane, to look after his family after he was dead. I've never told anybody about this before, but it might help you understand a bit better why he's like he is if you know about his past. . . ."

Kitty stiffened apprehensively. "I don't have a need to know anything about Travis's personal life, Sam. I'm not trying to be rude, but I just don't care."

He ignored her protest. He went on to tell her about Deke Coltrane finding his wife in the arms of another man and killing that man and then dragging her home and beating her to death while Travis and his sister cowered in a closet. And when he told her about Deke finally killing himself, she shook her head in horror.

"That was terrible for a young boy to experience," she whispered, shocked. Sam was right. She could begin to see why Travis was so bitter, so hard.

Sam reached into his coat pocket and pulled out a plug of tobacco, bit off a chew, then said, "Yep, it was terrible, and it was even worse when we come in from fishin' that day and he found out some slave traders had ridden through and carried his sister off. He just went crazy then —'specially when he finally tracked her down and found out she'd killed herself. The things those men must've done to her. . . ." He shook his head, spat, unable to go on for a minute. "Anyway, Travis has been through hell. He don't trust nobody. He's working out his fury in this war, and I just hope that when it's all over, the fury and the rage will be out of him, and he can live a normal life. He sure deserves it."

They were both silent for a moment. Kitty was beginning to fully understand the arrogance, the smoldering rage that filled Travis, made those steel-blue eyes glint so savagely when he was riled. "Sam, I'm grateful you told me all this. If I'm to be forced to be your Captain's prisoner for God knows how long, maybe it will make it a bit easier knowing he's got a good reason for being the bastard he is."

He looked at her and laughed. "Dang it all, Kitty, you just ain't got sense enough to realize that deep down, where you don't want to see it, you really do care about him— just like he cares about you."

She got to her feet, annoyed. "You're wrong, Sam. I still hate him, and I always will, and nothing is ever going to change that."

"War changes everything."

"And it looks as though this one is going to go on for ever," she sighed wearily, looking toward the hospital tents. It was time to return to the blood and the suffering and the dying.

"Well, the Rebs whipped us yesterday, but we're doing all right today. Their casualties are high, and so are ours, but the word is that the Rebs are falling back."

"You take care of that hand," she said in parting, "and it should be all right if you don't let it get infected. Pour some of that old 'red-eye' on it that you keep hidden in your haversack. That's enough to kill anything."

She heard him laughing as she walked up the hill toward the tent, her skirt swishing against her ankles. Suddenly she spied the body of a Yankee soldier, his throat blown open by the crashing thud of a Rebel ball. Keeping her eyes away from the raw, gaping wound, she quickly worked to remove his trousers, which were in good condition. Then she searched the bodies waiting for mass burial until she found one with a decent looking shirt. Stepping behind the shelter of a large oak tree, she changed clothes. Now she felt better prepared for the long hours ahead. Travis would never approve, but what did she care? He only wanted her in a dress to remind her she was a woman, and supposedly that made her humble to a man! Hogwash, she thought defiantly, using one of her father's favorite expressions.

She stepped into the tent, the scene before her garish and horrifying in the swaying light of the lanterns above. The surgeon she was supposed to be helping was standing beside a blood-slick table, sleeves rolled up to his elbows, bare arms, as well as the linen apron he wore, smeared with blood. He was holding a knife between his teeth as he helped Andy lift a wounded soldier onto the table. She stepped forward, watching as he quickly examined the wound and decided to amputate.

"No, Doc, God, no. . . ." the soldier shrieked, wrestling with Andy, who was trying to hold him down.

"Chloroform," he snapped to Kitty. To someone else he yelled, "Hold him in position."

Kitty reached for the chloroform and a paper cone that contained a sponge in its apex. Gradually, she lowered it toward the soldier's nose and mouth as someone tried to hold him steady. She began to drip the anesthestic into the cone, as he shrieked with pain and terror over what was about to happen to him. She judged him to be seventeen or eighteen years old—and if he lived, he would go through life with only one leg.

The doctor snatched his knife from between his teeth, wiped it quickly a couple of times across his bloodstained apron, and then began slashing into the mass of damaged, torn flesh. Holding out his hand to no one in particular, someone slapped a bloodied saw into his grasp. The grating noise began, followed by the awesome sound of bone cracking, breaking—then the thud of a leg falling into the dirt below.

A few more minutes to suture the wound, and the weary doctor stepped back and motioned them to move the boy on as he yelled, "Next. . . ."

God, Kitty thought in anguish. *How much longer? How much longer will this hell go on?*

She watched the procession—the two-way march that split at her table—some to the table, others to wait for death—and burial. If they were too badly wounded, with no hope at all to save them, they wasted no time on them. And it was a pity, Kitty thought with a wrench of her heart—to just lay them outside to wait alone for death. It was cruel, heartless—but they owed their time, their skills, to those who had a chance to live.

Someone stepped into the tent, glancing about wildly. Kitty recognized Sam through her weary gaze. He charged over to where the surgeon was amputating an arm at the elbow. "Doc, Captain Coltrane's hit bad, and he can't be moved. . . ."

Kitty felt a stab go through her chest. Coltrane was hit. She shook herself. What difference did it make? She wanted him dead—didn't she? Forcing herself to look downward, she did not want to meet Sam Bucher's eyes.

The doctor waved his bloodied knife in the air, impatiently dismissing him. "I can't help your Captain Coltrane, whoever he is, soldier. Can't you see I've got hundreds of soldiers waiting outside? You think I can leave them for one man? Now get out of here. You're blocking my light."

"Doc, you've got to come." He grabbed his arm, shaking him, and Kitty looked up to see that tears were flowing from the big man's eyes. The doctor signaled to his attendants, who stepped forward quickly to grab Sam by his arms and struggle with him, pulling him away from the table. Then he looked up and saw Kitty, and he brightened, "Kitty, you'll come with me and help him, won't you?"

"She isn't qualified to do much but damnit, man, take her and go if it will get you out of here!" the doctor cried.

Kitty froze. Help Travis? Again? After the way he had made a fool of her?

"Kitty, come on," Sam stood there, disbelief starting to show on his face. "He's in a ravine. A shell took his horse, maybe part of his leg. He's hurt bad, and he's dying. . . ."

It had to be done, she told herself, looking around for a bag and starting to throw instruments into it. Travis was hurt, and she had to go to him, but he was no more than just another soldier, she told herself. That was the only reason she was going. Yankee or Rebel, she would help anyone who needed her. That was why she was here. That was what had gotten her into the war to start with, because she believed in helping those who suffered, the way Doc did—the way Doc would want her to feel.

He took her arm, leading her out of the tent and into the woods. "I went looking for him, didn't know the Rebs had gotten this close. He was out looking for me. We always stick together. Then I got to this ravine and heard someone yelling, and I crawled down and found him beneath his horse. I didn't know what to do—he said not to move him. Said to bring you there."

"Me?" She stumbled, and he righted her. "It's a wonder. He knows I don't care if he lives or dies."

"Oh, stop lyin', Kitty," he gave her arm a jerk. "And hurry. He might already be dead, for all I know."

"Is it far?"

"Almost a half mile or so, I reckon. Let's just hope we get to him before those damned Rebel ghouls do. Ever seen the way they strip a Yankee soldier? They think he's a goldmine—especially a cavalry man. They know we've got unpatched boots and more supplies in our haversacks, and I think they kill us more for what they think we've got on us than because we're Yanks."

They passed a group of soldiers, and Sam yelled to them that Coltrane was hurt. They seemed to know him, Kitty thought. At least they didn't hesitate to follow just in case they were needed, or if any Rebels were in the area.

"We're almost there," Sam said, knocking the brambles and foliage aside. It was dark. Kitty wondered how he found his way, then reminded herself that he and Travis had tramped around the swamps of Louisiana all their lives and were quite adept at making trails and finding them again—even in the hysteria of war.

"Okay, we're almost there."

The sun was just starting to break through the haze of smoke and darkness, and now they could make out clearly the land around them.

"Here we are . . . just ahead."

Kitty stopped. There was no mistaking just where that Rebel shell had burst. They stood at the edge of the ravine and looked down to where Travis lay beneath the blasted bag of skin and bloody pulp that had once been his horse. The grass in the clearing where they'd fallen was burned a little bit, and probably would have blazed up to burn the captain to death had it not been soaked from the early dew.

"Move him gently from beneath the horse and get him up here," Kitty ordered. "Someone else get me a torch going so I'll have more light until the sun gets up a bit higher."

Sam took two men and slid down into the ravine. She heard Travis moan painfully as the shreds of the great horse were moved away.

Just then someone came crashing up behind them. "Wait! Stop! Dr. Gordon sent me!" He was yelling at the top of his lungs. "I'm a surgical assistant. He said there was a cavalry officer here wounded."

"That's right," Kitty said, looking at him curiously. He was young—probably a medical student when the war broke out. He was thin, wild-eyed, and nervous, and when he had first spoken she had felt relief at having the responsibility of treating Coltrane removed, but now, as she surveyed him, she began to feel a wave of apprehension.

Sam and the others brought Travis up from the ravine and laid him on the ground. The young doctor, or assistant, as Kitty decided was all he could be, knelt down. She did, too, fighting to keep from gagging at the stench. Travis had been soaked in the discharge from the horse's entrails as they had wallowed under the first impact. The assistant was pulling out a knife to rip open the uniform, baring the wound from thigh to knee.

He examined it quickly, then ordered in a high-pitched voice, "I'll have to operate here. Build up a fire. . . ."

"Hell, no, you aren't cutting off my leg," Travis raised his head to look at him, and Kitty saw that his face was smeared with blood, his eyes glowing with the intense pain he must be feeling.

"Well, that's my decision to make," the assistant snapped. "Do you want to die? Men, hold him down. I don't have time to argue."

No one moved.

"Did you hear me? I said hold him down! I don't have any chloroform. He's still bleeding. If we don't act now, he'll bleed to death. . . ."

Still no one moved. The nervous-looking young man got to his feet, dancing impatiently, fists clenched at his sides. "Damn you, hold this man down. Build up that fire. We're supposed to save lives when we can—not deliberately stand by and allow them to die!"

Kitty turned to see that Travis was watching her intently, his eyes now burning into hers with an unspoken message. What was he privately trying to convey to her? That he would rather be dead than spend his life on a wooden leg?

"Kitty, examine my leg and tell me what you think," he spoke quietly, no evidence of pain or apprehension in his voice. He was quite calm. "And whatever you say, I'll go along with."

"What? How dare you pass over my judgment for that of a woman!" The assistant's face was turning a fiery red in the early morning light. "How dare you? How dare you? I forbid this."

"Fuck you, jackass!" Sam shoved him aside roughly. He nodded to Kitty. "Go on. Do what the captain wants."

Kitty probed her fingers into the gaping flesh. *Look for the artery*, Doc had told her. *Look for the artery and see if it's severed. If it is, then there's no hope but to cut.*

There did not seem to be deep, penetrating damage to the muscle and tissue, and the blood that was oozing forth was not spurting. Of course, if it had been, and the artery had been severed, there was a good chance he would have bled to death by now. So it appeared that the artery was still intact. The next thing was the extent of the damage. If the flesh was hopelessly torn and shredded, the bone shattered and splintered, then the leg would have to come off.

"Give me more light," she whispered feverishly. She could feel Travis wincing with pain, but he did not cry out. She parted the torn, mangled flesh, saw the exposed bone of the thigh. Intact. Not injured except for a slight crack. Fracture. That was what Doc said it was when the bone is found to be cracked, not broken.

A fresh flow of blood was now coming from the wound. "Lint," she said to Sam, who was hovering nearby. "Get me some lint and some material for a tourniquet. Then we're going to suture and put the leg in a splint."

"You've got to cut that leg off!" The assistant was dancing up and down in his anger once again. "I forbid this. I'm the doctor in charge here."

He yanked at Kitty's arm as she fumbled in the bag she had brought, and that's when Sam sent his fist driving into his face. He fell backward onto the ground, and Sam pointed his finger at him. "Now you get the hell out of here. This woman knows more by instinct, and just plain givin' a damn about savin' lives, than you'll ever learn from a book."

Travis's head fell back, a grateful, relieved smile on his lips. Kitty worked feverishly, mopping up the blood, stitching the torn flesh together as best she could. She sent the men into the woods to search for something with which to make a splint, then she told Sam to get Andy and have him bring a stretcher. "We've got to get him back to the hospital where we can keep a watch on him. If the Confederates are going to overrun us, then we've got to be prepared to retreat."

At that, Travis opened his eyes and grinned, that cocky, arrogant grin that she hated. "Hey, Sam, did you hear the lady? She said 'us'—like she's one of *us* now."

"Well, damnit, Captain, she just saved your leg. Don't that mean she ain't mad at us anymore?"

They both laughed, and Kitty stiffened, glaring down at Travis as she said, "It only means that I don't hold to cutting off a man's leg, *any* man's leg, if it can be saved. I still hate you with everything within me, Travis Coltrane, and don't you forget it."

"And I still don't give a damn *how* you feel!" He snapped back at her. "Just get me out of here before you decide to show your true colors and cut my throat. . . ."

She was able to laugh, to taunt him. "You aren't going to be giving anybody orders for quite a while, Captain, because that wound is going to keep you down. If the Confederates do come, you just might be left behind and taken prisoner, and then you'll know how I've felt all these months."

"Maybe the other Southern women will treat a Yankee kinder than you. Maybe they aren't so hypocritical about their feelings."

"Hypocritical? I've never made any pretense of how I felt about you."

The stretcher-bearers arrived. They lifted Travis up, and he gritted his teeth against the pain. "No need to be gentle with him," Kitty quipped, following along behind. "You couldn't hurt him if you tried."

Travis raised his head, trying to look back at her. "Just wait till I get on my feet. You need a good sound thrashing, Kitty Wright, and I'll see that you get it."

Sam chuckled, and Kitty shot a sideways glance at him. "Just what do you think is so funny? You saw how I saved his leg. That young doctor's assistant didn't know what he was doing. If I hadn't been around, he would have cut that leg right off, and what thanks do I get? He threatens to beat me!"

"I'm laughing because the two of you are ridiculous. Both of you are so goldarned headstrong and stubborn that you refuse to admit that you fell in love with each other a long time ago."

It was Kitty's turn to laugh. The idea was absurd. No one could possibly know how much she hated that man moaning on the stretcher. No one could realize how she wanted to slap that smug, arrogant grin right off his face. Love? The idea was absurd—ridiculous.

When they reached the hospital area, Dr. Gordon was waiting for them, the angry assistant standing beside him. "Just who in hell gave you the authority to override my assistant?" He roared indignantly. "He said amputate, and that's what should have been done. You have no right . . . no authority. I understand you're a Confederate prisoner. I think it's time you were sent to prison."

"I think it's time everyone shut up and let me have some peace," Travis snapped as the stretcher-bearers set him down on the ground. "It's my leg, and I said it wasn't coming off. As for her, she's *my* prisoner, and don't *you* go thinking you've got any right to say what's to be done with her. Now if you want to examine my leg, I think you'll find she did the right thing. And I'm going to ask General Grant to look into your assistant's qualifications, because there's no damn telling how many arms and legs he's chopped off because he was too stupid to know of anything else to do to try and save them."

Sam seemed to be able to do more to calm Travis Coltrane than anyone else. He talked both to Travis and to the surgeon, and finally it was agreed that Kitty would go back into the tent and work as an assistant. The battle was raging. There was no time for arguing among themselves.

The air hung heavy with the odor of sulphur. It was a cloudy day, and made worse by the sun being shrouded from view by smoke and gas. The Confederates were bombarding. Many of the Federals, Kitty noted, were walking around dazed, eyes glassy, unable to speak except in monosyllables. Some were so addled by the horrors they had witnessed that they could not speak at all, merely sat and stared straight ahead, not seeing anything. Many men were lost from their regiments. Everything was a mass of confusion.

Day turned to night, then Kitty lost track of time. She

wondered vaguely how Travis was getting along, not because she cared, she told herself, but merely to reaffirm the correctness of her diagnosis in the field that his leg should be saved. It didn't matter otherwise. Sam Bucher was out of his mind. Love Travis Coltrane? She'd sooner love the devil himself.

Word had come that General Robert E. Lee's army had broken the Federal lines at Gaine's Mill. McClellan ordered his army to retire to Harrison's Landing, the Federal supply base on the James River. Kitty was moved along with the retreating forces. Lee's troops tried again and again to destroy the entire Federal army, but after hard fighting at a place called Savage Station on June 29, 1862, and Frayser's Farm on June 30th, White Oak Swamp the same day, and Malvern Hill the first day of July, McClellan was able to safely reach Harrison's Landing and the protection of a Federal river fleet. The dream of the north capturing Richmond had ended.

Kitty remained behind the lines, working in the hospital, but the news drifted in, along with more and more casualties, that General John Pope was moving overland from Washington with a newly formed army—his target was Richmond. Then Lee shifted his army northward to block him, and on August 9th, Jackson was able to check Pope's lead elements at Cedar Run, a few miles south of Culpepper, then he swept around the Federal right flank and captured Pope's all-important supply base at Manassas.

"We're getting out," Sam came to Kitty one night and told her. "We're getting our pants beat off, and we're pulling back. The Captain isn't in any shape to stand and fight, and he refuses to be moved with the other wounded men to Washington. Besides, Grant and McClellan both know that Travis is the best danged scout they got, and as soon as he's on his feet again, he'll be out again. We've had some new men assigned to us, and as soon as we can get our gear together, we're moving out."

"I'd rather stay with the hospital wagons," she protested. "I don't want to go with Travis and his band of cutthroats."

"Now, Kitty," he chided her. "There's no point in arguing about it. Travis sent me to get you ready to go, and you know when his mind's made up, there's no changing it.

You ought to know how it is, because you're just as stubborn. Now let's go."

"Only if Andy goes, too."

"He's already with the Captain, helping to load him into a wagon. Now get moving."

There was nothing she could do but go with him. But where? To what wilderness were they headed now? Why couldn't Travis stay and fight with the regiment? Why did he have to have a special band of men assigned to him just so they could get out and roam the countryside?

There were fourteen of them sitting on horses around the small wagon. And Kitty did not like the looks of any of them. Burly, grizzly, rough, mean—there was nothing nice she could say about any of them. None of their uniforms matched, and they were all dirty and blood-stained. And she didn't like the way their eyes raked over her, either, resting insolently on her breasts. She was glad she wore a loose-fitting shirt and baggy trousers.

Andy was loading water barrels onto the back of the wagon, and one of the men yelled, "Hurry it up, Johnny Reb, you want to get shot and left behind?" The others laughed, and Kitty bristled. She didn't like this—any of it. These men were hard, cold, cruel.

She had been riding behind Sam, and she slid off the horse and hurried to the wagon and climbed inside. Travis lay on a stretcher, his head resting on a blanket roll, and he frowned as she entered. "Just what kind of animals do you have traveling with us now? Do they assign the muck to you because they feel more at home?"

"I believe the Generals feel that I can control the more unruly soldiers better than they can. I've tamed you, haven't I?"

She stamped her foot, crying, "Oh, why can't you leave me and Andy behind, damn you! This is no place for us."

He ignored her protest, threw back the blanket that covered him. "I want you to check my leg, see if it's healing properly."

"You mean no one has checked it lately? Are you mad?"

"No. I didn't want McClellan to hear about it if it was worse than anyone thought. He'd send me to Washington with the others, and I want to stay in the war."

"Till you're killed?" She leaned forward and started unwrapping the messy bandage that Sam had obviously put on the wound. "What will happen to you if you *are* killed, Captain? Neither heaven nor hell would let you in, because you don't belong in either—not good enough for one, and too mean for the other."

He started to comment but instead howled with pain as she jerked off the last of the bandage. The wound was healing. The leg was still in a splint. In time, perhaps a few months, he would be as good as new. She said as much, and he nodded. "Then I suppose the thing for us to do is head into winter quarters. It's almost September, and cold weather will soon be here. I think we'll be safe in the mountains of Tennessee, and come spring, we'll be ready to fight. I'll use these months to whip my men into the toughest cavalry unit in the whole Federal army."

Sam came in, and Travis told him his plans. "Head for Tennessee. By the time the snows come, we'll be set for the winter."

Sam took a seat in the front of the wagon and picked up the reins, with Andy right beside him. The other men fell in line behind the wagon, and they started moving.

"I think I'd like to ride a horse," Kitty said quietly, staring straight ahead. "I don't think I want to be here with you."

"Well, those men back there would love to have you riding a horse with them, Kitty," he grinned in the manner she detested. "You just go right ahead. You tell Sam to stop and let you get on a horse."

And she did. And within a half hour, she was off the horse and back in the wagon beside Travis, who laughed at her. "They're animals," she said, furiously. "They have no respect for a woman. One of them even reached over and touched my breast!"

"And you slapped his face, of course. . . ."

"I certainly did."

"I told you, Kitty, those men are about the roughest there is. That's why they've been assigned to me. When I'm on my feet, I can control them, make soldiers out of them. But for now, stay clear of them. We're in for a long winter without my having to keep you out of their beds."

"I don't want to be in their beds!" she snapped indignantly.

He gave her a long look—a warm look, caressing her with those steel-blue eyes. "Would you like to share my bed?"

"Certainly not." She moved as far away as she could in the crowded wagon, but he was still able to reach out and touch her.

"Get your hands off me, please!" she said haughtily.

With more strength than she knew he possessed since he had been wounded, Travis wrapped his fingers around her arm and yanked her forward. The wagon was jouncing along, and she was unable to keep her balance and fell across his chest. Their faces were mere inches apart. "Tell me, Kitty Wright," his breath was warm against her skin. "Do you slap every man who tries to touch you? Would you slap me now, a poor, wounded soldier?"

Strong hands cupped her face, pulling it close. His lips brushed hers, gently at first, then hard, demanding. He slipped an arm down around her shoulders, pressing her forward until her breasts touched his bare chest. Strangely, she could not will herself to resist, and she melted against him, her blood surging hotly through her quivering body.

He released her, but he was not grinning arrogantly this time. His whole expression was serious. "I guess I've got you in my blood, you little spitfire. It's going to be a long winter, and we're going to have to keep each other warm. Why don't you relax and enjoy it?"

"Just wallow in the filth you call love?" She jerked away, passion quickly cooled by the flood of anger that washed over her. "Just sleep with you and be your whore? Is that it? Is that why you brought me along?"

Now his expression changed to one of anger, and he gave her a shake before flinging her away from him. "Damn you, girl, every time I try to love you, really love you, you remind me all too well that you're just another woman with a heart as cold as ice—good for only one thing. Let me get my strength back, and I'll give it to you, with no strings. You can be sure of it, if I have to tie you down to do it to you."

"I'm going to get back on that horse and ride beside

Sam," she started toward the front of the wagon. "I don't have to stay here and listen to this."

And once outside, on the horse and riding next to Sam on the driver's seat of the wagon, Kitty felt her head swirling. Why did he enjoy tormenting her so? What kind of animal was he? Didn't he know she didn't love him, didn't want him? Why, then, did he insist on keeping her with him?

And then she thought of her own feelings surging whenever he was near. It couldn't be love. Sam couldn't be right. She couldn't actually love that . . . that monster! It was all a nightmare!

But yet, there was no denying that his kiss left her breathless, and there was that little quiver that went through her whenever he flicked his eyes over her in a way that told her he found her beautiful—and desirable. Could she really be falling in love with him? Did the conflict come because they were both so much alike? She did not know. But as he'd said—they were in for a long winter. By spring, she would surely be all too aware of her feelings for Travis Coltrane.

✺ Chapter Twenty-two ✺

KITTY awoke, startled. Blinking her eyes, she tried to remember where she was. How long had they been traveling towards wherever they were headed in Tennessee for winter quarters? She couldn't remember. A week. Yes, it had been a week now. Already the air was cool and crisp, the leaves turning golden and drifting slowly to the ground. It was coming back to her. They had pitched camp beside a sleepy creek, and she remembered Sam and Travis talking over the supper of mush and bacon. Travis wanted to try to ride his horse for the first time, impatient to be back in the saddle. Sam had argued, but, as usual, the Captain had his way. It was a nice night for a ride, Sam had conceded, and Travis had smiled at her and asked if she would like to come along. She had declined, taking her blankets very far from the campfire, saying she was tired and wanted to sleep. She could have told them the last thing she wanted was to spend more time than necessary with the arrogant Coltrane.

But what had awakened her? Staring into the darkness, she strained to hear. And then it came to her. "You go to hell!" It was Andy's voice, reaching her from beyond the trees and dense foliage of the forest. "I'll never swear allegiance."

"The hell you won't. . . ." A Yankee voice boomed. "You'll swear allegiance, or we'll make you wish you had."

"Nail him to that tree." Another angry voice. "Nail his hand up if he won't raise it in allegiance."

Kitty was scrambling to her feet, legs twisting in the blanket that covered her. Kicking free, she hurried toward the clearing, where the campfire still burned. She could see them in the eerie glow, gathered around Andy, who faced them defiantly unafraid.

"Hold his right hand up against that tree!" The thickly bearded man with the long shaggy hair doing the talking was Wiley Burns. Sam had confided to her that he was the meanest of the lot. He was holding a hammer and a long nail. "You swear allegiance to the North, boy, or I'll crucify you like Jesus!"

"Stop it! Are you mad? Stop it, I say!" Kitty burst into the clearing, lunging for Wiley. The others were holding onto Andy, who was struggling for his life, but two stepped forward to grab Kitty, twisting her arms behind her back.

"Well, well, the little spitfire is awake!" Wiley's slitted eyes moved over her. "When we finish with Johnny Reb, here, I think we'll tame you and have you pledge allegiance. 'Course we'll have a little fun first, though." They all laughed, and it was an ugly sound—ominous, and Kitty shivered, frightened because she realized suddenly that she was all alone—and helpless against them.

"Now you take the oath, Andy!" Wiley turned to the wild-eyed boy who was struggling to get his arm down. "Repeat after me . . . I pledge allegiance . . ."

Andy spit in his face, and Wiley turned purple with rage. He yanked the boy's hand into position against the tree, and the others held him fast as Wiley drove the nail through the youngster's hand and into the tree. Andy screamed with pain, writhing and twisting.

"Damn you!" Kitty screamed, twisting with all her strength, but the two men wrestled her to the ground and held her firmly.

"Go on, take the oath," Wiley commanded, grinning. He was actually enjoying seeing the boy suffer, Kitty realized. He was Luke Tate all over again! She could hardly see through the red haze that clouded into her eyes.

"Andy, for God's sake, take their damned oath," she

begged. "It doesn't matter. It's only words. Take it before they kill you. They're animals. . . . they're. . . ."

Her words were cut off by the sharp blow to the side of her head. Dizzily, she fought to focus her eyes on the man straddling her. Wiley stood laughing down at her. "So it's just a damned oath that doesn't matter, eh? Suppose you take it, Rebel whore. Suppose you stand up now and take the oath of allegiance to the North. It's time you started getting treated like a prisoner, like the Rebel dog you are."

She could smell the rot-gut whiskey on his breath as he leaned over to yank her to her feet as the other men stepped back. Dear God, where were Sam and Travis? How long had they been gone, and why didn't they return?

"Say it!" he commanded. "Repeat after me. . . ."

Andy had ripped his hand loose from the tree and sat crumpled on the ground, crying as the blood rushed from the wound. "I'll say anything you want," she said then. What did it matter? She was no match for them. Whatever she said would be meaningless, anyway. Play their stupid game. They were drunk. When Travis came back, there would be the devil to pay, and she would have her revenge then.

Wiley said the words, and Kitty repeated them, spitting out each word with hatred smoldering, eyes flashing fire. The men laughed as Wiley reached out and ripped her shirt open, her breasts tumbling forth. She did not move to cover her nakedness as their eyes devoured the sight hungrily.

"Look all you want!" she said defiantly, facing them, holding her arms above her head. "Look and see . . . touch . . . I don't care . . . do what you will . . . because the more you do to me . . . the more Bucher and Coltrane will do to you when they get back! And I'll enjoy watching them cut you to pieces!"

Several of them realized the wisdom of her words and stepped back, unwilling to participate in the fun any longer. But not Wiley. He reached out and grabbed one of her breasts in his hand and twisted so hard she winced at the sharp pain. "Well, if I'm gonna get cut up, I might as well go ahead and have me some fun." He started fumbling with his trousers, reeling in his stupor. "I'll make it good to you. . . ."

No one had seen Andy reach for the carbine. No one saw him point it straight at Wiley's back. There was an explosion, and the Yankee soldier pitched forward, blood and intestines gushing from the gaping hole. No one moved as they watched Wiley's body jerk convulsively in the dirt and blood beneath him. And then he was still, eyes staring upward, a trickle of blood and mucus oozing from his gaping mouth.

Kitty moved quickly for another carbine propped against a tree, and she backed toward Andy, who was reloading. "No one move," she ordered. "I'll shoot the first one of you that moves."

"Hey, look," one of them held up his hands. "We were just drinkin', foolin' around, we never meant for it to go this far. There won't be no more trouble, honest. . . ."

But Kitty wasn't taking any chances. She and Andy made them all toss their handguns to the ground, along with their bowie knives. Then they were made to lie down on their faces, hands behind their backs.

"Kitty, what do we do now?" Andy whispered nervously.

She looked at his bloodied hand. "I've got to see to that hand. That's a bad wound."

He was staring at her thoughtfully, oblivious to his torn palm. "Kitty. . . ." he said in wonder as the idea came to him. "We can escape. . . ."

Her eyes widened. Yes, they could escape. There were horses, and they had the guns they needed. They could ride out right now, before Sam and Travis got back, and they would ride until they hit Confederate lines. It was over! They were going to be free.

"Get some rope and tie their hands while I keep a gun on them. Then we're riding out of here. I'll bandage that hand as soon as we get a little ways from here."

Andy moved as quickly as he could with his hand on fire with pain and bleeding badly still. When they were all tied, he went and brought back two horses. Mounting, they turned the horses toward the woods—and that's when Kitty realized that Travis was riding straight toward them.

"Don't come any closer," she cried, pointing the gun at

him. "Travis, I mean it. I'll kill you if I have to, but we're riding out of here."

Travis looked at the men tied on the ground, the body of Wiley Burns, the blood dripping from Andy's hand. His expression was one of serious contemplation—not anger— not bewilderment. He just stared as though deep in thought, eyes narrowed. "All right," he said finally. "Go ahead. I'm not going to try and stop you."

Kitty was surprised, but grateful that there was not to be a showdown. Digging her heels into the horse's flanks, she moved forward, Andy right behind her, both their guns trained on Travis, who sat watching them intently.

When they were right beside him, he spoke. "Aren't you going to ask where Sam is?"

For the first time, Kitty realized Sam was not around. "If he's hiding, I'll get you by the time he shoots me," she warned.

"We would have been back sooner, Kitty, but Sam's horse got spooked by a rattler. He got thrown, and the rattler got him. He's bad off. I came to get you to help. With my leg like it is, I couldn't get down off my horse and back up again by myself, much less try to lift him up in the saddle with me. If you don't go back with me, he'll die. You should know how to treat a snake bite."

"I do," she said anxiously. Sam Bucher was her friend. He'd never done her any harm, and now cold terror was once again coursing through her veins as she thought of him lying out there in the night, rattlesnake poison rapidly spreading through his body. "But couldn't he get on his horse himself?" she persisted.

"He thinks his ankle's broken. He can't move. I came back here quick as I could to get you."

"Kitty," Andy spoke softly, frowning with pain from the nail wound in his hand. "We can go see to Sam, and I'll hold a gun on the Captain, and then we can ride out."

She nodded. That was the answer. "You ride ahead," she ordered Travis. "And don't make any sudden moves, or we won't have any choice but to shoot. We're getting out of here and going back to our people, and nothing is going to stop us."

He said nothing as he reined his horse and started back

into the woods, moving as quickly as possible through the dense undergrowth and foliage. Travis knew she probably would shoot him, but the most important business they had to face was getting to Sam and doing everything possible to save his life.

He had shot the snake right after he struck—a Cane-break rattler—extremely poisonous he'd heard. Telling Sam to take off his belt and tie a tourniquet around his leg to stifle the flow of poison, there hadn't been much left for him to do but go for help. He knew if he had gotten down off his horse, he would never have been able to mount once again.

It took about fifteen minutes to reach the point where Sam lay on the ground, and while they were riding, Travis asked Andy what had happened to his hand. The boy told him, and Travis swore under his breath. "I'm glad you killed the son of a bitch. I knew the first time I laid eyes on him, he was a trouble-maker. I'm sorry it happened, Andy. If I'd been there, believe me, it wouldn't have."

"Why weren't you there if you knew those men were so dangerous?" Kitty snapped irritably. "Why did you go off and leave us unprotected."

He laughed, looking at her over his shoulder in the dim moonlight. "I never consider you in danger, Kitty. I always pity the people around you."

"Just keep moving. I want to do what I can for Sam and then be on my way."

They rode the rest of the way in silence, and as soon as they reached Sam, Kitty told Andy to keep his gun trained on Travis and shoot if necessary, and she slid off her horse and ran to his side. "Sam, are you hurting?" she asked him anxiously, reaching for the knife he held in his hand and cutting the pants leg away from the wound. Two pinhole fang marks oozed blood and yellow serum. Already it was beginning to swell.

He moaned softly, his head leaning back against the trunk of the tree he'd managed to drag himself to. "It hurts powerful bad, Kitty, and I think my other leg is broken. I think I'm a goner. . . ." Through glazed eyes he looked at Andy pointing a gun at Coltrane. "What the hell's going on around here, anyway?"

"We're escaping. Just as soon as I do what I can for

you. Now don't talk. Rest so that the blood won't pump the poison through your body so fast." She took the tip of the knife and stabbed down into first one fang mark, then the other, slicing open the flesh, then crossing it with another mark. He bit his teeth to keep from screaming, but the moans in his throat were agonizing. She knelt and began to suck out the blood and poison, spitting it out of her mouth.

Sam began to vomit, his whole body heaving convulsively. "He isn't going to make it, is he?" Travis asked quietly from where he sat on the horse. To Andy he said, "Boy, get me a limb or something for a crutch and let me down off this horse so I can be with my friend."

Andy did as he was asked, still holding the gun, and Kitty did not protest. She was working feverishly to suck out the poison. And when she had done all she felt she could do, she rocked back on her heels and looked at the now unconscious man before her. "We won't know for a while whether or not he'll make it. He's strong. He didn't jump and run around and move the poison to his heart, and I did get a lot out by sucking it. With God's help, he just might make it."

They all sat down to wait. The night wore on. Ever so often Kitty would reach to touch Sam's forehead, feeling that it was burning hot with fever. He would moan incoherently, and when his eyes fluttered open momentarily now and then, the look was glassy, dazed. The poison was working on him. Kitty knew that he might die in agony—or he might just go through this terrible period of sickness and then come out of it. There was nothing to do but wait.

"So you're going home," Travis said quietly, sitting beside her.

"I certainly am—back to North Carolina—back to wait for the man I love and want to marry."

"We're going to find winter quarters to train those men and get me and Sam back on our feet, and when spring comes, we want to get this war over with."

"I'm sick of hearing about the war." Her voice was weary.

He ignored her indication that she didn't want to discuss the situation. "A lot of good men have been killed so far—a lot more will die before it's over."

"How many have you killed?" she asked accusingly.

"By myself, maybe twenty, by my men, maybe a hundred."

"Are you proud of yourself?" She shot him a hateful glance.

"I'm not proud of much of anything, Kitty." He spoke in a tone of voice she'd never heard him use before—soft, tender, as though maybe, somewhere behind that shield of protection he wore, he might actually care about the dying and suffering that was going on all around them. "It's a sad war. Brother against brother. Father against son. It's hard to even pinpoint the exact reason that men are killing each other. Up North, I hear there have even been riots because of the new conscription law, and you know what the rioters do after they shout and burn and demonstrate?"

She shook her head. It really didn't matter. All she wanted was for Sam to come out of this so she and Andy could be on their way.

"Well, they go out and kill hundreds of blacks, sort of like they're saying 'Take the black man and get him out of the way . . . kill all the blacks and we won't have a war.' If they weren't one of the issues, I don't think Johnny Reb would even fight. What does the average Southerner care about government anyway? He cares more about God than government."

She had to laugh in amusement at his thinking. "And just what do you know about the Southerner and his religion?"

"I don't think there are any people on earth who are more religious than the Southerners. And they're basically kind people—but then they can turn around and be the meanest. A Northerner will most likely hurt a stranger before his own people, but a Southerner will hurt his father, brother, sister, wife, friends. He just hasn't learned to separate love and hate. He even blends his belief from the Old Testament into the New, saying one testament is thick with racial pride and war—yet the other is filled with love and forgiveness. They sort of think of themselves as chosen people in the promised land. And your father, he loved you, but yet he walked out on you to go fight for the North. That hurt you, didn't it?"

She really wasn't paying any attention to what he was

saying except to wonder why he was rambling on so. And then, just as she realized Andy had fallen off to sleep, Travis reached out and whipped the gun from the boy's limber hand, laughed, and said, "Now it's a whole different story, Kitty. The South will have to wait a long time for your return, because you're still with us." And his voice was no longer soft or soothing—but harsh and mocking.

Kitty did the one thing she swore she would never do in front of Travis Coltrane. She put her head in her hands and wept—wept for her plight—once again a prisoner, her chance of escape now a thing of the past. It was hopeless. She would never be able to go home. She would never see Nathan again, or Poppa, or her mother. She would probably be killed by a stray bullet in some battle in some unknown town or field. And what difference did it make anymore what happened to any of them? The world as she had known it—and loved it—and lived it—was destroyed. There was nothing left.

Travis reached out and touched her long, silky hair, glistening with golden highlights in the moonbeams that filtered down through the leaves above. "Kitty . . ." he whispered her name. "Kitty, look at me. . . ."

She turned her face to his, tears glistening on her cheeks. What did he want from her now? What new thing had he thought up to hurt her, destroy her?

He was not smiling. His eyes were burning into hers, his mouth only inches away. "I know you are a temptress, a lying, deceitful Rebel witch who would like to see me dead. I know you're like all other women, out to use a man, make a fool of him, but yet, you're so goddamned beautiful that I can't let you go . . . can't get you out of my blood. I know I'll hate myself for letting you go . . . I'll probably hate you, maybe even wind up killing you for betraying me . . . but for now, I want you as I've never wanted a woman before, and I think, if you'll be honest enough to admit it to yourself, you want me, too."

She watched, wide-eyed, struggling with the emotions churning within her, as he struggled to his feet, then drew her up against him. Hobbling along, he led her away from where Sam lay, breathing gently now, and Andy, who was still sleeping. He took her through some bushes, where a pine-needle carpet lay, closing them out from the rest of the world. He fell to the bed Nature provided, and she let him draw her down beside him. Wordlessly, he began to unbutton the shirt she wore, his hands warm, touching, seeking. His lips pressed against hers, and she received his probing tongue, yielding, her body aflame with the emotion, the passion, driving within.

He was gentle, loving, taking his time to arouse her and make her moan beneath him. But he did not torture her. For the first time in many years, he wanted to give a woman pleasure, not tease her into begging for his pleasures. And when he took her, they rocked together, murmuring sighs and words of love, and Kitty could not believe it was really happening—she could not really be receiving him this way. Was he right? Did she, deep down, want him this way—or was her body merely seeking animal pleasures?

And when they touched the stars together, he held her close for a long time afterward. "I think it would be proper to tell you I love you," he whispered against her ear. "But I won't, Kitty, because I can't be sure, and I don't want to lie to you. But I will say that you mean a great deal to me, and I desire you as I've never desired another woman, and if you'll let me, for the time we're together, I'll be good to you—I'll be gentle to you."

"I can't say that I love you either, Travis," she spoke honestly, her mind twisting with agonized memories of the love she was sure she felt for Nathan. "But remember this, in all honesty, I will not take an oath against my people, and when the day comes that I have the opportunity, I'll go to them."

He released her and sat up, and in the soft light of the first rays of dawn, he smiled that arrogant smile. "Then we understand each other, Kitty. We're honest with each other. And we can't ask for more than that, can we?"

"I guess not."

They adjusted their clothing and then returned to where Sam was propped against the tree, staring at them with clear, alert eyes. "Where the hell have you two been?" He greeted them. "Damnit, a man could die around here and nobody would care."

Kitty touched his forehead. The fever was gone. She

looked at his leg. The swelling was down. "Sam, I do believe you're going to be just fine."

"Hell, if the whole Rebel army can't kill me, I sure as hell ain't gonna let no damned rattlesnake take me to glory! Now how about fixing my busted leg so we can get back to camp?"

"There's something you need to hear about what went on in camp while we were out last night," Travis sat down and started rolling a cigarette. "And I reckon Kitty needs to tend to that nail hole in young Andy's hand. Then we'll get around to that leg of yours."

Kitty and Travis exchanged looks, and Sam saw and chuckled, "Well, I guess you two have seen what I been knowing all along."

Kitty had moved out of hearing range, and Travis asked him, "And what might that be, you old codger?"

"You two love each other," he said simply. "You might wind up shootin' each other before this dadblamed war is over, but for right now, you sure as hell are in love with that girl."

Travis looked to where Kitty was leaning over Andy, shaking him awake, telling him she had to see to his hand. She was beautiful. She was the finest-looking woman he had ever seen, the lushest, most appealing body he had ever held in his arms. And for the moment, until their world finished exploding around them—she was his. But love? No—he couldn't admit to love, not the way he felt about women, and if ever a treacherous woman lived, it was Kitty Wright.

"Sam"—he slapped his longtime friend on the shoulder and grinned down at him—"you're full of shit!"

❧ Chapter Twenty-three ❧

BY the first part of September 1862, the state of Virginia was clear of Federal forces. General Robert E. Lee felt that the time was ripe to invade the North as success might secure Maryland for the Confederacy and bring the needed official recognition to the Southern nation from England and France. Then both foreign powers would send supplies, perhaps even troops, to aid the Southern cause. So on September 5th, Lee's gray-clad regiments waded across the Potomac River. At Frederick, Maryland, Lee divided his army, sending General Thomas J. "Stonewall" Jackson southward to capture Harpers Ferry and keep the Valley avenue open, while Lee took the rest of his army and headed westward to Sharpsburg.

Meanwhile, President Lincoln assigned what was left of General John Pope's forces to join McClellan to pursue the Confederate invaders. And on the fourteenth day of September, McClellan fought his way through the passes of South Mountain, Maryland. The next day, as McClellan's troops converged on Lee, Jackson was busy seizing Harpers Ferry. Jackson then hurried northward and rejoined Lee at Sharpsburg on September 16th.

And then came the largest one-day blood bath ever fought on American soil. From sunrise to sunset, Federal units made repeated assaults on Lee's lines. Casualties were mounting frightfully in East Wood, West Wood, Dunker Church, and Sunken Road, and around Burnside's Bridge. By nightfall, General Lee's battered army was still holding its position, having lost nine thousand men. McClellan had lost twelve thousand.

Lee's invasion was ended by the battle of Antietam Creek, and he retired back to Virginia. It was five days later that Lincoln issued his preliminary Emancipation Proclamation, which promised freedom to all slaves in Confederate-held territory after January 1st, 1863. Thus, the war was converted into a struggle for human freedom and the European nations were deterred from granting aid or recognition to the Confederacy.

Coltrane's Raiders heard the news as they pushed on toward the Cumberland Mountains of Tennessee, rumored to be a haven for deserters from both armies.

"Damnit, I want to head back," Travis swore as they sat around the campfire after a meager supper of flapjacks. "Now's no time to be sitting around. We've got to strike while Lee's strength is weakened. How many men we got rounded up so far?" He looked at Sam.

"I reckon we've got about thirty-eight now." Andy spoke up from where he sat close to Travis, hanging onto his every word.

Kitty stared at them critically from where she sat in the shadows eating her small portion of the food. She didn't like the way Andy was looking up to Travis. She had seen it developing little by little, but after the shooting incident, when Travis praised Andy for killing one of his own men, telling him how brave he was, Andy was following the Captain around like a faithful old hounddog.

She also did not like the way that Travis and Sam were able to pull in deserters along the way to join their group. The Yankees were scared to refuse because they were threatened with instant hanging if they did. And the Southern soldiers were just grateful that they weren't shot on sight, and since they were deserting from their own regiments, they felt safer, Kitty supposed, joining up with the Raiders.

"Both of us are too busted up to think about fighting right now." Sam poked at the fire with a stick, his splinted leg stuck out in front of him. "The thing for us to do is hurry up and find decent winter quarters, and by spring we'll be better'n ever, and we'll have a hundred men ready to fight. We'll have the best gol'danged bunch of cavalrymen in the whole Union army!"

Travis dug at his chest furiously. "I'll be glad to see the cold come. Maybe these damned lice will freeze to death."

Andy started scratching too, then stopped to snap his fingers excitedly. "Hey, Sam, that new man just joined us today? Jack Wilson from New York?" Sam nodded. "He says he's got the fastest louse in the whole army."

"Naw, he don't." Sam grinned. "Old Pete can outrun anything he's got. Want to bet on it? Go get that scutter and tell him he's got a louse race!"

Kitty wrinkled her nose in distaste. She'd seen these contests before, and they never failed to nauseate her. So far, she had been lucky not to get any of the crawling white creatures on her body, but Travis constantly scratched and he forced her to sleep right beside him every night. Sooner or later she knew, she, too, would be infested. One night she had complained about it, but he very quietly explained that he had to keep her close by during the night. "I don't want to take a chance on what happened before happening again."

"Are you talking about the incident with Andy and me and your men the night Sam got snake-bit . . . or the time later on that same night when you took your pleasure with me?" She had looked at him mockingly.

Eyes flashing fire, he snapped, "You know damned well what I'm talking about, Kitty. The men we're recruiting are tough, and they wouldn't blink twice over raping you or any other woman. The only reason I can hold 'them in line is because they're scared of me. I've got a reputation for killing any man who crosses me, and that's the only reason they haven't taken you before now. If you want to play games, go sleep elsewhere, but don't scream to me when one of them crawls on top of you."

"You're disgusting!"

"No, just honest." He smiled wryly. "Which is more than I can say for you. You can't admit even to yourself that you enjoy my making love to you, but you sure let me know it when . . ."

She picked up a pot of coffee from the fire and threw it at him, and he ducked, laughing. "Wait till my leg heals, you little she-devil, and I'll have you running in the other direction."

But Kitty didn't laugh. Travis still had the power to infuriate her, in spite of the so-called bargain they had made to try to get along with each other as long as they were together.

Andy had run to get Jack Wilson, and Kitty looked up as he stepped into the clearing.

"Which one of you'ns thinks he's got a louse that'll outrun my champeen?" He looked at them, still grinning broadly. "Done won every race we ever been in." He pulled out a small container from his trousers pocket.

"Pete can whip anything you got," Andy shouted.

Kitty stepped close enough to where she could jab him with her elbow and whisper so the others couldn't hear: "What's wrong with you, Andy? Are you forgetting your loyalties? Why do you act so friendly to these Yankees?"

He looked at her, eyes gleaming quizzically in the glow from the fire. "Kitty, we might as well make the best of things, and it's a whole lot easier to be friends than it is to be enemies." He looked back to the others and said, "Come on, Sam, bet him that Pete can whip his louse!"

The bets were made, and Kitty went to bring Sam a tin plate, while Jack returned to where the other men were to fetch his own. A few minutes later, he came back with all the others, and they gathered around, placing their bets.

And then the race started. Sam's louse "Pete" was placed in the middle of a tin plate at the same time Jack released his champion. Kitty stared through an opening in the crowd circling the two men who were down on their knees, and she felt itchy all over just watching the tiny specks of white begin to scurry around. Sam's was moving slowly, lazily, but a cry went up from those watching as Jack's louse darted across the plate into his master's waiting hand!

"I don't believe it," Sam yelled above the din. "I dang well don't believe it. That louse was all but flying!"

"Told you," Jack crowed proudly. "I've got the *champeen!* Anybody else want to race? I'll beat every louse you creeps got crawling all over your bodies. Come on. I'll take anybody."

Travis was struggling to his feet. "I imagine you could, Jack, and so could anybody who put his louse on a heated pan." He reached out and snatched the plate and passed it among the men. "Feel for yourself. A louse is naturally going to run like thunder across a hot surface. A smart trick, my friend, but an old one, I'm afraid."

For a moment, Kitty feared there might be trouble, but the new member of the Raiders just threw his head back and laughed good-naturedly. "Well, I'll just save my critter till I join a new group, and then I'll clean up again."

The tension was eased, and Sam told Andy to bring out a hidden jug of "popskull." Kitty turned away, planning to take her blankets and go to bed beneath the wagon. She didn't like to stay around the men when they were drinking, and Travis usually told her to leave when it started, anyway.

She was ready to crawl beneath the wagon when she heard the shouts of the picket. A shot rang out, then a cry, "Don't shoot! I give up! God, help me, I'm through with fightin'. . . ." And whoever was doing the yelling was obviously crying.

The picket brought him in, jabbing him in the back with his gun to keep him moving. His clothes were blood-stained, the hanging shreds of a Union soldier. His eyes were huge dark sockets in his heavily bearded, sallow face. He fell to his knees, then buried his face in his hands. "God, God, don't kill me . . . please, don't kill me. . . ."

Travis signaled to one of the men to haul the stranger to his feet. He was so weak he had to be held up. He looked at Travis, squinting wearily. "Who you be, sir? I'm no Federal or Rebel soldier now, I swear to you. I've had my guts filled with dying, and I'm running to the mountains to get out of all of it."

"I'm a Union officer, soldier, and I think you'd better explain yourself. Where do you come from and why are you deserting your cause?" Travis's voice was firm, intimidating—with that heavy quality that made men instantly realize he was a natural-born leader, a man not to be taken lightly.

"Virginia . . . the fightin' in Virginia . . . oh, God, it

enemy or flies his flag, try to kill him. And what about your Rebel lover?"

"He wasn't my lover," she snapped. "I told you, Luke Tate was the first man who ever took me. Nathan was too much of a gentleman. He was waiting for marriage."

"And somebody else got there first." He chuckled, feeling strong once again. If he could still be so caustic, then the girl hadn't completely gotten to him with her beauty, charm . . . whatever the hell it was about her that kept him feeling heady and unbalanced whenever she was near.

At times like this, she hated him. Travis could show so many different faces—selfish, arrogant, ruthless, brutal, cold, hateful, impatient. Yet he could also be tender, kind, gentle, and, she remembered with a warm flush, passionate and loving. But it was this face that she despised.

"I was raped. I've told you that."

"*I* never raped you."

"Oh, goddamn you, Travis, I wish you'd just go on and kill me!" She turned her head away, sick at heart, hating him, hating the world and everyone in it.

They lay in silence, listening to the night noises—the owl, still hooting mournfully; a bobcat, snarling ominously from a distance too far away to worry about; an animal, possibly a possum, scurrying in the bushes near the wagon.

"I heard talk about a man with a patch over his eye and a hounddog forever at his side," Travis said quietly. He felt Kitty tensing up beside him, waiting for his next words. "They say he's the bravest man in the whole Union army—fearless—a real soldier. He fights like he's driven by a thousand demons inside him. I also heard he was from North Carolina, that he's got a deep hatred inside, and that's why he's driven. He won't accept a rank other than private. Told General Grant himself that he wasn't in this war for personal glory. He just wanted to see it over with as quickly as possible. But even without a rank, the men around him look up to him as their leader and follow him right into the thick of battle—and often straight to death."

Kitty rolled over, and he could feel her eyes blazing in the darkness. "Why didn't you tell me? Why didn't you tell what you'd heard, Travis? You've heard me talk about my father, and you knew it was *him!*"

"I guess I figured your allegiance was with the South, with that Rebel officer you want to marry—not with your father. Why make things worse? We're in the middle of a bloody, terrible war, and the thing I want most of all is to win it—and live through the victory. Your father wants the same thing. Had I told you he might be near, even if I'd thought you really cared, you'd have gone running out to look for him—right on a battlefield with a thousand soldiers shooting at each other."

"I don't care if you never trust me," she cried, trembling in her rage. "Just let me go. Let me get out of your life. Let me take Andy and go look for my father."

"And do what?" He laughed at such a ridiculous idea. "What are you going to do if you find him? You think he's going to go home with you? Grow up, Kitty, the man has made his decision."

"Then let me make mine." She was begging now. "Let me leave, Travis. My pa's mind isn't right. You don't know how bad the Vigilantes beat him. He's tetched. That's why he's doing what he's doing. Let me find him and try to get him home."

"I can't let you leave, Kitty. I've got a mission—it's my job to scout these mountains and gather up all the deserters I can find and whip them into some kind of army by spring. And I need you because a field surgeon can't be spared to roam these mountains with me. You're valuable."

"But what if you hadn't found me?" she pointed out. "What if Luke Tate had murdered me, and there had been no woman with a knowledge of doctoring for you to kidnap and drag around with you as your prisoner? What would you have done then? Do whatever you would have done, please, and let me and Andy go. . . ."

Sighing, he turned and tried to take her in his arms, but she pulled away. "Kitty, even if I wanted to let you go, I couldn't. We're in for a rough winter with a lot of sickness and disease. There are also going to be some skirmishes along the way, and I'll have men wounded or killed. And even if I did let you ride out of here right now, how long do you think it would be before you ran into a deserter? These mountains are crawling with the bastards.

They'd rape you and tear you apart and leave you to die. I can understand why you want to be with your own people, with your father, but you've got to understand that you're going to stay right here with me as long as you're needed. And then when the war is over, I'll personally see that you get home safely. I'll take you there myself."

"You'll be in a Confederate prison waiting to be hanged," she cried.

"Not with men like your father fighting on our side," he laughed. "If he's got the spunk and spirit you've got, then the South doesn't have a chance."

She turned her back on him, and she promised herself if he tried to touch her, make love to her, she would do something terrible to him—gouge the wound in his thigh—something, *anything*, but he had better not touch her this night.

In a few moments, Travis was breathing evenly. He had sensed her anger, her frustrations boiling within. And she lay there staring into the darkness, her brain burning with new determination. No longer would she cry with bitter defeat and resignation. Oh, no. Now there was a stronger reason than ever to live because she and Andy were going to escape. She did not know how, or when, but the time and the opportunity were going to come, and when they did, they would be ready.

Andy. She was worried about him. He was looking up to Travis *and* Sam. Too young to really know what the war was all about, the youth could not fully understand the issues and was easily being swayed to listen to the other side. Would he go along with her escape plan? She would have to find out because they would have to be ready to move at an opportune time. If they tried and failed, she knew that Travis Coltrane would make sure that they never had another chance—even if it meant keeping her tied to her horse!

But she would have to give the appearance of being completely subdued and bowing to the will of the enemy. Sam would be easily fooled, but not Travis. It would take much to convince him that she had ever given up, and he might possibly never trust her completely.

But she was going to do it! And this vow gave her the peace to close her eyes and give way to the weariness.

Kitty was going to find a way to escape and find her father and take him home. And she was going to wait there for Nathan to make her his wife.

She closed her eyes and slept, with a smile on her lips for the first time in a long, long while.

❦ Chapter Twenty-four ❧

FEBRUARY of 1863 found Coltrane and his raiders holed in during repeated blizzards in the Tennessee mountains. Kitty had busied herself during the winter months treating the soldiers for all manner of illnesses. Perhaps a hundred men had been rounded up once Travis and Sam Bucher were healed and able to ride, and out of this number, a third had died from dysentery.

The slush, the rain, the cold, and, finally, the frozen snow banks kept the men from going out and hunting for deer and other wild game. Blankets were scarce. Clothing was inadequate, and shoes were worn through, leaving the feet little protection against the snow-covered ground.

Things looked bleak. "What good does it do for us to gather men to be ready to fight in the spring if the men die before the snow thaws?" Kitty asked Travis one night as they sat together eating meat from one of the horses that had frozen to death. It was tough, tasteless, but it would quell the painful gnawing in their stomachs.

Travis eyed her, always wary when she spoke in terms of "we." Was it possible that, because of her father's allegiance to the Union Army, she, too, was swaying away from her loyalties to the South? He couldn't be sure, even though he had discussed it at length with Sam, who felt that the girl had changed. He also felt she had fallen in love with the Captain, an idea that Travis scoffed at.

"We'll have a few men left." His jaws were actually tired from the effort of chewing the stringy horse meat. Drinking from a tin cup, he washed down the gummy taste with melted snow. "Don't we have any coffee left, Kitty?" He slammed his cup down disgustedly.

"I've been brewing it from the last bit of corn we had—and now that's gone. In fact, all we have left is this horse meat. When that's gone, someone is going to have to go looking for game."

"And that means losing a few more men to the fever, if they don't freeze to death along the trail."

Sam sat near the fire, digging at the skin mange that covered his arms and legs. "I wish I had something for that," Kitty said sympathetically. She felt lice crawling on her own body, and perhaps she, too, would become infected with the mange. But how could she bathe in this freezing weather? They all had to gather around the fire to preserve wood and heat, and there was no privacy for a bath.

He looked at her and grinned. "Kitty, I reckon the mange varmints and the lice need something to do this winter, too, so they fight over me. That's better than the Rebs, I guess." His beard was now down to his chest. Travis didn't order the men to cut their hair or keep themselves up, but he vowed that come Spring they would quickly learn to look like soldiers.

"Sam, how far are we from Murfreesboro?" Travis asked quietly as though he were deep in thought about something.

"Dunno. Maybe two or three days in this snow, if we could even get down out of the mountains. Why, you headin' out?"

"No. Once the weather gets a bit warm, the deserters hid out will start coming out like skippers from a ham, and that's when we'll round them up. But in the meantime, we've got to have food. Look at Kitty. She's skin and bones now, and we've got to keep her strong so she can look after us."

"And is that the only reason you're worried about my health, sir?" She flashed him a grin that was forced, and she made her hand snake out to cover his across the table.

He lifted his eyes and met her gaze, puzzled. Was he fooled? Did he believe that she had fallen in love with him during the cold nights they had held each other close for warmth? How she prayed that he did, for only when he truly believed that she now gave her heart to him and her sympathies to the cause he fought for would she ever be given the freedom she would need to find a chance to escape and return to her own people.

Travis ignored her question, turning instead to Sam. "Do you want to go or would you rather I went? That last soldier that wandered in said that was quite a battle Rosecrans and Bragg had the end of December. The army might be completely broken up for all we know. There may not even be any Federals in Murfreesboro."

Sam thought a minute, scratched at his beard, then said, "Well, I tell you, Cap'n. I'd just as soon not try to make it down the mountain. These old bones of mine kind of got the creaks in all this cold weather. You just take as many men as you want, and I'll hold things together here."

"All right. I'd like to get back to civilization and see how the war is going. Let's pray it's already over with and we just haven't gotten the word yet."

Civilization. People. A town. A *chance!* Kitty hoped her excitement did not show. Forced to wait until Sam moved outside to relieve himself, she all but leaped on Travis once they were alone. "Take me with you, please, Travis."

He looked down at her and raised an eyebrow. "What for? You're needed here, Kitty. There are sick men."

"Please . . ." she forced her arms to reach up, clasping her hands behind his neck. Standing on tiptoe, her lips only inches from his, she could feel his desire beginning to swell against her thigh. "I want to be with you, Travis. Don't leave me here. I think . . . I think I'll go crazy if I have to stay behind not knowing whether you're alive or dead. I've fought it . . . this feeling . . . but it . . . it overwhelms me. And I have to be honest. I want to see if anyone has heard from my poppa. He might even be there, for all we know. Take me with you, please."

His eyes searched hers, looking for some sign that there was treachery in her motives, but then she was pressing her lips up, crying to be kissed, and he answered the plea, lifting her into his arms and carrying her to the bunk. It was cold away from the fire, and she wriggled beneath the blankets while Travis walked to the door, opened it, yelled to Sam to go play in the snow for a while, and then slammed the door shut, bolting them in away from the wintery world outside.

He slid beneath the blankets, taking her in his arms to taste the sweetness of her body. "I wish I were bathed and perfumed for you," she whispered. "I wish I were clean and womanly and could love you in the right way. Take me with you. Dress me in silks and lace and make love to me in a real bed, where we'll have room and comfort to love each other all night long. Please, Travis."

For the moment, he ignored her pleas as he slid on top of her body, entered her, plunged into the velvety depths of pleasure. He took his time, moving slow and gently so that she could fall into the rhythm of his passion. He felt her shudder against him, and only then did he allow his loins to explode inside her.

For a long time, he lay on top of her as she rained tiny kisses all over his face, her fingers moving frantically up and down his back as though she wanted him never to move away from her. "If only I could have you this way every night, my love," she whispered raggedly. "Do you know how I lie awake and actually quiver because I so desperately want you to take me?"

He moved away from her and rolled to the edge of the bunk. He never liked to be with a woman once his desire had waned, not finding anything manly about a limp organ against female flesh, and doubting that women did, either.

"It's difficult to make love when we're crowded like this," he said by way of making conversation, as he felt a slight twinge of guilt because he could not return her vows of love and affection. Damnit, it *had* to be a trick. She couldn't have really fallen in love with him. Somehow, it changed everything.

"But if you'd take me down the mountain with you, we could have a little time together—alone."

"We could also ride right into the middle of a war, Kitty. It wouldn't be safe to take you with me."

"How can you say that? You've certainly carried me right into the thick of battle before, with balls and shells exploding all around us! And it was different then because I hated you."

The smile he gave her was wry, almost to the point of mocking her words. "And you love me now, my sweet—is that it? And the *only* reason you want to go with me is to be by my side 'cause you can't stand the thought of being apart from me—is that it?"

She looked him straight in the eyes, feeling as though he were looking right into the very depths of her soul and could see it was all a trick, a lie!

When she did not speak, Travis said, "What if I told you that yes you could go with me and I'm going to send you south, to your people, and you and Andy can go free. Would you leave me then?"

She knew this was important, but then she reminded herself the wrong answer might be what he was looking for. Blinking, as though to hold back unshed tears, Kitty whispered, "I would have to leave you, Travis, if you sent me away. If that was what you wanted, then I would go. I'd feel an obligation to go back to my people regardless of what I feel in my heart."

Damn! He swung his feet off the bunk and stood up, yanking on his trousers. She admitted she would go—yet she wanted to stay with him. He shook his head, walked to the window, and peered out. The men *were* playing in the snow, racing their horses, exercising—anything to end the boredom that enshrouded them all.

He felt tiny feet scurrying across the floor, hands slipping about his waist, a bare body pressed against his in the chill of the small cabin. "Please, Travis. Let me stay with you. If you leave me here and never return, or if you send me home, then I'll always wonder what would've happened to us—the feelings that smolder between us. I'll never know any peace. I've stuck it out so far . . . let me see it to the end, please."

He turned around quickly, eyes blazing, his voice snarling as he looked deep into the pools of those lovely purple eyes. "Goddamn you, Kitty, don't lie to me now. This is a trick. You want to go with me to try and escape. I can

289

feel it. You haven't fallen in love with me anymore than I've fallen in love with you, and all of this bullshit is just that—bullshit!"

He shook her, and she reached to tear his hands from her shoulders and ran naked across the room, throwing herself down on the bunk and sobbing, "I do hate you, Travis Coltrane, when you treat me like a . . . a whore! Is it so disgusting to you? The thoughts of me loving you? Do you think I'm just some trollop to ravish when you will and then cast me aside? Don't you think I have some feelings, too?"

He watched her as she moaned and writhed on the bunk, and listened to her words of scorn. He had hurt her. And what had she really done to him? Once she had saved him from having his leg cut off by an over-zealous young field surgeon. She had also given up the chance to run away in order to save the life of his best friend. Even now she was skinny and lean, and he had seen her slipping the scarce food from her own rations to give to a sick Federal soldier who needed the nourishment. How could he believe she was only a deceitful female, out to catch him off guard so she could run away? In bed, she no longer lay limply beneath his caresses but returned his passion eagerly.

Had she even loved her Confederate fiancé, he wondered bitterly? So many soldiers had hurriedly married their sweethearts, or become engaged, when the war first broke out. Emotions and passions had run high—and still did, for that matter. Perhaps her betrothal to Nathan Collins had been made in the heat of the moment, faced, as she was then, with the threat of his going to war and never returning. And she loved her father. They had been terribly close. Perhaps she had been in a state of utter confusion when he walked out on his family to join the Union. She might not have known nor understood her own heart's desires.

And now he had hurt her when the girl might genuinely be in love with him. Damn his own soul to eternal hell, did he have to strike out and hurt every woman that ever crossed his path because his own mother committed the sin of adultery? Because a single woman in his youth betrayed him? Was he that cold, that callous, that damned *hard?*

He crossed to the bunk, reached down to gather her naked body in his arms and hold her against his chest, wanting to warm her as well as stop the tears that stained her beautiful face. "Kitty, I'm sorry. I didn't mean to tear you to pieces that way. The things burning inside me . . . well, I've got my own war going on deep inside and I take it out on you. I'm sorry."

"I'm not asking you to love me back." She hid her face against his chest, afraid to look at him lest he see the truth in her eyes. "Just let me love you and stay with you. That is all I ask."

For a long time he held her without speaking and then Sam banged on the door and bellowed, "Damnit, you two, I'm freezing my butt off out here while you two are in there playing like you hate each other. Open this door before I kick it down!"

Travis laughed and stood up as Kitty began to scramble into her clothes. "I'll get you that dress of silk, Kitty, and I'll see that you get some decent food in you and put some meat back on those bones."

"You mean you'll take me with you?" she cried exuberantly.

He nodded, walking across to open the door and let Sam in. "We'll leave first thing in the morning, soon as it's light. Do what you can for the ones who are sick before we go and tell Andy and Sam what you want them to do."

Andy!

She stared at his back, chewing her lower lip nervously. How could she insist on Andy going along without giving herself away? She couldn't leave him behind. Once she was gone and Travis realized she had played him for a fool, he might be so angry that he would kill Andy for revenge. Hadn't he threatened to often enough? But if she said much about taking him along, it was bound to arouse suspicion.

Sam walked in, shaking snow from his hair and beard, when suddenly a big ball of snow smacked him right on the back of his neck. With a bellow, he wheeled about and took off stumbling through the snow after Andy, who was laughing gleefully over hitting his target. Through the open door, she watched Sam catch him and throw him into a snowbank, covering his face with the icy whiteness.

Kill Andy? No, neither Travis nor Sam would kill the boy. Now it was obvious to her that they liked the youth. And he had grown extremely fond of them. Andy would be all right. They would keep him from harm as best they could. She had to go on now and take her own chances at freedom.

The next morning Kitty bundled up as warmly as possible. Travis gave her a warm woolen cape and a battered old hat to wear. He, himself, wore a poncho. The sun was shining, but the air was bitterly cold and their breath hung in frosty puffs in the air. They took a wagon, driven by two men with a team of four horses, and six more soldiers accompanied them. "Not much to fight with if we run into trouble," Travis told Sam. "But at least we won't look too dangerous ourselves. Let's just pray we get down and through the pass without a skirmish."

Everything was covered with a layer of freshly fallen snow. Trees bent down toward the earth, their branches weighted by ice and snow. All was still, the silence shattered only by the sounds of their horses struggling to move through the frozen forest.

"Kitty, are you warm?" Travis asked her, twisting in his saddle to look back. They were riding single file.

She managed to smile. "I don't think I've ever been so cold in my whole life. But it's okay. I'm fine. I'm just thinking about that warm bed in Murfreesboro." A look passed between them and for the moment there *was* warmth. Then Kitty reminded herself it was all an act and soon, if everything worked out according to plan, she would be safely across the lines and into Confederate hands. All she had to do was keep her ears open and find out where the Southern army was camped, and then one night when Travis went out for a drink or supplies, she would slip out, steal a horse, and ride! It seemed so easy— too easy, in fact—now that he wasn't having someone watch her every single minute.

They entered a pass cautiously. On each side, ledges weighted down by heavy snowbanks loomed ominously. They headed through slowly, downward into the valley and then up again, each of them gazing about intently for any sign of danger.

Suddenly, Travis's arm shot straight up, a signal for them to halt in their tracks. "Up there," he pointed, speaking to the soldier closest to him, Jabe Harris from Pennsylvania. "I saw something glinting in the sun when the clouds parted. We'd better take cover. It could be an ambush."

They moved into the trees on either side, while Jabe and another soldier rode cautiously up the side of the pass, moving slowly in the snowbanks. No one spoke. Kitty stared anxiously at Travis, but he was watching his men, eyes squinted in the glare of the snow and ice. The men disappeared around a bend, out of sight, but still he looked in that direction.

Perhaps ten minutes passed. Kitty waited tensely for the sound of gunfire. There was only silence, save for the mournful scream of the wind whipping down out of the mountains, swirling about them like some unseen fore-boding ghost telling them that only danger, and possibly death, awaited.

"Captain!" It was Jabe, unseen but clearly heard, and he sounded frightened.

Travis moved quickly forward, motioning everyone else to stay back, but Kitty, not about to be left behind, dug her heels into the horse's flanks. They plunged ahead, and the sight that greeted them as they rounded a bend made both of them gasp in horror.

There were four soldiers frozen at their post and com-pletely enveloped in ice. Their eyes were open, staring straight ahead, mirroring the horror of their deaths. Icicles hung from their rifles, their noses, their chins—completely frozen in death.

"Rebs?" Travis asked tonelessly.

"Yes, sir."

"Leave them be. We've got to move on."

They rejoined the others, moving ahead slowly through the pass, each lost in thought. A few talked about the bodies, the way they'd looked. Kitty and Travis were silent, not wanting to discuss the horror of the scene.

They rode through the day, stopping for the night to camp beside a fire that strong winds kept blowing out. Kitty snuggled next to Travis beneath thin blankets, and he held her close. She prayed once again that he believed she really and truly loved him, and she told her stinging conscience that actually she felt nothing. Nathan. She had to keep thinking of Nathan.

Suddenly, as dawn broke on the icy world around them, a voice boomed out, "Freeze, Rebs, or prepare to enter hell before breakfast!"

Eyes flashed open, but no one moved. Kitty stifled a scream, expecting a bullet to come ripping into her heart at any moment. All around them stood men in tattered blue uniforms, guns pointed straight at them.

"Want to know what happened to your picket?" said a burly man with a thick beard, grinning. He seemed to be the leader. "He fell asleep at his post, but little did he know it was to be an eternal sleep, because now he's got a Federal knife stuck in his throat."

The movement came as a jolting surprise. What man in his right mind with a dozen guns pointed right at him would dare to leap to his feet, red-faced with anger. The soldiers were so stunned they did not fire as Travis yelled, "You goddamned fool! That was a Federal soldier you murdered! We're Federals! Union soldiers! I'm Captain Travis Coltrane, U.S. Cavalry, under special assignment to General Grant."

"Sir, I'm sorry. . . ." The soldier quickly signaled to his men to put down their guns, while he kept his trained on Travis. "I will need to see some identification, sir. I hope you understand."

"Of course," Coltrane snapped, reaching for his haversack and bringing out some papers. When the soldier was satisfied with his identity, he put his own gun away. "Now suppose you tell me who the hell *you* are!"

"Sergeant Jay West. Third New York. We're patrolling for General Rosecrans. He's licking his wounds in Murfreesboro."

"And that's where we're headed." Travis motioned to his men to get moving. "We don't stop to eat. We ride straight into Murfreesboro before we run into some more bloodthirsty soldiers."

"Sir, I am sorry."

Travis brushed by him, yanking his saddle from the ground and throwing it on top of his horse.

"Sir, you know the penalty for falling asleep on picket.

That man could've been shot if he'd been found. You know Grant's rules."

Travis whirled about, eyes blazing. "My men are sick, cold, half starved, and it's no goddamned wonder he did fall asleep. That's still no excuse for you sticking a knife in his throat because you were so damned eager to kill somebody you couldn't take the time to find out which side he was on. Yours is the error, Sergeant, not my man's for falling asleep on duty!"

Sergeant West spurred his horse up alongside Coltrane's as they moved out. Kitty quickly moved close behind, eager to hear anything that might aid her plans for escape.

"You been up in the mountains all winter, Captain?" the Sergeant asked solicitously, anxious to make amends.

"Yeah. Rounding up deserters on both sides. But we've got to have supplies. We've had to start eating frozen horses."

West shuddered in revulsion, then quickly changed the subject. "You heard about Antietam? You heard about Mr. Lincoln replacing McClellan with General Ambrose Burnside?"

"We don't get much information where we're camped, but we've managed to learn a little bit now and then."

West plunged on eagerly: "Around the middle of December, Burnside ordered six big assaults against Lee's army that were up on the heights above Fredericksburg in Virginia. It was nothing but a useless slaughter, Captain. They say Burnside just sat down and cried over all the killing. They got over ten thousand of our men, I hear tell. The Rebs lost less than half that many. Then, a few weeks later, Burnside tried a secret march and got bogged down in mud and couldn't cover over a mile a day. Called it the 'Mud March,' they did, and it sure finished up Burnside. He just up and gave up his command to General Joseph Hooker."

They talked on about the war, but Kitty was unable to learn any information that might tell her where Nathan would be. He could be anywhere. The war was going on all over, it seemed. Somehow, some way, she had to find him.

They reached the town of Murfreesboro, and the first thing that caught Kitty's eye was the cattle pen next to the railroad which held Confederate prisoners. They wore tattered uniforms, and they looked thin, emaciated. Could Nathan be one of them, she thought with a painful twist of her heart, her eyes scanning the crowd of soldiers.

The prisoners shouted obscenities. She saw some of the guards hitting at them with the butts of their rifles. Travis turned once to look at her, but she kept her eyes straight ahead, pretending indifference.

Through the muddy, rutted street they rode, stopping finally in front of a ramshackle hotel set back from the other buildings and stores. "General Rosecrans is quartered here," Sergeant West said as they prepared to dismount. "There are ample rooms upstairs for you and your lady. The other soldiers can camp at the edge of town with us."

Travis helped Kitty from her horse and held tightly to her arm as they went up the steps and entered the hotel. To one side, there was a saloon, and on the other, steps wound upward. Travis introduced himself to a soldier standing guard, saying first he wanted a room for Kitty and then he needed to talk with Rosecrans right away. The soldier nodded, holding out his hand to Kitty, who brushed by him and walked on up the steps.

He led her to a room at the end of the hallway, and she stepped inside to survey the shabbiness. Worn, frayed carpets, a grease-stained bedspread on a sagging iron-postered bed. A chair and a rickety table were the only other furnishings. The windows were broken out. The soldier noticed her dismay and said apologetically, "You know we've had some skirmishes here, lady, and things are kind of in a bad way. We haven't had time to fix up, and nobody knew you were coming."

"This will do nicely," she said, her voice crisp. Already she had noted the window at the end of the hall and the outside stairway leading downward probably to a rear alley. When the time came for escape, it would be very easily accomplished—if she could make the right contacts.

"I'll have some food sent up." The soldier went out, closing the door behind him. She waited to hear it lock, but there was no such sound. Travis *did* trust her. There was to be no locked door. She hugged herself with delight and hurried to peer out one of the broken windows.

The stockade where the prisoners were held was in sight. Surely there would be one soldier down there among them who would know something about Nathan, where he might be fighting. And surely to goodness, one of them, if not more, would be willing to attempt escape and take her with him. It wasn't much of a plan, not yet, but she would quickly work things out. It was now or never!

The sound of the door opening made her whirl about, startled. Travis stood there, smiling, a tray of hot food in his hands—griddle cakes, coffee, bacon. It smelled heavenly. "I'm having a tub of hot water sent up. Then you can get that bath you've been hoping for . . ."

"And have you in my arms as I've been hoping for," she said meaningfully, lowering her lashes to look at him seductively.

He set the tray down, then took her in his arms and kissed her firmly. "That will have to wait, love. I've important business to discuss with Rosecrans. I may have some bad news for you, too, but let's wait on that until I'm certain."

"Bad news?" She stared at him, frightened. "Travis, don't make me fret. Tell me, please . . ."

He sighed, shaking his head. "I shouldn't have even mentioned it till I was sure. But I guess you will worry now. I've just been told that a man named Nathan Bedford Forrest, a general for the Rebels, has started attacks and raids that have to be checked. Colonel Ben Grierson is gathering as many Federal cavalrymen as possible in La Grange, Tennessee, and Rosecrans says Grant wants me to take my men and go with him. We're going to tear up railroads and supply depots all the way to Louisiana and help clear the way for Grant's campaign against Vicksburg."

"What does this have to do with me?" she demanded. "Do you think I'm going to shout it out the window? Are you about to tell me I'm to be bound and gagged to keep from telling what you plan to do?"

She stomped her foot, face red with anger, and Travis had to laugh. "No, princess." He grinned, kissing the tip of her nose. "I don't believe you'll do that. And who would you tell? Those Rebel prisoners down there who'll be off to prison as soon as the next train comes through? I'm telling you this because you may have to stay behind. The ride will be rough, and even though we may need your medical skills, it won't be any place for a woman. I'll have to go back and get Sam and the others and head for La Grange to meet Colonel Grierson. You'll have to stay here with Rosecrans. He'll put you with the field surgical unit."

"I don't want you to leave me," she cried, pretending to be heartbroken. "How can you do this to me, Travis . . . to us? Don't I mean anything to you at all?"

He grabbed her, holding her close against his chest. "Of course, you do, precious, but I can't endanger your life. Before, it didn't matter. I'll be honest with you. You meant nothing to me, but now you do, and I want you to be kept as safe as possible. Cavalry raids are very dangerous, and I just can't take you with me."

She hated herself for actually feeling regret that he would be leaving her soon. She hated him, didn't she? Oh God, the whole world was turning upside down! She had to get away—return to her people—before she completely lost her sanity!

"Sir, Rosecrans is waiting," a voice came through the door.

"I may be late." He kissed her again. "Enjoy your food. Take that hot bath. And wait up for me."

He walked out, closing the door behind him, and Kitty tiptoed to the door, pressed her ear against the thin wood, and listened. "Get the lady her bath and then clear this floor. I don't want any of these men getting ideas about peeking through keyholes."

"Sir, with you and the commander right next door, I think guards should be allowed to be on post," a strange voice commented worriedly.

"Place a guard downstairs. Hell, soldier, the only Rebs around here are at the stockade! I gave you an order, now follow it."

Next door, she thought feverishly. The conference between Travis and Rosecrans would take place right next door. And there would be no guards posted in the hallway because she was supposed to be taking a bath! Oh, it was all too easy, she thought, hugging herself with delight.

She ate ravenously, then pretended excitement over the

washtub of hot water that was brought in by two shiny-eyed soldiers. She waited about ten minutes, then slowly opened the door and stepped into the hallway. There was no sound except for low voices coming from the room next door, and she tiptoed in that direction, praying the floor would not creak beneath her feet.

"It's true that the Northern grip is tightening," she heard a strange voice saying as she pressed her ear against the door. "Grant's bogged down in that damned steaming low country north of Vicksburg, and I'm inactive here trying to get my men back together. It'll take six months or more. Hell, at last count I lost thirteen thousand men."

There was a low whistle, and then Travis's voice, saying, "What happens next?"

"Hooker's doing a fine job with the Army of the Potomac. You know, he's shown real talent as an organizer, which came as a surprise to many. He drinks a lot, but he's a leader, and that's what counts. He can whip his men into shape. Makes them shave, clean themselves up. I'm afraid I haven't been able to fret over such matters."

"Nor have I," Travis admitted doggedly. "I've been too worried about keeping them alive to worry about keeping them clean."

"Hooker's sent word to Mr. Lincoln that it's not a question of whether or not he can take Richmond—it's a matter of *when*."

"That's cocky." Travis laughed.

"Not if you know 'Fighting Joe' Hooker," Rosecrans said, also laughing. "He means it. As soon as the spring winds dry the dirt roads so the armies can start moving, he's going to head for Richmond with more men than McClellan ever had. He'll move along the Virginia countryside on the south side of the lower James River, apparently aggressive to the enemy to hold them in check and keep that part of the country open so that its bacon and forage can be used. But he won't repeat Burnside's mistake and butt head-on against the Confederate defenses at Fredericksburg. He'll leave a third of his army there to hold Lee's attention, and then swing up the rest of his men along the Rappahannock and cross the river to march on Lee's unprotected left and rear."

Kitty held her breath. Dear God, if she could only get this information to the Confederates! It could save the capital! But how far away was Fredericksburg, Virginia? She was in Tennessee!

"I'd rather return to General Grant, sir," Travis was saying.

"No," came the booming reply. "Grant says you are one of the best qualified cavalrymen and officers in the whole Union army, and a sharpshooter besides. You head on out and join Colonel Grierson's troopers like Grant wants you to do."

"And you'll look after the lady?"

Rosecrans chuckled. "So that's it. You're worried about your lady. A pretty thing she is, too. Yes, I'll see that she's taken care of, and if she's as good a nurse as you say, she'll be desperately needed. You haven't gone and fallen in love with a Rebel prisoner, have you?"

"Her father left her and her mother to join our side, sir," Travis spoke up quickly. "Kitty's changed. I'm pretty sure of it. As for love, I guess my reputation hasn't reached you, sir. I love no woman."

"Such a reputation is not important enough to reach me." Rosecrans's voice was cold and intimidating. "But I will see to it that she is taken care of. You can be sure of that. Now I want you to prepare to leave first thing in the morning to go get your men and head for La Grange. It's on the Mississippi line and you need to get started right away."

But Travis was not intimidated by the higher-ranking officer. "Sir, a few days can't matter that much if the Colonel has to wait for the roads to dry up. It's only mid-February, and my purpose in bringing Kitty down out of the mountains was to give her a respite from the hard winter. You don't understand what she's meant to me and my men. She's saved many lives, and she's gone without her own rations to give to a sick soldier who needed the nourishment, such as it was."

"I'll see that the lady is treated well . . . entertained . . ."

"No, sir." The voice was firmer, and Kitty felt a strange little shudder rippling through her body. "You don't understand. It's *me* she wants to entertain her, and if I'm to leave her behind . . ."

There was a moment of silence. Kitty tensed. Then there came a loud, surrendering sigh. "All right. Take three days' leave, Captain. I suppose you and your men are quite deserving."

Kitty hurried back to her room. She was a mixture of emotions. Travis had stood up to a man like Rosecrans, demanding that he be given time to spend with her before leaving her—and now an unfamiliar emotion was sweeping over her. Could he actually have fallen in love with her? Could she actually be in love with him? It was time to admit that the thought of escaping and never seeing him again caused a gentle ache deep within. But no! It hadn't happened—and it couldn't happen. The cause was greater! She was promised to Nathan. More than that, she owed a debt to her people—to Doc Musgrave and the thousands of other Southerners who had died for something they believed in.

And Poppa? Did she owe him a loyalty, too? "A man has to follow his heart"—he had said that to her many times. "A man has to have the courage of his convictions." He was following his—if he was still alive—and she had to follow hers. Travis was handsome, dashing, exciting, and he could make her body come alive in a way she never dreamed existed. But love? No. It couldn't be. Underneath the aura, there lay the coldness, the brutal savagery, of a man with no heart. Any emotion that existed between them was physical, and anything physical is fleeting, decaying like the flesh when committed to the grave. "Ashes to ashes, dust to dust," the Good Book said. And so would their feelings for each other be committed.

She did not have to wait long. The door opened softly. Kitty lay naked from the hurried bath. Travis undressed, stretching out beside her. He reached for her with a gentle hand, but his lips were hungry. He caressed her, touched her, made her body sing with a chorus of a thousand voices in joyful unison. And then they crested together, her head tucked against his shoulder, as she closed her eyes and pretended to sleep.

Travis dressed, tiptoed from the room. He would be joining his men downstairs for drinks and revelry. She would have a few precious hours to attempt her mission.

Someone had left a clean Union uniform, and she

dressed hurriedly, moved to the end of the empty, silent hallway, then crept quickly down the outside stairway. The streets were almost deserted. The sounds of music and laughter from inside the saloons along the way gave evidence that the soldiers were relaxing and enjoying themselves with the loose camp women who abounded.

She hurried along to the railroad stockade, picking her way through the shadows of the dark buildings. She paused just across the street to look over the situation. There seemed to be only two guards, and as Kitty watched, they passed a bottle between them. She could not distinguish their conversation but heard enough to tell that the speech was slurred. They were drunk!

Someone walked by, and she pressed herself flat against the doorway of the building and held her breath. The person went on by. It would be difficult to explain why a woman wearing a baggy uniform of the Federal army was spying on the Confederate prison stockade in the middle of the night.

The guards were soon slumped against the gate. Kitty moved across the street after checking to make sure no one was around. She kept a safe distance from the stockade where the prisoners were lying on the ground. Some of them were asleep. Others were sitting up mumbling and cursing. If they spotted her, they might give her away.

There was a deserted-looking building at the side, with a narrow pathway between it and the wire stockade. She slipped inside, and the first prisoner she reached was leaning back against a fence post, his head nodding.

"Please, don't make a sound," she whispered nervously, her voice quivering as she reached through the wire, gently touching his shoulder.

Whipping his head around, he gasped, "Well, I'll be damned. . . ."

"Please, not a sound!" It was a dark, cloudy night with no illumination from the moon. He could not see her face but could tell she was a woman by her voice. "I'm a Confederate like you and I'm held prisoner by a Yankee officer. I need help to get back to our people."

He turned around, straining to see her face. "I'm afraid I can't help you none, lady. I'm a prisoner, too, as you can see. You better not let them catch you here, either."

"I want you to ask questions of the other men. When do they say the train will come for you?"

"Dunno. Some say tomorrow. Some say day after. Nobody knows for sure."

"Listen carefully." She moved closer to him. "I'll come back here tomorrow night. You be sitting right here. You ask around. Find out if anyone knows anything about a Confederate officer—a Major, the last time I heard—Major Nathan Collins of the Wayne Volunteers, assigned to the North Carolina State troops under a Colonel named George Anderson. The last I heard, they were were at the battle of Shiloh."

"Glory, woman, that was almost a year ago. There's been a hundred battles since and thousands of men killed. He probably ain't even alive now," he added caustically.

Her heart wrenched painfully. "He has to be. Please, ask about. Someone might have heard something . . . know where he is. I have information that is vital to the South."

"And what do you aim to do, lady, if someone's heard of this man?"

"Go to him. I can slip away. They trust me. I have some freedom now, and I can get away."

He was almost shaking with interest. "And you'd let us out of here? There's almost a hundred of us, lady, and we'd make a strong band to take you where you want to go."

It didn't take Kitty long to agree that with a hundred men to help her, she would have a better chance of getting to wherever Nathan was. "All right. You find out what I need to know, and tomorrow night I'll find a way to free all of you."

"Find out where the horses are stabled. We'll need those. Now go before someone hears us talking."

She slipped away, across the street, through the shadows, and by the time she was back upstairs in the hotel room and beneath the covers, her whole body was trembling. It was happening! It was finally happening. She was going to be free. She was going to return to Nathan. Oh, please, God, she prayed, let someone know where he is!

Finally, she slept, and she did not know when Travis had come in during the night, but when she awoke, he was holding her tightly against his strong chest. For a moment,

303

she could only lie there, her pulses pounding as she told herself she was only doing what must be done. Travis did not love her. He could never truly love any woman. There was no need to feel any guilt. Hadn't he humiliated her? Used her?

Her body tensed, and the movement awakened Travis, who was trained to be alert to any move while sleeping. His eyes flashed open, and when he saw her staring at him, his lips spread into a lazy smile. "What a nice way to wake up," he murmured, reaching for her; and she gave herself to him wholly, completely, for what she prayed would be the last time.

Closing her eyes, the scorching thought pulsated through every fiber of her being: she was a whore, using her body willfully. But no, there was a purpose, and that purpose was to obtain freedom for herself and for almost a hundred Confederate prisoners and to take information to the Southern army that might very well save the capital of the Confederacy! Other women did what she was now doing for no reason at all, save their own lust and pleasure, so why should she feel any guilt?

That afternoon, Travis took her to a store where a few women's dresses were available. He bought her a beautiful gown of red lace and satin, whirling her about approvingly. "You are the most damned beautiful woman I've ever seen," he grinned. "I swear, Kitty Wright, you're *too* damned beautiful!"

The woman clerk standing nearby watched curiously, then asked cautiously, "Are you sure you want a *red* wedding dress, ma'am? I know with the war that dresses are scarce, but I could come up with something perhaps, ah, more conservative. . . ."

"A wedding?" Travis threw his head back and laughed, and Kitty felt her cheeks flaming. "Ah, my innocent woman, marriage is for fools. The princess and I merely love to make love, isn't that right, my lovely?"

Kitty was seething with rage. How could he embarrass her so? How could he dress her in flaming red like a harlot, then publicly announce that they were merely lovers with only scornful thoughts for the sacredness of marriage?

Stalking into the curtained-off dressing area, Kitty almost ripped the dress taking it off. Walking back into the main room of the store, she flung the garment across the counter and snapped, "I don't want it. I don't want anything from this man!"

And then she hurried out into the muddy street, not caring that her ankles sank down into the mud and slush and ice. A few soldiers yelled at her, but she held her head up and kept going. She did not stop until she was back in the hotel room, stamping the slush from her feet.

Suddenly the door banged open. Travis walked in, seemingly filling the room with his anger. "Just what in the hell was that all about?" He flung the red dress he was carrying across the bed.

He was wearing a poncho, which he yanked off and threw to the floor. He stood with booted feet wide apart, the shirt of his dark blue Federal uniform open to expose his massive, hairy chest. His mud-spattered blue trousers had a stripe down each leg, and he was rumpled and unkempt. Even his beard looked shaggier, Kitty realized, if that was possible. Did his ruggedness, his callousness, have anything to do with the mission he was about to undertake? She did not know and, at the moment, did not care.

"How dare you shame me so in public? Just who do you think you are? How dare you?"

She could have slapped him, but the gleam in his eye told her plainly that the move would not go unrevenged.

"I never promised you anything, Kitty, except to be kind to you, which I have been. If you're so damned sensitive that you can't stand a bit of jest . . ."

"Jest. You call it jest when you tell a total stranger that we are no more than lovers?" Her purple eyes were flashing, and her whole body trembled with rage.

"You'll never see the woman again. What difference does it make what she thinks? Every man in my company knows we're lovers, that we sleep together as man and wife, and you haven't minded them knowing it. Why make a big scene over a total stranger? Woman, I'll never be able to figure you out!"

He looked at her and shook his head. Would he never be able to figure her out? What had happened to make her behave so? Yesterday they were friends and now they were enemies once again.

She whirled and sat down on the sagging bed, turning

her back to him. "Just get out, Travis, and leave me alone. And take that harlot's dress with you! I never want you to touch me again. You can beat me, kill me, but I'll never give in to you again. I should have known you were no better than that scoundrel, Luke Tate, except that you're worse, because you're a . . . a damned *Yankee*!"

There was such a long silence that Kitty finally snapped her head around, thinking he might have actually left without her hearing him.

But he was still standing there, staring at her in such a puzzled way that she cried, "Well? Why do you stare at me that way? Get out and leave me alone!"

"All right." His voice was calm, quiet, almost ominous, as though he had figured out something was very wrong. "But this will be goodbye for now, Kitty. I have a mission that will take me somewhere you can't go. Rosecrans will see to it that you're sent to a medical unit and kept as safe as possible. I wish you well. Perhaps one day we'll meet again. . . ."

He stood there a moment as though waiting for something. Finally, Kitty stuck her chin up a bit higher, giving her long hair a flip as she turned her face to the wall. Travis was almost out into the hall when the question came in a whisper, "What of Andy?"

He paused, then said gently, "Kitty, Andy is one of us now. I think you've realized that. He pledged his allegiance in his heart to the Union a long time ago. Don't fret about him. I'll keep an eye on him."

He stepped into the hallway, closing the door quietly. Kitty almost called out to him. Her lips parted and her hand moved toward the closed door. This was not the way they should say goodbye, but then her hand fell to her lap, her lips closed. What difference did it really make? They'd never loved each other. It was better this way, better that they part in anger.

And, yes, she thought with painful remembrance, it was best he did not know that the crumpled red dress lying in a heap upon the bed had brought back memories of another dress—also red—and the happiness with which she had first modeled it, and the love she'd felt for Nathan. Could it be that she was experiencing similar emotions back there in that shop and that Travis's caustic remarks to the clerk had made her realize that she was a fool for even thinking love between them might be possible?

And then she heard the footsteps, finally retreating down the hall, and with the sound came the realization that he had been standing there, waiting for her to call out to him! Oh, the nerve and the conceit of that . . . that animal!

Travis Coltrane would never love anyone but himself and his precious Union. And she would never love anyone except Nathan—and the sooner they were married, the better.

She lay down on the bed and waited—for nightfall, for *escape.*

❦ Chapter Twenty-five ❧

KITTY opened her eyes to darkness. She did not know how long she had slept, but after groping her way to the window, she could see that all was quiet below. It was late. A supper tray had been brought and left by her bed. No sound came from the hallway.

It was time to act.

She put on the heavy boots which she hated—but they were all she had to wear—then the blue trousers, and the shirt. There was a woolen cape hanging on a nail, and she slipped that on also. It was bitterly cold. They would be traveling at night until they were safe behind their own lines. But where were the lines? Who knew where the war was being waged anymore?

Opening the door gently, she peered outside. The corridor was empty. Tiptoeing, she moved to the end, opened the outside doorway, then started descending the stairway. Once, she had to press herself against the side of the building and hold her breath as two drunken Union soldiers moved below her, slurring the notes of their song.

She made her way down the street cautiously, eyes ever alert for any movement. Finally, she was once again crouched in the darkness directly across from the stockade which held the Confederate prisoners. She noticed that most of them were sitting up or walking about, and she cursed silently. Word had spread! Didn't they know that the guards might be more alert if they felt the tension?

Her eyes watched the two guards sitting in front of the entrance gate, heads nodding. A cold wind was blowing, and they huddled together for warmth. She stood there for perhaps a half hour without moving, just watching, making sure that the guards were truly asleep. Every so often, one of their heads would jerk up, shake, then promptly the chin would fall to the chest.

Finally, she moved across the street and down the alleyway toward a soldier who sat propped against the same fence post. She knelt down, and in the dim light from a campfire, she realized it was not the same soldier she had talked with the night before. This soldier's right sleeve was doubled up and pinned to his shoulder—his right arm had been amputated!

"Please . . . don't make a sound," she said, repeating her warning of the previous night. "I'm here to help you escape."

The soldier turned slowly, and a voice filled with such pain that it wrenched her heart, spoke quietly. "Hello, Kitty."

For a moment, she felt herself swaying as she fought to hang onto reality. She had to be dreaming. Could it really be?

"David . . ." she whispered, tears starting to stream down her face as her fingertips reached through the fence to touch his dear face. "David Stoner."

"God, Kitty, we thought you were dead"—his own voice was breaking. "When that soldier passed the word through the stockade that a woman held prisoner by the Yankees was trying to find Nathan Collins, I knew it had to be you."

"Oh, David . . ." She put her face in her hands and wept, for the moment forgetting the dangerous situation she was in. To see someone so dear was like being home again. But she was *not* home, she reminded herself, far from it, and her head snapped up as her teeth bit into her lower lip to check the tears.

"David, do you know where Nathan is? I've got to get to him. We've all got to get out of here."

"I've got a general idea, Kitty, but our company took a

licking in a skirmish a few weeks back, and we got spread out."

"Is that how you lost your arm?" she asked cautiously, not wanting to remind him.

"No, that happened at Shiloh."

"A year ago? David, you could have gone home. The war was over for you."

"I didn't want to go home. If I can't do anything but help tote supplies with one arm or give a wounded man a drink of water, that's better than going home and not doing my part, Kitty. Then I had to go and get myself captured and hell, none of us want to rot in a Yankee prison for the rest of the war."

"Then let's get moving," she said quickly. "What about the guards? Are there only two of them?"

"Yeah. They figure since we're stripped of weapons and the whole town is crawling with Yankees, they don't need more'n two. Besides, Rosecrans is having a time keeping his men sober. But we've already talked about how we're going to work this. You find us any kind of a weapon— something to bust their heads with—and we'll do the rest. There's a pen full of horses not far from here, and we'll get to those and then ride out of here before they know what's happening."

"But what about guns?" she asked, frightened. "The other soldiers will hear the commotion and come running, and we'll be gunned down before we can get out of town."

"We're going to be quiet about it," he assured her. "We talked about it all night last night and all day today. We're going to be quiet—slip out a few at a time. Now you do as I say. Go find us a club or something and then try to find a couple of horses for me and you. We're going to leave the others. We won't attract as much attention traveling in a pair. Everyone will think we're husband and wife, me an amputee out of the war and you my wife, just riding along. I'll wait right here, and you go find us two horses. Now hurry, Kitty."

Kitty's heart throbbed as she darted through the night. Several horses were tied in front of a darkened store used now as a barracks. Untying two, she led them to the rear, down the side of the railroad track, retying them in the shadows. What David said made sense: with David an amputee the two of them could travel almost safely. With the entire group of escaped Confederate prisoners, they would make an easy target.

It was not hard to find two large rocks, which she passed over the fence to the waiting prisoners. Then she pressed herself against the building alongside the alley and waited.

There was the sound of loud thumps and sudden groans, and then—dear God, no—the men were shouting and screaming and running from the stockade in wild panic! They were fighting each other for horses tied along the streets, and Union soldiers, awakened by the noise, were stumbling out of the buildings and saloons.

Shots rang out. Confederates were falling in the street. Others were grappling for guns, returning the fire. Kitty crammed her fist into her mouth and tasted blood as her teeth bit down. It was over before it even began. Terror constricted her, froze her where she stood. She would be shot down like the others. Why did they have to run screaming through the streets in hysterics?

She felt a hand on her shoulder and looked up in the shadows to see David standing there. "I was afraid it would be like this," he said quickly. "Kitty, where did you tie our horses? There might still be a chance for us to escape."

She was unable to move. She was staring beyond him at the street where a Confederate lay writhing in the slush and ice, clutching his stomach. The Union soldiers had reacted quickly. It was a massacre!

She felt the sting of his remaining hand across her face, and she snapped back to reality. "Kitty! We've got to move. This way."

She turned in the opposite direction, toward the railroad track. In the shadows, the horses waited, pawing the ground impatiently. With his one good arm, David gave her a boost onto the saddle, then hoisted himself atop the other horse.

"Move easy," he ordered, "and when I give the order, dig your heels in and ride like hell, Kitty. I know you can do it. And if I get hit, you keep on going."

"But where? What direction, David? I don't know where to find Nathan."

"Find Pemberton, Lieutenant General John C. Pemberton, and you'll find Nathan. Head for Richmond."

They moved slowly. Out in the street, the fighting was still going on. The Confederates were being slaughtered, but a few had reached horses and were riding away into the night.

They moved slowly, behind the buildings. Suddenly, two men stepped out in front of them, one of them carrying a torch. "Now!" David screamed, spurring his horse, leaping across the railroad track and disappearing into the darkness.

But Kitty was frozen and could not move.

"Kitty, ride!" She could hear David yelling above the thundering hooves of his horse. "Ride!"

A gun was pointed right at her, and the gun was held by Travis Coltrane.

"You did this, didn't you, Kitty?" he asked quietly.

In the background, there was the sound of guns firing, men screaming, horses charging through the night in pursuit of the Rebels who had managed to escape.

Kitty's lips moved, but she could not find her voice.

"All of it, it was part of the plan, wasn't it?"

In the maddening, dancing flicker of the torch, his face looked wild, maniacal. The gun was trained straight at her, and at any moment, a bullet could go tearing right into her body, ending her life.

"I never swore allegiance to your cause, Travis," she said finally, wondering in the panic of the moment why she felt like crying. Was it because death was so near or because Travis was looking at her with such hate and disbelief in his steady gaze?

"Shoot her, Coltrane," the soldier holding the torch cried as Kitty dug her heels into the horse's flanks and reined him to a sharp right in the direction David had taken.

Tears blinded her eyes. Let the bullet rip into her flesh. She would not turn back now.

"Goddamn it, Coltrane, shoot her! She's the cause of all this."

"Kitty, stop!" The voice was cracking, almost pleading, but Kitty dug her heels in harder. The horse started to trot, then broke into a full run just as she heard the scuffle behind.

Giving the horse full rein, she whipped her head about just in time to see Travis wrestling with the man who had held the torch and dropped it—grappling for the gun. He was trying to keep the soldier from shooting her!

For one brief instant, she snaked her hands out for the reins to bring the horse around. But for what? To help Travis? To give herself up?

"Kitty, please, hurry."

In front of her, in the night, David was calling to her, waiting. He would see that she got to Richmond and to Nathan. Behind her, two men were grappling for a gun. One of them, she had foolishly thought she might have loved—and had dared to think he might love her. Go back? Back to what? Helping the Yankees? Give her body and soul to a man who only wanted to use her?

But then cold realization washed over her, and she yanked the reins so hard that the horse reared up on his hind legs, pawing at the air wildly. Had she not been an expert horsewoman, she would have gone sprawling to the ground, but she held on, brought the horse back down on all four legs and turned and started back. Travis was fighting at this moment for *her*—for her life—to keep his own man from shooting her to halt her escape!

And then the explosion came. One of the men was clutching his stomach as he fell to the ground.

"God, Captain . . ." She heard the mournful, agonizing cry. "I didn't mean it. . . ."

And then the body pitched forward to the ground.

She wheeled the horse around, dug her heels in harder and harder as the tears blinded any vision she might have had in the darkness, the terror constricting her throat, making her gasp for breath. She galloped right past David who was waiting for her, and he had to spur his own horse in pursuit.

How long they rode blindly in the darkness Kitty did not know. Finally, when the horse stumbled and almost fell, she reined up, leaped off before her mount had come to a complete stop, tripped, lost her balance, fell to the ground on hands and knees, and felt the flesh being torn away.

313

And only then did she give way to the great, gulping sobs that racked her body.

"Kitty, Kitty, for God's sake . . ." David was right beside her. "What happened back there? Why'd you stop? What happened to make you act this way? Why were those two men fighting?"

"Please," she gasped, feeling a knife-like pain in her side as she pressed her hands against the flesh there. "I . . . I don't want to talk about it . . . not now."

He smoothed her hair back from her face, then took his remaining arm to hold her against his chest. "It's going to be all right now. We'll find shelter and rest, and then we'll head for Richmond. We'll find Nathan there with Pemberton's army, I'm sure. He thinks you long dead, Kitty, and he'll praise God for sending you to him."

"And I've thought *him* long dead," she said, swallowing her tears. "I never thought I'd see anyone from home again."

They had reached deep woods, and David led her and the horses into a thicket where they sank to the ground, exhausted. For a while, they were silent; then Kitty asked, "How many of our men do you think got away?"

"Maybe twenty. I don't know. It's hard to tell. It was dark. They just panicked. I was afraid it would happen that way. The thoughts of escape—the gate finally opening—they just went crazy. Can't say as I blame them. I just wish it hadn't happened that way. Maybe we could have all gotten away."

"Have you been back home?" Kitty asked suddenly, thinking of her mother.

"Yeah, I went home after I lost my arm. I got married, too."

"Married?" Kitty's eyes widened in the darkness. "David, I never knew you were seriously interested in anyone . . ."

"Except you." He laughed softly, teasingly. Kitty felt herself blushing. Reaching out with his one hand, David touched her face, tracing his fingertips along her cheek. "It's all right, Kitty. I never made much of a secret about the way I felt about you. But I knew it was Nathan you really loved. I think I knew it even before you did."

There was a moment of awkward silence, then Kitty asked, "Do I know your wife?"

He snorted. "Doesn't everyone?" He lapsed into another mood of silence, and this time Kitty did not prod him to speak. She waited.

"I went home on leave after I lost my arm, like I said. Nathan went with me. It was after the battle of Shiloh. Everybody made a pretty big to-do over me, made me out to be a hero and all. Of course, Nathan's a big officer now and made a good name for himself, and everyone was paying a lot of attention to him, too. Well, we both asked a lot of questions about you, but nobody had ever heard anymore about you once they found Doc's body. We figured you'd been killed, too, only your body wasn't found.'"

"Well," he went on after a long sigh, "Nancy Warren really made it known to Nathan that she was after him, but he was taking it pretty hard about you. She turned to me to try to make him jealous, I realized later. At the time, I had my own sorrow to bear—realizing you were gone. I'd lost my right arm, and I came home to find out my pa had been killed in the Shenandoah Valley. I reckon I was about the most miserable man in the whole world. Nancy made me feel like somebody cared. The next thing I knew, I'd asked her to marry me and she'd accepted. Nathan went back to the war, and I tried to settle down to married life and working some land to try and grow enough to keep us from starving."

Nancy Warren and David Stoner? Kitty shook her head in disbelief. It didn't seem possible. David was so sweet and kind and gentle, and Nancy was—well, Nancy was just a witch, that's all, a snobby, conceited little witch who would make any man miserable.

"It didn't work out," David said, confirming Kitty's thoughts. "She said my stump bothered her. Said she didn't like being married to a dirt farmer. Next thing I knew she was running off to Raleigh to dance with the officers on leave. I just upped and walked out. Found my way back to the war—and Nathan. Then I got myself captured and was headed for a Yankee prison till God sent you to me."

"My mother . . ." she said then. "Is she well? David, it's been almost two years! Is she still alive? How does she get by all alone? Did Jacob stay with her?"

She was trembling with anxiety. This was the first chance in so long to hear any kind of news at all about her mother.

David was strangely quiet, and she reached out and gave him a shake, apprehension coursing through her veins. "Tell me, please. It's bad, isn't it? She's dead. . . ."

"No, she isn't dead," he sighed. "She lives in town now. Works there. Manages to keep herself from starving, I reckon. Every soldier that comes through, she asks about you and your pa. You should write to her, Kitty. Let her know you're alive. No one's ever heard a word from your pa except that he's one of the fiercest Yankee fighters alive. In fact, when word spread back home, some of the men who'd lost arms and legs and gone home to stay put a bounty on him. They got together and raised over five thousand dollars to bring him in—dead!"

"Oh, my God," she whimpered, and David quickly apologized for repeating such news. She shook her head. "No, I'd rather know the truth, David. I've heard the same tale about him being such a fine soldier for the North, and I'm not surprised to hear about the bounty."

"I know you're hungry," he said then, anxious to change the subject. "I'm going to look in the haversack on that horse's saddle and see if there's anything inside."

He returned with some corn dodgers and a canteen of water. "It's not much, but it will do till we can find better. We've got quite a ride ahead of us to find Pemberton's army—and, we hope, Nathan. I feel like I should just take you right on home. I can find some way to get you there. Nathan won't like you going into the thick of battle, even as glad as he'll be to find out you're alive. I can take you home, and you can write to him. It might be better that way."

"No!" she said sharply. "I've got to find Nathan. And I have to find General Lee and tell him about a Yankee named Hooker who plans to march on Richmond and about how he plans to do it. I overheard someone talking to Rosecrans back there."

The way she said "someone" with a certain touch of tenderness to her voice made David speak up and ask gently, "Would that someone be the soldier who died for you back there, Kitty?"

For a moment, she could not find her voice. Oh, Lord, the confusion flowing through her veins! Was Travis dead?

Had he died for her? And if so, was the ache, the pain, that she felt inside genuine? Would the gnawing demon eat into her very soul to destroy her with grief? Or was she actually numb because it did not matter that Travis Coltrane might be dead?

"Who was he? Who do you speak of, Kitty?"

"Travis Coltrane, a cavalry officer in General Grant's army," she said finally when she could trust herself to speak. "He . . . he rescued me from Luke Tate, but he wouldn't let me return south, not when he found out I knew something about medicine."

"Luke Tate?" He was shocked. "What's Luke Tate got to do with any of this?"

And then she realized that David did not know the whole story—how she had actually been kidnapped by Nathan's former overseer and held prisoner. She had to tell him the whole terrible story from beginning to end. And when she had finished, she could feel him beside her, shaking with fury.

"And he escaped?" he asked between clenched teeth.

She could only nod and mumble a feeble yes.

"I'll find him and kill him!"

He spoke so fiercely, so furiously, that Kitty reached out to touch him, to try to soothe some of the anger. "He's probably dead by now, David. And it's in the past. I try not to think about any of it anymore."

It was bitterly cold there in the thick Tennessee woods. "We'd better try to get some sleep and be on our way as soon as it's light." David got up and went to the horses, grateful to find a blanket laced onto the rump of each. "This isn't much cover, but if we huddle together, we won't freeze."

They curled in each other's arms. Kitty did not think about the propriety of such closeness. It was a necessity to try to keep warm. She snuggled with her back against David's body as they lay beneath the blankets. In only a few moments, she heard his even, gentle breathing and knew he was sleeping from exhaustion. A long journey lay ahead—a dangerous, long journey.

Kitty tried to sleep also. Closing her eyes, she listened to the night sounds—a gentle singing wind that moved through the longleaf pines above, an owl hooting mournfully from somewhere deeper into the woods, now and then the shriek of some wild animal in search of prey. Her eyelids grew heavy. She was exhausted, both physically and mentally. Even her jumbled thoughts could not keep her awake.

The dreams came—the sandy-blond young boy holding her close on the mossy bank beneath the draping shroud of a weeping willow tree, a soft, warm wind blowing across the flat land of the North Carolina countryside. "I love you, Kitty," he'd said. "Marry me . . . be my wife." And gentle hands had touched her body, caressing her, but moved away before the stormy sea of passion had engulfed them. "I want everything to be perfect for us always," he'd said. And she, so young and foolish, had dared to believe life could be just as anyone desired it to be.

But then the dream became distorted, and there were dark eyes fringed with thick lashes, eyes the color of a steel-blue gun barrel; a firm, set look to the gaze that devoured her; a thickly bearded face; lean, hard muscles that rippled as he reached for her, smothering her with his massive body, taking her body to pinnacles of joy she had never dared dream existed. Mocking lips, gentle lips, teasing eyes, and dancing fingertips; two hearts in unison, thundering with the wild river of hot blood flowing between the two—man and woman, fire and passion, love and desire, and hatred and loathing. He was kind, he was gentle, he was cruel, and he was ruthless. And there was the pain of seeing his leg gouged open with a wound; the panic of having to argue down a field surgeon and insist that amputation was not necessary; the pounding of her heart as he thanked her later—memories, washed away by the sands, the winds, of time.

And finally, that one heart-shattering moment with two men grappling for one gun, an explosion, a body falling to earth, blood unseen but somehow she knew it was gushing forth. It ended there, in the dirt, in the soil, in the sand and nothingness from whence it all began.

Someone was crying, sobbing, and then her name was being called and her body shaken.

"Kitty, wake up. You're having a bad dream. Wake up, please."

She opened heavy eyelids to the early cold light of morning. A raspberry-colored sky streaked the edges of the longleaf pines. David was staring down at her anxiously. "Are you all right? You woke me up, screaming. . . ."

"I'm sorry." She was contrite and scrambled to her feet, anxious to be on her way. "Let's go to Nathan quickly, David. Let's be on our way." She was fighting to hold back the tears; her insides churned with emotions—confusing, distorted emotions that she could not understand.

As they gathered the blankets and prepared to mount the horses, Kitty felt David staring at her. Unable to contain her annoyance, she asked rather waspishly, "What is it, David? Why are you looking at me like that?"

He smiled, a sad, secretive little smile. "Remember what I said about how I figured out you loved Nathan long before you did?"

She nodded.

"I think I've always understood you better than you understand yourself, Kitty."

"What are you getting at, David?"

"Well, I can't help wondering, are you running *toward* Nathan or *away* from Travis Coltrane?"

She had been about to mount her horse, but now she turned to stare at him incredulously. "Are you crazy? I love Nathan. I want to marry him. And Travis Coltrane is probably dead for all I know, and he never meant anything to me anyway. I told you—he held me his prisoner."

"I know that," he agreed with her. "But I also know that you sometimes don't admit your true feelings, Kitty, and I kind of think this Coltrane fellow meant more to you than you let on. You can't be sure he's dead, you know. You could still go back there."

"That's silly!" She mounted her horse, more than a little annoyed at this point. She was almost ready to explode in anger against her lifelong friend. "Let's ride, David. We have to find food and shelter before the night. We have to talk and plan this trip. We've no time for any of your foolish notions."

"Maybe you should turn back." He had not mounted his

horse but was standing there holding the reins and looking up at her with a very sad expression on his handsome face. "It *has* been a long time, Kitty."

"David, you do exasperate me! What's wrong with you? I told you, I want to find Nathan."

"Maybe you do, maybe you don't." He got on his horse, turning in the saddle to look directly at her. "Kitty, you can't ever go back to the way things were. Nathan has changed. You've changed. This blasted war has changed the whole country. If you think you found anything back there with that Yankee at all—anything—then you're never going to know a moment's peace until you go back and find out just what it is you think you want to leave—or maybe you don't want to leave at all."

"I think," she said sharply, "that you're the one who's changed, David. I told you, I want to get to Nathan as quickly as possible."

And she did. Travis could mean nothing to her. And if he had taken that bullet rather than see her shot, well, that was his choice. *Then why am I fighting to hold back the tears?* She cursed herself silently. *Why do I feel like a part of me is dead, gone, amputated like David's arm—a part of me that will never, ever grow back?*

David dug his heels into the horse's flanks and started forward with Kitty following right behind. "Just remember," he called over his shoulder, "I've always been able to figure you out, Kitty, whether you like it or not. And this is one trip you may very well wish you'd never made."

"I can't appreciate your saying that and neither will Nathan." She was getting more and more annoyed with David's attitude. "You know that I love Nathan. You said you knew it long before I did. Now you're behaving as though you don't want me to find him."

"Folks can't ever go back to what they leave behind." He kept riding forward, not looking back, and she had to strain to hear his words. "And what you think you're running toward, you might just be running *from*."

Jutting her chin upward, Kitty dug her heels in her own mount to move him faster. David didn't know what he was talking about. She was riding toward the one thing she did want out of life and escaping the man who'd kept her from it. Since that horrible day in the late summer of

1861, life had been one continuous hell. And now, God willing, the worst was over.

Life was cold, harsh, cruel, and in living it she was becoming the same. At that moment, pushing ahead into the wilderness of the mountains of Tennessee, toward Virginia, and, with luck, Nathan, Kitty felt that the snow and wind that whipped about her body could be no colder than the chill that enshrouded her very soul.

❦ Chapter Twenty-six ❧

KITTY soon realized that David had been right in his prediction: a one-armed man riding with a woman at his side would arouse no suspicion. Husband and wife. Seeking a new life together, not knowing exactly where they were going, but keeping on the move, trying to put the horrors of war behind them.

But the ride itself was hard, and the weather was against them from the beginning. Sometimes they were able to ride only a few miles a day before they were forced to seek shelter from the cold. Sometimes they would find refuge with kindly settlers along the way. At other times they were forced to camp in the woods, in a cave if they had the good fortune to find one. Food was scarce, and both of them grew weak and weary.

It was toward the end of March when Kitty felt the fever creeping upon her. She tried to move onward, but one day she felt herself falling from her horse and when she awoke, she found herself looking into the face of a kindly, concerned mountain woman who, much to Kitty's astonishment, told her that between the fever and diarrhea and just plain being nearly starved to death, it was a wonder she was even alive. But the "wonder" to Kitty was the fact that it was then mid-April.

David seemed in no hurry to move on, saying that she needed to regain her strength. "We were pushing too hard.

That's why you fell ill. We're just blessed that we were near folks as kind as the Gentrys. I've gotten to know Lucille and Mark, and they're good, Christian people. You just don't know how many hours they've taken turns sitting by your bed, spooning broth into your mouth when you were so sick you didn't even know you were even swallowing!"

"I am grateful," Kitty assured him, "but David, we've got to get to Nathan. I told you, I have news that the Confederates need to hear!"

"You're too weak to travel just yet," he said sharply.

"True, I am weak," she conceded. "But David, when I'm strong enough to travel, if you don't go with me, so help me, I'm going alone."

He nodded, eyes dark with anger. But why, she wondered, did he hate the thought of reuniting her with Nathan? It was certainly obvious that she loved no one else, and whether David was happy about the situation or not, he was married to Nancy Warren. Something was not quite right, something she could not put her finger on.

The cabin sat on the side of a gently sloping hill. The mountains were bursting into fragrant blooms of laurel and honeysuckle, and Kitty, sitting on the front porch, inhaled the sweetness. She liked the nighttime best, when the others were asleep, and she would sit alone and listen to the night noises—the crickets, the owls, and the frogs in the pond below. And these were the times when the memories would come flooding back—Travis, always Travis, who could make her wild with fury one moment and delirious with passion the next. She thought of the strength of his powerful arms when he held her close, the way he would lie on top of her, resting his weight on his elbows as he smiled down, eyes misty with the warmth of passion spent, and whispering that he wanted her again and again and again.

Tears would sting her eyes. Travis was dead, and if he weren't, he hated her. She could not dwell on anything in the past except the love she surely felt for Nathan. That was the importance of her life in the future, not the bittersweet thoughts of splendor in the arms of a wild, reckless, dangerous man.

Sometimes Mark Gentry would sit with her on the

porch until he grew sleepy. He was an old man and he'd lost two sons in the war. He recounted to her over and over again what he knew of the war. Some of it she already knew, but she politely listened to the old man's lament. He told about how Wednesday, September 17th, 1862 was the largest one-day blood bath so far and how from the time the sun came up until it went down again, Federal units made repeated assaults on General Lee's men. McClellan lost twelve thousand soldiers, they said, and the Rebels lost about nine thousand. Mark Gentry's son had been one of them.

They had called it the battle of Antietam Creek, and it had ended Lee's invasion. After the battle, he retired to Virginia. Kitty remembered hearing about it, hating it.

"Now they've started cavalry raids, I hear tell," the old man said. "A Yankee by the name of Grierson is burning and looting and tearing up railroads and supply depots all over."

Kitty's heart constricted when she heard the name of "Grierson"—that was the man Travis was to have gone with.

"But we're a'whooping 'em right back," Mark Gentry went on. "We've got a General by the name of Forrest, Bedford Forrest, yep, that's his name, and he's showing them Yankees a thing or two. Goddamned bastards. . . ."

"Pa, watch your tongue," Lucille Gentry called from an open window. "Let God punish the Yankees and heap his wrath on them. It's not your place to use his name in vain to curse them."

"Yes, Ma," he sighed wearily. He waited a few moments then went on with more stories about the war, cursing the Federals in a whisper, lest his wife overhear again.

It was the first of May when Kitty told David she was ready to be on her way. He had been preparing to ride to a nearby settlement for supplies, and he merely frowned when she told him to try to get the things they would need to continue their journey.

When he and Mark Gentry returned later that day, David stormed into the cabin and practically screamed, "You can forget about leaving here, Kitty. All hell's broke loose. . . ."

Lucille looked up from the table where she was cleaning a chicken. "I'll ask you to watch your tongue, David. You know I don't hold to no cursing in this house."

"It's time to curse," Mark thundered as he came in behind David, his wrinkled face red, his breath coming in gasps. "We heard all about it down at the store."

"The Yankees are moving through Virginia and headed straight for Richmond," David said, eyes shining, staring straight at Kitty. "We've got to stay put right here and hope they pass us by. We head for Richmond now, and we'll be killed or taken prisoners for sure. We'll be safe here."

"David, don't you see?" Kitty wrung her hands, her whole body shaking. "This was why I wanted to get to Nathan, to someone in the Confederate army. I *knew* that a Federal General named Joseph Hooker was going to march on Richmond. I heard Rosecrans telling Travis about it. I listened outside the door. But *you* wouldn't listen to me, and now it's too late!"

She turned and ran through the cabin and down the front steps, flinging herself into a soft, fragrant bed of periwinkles. But she didn't care about the flowers or their sweetness. The tears that came were bitter, angry—with herself for being so weak as to fall sick and delay their journey and with David for not caring about any of it anymore.

She felt someone behind her, turned her head to see that it was David, then looked away as she said, "You don't care anymore what happens to anyone, David, but yourself."

"Maybe." He spoke quietly, almost apologetically. "But I do care what happens to one other person, Kitty, and that's you. That's what I'd hoped you'd see before now, that I'm only trying to protect you, keep you from danger."

He sat down, and she turned to stare at him incredulously. "You never meant to take me to Nathan, did you? You only pretended to be taking me there, until you could find a place to . . . to *squat*, like the nesters back home—and you found the Gentrys, after they'd lost two sons, and they took you in because I was sick and you were like a son come home wounded from the war. You took advantage of them."

It was all falling into place. She pulled herself up to a

sitting position, and he wouldn't meet her gaze as she rushed on. "You couldn't take me home, because you've got a wife there! So you wanted to stay here, pretend the war didn't exist, your wife didn't exist, or Nathan—any of it!"

She was gasping for breath, body heaving, overcome with the realization of the trap she had fallen into. Finally, he lifted his watery eyes to meet her cold stare and said, "I've always loved you, Kitty. Nathan's not good enough for you. He never was. And you don't know what he's like now, but I do. He's a coward, hiding behind the uniform of an officer and seeking glory in other men's blood. I didn't want you to see that, and I didn't want to lose you. We can be happy here, all of us. I've told the Gentrys the whole story, and they want us to stay."

"You are mad!" She got to her feet, afraid that if she didn't get away from him she would rake her nails down his face. She fought to remember that his mind was warped.

She began walking toward the cabin, but David was right behind her, screaming like an angry child in the midst of a tantrum. "Just where do you think you're going? War is all around us. Our only hope is to stay here, give aid to both sides, and stay out of the war completely. Hooker's got over a hundred thousand soldiers, they say, and he's headed straight for Richmond. The Yankees are going to win, and Nathan and all the other fools are going to die!"

Kitty lapsed into an icy silence, refusing to speak to David, Mark, or Lucille. They left her alone, whispering that she would come around. They went to bed early that night, leaving her alone on the porch. They were all mad, she thought, terrified to stay another minute in the cabin. Her heart went out to David, but she had her own life to live. And she ached for the Gentrys, who'd lost their family and now thought they'd found another, ready-made. But it was not time for sympathies. Kitty felt that she had to get away as quickly as possible, and as soon as she was confident they were all asleep, she led her horse from the barn and rode east toward Virginia and, she prayed, toward the Confederate lines.

Meeting settlers along the way, Kitty received enough food and water to keep her going. She would rest only a few hours at a time, wanting to keep on the move. Finally, after riding for almost five days, she came upon a company of soldiers dressed in tattered gray uniforms. When she told them she was a nurse from North Carolina, some of them broke into tears of joy. They'd gotten separated from their main brigade and they had many wounded. She was put to work with a hospital wagon as the company tried to find its way back into battle. Their only doctor had succumbed to disease, and Kitty was all they had to treat their wounded.

Bone-tired and so weary that day turned to night without her even noticing, Kitty was shocked the day someone shouted they were outside Richmond.

"Richmond?" She left the side of a soldier with a gaping head wound, who would soon die. "But I thought Richmond would have fallen by now."

"Hooker got his ass beat!" A grizzly soldier with one leg called out jubilantly from the roadside where he stood leaning against a crutch, watching the company move slowly by. "General Lee done run him off!"

The soldiers were ecstatic. Kitty was anxious to hear more, but the dying soldier needed her attention. She sat next to him, straining to hear his last words. Send his Bible to his mother, he instructed in garbled words. Write her and tell her he was ready to go and meet his God. She was not to worry. He was ready to die. Kitty could not be sure that he understood that she was promising him she would carry out his last request. Somewhere in a little town down in south Alabama, a loving, fearful mother would weep over the bloodstained Bible Kitty would send to her, comforted only by the knowledge that her son felt he was ready to go and meet his Maker.

The soldier gave one last gasp and died. Kitty pulled the bloodied blanket over his face and then climbed down out of the wagon. The company had stopped, eager to hear news of the war.

They were saying that Hooker got more than seventy thousand men placed around Chancellorsville, a crossroads about a dozen miles back of Lee's left flank, and his cavalry went swooping quickly down to cut into the Richmond, Fredericksburg, and Potomac Railroad farther south. General Lee, however, ignored the cavalry raid and used Jeb Stuart's cavalry to control the roads around Chancellorsville—and Hooker had been unable to find out just where the Rebels were. Bewildered, Hooker had called a halt and sent his troops out into sketchy fieldworks near Chancellorsville, instead of going on to more open country a few miles to the east.

It was then that General Lee split his army up into three groups and gave the cocky Joe Hooker a lesson in tactics. Everyone was singing Lee's praises. He had left part of his men at Fredericksburg, Virginia, to make sure that the Union army left there could not do anything damaging. Then, it was said, he took about forty-five thousand men into Chancellorsville to face Hooker. And, sizing up the situation, he gave Stonewall Jackson over twenty-five thousand men, sending him on a long swing around Hooker's exposed right. And two hours before dark on the second of May, 1863, Stonewall Jackson hit that right flank with the force of a million sledgehammers, shattering it to pieces and driving a whole Yankee army corps into wild rout—knocking Hooker's army apart from its readied position.

Several more days of confused and desperate fighting went on all around Chancellorsville clearing and back to Fredericksburg. The Federals forced a crossing but found they could not accomplish anything, and Hooker quickly retreated, pulling his troops north of the Rappahannock.

"Bet he lost over fifteen thousand men and more," someone cried out. "He let an army half his size cut him all to pieces. How about the old fool? And he thought he could take Richmond!"

Cheers went up. Chancellorsville was easily General Lee's most brilliant victory, they were all saying, but then another voice cut into the joyous description of the battle and a quiet sadness spread like a giant shroud over everyone present.

"Stonewall Jackson is dead," came the word. The irony was, Kitty realized painfully, that the great General had been accidentally shot down by his own troops in the confused fighting of the thickets.

A great, great man had died.

They moved on toward Richmond, and when they arrived, Kitty was greeted by an officer who welcomed her and stated how sorely she was needed in the hospital compounds.

"And I'd like nothing better than to get right to work," Kitty told him honestly, "but I'm so tired I would do no one any good, sir. I can't even remember the last time I slept." Even as she spoke, she was swaying where she stood.

"That's right, sir," the driver of the hospital wagon she'd occupied was saying quickly. "She's been with our men day and night for days. I can't remember how long exactly. We picked her up along the way."

The officer was instantly apologetic. "Forgive me. I had no idea. We've been in such a turmoil here the past few days." He turned to the driver. "Take her to my tent. See that she's given food and water. Place a guard outside to see that she isn't disturbed for as long as necessary."

Kitty leaned against the soldier, closing her eyes wearily. Had she ever been so tired? But at least she could be thankful that at last she was among her own people. Hooker's plan had not worked. Richmond still belonged to the Confederates, and perhaps somewhere she could find Nathan, even though the city, a bustling hub of activity, was big and filled with civilians and soldiers.

She was not aware of how long she had slept, but suddenly she awoke, her stomach rumbling from hunger. A delicious odor reached her nostrils, when suddenly a soldier entered with a bowl of hot chicken stew and a cup of steaming tea. She devoured the food greedily, and was almost finished when the officer who had greeted her appeared.

"Miss Wright, how do you feel?"

"Much better, now that I've rested."

He nodded. "I've been asking some questions and I hear you've really done a fine job for the Confederacy. I want you to know that we appreciate all you did for those soldiers."

He was a stout, balding man, with a dark beard and deep, piercing eyes that boasted of his command and authority. "I understand you're looking for an officer, a Major, named Nathan Collins from North Carolina. Is this true?"

"He may be dead now," she said dully, hopelessly. "I don't know what to do. I'm just thankful I'm here, back with my own people, away from the Yankees. If you'll let me, I'd like to work at a hospital here."

"I'm quite sure that can be arranged. What I would like to do now is have you taken into town and given a room at a hotel there. Rest is what you need, and comfort, and you'll find neither here in this camp at the moment. I've arranged for one of my men to take you, if you feel like traveling a few more miles."

Rest? Comfort? It seemed like a dream, but nothing had seemed real for the past few years.

Once she was in her room, Kitty walked about and touched each piece of furniture lovingly. There was a marble-topped washstand on which sat a delicately hand-painted porcelain pitcher and bowl, and a high, four-postered bed with a dainty blue spread and a lacy canopy to match. The chairs were carved in ornate designs, the seats were covered in fancy tapestry, and upon the floor there were imported velvet rugs. It was so beautiful, all of it.

She thought of the months spent sleeping on beds of prickly pine needles, with a saddle for a pillow and only a thin blanket for cover.

She fought to hold back the tears. Lately, she was given more and more to crying, a weakness she detested. But what difference did it make? If Travis had lived, he was nothing to her, and he would also hate her for tricking him as she had.

Think of something else, she commanded herself. Walking quickly to the little wooden writing desk standing against a far wall, she remembered that she could write to her mother and let her know that she was alive and well and would come home when she could. Right now, she had to remain in Richmond and wait, and pray, that Nathan would come and find her.

There was an open Bible on the desk, and a small newspaper clipping lying in the center fold. The clipping had been torn from the pages of the *Richmond Daily Dispatch* on May 12, 1862, almost a year ago. Her eyes read the printed lines:

Then call us Rebels, if you will,
We *glory in the name*,
For bending under unjust laws,
And swearing faith to an unjust cause,
We count as greater shame.

Eyes misting, Kitty no longer tried to hold back the tears. She sank down onto the bench and cried, letting all the pent-up frustrations and grief pour out. She was crying so hard that she did not hear the knock on the door nor the sound of it opening behind her.

"Oh, dear, are you ill?"

She whirled about. A small, thin woman, perhaps in her late thirties, stood there with several garments across her arms. Her hair was drawn back in a tight bun, and she wore a plain gray muslin dress. The eyes were kind, concerned, and Kitty could already feel the warm friendliness emanating from the woman's presence.

"I guess I've been holding it back. I'm sorry." Kitty dabbed at her eyes with her bloodstained hem.

The woman walked on into the room, spread the dresses upon the bed, then stepped back. "I'm Mary Culpepper. My husband is Captain Dawson Culpepper, a member of General Lee's staff. He brought you here, I believe."

"Oh, yes. He's very kind."

Mary Culpepper smiled. "Now don't you go praising others, Kitty Wright. We've all heard about you and what you've been through. We also know you've worked day and night helping the sick and wounded, and we're all so very grateful."

"Thank you," Kitty murmured, instantly liking the woman. "Where I come from, back in North Carolina, people thought I was crazy because I wanted to be a doctor."

Mary laughed. "Wait till you meet Sally Tompkins. She's taken over an old mansion here in Richmond and made it into a hospital. She's been running it since right after the First Battle of Manassas, in July, back in sixty-one. It's called the Chimborazo Hospital. President Davis is so impressed with her work that he made her a cavalry Captain to regularize her status so she could continue working

331

under government auspices. So far, she's the only woman who holds an official military commission."

"That's wonderful! I can't wait to meet her. I've never had the pleasure of being in the company of another woman who was interested in medicine also." Kitty was almost exuberant. "Perhaps she'll let me work there, too."

"Just you try to get out of working there," Mary laughed. "There are nuns who help out, the Sisters of Charity. Oh, the hospital has grown so much since it was first founded. Some say the count of those treated so far is over forty thousand, maybe even fifty thousand. Can you imagine? I read in a newspaper that it's believed to be the largest hospital in the whole world. I'll see that you get to visit out there as soon as you've had some proper rest. My, you look pale, child."

There was another knock on the door, and Mary hastened to answer. Then a parade of servants began. First came the large tub, then buckets of hot water to be poured into it.

"I'll leave you now," Mary said, pouring a bottle of perfume into the bath water. "You choose whichever dress you'd like to wear tonight. My husband is coming for you, and you're to dine with us."

Slipping into the water, Kitty sighed deliciously. Soaking till the water turned too cold, she toweled herself dry, rubbed her hair until it was only slightly damp and able to be twisted into a bun at the nape of her neck.

She tried on a yellow silk dress with lace trim, and the fit was not too bad. Surveying herself in a full-length mirror, she found it difficult to recognize the woman who had dressed as a Yankee soldier, ridden a horse like a man, worked endless hours trying to piece bodies back together —and lain naked in the pine straw bed in the mountains of Tennessee in the arms of a Federal cavalryman.

But she was *here* now, she reminded herself, here with her own kind, where she belonged. And the little flicker of hope was starting to come alive, the hope that maybe, just maybe, Nathan might be alive—somewhere close by!

What would she tell him about her past? He would know that Luke Tate had raped her—that she was no longer pure and innocent. But Travis was another story. That was a memory that had to remain locked in her heart forever. She was afraid that if she tried to explain how it was, then something might come out that would show her own confusion as to her real feelings for the man. Nathan might wonder and, dear God, he already would have enough to absorb if ever they should meet again.

❧ Chapter Twenty-seven ❧

KITTY found herself in the midst of another world. Richmond, Virginia, while very aware of the hellish war going on all around it, still continued to flourish with social activities. When units departed for camp, there was a whirl of parties, balls, and religious services. Once the volunteers were in camp, the ladies busied themselves with suppers, bazaars, dances, and other projects to raise funds for their brave defenders. And when soldiers returned home on furlough, they were always treated to a round of social events. They were invited into private homes to talk, sing, and play parlor games.

Kitty heard, also, that the glamorous and gregarious Generals like Stuart, Beauregard, and Morgan—always honored guests at parties and dinners—were showered with attention by females wherever they went. She wondered, a bit jealously, if Nathan were also treated in such a manner. He was handsome and dashing. Women always glanced at him a second time; some flirted openly.

There was a side to life in Richmond, despite the war, that Kitty had never participated in—dances, charades, tableaux, theatricals, musical concerts, receptions, fancy dinners. But as Mary explained about these, Kitty was unimpressed and not interested. How could she make merry and seek entertainment when her heart was breaking?

Andy was somewhere out there fighting with the Yankees; David Stoner, whose mental state was questionable, had stayed behind; she worried about her mother and feared for her father; and beneath it all lay the smoldering love for Nathan, mingled with the twisting guilt she felt over Travis's death. And if he were alive, by some miracle, he must surely hate her, and she had to keep telling herself it did *not* matter. She could not let anything in the past matter. Work was important, helping the sick and wounded. Think about the war, the future. She could not dwell on the past and keep her sanity.

It was almost a week before Captain Culpepper arrived with the news that General Lee had requested that she visit with him.

"You look frightened," the Captain said, laughing as she stood there wide-eyed and open-mouthed.

She blinked. "I guess I'm stunned that he really wants to help me. After all, I'm just another civilian, and General Robert E. Lee has the weight of the whole South on his shoulders right now."

"You don't know much about him if you think you're just another civilian to him." The Captain spoke with a touch of reverence. "He's one of the most thoughtful men I've ever known. He has great compassion for his fellow man. When I told him how you've been helping with the wounded, and what little I know of the suffering you've endured at the hands of the Yankees, well, General Lee felt that the least he could do was talk with you about your Major, whom you're trying to locate."

The next afternoon Kitty found herself in a carriage being taken to the site where Lee's army was encamped. She was surprised to learn that he lived in a tent. Captain Culpepper explained that the General insisted upon a tent, due to his fear that the enemy might take reprisals on any family whose hospitality he might accept.

"I think," he added, "that he might just want to be easily accessible to his staff and his men. There's never a sentry or an orderly needed to protect the cluster of our headquarters' tents from any intruders. The men have such a reverent respect for Lee that it forms an invisible wall around him."

Richmond was the heart of the Confederacy, and however inadequately the supply system operated, Richmond was the supply center for all of Lee's army, with roads and railroads leading to all points of the compass and with a canal to the west. It was the medical center which had grown to accommodate about twenty thousand sick and wounded, and it was also the center of the interlocking system of private and government manufacture of arms, ammunition, and war materiel.

As the carriage moved through the city, Kitty viewed the houses, some lovely, some giving way to decay due to the men of the house being away at war. There were many warehouses and office buildings being used by the government, and the streets were filled with horses, buggies, men and women bustling about. It was a busy place, and Kitty felt dizzy just being there, much less on her way to meet with General Robert E. Lee.

The army tents seemed to sprawl for miles in all directions. The soldiers hardly glanced at the woman passing by in a carriage. Many wives visited their husbands in camp, coming from faraway places by railroad when possible. Some of the young ladies in town, even, boldly visited their sweethearts unchaperoned.

The soldiers, she noted, were dressed quite differently: in the early months of the war, their visored caps, gilt-buttoned frock coats, and stripe-legged pants made privates look like European courtiers. Now most of them were wearing a weather-stained slouch hat, with dented crown and brim turned up in front and back. Their hair was longer, and they mostly had on gray or butternut-colored single-breasted jackets. She had noticed that the buttons on the jacket of the soldier driving the carriage bore the seal of his state. He was from Georgia, he said. The letters "CSA" were embossed on his belt buckle.

Most of the men wore cotton shirts, of which some had collars and some had none. They wore no cravats. Their pants were patched in the seat, frazzled at the cuffless bottoms, and often of a color that did not match their jackets.

But it was their shoes that broke Kitty's heart and made her realize just how greatly the Southern army lacked funds and supplies: the soldiers wore pitifully worn-out shoes, and several, whose feet were propped on barrels as she passed, hardly had any soles left at all. A few even had shoes that actually looked as though they had been carved out of wood!

The soldier driving the wagon reined up the horse in front of a large tent over which the Confederate flag was flying in the gentle June breeze. He stepped down first, then moved to the side of the carriage and held out his hands to encircle Kitty's tiny waist and set her on her feet. Mary had insisted on buying her a new dress to wear to meet the General; it was pale blue organdy and had a modest, high neckline trimmed in lace. She carried a parasol and felt ridiculously uncomfortable with the high neckline scratching under her chin. Every time she turned her head, it rubbed against her flesh.

She was still glancing about the camp, looking at the other tents and the men sitting about playing cards or strumming at banjos, when suddenly the flap of the tent swung back and out stepped a gray-bearded, stockily built man with thinning white hair. But the one feature that impressed her most was his eyes—they were so warm, so compassionate.

"Miss Wright," he said, bowing slightly to kiss the tips of her gloved hand which she held out nervously. She didn't like the custom of men kissing women's hands and never had, and she felt positively awed in front of this man anyway. Why, she felt with a flutter, she should be kissing *his* hand, kneeling before him!

"I'm honored," she murmured, as he stepped back for her to enter the tent.

She was impressed with its neatness and surprised by the starkness of the furnishings. There was a plain, uncomfortable-looking cot, a few chairs, and a large table on which dozens of maps and papers were strewn about. A washbasin and pitcher sat on a smaller table near the cot, and other than a little wood stove, there was nothing to give the room a really lived-in look. But, she reminded herself, this was not an ordinary room—it was a military tent, meant not for comfort but merely for convenience and operations of military forces.

Lee gestured to a chair, and after she was seated, he

placed himself on a bench nearby. He coughed, apologized, and said, "I'm afraid I'm still recuperating from a throat infection I suffered in March, a rheumatic attack, I'm told.

"Now then," he placed his hands on his knees and smiled at her. "Will you have lunch with me? I'm afraid I can only offer you cabbage, corn bread, and buttermilk. These seem to be the only foods that cause me no stress of late."

She declined, too nervous at the moment to even think about eating, but she did accept the cup of hot tea which a soldier brought to her in a tin cup.

Lee watched her quietly, thoughtfully for a few moments, then said, "Captain Culpepper has told me that you have been through a great ordeal, Miss Wright, having been taken from your home in North Carolina against your will, held prisoner by first a Southern traitor and then a Federal cavalryman. I am told also that you seek to find a man named Major Nathan Collins to whom you are betrothed."

She nodded, her heart pounding. Was she really here in the presence of this great, respected man?

"The Confederate army is grateful for the services you have rendered on the battlefield in the hospital tents, and we also grieve over the suffering you have endured. I asked you to come here today . . ." he paused, coughing again briefly, then cleared his voice to continue. "I asked you to come here so that I could personally thank you on behalf of the Confederacy for your services."

"That isn't necessary," she blurted.

He held up a hand for silence and smiled gently. "I want you to know, also, that I have asked a member of my staff to try to locate your Major and have him sent here. The two of you can then decide what is to become of you. If you wish to remain in Richmond, I will see that you are looked after. If you wish to return to North Carolina, I will have you personally escorted by a member of my staff."

She was overwhelmed, and when she could find her voice, said, "I thank you for everything, General . . . sir . . . but what I really want . . ."—she paused, swallowing hard—"is to stay here and wait for Nathan and work in the hospital. I pray to God he's alive, that he will come, but if he's dead, then I still want to remain for a while, anyway, and sort out my thoughts on many things."

Nodding, he said, "We will be proud to have you working in the hospital—and quite grateful. And do pray, my child, for God alone decides our fate. But tell me, do you have family that will worry about your safety? How long is it that you have been away?"

"Since late summer of 1861." Then she told him about her mother, one thing leading to another; and because he was so kind, seemingly so concerned, she found herself telling him about how her mother had turned to drink and her father had left the South to join the Northern army, and finished by apologizing for his actions.

"You owe me no apology, young lady." His voice was stern, eyes grim. "In this war, I have seen father fight against son, brother turn against brother. Each man does what he must when duty calls. Duty must be the guiding rule of any man's life. There is a true glory and a true honor and that is the glory of duty done and the honor of integrity of principle. That, my child, is all the pleasure, all the comfort, and all the glory that man can expect to enjoy on this earth. So do not condemn your father nor apologize for him. He did what his conscience led him to do, as we all must."

She stared at him in respectful wonder and awe. How like her father he was in his principles!

They had talked for almost two hours about the war, about some of her experiences but not the painful ones. He asked her no embarrassing questions, seeking to learn only what had happened to her in relation to the war while with the Federals in an effort, she supposed, to obtain new information about the inner workings of the enemy. It was doubtful she could tell him anything he did not already know, she thought, but he did seem very interested in the conversation between General Rosecrans and Captain Coltrane that she had overheard and her attempts to get to the Confederates with the information.

"A pity you did not," he shook his head sadly, "but what is past is past. Try not to look back. You did what you could.

"Now you rest assured," he told her in parting, "that I will try to locate your Major for you. The agonies of war are enough by themselves without two young people having to worry whether the other is alive or dead."

So Kitty reported for duty at Chimborazo Hospital. Male members of the staff accepted her as another female nurse, until she noted the need for surgical assistants and applied for one of these positions. Then the men gave unmistakable evidence that they resented her presence, but she was able to win most of them over by efficiency and charm, even though a few remained openly hostile. These she ignored.

Kitty hated assisting in the many amputations. To sever the shredded remains of a man's arm or leg was always a heartbreaking experience. Some of them screamed when told amputation was necessary to save their life, and they would beg and plead to be allowed to die. Others would stoically accept the decision, grateful to be given some semblance of a future.

Kitty made rounds at the hospital to visit the patients when she was not with the surgical team. She was called on to write letters for illiterates; sometimes prepared special dishes for those of poor appetite who had to be coaxed to eat. She tried to comfort the homesick, bathed the brows of the feverish, and many nights knelt beside the bed of a dying man and prayed for his immortal soul.

Tragedy . . . misery . . . these passed before her eyes as a part of her daily routine, but she had long ago developed a strength which enabled her to maintain her composure under the most trying and difficult of circumstances. She did not fancy herself as any kind of stoic heroine; she felt she was merely doing a job, a service, and expected no praise, no compliments, wanting only to do her job and be treated as an equal of the men staff members. She never tried to get out of any of the dirty work involved in the hospital operating procedures. She would take up a shovel and help dig ditches in which to bury amputated limbs, and several times, when help was scarce, she had dug trenches for latrines. Of course, she lacked the physical strength of the men, but her spirit was never lacking.

For a few weeks, she had lived in the house with Mary and her family, but she soon tired of the social activities and requested permission to live at the hospital. She was given a small room which she shared with another nurse and all her waking moments she spent working. She was able to keep her mind occupied, so there was little time to think of Travis or wonder if Nathan or her father was alive.

The news of the war flowed through the hospital like the blood on the battlefield, fast and furious. Lee's army had begun a second invasion of the North. The South hoped that Lee could capture an important city such as Harrisburg, Baltimore, or Washington, relieving the pressure on Vicksburg in the west and possibly bringing a victorious peace and an end to the war. There was hope, too, that a great victory on Northern soil would cause England to offer mediation and aid, and there was also the strong desire to transfer the war from the ravaged state of Virginia. Supplies were also terribly scarce for Confederate soldiers. Some were out of shoes. There were reports of starvation. Desertion was becoming more and more common. Morale was getting lower and lower.

With an army at a peak strength of seventy-five thousand men, Lee crossed the Potomac River in the middle of June. Word came that Lincoln had replaced "Fighting Joe" Hooker with a Pennsylvanian named George G. Meade, a General. And by the end of June, a Federal army with a strength reportedly totaling over ninety thousand men was said to be moving northward from Maryland into Pennsylvania in search of the Confederates who had turned southward in search of supplies. Advancing from opposite directions, the two mighty forces collided head-on at Gettysburg, Pennsylvania.

Richmond and the hospital staff waited anxiously for news of the terrible battle said to be exploding. On July 3rd, General George Pickett's men charged across an open field directly against the center of the Federal line. But Pickett's assault failed and half of his men were killed. The battle ended. Vicksburg fell the next day, and Kitty, along with everyone in the South, felt more defeated and emotionally stunned than ever before in the war.

Lee retreated back to Virginia, and both armies took up strong positions on opposite banks of the Rapidan River, each awaiting possible movements by the other. And the wounded poured into the hospital at Richmond, and once again, the world of blood and tears melted into time that seemed to stand still.

It was a hot August afternoon. Kitty sat at the bedside of a young man who had lost both his arms, writing a letter for him. One of the nuns appeared in the doorway of the long room, her eyes searching for someone and then falling on Kitty. She waved frantically.

Kitty got to her feet, told the soldier she would return later to finish his letter.

"Don't hurry," he quipped with amazing good nature. "I might get impatient, though, and finish writing it with my toes."

Impulsively, she leaned over and kissed his cheek, smoothed back his tousled red hair, and then hurried down the aisle that separated the rows of beds to the wide-eyed nun who stood wringing her hands impatiently.

"Kitty, several wagons have arrived crammed full of wounded soldiers, and more are due to arrive any minute." The nun's voice was shaking. "There's been a skirmish somewhere, and our men took quite a beating. The doctors are frantic and have to have help. . . ."

"Well, of course, let's go."

Kitty started through the door, heading for the building where the operating rooms were. The nun reached out and grabbed her arm. "No, please, there's a boy . . ."

Kitty paused, noticing that the woman was crying.

"They say he's done for. It . . . it's my nephew, and the doctors say there are others who are in greater need of help. Please, in the name of God, Kitty, won't you see what you can do?"

Her heart went out to the grief-stricken woman, but Kitty reminded her she did not have the skills of a professional doctor.

"But won't you at least look at him?" she begged, her nails digging into Kitty's arm. "He's out there in that horrible building where they leave them to die so their screams won't be heard over here and frighten the others."

She knew the building and always dreaded having to go there herself. It sat way back at the edge of the hospital compound, and the stench of the dying was overwhelming. Twice she'd had to stumble outside and vomit before she could force herself to tolerate the odor.

"I'll do what I can," she said quietly, knowing in advance

that if the surgeons had turned the boy away, there was nothing to be done for him. There were hundreds of men, all terribly wounded, all waiting their turn for treatment. There was not enough time, or manpower, to try to save the life of a man when it was obvious that his life could not be saved. Word spread about the building known as "The Coffin," and when a soldier realized his stretcher was being taken in that direction, he would sometimes go into such fits that he would have to be tied down. There were reports that several had been so stricken with terror that their hearts had just stopped beating; the soldiers were dead before they ever reached the building.

Kitty paused outside the door and turned to the nun. "Do you think you should go in?" she asked compassionately.

"Oh, yes," the nun answered, nodding quickly. "I spend quite a bit of my time here. My only medicine is prayer, Kitty, and that is all that helps inside. God is the almighty doctor here, and with His help, and yours, a miracle could happen."

Kitty stepped inside. Flies seemed to be everywhere. The air was thick and pungent with the odor of decaying flesh. A few nurses, their faces covered with masks, moved about cleaning up vomit and blood, giving morphine to ease the pain and suffering as much as possible.

The nun led the way to the third bed on the left. A young boy of perhaps sixteen or seventeen lay there. Even with the sheet covering him, Kitty could make out the outline of bowels protruding from the gaping wound in his abdomen. Taking a deep breath, she called to a nurse to bring bandages and morphine.

"They just brought him in a little while ago," the nurse whispered as she handed the items to Kitty. "He's in shock, doesn't know what's going on. Why waste bandages and morphine when it's going to be over soon?"

"Because sometimes you have to think about the living!" Kitty said, more sharply than she intended, nodding to the nun who had fallen to her knees, her crucifix clasped in trembling hands as she murmured her prayers.

She drew back the sheet, swaying at the sight of the exploded belly. How had he lived this long, she wondered.

There was nothing to be done. Most of the lower extremities had been blown away. And, too, both legs would have to be amputated all the way to the trunk.

As Kitty stood there, wondering what to do next, the boy's eyes opened and he looked up at her. She noted they were blue—as blue as the huckleberries back home that grew on the vines around the old barn.

All around them was the smell of death, the sound of men weeping and calling for loved ones, God, or Jesus, and the cries of agony and pain. Flies buzzed noisily in the midsummer heat. Someone vomited. The nun was praying quietly, her words inaudible.

Kitty started to speak, but the boy was moving his lips, his eyes rolling upward. "I . . . see . . . Jesus," he whispered. His head lolled to one side. And she knew he was gone. She felt for a pulse. There was none. She placed her hand over his heart. There was no movement.

Placing her hand on the nun's shoulder, Kitty said quietly, "He's gone. I'm sorry."

The woman stood up, tears streaming down her cheeks as she fingered her rosary, hands still trembling. "What . . . what was that he said," she asked, "just before he died?"

"He said," Kitty repeated for her, "that he saw Jesus."

"Praise God. Jesus took him home. We'll meet again one day." And a joyful smile spread over her face.

Kitty felt the same sense of peace. She had seen men die in agony, and she had seen them pray their agony into the release of a peaceful death. She wondered sometimes which hurt the most, the fight to the end or the quiet acceptance; but she knew that when her time came, she would hope to have the kind of faith that carries a person into eternity with the knowledge that life is not over—but merely beginning.

She pulled the sheet up and over the boy's head. It was then that she heard the voice behind her, speaking her name. At first sound, it was like a dream, a stupor brought on by the shock and tragedy of death and the whole macabre atmosphere of the "Coffin Room."

"Katherine . . . dear God, it *is* you."

She could not move. She continued to stare down at the covered body of the dead soldier, fighting to control the sudden nausea churning in her stomach. It was not real. It was not happening. It could not be so.

A hand touched her shoulder, then fingers tightened to make her turn. Closing her eyes, she would not allow the hope that was rippling through her body to kindle into a flame that would be doused into nothingness.

"No . . ." she whispered, a half-moan rising in her throat. "No . . . it isn't so."

"Katherine, look at me, please . . ." the voice begged.

When she opened her eyes, she was looking at the floor and the first thing she saw was the spit-polished Jefferson boots. Gaze traveling slowly upward, she took in the dark blue trousers with black velvet stripe on each side and edged in gold cord, a bright red sash of silk about the waist of the gray officer's tunic with its black facings on the stand-up collar, gold stars, and the initials "CSA."

And then, realizing that she had to get it over with—face this man and know once and for all that it was just a dream—she lifted her eyes to his face.

Nathan was staring down at her.

❧ Chapter Twenty-eight ❧

FOR over an hour they sat silently beneath the spreading chestnut tree on the little knoll overlooking the hospital compound, too overcome with emotion to speak. Finally, Kitty raised her head, which was pressed against his chest as he held her, and with trembling fingertips traced the dear, familiar lines of his face.

"It is you," she whispered. "How I've prayed for this moment."

"And so have I. Katherine, when I went home after hearing that they'd found Doc's body, and there was no trace of you, I . . ."—his voice shook with emotion—"I wanted to die myself. God, how I've lived in agony these years."

"General Lee told me he'd try to find you for me, but I couldn't believe that a man so important would really find the time, the means, with the war going on."

"I was down in Mississippi with Pemberton's army, and General Lee probably found that out. He probably also thought that I was one of the thirty thousand soldiers who surrendered there on the fourth of July when Vicksburg fell."

She heard the bitterness in his voice. She had read of Pemberton's surrender to General Grant in the *Richmond Daily Dispatch*, and had cried, wondering if Nathan had been among those sent home promising to retire from the

war—or if he was even still alive. Then it dawned on her
that he had been there—and he hadn't gone home. He was
here—in Richmond. Sitting up to stare at him curiously,
she asked, "Then what are you doing here? I read that
Pemberton sent out a white flag through the lines and
asked for terms, and General Grant sent back word there
would be 'unconditional surrender,' but when he realized
Pemberton would not agree to that, Grant said the Confederates could surrender and go home. He was criticized
by Mr. Lincoln for not sending you all to prison."

"I wasn't there *then*," he said meaningfully, and she
blinked, puzzled. "I wasn't going to wait around to see
what would finally happen and maybe wind up rotting in
some Yankee prison for the rest of the war, so me and
some of the other men slipped away."

"Deserted?" she asked cautiously, hating that she remembered David's warning that maybe she wouldn't want
to find Nathan after all. In just the short while they had
been reunited, she sensed the drastic change that had
taken place. Somehow, he was not the same. Of course,
the war had made men of boys, heroes of cowards, and
some just the opposite. And then there was the bitterness.
Who could witness the tragedy of death, the agony, the
horror, and remain the same throughout? She had changed,
also. They would have to get to know each other all over
again, and it would happen because the mutual feeling of
love was still there. She could *feel* it.

"No, I didn't desert." He looked at her as though the
subtle accusation had hurt. "I just didn't want to be a part
of any surrender terms. I didn't go home, did I? I came
here and reported for duty, didn't I?"

"I'm sorry." She was instantly contrite, ashamed for
thinking such thoughts. But she had heard that General
Lee had sent word to the Secretary of War that there had
been frequent desertion from the North Carolina regiments, and only three months ago, Lee had written to the
Secretary to say that unless something was done immediately, the number of North Carolina troops in his army
would be drastically reduced. But morale was extremely
low, and desertion was common among the soldiers. She
was just glad that Nathan was not himself a deserter.

He hugged her, pressing her back against his chest.

"Thank God, I did come here instead of heading home. I wouldn't have gotten word that you were here. I just reported in, said that me and my men had somehow gotten separated from our unit, and then someone told me about you and how General Lee had asked that I be located, if possible. I can't believe you're really here, Katherine, in my arms." He kissed her forehead gently. "Tell me, all of it."

She took a deep breath and said, "It's been a nightmare that I'd just like to forget, Nathan. Let's just be thankful that we're together again."

"But *how* did you get here?" he persisted, his voice firmer, almost commanding.

She chose her words carefully, telling him only that she had been held prisoner by the Yankees, made to work in their hospitals, and finally escaped, thanks to the help of David Stoner. She explained how David's mental state had changed since he lost an arm, how he had stayed behind with the grief-stricken family in Tennessee that had "adopted" him as their own.

"He married Nancy Warren, you know," she added.

When he didn't speak, she looked up to see the faraway look in his eyes, the glint of suppressed anger. Wanting to change the subject, she asked, "Nathan, when were you last home? I haven't heard from my mother, though I wrote to her after I reached Richmond. Andy told me she was drinking a bit heavily."

"Andy?" He raised an eyebrow.

"You remember Andy Shaw."

"Yes. I thought he was killed at Shiloh."

"I found him on the battlefield."

"What I want to know"—he sat up straight, releasing her from his arms, his eyes blazing furiously—"is what happened to you and Doc Musgrave? Did the Yankees kill him?"

When she didn't, couldn't speak, he grasped her shoulders with his white-gloved hands and shook her. "Tell me, Katherine. What happened? I have a right to know, damn-it."

"Talking about it brings back the pain," she said, fighting back the tears that were once again stinging her eyes. "It's best to leave everything in the past where it can't hurt anybody."

But he insisted, and finally she began to cry and the whole story tumbled out in choking sobs. And then for a long time there was no sound, except Kitty crying softly, until an agonized scream drifted up from the hospital below. She shuddered. Someone had died or was dying, or had been told an arm or leg would have to be amputated. There was suffering and torture down there . . . and also here on the wind-swept hilltop in the late August sunshine.

Suddenly Nathan was leaping to his feet, his gloved hand knotting into a fist that went slamming into the tree trunk so viciously that when he withdrew it, blood was already seeping through the white cotton. He swore beneath his breath, and Kitty, frightened, stepped back.

"After all this time," he said through gritted teeth, "I find you, Katherine, and you're still the most beautiful girl I've ever seen, and I still love you and want you for my wife. But goddamn it, it's hard to take, realizing that you've been raped—and don't try to tell me you haven't!"

His eyes blazed into hers. She hadn't told him the details —just that she'd been held prisoner first by Luke Tate, then Travis Coltrane. "I'm no fool!" he raved. "I know you weren't with those men all this time without them raping you."

"Do you think I liked it?" she screamed at him, angry herself. "You think I wanted it to happen? Any of it? You were the one, you and all the others, who thought war was going to be so great, so glorious. You couldn't wait to march off in your fancy uniforms with the bugles blowing and the drums beating and everyone cheering and waving. And I've seen the blood and guts on the battlefield, and I've seen the suffering and the dying and the mutilated and the maimed—and I've suffered, too, and I've died a little, too, and I've hated every damn moment of it, and you stand there and act like I've committed some heinous crime because I was kidnapped against my will and raped?"

She turned away from him, trembling in rage. Why had she allowed herself to lose control? This wasn't the way it was supposed to be! This was supposed to be a tender, beautiful time, not an angry exchange.

She felt his hands touch her shoulders gently, heard the huskiness of his voice as he said, "I'm sorry, Katherine. I didn't mean to hurt you. It just tears me apart to think of what you must have gone through. God, don't you know I would have fought to my death to defend your honor? But I'll try not to think about any of it. We'll pretend it never happened and go on from here together."

He turned her around. "Oh, Katherine, if you only knew how much I love you!" And he grabbed her, kissing her until her lips felt bruised, and she tried to return the kiss with equal fervor.

Why, she wondered with a flash of guilt, did she not feel the feverish surge of passion that Travis had been able to arouse so easily? Travis had not been the marrying kind, had known many women's bodies, knew how to make them wild with desire. Yet, she had allowed herself to enjoy his lovemaking, and it was remembering this that made her feel ashamed to be in Nathan's arms, receiving his kiss. But the guilt would pass. It had to. She could not let it destroy the future.

When at last he released her, they sat back down under the tree and he told her about the men from Wayne County who had been killed. She grieved for each but rejoiced that others had returned home, even if they were injured. At least they had lived. Nathan told her that there were not many left of the original Wayne Volunteers, that they had spread out into other units in the confusion of so many different battles and skirmishes.

"The war doesn't look good for the South at all," he said gloomily. "I hear things aren't good back home, either."

"You never did tell me if you knew anything about my mother," she said quietly.

He dug the heel of one boot into the ground, and she could tell he did not want to talk about it. Finally, he said, "The last I heard, in a letter from my mother, your mother has turned into the town drunkard."

A stab of pain went through her. "I . . . I can't believe that. Maybe she's heard that Poppa is dead and she's turned to the bottle. I mean, a woman can be so grief-stricken she could turn to whiskey to dim the pain of losing her husband. . . ." She was babbling, shaking her head from side to side, not willing to accept either the realization of her mother's condition or the possibility that her father might be dead.

Nathan, beside her, took a deep breath. "No, Katherine, your father is not dead. In fact, from all I hear, he's very much alive. But if he ever returns to Wayne County, he'll be hanged."

"I don't understand." She looked at him in astonishment.

"Have you heard about the cavalry raids going on in western Tennessee? Have you heard about Grierson's raiders? Well, your father is said to ride with him, wrecking railroads, killing anyone who gets in their way. General Nathan Forrest is making some attacks for our side, thank God, but Grierson is doing a lot of damage, and your father is riding right alongside him."

Kitty felt herself swaying. Grierson was the cavalryman whom Travis had been assigned to ride with. Had he known then that John Wright would be riding with them also? Dear God, if so, why hadn't he told her? Or maybe he had planned to, had she not escaped, had he not been killed.

"Katherine, are you all right?" Nathan was gathering her in his arms, concern etched in his face. "I'm sorry. I shouldn't have been so blunt about it, but everyone back home knows about it. Your father was seen by one of your neighbors, Wiley Cox. In fact, he even shot at Wiley, but missed, and Wiley got away."

"Travis was to have gone with Grierson . . ." she said, speaking more to herself than to Nathan. "I heard General Rosecrans give him his orders. He must have known Poppa was with them. Why didn't he tell me?"

"Travis? Coltrane? The Yankee who kept you prisoner? How'd he know about your father? Just what all did you tell him?" He was getting angry again and Kitty no longer wanted to argue. Her mind was whirling dizzily as she tried to sort out the bits and pieces of all that had happened in the past few hours.

"Travis is dead," she said finally. "He was killed by one of his own men, trying to keep him from shooting me . . . as David and I were escaping . . . running away. Try to understand, Nathan, I kept those men alive—some of them. Many of them died. I was all they had for medical aid of any kind. I nursed Travis through an illness, saved his leg from amputation, saved his best friend from a snake bite. We grew to be friends. In the end, even though he was my captor and I, the prisoner, he couldn't kill me when I was escaping. He saved my life—and lost his own."

Her voice caught on a sob, and Nathan snapped, "Katherine, I just don't want to talk about any more of this. You make me feel like there was something between you two. I've already got horrible images dancing around in my head of you with all those men. . . ."

"There were only two!" she snapped, jerking her head up to glare at him. "I don't grieve for Travis, but I owe him my life. After all is said and done, he was still the enemy and I still pledge my allegiance to the Southern cause. And if you will let me, and let yourself, I'd like nothing better than to mention none of this ever again."

"We'll go on from here." He got to his feet, pulled her up once again. "And we'll concentrate on the war around us and the future, if there is one."

He began to lead her down the hill. Somewhere a bird was singing, but Kitty did not take it as an omen of happiness to come.

❧ Chapter Twenty-nine ❧

TRAVIS reached inside his greatcoat, then under his shirt. His fingers were wet with blood. The ball had entered the flesh below the ribs on the left side and gone right through tearing a rough hole in his back as it ripped its way free. Shuddering, he felt the exit hole. The wound wasn't all that bad. At least the ball wasn't still in him. He'd been in the war long enough to know it was rougher when the ball stayed inside a man. There was a lot of bleeding, but the pain wasn't so bad—not yet. Fingers probing around the edge of the wound, he felt numbness.

Well, if I've got to be hit, it's the best kind of wound to have, he thought realistically. But it hadn't come with bugles blowing and drums beating in some kind of glorious charge. No, when Grant had ordered a brigade of cavalry to come down from the Tennessee border, riding between the parallel north-south line of the Mississippi Central and the Mobile and Ohio railroads, it was no glorious charge. Led by Colonel Benjamin H. Grierson, they had hit hard and fast without warning.

And it had been successful, Travis thought with a wry grin. They had sliced right through the length of the state, cutting railroads, fighting detachments of Confederate cavalry, and finally reached the Union lines at Baton Rouge. For the few days when it had counted the most, Pemberton's attention had been drawn away from General

Grant and kept him from figuring out what the Yankees were driving at.

Pemberton had surrendered Vicksburg on the fourth of July. Grierson and his men could head back into Tennessee to continue their cavalry raids and try their damndest to track down Nathan Bedford Forrest and his Confederate cavalry.

Only Travis had decided to do some scouting on his own, and some stinking Rebel had ambushed him, but not before he fired his own rifle and killed the Rebel. But here he was lying in a muddy ditch and the pain was starting to come. And I'm going to die in this goddamn ditch, he thought, as blackness began to sweep over him.

Opening his eyes, he reached down dizzily and scooped up some of the brackish water to rub across his face.

Damn! There she was again. Kitty's face swam before him. He swore to put all thoughts of her out of his mind. Then, just when he thought he'd succeeded, she would come creeping up on him again. He should have let that soldier shoot her when he didn't have the guts to. Hell, he should've shot her himself. Murfreesboro had been crawling with Federals. Who would have thought that two soldiers couldn't guard a hundred Reb prisoners inside a stockade? Who would have thought that a woman would succeed in helping them escape? Maybe fifteen or twenty had gotten away. The rest had been shot down in the street. And Kitty wouldn't have succeeded in her plans if he hadn't let his guard down.

But those eyes. He could almost see them in the darkness, shining with either passion or anger, flashing like a thousand lightning bolts on a stormy night. He could almost feel her body against his—warm, supple, giving, taking. He could smell the fragrance of the pine needles in her hair. Clean. She always managed to stay clean when the rest of them were practically rotting in their own filth.

Damnit, why couldn't he get her out of his mind? She'd almost gotten him killed. The soldier he'd grappled with that night was probably nothing but bones by now—and it could have been *him*. Why hadn't he shot her? All that time she was pretending allegiance to the North and it had been a trick to catch him off guard. All along she'd planned to escape at the first opportunity.

He leaned his head back against the rocky wall of the shallow ditch. Damnit, here in the silence of the night he had to admit to himself that he had loved her. Maybe he still did. But the hate, the anger were stronger. He prayed that someday their paths would cross and then he would make her pay for double-crossing him and for making him love her and then betraying him.

The wound was not so bad, he thought. Maybe he could still ride if he could get out of the ditch and find his horse. He might make it back to the camp. Hell, what had he wanted to go out scouting for anyway? Nobody asked him to. He just liked to be by himself, knowing that visions of Kitty would come to his mind. Why did he torture himself this way? She was probably back home with her Rebel boy-friend, married, maybe even going to have a baby. He hoped she *was* carrying a baby. *His* baby. Wouldn't that be funny—for her to escape and run for home with a Yankee growing inside of her?

The pain was getting worse. Damn, if he could get up, get to a horse, and get back to camp, someone could patch him up, stop the bleeding. If he stayed here, he was going to die. Forcing himself, gritting his teeth against the pain, he pulled himself out of the ditch, slowly crawling on his hands and knees through the scrubby underbrush. Would that fool horse come when he called her? He hadn't had her long and she wasn't all that well trained.

Suddenly he heard voices and then saw a pine torch flaring in the darkness. They're Rebs, he thought in panic. The drawl of the voices was deep, slow, and then he heard one say, "I swear, Cap'n, I know it was a Yankee and Zeb shot him and he shot Zeb deader'n hell."

And now they're going to find me and finish killing me *deader'n hell*. Travis silently mocked the Southern accent. They'll finish killing me. They won't take me prisoner, he thought. They'll want their revenge. Out here, away from the order and precision of planned battles, few prisoners were taken, he remembered. He'd shot a few Rebs himself rather than fool with taking them prisoner.

He flattened himself in the underbrush, holding his breath as he heard the soldiers pass within a few yards of where he lay. "Go look along the ditch," someone ordered. Travis was absolutely still.

It seemed like hours but was only a matter of minutes before the Confederate Captain told his men to discontinue their search. "Zeb probably didn't hit him. If he had, he wouldn't be dead himself. Let's take his body back and bury him before we move out."

The footsteps and voices faded away. So they weren't that far off, Travis thought. When daylight came, he had to be away from here or they would find him. And if he could make it back to camp and report their location, Grierson and the others could attack and clean out a hornet's nest of Rebs.

Blood seemed to be pouring out of the wound. How much longer did he have? How long was it before a man bled to death? He didn't know. Maybe he should have called out to the Rebs, taken a chance on them taking him prisoner. He was getting weaker. He would never find his horse and be able to get out of there.

"Coltrane . . ."—it was a barely audible whisper—"you out here?"

If he knows my name, then he has to be one of us, Travis thought excitedly. "Here," he answered. "I'm hit."

Footsteps moved through the brush; a figure squatted down beside him. "How bad?"

"I think the ball went all the way through, but I'm bleeding bad." It was the man with the patch over his eye, Travis realized. He felt a wet nose nuzzle his cheek. Killer, the old hounddog that the one-eyed man kept at his side at all times, was whimpering his sympathy.

"There's a nest of Rebs close by," Travis told him quickly, afraid he might pass out and die before he was able to give the vital information. "Tell the others."

He felt himself being lifted in the man's arms, and then closed his eyes.

"You missed all the fun."

Travis opened his eyes to see the one-eyed man peering down at him, his face covered almost completely by the beard and the patch. One jaw protruded, filled with tobacco juice; he spat on the ground and then turned and held out a tin of coffee. "We routed them Rebs and killed every last one of 'em. Body count was twenty-three. Even got some right nice guns. Horses, too. Grierson says he's

356

much obliged to you for finding 'em, even if you did nearly get killed doing it."

"How bad am I hit?" Travis moved his left hand to his chest and felt the bandage.

"Clean wound. We got the bleeding stopped, packed you full of lint after filling it with whiskey. You'll make it. Probably be laid up a few weeks, but the Colonel says there's a little settlement nearby that our boys have taken over, and we can rest up there for a spell. He's going to wait for further orders from Grant before moving out."

Travis sipped at the coffee, wrinkling his nose in distaste. "Damn, what was this brewed out of? I can't remember the last time I had a decent cup of coffee."

John Wright chuckled. "I believe they brewed it from potatoes and parched peanuts. You better hope we get to that settlement. I hear supper is going to be stew."

"That's not so bad."

"It is when the meat for it is pulled off a horse so dead that the bones were pulling apart."

"Suddenly, the coffee tastes real good and I think it will hold me till we get to town."

Travis was lying on a blanket and covered with another, his head resting on a saddle. He looked around and saw that the other men were working on their rifles or playing cards—relaxing after killing twenty-three Rebs.

"How come you found me?" Travis remembered the night before, when all seemed hopeless. "What were you doing out there and how'd you know where I was?"

John nodded his head to where his dog lay sleeping, head on his paws. "Killer can track anything that walks, even your horse. I got there just before the Rebs did and I hid and heard them talking. When they said a Yankee had shot one of their men, I figured it was you. I'd heard a couple of shots a ways back."

Travis could tell by the way the man was looking at him that something was on his mind. "You had a reason for following me. What was it?"

He spat again, then looked him straight in the eyes and said, "I've been meaning to talk to you for quite a spell, Coltrane, ever since Andy Shaw told me about Kitty . . . and you."

Travis sighed, stared up into the branches of the tree

above. It was a hot day and the sun was blazing everywhere but there in the shade. He had known for quite a while that John Wright was Kitty's father, even before Andy told him. He knew the day he reported to Colonel Grierson and saw the man with the patch over his eye and the hounddog at his side and heard his soft Southern drawl, not quite as deep as that of the men from Alabama and Georgia, but Southern just the same. He had kept his distance for several reasons. First, he hadn't wanted to discuss Kitty, and he didn't figure her father would take kindly to him for having kept her a prisoner of sorts instead of sending her home when he raided Luke Tate's hide-out.

He looked back to meet John's gaze and he couldn't tell whether or not he was angry. He just looked like a man who had something he wanted to settle. "I knew who you were, Wright, and I had all ideas you knew about me and your daughter," he said finally.

John nodded. "I was surprised to see Andy Shaw riding with the Federals, you can be sure of that. I've known the boy since he was born. Naturally, I asked him plenty of questions and I felt like he was holding something back. Finally, he had to get it out of him and he told me about Kitty—and about you. At first, I was plenty mad. It hurt like hell to know she was mixed up in this damned war. Sure, I went off and left her and her ma, but a man does what he has to do."

"She told me about what happened to you."

John didn't acknowledge the statement but continued: "I was plenty burned up about Luke Tate kidnapping her. I'm no fool. I know why he did it and what he done to her. If I ever meet up with the son of a bitch, one of us will die, you can bet your life on that. But then I got to thinking about how you didn't send her home. I know she knows plenty about doctoring. Hell, she followed Doc Musgrave around from the time she could walk, almost. But she's still a woman, a young woman, and you should have sent her home. And she's also a *beautiful* young woman and I've got my own notions as to why you *didn't*."

Now Travis could see anger beginning to smolder in the man's eyes. He started to speak but decided it best at this point to let him have his say.

"We had a job to do and we did it; and I made up my mind that if I came out of it alive and you did, too, we'd have this talk. I want to know what you did to my girl and where she is now. All Andy knows is what you told him—that she escaped with a Confederate prisoner."

Travis nodded. "I don't know what happened to her, John. She tricked me, made me think she might be falling in love with me. I got careless, gave her too much freedom, and the next thing I knew, she'd helped set free a compound full of Reb prisoners. I could have killed her, had a gun right on her, but she kept on riding. I wound up having to kill one of my own men because he was about to do what I couldn't."

If he had expected sympathy, Travis was in for a surprise. John laughed. "That sounds like my girl. She's got more spunk than most men. She would've kept on riding no matter what if her mind was made up. And I'm not surprised that she tricked you into thinking she loved you. She's smart, that one."

His eyes grew stormy again, and he pointed his finger at Travis. "You better hope she's alive. You better hope I don't find out she's dead. If you'd sent her home when you first found her, she'd be back home in North Carolina where she belongs instead of God only knows where. There's a war going on now and I turned my back on my people, but I'm not going to turn my back on the army I've joined and start shooting at you. But you can believe one thing, when it's finally over, I'll settle up with you on the matter of my daughter's honor. You heed me well, boy."

Travis tried to sit up but couldn't. His head fell back and he took a few deep breaths. He was weak, but he had to say what was burning inside. "John, I'm going to admit to you what I haven't been able to admit to myself. I did fall in love with your daughter, but right now I could kill her myself for using me the way she did. I guess I thought she'd fallen in love with me, too, but I was dead wrong. Now I didn't hurt your girl, not the way Luke Tate did, and I'm going to settle a score with him, too, if ever we meet.

"As for how you feel about me, I can understand your resentment. But if you want to kill me, you do it now.

Don't shoot me in the back in the middle of a skirmish. I've got enough on my mind without worrying about another traitor."

John snarled at him, "Goddamn you, boy, you better be glad you're flat on your back wounded, or I'd whip you with my bare hands for calling me a traitor."

"You raised one." Travis grinned. "I figured you two were alike."

"You'll probably have to answer to someone else besides me," John warned him then. "Kitty was betrothed to someone, and he won't take kindly . . ."

"Nathan Collins," Travis sneered. "I've heard about him from Kitty. I'm not worried. I doubt any of us will ever meet again anyway unless it's in hell."

They were silent for several moments. Then John lifted an eyebrow curiously and asked, "You still love my girl?"

"The resentment over what she did is too fresh, too bitter, for me to think of much else. Maybe it's best things turned out like they did. I'm not the marrying kind."

"Can't say as I'd want my daughter marrying your kind anyway."

Travis retorted angrily, "What in hell makes you think you can look down on me, Wright? You walked out on your wife and your daughter, never looked back. Andy tells me your wife was turning into a drunk when he left to join the war. Don't you care?"

"Man does what he has to."

"You've said that before."

"I'll say it again. You're from the South. How come you're killing your own kind?"

"That's my business."

"Then don't pry into mine. Just remember, we've got a score to settle one day."

"Just let me know when."

They glared at each other. John got to his feet. His dog got up also. They started walking away and Travis called out, "By the way, thanks for saving my life."

John kept on walking and Travis closed his eyes wearily. Well, it had finally happened, he thought with some semblance of relief. He had known it would come sooner or later—the time when it would come out about Kitty. Damn Andy Shaw. Why did he have to go and tell John about it anyway? But it was only natural, he supposed. Well, at least he didn't have to dread anything any time soon. They both knew where the other stood and neither was afraid. Travis had great admiration for John Wright's courage and bravery. He'd seen him in battle, knew he was every bit the fighter people said he was. But he had a good name, too, he reminded himself. If they ever did have it out, it would be a match all right.

Someone came to tell him that the Colonel was moving out, and Travis was grateful. Maybe in the little town they would find a bed for him, a real bed, where he could rest and regain his strength.

When they moved him, he cried out in pain and the trip into town was rough and uncomfortable. Colonel Grierson came and told him there was a young woman in town who was caring for sick soldiers. The only doctor around had been killed a few weeks before. She agreed to take Travis in and look after him. Her cabin was small and shabby, but there were a few beds. Anything, he figured, was better than sleeping on the ground.

When Travis first laid eyes on Bonnie Pelham, if he had been a praying man, he would have given thanks right then and there for his good fortune.

"Just bring him right on in here," she had said, grinning at the soldiers carrying the stretcher. "I'll take extra good care of him because my last patient reported back to duty this morning. Less'n some of you get sick, he'll be all alone here."

"Make sure you bastards stay well," Travis had quipped.

One of them laughed, saying, "You won't be up to any action for a while, Captain. And we'll see to it you have plenty of visitors."

Bonnie tucked him into bed and he looked around the room. It was sparsely furnished and smelled of pine wood.

"You like my little cabin?" she asked as she handed him a cup of fresh cool water. "Me and my husband built it with the help of our neighbors before he went off to war and got himself killed."

Travis sipped the water, looked up into her big, brown eyes, and said bluntly, "You don't sound like a grieving widow."

"Oh, you know how it is," she replied. "You grow up in

the mountains and you don't have much say-so about who you marry up with. It's mostly always arranged by the old folks. I knew I was gonna have to marry Bill-Bob by the time I was old enough to know what marrying was."

"Didn't you love him?"

She shrugged. "Don't rightly know. I never really knew much about love. I was told a proper girl gets herself proper-married, has babies, and takes care of her husband. That's what I was aiming to do, but Bill-Bob went off and got himself killed and now I reckon I'm about the youngest widow in the mountains."

She walked around the room as she told him how she'd used a mixture of flour and water to paste paper over the boards to keep out the winter chill. In the corner there was an oak chair that her father had carved and a dressing table that her husband had made from cherrywood that had since lost its redness. There was a bench of hickory and propped in one corner, a broom made of hickory splits.

"See my linen curtains?" Bonnie asked proudly, holding one out for him to view. "I made them from flax I broke myself, and I dyed them myself, too, from blue dye I boiled out of alder bark. I even made that quilt that's covering you from cotton my daddy grew. And that blanket? My daddy's got some sheep if you Yankees ain't butchered them all by now, and me and my momma carded and spun that wool from those sheep and made that blanket. And those sheets you're lying on? I made them, too. Even stuffed that mattress with feathers I pulled from many an angry goose!"

Travis suddenly wondered if he should be so thankful for his plight after all. "How come you're telling me all this?" he asked curiously.

"Well, I'm a widow-woman now," she said with the frank honesty of a child. "And I've got to get me a husband quick, Poppa says. Poppa says it ain't proper for me to be keeping men here when I ain't married to 'em, even if I am doctoring. I figure maybe some lonesome Yankee will come through here and be right proud to marry up with a widow-woman who can fix up a cabin the way I have this one."

"Maybe one will one day." He closed his eyes and prayed for quick recovery.

He felt her sitting down beside him on the bed and his eyes flashed open. "I have to check that wound of yours," she said, as she reached and pulled the bandage away from his side, making a face. "I've got to make some salve to go on that. And you're going to need to rest so's you won't start bleeding again."

She went and got a jar and spread some foul-smelling paste onto his wound. He winced beneath her painful touch. Then she got some clean linen and made a new bandage.

"Now then. I'm going to fix you something good to eat. How would you like some chicken stew? I've some in the pot cooking, but when those soldiers outside start smelling it, they're going to be in here."

He nodded. She was probably a good cook.

He was right. The stew was delicious, and it was the best meal he'd had in quite a while. She even brought him fresh milk that was cooling in a nearby mountain stream. He felt stronger already. Maybe it wouldn't take so long to heal after all.

She sat on the side of the bed and stared at him.

"Why are you looking at me like that?" he asked, a bit annoyed. She wasn't really unattractive, but when she grinned it was more of a grimace.

"I know how to make a man happy," she said meaningfully, running her fingertips down the side of his bearded face.

Then she laughed. "You know, you're about the handsomest fellow that's come through here. You got the prettiest eyes. Not really blue, not really gray. And you got a nice body, too."

Travis squirmed uncomfortably. "Will you ask Sam Bucher to come in, please? I need to see him." He knew he had to get her out of there.

"But I'll be right outside if you need me," she said, smiling.

When she'd gone, Travis looked up at the roof of the log cabin and cursed. He had to get out of here—and soon. What were the orders? Sam would have to find out from Colonel Grierson. He was anxious to get back into the fighting as soon as possible. And maybe he was even anxious to ask questions and find out what he could about

Kitty. But that was ridiculous to even think about, he thought, admonishing himself. They would probably never meet again—and maybe it was just as well. He couldn't be sure of what he would do if they *did* meet!

The door to the cabin was kicked open and Sam Bucher walked in, grinning broadly.

"If I were able, I'd wipe that grin off your ugly face," Travis snapped.

"But you ain't able," Sam laughed, straddling a chair and leaning his chin on the back of it. "You been fixed up yet? I hear Bonnie knows how to nurse a man back to health." He laughed again.

"Sam, you listen to me." Travis tried to sit up but couldn't. "You talk to Colonel Grierson and tell him to get me out of here. I'll sleep on the damn ground, anything, but if I stay here and he doesn't run that trollop out of town, the whole camp's going to have the pox."

Sam allowed as to how this was possible. "I'll see what I can do. He's probably had time to hear as much about her as the rest of us by now. We thought she was some kind of nurse, but when I started hearing from the others how she is, me and the rest of the boys laughed our heads off thinking about you here at her mercy."

Travis reached out for the tin cup of water left on the stool by his bed and sent it sailing across the cabin toward Sam, but Sam ducked, still chuckling. "Now don't be mad at me, old friend. It's not my fault you're here, and I'll do what I can to get you out. Now, is that all you wanted with me? We're fixing to get a hot keno game going. Some of the boys found some 'red-eye' and we're going to have ourselves a time tonight."

"You can find out what's happening in the war. I'd like to know where we go from here."

"Well, with Lee getting his tail beat at Gettysburg and Pemberton surrendering Vicksburg, I'd say things are looking up for us and down for the Rebs. Lee's retreated to Virginia and our armies are both holding strong positions on the opposite banks of a river called the Rapidan, waiting for the other side to make the first move. From what I hear, it's going to be one skirmish after another as we run into Reb patrols."

"I just want to get out of here."

"Well, I'll see what I can do. . . ."

"I just want the damned war to end."

"And then what will you do? Go look for Kitty?"

Travis glared at him. "You know, Sam, you're my best friend, but you've got a way of griping my ass at times."

"I've got a way of hitting at the truth, old boy, and you know it. You love that girl, and she loves you."

"Yeah, well then why did she run away? For all she knows, she left me behind to die. She didn't know who got shot—me or that other bastard."

Travis pursed his lips and waited for an answer to that one. Sam was not long in firing one back at him. "I can't blame her for escaping when she got the chance. After all, did you ever admit you loved her? Did you two ever do anything besides fence with each other about your real feelings? And don't forget, she's a Rebel at heart and she's a stubborn gal, too. She's also been through hell, and she was confused and didn't know what she wanted. Don't fault her too much. War does strange things to people."

Travis scowled. "Just why do you keep insisting I'm in love with her?"

Sam got to his feet, pushed the chair aside, hooked his thumbs in his belt, and smiled. "Well, if you don't love her, you sure do think about her a lot."

"And just what in hell makes you think that? You so damned smart you see inside other people's minds?"

"No." He walked toward the door. "But I sure hear folks when they talk in their sleep, 'specially when they're calling names."

And he walked out, closing the door behind him.

❦ Chapter Thirty ❧

KITTY was reluctant to take a furlough from her work at the hospital. There were so many hundreds of wounded soldiers who needed care, and doctors and nurses were in short number. Nathan kept urging her to go away for a while, so they could get to know each other all over again and regain some of the closeness they had lost. He also pointed out how weary she looked, how he feared for her health and well-being. When she repeatedly resisted, he went to one of the doctors in her unit and insisted that he grant Kitty the furlough that she did not want.

"I wish you hadn't done that, Nathan," she said when he came for her in the carriage. "I don't like you meddling in my business this way."

He shrugged. "Katherine, you always were a stubborn young woman. You just can't see how you're wearing yourself out. Have you looked in the mirror lately? You're showing signs of age all because of the long hours you work in that hospital. And you know I don't feel that a woman belongs in such a place."

"You're still bossy," she pointed out. "You refuse to believe that a woman might have some other purpose in this life besides pleasing a man, having his babies, and sitting at home sewing and cooking."

"You're forgetting that I love you." He leaned over and kissed her cheek as the carriage bounced along the rutted road. "And if I'm selfish, then so be it. I want you all to myself—as my wife."

She frowned. In the past weeks ever since their reunion, they had talked about marriage, but something deep within told her that the time was not right. Not now. Not in the middle of the war. Still, she reminded herself that Nathan was her true love and they were pledged to each other. Maybe he was right. Going home—as Nathan's wife—to wait for his return seemed more and more appealing to her: had she not seen too much suffering and dying, and endured such nightmares herself?

He told her that he had been able to find a room for her at the hotel in Richmond where he was staying during his furlough. "Prices are so high and the hotels are so crowded, what with families flocking in either to seek shelter from the foraging Yankees or to visit kin at the Chimborazo. I hear coffee is selling for a dollar fifty a pound now and tea for fifteen dollars. Writing paper is even selling for fifteen cents a sheet. Some of the men are even writing home on shreds of wallpaper or wrapping paper—anything they can find. And tobacco! If you can find it, it's too high for an ordinary soldier."

"I wonder if things are any better at home."

"I don't know, Katherine." He sounded worried. "I want us to go there as soon as possible and find out. We can read the papers, but we won't know the whole story until we go there ourselves."

Kitty had only one other muslin dress besides the one she wore and both were hopelessly bloodstained. Nathan insisted that he take her shopping right away. "There's a ball in the hotel tonight and I intend to have the most beautiful girl in all of Richmond on my arm."

"I can't let you buy a dress for me, Nathan. It seems like old times, though, doesn't it?" she remembered sadly. "The first time you ever came calling, you invited me to a party and I didn't have a dress to wear."

He patted her knee, smiling. "One day, my love, you shall be the best-dressed woman in all of Wayne County. Your clothes will come from the finest fashion houses in Europe, designed just for you. Every woman around will look up to you—your style, your position, your beauty. For now, I want to buy a dress for you to wear tonight, a special night for both of us. I plan to present you to all my friends in Richmond and announce that soon we'll be married. Soon we can put the past behind us."

She glanced at him curiously. There were times when Nathan would stare at her moodily, lapsing into a deep silence, and she would wonder if he was remembering Luke Tate and Travis Coltrane, perhaps conjuring up an image of her in their arms. Was this the reason he talked of marriage as though it was something that had to take place quickly? Did he, perhaps, think that once they were legally wed, her body would belong to him and him alone and he could forget about the other men in her life? If so, then it would be a mistake. Nathan was a proud man, and it would take much for him ever to forget. She doubted that he ever would.

He was different somehow. He stood in his uniform with military straightness, his pistol in its holster, his scabbard smartly slapping his polished high boots, the spurs gleaming brightly. Major Nathan Collins, C.S.A.—proud and, in a way, arrogant. She had seen the way he barked orders to soldiers when they were around and the way some of them snarled at him behind his back. He was obviously disliked by those under his command. And once she did ask him about it.

And he laughed.

"Everyone is out to get an officer, Katherine. Especially the Yankees. Just like we tell our soldiers: officers don't live in heaven. Shoot them first. Aim to wound and not to kill because a wounded man is more of a problem to an army than a dead one—especially a wounded officer. No one is going to leave him behind."

"But why do your men dislike you?" she persisted.

He frowned, obviously annoyed that she was pursuing the subject further. "Katherine, I have to command my men, not coddle them. They have to learn to do what I tell them to do, *when* I tell them to do it. If it means a whipping, putting them in stocks, tying them to a caisson— whatever—I will do it and they know it and they dislike me. But they respect me and that is more important."

And she wondered.

When they arrived at the hotel, Kitty felt extremely

tired. "Please, just send up the dress you'd like for me to wear. If I'm to attend a party tonight, then I must rest." She could not remember when she had last slept, although she did recall that a young soldier, of perhaps only fifteen or sixteen, had been dying. In his delirium, he had thought Kitty was his mother and begged her not to leave him. And she hadn't. He had lingered for two nights, and she had sat wearily by his bed, holding his hand, comforting him when he screamed out in agony. When Nathan had found her slumped over the dead boy's bed, exhausted, he had gone to the officer in charge to demand that she be given a furlough.

"Very well," Nathan agreed. "I'll send up a bath and a servant to help you dress later."

The moment she was alone, Kitty fell across the bed and was instantly asleep. Several hours later—though it seemed to her that she had slept only a few moments—she awoke to the sound of rapping at the door.

A black woman was outside the door; behind her were two more servants carrying a large tub. The procession began once again as buckets of hot water were brought in for her bath. Kitty insisted she could bathe herself, but the woman was firm. "Major Collins told me I got to bathe you myself, 'cause you is too tired, and he wants you to feel good tonight. Ever'body talking about that party. He got you a fine dress, and I gonna fix you up pretty. You just leave it all to Maybelle."

So for the first time in her life Kitty allowed herself to be bathed. She was washed and then powdered with something that had a delicate, subtle fragrance, like the magnolias back home when they bloomed in the summertime.

Maybelle brought in the clothes Nathan had purchased. There were silk drawers, a silk chemise, silk stockings, and shoes. The fit was perfect. Nathan knew her size just by looking at her—and holding her in his arms, she thought with a smile.

And then the woman brought in the dress, a mist of blue taffeta trimmed in delicate lace.

"You sho' got nice breasts," Maybelle said bluntly, helping her with the dress. "You don't need no stays. Lots of women would give anything for breasts like yours. You sho' better make sho' when you have the Major's babies that you got somebody to suck them young'uns, or you won't keep yo' shape. You can be sho' of that."

Nathan's babies. A warmth spread to her cheeks, but it was not a feeling brought on by desire. Actually, it dawned on her that she was embarrassed to think of having Nathan's babies. And why she felt this way, she did not know. It was only natural when you loved a man to want to have his children. Or so she had been taught.

When she was dressed, Maybelle grinned broadly. "The Major gonna have a fit when he sees you, Miss Katherine. You is one pretty woman. I dress a lots of women, but you is the purtiest I ever dressed. And the Major, he's so handsome. You two gonna make the finest couple in all of Richmond tonight. I gonna sneak in from the kitchen and take a peek when the dancin' starts, just so's I can see the two of you together. I gonna ask the Major, too, if I can come back and be your own special maid."

Kitty did feel embarrassed then with so much fussing over her. She thanked Maybelle, then asked her to leave, saying she wanted a few moments alone before going downstairs.

She stared at her face in the mirror. There was no color in her cheeks. Nathan was right. She was tired. She pinched the flesh, watching the soft redness appear.

Then, slowly, her gaze moved down to her breasts, very exposed in the low bodice. An average-sized dress would not hold her large bosom, she realized proudly.

And then the memories came flooding back like the flash floods in the North Carolina mountains when the snows melt. It was vivid now, somewhere in the hills of Tennessee, moonlight spilling down on two naked bodies lying on a bed of grass and moss. Travis had stared at her breasts hungrily, murmuring, "Christ, woman, I've never seen such beauty! You drive a man wild, do you realize that?"

She had been unable to speak, her chest rising and falling nervously as she breathed heavily in anticipation of the ecstasy that was sure to come.

He had traced a line about her breasts with his fingertip—first one, then the other, squeezing the nipples between thumb and forefinger until they were taut and firm. And then he had bent down, tongue slipping from his lips to touch each rosy tip in turn. Kitty had moaned as a convulsion of desire spread through her body in a giant wave. Why didn't he go on and take her? She could feel the pulsating throb of his manhood against her naked thighs . . . knew he wanted to enter her and know the sweetness of release. But he seemed to enjoy touching her this way, teasing her into a quivering mass of sobbing flesh, begging to be taken again and again.

Lips parting, he sucked one breast inside his mouth, as much as he could hold. Kitty's toes had arched downward with spasms of joy moving through her legs. His tongue moved around and around teasingly, the warm moisture causing her back to arch, strain to get even closer, give him more of her to devour and consume. His hand moved downward, touching where the flames were already burning . . . the fire spreading upward seeking to consume her whole body.

"Take me . . . please . . ." she had begged shamelessly. "Travis, take me. Oh, why do you torture me so?" Her nails dug into the flesh of his back and shoulders, pressing him closer as she sobbed his name over and over again.

He had moved ever so slightly as his lips moved to her other breast, deliberately letting his swollen organ tease the flesh of her inner thighs, thrusting gently, probing, letting her know that soon, very soon, she would have all of him. But not yet. Oh, no, not yet. He would make her dizzy, make her beg and whimper and plead. He was not like other men, believing a woman was only to give herself to a man and never take from him. Once they had talked at length about it, and he told her that he felt a woman should enjoy sexual pleasure as much as a man did, and she surprised herself when she finally agreed. Sex was not the unpleasant chore her mother had said it would be once she was married. Certainly it was forbidden before, but Kitty was not so certain about that anymore, either.

That had been the night Travis laughed and rolled over on his back, holding out his arms to her as he said, "Tonight, princess, you shall make love to me and give me pleasure."

She had stared at that teasing smile in the moonlight. "I don't know what you mean," she said, bewildered.

And he had showed her, grabbing one leg to pull it over his stomach until she was straddling his body. Then he guided her down onto him, hands clasping her buttocks firmly as he began to rock gently up and down, to and fro, rhythmically. Falling forward onto his powerful chest, Kitty felt his arms go about her back, holding her even tighter against him.

And like the crashing explosion of the artillerist-fired canister gun, they came together, and the roaring in Kitty's ears and the pounding of her heart were like the great thundering guns of war.

She had cried out loud in her passion, and he had gently cradled her head against his shoulders to muffle the sound in the still night. And they had lain together for a long, long time, neither of them speaking.

Kitty shook herself. She was warm all over, a gnawing hunger creeping up into her loins. Goodness, what was wrong? Was she sick? She had found once again the man she truly belonged to—Nathan—and they were going to be married. So why was she wasting her time thinking about a man who never had the right to touch her in the first place? Why was she remembering the way he made her enjoy it?

Tears were stinging her eyes, and she dabbed at them with a lace handkerchief. Maybe she was even thinking about a dead man. But was Travis dead? And if he was alive, what difference did it make? They would never meet again. That part of her life was over forever. It should never have happened. When she married Nathan, they would know the same joy and ecstasy that she had shared with Travis.

And besides, she reminded herself, the times with Travis had only happened because they were in the midst of war with death hovering all about. They had to take what pleasures they could where they found them. There was no need to feel shame and guilt—unless she dwelled upon the pleasurable memories as she was doing right then while Nathan waited for her downstairs.

Opening the door, Kitty could hear the violin, a banjo,

and drums. Someone was playing a piano. The sound of the music had a persuasive urgency, and the beat was pulse-stirring. Over it, there was the murmur of a crowd, and she realized the party had already begun. How long had she been woolgathering over Travis? How was she going to explain her dawdling to Nathan?

Walking to the landing above the big staircase, she felt suddenly conscious that something was awaiting her that she had no power to control. Something was pulling, beckoning. She walked to the stairhead, placed a hand on the balustrade, and with her other hand held her skirt up so she would not trip.

And then she was aware that the music had stopped as she descended, and people were standing at the foot of the stairs, looking up at *her*. She noted envious stares from the women, admiration from the men.

She heard Nathan's voice ring out above the silence, the words a bit slurred as she realized he had obviously been drinking; but he sounded proud, almost defiant. "My future wife! Isn't she beautiful? I am so proud to present to you the most beautiful woman in all of Richmond, the flower of North Carolina—Miss Katherine Wright."

And there was an answering ripple of applause, the murmur of agreement from a few men brave enough to do so in front of their wives and sweethearts.

Nathan moved to the foot of the stairs and waited for her with his hand held out. The violin came alive in a lovely, sweeping arpeggio and then steadied itself into a moving minuet. Nathan led her forward, his thick voice whispering over and over again, "Katherine, Katherine, my own sweet, lovely bride-to-be . . . lovely, wonderful . . ."

Kitty was conscious of the outrageously deep cut of her dress, the beauty of her naked shoulders, and the swell of her bosom. Proud, at the moment, she was very proud.

The minuet ended. Then music began again and men were stepping up to dance with her, but Nathan refused to allow them the privilege. "Mine . . ." He sounded drunk, Kitty realized with a start. "All mine and I refuse to share her with any of you."

A few of the men arched their eyebrows; others glared

angrily. Nathan was not being a gentleman. People were beginning to stand along the walls and whisper among themselves, staring reproachfully in the couple's direction.

"Nathan, what is the matter with you?" Kitty hissed at him in disgust. "You . . . you're intoxicated."

"Intoxicated with the beauty of *you*." He laughed as he stumbled against her.

"Nathan, you're making a fool of yourself—and me."

"It's hot in here." He grabbed her hand suddenly and led her toward one of the open doors leading to the veranda of the hotel. The murmur of those staring grew louder as they moved across the floor, beneath the crystal chandeliers, past the raised stand where the musicians played, beyond the potted plants, and out into the Virginia summer night.

Nathan leaned against the marble railing, swaying momentarily, then he whipped around to look at her with bleary eyes. "Katherine, you don't know how much I love you," he moaned. "I thought I'd memorized everything about you—the way your hair dances with fire when the light shines on it and your eyes, so blue they're almost purple, and how they flash with red sparkles when you're angry. And your eyelashes . . ."

He reached out to touch her, but she jerked her head back. "Your eyelashes look as though they're dusted with pure flakes of gold. When you walked down those steps tonight, it was like I'd never really seen you before, never known you were so beautiful. God, you were glowing. You looked the way I hope you look when I finally get to make love to you the way I want to. . . ."

Perhaps the words would have meant everything had his speech not been slurred, his breath thick with the odor of drink. He reached out, grabbed her, hands mashing against her breasts as he swung her around to pin her against the railing. "I can't wait to have you lying beside me, naked, my hands all over you . . . like this. . . ."

"Nathan!" She tried to push him away, but he was holding too tightly. "Nathan! Stop it this instant! Have you gone mad? What is wrong with you? I've never seen you so . . ."

"I'm sorry." He was instantly contrite, his hold slackening to a point where she could wriggle away. "I just love you—want us to get married quick as we can. . . ."

"So we can have sex?" she snapped. He stared at her in the dim glow from the lights inside the hotel ballroom. "That's all you talk about, it seems, making love to me. Is that why you want to marry me?"

"What's wrong with that?" He swayed, hicupping.

"There's more to marriage than just making love."

"Well, maybe." He lurched against the railing and hiccupped again. "But maybe once I have you, know you're legally mine, I won't see you doing it with another man every time I close my eyes. It'll be *me* doing it to you and I'm going to do it to you so goddamned good, *you* won't think about those other men anymore, either."

She turned to walk away, but his hand snaked out to grab her once again, this time slamming her to the railing so hard she almost fell, a sharp pain moving up her back. "How dare you!" Her hand came up, ready to crack across his face, but he caught her wrist, twisting it painfully to her side.

"You listen to me," he snarled, a complete stranger now —an angry, hurting stranger. "I can't stand it, knowing what happened to you. I never wanted you in this war to start with, remember? If you'd stayed home, like I asked you to, left Doc and his hospital alone, none of this would have happened! But no, you had to play the stubborn, independent woman and look where it's got you. Look what it's done to me, or don't I matter anymore? Tell me, Katherine my sweet, which one was the best? Tate or Coltrane? Or have there been so damned many you can't remember which you liked the best?"

Her hand ached to slap him, but he now held both wrists tightly. "You think a woman is only fit for one thing—a man to take her when he wants to so she can have a baby every year and get fat and ugly and sit at home like a crow and sew and tat and think empty-headed thoughts. You think it's wrong for a woman to want to be herself, have hopes and dreams of her own, have a life for herself! Well, I tell you what you do, Major Collins, you go back to Wayne County and find Nancy Warren. Maybe she's pure and goody-goody, maybe she fits your image of the ideal wife and mother. And you just leave me alone. Leave me to live my own life the way I want to. I've had my fill of men, including you."

Her nostrils flared, her eyes danced like coals of fire— every fiber of her body wanting to strike out and hurt, hating, despising. This was not the man she had known and loved. This man was a selfish, jealous stranger, a man she no longer knew or wanted to know.

For an instant his eyes, too, flashed fire, but then he laughed. "Nancy Warren? I rolled her in the hay before we were ten years old. I had all of that I wanted, and then some, because she loved me, still does. She'd do anything for me, which is goddamned more than I can say for *you*."

He released her and she slapped him—once, twice—and he stood there, lurching, hiccupping, grinning. And finally, pressing her fist against her lips to stifle a sob, she ran from the veranda, through the crowded room of faces staring curiously; she ran up the steps and into her room, slamming the door behind her.

She flung herself across the bed and then the tears came —tears for Nathan and what was but never could be, and for Travis and the realization of what *might* have been but never *should* have been. And yes, she cried for herself, also, and whatever the frightening future might bring her way.

War had done this to all their lives. Nathan was not the same; she had sensed it that first day but refused to acknowledge it. Her father's life had been destroyed—and her mother's and Andy Shaw's and David Stoner's, and, yes, Travis's as well. As for herself, did she even have a life left? She could return to the hospital, care for the wounded, give what she could to those who needed her. And then what? Did she even have a future? And what if the North won the war, what would happen to all of them then?

It all seemed so hopeless. A headache began to inch its clutching fingers around her forehead, but still the tears came. Feeling weariness creep over her body, Kitty gave way to the sweet oblivion, hoping for release, freedom, to leave behind the shreds of the world about her.

Out of the mist, he came to her, arms outstretched. It was difficult to see through the gray-orange shroud of light that swept over their bodies. His lips were warm, seeking, possessive, and his hands were deft and quick as he ripped her clothes away until she lay naked beneath him.

"Mine . . ." she heard the voice straining to reach her through the shroud of mist. "All mine . . . forever and ever . . ."

Who was this stranger in the night, this faceless lover who came to claim her in a dream? The touch was familiar. And then there was a parting of the clouds and she saw the familiar Federal blue, the dark beard, the gun-steel eyes hot with desire. Travis . . . Travis was not dead. He was here, alive, consuming her, ravishing her body, plunging into her, and she wanted him—had to have him. She moved against him, answering the rhythm of two bodies locked in unison, legs reaching up to wrap around his hunching buttocks, heels digging in to lock him even closer against her throbbing form.

"Travis . . . Travis . . . I want you," she whimpered shamelessly. "Travis, you live . . ."

Suddenly the movement ceased. There was a sound like that of a wounded animal snarling in the night. She felt a sharp crack across her face, opened her eyes to awaken from the dream to shocking reality. "You bitch!" The voice screamed down at her, and she stared up, straining in the pitch-darkness to make out the hulking form above.

It was slowly coming back: she was here in the hotel room and there was a real man above her and she was naked and he had been ravishing her—but who?

"You lying bitch!" Again the crack across her face. "So it was Travis Coltrane, the son of a bitch! He was the one who took you away from me."

Nathan. It was Nathan moving quickly to the edge of the bed. Her whole head ached from his blows. Quickly, frightened, she slid away from him in the darkness. She could feel his heavy breathing, his body shuddering with rage.

He reached out for her, slapping at the air, and she cowered in the darkness, trembling with terror. Was he so drunk he had lost his mind? Was he going to kill her here and now?

He threw himself across the bed, reaching out, hands entwining in her hair, yanking her down on the mattress, bouncing her up and down furiously.

"Nathan, please, stop," she screamed, her teeth rattling inside her mouth as he continued to bounce her upon the mattress violently.

"Hey, what's all that yelling about in there?" Someone was pounding on the door furiously. "What's going on? Let me in!"

Instantly, Nathan withdrew his hold, moving off the bed. A small shaft of light filtered through the window from a lantern burning on a street light below. Kitty realized blearily that he was stark naked.

"It's okay." He was instantly contrite, his voice slurring the words. "Had too much to drink, that's all."

"Well, keep it quiet," the voice cried through the door. "I've had some complaints. One more peep out of you tonight, soldier, and out you go."

"I'm an officer, not a soldier!" Nathan yelled back, angry once again. "And you go to hell!"

"I'll kick this door down, you son of a bitch."

"Please," Kitty cried then, pulling the sheet up around her, eyes still on Nathan as he stood in the gleam of light. "Please don't come in. It's all right. He's had too much to drink."

There was a momentary silence, then the voice again: "All right, lady, since *you* asked me, but tomorrow I think it's best the two of you get out of here. I try to run a decent place."

"Yes, yes, we're sorry. We'll get out."

Footsteps echoed down the hall.

Nathan stooped to snatch up his clothing from the floor. Slinging them over his shoulder, he walked naked across the room to a door Kitty had not bothered to notice before. Their rooms adjoined, and she had not known it! He opened the door, then slammed it loudly behind him.

For a moment, she could not move. Then she forced her shaking legs to walk to the little wooden desk that stood near that door, sliding it in place to block the entrance. True, it would not keep Nathan out should he decide to enter once again, but there would be enough noise so that she would have time to get up and run out the door leading into the hall.

She walked back to the bed and lay down, turning her face to the wall.

There were no tears left to be shed.

✌ Chapter Thirty-one ✌

FOR a time, Kitty did not hear the urgent knocking. Exhausted both physically and mentally, she had fallen into a deep, though restless, sleep. As she opened her eyes, reality was slow in coming. There was the taste of old blood, the feeling of soreness in the jaw. And then it came, first hurt, then deep anger.

The knocking continued, louder, insistent.

Finally, she asked suspiciously, "Who's there?"

And she knew, before the voice replied, what it was going to say. "Nathan. Let me in, please. I must talk to you, Katherine."

"Go away. I never want to see you again." She turned her face to the wall, pulled the covers up tightly around her neck. How could he have done it? How could he have sneaked into her room and removed her clothing and . . . *raped* her? Yes, that's exactly what it had been—*rape*. Nathan—who had always been the perfect gentleman, the aristocrat, the fine image of decorum and good breeding— like an animal gone mad, he had *raped* her.

"Katherine," the voice through the door sighed wearily. "I know you're angry with me and for good reason, but please don't make me stand out here in the hall groveling for everyone to hear. Let me in even if you hate me. Have some feeling for what we used to mean to each other. Please."

Feeling? What did she feel now but complete hopelessness? And he was right. There was no use in letting everyone in the hotel hear him begging, for after all there had been enough to attract attention last night. Wrapping the sheet about her, she got up, opened the door, and then retreated to the bed.

He looked terrible, as terrible as she *felt*. His hair hung down in his face, his eyes were bloodshot, his hands trembled. He drew up a chair and sat down near the bed, staring at his feet miserably. "I know how you must hate me."

She did not speak.

"Katherine, hear me out. I beg of you. I was drunk. I cannot deny that fact. It was getting to me—this . . . this *thing* I feel between us. It's not like it used to be. Perhaps it can never be again. Thinking about those men, what they did to you . . ." he shuddered.

"I couldn't help any of that," she reminded him bitterly.

The voice changed. Gone was the humbleness and in its place was angry reproach. "You can help dreaming about this Coltrane fellow, damnit. You can help calling out his name when it's *me* making love to you. Just what the hell was he to you anyway? He's a Yankee, a marauding, no-good Yankee soldier who held you prisoner. And as wrong as I was to do what I did last night, it was wrong of you to pretend all this time that you didn't enjoy what he did to you. Maybe you even enjoyed what Luke Tate did, too. Maybe I never really knew you, Katherine."

They faced each other, eyes blazing, and then his gaze moved downward and he snapped curtly, "Cover your shame, woman."

She looked down as his words washed over her. Snatching up the sheet, she screamed, "Shame? My body is shame? Something to hide? You wanted it last night, Nathan, all of it, because you couldn't live with the fact that another man possessed me!"

In a rage, Kitty leaped from the bed and reached for one of her old muslin dresses. "Let me tell you one thing, Nathan Collins, I don't consider my body, or sex, something to be ashamed of. The shame comes from your wanting me and then putting the blame on me."

He stood up also, slamming the chair across the room

loudly. "You don't consider it shameful that you cried out the name of the man who raped you, who held you prisoner? A goddamned son of a bitch Yankee?"

And then it came, the explosion that had been bubbling from the depths of her soul and that she could no longer control. "I dreamed it *was* Travis," she cried furiously. "I think I wanted it to *be* Travis. He wasn't all that bad, not toward the end. I don't know how I feel about him, whether it was love or whether we were just two people reaching out for something to hold onto in the middle of all the suffering and dying. I don't know what I feel for you now, either. At this moment, I *hate* you."

He stared at her a long time without speaking. Kitty finished dressing, moved to the mirror, and eyes blazing, began brushing her hair with short, quick strokes.

"I think," he said finally, evenly, his voice low and ominous, "that you have developed a sickness from your experiences in the war, Katherine. It's been too much for you. There is a train leaving for Wilmington in an hour that will have us in Goldsboro by late evening. Get together what few belongings you have and I will be back to take you to the depot. We're going home."

Whirling about, she threw the hairbrush at him. "You can go to hell, Nathan! I'm not going anywhere except back to that hospital."

"No." He still spoke quietly, as though she were, indeed, mentally ill and had to be dealt with thusly. "I will speak to the people in charge there, explain that the place for you now is home, around familiar people and things. If necessary, I will have you forcefully taken to the depot and put on the train. Don't make me embarrass either of us this way. Now you just go on and get ready. I'm going to do what's best."

He walked out and closed the door, and Kitty stood there, shaking in her rage. He would do it. She knew he would do it. He would have his men carry her bodily to the depot. He would also go to the hospital and make sure she was not allowed to work there any longer. They would believe him. Who wouldn't? After all, *he* was a respected major and *she* was merely a poor war refugee who'd dragged into town after having been held prisoner by the

Yankees till it drove her to madness. Who would believe she was sane when Nathan got through with his lies?

There was nothing to do but prepare to leave.

And what difference did it make, she thought dully. What was left here? Nathan had changed. She doubted she could ever forgive the events of the night before nor the way he had just talked to her. Her father was probably long dead. Travis Coltrane, if he existed, hated her—and all of that had been a mistake that never should have happened, anyway. There was nothing to do *except* go home and try to pick up the pieces. If the stories about her mother were true—that she was a drunk—then perhaps there would be something to be done there. And there was also a hospital in Goldsboro now, the one Doc Musgrave had helped to begin—"Way Hospital #3," it was called. She could go to work there after Nathan returned to Richmond.

But here, there was nothing. The past was dead and only the future remained, for the present, with Nathan, was unbearable for both of them.

❦ Chapter Thirty-two ❧

THE train ride had been agonizingly slow, averaging only a little over ten miles an hour. Kitty did not speak to Nathan, who sat next to her, an anxious look on his face as though he expected at any moment that she would leap through the open window.

The air was hot and humid, and the ashes and cinders from the wood-burning engine up front whipped through the window which had to remain open, for in the humid late summer weather, the closeness would be unbearable. At the rest stops along the way, Nathan would ask a soldier nearby, or some other passenger, to leave the train and bring back cool drinks for them—as though he were afraid to leave her alone. She took the drinks but refused the food, and he would urge her to eat.

Finally, she snapped, "Nathan, for God's sake, just leave me alone. I want to go home and never see you again, so stop hovering over me or so help me, I'm going to start screaming and not stop, and everyone will think I *am* crazy!"

He shifted away from her, his brows knit together tightly and his chin propped on a knotted fist as he stared moodily straight ahead. Kitty fought the childish impulse to stick out her tongue. How she hated his pompousness, his self-righteousness! At that moment, it was hard to remember a time when love had existed between them.

When the train finally chugged out of the mountains and sloped down into the flat lands of eastern North Carolina, Kitty finally felt she was truly getting near home. Tall pine trees with thick scrubby underbrush stretched as far as the eye could see. Here and there plank farmhouses stood, some deserted by inhabitants who sought to flee the threat of invasion from the North.

Directly in front of Kitty and Nathan, a bald-headed man held a newspaper in front of him.

To agitate her further, Nathan, bored with having no one to talk to, addressed the man. "Sir, I see you have a copy of the *Raleigh Standard*. What do they write about the war?"

Eager to engage in conversation, the man said, "They're carrying on an active campaign to bring the war to a close. The editor, a man named W. W. Holden, is leading it, says the war should end—at any cost."

"At any cost?" Nathan frowned.

The man nodded. "Peace meetings are being held all through North Carolina and they say soldiers are deserting right and left. They're fed up. Have you heard about the trouble up in the mountains, in the western part of the state?"

"No." Nathan shook his head and looked at Kitty meaningfully before turning his attention back to their traveling companion. "I've been in Richmond and unfortunately, I've had other matters to draw my attention besides the war back home."

"Well, there's a civil war going on there between the Confederate troops. Terrible, just terrible," he clucked. "Paper says they're even organizing—deserters against bushwhackers. And there are Federals in the area who are stripping the region of anything of value that they can move."

He looked from Nathan to Kitty. "You know, you're heading into a dangerous part of the state. The enemy is making raids in the countryside, foraging, doing God knows what to the womenfolk when they can. You'd be smart to turn and head back to Richmond."

"I have family in Goldsboro," Kitty said quietly. "I have nothing in Richmond."

"Ever hear of the 'Buffaloes'?" he asked. Nathan shook

his head, and he went on, "They travel in gangs of a dozen or so men—Union bushwhackers who infest the swamps. They used to live around here, they say, and went to join the Yankees, then deserted. Their hometown folks are itching to lynch 'em, so they've got no place to go but to the swamps to hide out and run their raids at night. They like to visit their old neighbors and take revenge for being unable to go home."

"Perhaps," Nathan said, turning to Kitty with a sneer on his face, "you will find your father among them."

"I doubt that," she snapped. "He'd never desert the Union army. He'd sooner die."

"A loyal traitor." Nathan snickered. "How noble."

She bit down on her lip until she tasted blood, not wanting to unleash her fury in front of strangers.

The man was watching with interest. He leaned forward and said, "That true, lady? You from North Carolina and your daddy is fighting with the Yankees? It's a wonder folks in your hometown don't run you out! And you hooked up with a fine Confederate officer here." He nodded to the single star on the tunic of Nathan's uniform. "I see you're a Major, sir."

She turned her head slowly and stared at him with such vehemence that he sank in his seat. "I'll thank you to mind your own business," she said icily.

"Katherine!" Nathan admonished.

"And I've had about all I'm going to take from you, Nathan!" She stood up and with a swish of her skirt, moved past him, fighting to maintain her balance against the lurching of the train as she walked up the aisle to take a seat beside another woman.

When the train arrived at the Goldsboro depot a short while later, Kitty hurried to be the first to descend onto the platform. She stood there, gazing about at the familiar buildings, searching for the face of anyone she might know.

"Katherine, where do you think you're going?" Nathan rushed up to her side and grabbed her arm tightly.

"Take your hands off of me, Nathan."

"I asked you where you are going!"

"It's none of your damned business!"

Shocked by hearing such profanity from the lips of a Southern woman right out in public and seeing that others heard and turned to stare, Nathan dropped his hand and stepped back.

Kitty walked over to a black man standing beside a wagon. "I have no money to pay you," she said curtly, "but I would appreciate your giving me a ride out in the county to my home. Perhaps you know where I live. My name is Kitty Wright. My father's name is John Wright. My mother is Lena Wright."

The man's eyes widened with each word she uttered and now he was actually stepping back away from her, as though frightened.

Kitty asked him what was wrong and he started to shake his head. "I don't wanna ride you out there, Missie. You don't wanna go out there."

"What is wrong with you?" she demanded.

Nathan had followed her. He nodded to the man. "I'm Major Nathan Collins. I believe you know my people?"

"Yassuh." He bowed respectfully.

"Would you give both of us a ride into the county? I live just beyond Miss Wright's home. You can drop her off there."

"Suh, this ain't my wagon, no how. It belong to Mistah Carter. He inside the hotel. He tol' me to wait heah."

Nathan sighed, turned on his heel, and walked across the street to the hotel. He returned in a few moments and told the man Mr. Carter had been paid for the use of his wagon and it was quite all right for them to be given a ride home. Turning to Kitty, he said, "You can either ride with me or walk—whichever you prefer. You're trying my patience, Katherine, and I really don't care what you do."

She let him help her onto the wagon. The thing to do at the moment, she realized, was to get home, not stand around in the middle of Goldsboro without a cent to her name.

Down the familiar road they went and when they got to the front of Andy Shaw's house, Kitty cried out, "They burned it. It's burned to the ground!" She stared in disbelief at the charred remains. "What happened? Have the Yankees been through here?"

"No'm," the black man answered, staring straight ahead. "Folks 'round here burned lots of folks' houses what they thought was Yankee lovers. They heared 'bout Mistah Shaw ridin' with Luke Tate and his bunch, and they burnt his house down."

"But what about his wife and his children?"

The man did not speak. Nathan reached for her hand, but she snatched it away. Sighing, he told her that his mother had written to him about the night the townspeople burned the houses of those they felt were Union sympathizers. "Mother also wrote that the Shaws moved somewhere to the central part of the state where Mrs. Shaw had relatives. They were unharmed."

"Thank God for that," she said. "That woman couldn't help what her husband did."

And then, as they rounded the curve in the road, flanked on both sides by plums ripening in the bushes, Kitty cried out before the farm even came into view, "Our home! If they burned the Shaws' . . ."

And there it was, all that remained of the farmhouse and the barn—black, charred ruins in a pile of rubble. "Didn't want to bring you out heah," the old man mumbled. "This'n was the first they burned."

Kitty put her hand on his shoulder, made him pull the reins of the mule until the wagon stopped. Nathan did not try to stop her. Climbing down, she walked as though in a daze, stumbling now and then, but moving forward to the blackened heap that was once her home. Nothing remained. Even the fields had been burned and the woods all the way back to the swampland. There was nothing left. Nothing.

Unaware that Nathan had followed her, Kitty jumped when he placed a gentle hand on her shoulder. "I'm sorry, Katherine, truly sorry. It was bound to happen. The war news is not good. People are becoming discouraged. They're taking drastic steps to fight back. Your father's home represented everything that they hate. When Mother wrote me that it was burned to the ground, I was not surprised."

"Why . . . why didn't you tell me?" Her eyes were starting to burn with tears. Desolation and loneliness such as she had never known was moving across her body in a giant, consuming wave. "Nathan, why did you bring me home—to *this*?"

"To make you see for yourself that everything in the past is dead, Katherine." She allowed him to place both his hands on her shoulders and turn her around to face him. His touch, like his voice, was gentle. "You had to see for yourself what the war had done to all our lives. I'm truly sorry for the way I behaved, the things I said. But you had to come here, had to see what your father's behavior has done to what life you thought you had left. It's over. All of it. There's nothing left for you now but to regain control of yourself, your morals, your values. When the war is over, when we finally win, if you have changed, then we'll be married.

"Now I'll have to return to Richmond soon to receive new orders for where I'll report to duty," he continued. "Right now, we're going on to my home, where you will stay for the remainder of the war. You'll be taken care of there."

"My mother," she moaned, remembering, "where is my mother?"

"That is another shame you must live down," he said crisply. "She's beyond help, Katherine. She's back there in town, a prostitute, a drunk. Now listen to me. I'm willing to try and forget your past, forgive it, overlook your background. I'm giving you a chance at decency if you will only listen to me and cooperate. Now let's go back to the wagon. Hold your head up and don't look back. It's the only way."

She stared at the black, empty fields. This was her father's land. This was where he'd had his hopes and dreams. It had been his life, however unhappy due to a nagging, dissatisfied wife. It had been his. And now it was gone. And why? Because he had dared to help slaves escape? Because he refused to believe one man had the right to hold another man in bondage? Those men had beaten him almost to the point of death, cost him the loss of vision in one eye, driven him to fight for the North, and now he, like herself, had no reason to come home. *They* had stripped them of everything.

"Come along now." Nathan spoke to her once again as though speaking to a child. "Here, take my hand. You're tired from the trip. Mother will put you right to bed. We'll talk tomorrow. Come along now. It's over, Katherine. There's no need to look back or think about unpleasant things."

She took a deep breath and turned on him with all the fury of a cornered animal. "Yes, there is a need to look back, Nathan. It's looking back and seeing what you, and those who think like you do, have done to me and to my father! Go to your home? Live with your people? Wait for you to come home? Be your wife? No, thank you, I'll have no part of it."

"Katherine, you're ill . . ."

She slapped his hand away. "No, I'm not ill. I think I'm stronger now than I've ever been in my whole life. I think I needed this to give me the strength to go on. I don't need you, Nathan. I don't need anybody!"

She turned and walked across the field, cutting along the ruts and gulleys to reach the road leading into Goldsboro. Nathan called to her, but she put one foot in front of the other. This time she wasn't looking back because she didn't want to see him, because the sight of him and all he stood for—that was what made her sick!

❧ Chapter Thirty-three ❧

KITTY moved between the beds. A soldier, sitting up
and rubbing at the bandaged stump below his thigh,
called to her, "Think I'm going to be getting out of here
soon? The war's over for me." Despite his handicap, there
was a touch of joy to his voice.

"That's up to Doctor Holt, soldier. I'm just a nurse."
She started on by, then turned slowly. "Aren't you the
soldier who stuck a foot out to try and stop a cannon ball?"

"Yep," he answered proudly. "Damned thing was moving
so slow I never knowed it would tear my leg off. Now the
war's over for me and I reckon I'll be headin' home soon's
I get a crutch and you folks let me outta here. Goin' to
Smithfield. Got a wife and three young'uns there."

Kitty nodded, kept on moving, unable to have much
sympathy for the grizzly-faced soldier. She heard the surgeons talk about those who stuck their foot out in front
of a cannon ball. Usually, they did it hoping for a wound
that *would* put them out of battle—even if it did mean
amputation of a leg. Some of them would rather lose a limb
than their life, and so terribly many were despondent over
the war that they were willing to do anything short of
dying to escape from all the suffering.

Once, when she had asked a surgeon about it, he had
explained, saying, "They see a stray cannon ball come
bouncing through camp, leisurely skipping along through

wagons, mules, and infantry ranks. Then someone decides to stick his foot out and stop it. Some of them might be fooled by the way the ball is traveling and not realize what will happen. Others, I'm ashamed to say, deliberately do it. Even at the slowest speeds, a moving cannon ball can tear a leg off at the hip!" He had shuddered. "I've seen some gory messes that had to be amputated. The shock isn't transmitted through the leg because of the rate of motion—the projectile is faster than the propagation of the stress through the limb—so the limb is torn off."

Kitty stepped out of the hospital into the crisp fall air. The pace here at Way Hospital #3 was not as hectic as it had been at Chimborazo. These soldiers had received emergency treatment on the battlefield and had been sent here either to recuperate and return to battle, or to be sent home.

Looking down the street with its trees casting gold and red highlights as the sun filtered down through the autumn foliage, she thought of her mother. The scene in the hotel saloon had not been pleasant. In fact, it had been horribly embarrassing. She had walked part of the way back to Goldsboro before a wagon came along to offer her a ride and on arriving in town, she had gone in search of Lena.

She found her, drunk, leaning against a bar, surrounded by shabbily dressed men. For a few moments, Kitty had stood inside the door, staring, unable to absorb what she saw—her mother in a sleazy, low-cut red dress, leaning on the arm of the man closest to her. Her laughter was loud, shrill, filling the whole room, screaming about Kitty's shocked ears.

"Lou, you give me five dollars last night and took an hour to get it off," her mother was taunting someone. "Now Zeb, here, has offered me ten and he don't take long. I can make more money with faster studs."

"Hell, I'll give you ten," someone snarled—probably the man named Lou, Kitty reasoned. "And I won't take so long, the way you been rubbin' your tits all over me this afternoon. Besides, you passed out drunk, so how do you know how long it took?"

There was a round of laughter quieted by Lena's curses. "Goddamn it, if you ain't good enough to keep a woman awake, I'd damn sure not let everyone know about it, if I was you."

More laughter.

And then someone spotted Kitty and there was a rippling wave of silence throughout the saloon as all eyes turned to stare. Lena was downing a drink and as she slammed the empty glass onto the bar, she realized everyone had grown silent. She followed their gaze and her face paled at the sight of Kitty standing there, watching.

For a moment, Lena froze and then her face screwed into a mass of sobbing wrinkles as she stumbled forth, blubbering, "My baby . . . my little girl . . . thought you were dead . . ." She came forward and Kitty caught her as she threw her weight against her and struggled to hold her up. Someone stepped forward to help her lower the crying woman into a nearby chair.

"Thought you was dead . . ." Lena cried over and over, blubbering. Kitty could only stare down, dazed. It was true. Her mother was a drunk—and a prostitute.

"Nearly went out of my mind . . . gave you up for dead . . . never heard from your pa . . . didn't have nothin' left. The bastards burned me out of the house . . . all because of the war . . . everything gone . . ." Sobbing again, she bowed her head and then raised it to look at the man in the white apron who stood behind the bar staring. "Joe. Get me another drink. Damnit, I need one bad."

"I think you've had enough, Momma."

Lena lifted bloodshot, swollen eyes. "You don't understand, child. I ain't got nobody, not even you. I see it in your eyes, the way you're lookin' at me. You don't understand."

The bartender approached, but a look from Kitty halted him. He spun on his heel, the drink still in his hand.

"I want you to come with me to the hospital. You're sick, Momma. You need help."

She held out her hand, but Lena slapped it away as she lurched to her feet. "How dare you sound so high and mighty? I hear things! I hear how you lived with the Yankees. I hear how Nathan's bitchy mother told the whole town about it—how you never was good enough for her son and now he wouldn't have you."

393

Kitty was surprised at her own calmness. "Then you knew I was alive. You knew I was back in town."

"Somebody saw you get off the train. I didn't believe it." She lowered her head once again, then raised it to yell, "Damnit, Joe, where's my drink?"

"And you got my letters, didn't you? But you wouldn't answer. You were ashamed for me to know what you've become and now you're going to refuse my offer of help to get you out of all this."

Lena was holding onto the back of the chair, trying to steady herself. Lips curling back, she snarled, "Yeah, I got your letter and Nathan's mother got one from him telling how he's ashamed of you, the way you lived. Where do you get off comin' in here lookin' down your nose at me? You're just like your no-good daddy, always was . . . thinking you're better'n everybody else. Both of you walked out on me. Well, I can take care of myself . . . don't need you or nobody else. Now get the hell outta here and leave me alone."

Kitty felt herself swaying. Dear Lord, she thought in anguish, was it possible to experience such heartache without the heart actually breaking? Could she go on living in the face of all that had happened in the past two days? This was her mother, standing there drunk, screaming obscenities in front of all these men as they snickered approval.

And then Nathan had come through the door, seeming to fill the room with his stature, his uniform, his pride. "Katherine, come out of here!" he ordered.

Turning her head slightly, she hissed, "Will you stop following me? I don't need you, Nathan. Now leave, please!"

"Go with him," Lena hiccupped. "You ain't needed here. You ain't wanted. I got me a room upstairs, get all I want to eat and drink, and make money besides. Leave me alone."

She waved her hand, turned and started toward the bar. She was halfway there when she stumbled and fell to her knees. Kitty started to move forward, but Nathan grabbed her, holding her back as two men lifted Lena in their arms and carried her up the stairs.

She let him lead her outside, shocked and dazed by what she had just witnessed.

Finally, she came alive again and whirling on Nathan, she hissed, "I told you to leave me alone. I never want to see you again."

"I love you, Katherine," he said quietly, his eyes misting. "I know right now you hate me, but I do love you. I'm going back to Richmond right away. I can't bear to stand by and see what's happening to you. But one day, we'll meet again and perhaps by then you'll realize you love me, too."

And he had left her standing there in front of the hotel and she moved in the direction of the hospital where she would be needed, where they would accept her eagerly.

As Kitty's mind came back to the present, she realized she was no longer alone. Turning, she saw that one of the other women who worked as a nurse, Judith Gibson, was standing beside her, concern etched in every line of her face.

"Why don't you go see about her?" she asked quietly, knowing without being told what Kitty was brooding about. "I hear things and I've heard that your mother isn't well."

"Not well? Where . . ."

"Where did I hear it?" The petite dark-haired woman smiled wryly. "Tom goes to the saloon a lot since he came back from the war, Kitty, if he can get there. It isn't so easy for a man without legs to get around, you know. But he manages and he tells me some of the things he hears— like the way no one has seen your mother for several days now and Joe, the bartender, is grumbling about how she's not . . . earning her keep." Her voice trailed off, embarrassed.

Looking down the street, Kitty said, "I appreciate your telling me, Judith. I worry about her a lot, the way she is, what she's become. Maybe if I hadn't been forced to leave, things wouldn't have happened to her the way they did. If she's sick, then I'll go to her, of course."

Suddenly the door to the hospital banged open, and one of the younger, less-experienced doctors poked his head out, a panicky look on his face. "You." He pointed to

Kitty. "That soldier, the one that developed gangrene in his arm, he's worse and he's calling for you."

"I'll go to him if you'd rather go see about your mother right now," Judith said.

Kitty shook her head and started for the door. "We've grown rather close. Norman knew all along, I think, that he was going to die from that wound. He asked me to be with him when his time came, and I promised. I'll go see about my mother later."

Kitty followed the doctor down the dimly lit corridor, turning into a room at the end. The air was close, smelling thickly of chloroform and turpentine—and death. Beds were shoved so close together they were almost touching. Some patients had to lie on blankets upon the floor. With so many skirmishes going on in Virginia, Tennessee, and even in the western part of the state, all hospitals were filled to overflowing.

Private Norman Herring, a stocky, prematurely bald soldier in his late thirties, was moaning softly and writhing on the stained sheets. Hurrying forward, Kitty took his left hand, frowned at the yellow oozing from the bandage on the stump of the right arm. It mingled with a greenish pus. Gangrene. And it was bad. The surgeon had amputated as high as possible to the shoulder. Day and night the nurses had kept the dressing wet with iodine and tannic acid solutions, as well as camphorated oil when they could get it. Medical supplies were getting so scarce that in the past week three amputations had been performed without the comfort of anesthesia.

"Norman, I'm here," she whispered gently. "Is it bad?"

He opened swollen, bleary eyes, trying to focus on her face. A wry smile twisted his puffy lips. "Ain't bad. It's about time for me to kick the old bucket, though, Kitty. I reckon an old man like me did pretty good to last in the war this long . . ." he paused, gasping for breath, and Kitty interrupted.

"Who says you're dying? You just want some attention." Judith had followed behind and stood squeezed in on the other side of the bed. Their eyes met and held, sending a silent message of agreement that the soldier was almost gone. Kitty could feel the heat of his fever as she held his hand.

"Get me a cloth and a pan of cool water, please," she said to Judith. "Maybe we can bring his fever down."

"No use . . ." he moaned, "almost over. Need to write a letter home, please, to Fayetteville."

Kitty called to Judith, who was almost out of the door, and asked her to stop by the little room where she lived and bring back the fresh bottle of ink she had made from pokeberries, and a goose quill.

Judith was only gone a moment, and while she bathed Norman's head with the cloth, repeatedly wringing it out in a pan of cool water, Kitty tried to write the words as he dictated them: "Dearest Mary, I am going. I love you. Take care of the boys . . . remember me . . . remember our cause. I ain't died for no good reason. If God will have me . . . I'm ready to go."

He paused, gasping for breath as he did after every few words, and Kitty waited, pen poised in her hand, body rigid. She was about to look up when Judith whispered, "He's gone, Kitty."

She looked at him: his eyes stared upward, his mouth gaped, his head slumped back. Quickly, Kitty pulled his eyelids down, propped his mouth closed with the cloth that she took from Judith's trembling hand, then pulled the foul-smelling sheet over his head. Kitty's hand held the unfinished letter as they left the room together.

Judith and Kitty walked out onto the porch. The sun was almost down and gentle darkness spread over the earth. Somewhere, a bird sang his goodnight lullaby. An owl hooted way off in the distance. Peaceful, it was so peaceful, Kitty thought wearily, even in death.

"I guess I'll never get used to the dying." Judith sounded as though she were about to cry. "I've been here six months and I've seen a hundred soldiers die and it never stops hurting. Even when I don't know their names or anything about them. Some of them scream for death because they hurt so bad. Others scream in terror because they feel the flames of hell licking at their souls, they say. Some just lie there, like Norman, and wait. I don't think I'll ever get used to it . . . ever."

Her voice broke and Kitty put an arm around her tiny waist. Judith was not meant to be a nurse, she knew, but it occupied her time away from Tom, her husband, who had never been the same since he had been sent home from Fredericksburg with both his legs amputated above his knees. She'd had three children, but they had died of smallpox. Her work at Way Hospital #3 was all that kept her going.

"Think of the living," Kitty said, hoping to console her. "Think of the soldiers who come here sick and wounded and leave to go back to their loved ones."

"Back to what? The South is losing the war, Kitty. Why pretend? Our soldiers desert by the hundreds. Governor Vance says there are over twelve hundred in the mountains right now. Ever since that Conscription Act was passed in April of sixty-two, it seems our people are rebelling. All white males between eighteen and thirty-five have to report for duty for three years. My God, they turn and run the other way!"

She paused to take a deep breath, wanting, Kitty figured, to get out everything that she had been holding back. "And they rebel against the tax law, saying they have to tithe one-tenth of all the produce for distribution by the army at Richmond. And now the government has the right to take livestock, slaves, provisions, wagons, anything they want, and they set the price they pay for them. What's going to happen to us, Kitty? They take our men, our food, our supplies, our homes. We're losing. And what's going to happen to us then? Will the Yankees kill us or make us rot in their prisons till we die?"

Her shoulders were shaking and Kitty patted her awkwardly. Everyone had their own despairs, she was reminded. Every single human being in the North and South had his own particular bitterness over the war. For Judith, it meant her husband's legs and the subsequent collapse of their marriage. For Kitty, it had meant her whole world as she had known it.

"I think I will walk down to the saloon . . . if you'll be all right." She touched her shoulder.

Judith dabbed at her eyes with her bloodstained apron, nodding. "Of course, you go right along. I have to help with the supper tonight—what little there's going to be. Dried beef and hot cakes. No molasses. No coffee. Those poor men. If we can't feed our wounded, how can we expect to feed an entire army?" Turning, shoulders slumped, she disappeared inside the hospital building.

Gathering her worn shawl tighter, Kitty started down the steps. She hadn't reached the bottom before an anxious voice called out from the shadows, "Miss Kitty, may I go with you, please?"

Startled, she whirled about to see Lonnie Carter limping from the shrubbery shroud at the end of the porch. He still stooped with pain from the operation that removed from his side a ball whose impact had crushed several ribs. He wore a ragged, mismatched uniform, and his feet, like so many others these days, were bare.

"Lonnie, you startled me. I didn't know you were over there. You should be inside, resting, so you can go home soon."

"Home?" He sounded contemptuous. "Where is home, Miss Kitty, besides the grave? I'm from below New Bern, remember? The Yankees have my home. I've no place to go."

Not knowing what to say, Kitty moved on down the steps, looking at him over her shoulder as he leaned over the porch railing. "I have to go into town now, Lonnie."

"I know. I heard. And I want to go with you. You have no business walking down the streets unescorted. What if the damn 'Buffaloes' are around? It ain't safe, Miss Kitty."

She kept on going, looking straight ahead. She didn't want Lonnie to see her mother. This was something that had to be done alone. From the hospital, there was a distance of only one block to reach Center Street which led to the Griswold Hotel on Walnut—and the saloon just beyond.

Few people were out. Goldsboro had changed so much that decent folk didn't venture out after dark. The town was crammed with those running from the fighting or recuperating from wounds or seeking refuge from the bush-whackers. The atmosphere over the town was one of desperation and hopelessness, with death and destruction moving closer in an ever-tightening ring.

She thought about Nathan's furlough of two weeks before. Their meeting on the front porch had been brief. She would not even have met with him had he not sent word to her that he would wait until she came out. Embarrassed, Kitty had no choice.

He had told her that he had been assigned to the Army of Tennessee under the command of General Joseph E. Johnston. His eyes shone with excitement as he spoke and she realized that Nathan had not yet grown weary of the fighting and whatever glory he had found in the war. He told her that President Davis had removed General Bragg from command of the army because of his hash of the Kentucky invasion the summer before, the way he had let victory slip through his grasp at Murfreesboro, and how he'd failed to make good use of his great victory at Chickamauga. And, afterward, Davis removed him, installing him as chief military adviser to himself, as president, and placing Johnston in his place.

"President Davis doesn't have a lot of confidence in General Johnston," Nathan had said. "We hear that he dislikes him a great deal personally, but there's no great love for Davis from General Johnston, either. But one thing is for sure, the Army of Tennessee can fight but it's never had adequate leadership. The men know Johnston and they trust him. And now they have their morale back. I'm anxious to join them in Georgia."

"God speed," Kitty had said tonelessly.

And he had grabbed her, crushing her in his arms, bruising her lips with his kisses. At first, Kitty did not respond, but then, slowly, felt herself weakening, yielding to him. And afterward, when he released her and stood looking down at her with a gleam of satisfaction in his eyes, she hated her body for once again betraying her.

"Everything is going to work out for us, Katherine," he had told her with confidence. "Just you wait and see. This war is going to be over and we're going to be married— and we'll forget all the unpleasantness of the past."

Quickening her step, Kitty remembered his prophecy that "things will be like they were before the war."

Shuddering, she knew that nothing would ever be the same for any of them again. It was hard to look back and remember the beginning when everyone seemed to want the war. In the spring of 1861, no one thought about the horrors of war. It all looked like a great adventure after the excitement of Fort Sumter, and the waving flags and loud brass bands, along with the chest-thumping orators, all combined to cast an aura of romance over everything and everyone. Thousands and thousands of young men had hurried to enlist, she remembered, feeling lucky to have the chance to fight. There was even news in the papers that neither government—the North or the South—was able to use all those men who crowded the recruiting stations in those first glittering weeks of the war. There were those who were rejected and returned home broken-hearted. And there were those who went off to camp afraid that the war would be over before they, themselves, joined the action.

And that was all over two years ago, Kitty thought grimly. And they had all had a taste of the war—or would, before it was over, it seemed.

Go back to the way it was? Nathan was a fool. No one can ever go back, especially after so much killing and bloodshed and hatred and agony. They would be hard-pressed to go on living when the war finally ended, which-ever side was the victor. No one could turn and go back; rather one could stumble forward and try to meet the future as best he could.

Drunken laughter from the shadows made her wish she were not alone. But, if Lena was sick, there would be no one else to help. The men in her life would not—they only wanted to use her.

Pausing to take a deep breath, Kitty pushed the slatted, swinging saloon doors open and stepped into the smoke-filled room. There was instant silence as all eyes fell on her curiously.

A scowling yellow-haired woman with orange-painted cheeks stepped forward, blocking her path. "He ain't here!" the woman said sharply.

Kitty snapped in reply, "I'm not looking for a man."

"Ain't one lookin' for you, either, so get the hell out of here."

There was a round of laughter and Kitty felt her cheeks burning.

"Hey, I know you." She whipped her head about to see a man standing at the bar. "You work at the hospital. Your mother works upstairs."

There was a fresh round of laughter.

She crossed the room boldly to where he stood. He was tall, gangly, his clothes thin and patched like every other man's these days. His beard was thick and his eyes were hard and cold, but something in his voice told Kitty he might be willing to help her—and she was desperate.

"I hear my mother hasn't been seen for a few days." She spoke quietly so that the others wouldn't hear. Gradually the din was picking up again as the talking, the clink of glasses, and the piano playing resumed. "Would you help me find her room? If she's sick, I need to go to her."

"Yeah, I guess you do." He turned up his glass, and gulped down its amber contents, then slammed it down on the counter. The bartender quickly stepped forward to pour more liquid from a bottle. As he took another sip, Kitty waited, trying not to be impatient. Finally, he spoke again. "Yeah, Lena's sick. Bad off. Leastways, I heard she was. I ain't seen her. Don't go for old women, myself, no matter how long it's been since I took my pleasure. I like my women young . . ."

He winked at her. "Now then. I reckon I can take you upstairs to your momma's room, *if,*" he added meaningfully, "me and you can get together later on."

"You can go to hell!" Kitty whirled away from the bar and moved toward the stairway. She would find the room herself if it meant beating on every door up there.

The yellow-haired woman stepped forward. "Hey, you can't go up there. It's private up there. I got girls workin' . . ."

Turning to give the woman a glare to let her know she was not about to be stopped, Kitty froze where she stood. It couldn't be! Not those evil, staring eyes from the shadows to one side of the room. The face was thickly bearded. But still, there was something familiar about the eyes that had turned quickly away. Icicles of fear began to freeze along her spine and she had to force her legs to move, to take her on up the steps.

Evil, foreboding, whoever that man was, he hated her—but why? He reminded her of Luke Tate, but he was probably killed a long time ago, she hoped—and if he lived, he would surely have more sense than to return to Wayne County.

Shaking herself, Kitty turned to the moment at hand. Lena had to be found. Whether she wanted help or not, she was going to get it.

The hall was dark and smelled musty. Tiny gas lanterns illuminated the worn, slick carpet with its patches of dried vomit. Kitty had worked around the smell too long not to recognize it. The walls were badly stained. It was a wretched place, she thought with revulsion.

Kitty knocked on the first door on the left. A man's voice boomed out nastily, "I'm not through yet, and my time ain't up anyway, so quit poundin' on the goddamned door!"

She hurried to the other side of the hall. "Yeah, come on in," a man called out happily. "I can take on two at the same time." A woman giggled.

Disgusted and with a heavy heart, Kitty moved to another door. How could her mother live this way? How could she have done it? She knocked loudly and a few seconds later the door was yanked open. A naked woman stood there scowling. "Well, what the hell do you want?" she demanded. "I'm busy. See Big Bertha downstairs if you want a job."

"I'm looking for Lena," Kitty was barely able to whisper as her eyes fell on the naked man stretched out in the rumpled bed. Her gaze quickly moved back to the angry woman's face. "Please can you tell me which of these rooms is hers?"

"Try the last door on the right!" The door slammed shut in her face.

She moved on down the hallway, hesitating outside the closed door before knocking gently. There was no sound from inside. She knocked harder, then leaned forward and called out softly, "Momma . . . it's me . . . Katherine."

There was only silence from inside. Grasping the knob, Kitty was relieved to see it turn. The door squeaked open to display a black hole of darkness. "Momma . . . are you in here?"

Kitty jumped, startled, as a feeble moan came out of the blackness. "Momma, is that you?" Her heart pounded fearfully. What if the sound was coming from a drunk man who might leap on her at any moment? This was a terrible place. Anything could happen. Why, oh, why had her mother degraded herself so?

"Here . . ." the voice was barely audible, but it was Lena's.

"Wait . . ." Kitty hurried back into the musty hallway, stood on tiptoe to take down a lantern from a nail hanging on the wall, then approached the bed. In the flickering light, she saw her mother's pale, stricken face, her eyes sunk deep into her head; and when she reached out to touch her forehead, it was hot with fever. "Momma, how long have you been like this? Why didn't you send for me?"

"Didn't . . . want you . . . to see me . . . like this," Lena gasped, obviously in pain. "Knew . . . it was . . . gettin' bad. Didn't know . . . what to do . . . for my kind of sickness."

Kitty realized right away what her mother was talking about. She obviously had the dreaded disease that some people got from having sex and not being choosy about who they had it with. That, and becoming pregnant, had been fears she herself had lived with. She'd seen many soldiers with it, too, some of them in agony, their bodies broken out in open, pus-filled, draining sores.

"I'm going to go back to the hospital and get some rosin pills, sassafras . . ." Kitty babbled in fright, pushing back the damp hair from Lena's forehead. "We have some pieces of blue vitrol, too. I'll come back and sponge down that fever, and we'll move you to the hospital in the morning." She was speaking more to herself than to her mother right then, her mind frantic, knowing how sick she was.

She had been sitting on the side of the bed and moved to get up, but Lena's hand crept across the sheet to touch hers, to clasp it weakly. "Want you to know . . . I always . . . loved you. The war . . . the war did this . . . to all of us . . . your pa . . ."

"Momma, the last I heard, Poppa was alive," Kitty said through her tears. "Now don't you fret. I won't be gone long. I'm going to get some things I need and in the morning I'll have someone help me take you to the hospital. I live in a small room there, but there's room for another cot. You can stay with me, Momma, and together we'll find a way to make it. The house may be gone, and the barn, but it's *our* land. We'll make it—I know we will." She was babbling, frightened. Lena looked terribly sick. It was plain now why one one had helped her or wanted to go near her, even if they had cared just a little. Everyone was afraid of what Lena had.

"No hope . . ."

"Yes, there *is* hope, Momma. There's always hope. We have to believe in that. Now I have to leave you for a little while to get some medicine for you. We have to get that fever down."

Lena was crying. "I only wanted . . . the best for you."

"Momma, I know, I know," she said, patting Lena's hand. Kitty stood up. "Now I have to leave. I won't be gone long."

"Forgive me . . . ," she said, breaking into great, racking sobs.

"Now you stop that!" Kitty said fiercely, sitting down again and leaning over to place her hands on Lena's shoulders and giving her a gentle little shake. "Poppa was alive the last I heard, fighting with the Yankee cavalry up in Tennessee. They say he's the strongest, bravest, fiercest soldier in the whole Union army. He's going to come out of this alive—I know he is. And if he doesn't want to come home, if they won't let him, then we'll sell the farm and go to him. We'll start a new life somewhere else. Now stop that crying, you hear? You need your strength. You have to get well—get out of this place."

The sobs quieted. Kitty stood up and waited. Her mother was now very still, her eyes closed. She was either asleep or had fainted—for the moment, the suffering was gone. Hurrying from the room, Kitty made her way downstairs once more, pushed through the crowded room, and stepped out into the street.

She ran most of the way back to the hospital, and when she bounded up the steps, lifting her skirt so as not to trip, Lonnie stepped quickly out of the shadows to stare at her in alarm. "What happened? Is someone chasing you?"

Brushing by him, she mumbled only that her mother was ill, then hurried into the hospital to get the items she needed from the supply closets. When she returned, carrying a doctor's borrowed satchel, Lonnie blocked her path.

"I'm going with you."

"No, I don't want you to go with me, Lonnie. Not now."
She didn't want anyone to see the filth her mother lived
in, the degradation surrounding her.

She pushed by him, then paused apologetically. "Lonnie,
I appreciate your concern, honestly I do. But this is something I have to do myself."

"But a woman has no business out there on the streets
alone, this time of night."

"Please. I can take care of myself."

She hurried on down the steps, impatient to get to her
mother. How sick was she? It was hard to tell. All the
doctors were busy. A trainload of wounded had just arrived
and everyone at the hospital was bustling about treating
the new patients. She needed to be with them but for the
moment, Lena had to come first. She couldn't even ask one
of the doctors to leave and come with her. Not now. It
would be much better if she could bring the fever down
herself and then have one of the men at the saloon help
move Lena to the hospital. Perhaps Joe, the bartender,
would help. He didn't seem too bad a sort.

So many thoughts were whirling about in her head.
Could the terrible disease be cured? She doubted it. Some
were, some were not. Lena's case seemed pretty advanced.
The house and barn were gone. There was no home to
go to. The hospital was the only refuge for the moment.
Would the South win the war? And if it lost, what then?
What would happen to all of them? And Nathan, was it
really and truly over between them? Could they ever love
again? Or were they merely suffering agonies of love caused
by the grimness of war? And Travis, if he lived, if she
ever saw him again, what would she feel? What would he
feel? Oh, God, there was so much confusion and turmoil
both around her and within her.

She was approaching the vacant lot, overgrown with
shrubs and weeds and thick undergrowth. Shivering, she
almost crossed the street but instead chided herself for
being so foolish and continued on her way. It was but a
short distance to the main street and she was almost running in her haste to get out of the darkness and into the
light.

It happened so quickly that there was no warning of
danger. Suddenly a figure loomed up out of the shadows,

blocking her path. At the split second that the scream bubbled its way up and into her throat, ready to emerge and split the stillness of the night, a hand clamped tightly over her face, stifling any sound. The satchel tumbled to the ground as an arm went about her chest, pinning her hands to her sides.

And then he was there, sour breath falling hotly on her face, eyes blazing ominously in the darkness. "We meet again, you little tiger, and I've got quite a score to settle with you."

Above, in the inky sky, a cloud moved slightly, parted, and a thin shaft of moonlight filtered down through the night.

And in that moonlight, she recognized the hated, leering face of the one man she feared above all others—Luke Tate.

❧ Chapter Thirty-four ❧

KITTY struggled in vain against the man who held her.
Finally, she was able to twist her face to part her
lips and bit down on a finger that slid between her teeth.
Yelping, he let her go, and she was able to scream.

"Goddamn you." Luke reached out for her, but she
twisted from his grasp, then lost her balance and tumbled
to the ground. She was struggling to get to her feet when
she felt him grabbing her from behind. And just at that
moment footsteps came thundering down the dirt street.
Someone was yelling.

Luke shouted to his men to bring the horses. Kitty
felt herself being lifted in his arms and she struggled with
all her might, kicking, scratching. A gun exploded somewhere close by, then another. More yells and screams, and
then something crashed into the side of her head and
everything went black, dissolving into a vast nothingness.

When she opened her eyes, it was daylight. She was
lying on her stomach across the back of a horse, her body
painfully jostled as the animal galloped. The ground sped
by in a blur beneath her gaze. A dull, throbbing pain
spread from the back of her head all the way around to
her cheek. Her hands were tied behind her back. A sharp
throb ached along her legs. Turning her head slightly, she
could see and hear more horses, thundering along beside
her, around her, in front and in back.

"Hey, she's awake," someone yelled.

"We need to stop and rest a spell." There was another voice. The jostling slowed. Kitty was gasping for breath. Mercifully, the horse stopped. She felt herself being pulled back, set on her feet.

Gazing into the mocking face of Luke Tate, Kitty felt anger so strong that it constricted her whole body, making her quiver and shake.

"Ain't you going to say hello to an old friend, my pretty little tiger?" He grinned that yellow-toothed smirk that made her cringe in fearful anticipation of what lay ahead. God, why did this have to happen—and now? For an instant, she closed her eyes, lifted her face to the skies, and silently asked her Maker what had ever provoked Him to send down such wrath.

Then she faced him. "Why did you do this to me, Luke? Why couldn't you leave me in peace? My mother is sick, very sick. She needs me."

"You knowed it was me back there in that saloon. You think I was going to let you put the Rebs on my ass? Tell them I was the one that killed Doc Musgrave and all the rest? Hell, no. That's why I brought you with me, my pretty, that and the memory of all the good times we had together." He chuckled and it was an evil, nasty sound.

"Don't you touch her!"

Kitty snapped around to gasp at the sight of Lonnie Carter, sitting atop a horse, hands tied behind his back.

"I remembered how you tend to cooperate when you have a buddy along," Luke said matter-of-factly. "He came tearing out of that hospital with some more Rebs. We killed them and brought him along."

"But why?" Tears were stinging her eyes. "Just let us go, please. Let me go back and take care of my mother, and I swear to you I'll never mention a word about you, Luke."

"I doubt you could be trusted. Besides, there's probably a posse out after us since we killed a few of those bastards."

"That's right, Luke. You've got us in one hell of a mess. So what do we do now?"

The man speaking was big and dirty, and as he stepped forward, Kitty fought the impulse to gag at the filthy odor that emanated from his body. There was a purplish scar winding its way across his face, pulling down the corner of one eye to give him an ugly, grotesque look. He towered above Luke and when he spoke, a gravel-huskiness to the tone, it was obvious that Luke stood a bit in awe of him.

"She would've told. I know she would. I had to do what I did."

"So what do we do now? These parts is crawling with soldiers looking for bushwhackers and 'Buffaloes,' and here we are travelin' with a Reb and a woman. You think we ain't going to attract attention? I say head for the hills and leave these two right here."

Kitty was silently counting the men with Luke. Besides him and the scar-face, there were fourteen others. And they were all heavily armed. Then her eyes fell on the borrowed satchel tied to the saddle of the horses she'd been lying across. In the bottom of that satchel was a tiny surgeon's scalpel—beneath the medicine she'd stuffed inside. At the time, it had occurred to her it wouldn't be needed, but why take the time to remove it, either? Now she was glad it was in there, for it gave her some feeling of self-protection, however slim it might be against sixteen men. Still, she thought with a chill of anger, if Luke touched her—even if it meant her own life—she was surely going to take *his*.

"Listen, Jabe," Luke was saying, "I know what I'm doing. This woman's smart when it comes to doctorin'. We can use her if we get into a skirmish."

"Ain't plannin' on gettin' in no skirmish, Luke. I'm headin' out west to California, out of all this goddamned fightin' and killin'. Now you comin' with me, or you goin' to hang around here and wind up with a bullet in your gut or a rope around your neck? We're hated by both sides, you know! I'm gettin' out while I still can . . . headin' straight for the mountains and then due west!"

A cry of approval came up from the others. Kitty watched as Luke's gaze darted around; he realized he was outnumbered. Finally, he looked back at Jabe. "Okay, I'm comin' along. But let me take the girl for a little while at least. She's good, I tell you, and she'll warm your bed like no other woman can," he added with a meaningful snicker.

Jabe's eyes flicked over her, falling on her heaving bosom as he ran his tongue across his lips. "Yeah, I guess so. We'll keep her awhile, just for fun, but when I say she goes, she goes. Understand?"

Luke nodded eagerly. So he was no longer the leader, Kitty thought with satisfaction. The scar-face was obviously in control.

Luke was pointing his finger at her. "Get back on that horse and don't try nothin' funny," he barked. "For now, you ain't got nothin' to worry about 'cept keepin' me and Jabe filled with our pleasures. You try anything and that Reb soldier-friend of yours will suffer for it."

"You son of a bitch, I'll gladly die for her," Lonnie cried, straining at the ropes around his wrists, his face purple with rage. "I'd rather die than see you lay a hand on her!"

"And I'd rather die than let you touch me again," Kitty screamed, reaching out to rake her nails down one side of Luke's face before he sent her sprawling to the ground with one slap of his hand.

Stepping forward, he placed one booted foot on her chest to hold her firmly on the ground. Gasping, she clutched at the boot, trying to remove the heavy weight, but he laughed down at her and pressed harder. "Now get something straight once and for all," he barked gruffly. "There's worse things than death. You give me any more trouble and so help me, God, we'll hold that Reb down and cut both his legs off and let him bleed to death. You understand? And then I'll cut your face up so no man'll ever have you again—once I let my men take turns with you. So which is it goin' to be?"

She looked at Lonnie whose face had turned pale. A man sitting on a horse next to him was turning a large knife over and over in his hands. Then, while Kitty watched in horror, the man reached out with one quick swipe and slashed across the top of Lonnie's right thigh. Lonnie screamed as blood began to spurt forward.

"It ain't deep," the man with the knife snickered. "But it can be."

"Now what's it going to be?" Luke snarled.

She nodded helplessly. For the moment, it was all she could do.

Night fell and still they rode on, wanting to put as much distance between them and Wayne County as possible. When they stopped, it was only to water the horses and sip themselves from the muddied streams. The only food was hardtack and a few corn dodgers. Kitty was so heartsick over her plight and so worried about what was to become of her mother that she could not swallow, even though her throat was parched and her stomach rumbled with hunger pangs.

Finally, toward the evening of the second day when they stopped to rest, Luke wrapped his beefy hand around her throat and forced her to her knees. As he plunged her face into the stream, she saw the wiggle-tails, the mold, and the slime along its edge.

"Drink, damn you." Luke pushed her head into the water as she choked and gagged. "You think I'm goin' to let you die on me? Drink, I say."

He raised her head, then pushed it down once again and over and over until he was obviously satisfied that she did, indeed, swallow some of the water. Then he thrust a corn dodger into her hand. "Eat this, or I'll force it down your throat."

Obediently, she began chewing the tasteless morsel as Luke knelt in front of her to make sure she did. Somewhere a gun exploded, and both of them sprang to their feet just as one of the men came crashing out of the woods to cry jubilantly: "A deer! We shot ourselves a deer! We'll feast tonight!"

A fire was built and the venison roasted. Someone brought out a jug, then another, and Kitty hid in the shadows, watching as the men drank themselves into a stupor. Something told her that tonight would be the night that Luke would force himself upon her.

Tied to a tree, Lonnie leaned over and motioned with his eyes for her to come to him. She crept to the tree and he whispered, voice quivering with emotion, "Miss Kitty, I don't care what they do to me. Don't let them hurt you if you can help it. I'd rather die. It's a matter of honor."

"I think . . ."—she said, speaking with such amazing calmness that it stunned her when she thought about it later—"I think that I, too, am ready to die, Lonnie. It's all over."

Nimbly, she stole through the night to where the horses were tied. The satchel was still hanging from the saddle. Reaching inside, fumbling through the medicine intended for Lena, her fingers closed around the scalpel. Bending over, she slid it carefully into the side of her high-top shoe. She would have to walk cautiously lest it cut into her own flesh.

She knew what had to be done. Returning to the tree and sitting down next to Lonnie, she whispered, "Do you think they will leave you tied here all night?"

"I haven't been untied since the night we left Goldsboro." He sounded defeated. "They force water in my mouth and stuff food down my throat. I don't have any idea they'll do otherwise now. God, Kitty, I think death would be sweeter. They're going to wind up killing us anyway."

Slowly, she pulled the little knife from her boot and snaked her arm around behind the tree. Feeling for the ropes that bound him, she told him she was going to cut him free, but he should wait until the time was right before making his move. "Luke Tate is getting drunk right along with the rest of them, but I have all ideas he's going to rape me tonight. Now when he tries, I'm going to put this knife in his throat. When you hear the commotion, you run for a horse and get away. Don't worry about me."

He looked at her, shocked, face glistening with perspiration in the soft glow from the dying embers of the fire nearby. "You know I ain't gonna leave you behind."

"Oh, I have an idea that when they realize what I've done to Luke, they're going to kill me right away." Again, she was surprised at her calmness. "If there's a chance, I'll try to escape, too. Otherwise, you go on and just do me one favor."

He watched her intently.

"I want you to promise me you'll head right back to Goldsboro as quick as you can and find my mother and get her to the hospital. If you don't, she'll die. She may already be dead."

"I promise," he whispered huskily.

She finished cutting through the rope, then placed the knife back in her boot—and they waited.

And she did not have long to wait.

The men were singing, jostling each other, turning up their bottles and jugs. One by one, they passed out, until only Luke Tate was left swaying. He stumbled toward the tree, a jug still in his hand. "Betcha been waitin' on me, haven't you, pretty tiger?" His voice was thick and heavy. "Been rememberin' all those good times we had, huh?"

"Damn you, Tate, leave her alone," Lonnie cried.

With a loud snort, Luke whirled to send his foot crashing into the soldier's stomach. Kitty felt a wave of panic. What if he knocked him unconscious? It would not be hard to do. Lonnie was not fully recovered from his wound. If he should slump forward, hands untied for Luke to see, then it would be obvious she had cut him free. And with what? Luke would naturally search for a knife. Her plan would fail. And he would make her suffer even more.

Miraculously, Lonnie fought the pain. Gritting his teeth and pressing his back against the tree trunk, he said nothing more. Satisfied that he had conquered once again, Luke reached down and brutally dragged Kitty to her feet, wrapping his fingers in her long hair.

"Beautiful, you are . . ." As he spoke, she fought the wave of nausea that rose in her body at the smell of his sour breath. She tried to turn her head away, but he held her tightly, his lips moving across her face, covering it with wet kisses.

"Come on . . . got somethin' for you." He laughed. "Been a long time . . . probably be quick the first time . . . make it up again and again and again." He dragged her along, away from the dying campfire and the loud drunken snores of the other men.

When they had walked perhaps fifty feet into the woods, Luke stopped in a small clearing and glanced upward through the bare branches of the tree above. "Ain't much moonlight tonight, damnit. I wanted to see you naked. Best damned body I ever seen on a woman."

He gave her a shove that sent her sprawling to the ground and he started fumbling with his pants. "Now get them clothes off . . . no, just shove that skirt up . . . let me have it quick. Then we'll play while I get ready again. We'll do it all night long."

With her skirt covering her ankles, Kitty was able to slip the scalpel out of her boot, clenching it inside her fist. Luke fell to the ground beside her as she lay motionless, seemingly frozen. Grumbling as he shoved at her skirt, he pushed the material up and yanked her drawers down. She felt his hands pulling her thighs apart and then he probed, about to make his first savage plunge into the recesses of her body.

And then it happened. She came to life as she felt that first hot stab. And the indignity of what she was forced to endure, of what was being inflicted upon her, woke her from her trancelike stupor. She brought up the knife, intending to stab him right in the back of his neck; but Luke felt the motion, the hysteria of it, and just as the blade came slashing down, he jerked quickly to one side and Kitty felt the flesh of his shoulder being ripped apart— felt the gush of warm blood splash down onto her face as he screamed in agony.

Footsteps came crashing through the fallen leaves, and voices were yelling. Luke rolled to one side, clutching himself, cursing. Kitty was on her feet, still holding onto the scalpel, holding it above her head threateningly as the men rushed into the clearing, one of them holding a torch high.

"What the hell . . ." It was Jabe, stepping forward to look in shock at the blood rushing from the wound in Luke's shoulder. "I'll be damned. You bitch . . ." He whirled on Kitty whose face was illuminated by the flickering torch. Her eyes shone purple, glittering yellow darts, like a caged, trapped animal staring out of the darkness. Her lips were trembling wordlessly, but the hand she held above her head was steady: it held the knife firmly.

"You put that knife down."

She did not move.

"Go get that soldier—that Reb—and kill him."

One of the men moved back toward the camp. Kitty still stood her ground, holding the knife menacingly. No one took a step forward.

"Somebody help me, damnit, I'm bleedin' to death," Luke moaned. "She bared me to the *bone*."

The sound of shouting came from the woods beyond where one of the men had gone after Lonnie. She prayed he had escaped as she had told him, prayed that he would not stay behind in an effort to save her. If need be, she was prepared to die.

But that hope was short-lived as someone yelled that the Reb was untied and had been knocked unconscious. "Want me to kill him?" a soldier asked.

"Wait . . ." Jabe was smiling, a slow, taunting grin, his scar twisting grotesquely in the glow of the torch. He took a step toward Kitty. "Hand me that knife, girl, or I'll go back to camp and cut that boy's legs off—one by one—and then his arms and his hands and . . ."

"Stop it," she screamed, unable to envision the horror any longer. "Stop it, please." But still she held the knife and then the thought washed over her: plunge it into her own chest. End this madness, this nightmare, once and for all.

She brought the knife down, but then, at the last instant, flung it to the ground. "I can't," she sobbed, burying her face in her hands. "I can't even kill myself."

Jabe stepped forward quickly to yank her to her feet, then he slapped her once, twice, three times, snapping her head to and fro. "Now you listen to me," he roared. "You're going to sew that cut up. You're going to fix Luke up or so help me, woman, we'll kill that Reb and then kill you. Now what's it going to be?"

He yanked her along, not waiting for an answer, and snapped at the others to bring Luke back to camp. When they reached the clearing, he barked orders to build up the fire. She saw Lonnie lying on the ground unconscious. Jabe told someone to throw water in his face to wake him up and then tie him tight. "We're going to start chopping on him—toes first. Get me an ax."

"No!" Kitty shook her head from side to side, her whole body heaving with terror. "No. Don't do it. I'll . . . do whatever you want."

Jabe laughed, a nasty, ugly sound. "That's better. I kind of figured you'd see it our way."

❧ Chapter Thirty-five ❧

KITTY was mad—with herself, with the whole world and everyone in it. She sat beside a rushing stream, watching the sparkling waters dance along the rocks, and thought about the hell her life had become. The night before she'd held a knife to her breast but at the last moment could not make that final plunge. There had been too many times in the past months when she had succumbed to tears. Weak. Damn it to hell, she was getting weak!

Picking up a nearby pebble, she sent it splashing into the stream, a scowl on her face. Had she been noble in sewing up Luke Tate's shoulder to keep his men from mutilating Lonnie? If so, there was no chest-swelling over saving his life. Instead, there was only a heavy shroud of defeat, hopelessness—and that shroud was, at the moment, smothering her. The wound had not been deep, but there was a blood vessel that had to be tied off. Doc had taught her how to use boiled horsehair for ligatures in an emergency. He had even been using flax thread to sew the flesh together. Luke had allowed her to do this, all the while howling with pain each time the tenaculum she'd found in the satchel entered the skin. And after it was over, as she prepared to bandage the wound, Luke had insisted that a red-hot knife be applied to the flesh to cauterize it. Kitty felt it wasn't necessary but said nothing, feeling actually gleeful when the searing blade made the flesh burn and sizzle and Luke screamed and passed out. How she hated that man!

At sunrise Kitty went to the stream to bathe and she sat there, brooding. What would happen next? Luke and the others were heading west. Did they plan to take her along, raping her at will? God, she might as well do what Travis's sister had done when faced with the same future —commit suicide. But no, she'd had her chance for that and was angry now that it had even been contemplated. That was not the way out. No. She was not an ignorant farm girl and certainly she was not about to give in to the weakness of being female and do nothing about her plight. There had to be an answer somewhere.

From behind, up the little sloping hill, there was laughter. The men were drinking again. Feeling eyes upon her, she turned in time to observe one of them checking to see if she was still there. They were keeping a closer watch on her than on Lonnie, who had not even been re-tied since the events of the night before and was now sitting listlessly against a tree trunk nursing a throbbing headache from the blow he had received. Why did he have to be so damn noble, Kitty cursed. Why didn't he go on and leave when he had the chance and find help for her? It was extremely doubtful they would have killed her so quickly. Then she checked herself. They might have, for had it not been for Lonnie, she knew there was no power on earth strong enough to have made her tend to Luke's wound. And they might very well have been angered to the point of shooting her.

So what difference did it make? Digging her bare feet into the mud, she watched the reddish-brown slime ooze between her toes. On how many summer days had she done the same childish thing back home in North Carolina? But that was a lifetime ago.

A cool wind was blowing. Her skin felt chilled. How she hated to put on those uncomfortable ankle-high shoes. *The next dead Yankee I find, I'll steal his boots*, she thought defiantly.

Footsteps crackled in the dead leaves that covered the slope behind. Whipping about, Kitty saw Jabe coming toward her and a wave of defiance swept through her. If he made one move to touch her, she would jump right into the stream and let it carry her to the thundering falls below. Better to take a chance with nature than with this evil man, she figured.

"Kitty, I think it's time me and you had a talk." He sat down beside her, his voice somber, his eyes stormy.

"I have nothing to say to you or any of your hoodlum friends. I just wish I'd had the guts to let that bastard die . . . that I'd cut his throat like I tried to. . . ."

"Shut up! I ain't interested in listening to the ravings of some fool woman. I come down here to talk to you and tell you that I'm gettin' rid of you."

She blinked. He was talking so *calmly* about getting rid of her? It was unreal. "If you're going to kill me"—she managed to find her voice—"then go ahead and do it and not sit here and talk about it." Strangely, she was unafraid.

"Ain't gonna kill you, Kitty. I'm gonna trade you off in exchange for quick passage through these mountains. You see, you're big trouble for me. Luke's got quite a hankerin' for you and you are a right smart pretty woman. I wouldn't mind having some of you myself. But the thing is, Luke's got this hankerin', like I said, and he ain't ready to pass you around yet. My men ain't gonna like riding with a woman and not being able to take their pleasure with her. It'll get harder and harder. Sooner or later, there'll be some bad trouble and I don't want any of my men killed over some damn woman. So, the only thing to do is get rid of you."

She shook her head from side to side, puzzled.

He grinned, his scar twisting his eye downward in a grotesque grimace. "I'm gonna trade you off to the Indians. Talked to a scout this morning that says, as best I can understand sign language, that he'll go back and see if his chief agrees. Winter's comin' on and if them Indians will show us an easy way over these mountains before the snow comes, we'll be that much ahead. The war can't last much longer and whichever side does win, me and Luke and the likes of us will be better off if we ain't around."

"Indians . . ." Kitty turned her head to stare at the rushing waters, which seemed to be crashing toward the falls along with any hope she might have had for freedom. "Why? Why do you have to do this to me? Why not set me and Lonnie free—here? By the time we found civilization in all this wilderness, you and your men would be far, far away. Why do this thing?" She shook her head from side to side, not frightened, not pleading, but merely bewildered by the sudden turn in events. She thought of her mother back there in that hotel room. Would she die? Would anyone help her? And she thought of her father. Would she ever see him again? And then there was Travis who was probably dead, but was ever present in her thoughts and memories. And Nathan. Had the war destroyed their love? Would there have been a chance for them later? Now she would never know—not living with Indians.

Indians. What was it she had heard about them? Savages, some said. Killers. Murderers. But they had been moved out west to reservations, or so she had been taught in school. She could remember her teacher in the community school telling about the "Trail of Tears" which began in October of 1838 and ended in March 1839, when the Cherokees in the western North Carolina mountains were forced to walk to their reservation in the state of Oklahoma. Of the twelve thousand who started the twelve-hundred mile journey, four thousand had died. A great tragedy, her teacher had said, both for the Indians and the American people.

Frantically searching the recesses of her mind for any other information she might remember, it came to her that some of the Indians had hidden in the hills and caves of the mountains and managed to escape the troops rounding them up. Were these the Indians, or their descendants, to whom she was being traded almost thirty years later?

"There's no other way," Jabe was saying tonelessly. "I don't say it's right, trading a white woman to the Indians, but I got myself and my men to look after. Now we'll do it quiet, so's not to rile Luke. I'll tell him about it later when it's too late for him to do anything about it. 'Course the shape he's in, he couldn't do anything now if he wanted to 'cept holler when the Indians come for you, and that might scare 'em off, make 'em think you're bad medicine."

Kitty felt as though everything within her had just died. Then she remembered Lonnie. "What will you do with him?"

"Lonnie? Don't rightly know. He ain't good for much. We might keep him around to fetch wood for campfires, stuff like that. We don't have to worry about him giving us no trouble. Hell"—he threw back his head and laughed —"Pete says when he went back to the camp and aimed to kill him, he didn't have the heart 'cause the son of a bitch was down on his hands and knees scared shitless and beggin' for his life. So Pete just knocked him in the head 'cause it made him sick to see all that grovelin'. Naw, we ain't got to worry about old Lonnie, not as big a coward as he is." He laughed again.

Kitty felt sick. Was there no hope? She had always taken pride in being a bit above the average mealy-mouthed woman who merely accepted her lot in life without question. She had looked in scorn upon the women who were content only to have a baby every year and sit around and sew and tat and do the "proper" things. She had wanted more—had wanted most of all to be free and independent to do what she wanted to do with her life, not to be destined to do as others of her sex had done before her merely because she was born a woman. She remembered thinking defiantly that it didn't take a penis and a pair of testicles to be a doctor, but merely a good brain, and she felt she was equipped with sufficient intelligence to pursue the education required to practice medicine. And there had been those who were appalled at such an idea. A woman's place was to marry, give her husband pleasure, have his children, keep his home. Kitty had defiantly thought otherwise. But now, what did any of it matter? She was about to be traded off to a bunch of savages, probably to be raped over and over till she became pregnant with some buck's child and then she would sit among the ranks of squaws for the rest of her life. Bitter tears filled her eyes.

"This young buck rode right into camp this morning, brave as could be," Jabe was saying. "He was hopin' we'd have some whiskey or guns we wanted to trade. We let him know we were poor on both counts. Then he got to lookin' at Luke's arm, the way you sewed it. He started askin' a lot of questions in sign language and I got him over to one side and started trying to make the swap, because already the idea had hit me that here was a great way of getting rid of you quick."

Kitty had to make her choice: to leap into the madly rushing stream and perhaps be dashed to death on the rocks below the falls, or to stay and be given to the Indians. She put one foot into the water, felt the strong current rushing against her ankle. Already her toes could feel the slope of the land. Another few feet and the bottom would drop off sharply and she would plunge right into the charging water and be swept away. But perhaps, she thought frantically, she might be able to make it to the other side. She'd taught herself how to swim—and she'd been able to outswim any of the boys back home as a child. There might be a chance and she had to take it.

She lunged forward. The waters closed about her head for one quick instant. The current wasn't all that strong, she realized, and she was able to move her arms to fight against it. The thing to do was move away from shore toward the other side and try to make it to the opposite bank. Whatever awaited her there—wild animals, Yankees—anything was better than what lay behind. Gasping for air, filling her lungs, she found it extremely hard to keep the current from taking her away completely. In spite of her struggling, she was being carried down. Jabe was running along the bank, yelling that he was going to kill her if the falls didn't. Some of his men were scurrying out of the woods to see what all the screaming was about.

A few feet. She had made a few feet of progress toward the opposite shore. How much farther? It was difficult to gauge distance in water. From the bank, it had appeared to be fifty or sixty feet. Now it seemed miles away. Suddenly, she was slammed against a rock and she lay there, pressed back, gasping, resting against the current that gurgled and pushed about her neck, splashing into her face. It was a welcome rest for the moment, but then she realized that Jabe was standing at an angle to her right with a rope in one hand and his hand gun in the other.

"It's your choice, Kitty," he yelled across the thunder of the rushing waters. "You grab this rope when I throw it and let me pull you in, or I'm going to shoot you here and now."

She could tell by the grimace on his face that he was serious, but there was no way that she would grab the rope and be hauled back in. When he lifted his arm to fire, she would duck her head and let the current take hold. Her fate would be in the hands of the Lord and the stream with the falls waiting not far away.

"What the hell's goin' on here?" Luke came charging out of the woods, eyes bulging, shoulder wrapped in blood-stained bandages that would soon need changing again. His gaze took in Kitty, pressed against a rock in the middle of the stream with the water swirling all about her face, and Jabe, on the bank preparing to throw a rope out and holding a gun in one hand. "You hear me, Jabe? What the hell's goin' on? Get her outta there!"

He started down the sloping bank, his face pale. He had lost much blood during the night. Once he stumbled, grabbed at a nearby tree trunk to right himself, then continued on down. Kitty felt sick at the sight of Lonnie peeking out from behind a tree, his eyes wide with terror. If the boy had ever had any grit, it was gone now.

Jabe swung the rope above his head and then snaking his arm out, he threw it. It landed with a dull plop less than a yard away from the rock. Kitty could have reached out and caught hold—but didn't. "Damn you, girl, I said grab the rope. You think I won't shoot? I'm givin' you one more try."

"You ain't shootin' her, Jabe," Luke cried, reaching his side and struggling for the gun. There was a brief scuffle and Kitty watched as Jabe easily threw the wounded man aside. He yelled to his men to keep him down on the ground, then he hauled the rope in and made ready to throw it once again.

This is it, Kitty told herself, filling her lungs with great gulps of air and making ready to plunge beneath the water. When she failed to grab the rope, Jabe would surely raise his gun and fire. How high were the falls? She guessed it would be about a hundred-foot drop. There were rocks in the pool below, sharp rocks. The thing to do was fight for consciousness, try to leap off the falls away from the rocks, and guide her descent. She could do it. She knew she could. Damnit, this was her life and she was not going to give up ever again—not as long as there was breath in her body. She would never let the war, or any man, take the spirit from her again. By God, she had fallen to her knees and begged for mercy for the last time. If death waited, then so be it. That would be faced as stoically as possible. But she would fight it to the end. No longer would she be pummeled through life as was her body now threatened by these swirling waters which were drawing her into their dictating grasp. Whatever happened, it would not be due to her allowing the current of life to sweep her up and along without a struggle.

The crashing sound of rushing water was deafening. Blinking against the stinging sprays of the torrent, Kitty saw the rope making its final arch through the air, landing just beside her.

"Grab it, goddamn it," Jabe screamed. "Grab it, or I'll kill you." One of his men had taken hold of the end of the rope. Jabe was lowering his handgun, pointing it straight at her.

She took one last great swallow of air, filling her lungs till they ached. Her arms moved, projecting her body around and into the gushing, gurgling waters that waited to gobble and consume like some great predatory creature of the wild.

And just as the waters closed, she heard the great explosion.

Kitty opened her eyes, closed them again. She was dreaming. A man with feathers in his hair was staring down at her. Silly dream. That's all it was. Feathers, indeed. Soon her mother would be in to tell her to get up, and if she were lucky, this would be another day to slip off with Doc Musgrave in his old buggy, going around to visit the sick in the county. Or maybe Pa would want to go hunting, letting her tag along. And there was that handsome Nathan Collins coming to call. His kisses left her dizzy. Blue skies. Warm winds across the sandy plains of eastern North Carolina. Cotton fields with white puffs ripening in the sun. Green tobacco leaves swaying to and fro in the fields. A good life. A rich life. So much happiness, so much joy. No grief here. Not in dreams.

She opened her eyes to reality. A man with feathers in long, shiny black hair was staring down at her. His eyes were like tiny dots beneath bushy brows. His nose was large and hooked, his mouth a grim, set line surrounded by red skin. An Indian. It was an Indian. Kitty struggled to get up, but there was a fierce pounding across her forehead. Touching it tenderly, her fingertips became tinged with blood. The Indian frowned.

She realized her clothes and her hair were dripping wet. Slowly it was coming back. The stream. Jabe. The choice she'd made. The determination. Dizzily, she did manage to sit up, gasping at the sight of several Indians surrounding her. Bare-chested, they wore buckskin pants; some had hair streaming down, others wore theirs tied back in a queue. A few wore earrings and all had on moccasins.

"Speak."

She blinked. Was the Indian squatting right beside her speaking English?

"Speak," he repeated, pounding his fist into his open palm.

"My name is Kitty," she began to blabber nervously, aware that all those dark beady eyes were glaring at her. "I must've gone over the falls, hit my head. Did you pull me out? I . . . I thank you."

The wind had become brisk and she shivered in her wet dress as the chill passed through her body. The sky above had grown dark, with great gray clouds rolling in ominously across the mountains.

The Indians continued to stare silently. What else was there for her to tell them? Maybe they didn't know about any intended "trade" with Jabe. Perhaps she could just get up and walk quietly away into the woods. These were obviously Cherokees. Surely they were civilized to a degree and knew about the war going on all around them. She had heard about how the Sixty-ninth North Carolina Regiment had recruited two Cherokee companies of men; their chief contribution was a savage shriek that made the Yankees quake in their boots, she recalled. Their only major encounter had been the battle of Pea Ridge back in 1862. They fought well, charging into battle with that soul-squeezing war cry and carrying bows and arrows, guns, tomahawks, war clubs. But the Confederates experienced a major problem with them: They mutilated the dead, which was condemned. In desperation, some Cherokees were being used as scouts, or for raiding when absolutely necessary, and the Choctaw and Chickasaw tribes were used also.

The Indian closest to Kitty reached out and touched her wet hair, and she snapped her head back away from his touch. "Leave me alone," she hissed, struggling to her feet. She began to back away but one of the braves blocked her path.

"Come." The first Indian, that same stony expression on his face, held out his hand. "We go."

He was speaking English. She felt her eyes bulge with astonishment. Seemingly sensing her puzzlement, the Indian said tonelessly. "I fight in war. I come home. I know of white man's war. You go with us. You make medicine."

Then they did know about her, she thought with sagging shoulders as she trudged along followed by those few Indians whose task was to make sure she didn't escape. Where were they going? God only knew. She didn't. But at least she was still alive, and there was still hope for getting out of all this.

The sound of rushing water made her turn her head sharply. They were on the opposite side of the stream's bank now, and she could see Jabe's men standing around, scowling, shaking their fists at the Indians. One of the braves fired a gun in the air and all of them laughed as the white men scattered into the woods, yelling in fright.

And when they scattered, Kitty froze there where she stood. A body lay in a bloody puddle beside the rushing stream. It was Jabe. So that had been the explosion she heard as the waters closed over her: the Indians had shot Jabe, probably saving her life.

But for what reason had it been saved?

Suddenly, the Indian with the most feathers was standing beside her. "Chief's son sick. You come . . . hurry."

"I don't have my satchel," she blurted out. "I need my bag." She motioned with her hands, trying to show him the size of the satchel. "It has medicine . . . a few things. I'll do what I can, I promise, but I need my satchel. Without that, I have nothing."

He turned to the others and barked orders in the language of the Cherokee. Screaming war hoops and brandishing tomahawks, war clubs, and guns they'd stolen from soldiers here and there, the Indians leaped down the bank and headed for the stream. Kitty watched as they ran up the side a little ways and then leaped across the rocks to

427

reach the other side—traversing spaces perhaps as great as six-feet wide—with grace and ease.

He touched her arm. "We go."

Slowly, she turned to follow, and in the distance, over in the woods across the stream, she could hear the sounds of the ear-splitting war whoops, the gunfire, and the screams of dying men.

✣ Chapter Thirty-six ৩%

THE air was heavy with the smell of sulphur. Travis wondered if he would ever know another living moment without the familiar stench in his nostrils. Looking around him in the shadows of the sunset, he noted that everyone in the camp seemed lost in his own thoughts. Were they brooding, as he was, over whether they would live to see another sunset in the Tennessee mountains—or even a sunrise? So many had died. Others would surely follow. Who would be next? Only God knew.

God.

He looked at the sunset, its last rays of orange and pink fading behind the towering pines in the west. God made the sun rise and set, didn't He? He made those trees, so tall and sturdy and proud. And He made him and everyone else about. The wonder of life—the sheer miracle of being alive. Why, then, did he not think very much about God or the hereafter? He'd seen men die in peace, their guts busted open and innards spilling onto the ground, yet they could whisper about hearing beautiful music and seeing blue skies while the rains poured onto their blood-soaked faces. They saw something in death he didn't think he would see when the time came. Evidently they'd seen more in life than he had, too. But what? Living. Dying. That's all that ever happened to a man, wasn't it? And whatever happened, a man had to do the best he could.

He couldn't go around thinking about sunsets and trees and wondering how one person, God, could make everything. But He wasn't really a person, according to the preachers he'd heard in camp occasionally, or *overheard*, actually. He had never gone to a service; but once in a while a parson would deliver a sermon so loud that the very ground shook with his yelling and a person would have to be deaf—or dead—not to hear. The parson talked about the hereafter, how a person who doesn't live right will not be in the Lamb's Book but will burn in hell forever and ever because God won't take him into heaven.

Travis had never thought much about hell—or heaven, either, for that matter. He worried about survival, food in his belly, clothes on his back, a drink when he needed one, and a woman to answer a different kind of need. He'd think about dying when the time came—maybe.

He thought about the other kind of dying, the screaming and cursing and shrieking that went on with some men who weren't really hurting that bad at the last. "Scared to die," someone once said of such a man. "He sees the fires of hell." Bullshit. Travis didn't believe in heaven or hell or God or the devil. He believed in very few things, but those things he defended with his life. Freedom for every man and the preservation of the Union at any cost, those were the things that mattered because those were the things that affected him here and now. He'd worry about this God and His heaven and hell one day when everything else was taken care of.

He wondered suddenly whether Kitty believed in God. Somehow, he felt that she did. She was a peppery one, that woman. Just thinking about those dancing eyes and the saucy grin made him smile to himself. They'd had their bad moments, but there had been some good ones, too. Then, damn it, right when he let his guard down, actually thought that the little vixen was in love with him, she stabbed him in the back like every other female he'd ever let get to him.

It was cold. He wished the fires were burning, but General Grant had said no lights, not with the Rebs all around. Pulling his poncho around his shoulders, he still felt a spot of tenderness where he'd been wounded. But it had healed, thank God, and he had finally gotten out of that horrible house with that crazy woman pulling at his crotch all the time. He shuddered, remembering.

Kitty. Damnit, why did he have to keep thinking about her? She probably hadn't given him a second thought since that day she'd ridden off with her Rebel boyfriend or whoever the hell he was. For all she knew when that shot was fired, it tore into him instead of the soldier he was struggling with. Maybe he should've let him shoot her. Hell, what difference did it make? She hadn't cared. She'd used him. And if he ever got the chance, he'd make her pay for it. How he'd love to wrap his hands around that smooth-skinned neck and twist until those funny-colored eyes of hers popped out.

No. He shook his head, picked up a rock, flung it to no place in particular, then ran a weary hand through his long ragged hair. He could pretend with Sam and everyone else, but the truth was he'd let himself care something about her. He couldn't hurt her. Not that he wanted her again. Oh, no, should they ever meet, he'd turn and keep on going, but he wouldn't hurt her. That funny, warm feeling he got whenever she came to mind would keep him from actually hurting her.

A twig cracked nearby and Travis automatically reached for his rifle. "It's me. . . ." The familiar voice of John Wright cut into the silence. "Don't shoot."

". . . shouldn't be sneaking around on a night like tonight," Travis grumbled as the one-eyed man sat down next to him. "Everybody's on edge."

"And well they should be with these mountains crawling with Confederates."

"You don't like to call them Rebels, do you, John?" Travis said, suddenly aware of this peculiarity.

John snorted. "What's a 'Rebel'? A man who rebels against something? Hell, we're all rebelling against something, aren't we? But what difference does it make? This time tomorrow we may be lying in a ditch rotting."

"You sure are a grim man to have around."

"I feel grim. You heard the news? We're attacking Bragg at sunrise. He's dug in along the slopes, and we've got him outnumbered, we think, but a lot of us will die. I keep wondering if I'm ready to go."

"Go where?" Travis laughed, philosophically proclaiming, "Where do any of us go when it's all over, John? I've been sitting here thinking about that very thing. When the last battle is over, where do we wind up? And don't feed me that bullshit about heaven and hell because I don't accept it."

"I reckon I've had my doubts at times, too, Coltrane, but I'll put it to you this way. If there isn't a heaven or a hell, then what's the point? I mean, what's it all about? What difference does it make how we go through life if we wind up at the same place—all of us together. And if that place is no place, then a lot of men wrote a lot of lies a long, long time ago when they wrote that book called the Bible. Can you sit there and say that a man is born and he lives and he dies and then nothing happens? I don't accept that."

"Then you believe in God."

"Man's got to believe in something, or else why struggle to live? I'd hate mighty bad to think that if I get killed tomorrow when we charge that mountain it's all over. I have to believe that it would really be the beginning, that somehow God finds me good enough to go on to heaven and be at peace through all eternity."

Travis pulled out a cheroot and sniffed it. Damp. He threw it away. "Didn't know you were a religious man, John. I guess I always figured you were a hell-raiser like me with no thought of tomorrow except getting through it."

"Then you don't know me very well. Maybe we should have taken more time to get to know each other, seeing as how I'd kind of gotten the notion that you love my little girl."

Travis's eyes widened as he stared at the shadowy figure. "Love your little girl . . ." he sputtered. "Kitty? Now wait a minute. I've never loved any woman. Granted she's beautiful and I was fond of her—but love?"

John ignored his protest. "Kitty believes in God."

"She does?"

"Yep. We used to sit by the fireside and read from the Bible. We'd talk about God and heaven and living and dying. Kitty's got spunk, no doubt about that. And she's got a temper that would try the patience of a parson, but she's a fine woman."

"Depends on how you look at it," Travis snapped defiantly. "Don't forget, she betrayed me."

"Sure she did because she believed in something. I can't blame her. That's the way I brung her up—to believe in something and stand up for it. She didn't ask to go with you, boy, you dragged her along, remember? I could've told you what she had in mind." He chuckled. "Kitty's a cagey one. I pity the man she marries. He'll have his hands full."

In more ways than one, Travis thought, a warm wave creeping down into his loins, but he didn't dare make such a remark. "I imagine she's married by now, anyway, to that Reb she told me about. She's probably safe and snug back home in North Carolina waiting for him to come marching home from the war."

"No. She didn't marry Nathan."

Again Travis stared incredulously through the shadows at the one-eyed man sitting beside him in the chill of the night. "How do you know? You haven't been home. You told me so yourself."

"Andy got a letter from his mother."

"You told me Andy found out his mother's house was burned and she left and went to live with relatives."

"He found out where she was from a Reb prisoner we took that came from our neck of the woods. Andy let him go in exchange for information from home. Can't say as I blame him. He can't exactly go find out what's going on for himself since everyone knows by now he took an oath to the Union, now can he?"

Travis wasn't interested at the moment in Andy's oath of allegiance or his inability to take a furlough and go home. He wanted to hear whatever Andy had heard about Kitty but didn't want to appear anxious. John would laugh, say he'd been right in accusing him of being in love with his daughter. So he just sat in silence, waiting.

"What's the name of that mountain up yonder? The one we're going for in the morning."

"Somebody said it was called Lookout Mountain. What difference does it make?"

"Well," he said, not sounding at all worried, "if I die up there I'd kinda like to know where I died."

"Ask God when you get to heaven," Travis said sarcastically.

"Well, He'd be able to tell me. He marks the sparrow's fall, you know."

"What the hell does that mean?"

"It means that God has things so organized that He knows when even a little sparrow is going to die."

Silence. Some of the men were stirring about, digging out sow belly and hardtack. They hadn't had much else in weeks. Food was scarce. Travis's stomach rumbled. He thought about the hardtack in his own haversack—a six-inch square cracker, not an inch thick, and solid as a board. The damn things had been made in Boston and they had the initials "B.C." stamped on each one. "Before Christ," someone had remarked once, "that's why they're so goddamned stale. They were made before Jesus was!" They weren't too bad, though, if they were soaked in cold water overnight and fried in grease the next morning.

He snapped back to the present and John Wright and what news he'd had of Kitty. He wanted desperately to ask but forced himself to be silent.

"I think we might just take that mountain," John murmured. "I don't think Bragg's got that many Confederates up there. And we got the Army of the Potomac and the Army of the Tennessee units—and us! General Thomas's soldiers are going to be out for blood, too, considering the way both Hooker's and Sherman's men been jeering 'em for more than a month over the shellackin' they took at Chickamauga, not lettin' 'em forget they had to have help to get 'em out of there."

"Damn it, Wright, what have you heard about Kitty?" Travis yelled, making some of the soldiers about turn and stare.

He was smiling. In the darkness, Travis couldn't see his face, but he knew, without a doubt, he was smiling because he had done what he set out to do: proven that Travis cared about his daughter. "Andy got a letter from his mother, like I said. He'd written to her, told her he had changed over to fight for the Union and couldn't write all those months he was a prisoner."

"That's right. Hell, you don't haul a prisoner around

with you and let him write letters all over the countryside telling everyone where he is."

"Anyway, he told her that Kitty had been held a prisoner with him till she got away. She wrote him back, told him his father hadn't come back."

"You never told him about Orville Shaw?"

"No. You said Kitty told you that was Andy's father your men killed. I never told him. The boy worships you, Travis, looks up to you. True, his pa was a no-good bastard that beat the boy and didn't do right by none of his family, but he was still his pa and it might make him feel different toward you if he knowed it was you what ordered him shot. Some things is best left unsaid. Anyway, his ma wrote him about being burned out and about my place being burned, too. I'm not surprised at that. I figured they'd get around to it sooner or later. Then she went on to say that Kitty had come home, she'd heard, and the reason she heard about it was because what happened was the talk of the town and her cousin heard about it and wrote her."

John's voice had changed pitch, becoming strained, husky; continuing, it appeared, would be difficult. Clearing his throat and taking a deep breath, he plunged on, the words coming rapidly, as if he were anxious to have it out and all said now that he'd gotten started.

"Kitty went home and went to work in the hospital, but one night she was attacked on the street and carried off. Some men were shot and killed. One was taken with her. Somebody who saw them riding out of town swears it was Luke Tate that had her."

Travis's heart was pounding with the flow of angry blood that ripped through his body. Tate! Tate had Kitty! He smacked his fist into the ground again and again, feeling the skin tearing, bleeding, and not caring. Tate had Kitty! Damn it, the son of a bitch had her, and there wasn't a damn thing he could do about it here in the mountains about to go into battle.

John touched his shoulder. "I know, boy, I'm hurtin' just like you are. My girl's been through hell and it don't look like it's ever gonna end. And right now, there's nothing either one of us can do about it. Andy wrote his mother and asked her to get in touch with her cousin and find out everything she could, but that will take a while, the way letters travel so slow these days. It isn't easy getting a letter out of the South to a Northern outfit, either. It has to go through the underground and that does take right smart time."

"So in the meantime, we do nothing." Travis let his breath out. He felt dizzy, not realizing he'd held it so long.

"We try to keep from gettin' killed so when the time comes we can help Kitty—we'll be around. But we can pray . . ."

"Pray?" Travis laughed. "Old man, my prayers wouldn't get above the tree tops. And I don't remember ever having prayed in my whole life."

"You don't have to reach above the tree tops. God will come down here to listen. He moves around quite a bit, I'm told. And there's always a first time. And if you're a bit rusty or can't get started, it'll come to you. The Lord has a way of taking care of that, too."

"Why didn't Andy come to me about this?"

"I don't think he figured you'd care. We talk a lot, Andy 'n me. He says you two fought a lot and at times he thought you hated each other. Toward the end, just before Kitty left, he said he wasn't so sure but he didn't think you wanted to talk about it."

"And what made *you* think I did?"

"Well, I may not have but one eye, Coltrane, but I see more'n most folks think I do."

Tate has Kitty—the knowledge burned into Travis's brain like a thousand branding irons. The son of a bitch had Kitty. Thinking of what he must be doing to her, God, he now wished he had gone on and killed her. Death would have been better than what she was probably being forced to endure! At least he had been gentle. He might have teased her, made her want him, beg for it, but he'd never brutally raped her—and if he did get a bit rough, at the time, she had enjoyed it. He'd made it good to her. However else she might have tricked him, he didn't think she was putting on an act when he was making love to her.

"Want to get some sleep," John asked, "or try to find some hot coffee? Though I don't imagine there's any to be had with no fires going."

"No. I can't sleep and I'm not hungry. I do have one question, though."

John had started to get up but sat back down. "What is it, son?" The voice was gentle, compassionate, as though he knew Travis shared his anguish and concern over Kitty's fate.

"Why aren't you surprised she didn't marry that Reb?"

"Nathan?" He snorted. "Those two grew up together. Kitty was so damned pretty she could have her pick of the boys, but she wasn't interested in boys or in growing up to just get married. We used to talk about that a lot when we was out huntin' or fishin', and she'd tell me how she didn't see why a woman had to grow up and get married and have babies just because she happened to be born a woman, and I agreed with her. She felt like a woman should be able to do what she wanted to do with her life, and from the time she was knee-high to a billy goat, she'd toddle after Doc Musgrave, making rounds with him. She could doctor almost as good as he could. She wanted to go away to school, be a nurse, maybe even a doctor. She didn't hold to sewin' and tattin' and doin' what she called 'women things.' She wanted to be her own person and I agreed with her all the way."

John paused to stick a plug of tobacco in his mouth. "Nathan came from a proud, rich family and had his own notions about what a woman was supposed to be. I knew he and Kitty would lock horns sooner or later over her thinking the way she did, but I didn't discourage him from courtin' her. I know my girl, and I knew when it came right down to it, she wouldn't be pushed around—even if she did think she loved him. And it seems I was right. Andy's momma wrote that Nathan brought her home from Richmond, but they didn't get married. He went back to the war and she went to work in the hospital at Goldsboro, like I said."

"And now she's God-only-knows-where."

"Kitty can take care of herself." John sounded as though he believed it. "If it was any other woman, I'd say by now she was whipped, beaten—but not my girl."

Travis nodded in silent agreement. Kitty would do her best to fight back, try to escape. She would never be beaten into submissiveness. Not her. He looked in the direction of the dog tent he shared with Sam Bucher. Sam's musket had been stuck in the ground with bayonet fixed, holding up the half-shelters. His friend wouldn't be alseep, he knew. He was probably still mumbling and cursing over being ordered to fight on foot with the infantry, but this was the way it had to be. A charge up that mountain couldn't be made easily on horseback, and besides, they'd had the misfortune of getting their mounts shot out from under them, and horses were scarce.

Get the battle over with quickly, he thought fiercely— and then what? There was no way of knowing where Tate had headed. The war was boiling all around, and he couldn't take off to look for her anyway. And if he found her—what then? Send her back to North Carolina to treat wounded Rebs and wait for her Reb boyfriend to patch things up and get married? Hell, nothing made sense anymore. He pounded his boot into the ground.

He remembered something. Turning sharply, he said, "Since when did you want to sit around and chew the fat with me, Wright? I've had the feeling all along you'd shoot me in the back if you got a chance."

"I don't shoot men in the back, Coltrane. I'll admit, at first I thought about it. I hated you for what you did to my little girl. Then I talked to Sam and Andy, and I started figuring out a few things for myself. I've also watched you fight. Takes a man with plenty of courage to fight the way you do. I have to respect that. I figured if anybody could help me find Kitty, it'd be you. When Tate took her before she wound up with you, I didn't know about it—couldn't do anything about it. I guess I went a little crazy when the war first broke out; anyway, I wasn't thinkin' too straight. But now I am straight and I do know about my girl being taken by those sons of bitches and as soon as we whip Johnny Reb tomorrow, I'm going to find her." He paused, gave his words time to soak in, then added, "I kind of hope you'll go with me, Coltrane."

A Sergeant walked up just then, addressing them gruffly: "The General says for everybody to write his name on something and pin it to his shirt. If you get killed, we need to know who you are so we can send word to your family."

Travis smiled sardonically. "What's this 'we' stuff, Sarge?

What makes you think 'we' won't be sending a letter home about *your* guts being blown out?"

John Wright laughed and the Sergeant bellowed, "Just pin your goddamned name on your shirt, soldier. And make sure you're keeping your cartridges dry and the nipple on your musket's firing pin is dry and there ain't no mud stopping up the barrel."

"You're talking to a cavalryman, Sergeant, and I've got a breech-loading repeating rifled carbine."

"I don't give a shit what you got, soldier. You just make sure it's ready to fire when we start shootin'. Damned cavalry!" He stomped away into the night, cursing: " . . . think they're so goddamned great and glorious. Hell, whoever saw a *dead* cavalryman, anyway."

Travis and John laughed, and the tension was gone. They sat together through the night, beneath the tree, talking about Kitty, how they'd find her, how they would make it through this battle and the next and the whole damned war. John had a jug of red-eye and the more they drank, the better they felt about the whole world around them— waiting for it to end.

"You going to pin your name on?" Travis asked as the first pink hem of dawn began to appear over the trees.

"No. I don't see where names matter so much right now, Coltrane. Me and you will be the only ones who go to look for Kitty. If we don't, she won't get found—and who else cares if I get killed?"

"I'm not pinning a name on either, John."

They were called together for briefing. The officer in charge stood before them and repeated the words they had heard before. "Do not shoot till you are within effective musket range and fire deliberately, take care to aim low and don't overshoot. If you wound a man, so much the better—they'll have to be taken off the field, by un-wounded soldiers and they make good targets. Pick off the officers, especially the ones on horses. Hold your ranks and don't huddle together when the firing gets heavy. When you hear the order to charge, do so at once and move fast. You're less apt to get killed moving steadily forward than if you hesitate or retreat; but if we have to fall back, do it gradually and in order. More men are killed during a dis-organized retreat than at any other time."

The officer looked around him; he was young and Travis thought he seemed nervous. Well, he had reason to be. They all did. Whether they drove Bragg off the mountain or not, one thing was for certain: a hell of a lot of men were going to die this day.

"Don't be afraid of the artillery," he went on, trying, Travis knew, to sound fierce and authoritative, making his voice gruff and stern. "Artillery is never as deadly as it seems. A rapid movement forward will reduce the battery's effectiveness and hasten the end of its capacity to destroy. Do not—I repeat—do not pause or stop to plunder the dead or pick up the spoils. Battles have been lost by this temptation. And as cruel as it might sound, do not heed the pleas for assistance from your wounded comrades. The best way to protect your comrades is to drive the enemy from the field. Straggling under any guise will be severely punished and cowards will be shot!"

He paused again and took a deep breath, pushing his chest forward a bit. "Do your duty in a manner that befits the heroic example that your regiment has already set in earlier fields of combat."

Somewhere the snare drums began the long roll. The color bearers moved forward. In the early morning mist, intense activity could be seen all around. Surgeons were preparing their kits and litter bearers and ambulances were grimly waiting. Some of the soldiers were down on their knees praying; others read from their testaments. And some, like Travis, bit off a chew of tobacco, jaws working furiously. Everywhere, suspense was bearing down with a crushing force—and the silence was overwhelming as they waited after the drum roll ceased.

Travis looked at the red-haired boy huddled beside him. Andy had grown up quite a bit since they had been together. He could fight like a man and would never be the kind to turn and run from a battle. They had grown close and he never failed to feel a spirit of big-brother protectiveness when danger prevailed. "You all right, boy?" he whispered, noting that he had pinned his name on his shirt while Sam, John, and Travis himself had all neglected to do so.

"Yeah. I'm fine." He spoke quietly. Too quietly.

"Are you worried, Andy? This is just another battle, you know. You've been through them before. You'll do fine."

"It ain't just another battle." His tone was clipped, short, almost defiant, and the three of them, Travis, Sam, and John, all turned to stare at the boy. "It ain't just another battle to me. If I get killed in this one, it ain't all over. None of it."

"Boy, you ain't makin' no sense," John said worriedly.

"Yeah, I am. The parson come by my tent last night and prayed with me. I'm saved."

"Saved?" Sam Bucher spit out a wad of tobacco and wiped his lips with the back of his hand. "What do you mean, you're *saved*? You ain't saved from fightin' today, boy. You're goin' into battle just like us. If you sit here and don't fight 'cause some preacher thinks he got you out of it, General Grant will have you shot quicker'n Johnny Reb skins boots off a dead Yank."

Andy's sigh was impatient. "Sam, you don't understand what I'm saying. I'm not talking about the parson savin' me from going into the battle. I *am* going and I intend to fight, but I'm *saved*, Sam! My soul is saved. I'm a born-again child of God, and if some Reb ball tears into me today, I'll still be alive, don't you see?"

He looked at each of the men in turn, his gaze imploring them to understand his words. "The parson says my sins are washed away; if my times comes to die, I'll die in peace. He says if I get killed today, I'll dine with the Lord tonight."

Sam slapped his knee, roaring with laughter. "Well, ask the good preacher if he's hungry and would like to go along and eat, too. I already seen him ridin' in the opposite direction, heading out of here like the devil himself was after *his* immortal soul!"

Travis managed to hold back his own laughter and kept a straight face as he said: "Leave him alone, Sam. If the boy feels better going into battle now that the preacher says he's saved his soul, then don't make light of it."

Sam and John exchanged incredulous looks. Andy smiled appreciatively. Travis knew that the boy had only pledged his allegiance to the North because of the way he had attached himself to him and looked up to him. And he felt a responsibility for him. True, he didn't understand a lot about God and heaven and hell, but he wasn't about to make light of those who did. And just the expression on Andy's face mirrored some kind of inner peace that he himself could not identify with.

And then they heard the rattle of musketry in front. The Confederate pickets had been alerted that an attack was about to come. Everyone stretched to immediate alertness. A signal gun fired, then the artillery guns began to explode in all their fury. Someone screamed, "Charge!" And the battle was on.

They moved forward, aware that comrades were already falling right and left. Travis paused, took aim, and fired. A soldier in gray toppled screaming from his perch high in a pine tree. A feeling of exultation filled him as he surged forward with the others, anxious to get to the enemy now.

Smoke rolled in torrents, spreading darkness about them. The Federals were firing their ten-pound Parrotts, ten-pound rifled ordnance, and twelve-pound Napoleons. They were using projectiles—conical, spherical, spiral. The smoke was becoming so thick that it was hard to see where they were going, but still they kept moving, shooting as they ran.

And the Confederates fired back—twenty-four-pound shells, twenty-pound, twelve-pound, ten-pound projectiles; they fired everything they had, and each had its own breath, its own voice, its own message of death.

Travis stepped over a soldier he recognized as having been a player in a card game with him a few days before, but now his stomach was gaping, his eyes staring blankly upward. Trees were breaking away everywhere. Horses fled in panic through the woods. A few men were wandering around dazed, completely unaware of what they were doing. An officer snatched at one soldier, shoved him forward, threw him to the ground, cursing. Travis kept moving. The noise all around him was deafening. Blood, smoke, sulphur, explosions, screams of the dying and wounded. This was the world, and it wrapped itself about him like a giant fist, squeezing, choking. He fought to breathe, to survive.

He came upon a good-sized boulder, crouched down behind it as Sam, John, and Andy fell in behind him. They were able to take aim and fire at the Rebs in the trees on the mountainside above, dodging when an enemy shell exploded nearby. "We've got to keep moving," Travis said finally. "We've got to get to them. We can't wait for them to come to us."

"Travis . . ." He heard Andy shouting in his ear as they prepared to move out. "When this is over, I've got something to tell you. I was afraid to before . . ."

"Hell, boy, *move!*" There was no time for talk. What was the matter with him, anyway? They were out in the woods, running, dodging the exploding trees. A wounded soldier called out, pleading for help, but they kept moving, doing as they had been told. There was no time to help the wounded. Not now.

General Bragg had only a skeleton Confederate force, dug in on the slopes of Lookout Mountain, rather than on the crest. The day, Tuesday, November 24th, 1863, was cloudy and bleak. All day they fought, but midway through the afternoon there came a break in the cloud cover and the sun shone through.

"Look at that!" John Wright saw it first, and he pointed above them, a grin spreading across his sooty face.

And there, waving proudly in the breeze, the Northern flag proclaimed victory.

Word spread that General Sherman had taken his Army of the Tennessee units upstream and attacked the Confederates on their right, making some progress; but he still had a grim fight on his hands. The top of the mountain might have been taken, but the battle was still on.

Darkness fell, and the four men huddled together behind a large boulder, firing when anything moved that might be the enemy. There was no food, no water, but no one complained at the moment. Travis felt his stomach rumble once and wondered if it were hunger or fear. He couldn't remember having ever been afraid before in his entire life. But here, with death all around, something was clutching right at his gut.

Someone passed the word that Grant had told General George Thomas to push his Army of the Cumberland forward in an attempt to take the Rebel rifle pits at the base of Missionary Ridge, exerting the necessary pressure to force Bragg to recall troops from Sherman's front.

And as dawn once again streaked across the smoky skies, it became obvious to Travis and the others that Thomas's soldiers had taken things into their own hands. They had suffered a long, slow burn for over a month as both Hooker's and Sherman's men had jeered them for their defeat at Chickamauga, not letting them forget that other armies had gone to their rescue. The Army of the Cumberland had had enough, and they were moving forward, taking the Confederate rifle pits as ordered. By midday it became obvious that without further orders from either Generals Grant or Thomas, they intended to charge straight up the steep mountain slope to try to hit Bragg's right line, which was the strongest.

Travis and his comrades followed. They were in the thick of the fighting when suddenly Andy screamed and fell to his knees, clutching at his stomach and toppling forward. And orders previously given about stopping to help the wounded were thrown to the winds as the three men gathered quickly around the boy, lifting him to carry him quickly to the shelter of a nearby rocky ledge along the incline.

Travis bent quickly and looked at the wound, then lifted his gaze to the waiting eyes of Sam and John. Without a word, he conveyed the grim message. Andy was dying.

Andy gasped, blood gurgling from his lips. Feebly, he clawed at his shirt pocket.

"What is it, boy? You want your Bible or something?" Sam asked anxiously, tears unashamedly streaming down his face.

"Didn't tell you . . ."—the words were barely audible, gurgling in the blood oozing from his throat—". . . 'fraid you wouldn't stay . . . and fight." Andy clutched at his pocket again. Sam reached for him, withdrawing a crumpled, bloodstained letter.

"Travis," Andy moaned. Sam handed Coltrane the letter.

"Tonight . . ."—the boy's face contorted with pain—"I'll eat with the Lord."

His eyelids popped open as he stared straight up, his eyes glazing over. One final gurgle of blood bubbled from the corner of his mouth as his head lolled sideways. Sam turned away, sobs racking his heavy body. John Wright cursed beneath his breath, slammed his fist into the rocky ledge and brought it away, bloodied.

Travis was struggling for self-control, biting down on his lips. He pulled the sheet of paper out of the envelope to give himself something else to fasten his attention on. He was fighting to hang onto his sanity. He loved the boy like a brother. Damnit, without realizing it, he'd really come to love the boy and in that moment the pain burned as it had when he learned of his sister's death. It burned and it hurt, and he gritted his teeth so tightly that his jaws ached.

And then his eyes scanned the bloodstained letter, and every nerve in his body was inflamed. It was from Andy's mother. She was writing to say she'd received word from the cousin in Goldsboro that a soldier who had been taken along with Kitty had returned. And he told a story about how a band of Cherokee Indians had attacked them, killing all of them. He managed to escape. And the next words leaped out like giant fingers of blood: "The Indians took the Wright girl with them!"

"What is it, Coltrane?" John Wright barked. "What's wrong with you? You look strange."

"Travis!" Sam nudged him, tears still streaming down his cheeks. "What is it?"

And he told them in low, guttural moans. John rocked back on his heels, stunned. Then he sprang and the two men leaped to pull him down to keep him from getting shot as the air sang with bullets and shells all around them. "I'm goin' after my girl," John screamed. "I've got to get to her."

"Listen to me!" Travis shook him fiercely and yelled: "Don't you see, John? This is the reason Andy didn't let us know he had even gotten this letter! He knew we'd take off and try to find her—and he knew we had to stay here and fight. Now get hold of yourself. I want to go after her just as damn bad as you do, but we can't go running off half-cocked in the middle of a goddamn war. You want to get shot in the back for desertion? Now get hold of yourself."

"Besides, you got to have more facts," Sam spoke up

quickly. "Find out exactly where they were so we can get an idea of whereabouts the Indians are. You can't just go riding off and not know where the hell to look."

John slumped and they released him. "Look, we'll finish this fight and ask permission to go after her," Travis said quickly. "We'll find her. I promise you we will."

John nodded, tears swimming in his one eye.

"All right." Travis patted him on the shoulder, his voice an ominous rasp against the noise that surrounded them. "Now let's get this fight over with so we can go after her."

They picked up their guns and stood for one last, somber moment, staring down at Andy's lifeless body.

"Since the Rebs sent Andy to eat with the Lord tonight," Travis said, biting out the words, "let's send a few of them to eat with the *devil!*"

And with loud shrieks that split the air around them, the three charged on up the mountain.

❦ Chapter Thirty-seven ❦

THE beaten Confederates withdrew into Georgia and General Burnside's Federal forces were secure in Knoxville. Everyone was singing the praises of Grant. Word spread that he would soon become General in Chief of the Union armies. It was obvious that the South had lost the war in the west. For the time being, there seemed to be nothing left except scattered skirmishes through the winter months and both sides dug in to brave the bitter weather.

Travis Coltrane, John Wright, and Sam Bucher asked for, and received, permission to take furlough and find Kitty Wright. And while John waited a safe distance away, Sam and Travis rode right into Goldsboro, spending several days discreetly asking questions before they cornered Lonnie Carter in the alley behind the saloon and made him tell his story. From what he told them, they were able to calculate the approximate location where the Indians had captured Kitty.

"You tell anybody we were here, that we asked questions," Travis hissed, holding the blade of a bowie knife against the shaking man's throat, "and we'll be back. You understand?"

Lonnie understood, but the blade was pressed so tightly into his flesh he could not give an affirmative nod. But Travis read the message in his eyes, released him, and flung him to the ground. "Just what kind of man are you to let

447

them take her away? Hell, what did you do? Hide behind a goddamned tree and watch?"

"They . . . they would've killed me too if I hadn't!"

Travis turned on his heels and walked away. Sam kicked the trembling soldier in the side, then followed.

It was winter and it was cold. Snow and ice made moving through the mountains slow, tedious, and all but impossible, and several times they were faced with the prospect of having to hole in until the spring thaw. But something deep within forced them to move on, if only a few miles a day.

And then they encountered a small band of Cherokee Indians high in the western region of Tennessee. The Indians were friendly enough. Speaking in broken English, they told them of hearing about the white woman with "big powers" who could bring people back from the dead. They spoke with reverence and awe, and it was obvious that Kitty was held in deep esteem by the Cherokees.

"That means she's probably treated fairly well," Sam said later, when they talked about it. "If they think she has the power to raise the dead, they'll be scared of her."

"Kitty ain't raised no dead," John said, chuckling. "She's probably brought a few out of fever that looked like they were dead. But I agree. It sounds good. She might just be all right. We've got to hope for that, anyway."

They were sitting in a cave high up in the mountains, with the snow whipping outside as the wind howled in all its fury. The fire they'd built from rotting wood found in the cave crackled and popped and cast eery shadows along the damp walls. The rabbit Sam had shot was being turned by John as he held the end of a spit over the flames.

"What happens when we find her?" Sam asked suddenly, looking from John to Travis. "If she's all right, unharmed, how the hell do we get her away from the Cherokees? If she's big medicine, they won't let her go. And we can't take on a tribe of wild Indians."

"If we have to, we will." John spoke quietly, his eyes fixed on the slowly browning rabbit. "I aim to find my girl and get her out of these mountains."

"And then what?" Sam prodded him. "What do we do with her? You know they're saying Grant is going to be named Commander of all the armies. The war is going to really get going once spring arrives. We've got to get back in it. I aim to see it through. What do we do with Kitty if we do get her back?"

"Let's just worry about getting her back," Travis said shortly. He knew it was going to be a problem, but it had to be done. He blamed himself, after much concentration, for the way in which it had all come about, for her even being in the thick of things. Had he allowed her to return to North Carolina when he first rescued her from Luke Tate's clutches, she would probably be there now. Maybe if it hadn't been for him, she and that Rebel officer would be married, and she'd be tucked away on some Southern plantation—and safe.

Safe! He shook his head. No one was safe anymore, not in this war. And he knew what Grant's plan would be: attack! Attack at all points simultaneously and apply constant pressure on the ever-weakening Southern states. Attack and fight and get it over with.

And where was all of this going to end? How was it going to affect each of them—particularly Kitty? And how was he going to feel when he faced her again? One minute he hated her and in the next he remembered the joy of holding her in his arms, possessing, touching, feeling—and he felt a warmth creeping into his loins.

"When we get her back," John said, cutting into his thoughts, "we'll do whatever she wants. If she wants to go home, then by God, I'll take her there myself. If she wants to go find Nathan, then I'll set her in that direction. It's up to her. She's been through hell. I just want to make some of it up to her. She never asked to be brought into this war. All she wanted to do was stay home and do what she could in the hospital there. And look what it got her."

"What gets me is the fact we're almost exactly back where we started from," Sam said disgustedly. "We took a chance on gettin' killed riding right into that town in North Carolina and finding out where she was first captured. Then it turns out we were almost right there when we were at Missionary Ridge. Couldn't have been over a day's ride, two at the most."

"We didn't have any way of knowing that." John pulled

449

the skewered rabbit from the fire, propping the stick against a rock to allow the meat to cool. "With all this snow, we can't move around and do much looking, anyway."

Sam nodded. "We've got to duck Rebs, too. I hear the mountains are full of deserters."

John shot a sideways glance at Travis, who was listening in silence. "What about you? When we find her, what's it going to mean to you?"

Travis looked at him, chewed at his lower lip, the muscle in his jaw twitching. Finally, he said, "Well, it will mean she's safe. If I can get her back home, where she belongs, then I'll quit blaming myself for her getting this far to start with."

"What if the North wins? What if we march right straight through the South and kill everybody?" John's tone was sharp, his one eye glaring at the two men simultaneously. "You two thought about that?"

"I think only about getting the war over with so I can . . ." Travis paused abruptly, realizing that he didn't know how to finish his sentence. So he could what? Go home? What home? There was nothing back there for him. Sam could do as he wanted. That was up to him. But what did the future hold for *him*?

Sam told John he should have thought about the possibility of eventually invading the South when he first joined the North. "You knew you were fighting against your own people, John. This isn't the time to question your decision, not at this late date."

"I didn't really want to fight against my people. I wanted to fight for a final peace, for the Union, to strike back at slavery and all that goes with it. I just hate the thought of destroying what I left behind."

"You can't go back to it," Travis said soberly. "You can't ever go back to what you left behind."

John squinted his one eye at him and scratched at his beard. "Then why are you going back to Kitty? What do you think there is to go back to?"

"Probably nothing. I just feel responsible."

"He feels love, don't let him fool you," Sam guffawed. "I watched the two of 'em. Oh, they put on a good show of hatin' each other, but I knew."

"Sam, the girl betrayed me," Travis reminded him sharply, and the grin left his comrade's face quickly. "One of my own men got killed over her, with a ball he intended for me if it came right down to it. She tricked me. I don't take that lightly. Now, true, I feel responsible for her being messed up in the war, but as for love . . ." He shook his head.

Sam looked at John, winked, and then said, laughingly, "John, you one-eyed son of a bitch, how can I tell if you're winkin' or just closing that one eye of yours?"

The two men laughed, but Travis continued to stare at them soberly. Love? The idea was ridiculous. He might love Kitty's beauty, her body, the feel of entering that body and plunging into its warm delights, but love her as a woman? Like a man loves a woman he wants to marry?

John and Sam were pulling the roasted rabbit apart, still laughing over Sam's joke about the one-eyed wink. Travis pulled his greatcoat around his shoulders and walked toward the cave's entrance and then straight into the wind and snow of the storm that swirled in the world beyond. It was time, he reckoned, to reflect on a few things that were whirling around inside him, to sort things out and think about the future—if he had one—and what it held for him. The last they figured, they were maybe fifty miles or so from the Indian camp where Kitty was said to be living. That meant that soon, weather permitting, they might reach that camp—and Kitty. And when they did, he wondered if he even wanted to see her, talk to her. True, most of the Indians around were friendly, but the ones who had Kitty reportedly slaughtered over a dozen Reb marauders. No great loss, true, but they appeared to be savages, from all reports. There was no way of knowing what to expect when they reached the camp, and they planned to be on their toes. But he still thought about Kitty and the image of her betrayal and escape blotted out any memory of happiness between them.

When the time came for an actual confrontation, perhaps it would be better if he just turned and rode away, heading back to the battlegrounds and letting Sam and John take over and get Kitty wherever the hell she wanted to go. There was no way of knowing what she wanted, either.

Who could predict the whims of a woman that strong-willed and conniving? He didn't intend to try. All he wanted to do was forget they'd ever met.

Travis was so lost in thought that he didn't see the shadowy movements coming up on him in a blur of snow from his left. The howling wind absorbed any sound the figures might have made. But suddenly he was very aware of their presence as a shot rang out, then another. But the first had missed, its explosion instinctively making him hurl his body to the ground. The next went straight over him. Rolling in the snow over and over, trying to make it to the dark outline of the thicket beyond the cave entrance, he heard John and Sam shouting, calling out to him.

Struggling inside his tangled greatcoat, he reached for his holster pistol. Bringing his hand out, holding the gun, he wallowed on his belly in the snow, trying to see his target, not wanting to shoot blind for fear of hitting his comrades or missing the enemy and thus wasting the ammunition.

"Stay back," he yelled, but his warning was drowned out by the sound of more gunfire. With the fire from within silhouetting them, John and Sam had made perfect targets —and they were now both falling to the ground. Travis leaped to his feet, throwing caution to the winds as he plunged forward, firing at the men running toward the shadow. With screams of pain, they fell, Travis's shots hitting them squarely in the back.

Bending over Sam, he noted a small trickle of blood along his forehead. "I think the bastards just grazed me." He rubbed at his head, struggling to sit up. "But see about John. I think they might've got him."

John was hit. They moved him gently inside to the warmth and light of the fire. Sam wanted to know if there were only two of them and Travis said he was pretty sure of it. "Just Reb deserters, no doubt. We've known these mountains were crawling with them and I let my guard down."

The front of John's coat was soaked in blood, and when it was pulled open, they saw that the ball had landed in the fleshy part of his shoulder. "You ain't gonna take my arm off," he said in a hoarse whisper. "They got my eye. They ain't getting my arm."

Travis told him he didn't think that would be necessary.

"But you are losing a lot of blood, old man. And that ball has to come out, and we're out here in the middle of nowhere with no doctor to be found."

John looked up at him, his one good eye watering painfully. "Then you got to dig it out, Coltrane, and get me up and out of here. I can't rest knowing my girl is with those savages . . ." He gasped, gritting his teeth against the agony. "Get the damned thing out, please . . ."

Sam and Travis locked eyes over the groaning man. "You ever dug a ball out?" Sam wanted to know.

"Hell, no, and I'm not going to try now." He yanked off his greatcoat, tore at his own shirt, wadding it to make a thick bandage which he pressed against the bleeding wound. "We've got a pretty good idea where there's a Federal winter camp located not too far from here. If we start out at daylight, we should make it by mid-afternoon if the snow lets up. We can probably hold the bleeding down, but if that ball doesn't come out, he'll likely get gangrene and die."

"No!" They looked down at John, who protested in spite of his pain: ". . . got to get to Kitty. Too close to turn back now."

"If we don't get you to a doctor, John, you're going to die," Travis pointed out bluntly.

"Sam can take me. You go on."

"You think I can take on a tribe of Cherokees?" His laugh was brittle, cold. "John, thanks for the faith, but I can't do it."

"You can try. They might not be hostile. You can at least go on and scout 'em out, make sure Kitty is still there, that she's all right, then ride back for a patrol to go with you."

Travis swore under his breath.

"He's right," Sam pointed out. "If we turn back now, we may regret it. I'll get him to the camp, and you go on ahead."

Travis chewed his lower lip thoughtfully, finally deciding to be completely honest with them. "I had decided I'd just back you all up if you needed me. I wasn't going to see Kitty. I still don't know what my reaction will be if I come face to face with her again."

With amazing strength in spite of the wound, John

raised his head, glaring out of his one good eye. "I know what *my* reaction will be if you don't. If I get well, then I'll make you wish you had gone on and found her, Coltrane." He fell back, gasping. "You should've let her go home back in sixty-two. . . ."

He was right. Perhaps she wouldn't be here now if he hadn't kept her a prisoner. All right. He would go. And he would find her, and then his obligation would be fulfilled and he wouldn't have to feel any remorse for any of it. Straightening, he motioned to Sam to get ready for the ride. "I want to finish this business once and for all," he said grimly.

And maybe then, he thought silently, *when my debt, if there is one, is paid, I can forget the damned woman.*

❧ Chapter Thirty-eight ❧

KITTY spooned broth into the Indian boy's mouth. It was cold, freezing cold, and the braided blanket she wrapped tightly around her shoulders did not give enough warmth. Neither did the fire just outside the flimsy tent. Trapped on all sides by the war, the Cherokees did the best they could for their winter encampment. Kitty learned from those who spoke broken English that when the snows melted and passage was possible, they were planning to move further west to try to escape the war.

The war. It seemed a lifetime away. True, the Indians had been good to her, even worshipping her as "big medicine"—and that, alone, had saved her from suffering at the hands of the braves who had eyed her so lustily at the beginning. The Chief's son had been quite ill with a very bad cold, Kitty had noticed right away. But because he was burning with fever and lying quite still, the Indians feared the great spirit was taking him away. With what few supplies Kitty had in her bag, she was able to nurse him out of it. And since, they had held her in high esteem.

But if only they would take her back to her people, she thought dismally. She'd tried to teach them what she, herself, knew about "big medicine" so they could minister to their own people. Their reaction was to think she was tetched to want to leave them when the "spirits" had sent

455

her to them. And all she could think of over the long, cold months had been that other world, wondering if the South was winning or losing, if her father was alive, what had happened to her mother—and yes, huddled in her blankets on the ground at night when she tried to sleep, she thought of Nathan and Travis, the two interspersed in her dreams. Did the war change Travis or had he always been so callous and brutal? And had the war changed Nathan to the point that all between them was lost forever?

So many questions, questions that would probably never be answered because Kitty strongly doubted that she would ever be allowed to leave the Indian tribe, small as it was. They watched her constantly. Oh, they were good to her, but they still kept her captive.

It could have been worse, she thought with a tremor of fear. She would never forget the night the brave called Long Foot became angry with his squaw and stripped her naked and raped her right out on the ground in front of all the teepees with people watching from inside. Kitty had watched, too, horrified, as the young buck plunged into the woman again and again, shrieking like a wild banshee as she screamed in pain and terror. When he'd finished, she lay there, bleeding profusely between her legs. Kitty had treated her, but could do little for the lacerations. She bathed the area and applied some salve that she mixed with pine-bark drippings. The young woman became ill, her wounds filled with pus, and after two weeks, she died. Kitty suspected there was internal damage, too—damage that could not be seen.

Still, the memory was vivid. So she felt fortunate that the braves didn't bother her, that she'd been treated well. And one day, perhaps a miracle would come and she could leave this place and go home.

The little boy slept. Kitty stood up, gathered the blanket about her shoulders and stepped out into the chilly night. Looking up, she saw that the stars were out. It was clear. Good. Maybe the snows would stop and it would warm up some. At least for now she could go to her own teepee and pull the bearskins over her body and be a little warm, if only for a few hours. When the sun rose, there would be more sick children and the older Indians to treat. They expected her to work from sunrise to sunset—and even more if there were many sick. And the Indians had been plagued with illness. Some Kitty could help. Others died. With practically no medicine at all to use, and no facilities or instruments of any kind, Kitty just had to depend mostly on the Lord's will in treating the sick, hoping that not too many would slip by her, lest the Indians decide she really had no magic powers after all and should be used as just another squaw.

She curled into a ball, the warm bearskins pulled around her shaking body. Her stomach gave a rumble. There was never enough to eat and she would never get used to the unpalatable food, anyway. Her own body could not stand much more of the terrible diet, the exhaustion, and the cold weather. How much weight had she lost? She tried to guess. Thirty pounds at least, maybe more. There were no mirrors for her to see herself, but she knew she probably looked a fright. When possible, she heated water to bathe and attempt a semblance of cleanliness. She washed her hair and tried to keep it tangle-free, which was difficult. It would be easy to lose all desire to be attractive, to become dull and dirty and ugly. But she was determined to hold onto something, if only her looks.

Closing her eyes, every bone in her body ached with cold and weariness. And, as always, the vision of Nathan and Travis came to her. Nathan—what they had once was beautiful. Travis—cold, brutal, yet gentle and compassionate when he wanted to be.

To wile away her moments of misery before falling asleep, Kitty tried to imagine what it would be like if she were Travis's wife. Would he stand in the way of her pursuing her own goals in life—her own ambitions? Would he want her to sit at home and be just a wife and mother to his children, as she knew Nathan would? Travis was strong-willed. If he had opposed her, they would have locked horns just as she'd done with Nathan.

Her eyes grew heavy. She was drifting. There was the feel of warm lips pressed against hers, moving, searching, seeking. Nathan's kiss. No, Nathan never kissed that way. The only time he had ever kissed her with his mouth open was that night when he was drunk and raped her. But Travis kissed this way, forcing her own lips to part as his tongue probed inside her mouth. It always made her feel dizzy, and suddenly the bearskins became unbearable as great waves of warm passion moved over her body.

And then he was no longer kissing her. She felt a firm hand pressed over her mouth. This was no dream! She opened her eyes, fighting to see in the darkness, struggling against the strong grasping hand across the lower part of her face.

"Don't make a sound," a familiar voice hissed in command. "You want to wake up every goddamned Indian around here?"

Slowly, the pressure of the hand released enough to enable her to whisper, "Travis."

"Right. Now, you come with me and be quiet, damnit. I slipped in here with nobody seeing me and I can get out the same way if you don't fall down and wake everybody up."

Dizzily, she let him take her hand and pull her to her feet. Tiptoeing on moccasined feet, she followed him out of the little teepee, around to the back, and into the scrubs and underbrush beyond. Her heart was pounding like the giant drums of the Cherokees. Travis was here! Really here! He was rescuing her. Oh, God, she prayed, don't let it be a dream. And if it is a dream, then don't let me wake up. Let me stay asleep forever if sleep is this much sweeter.

When they reached the brush, Travis made her move faster. "I've been watching this damn camp for two days," he told her, "watching for you to make sure where the hell you slept at night. I figured you'd be married up with some buck by now, and I'd have to slit his throat to get you out of here."

They kept moving. Kitty had a thousand questions but she was unable to speak. Travis was here! He had come for her! That meant he cared. And he had been kissing her—she was sure of it. And now her insides were all twisted around. What was happening? Why was he here?

He'd never loved her, never really wanted her. Why did he risk his life?

Finally, after perhaps a half hour of tramping through the woods and snow, they reached the thicket where Travis had tied his horse. He hoisted her up behind him, then moved out, back to the deeper woods, wanting to put as much distance as possible between them and the Indians. The sky was clear. There was no more snow. They would leave tracks, for sure. If they didn't run into any problems, they could make the small camp of Reb deserters he'd spotted earlier within a couple of hours, then skirt around them and disappear. When the Indians tracked them, they would naturally think the Rebs had stolen Kitty—and there would be a fight. But Travis planned to be a hell of a long way away by daylight when the Indians discovered their "big magic" princess had escaped.

Kitty rode in silence for a while, then knew she had to begin getting some answers. "How did you find me, Travis?"

Holding onto his waist as they rode, she felt him tense. "Me and Sam and your father have been tracking you for quite a while."

"Poppa?" Tears sprang to her eyes, her heart constricting joyfully. "You mean Poppa's here, too? Alive? Well?"

"He got hit by a Reb bushwhacker a few days ago. Sam took him to a Union camp to get him patched up. He made me promise I'd go on and find you." He spoke in clipped, curt tones.

"But he is all right" she persisted. "The wound wasn't severe?"

"A ball had to come out. He should be fine."

A moment of silence passed. Kitty's mind was whirling, and finally she exploded: "Travis, thank you for coming for me. They . . . the Cherokees have been good to me, in their way, but there was no chance for escape. I started thinking I never would get back to civilization. I . . . I didn't even know if you were still alive."

There, she had said it, brought it out in the open. She felt him tensing once again. Then he ground out the words: "You didn't bother to check and see, did you, princess?

You kept right on riding, didn't you?" He dug his heels angrily into the horse's flanks as the animal bogged down knee-deep into a snow drift. "And I think you would have made it back to civilization. As cunning and resourceful as you are, sooner or later you would have made it. You could always trick the Chief into thinking you were in love with him."

She felt as though she'd been slapped. Flaring instantly, Kitty fired back: "You asked for it. You kept me prisoner against my will. It was the only way I could escape you and get back to my people, where I belonged. I even had to leave Andy. You think I wanted to? You were cunning enough to make him idolize you, you know."

"Andy's dead."

Kitty blinked, feeling a thud in her stomach as his words washed over her. "No . . ."

"Killed on Missionary Ridge last November. He'd taken an oath of allegiance to the Union and been fighting with us for quite a while. He's the reason we found out where you were. His mother heard from a relative in Goldsboro." And then Travis told her about the visit back to see Lonnie Carter and find out where the Indians had been encountered.

It was all too much. Kitty's head swam dizzily. Andy was dead. Poppa was alive. Travis was here. She was free. Without realizing what she was doing, she lowered her head onto Travis's back as the tears began to trickle down her cheeks.

Travis felt as though someone had kicked him about six times right in the gut. The girl was pressed against his back and he didn't like the response from his body. She was still pretty, even with her hair hanging scraggily down her back, her face pale and drawn, and her body almost skin and bones—she was still pretty. And damn it, he still wanted her. But he also knew she was still as treacherous as always, and he wasn't about to be taken in by her because of any pity he might feel.

Her voice was lifeless as she asked, "Where are you taking me?"

"Don't worry. I'm heading straight for the camp where

your pa is. I'm not going to stop along the way and rape you."

"I didn't say you were!" Her head came up off his back. "But you were obviously thinking about it since *you* brought it up."

"Maybe that's because I figure that's all you're good for —you or any other woman."

"I wish . . ."—she was fuming—"I wish you would go to hell! I wish you had died. I wish . . ."

Suddenly, abruptly, he'd had enough. He yanked the horse to a halt and slid down off the saddle, turning quickly to pull Kitty down with him. His arms grabbing her against his chest, he glared down at her in the blinding whiteness of the moon reflecting off the snow. "You wish I were dead?" he snapped, bending to kiss her so hard she felt his teeth cutting into her lips. Then he raised his head to whisper, "You wish I were dead, princess? Then you couldn't feel this, could you?" His hands reached around her to clutch at her breasts, squeezing until she cried out in pain.

With one quick swoop, he lifted her up, tramping through the snow toward a rock ledge hanging over a small hollowed-out place in the side of the mountain. He threw her down, then fell beside her. He ripped at her clothes until she lay naked before him, then his hands moved swiftly to set every fiber of her body on fire. Kitty lay there passively, determined not to do what he wanted—not to fight or beg him not to take her. But Travis had no intention of making her beg him not to have his way with her. Instead, his hands and lips moved over her body, and against her will, she began to writhe as the giant fingers of passion played along the keyboard of her body. She wanted him. Damnit, damn her body and soul to hell—she wanted him.

He moved between her thighs, probing with his warm tongue. Kitty clutched at his long, thick hair, twining it in her fingers. This was a dream. None of it was real. When she awoke, she would be back in the Indian camp, facing another day of ministering to the sick and old. She was not here in the arms of the only man who could ever turn her heart to butter with just a look or a caress.

"Hurry before I awake," she moaned in anticipation, "Travis, hurry, please."

He didn't want to take her. No, he wanted to get up, to leave her lying there on fire with desire for him, to laugh at her prostrate form and then throw her across the horse and take her to her father. And then he would ride the hell out of her life forever. But she was there, naked beneath him, begging him to take her—and he wanted her, God, how he wanted her as he'd never wanted a woman before. She was everything a man could want. He felt as though his loins were filled to the point of bursting. He had to have her, despite the promises he'd made to himself to remain in complete control once they were together. Damn it to hell, he had to have her!

Plunging into the velvet recesses of her moist, receptive body, Travis felt himself exploding at once—and Kitty twisting in spasms of pleasure. It was over quickly, and it was just as well. He withdrew and then fumbled with his clothing, hating himself for his weakness.

And Kitty was pulling at her own clothes, cursing herself, cursing him. Animals. That's all they were and ever had been to each other. Animals.

"Let's get going." He sounded miserable. "Your father is probably worried sick over what's happened. And we've still got to get around those Rebs so the Indians will stop looking for us there."

He led her back to the horse. Anything, Kitty thought feverishly, talk about anything but the animal lust between us.

"Tell me about the war," she said quietly, once they were plodding through the snow once again. "I haven't heard a word for months. I hope you Yankees are getting soundly whipped," she added caustically.

He snorted. "Now how can you say that, sweet lady, when your own father is one of the best Yankee soldiers around these parts? And especially after young Andy Shaw took the oath to the Union and died for it."

"Poppa has his reasons for doing what he's doing. And Andy was too young to know and understand what it's all about."

"Hell, Kitty, you don't even know yourself."

"I know that my heart belongs to the South and always will. And as proud as I am to be seeing Poppa once again, I want to go home, back to North Carolina. I hope you won't try to stop me because I'm going to keep trying to escape."

"Hell, I don't want you around me messing up my life! The last thing I need is some bossy, half-crazy woman. But don't be sure you can make it home. The war is picking up speed."

A prickle of apprehension moved along her spine as he began to tell her the news that she had been unable to hear for so long, the news she actually did not want to hear.

Travis told her about how, during the last week of November of last year, 1863, Grant, with General Tecumseh Sherman as his strong right arm, had avenged a previous Federal defeat at Chickamauga by trouncing General Braxton Bragg and his Confederates at Lookout Mountain and Missionary Ridge in the state of Tennessee. Now the Union army was going to start an advance toward the South, Grant's goal being to destroy the southern part of the Confederacy piece by piece.

He told her how supplies of all kinds had been growing shorter and shorter for the Confederacy, especially after England finally took a firm stand in favor of neutrality. As a result, loans from England had promptly dried up. And the South, lacking the necessary funds, was finding it more and more difficult to get goods from Mexico.

"We've heard that Grant's been given command of all the Union armies," he went on. "And now he's going straight ahead with plans to invade the South and crush it once and for all. If you're smart, Kitty, you'll sit it out, because it can't last much longer."

"Sit it out where?" She was close to tears. "You think I can sit back and watch the Confederacy fall? It makes me want to take up arms and join the fight, too. But I can't do that, can I? Because I'm a woman! I can ride and shoot as well as most men, but because I'm a woman, I'm expected to sit safely behind the lines and tear petticoats

463

into bandages. Well, no thank you. I'll escape if you try to hold me prisoner and I'll find a Confederate brigade and I'll join them as a nurse . . ." Tears were streaming profusely down her face now and the wind was turning them into droplets of ice. Not because she wanted to, but because of the chill, Kitty once again pressed her face against Travis's back.

They rode along in silence for a few moments and then he said quietly, "For a girl who professes to love her father so much, I can't understand your loyalty to the South when he so obviously sees no reason to stand up for it. Maybe it's not your patriotic juices flowing at all, Kitty. Maybe it's your Reb boyfriend, Nathan Collins."

"Maybe it is," she said, more to herself than to him. "Maybe I'm just now understanding how I really do feel about everything."

Stiffening, raising her head once again, she said, "Please, just take me to my father, let me make sure he's well, and then I want to be on my way. I don't want to be around *you* any longer than necessary."

She didn't care whether she believed the words or not. They had to be spoken. Travis Coltrane loved no one but himself and his precious war. He had used her, violated her, and at the moment she didn't know whom she hated most, him for what he had done or herself for not being strong enough to withstand the power he exercised over her body. She had wanted him, damnit, wanted him with every fiber of her being. And she had enjoyed his love-making—if it could be called love. Animals. They were merely animals mating out of need and lust, and not love. And just his very presence at this moment, the warmth of his body permeating into her own, was overwhelming. Get away from him. That's what she had to do. Get away, as far away as possible. Never see him again. Control the animal instincts of her body. There could be no denying that she had sensed only joy over seeing him again, knowing he was still alive after months of *not* knowing. And ecstasy. There had been only painful ecstasy moving through her loins as he took her so savagely. Just remembering the waves of passion made her tingle instinctively. It was physical attraction: the male seeks out the female to mate. And since he made her so weak, the only way to control it was to get away from him at any cost.

He laughed, a low, guttural sound that infuriated her. "You want to get away from me, pretty baby, because of the hold I have on you. There's no denying you enjoyed what we just did. Tell me, did you enjoy it with the Indian braves, too? I hear Indians don't waste time with the pleasurable preliminaries—the kisses, the touching, and you glory in them. You . . ."

She began to beat on his back with her fists, crying "Damn you, Travis Coltrane, I hate you! You *make* a woman want you. You have hundreds of ways you've learned in the brothels, no doubt."

He reined up the horse, sliding off once again, jerking her down. She reached to slap his face, but he caught both her wrists, holding her, shaking her. "Now get this straight, you little spitfire"—his steel-gray eyes gleamed and glittered in the moonlight reflected upon the snow-covered ground—"you're nothing to me, understand? You're just another whore! A Southern whore! The worst kind! I want to get you to your daddy and let him send you home or wherever the hell you want to go, but you get off my back, you hear? I've had my fill of you! The only reason I even agreed to go after you was because of your father. I happen to respect and like him. He isn't like *you*, thank God."

"And you aren't like him and never could be!" Her face twisted into an angry grimace, but even in anger, Travis noted, she was the most beautiful woman he had ever laid eyes on. "I should have married Nathan. He's a gentleman. Something you can never be!"

"A gentleman?" He raised an eyebrow, that crooked smile appearing that never ceased to infuriate her. "Let's see, a gentleman is one who fornicates with the lights off, right? I don't think you'll enjoy that, pretty baby. I've seen the way you sneak looks at my body beneath those long lashes of yours."

"Ohhhh!" She struggled to get away, but he held her tightly.

"Now get on that horse and keep your mouth shut the rest of the way or I'll let you walk behind like the squaw you've turned into!"

He let her help herself onto the horse, and if he hadn't reached out and snatched the reins and held them, she would have kicked the horse into a run through the snow, leaving him behind. But Travis had foreseen what she planned. Laughing, he mounted himself and they rode on through the night in silence.

❧ Chapter Thirty-nine ❧

T HE one-eyed man sat next to the young girl. Her long golden red hair moved gently about her face in the early spring breeze. Below them lay the winter camp, spread out on the sloping hillside. There were several thousand tents and lean-tos, and huts thrown together and crudely made from logs, rocks, blankets, canvas, saplings, mud, and string. Some had squat chimneys of mud and stone. Sharp, distinctive noises emanated from the life going on within the camp—a cavalry horse nickering, a bell ringing somewhere, the distant note of a bugle, an artillery mule braying, dogs barking, the plodding of horses' hoofs, a belch, an angry curse, and a short scuffle with fists. A train approached, bells tolling, bringing in more soldiers to the sprawling city of men and animals and tents and huts.

The April sunshine peeked through the clouds momentarily, then receded once again, casting a sheen of gloom over the camp, an appropriate shading for the invisible air of tension and apprehension that touched each inhabitant's heart. The Federal war machine was moving into high gear. General Grant's master plan of attacking the South was moving right along. General Sherman had taken over command of the western forces and Federal drives in both the East and West would now proceed from one consistent strategy: Attack simultaneously at all points to apply constant pressure on the ever-weakening Southern states. But recent news had cast a depressed cloud over the North. While Grant and Sherman mapped out the details for their joint offensive, a third Federal force had met defeat when General Nathaniel Banks and forty thousand troops and fifty ships started up the Red River on March 14th, attempting to gain control of Louisiana and East Texas, to counteract threats from Emperor Maximilian of Mexico, and to seize large stores of cotton. The expedition had been a failure.

And, to make matters even worse for the North, Nathan Bedford Forrest and his Confederate cavalrymen had stormed Fort Pillow, Tennessee, on April 12th and killed most of the black troops that had been garrisoned there. Sherman had sent all his available cavalry to rid the West once and for all of Forrest.

John Wright held his daughter's hand. Their reunion had been deeply moving for both of them. Travis had taken Kitty the rest of the way with hardly a word spoken between them. And on arriving at the small camp, she had burst into tears at the sight of her father. They had spent hours talking of the years in between, the strong bond that had always existed between them once again in evidence.

And then they had moved to the huge winter camp on the banks of the Rapidan River to wait for spring—and for Kitty to decide what she was going to do with her life until the war ended.

The main Confederate defenses extended from northwestern Georgia along the eastern edge of the mountains into Winchester, Virginia, then southeastward across Virginia and into Fredericksburg and Richmond. The word was that Grant and Sherman would make their move sometime in early May.

John was recovering from his wound and he told Kitty that he intended to stay in the fight until the end. "And then what?" she had asked him point-blank. "What happens in the end, Poppa, to all of us?"

He had shrugged. "Who knows except the Lord? I don't see how the South can hold up under a constant invasion, Kitty. They're starving—troops half-naked—no supplies. It looks bad for them."

"And what about your land?" she pointed out, remembering the farm. "Do you just plan to forget all about that, never going home, Poppa?" She sounded bitter.

"If the North wins, I'll go home. Sure, there'd be hard feelings, maybe even a bit of trouble now and then, but I could handle all that. I'd go back and pick up the pieces, try to work the land and make a living. If your ma is still alive, well, if she'd change, we'd work things out."

He sounded less than convinced that Lena was still alive, much less that she would ever change. Kitty had had to tell him the truth about her, each word, she knew, stabbing into his heart painfully.

He scratched at his beard thoughtfully. "You've been asking an awful lot of questions about me, girl, and what I've got planned for the future—if the good Lord gives me one. But I've got a few questions for you, questions you haven't answered these past few weeks we've been together. What do you plan to do? Not only in the future but right now. We're going to move out of camp soon, and I told you, you can go with us and work with the hospital units or you can be sent home—or you can cross the river to Richmond and join the Confederates. It's your decision, but it's one that has to be made soon. Things are going to start jumpin' around here before long."

"I know." She stared down at the camp. Each day, more and more men arrived as the Army of the Potomac built its strength for invasion of the South. She could not be a part of it. No matter how much she loved her father—and even felt in her heart that slavery was very wrong—she could not turn against her homeland. An image of honeysuckle and sweet gardenia came into focus . . . lying in Nathan's arms beneath the cloak of the weeping willow tree alongside the gurgling creek. Hopes . . . dreams . . . promises . . . a young boy and a young girl, falling in love, untouched by war and the madness that went with it. Could the sweet overshadow the bitter? She did not know. Even if the South were to win the war, could anything be the same again, especially where Nathan was concerned? Was he out of her heart and mind forever?

A lone figure emerged from the fringes of the camp to stare up at the man and woman on the hillside looking down. Spotting them, he began trudging upward. "That's Travis," John said tonelessly. "I've got a feelin' he's been with General Grant, and now he's got news. I ain't so sure I'm going to like that news."

Kitty stared at the approaching figure, hating the way her heart began to pound. He had that effect. No matter how much she hated him, the sight of him could always start her pulses racing. He was handsome—there was no denying that—and when he looked at her with those steel-gray eyes through thick, half-lowered lashes, she always felt a warm glow spreading throughout her body. Since arriving at the winter camp, he had trimmed his hair till it just touched his collar and he had shaved his beard and trimmed his mustache neatly. He was a fine figure of a man, and as he walked up the hill, Kitty watched the muscles ripple along his thighs. He walked like—she tried to think of a fitting description—like a cat, lean, sinewy, deliberate, as though nothing would dare to get in his way. He was dangerous. He was brutal and cold. And she hated him. But more, she hated the way he made her feel.

"He's not all that bad."

She glanced sharply at her father, who was staring with his one eye down the hill at Travis.

Chuckling, he added, "I know right now you're thinking about how mean he is, how much you hate him 'cause he's cold, hard. I used to think the same thing when I first met him. I guess I hated him, too. It wasn't hard to figure out why he kept you with him instead of sending you back home."

She blushed, feeling humiliated.

But he went on, not dwelling on Travis's reasons. "But I fought beside him and got to know him. And that wall he's got bricked up around him—the one you can't see but you know it's there just the same—that was brought on by what happened to him a long time ago. It made him hard on the surface, but underneath it all, he's a good man."

"I saw him shoot one of his own soldiers once," Kitty pointed out. "He was wounded and there was no time to help him and he would probably have died anyway, but Travis took his side arm out and killed him."

"I've done that," he said simply, as though it were of no major significance. "I've killed men I knew well because

470

they were dying. I put them out of their misery. It hurts to do it—God knows, it does—but a man does what he has to do."

She was finding it hard to believe her father had done such a thing. But Kitty was also realizing that she had not known the real man, either.

"I saw Coltrane stop beside a wounded Confederate once and give him a drink of water. The boy died in his arms. I saw him help stop another from bleeding to death. I've also seen him go without rations to give his portion to the sick and wounded 'cause he figured they needed it worse than he did. No, girl, Travis ain't as bad as you think he is. He's just got that wall around him to keep from gettin' hurt again like he once was. Every man has his own kind of armor but he's just been hurt more than most."

"I'm not arguing your point. But I know him in a way you don't. I know what he did to me, my life, and the two of us hate each other. There's this . . . feeling between us . . . something I can't quite define, and we just hate each other. I have no respect or admiration for the man and I live for the time when I'll never have to see him again."

He chuckled. "You know, if two mules try to pull a wagon in the opposite direction, they ain't going no place. But if they pull together, it's a pretty good ride. I'd say you and that man walkin' up this hill are both about as stubborn as two mules trying to go in opposite directions. I think you've met your match, girl. You're a damned pretty woman and all your life men have all but laid down and died over you. That one didn't. You couldn't twist him around your little finger and make him do just like you wanted him to. That's when you locked horns."

"That's not fair!" she exploded then. "I told you about my problems with Nathan, how he insists I do nothing but be a wife and mother and not think about a life of my own. *He* didn't give in to me."

"That's different. He's raised to believe a woman ain't fit for anything 'cept havin' babies and bein' a wife. He was fightin' to protect the way he thinks, too. But when it came to other things, he gave in, I imagine. Most men give in to the little whims of a woman. Not Coltrane. He's a constant master of any situation, and you just can't stand up to that, girl, and you'd never be able to."

"I don't want to!" she screeched. "I told you, Poppa, I hate him. He hates me. We hate each other. It's that simple!"

"Oh, nothing in life is simple, Kitty. But you manage to make the easy things hard. Me and Sam talked it over . . ."

"I'll thank everyone to mind his own business." She leaped to her feet, tears stinging her eyes furiously. It wasn't fair that Travis was causing them to argue this way. He was putting a wedge between them and the closeness they'd always shared. So much had happened since last they met and they had so much to make up for without him casting a shadow over their lives.

John continued to chuckle as Travis approached. There was no time for further discussion. He didn't even nod in Kitty's direction but sat down beside John and said in a grim voice, his eyes serious: "I just talked with General Grant and I have our orders."

John nodded. "I figured as much. Well, let's hear it."

Travis turned his gaze on Kitty then, cold and accusing. "This is confidential. She may be your daughter, John, but she still has her allegiance to the enemy. I can't tell our strategy plans in her presence."

Kitty stamped her foot. "Oh, damn your strategy, Travis Coltrane, and damn you, too!"

"Kitty!" John admonished her.

"I'm sick of all of this. I'm going to ask to be taken to Richmond and I'm going back to help my people. You stay here and do what you have to do, but there's no point in *my* staying. Can't you see what he's doing to us, Poppa? He's trying to put a wall between us, drive us apart. I'm leaving because I can't bear to watch it happen."

She turned and started walking down the hill, then turned, tears streaming down her cheeks. "I'll say my goodbyes to you later, Poppa, privately!" And casting one final icy glare in Travis's direction, she hurried on down the hill toward the camp.

"I'm sorry," Travis said finally. "It's been a bad situation for you, I know."

John nodded thoughtfully. "She's doing the right thing. Her heart is in the South and always will be. It ain't right for her to be here with us. And I take it from the look on your face that you have news that's going to end the calm days of weeks past."

"Right. We're heading south with Sherman toward Atlanta. He's taking an army of over a hundred thousand men and he wants experienced cavalrymen for scouts. He personally asked for the three of us. Sam says he's ready to go. General Grant requests that we go also."

John picked up a small stone, sent it skipping down the hill. Kitty, hearing the noise, turned in annoyance. He waved. Travis gave her a mock salute. With a swish of her skirt, she quickened her pace, stumbled, righted herself with as much dignity as she could muster, and continued on her way.

"Travis," John spoke in a voice evidencing his pessimism. "Just what do you think is goin' to happen? You think Grant's plan will work? Do you think the South is ready to buckle under pressure now? You think the time is right?"

"Yes, to every question. We're going against the Confederate General Joseph Johnston. Our spies tell us he's reorganized the Army of Tennessee. We can't be sure of how many men he's got, but we suspect his strength is nowhere near ours. You and me and Sam will leave soon to do some scouting and try to find out just what kind of strength Johnston's got. I think this is it, one way or the other. The war can't go on much longer."

"I keep asking myself and everyone around me what happens when it does end. Maybe I'm trying to convince myself I'll be around when it's over. A lot have died and more will fall. I could well be one of them. So could you. We don't like to talk about death, but it's the only certainty we've got in life. You ready to die, Coltrane?"

He shook his head firmly. "Nobody is. You can talk about your God and heaven and hell, but when it comes right down to it, no man is sure of what happens when his time comes and he's scared to face it."

"Believin' in a hereafter makes it different. You got to believe in something, Travis, else why make the effort to even get through life?"

"Because we're put here and we've got to live the best we can. We don't have any choice about living or about dying. If you want to know the truth, I don't think we've got any say-so about how we do either. It just happens. I didn't ask for this war, but I sure didn't run from it. And when it's over, I won't see how my life has changed too much."

"And what will you do when it's over? Do you think about it much?"

Travis shrugged and watched Kitty retreat in the distance, entering a cabin. "Sam will go back to the bayou, I guess. Me, I'm heading for California."

"That's a long way off. Why California?"

He grinned. "Because it's there. But enough about me, old man. What about you and that farm of yours back in North Carolina? You think if we win you can go back there without getting lynched?"

"Oh, I'd try, I reckon. It's good land. I've no place else to go. The war will leave a lot of wounds, true, but I'm hoping everyone will be so grateful to see it end that they'll want to live in peace from now on."

They were silent for a moment, then Travis asked the question that was burning in his brain: "What about Kitty, John? What will become of her?"

Sadly, he shook his head. "I don't know. I'm afraid I goaded her into making a decision to cross the Rapidan and go back to the Confederates. I was afraid she would want to stay with us because of me. We're going to be on the move and it's no place for a woman, no matter how strong she is. Kitty's been through hell but I want her out of it. I figure she'll run into Nathan, and maybe she'll be so hurt and disappointed with me—and with you—that she'll listen to him and do what he tells her. He ain't much of a man in my opinion. I never did care much for him or his snotty family but I think he's got balls enough to look after my girl. If he don't, then when this war *is* over, if I'm still around, you can believe he'll answer to me. But I am worried. I've got to be honest with you. Wherever she goes, she's sure to be in the way of the army on either side. No one is going to be safe, I'm afraid, the way things are looking."

"What makes you think this Nathan will look after her? Andy told me his men under him were starting to think he's a bit on the cowardly side."

"For one thing, he's a gentleman, something he prides himself in being. He'll look after her. And he wants her.

That makes a lot of difference, too, Travis. He's always wanted her not because she's so damned pretty but because she was the one thing his daddy's money couldn't buy. Do you understand what I'm saying?"

He nodded.

John squinted his one eye and looked at him. "You love her, don't you?" he asked bluntly.

Travis forced a laugh. "Why, John, I don't think I've ever truly loved any woman. I've had bad experiences. . . ."

"I ain't talking about your past. I'm talkin' about you and Kitty. How do you really and truly feel about her? And I want you to give it to me straight. I'm not so old that I can't remember how it was when I fancied a woman. I can see it in your eyes. And you can't tell me you braved all those Cherokee Indians because an old one-eyed man asked you to. You had to have cared."

Sighing, Travis nodded his head. "Yeah, John, I do care. But it's something I have to get over. It would never work out. Maybe at another time or place, under different circumstances, Kitty and I would have fallen in love in the right way and been happy together. But we got off to a bad start and everything has worked against us. It's best she cross that river and we never meet again."

"I disagree."

Travis looked at him sharply.

"I have to disagree with you," John repeated himself. "I know my girl and I know Kitty cares about you, too. I don't like seeing it end this way."

"You just got through saying you forced her into making the decision to go back to the South."

"For her own damn good, Coltrane! You think I want her with *us*? Let her go back to the South but the least you can do is send her back with some kind of understanding between you two. You can let her know you care."

"Well, why in the hell are you so concerned?" Travis felt anger starting to course through his veins. "She can go back to her Reb officer and probably live a damn sight better life than she'd ever have with me."

"I'm concerned," John said patiently, "because I know my girl and I know she loves you and she'll never be happy with Nathan. And damn it to hell, it's been pretty hard for me to keep quiet about what I know about him. I haven't said anything because if he's the man she wants, then I won't stand in her way, but I don't believe he *is* the man she wants."

Travis leaned forward. "What are you talking about? What do you know about him that you're keeping hidden from Kitty?"

John's face twisted angrily, his one eye squinting in fury. "Nathan rode with the Vigilantes that night." He ground out the words, almost choking on his anger. "I struggled, tore at a hood. It slipped, not much, but enough for me to see it was him. I didn't let on. I was afraid if they knew I recognized any of them, they would go on and kill me. 'Vengeance is mine, sayeth the Lord' but if He don't finish off the scoundrels that took my eye, you can bet that *I* will one day."

Getting to his feet, Travis dusted off the pants of his uniform. "Well, I'm glad you told me. I guess maybe I kept telling myself that this fellow had background, breeding, money—everything I don't have—and that he was more suited for Kitty than I ever could be. But knowing this, that he's the type who would hide behind a mask and beat and kill, well, I can't see how he's better for her than I am." He took a few steps down the hill, stopped, and wheeled around. "I'm not saying I'm good enough for her or that, damnit, I even want her. I'm just saying that I'll . . . oh hell, I'll tell her goodbye. That's the best I can do for now."

John's chuckling echoed in his ears as Travis stormed down the hill following the direction Kitty had taken. When he reached the closed cabin door, he pounded on it roughly with his fists, shaking the walls.

The door flew open and Kitty stood there, wide-eyed and surprised. With one quick step, he was inside, kicking the door shut behind him. Looking around the small room, he saw that they were alone; then he reached out and placed his hands on her shoulders, spinning her around to pin her against the wall. Leaning forward, so close that she felt his warm breath on her face, he said in a low but firm voice: "Kitty Wright, I came here to tell you that I care about you. I'm the way I am, and I'll never change, but I couldn't say goodbye without telling you that no matter what's happened between us that might leave a bad taste in your mouth, I do give a damn about you."

Their gaze locked and for a moment, Kitty could not speak. Then she began to sputter, finally exploding: "Do you think I give a damn?" She clawed at the hands clamped so tightly upon her shoulders, but he held them there. "You think it matters to me for you to stand here and say that yes, you *do* care about me . . . all those times you . . . you *raped* me and mistreated me, that you *cared* about me? Well, damn you, Travis Coltrane, it doesn't matter! You are a no-good Yankee dog and I hate you now and I always will. I . . ."

His lips crushed down on hers, silencing the outpouring of her wrath. Her nails dug into the flesh of his hands, but he continued to hold her shoulders firmly, his mouth moving across hers as he pressed down to keep her head pinned back against the wall. And slowly, ever so slowly, her nails released their grip, her lips began to yield and respond.

And then he bent to scoop her up into his arms, carrying her across the half-darkened room to place her gently upon the bed. He began to remove his clothing, and their eyes still fastened in a piercing gaze, Kitty began to take off her clothes, as well.

Travis lay down beside her, his hands gently stroking the firm, supple lines of her tantalizing body. He wanted her. God, how he wanted her. Never had he wanted one woman so much. But he was not about to take her roughly, savagely. No. He wanted to show her once and for all that in his own way, he did care. Maybe he couldn't express himself in words or gestures in daily contact, but here, here in bed, lying naked together, he could show her that he did care, that he did want her, and that in his own way he needed her beside him.

His lips moved to her cheek, then his tongue darted out to trace the inner lines of her ear. She moaned, twisting beneath him, and he whispered huskily, "Am I raping you now, Kitty? Do you want me to stop?"

"No," she cried, thrusting against him. "No . . . no . . . no. . . ."

His lips, his tongue, his hands conspired to tease her into a sobbing mass of frenzy. Her nails dug into the firm flesh of his back and buttocks, drawing him closer. "Take me," she begged shamelessly, "take me now, Travis. Oh damn you . . . damn you."

He prepared to mount her, then paused. "*You* take *me*, Kitty. You take me and put me where you want me, where I belong—all of me, into all of you . . ."

For a moment, she hesitated. But the heat of her desires forced her hand to move slowly and her fingers wrapped around his swollen member. Raising her hips to meet the thrust, she took him inside her and their bodies crashed together in a crescendo of passion.

And as they crested together, the giant wave of fulfillment washing over their heaving bodies, Travis's breath seared against her flesh as he gasped, "I care, Kitty. In my own way . . . I do care."

And they held each other and slept the slumber of contented lovers.

❧ Chapter Forty ❧

KITTY opened her eyes. Someone was pounding on the door impatiently. She shook her head, trying to awaken fully. "Hey, girl, you all right?" It was John Wright calling. "Time to eat. Hey, don't you hear me?"

Her eyes went to her naked body. "Yes, yes, Poppa. Give me a minute. I'll be right there."

It was coming back, fully and clearly, and a turn of her head brought the shocking reality of Travis's having left her without another word. The warmth she had felt was slowly being replaced by stark, cold indignation. How could he? How could he have made love to her so sweetly and whispered how much he cared and then stolen away while she slept without a word, as though she were something to be used and discarded. And how could she have been fool enough to fall for his trickery? Damn! Damn! Damn! She cursed herself for being so weak!

Yanking on her clothes, smoothing back her hair, Kitty hurried to the door, opening it against the late evening sun. "You've been asleep," John said, puzzled, his eye taking in her rumpled appearance. "Are you ill, girl?"

She told him she was fine, only tired. Her eyes anxiously surveyed the soldiers lining up for meal call. Travis was nowhere to be seen. What would her reaction be when she saw him? Perhaps she was overreacting. He might have had to report for duty and did not want to awaken her. She was playing the role of the scorned woman, being weak, and this made the anger rise again—this time for herself. Forcing a smile, she said, "Let's eat. I'm starving."

They walked toward the line. Hesitantly, John touched her arm and said, "You still going across the river tonight? I can make the arrangements for the crossing. It will take a small patrol of men, a white flag. The Confederates will honor it and you can go over safely into Richmond."

"Poppa, I don't want to leave here." She looked at him incredulously. "There's nothing for me in Richmond."

He raised an eyebrow. "Nathan is in Richmond. What's here?"

"You. And Travis. Oh, Poppa"—she hugged him then, relieved that she had realized her anger earlier was ridiculous and unfounded—"would you be very unhappy if Travis and I loved each other? I didn't think it was possible."

For a moment, he stood there gaping in surprise, then cleared his throat and said, "I don't know what to say, Kitty. You know I've always told you to make your own decisions. But this is one I think you should give a lot of thought to. The war is about to bust wide open, and you won't be safe traveling with us."

"Everything will work out. You'll see." Happily she took a wooden plate and held it out to be heaped with foul-smelling stew. Things *would* work out. She was sure of it. She would find Travis and they would talk some more and the war would be over one day and they would be happy together. It had been there all along, only she hadn't seen it. And Travis had known it, too. They would be happy together. She was sure of it.

Hurrying through her meal, Kitty excused herself from her father and began walking through the enormous camp in search of Travis. Here and there she stopped to ask soldiers if they knew where he was. Some of them did not even know him, but she kept smiling hopefully, inquiring. She felt a desperate need to be with him and she intended to keep searching till she found him. So what if he was on picket? They could talk there privately, in seclusion. He wouldn't mind. He loved her!

She was approaching the outer fringes of the camp, feeling apprehensive with the realization that this was the seamy side, where the officers turned their backs on the cabins and tents that were being used for saloons and gambling and the women for sale that were smuggled in. Travis would not be here. Turning, she started back and then spotted Sam sitting outside a tent.

Relieved, she rushed up to him. "Sam, have you seen Travis? I've got to find him."

He looked at her a long time before speaking, and she was about to ask him why he was behaving so strangely when he said, "Kitty, just go back to your cabin. Get out of here."

Forcing a laugh, she said, "Sam, whatever is the matter with you? Travis and I have finally done what you knew we'd do all along, we've admitted we care about each other. And I want to find him, be with him."

He shook his head, a sad expression on his bearded face. "Please," he was begging her. "Go on back to your cabin. It would never work out for you and Travis."

"Sam, I don't understand you." She was uneasy, puzzled. "Do you know where he is?"

He nodded in the direction of a large tent behind him being used for a saloon. "But don't go in there, girl. You're only asking to be hurt. I guess I didn't know him as well as I thought I did."

He stepped to block her way, but she darted around him, looking inside the tent to see Travis sitting on a barrel, a bosomy yellow-haired woman on his lap. He was bending over, kissing the swell of her breasts. "Honey, I sure do want some of you . . ."—Kitty's heart constricted painfully as she heard him speak. "I just had me a woman not long ago, but she didn't have what you've got. It takes you to fill my need for a while, you know that."

The woman laughed, running her fingers through his hair, lifting his head, and moving to press her bright, red lips against his. Kitty could hear him groaning as he gathered her tightly in his arms: "I want you, baby . . . got to have you."

Stricken, she turned from the tent. Sam was standing

there looking pained and hurt. "Kitty, I'm sorry. Travis is all mixed up."

"Well, I'm not," she said tartly, "not anymore." With head held high, she moved back through the camp. Sol She had made a fool of herself. And why? Because she had behaved like a woman! An empty-headed, giddy woman who fancied herself in love with a man. She had asked for it. She had allowed herself to be weak. There was no one to blame but herself. She had it coming.

Reaching the spot where John sat playing cards with some of the other soldiers, Kitty asked if she could speak with him alone. He followed her inside the cabin. "I want to go to Richmond," she said tersely when they were alone. "I think I need to leave here, to sort out my feelings, Poppa. I hope you understand. I love you and I'll worry about you, but let's pray to God this war ends soon and we can be together soon."

She had to turn away, blinking back the tears, not wanting him to see the hurt.

And she was surprised to hear him calmly say: "All right, Kitty. I'll make the arrangements. You get your things together."

Within an hour, Kitty sat upon a horse with two Federal cavalrymen on each side of her, one of whom rode just in front waving a white flag on the end of his rifle. The Rebel picket yelled out that they could cross the river—but God help them if it was a trick. "I got my gun trained right on you bastards. . . ."

"Shut yer mouth, Johnny Reb," the soldier carrying the flag yelled as he kneed his horse forward in the shallow crossing of the river. "Can't you see we got a lady with us? Don't none of you Southerners have no manners?"

"You shut up," the picket cried angrily. "I didn't see no lady. All I saw was a bunch of dadburned Yankees. Now you go slow and easy 'cause I'm just itchin' to kill me a Yank today!"

Kitty tensed. If the picket did shoot, they would probably all be slaughtered. But the Federal soldiers knew how far they could go in their riling and when they were almost to the shore, they halted. The one in front called out: "Here we are, Johnny Reb. We're supposed to leave this woman here with you. She's from the South, one of yours, and there's an officer in Richmond by the name of Collins who will see she's escorted back to North Carolina."

The soldiers tipped their hats to Kitty and started back across. Swallowing hard, she felt the impulse to cry once again. Yankees. They were Yankees, but her father was one of them, and she had left him behind to return to . . . what? She did not know. Perhaps she was running from, not toward, her destiny.

Out of the bushes came six Confederate soldiers and in the dim moonlight, Kitty saw how shabbily they were dressed. One of them had rags tied around bare feet. Another was completely barefooted and had a ragged blanket tied around his shoulders. How different they were from the soldiers she remembered who had marched off to war so proudly when it all began.

She told them where she wanted to be taken, whom she wanted to see, and they eyed her with suspicion. A woman riding out of a Yankee camp was not a usual occurrence. And as they rode along in the dim moonlight, Confederate pickets came out to stare. But Kitty was too lost in thought to worry about being the object of so much attention. She was busily chiding herself for being so weak as to put herself in a position to be hurt by a scoundrel such as Travis Coltrane. It had to be forgotten once and for all, the whole torrid, seamy affair. They had been lovers in a physical way only, nothing more. There was no future and there was no need to brood over what was past. So she had made a fool of herself. Other women before her had made the same mistakes. Others would follow. She would merely have to be careful not to be so weak ever again.

And then her shoulders slumped as she admitted to herself it was all a game. Travis did mean something no matter how sternly she told herself he never had and never would. In spite of the bad memories, there had been good times, tender moments, reflections that overshadowed the bad. Kisses, caresses, murmured words of endearment, shared laughter and sorrow. In spite of the bitterness, there was sweetness that could not be denied—nor forgotten.

The ride took longer than Kitty had thought it would, but then she'd never been quite sure of just where the Federals were located, nor the Confederates. Virginia was still unknown territory and she was quite turned around. But then it dawned on her quite suddenly that they were nowhere near a city or even a town. They seemed to be melting further and deeper into the wilderness.

She kicked her horse's flanks and pushed forward, calling out to the soldiers, "Where are we going? We aren't headed into town."

They both laughed at once. One said, "Lady, do you really think we're just going to ride you right into Richmond after you come out of a Yank camp? No siree bobtail. We ain't stupid. We're takin' you to our Captain."

"I don't want to go to your Captain," she protested angrily. "I told you, I want to go to Major Nathan Collins."

One of them reached over and grabbed the reins from her hands, giving them a vicious snatch. And when he spoke, he almost snarled. "You're goin' where we want to take you. Now you just ride along and keep your mouth shut."

"You have to listen to me! I am a true Southerner. . . ."

"Tol' you to shut up!" He raised his voice, whipped around in the saddle. "Want me to make you shut up?"

A voice boomed out of the darkness at the shrubbery-thick to the right of the road: "We don't hit women, soldier. Now you just get hold of yourself."

They all stopped instantly. The soldiers slid down from their horses and stood at attention, giving the man who stepped from the shadows a smart salute. Kitty tried to make out his features: he was bearded, stout, on the short side. He wore a uniform tunic, but she could not tell his rank.

The soldiers were pouring out the story of the Yankees sending her across the river. "A spy no doubt," they said anxiously. "We weren't about to take her into Richmond. It's a trick, Captain."

The officer stepped closer. Someone near him was carrying a lantern and in its illumination, she could make out his expression of concern. "I'm Captain Ben Allison and I would like to hear from your lips, madam, what brought you across the river from your Yankee camp."

She slid from the saddle unceremoniously and faced him defiantly. "It isn't 'my' camp, sir. I happen to be from the state of North Carolina and I am a Southerner." Then she told him her story and asked for his services in seeing that she reached Nathan.

He held out his arm to her. "I will send a courier immediately into Richmond to find your officer, but until then, I will have to ask you to be my guest. I assure you, every effort will be made to provide you with comfort and respect while we verify that you are, indeed, telling the truth. In times like these, I am sure you can appreciate our being so cautious."

Kitty had four days to appreciate the Captain's reluctance to accept her word as truth. Finally, the courier returned with the news that yes, indeed, there was a Confederate officer by the name of Nathan Collins, a Major, and he was, unfortunately, no longer in Richmond. Assigned to General Johnston's Army of Tennessee, he was somewhere along the low mountain ridges northwest of Dalton, Georgia. The courier had also checked out Kitty's story about having worked at Chimborazo—and it had been verified by doctors there who remembered her well—and the fact that she had, indeed, been engaged to a Major Collins.

Captain Allison was very unconcerned as he gave her the news, adding, "If you are unduly distressed, I apologize, but we are in the midst of a war, and . . ."

"Oh, I don't want to hear anymore." Kitty waved him to silence, chewing a fingernail as she tried to rationalize her next move. They would, undoubtedly, escort her to the hospital in Richmond if she wanted to go back to work there. Or, they might even take her all the way to Goldsboro. But she had this unexplainable urge to get to Nathan. She did not want to admit it, but it was there, smoldering just the same—the compelling thought that if she were with Nathan once again, they might find what they had once lost and she could then forget Travis wholly and completely.

Captain Allison almost choked on the brandy he was sipping when Kitty faced him defiantly, eyes sparkling little purple dots of determined fury as she said crisply: "I wish to be escorted to Dalton, Georgia, *and* the Army of Tennessee *and* Captain Nathan Collins."

"You cannot be serious . . ."

"Oh, I am quite serious, sir. The war is coming to a festering head. I can see that. And when it does, I want to be at the side of my fiancé."

"But a woman's place is not on the battlefield. It's . . ."

"Damn it, don't tell me where my place is!" Kitty exploded, turning on him with all the fury of a defending tigress. "I imagine, sir, that I have seen more battle than *you* have. I can tell you tales of blood and gore that will make your eyes bulge out even more. I may be a woman, but I do not need a man to remind me. And I certainly need not be told where my place is, for my place is where I want to be and right now that place is with General Johnston's army, and if you do not provide me with an escort, then I will steal a horse and ride out of here by myself and try to find a place called Dalton, Georgia!"

The Captain looked at her, stunned, amazed. And he could only nod. "Yes, of course. Whatever you wish. I'll have my courier return to Richmond and find out if any troops are leaving to join General Johnston. You may certainly go where you choose."

Swishing her skirt, Kitty left his tent to return to the one assigned to her. Her place was where she wanted it to be, not where someone thought it should be. Once and for all, she was through with being mentally placed in a pen like a cow or a fat hen merely because she was a woman. Men like Travis had used her, scoundrels like Luke Tate had abused her—and now it was over. Nathan could accept her like she was or she would walk away from him finally, for good. But at least he would be there to help her through the rough spots, get over the burn Travis had so freshly given to her. Staying in Richmond alone would give her too much free time to brood and remember and blame herself and possibly regret and, worse, grieve.

At supper call that night one of the soldiers asked her if she was afraid to go near the battlefield. She merely shook her head, not wanting to discuss it. But she could have told him she was afraid of *not* going for the real battle was waging where no one could see it—within the recesses of her own soul.

❧ Chapter Forty-one ঙ

THE Confederate company had been told to avoid skirmishes and battle. Not only did they have a woman traveling with them, but the few supplies and ammunition they carried were valuable to General Johnston's Army of Tennessee, which lay entrenched northwest of Dalton, Georgia. So they had to move slowly, riding the lower hills of the Blue Ridge Mountains along little-traveled rocky paths and through jungle-like stretches of second-growth timber.

Two weeks into their journey their advance scouts came across a small band of Confederate deserters and brought them back to the commanding officer as prisoners. Kitty stood nearby and listened to their hysterical tales of horror.

"Lord, it was terrible. Gen'rul Grant and Gen'rul Lee fought it out in the wilderness. Then the woods, they caught fire and you could hear the wounded screaming as they burned to death. They couldn't move . . ."

"I seen one man with his legs blown off and both arms hit, and he couldn't do nothin' but scream when the fire caught hold of his clothes."

The officer in charge, a Major Jack Boykin, glowered at the five bedraggled men. "You boys look fit."

"We were lucky, sir," one of them spoke up.

"I guess you were, you sons of bitches!" he exploded

furiously. "I wonder how many of our men died because you bastards high-tailed it and ran at the first shot? You make me sick. You know the law! Take them out and shoot them before a firing squad."

The men screamed, tried to run, but were quickly surrounded by soldiers who dragged them away. Posts were quickly made from trees rapidly hacked down. Kitty watched in horror, and finally finding her voice, she clutched the Major's sleeve and said, "You can't just shoot them."

"Oh, yes I can. And we'll leave their bodies here for the vultures to pick. Goddamned deserters! I'm sick of them. I intend to shoot every son of a bitch that runs. It'll make a fitting example for my men, too. We're heading straight into the thick of the war and I want them to stand and fight Yankees, by God."

"But you need every man. Talk to them. They'll promise never to run again. They probably got scared. Let them join this company. . . ."

He wheeled on her, a weary-looking man who showed the reflection of seeing the anguish of many years in battle. "Miss Wright, I am in charge of this command and I will command it as I see fit. I do not need, nor want, your advice. Now I suggest that you take a walk until after the executions take place."

"No," Kitty said, quite calmly. "I'll stay. I want to see just how cruel you can be, sir."

"Oh, hell, woman, I'm merely following orders. How would you feel if your fiancé were killed because the men fighting in front of him turned and ran and left him exposed? Would you be so concerned then?"

She thought a moment. "Perhaps not," she said finally, deciding that perhaps she had been guilty of thinking like a woman again. They were at war and it was a cruel, ghastly war; and men could not turn and run away like cowards. They had to stand and fight. She looked around at the soldiers lining up for the firing squad. It was obvious they didn't like what they were about to do. The others watching looked frightened, as though they had never been sure of whether or not they would desert until this moment, this hour—and now they knew they would never run from fire and were frightened because they had even toyed with the idea.

The five deserters were tied tightly to the posts which had been driven into the ground about a foot apart. Scarves, rags, shirts—anything to keep them from seeing— were tied around their faces. At a distance of perhaps fifty feet, the firing squad stood at attention.

"Please, God, no . . ." one of the men screamed. The others were sobbing hysterically.

"Ready!" the Major barked. Rifles clacked.

"Aim!" A dozen guns pointed at the men.

"Fire!" The air split with the sound of gunshots.

The men tied to the posts slumped. Blood oozed from their chests and stomachs. Kitty gasped as she realized several of them were still alive.

"Again," Major Boykin roared. "Ready . . . aim . . . fire."

And when the last explosion quieted, no sound came from the men. "Leave them there," the Major ordered, "so others may see and know the fate of deserters!"

Would the horror ever end, Kitty thought as they prepared to continue their journey? Would all the pain and anguish ever cease. Perhaps somewhere along the way the war had ended and all had died and gone to hell and throughout all eternity they would walk in agony and in bloody war. Life no longer existed. Only war. Only hell.

Receiving word along the way that Johnston's army was moving down through Georgia, Kitty traveled with the company trying to get to them. A report came of a battle on the slopes of Kennesaw Mountain and Sherman's men were said to have been pushed back.

"We'll overtake them soon," Major Boykin told Kitty one night. "It's just a matter of days. They're all around Atlanta and we're going to be right in the middle of the fighting. How you will ever find your Major Collins is beyond me, Miss Wright, because once we reach the battles, I must admit I will have little concern for seeing that you reach him."

Kitty told him not to worry. "I'll work with the hospital units as I've done in the past. I just ask that when your courier reaches General Johnston that he ask the Commander that word circulate that I am present. Nathan will find me, I'm sure."

And they moved on toward Atlanta, Georgia, the thick woodlands and the red clay hills beckoning amid the smoke and sulphur clouds. Several times Kitty would be yanked from her horse by a nearby soldier and thrown to the ground for cover as shots rang out and a brief skirmish ensued. Then, without really being aware that they had reached the core of the war, Kitty saw suddenly that it was all around them. Major Boykin sent a soldier to take her to the ambulance wagons. There was not even time for a goodbye or a promise to try to get word to Nathan that she was in the vicinity. Things happened so fast. The war was exploding all about. There was no time for concern over a young Southern woman seeking a Confederate officer.

She was taken to a wooded area where hundreds of men writhed on the ground in wounded agony. Her escort could not lead the horses further and they dismounted. Taking her arm, he all but jerked her along, stepping over the bloodied bodies which reached out, pleading for help. Several were already dead, Kitty noted; flies crawled about their faces and into their oozing wounds while the victims lay still, mouth gaping, eyes staring upward blankly.

"This here woman knows somethin' about doctorin'." The soldier thrust her into the first tent they came to. "She's all your'n." And then he was hurrying away, back to Major Boykin's company.

A man with a thick beard and wearing a bloodied apron was hunched over a board set up between two barrels. He barely glanced in her direction as he barked: "Get the hell over here and get to work. We're shorthanded and even if you don't know *anything*, you can do *something* to help."

She moved forward, not flinching at the sight of the bowels protruding from the soldier on the table. "Hell, I can't do nothing for him." The doctor sighed wearily. He snapped to a soldier standing nearby who looked as though he might faint at any moment, "Get him out of here. Give him a dose of whiskey to ease his pain. He'll die soon."

The boy was unconscious and did not hear the grim

diagnosis. As he was carried away, the doctor yelled, "Bring me another one."

All around were the sounds of anguish and dying. Shells exploded in the distance. Guns barked. The Rebel Yell echoed in the hills. The war was on. Kitty melded into it, helping the doctor, helping others, ministering to the wounded with precision, moving as though she were another entity, with no thought of her own except to help the victims of the cruel war.

Gradually, the doctor in charge of the tent realized that Kitty had a good medical knowledge and he began to turn minor cases over to her to handle alone. A table was set up strictly for her work. "Do the best you can," she was told. "The casualties are mounting and the wounded are piling up outside like flies on a dead mule's carcass."

But then the ambulance wagons brought in a fresh load of wounded men and there was no time to sort out the minor wounds for Kitty's table and she was now finding herself faced with the most serious of wounds. Whenever she turned helplessly to the doctor, who was up to his elbows in blood, he would yell: "Do the best you can, woman. Try to stop the bleeding and move 'em on out. Can you amputate? Do that if it means saving a life. We have no time to worry about professional experience here. Just try to save lives and ease suffering."

Day turned to night and dawn came without anyone noticing. The air was thick, hot, humid. Kitty's clothes were soaked with blood and perspiration. Long ago her hair had tumbled down around her face, which had become splotched with blood as she constantly pushed the limp hair back out of her way. In a rare moment of respite between patients, a soldier helping her gave her a small ribbon. "You can tie your hair back with this, ma'am," he said respectfully. "I seen how it's gettin' in your way."

She gave him a weary smile, as she reached for the pink ribbon. "What are you doing out here in the middle of battle with a pink ribbon, soldier?"

He bit his lip. He couldn't have been much over fifteen or sixteen years of age and he reminded her so much of Andy, with the light sprinkling of freckles across his nose and cheeks. "My sweetheart," he said quietly, "she sent it to me. I reckon you need it more'n I do."

"I'll be sure to give it back," Kitty said gratefully as she tied back her long, blood-matted hair. "She might not like you giving it to another woman." She winked teasingly, trying to brighten up the dreary, grim world, if only for a moment.

He shrugged and she saw the glimmer of tears in his young eyes. "I reckon she won't know about it. She's dead. Yankees killed her when they raided her folks' place in north Georgia."

"I'm so sorry . . ." Kitty's words were drowned out by the sounds of another soldier screaming as he was brought in that he would rather die than have his left cut off. Kitty took one look at the exploded leg and reached for a scalpel and saw, tears stinging her eyes.

Kitty would work in the hospital tent as long as her legs could hold her up, then, overcome with weariness, she was forced to go to the rest tent set up nearby for the worn-out medical staff. The night one of the soldiers came to awaken her, she had lost all conception of time.

"Everybody is ordered to report to the hospital tent," the soldier told her in a frenzy. "There's a bunch of wagons coming in with hundreds of wounded."

Wondering if she could will her aching legs to move from the cot and stand up, Kitty struggled to sit up. Every time her eyes closed, she saw torn, ragged limbs, gouged wounds, crumpled, broken bodies, the dead covered in flies and maggots. The hot, humid July skies blended as blood red as the clay beneath her feet. All around were devastation, confusion, bloodshed. When would the nightmare ever end?

One knee buckled. She straightened. The soldier saw and timidly held out a bottle partially filled with an amber liquid. "I know ladies don't drink, Miss Kitty, but this might give you a little push."

"It probably would." She managed a weary smile in the glow of the lantern he was holding to dispel the inky blackness of the tent. "But save it for the wounded. I hear the chloroform is getting low."

493

"We got some hot coffee made from parched peanuts. It ain't the best in the world, but it might help."

They made their way through the piles of moaning, wounded soldiers, their screams of pain giving the night an eery echo. As they entered the hospital with oil lamps flickering as they swung from tent posts and the surgeons casting hulking, ominous shadows against the walls as they worked, Kitty winced, stomach heaving with nausea as she saw a stack of amputated arms and legs lying in one corner. They were being removed quicker than the soldiers assigned to dig a hole for them could take care of the grisly task.

The endless parade began. Kitty did what she could: stopped the bleeding, cleansed the wounds, set broken bones in splints, and amputated when absolutely necessary. By sunrise, she was so weary she could no longer muster the strength to wield the saw back and forth across the bone to be severed. She would make the necessary incisions through skin, tissue, and muscle, then step back while an assistant came forward to do the actual bone-cutting. The agonizing screams of the soldier held down upon the blood-slicked board pierced the air. There was no time to try to stitch the skin flaps in place. Nearby, a cauldron of tar bubbled, the smell mingling sickeningly with the odor of blood. Once the limb was severed, Kitty would swab the stump with tar to seal and stop the hemorrhage. Usually at this point, the victim would faint and be spared the agony of the hot-tar application.

"Lady, God, please, don't take my legs off," a soldier screamed, clutching at Kitty's bodice as he was placed on the board. "Please, I'd rather die . . ."

An assistant ripped his hands loose, pulling them to the side where a nail protruded. Quickly, he wound a rope around it so that the soldier could not move his arms. Kitty closed her ears to his pleas. She knew if she let herself hear them, she would not be able to function in a proper manner. Later, if there was to be a later, in peace, if there was ever to be a peace, she would remember the agony, the screams. But now, there was a job to be done, with no time for pity if that pity stood in the way of duty.

She picked through the torn flesh of what was left of

the soldier's legs. The bones were badly smashed, the muscles hung in shreds. There was nothing to do but amputate. It would not take long. A few slices of the knife's blade to finish severing the muscles, a few quick chops with a hatchet, then a swab of hot tar, and the war would be over for this young boy. He would be sent to rest in the fields outside, then transported home—wherever that was—to live out what was left of his life.

Motioning to the assistant, Kitty started working. The boy on the table lifted his head, saw what she was doing, then fainted. When it was over, she stepped back, heard the sound of gasping and retching, and looked at the wounded soldier. But he was lying quietly. The sound was right at her ear. Spinning about, she fought for consciousness as a dizzy wave washed over her weary body.

The retching was coming from Nathan, who stood behind her, covering his face with a handkerchief.

Her lips moved, trying to utter his name.

"Katherine, my God, get out of here." He was grabbing her arm, yanking her outside.

"Hey, we got another coming in," a voice yelled from inside the tent. "Miss Kitty, we need you. . . ."

"She's going with me, goddamn it!" Nathan screamed. Numb, Kitty let him lead her away into the night and they stumbled along until they reached a place where miraculously, no bodies lay.

His arms went around her, crushing her against him. She had briefly noted inside the tent that he had not changed. His uniform was hardly dirty, certainly not torn and ragged. He was still the portrait of a dignified officer and gentleman.

"I've been trying to find you for days, Katherine," he murmured, lips nuzzling her bloodstained cheek. "Dear Lord, how did you get here? What are you doing here?"

She told him. She had not wanted to go home and she had not wanted to remain with the Yankees. "I wanted to come where you are, Nathan. There was no place else to go." She said it quite simply, as if there it was, the only decision to make.

"Thank God, you're safe." He kissed her briefly. "But you aren't staying. I've asked General Johnston personally for permission to escort you back home and there is where you will stay."

"Nathan, no," she protested. "I'm needed here."

"Damnit, I know you are," he cursed in exasperation, "but the battleground is no place for a woman, Katherine. You're in danger, don't you see that? I want you at home where you have some chance of being safe."

Shaking her head from side to side and blinking back the tears, she whispered, "Oh, Nathan, don't you see? I've got to do something for the Confederacy. Sitting at home with the women is not for me."

He gave her a gentle shake. "Tell me. Do you love me?"

"I . . . I don't know." She knew she *wanted* to love him, wanted with all her heart to forget the past and Travis Coltrane and go back to the hopes and dreams she and Nathan had once shared. Could it be? She did not know. She could only hope.

"If you love me, you'll do as I say, Katherine. I'm going to leave with you at once and get you out of this. I'll take a small patrol of my men with me. We should make it in three days easy. You can stay with my mother. She writes that she is gathering up all the womenfolk from out in the country to make bandages and get together supplies. You can work with them, help them. If you refuse, then as much as I love you, I'm going to turn and walk away from you here and now."

She knew by the tone of his voice that he meant what he was saying. If she refused, and he did walk away, then she would be truly alone, with no one to cling to. And though she hated to admit it, being alone meant clinging to memories of Travis. She could not let her heart drift free. No, she would have to give her devotion to Nathan to ever know any peace. "All right"—the words came quietly, obediently—"I'll do whatever you want."

Raining kisses all over her face, Nathan was jubilant. "I knew you'd see it my way, darling. If you had only obeyed me before and not gone near that hospital in Goldsboro, you would not have been abducted again. Oh, if I could only erase the misery and suffering you've endured."

"It's in the past, Nathan. We've got to stop looking at the past if we're to have any kind of future. That's what ruined things for us in Richmond, your not being able to overlook what happened to me in the past."

"That's partially right, Katherine, but the final blow came when you called out the name of Travis Coltrane when it was me making love to you. I don't think I have ever been so hurt."

Kitty felt a wave of anger. "You were drunk, Nathan, and you slipped into my room and started . . . raping me while I slept!"

She started to pull away from him, but his arms held her tight. "Katherine, my darling, I'm sorry. We can't think about anything beyond right here and right now. Let's think only about the good things between us and from there I feel only love can grow between us, the love we once had and lost."

A scream of agony split the silence around them. War. It all came flooding back. "Nathan, things don't look good for us, do they? Soldiers die by the thousands and they get wounded and blown to bits. It's the same over and over. Will it ever end?"

"It will end one day, Katherine, and then life, real life, will just begin for you and me. Things aren't as bad as they seem. President Davis has relieved General Johnston of his command and replaced him with General John Bell Hood. I found this out when I went to Johnston personally to ask for leave to take you home."

"General Hood? But he lost a leg at Chickamauga I heard."

"That's true. He rides strapped to his saddle but he still has courage and valor. He was even wounded at Gettysburg in his arm but he doesn't give up. He's been a Corps Commander under Johnston and the two didn't get along. Anyway, Hood's been quite critical of Johnston's retreats and he wants to fight. We just heard that Sherman is crossing the Chattahoochee River and heading for Atlanta, and Hood is going to move out and attack."

"General Hood is planning an attack?" She pulled back to try to meet his gaze in the dim light from the fires burning in the distance. "Then how is it you can take me home, Nathan? You will be needed here and so will I. Later, when Sherman is beaten . . ."

"No!" His voice had a sharp edge to it and she could

make out the anger on his face. "No! We leave in the morning. I already have a patrol of men . . ."

"Nathan, I can take the train. I hear it runs from Atlanta into Augusta and up through South Carolina and into Wilmington. You are an officer. Your men will need you."

"I told you General Johnston gave me permission to see you home safely and I intend to do so. I will personally escort you right to my mother's front door and have your promise that you will not leave her house until you leave with me one day! Is that understood?"

Kitty did not understand. Why did Nathan insist on taking soldiers and riding her all the way to North Carolina when she could take a train? Why was he able to leave now when General Hood planned to ride out and attack Sherman's advancing army? It made no sense.

His arms were tightening about her again and she could feel his breath, warm on her face as his lips moved closer to brush against hers. She closed her eyes, yielded—but the image of a crooked smile and laughing gray eyes blotted out the sweetness of the moment. Would it always be this way? Even if she did not marry Nathan but one day wed another, would the image of Travis forever be there, burned into her mind for all eternity?

Damn him! Why did he have to command such power over her? A curse, that's what it was. He had used her the way he chose, then trampled upon her. Nathan offered love, devotion, all in exchange for her giving up what he considered "fool" notions. He wanted a wife . . . at home . . . in her place. She had tried to be independent, to think for herself in a world dominated by men and their ideas of how a woman should live her life.

And she had failed. It would be foolish not to accept what Nathan was offering. He would be good and kind, and once the war was over, they would have a future together.

Nathan raised his head, still holding her close. "I love you, Katherine, and I always will. Let me take you home tomorrow and I want you to wait for me there. And every time the past comes back to hurt you, I want you to think only of the future and this . . ." And once more he kissed her.

And Kitty closed her eyes and once again saw the smile, the gray eyes—like a whispering ghost gliding softly through the swaying leaves above. She felt a warm shudder —and knew the power still held her in its clutches.

✵ Chapter Forty-two ✵

A half-moon peered through the gray clouds, casting an eery sheen on the bare, gaunt fields that surrounded the Collins mansion. Only memories remained of the wealth that once surrounded the plantation. Kitty could remember the gala parties on the lawns, the field hands singing as they brought in the cotton from the fields. Gone. All of it. The slaves had long since run away and there had been no menfolk about to stop them. The silver and crystal had been sold for whatever heirlooms would bring, the proceeds sent to the starving Confederate army. No semblance remained of the prosperity that was once overwhelming.

Behind her, at the center of the wide veranda, a creaking door slammed.

"Kitty, are you out here? You know Mother Collins said to stay inside. There are foragers about. Kitty? Do you hear me?"

She turned her gaze in the direction of the whining voice. "I'm over here, Nancy, and I don't need you to tell me when to come inside."

Nancy Warren Stoner padded across the floor. "I do declare, Kitty, but you are a stubborn one. Everybody knows the foragers are about and General Sherman doesn't care what they do. If Mother Collins weren't stubborn, we could evacuate to the mountains. I can't see staying here, just waiting for those horrid Yankees to come marching up the road."

Kitty looked at the young woman leaning on the railing and tried to remember the time when she had been a social queen in Wayne County. Now she wore ragged dresses like the others housed in the mansion, her hair hung limply about her shoulders. Dresses had been ripped to shreds and sent off to the hospitals to use for bandages. There was no time, nor need, for curling irons and other frivolities. Food was scarce and so was time, and they had to do a bit of foraging themselves to exist.

"Lavinia isn't being altogether stubborn, Nancy," Kitty said patiently, as though speaking to a child. "She happens to be sick . . . too sick to be moved."

"Oh, I forgot," Nancy whined sarcastically. "*You* know so much about doctoring, don't you? You're the one folks talk about, the one who went off to the war and doctored the Confederates *and* the Yankees. Too good to sit home with the womenfolk and quilt and sew and make bandages, weren't you? And now you sit around all puffed up because Nathan won't let you go to that nasty hospital in town. . . ."

The girl had hit a sensitive spot. "Shut up, Nancy. I've listened to your bitching mouth for almost six months and I'm sick of it. The only reason you harp at me is because you know it's me Nathan is coming home to and not you. Where's your pride? And by the way, where's your husband? He chose to stay with strangers rather than come back to you because he couldn't stand your nagging."

"How dare you?" Nancy took a few steps forward, sneering. "Everyone knows what you did when you went away, how you slept with all those Yankees. When Nathan realizes how foolish he is, he'll be sorry he ever asked you to live here! Just wait and see. I wish you'd never come. It's embarrassing to the family to have you here."

Kitty laughed. It might be embarrassing but they had certainly made use of her. None of the high-bred women who had gathered at the house knew anything at all about cooking. She'd had that chore to do, for they were helpless once the slaves ran away. She was aware of how Nathan's aunts and cousins felt about her, but that was the least concern. She had made him a promise and she would keep it. And where else was there to go, anyway? She had learned upon returning that her mother was dead and even though the news hurt, it did not come as a surprise. Kitty had never expected to see Lena again after Luke Tate forced her away that night when her mother lay so deathly ill. With her father still away fighting for the North and their homeplace a pile of burned-out rubble, there was nowhere to go—and she had promised Nathan she would remain at his home till the war ended. Aching to go to Goldsboro and work at the hospital there, it was all she could do to stay out in the country away from everyone and all the war news. And most of all, she wanted to be back with the hospital staff.

"I'm going to tell Mother Collins you refuse to come in."

"Nancy, I don't care what you do. I wish you'd just go away and leave me alone. You're so childish, so hateful. I can't communicate with you and I don't see that we have anything to talk about, anyway. Now please, just go away."

Kitty knew what she wanted—an argument. Nancy loved to goad and needle, but she was determined not to let her succeed in getting her riled. She had noticed how it infuriated the conceited girl if she just brushed her aside like a pesky mosquito.

"Just you wait!" Nancy swished around and stomped down the rickety porch steps. "Just you wait till Nathan comes back and I tell him how you've behaved here, in his home—the way you've treated his relatives. A fine hostess you'd make for the Collins mansion, fine hostess, indeed! You haven't got as much polish as a stinking nigra field hand!"

Kitty hadn't been paying much attention to Nancy's ravings—she usually repeated herself every day, at least twice. But suddenly she sat up and saw the girl walking toward the road in the moonlight, head up, feet stomping her on her way.

"Nancy, you come back here," Kitty called apprehensively. "If there are foragers around, you have no business out there. You know the rules Lavinia gave us—no women out of the house after dark . . ."

"Well, look at you," she screamed into the night. "You sit out there brooding over all your Yankee lovers! Don't tell me what to do!"

Leaning back in her chair, Kitty said to hell with her.

Let her wander around out there in the dark. If an owl hoots, she'll run all the way back to the house, terrified. Maybe she deserved a good scare, anyway, to take her off her high horse.

The days since Nathan left had dragged endlessly, slowly becoming weeks filled with terrible war news. Sherman had finally attacked and taken the city of Atlanta, leaving it in flames. Marching south to Savannah, Georgia, it had been said, the fierce General had telegraphed President Lincoln that he was giving him the city with one hundred and fifty guns and twenty-five thousand bales of cotton—for a Christmas present!

Kitty shuddered. What of Nathan? Where was he? The last letter they had received arrived weeks ago, just before the occupation of Savannah. He had said they were fleeing Sherman, trying to regroup and gain strength before attacking. He hoped to be home soon. The letter was hurried, difficult to read. But where was he now? He could have been killed and in the confusion, his identity lost. They might never hear what happened to him.

I've got to stop thinking this way, Kitty chided herself. The war would soon be over, and even if the South lost, somehow they would rebuild, unify; and Nathan would come home and they would marry and one day the searing memories would fade to a cold gray ash.

The door squeaked. "Kitty, are you out here?"

Recognizing the voice of Nathan's Aunt Sue, Kitty acknowledged her presence. "Lord, child," the woman hurried over. "You know Lavinia don't want you outside like this. It isn't safe. At least inside we do have a few guns, and we could barricade the doors and try to defend ourselves. If you sit here alone like this, some Yankee forager could come along and snatch you right off the porch, and . . ."

"I'll be fine, Aunt Sue. You go inside and see to Lavinia. Tomorrow I'm going to go to the hospital in town and get the medicine she needs. She's very weak and frankly, I'm afraid she won't live much longer."

The woman gasped, hand flying to her throat as the moonlight spilled out from behind a cloud bank. "Oh, Lordy, don't say that about my blessed sister. She lives to see this war end. Don't let her die. . . ."

Kitty spread her hands helplessly. "I've done all I can

do. She was too weak and feeble before the fever ever set in. She hasn't eaten properly, has let herself go. . . ."

"We all have." Her voice cracked. "When my Lymon died at Gettysburg, all life ended for me. And when Lavinia lost Aaron, she just gave up. Sometimes I think we'd all be better off if we died—before the Yankees get to us first."

"We can't give up hope." Kitty tried to comfort the crying woman. "We have to have faith that all will be well one day."

But her words were of no comfort. The woman turned and fled back into the house. Kitty looked in the direction where Nancy had gone—toward the wooden farmhouse that stood just beyond the pecan grove. Sighing, she got up, went down the steps, and crossed the bare yard. The girl was so immature, so selfish and self-centered: she would have everyone worried half to death if they discovered her missing. And Nancy was certainly no outdoors person. She might have been raised in the country, but she knew nothing about the woods and scrublands about. She could get lost quite easily.

The pecan trees were bare, their branches swaying slightly in the chilly night. Underneath, green hulls crunched beneath her feet as she scurried along, trying to watch where she stepped. And she cursed herself for vowing to Nathan that she would stay with his mother until he returned. This was not the place for her. She belonged in the hospital wards, helping the wounded, doing her part. What good was she doing here? Cooking, trying to find food. Certainly if hard-pressed, Nancy and the other pampered women would have the courage to get out and do for themselves.

She saw the figures scuffling in the shadows before she could make out Nancy's muffled screams. Heart thudding, Kitty plunged ahead toward the struggles, crying out, "What are you doing to her? Stop it, I say. Stop it."

And then they turned and she could make out the angry, chiseled features of three men dressed in mismatched Yankee uniforms. Foragers! Damned Yankee foragers who would steal, burn, plunder—and rape, at will!

Nancy was trying to scramble away, but one of the men stepped down on her long hair, pinning it to the ground as she screamed with pain. Too late, Kitty realized she should have returned to the house for a gun. Perhaps she could outrun them. Turning, she started running across the grove, but the men were right behind her, grabbing her and slinging her to the ground—hard.

One of them fell on top. "Well, well, I do believe we've got us some real treasure, boys. Best I can tell, this Rebel wench has a body to behold."

Ugly, nasty-sounding laughs ringed the air.

"Let's get the other one, too. We can have us a little party."

"Let's take our pleasure and then move to the house and see what these Rebs have hidden."

"Yeah, maybe they have some liquor."

"Let's go ahead and get some lovin' right now. I ain't had a woman since I screwed the eyeballs out of that nigger wench down in Georgia."

"These look prime . . ."

Kitty was trying to scream against the nubby fingers pressed tightly over her mouth. She could make out the dim figure bringing Nancy forward. Nancy had stopped struggling and was crying instead, deep, racking sobs shook her whole body.

"Get 'em naked. Build a fire. I want to see this stuff."

"Can't have no fire. Might be some yokels around who'd come running with a musket. We'll make a fire later, though, when we burn that goddamned house down."

"Please, no," Nancy whispered hoarsely. "Don't take *me*. I . . . I just had a baby. I . . . I still have a . . ."

Her words were barely audible: ". . . bleeding . . ."

"Oh, shit." One of the foragers gave her a shove away. Then he turned to Kitty. "This right? This woman got a new baby? That means you got to please all of us."

"Oh, she can pleasure all of you," Nancy was babbling, still backing away. "She used to be held prisoner by some Confederate deserters and I know they raped her over and over. She . . . knows what it's all about. Spare me, please."

Kitty's body was shaking with white-hot fury. How could Nancy do this to her? How could she lie to protect her own body, knowing full well the Yankee bastards would ravish her over and over again. How traitorous could that girl be?

"You put up a fight and we'll cut your throat, you hear?" A burly, sweat-stinking man was straddling Kitty, his uniform damp with perspiration. "Now, let's get these clothes off. . . ."

He held a knife and picked at her bodice, then with one quick slash, tore it open. Her breasts spilled forward and he gasped: "Boys, come look at these. Oh, Lordy!"

They gathered around. Kitty struggled, opened her lips to scream, but a dirty cloth was stuffed down into her mouth. She was helpless.

"Oh, Bart, you hurry up and do it. I want some so bad."

"Yeah, Bart, you always get it first and don't leave much for anybody else, the way you fuck your women. . . ."

The man above her was ripping at her skirt. "I'll leave some of this, boys. It looks too good not to share. And I got a feelin' from what I'm lookin' at that she can take a whole hell of a lot of good, hard fuckin'."

"Hey!" someone shouted. "Get that other one. She's running away."

Kitty twisted her head to see Nancy being thrown to the ground. "Tie her up," the one on top of her ordered. "We don't need no sick woman, but we don't want nobody to come running outta that house with no gun. We can take care of what's inside that place later. Right now, I got other business to take care of."

She was naked, her arms pinned painfully behind her back. The man called Bart moved his free hand up and down her body—pinching, squeezing, probing roughly. He was up on his knees, pants down around his ankles. "Leamon, come here and hold her arms above her head. I want to be free to really get goin' here in a minute."

Someone stepped forward, yanked her arms up. Bart reached down, grabbed a handful of pubic hair, and squeezed, laughing with delight as Kitty gagged trying to scream out in pain. "Now I'll make it good for you," he hissed, blowing foul breath into her face. "I'll make you feel good . . . real good."

He began to caress her, and in spite of her terror and loathing for him, a sweet-hot fire began to spread through her body. Against her will, she felt herself yielding. *No,* she told herself over and over, *don't react this way . . . don't yield to his filth . . . no . . . don't.*

She went limp. The man above her released his hold, moved back. Bart was entering her roughly, starting his thrust. A wave of panic went through Kitty. She could not stand it—his violation of her body—nor the way she had been so weak. Damn it to hell, she had vowed never to give in to the weakness that plagued womanhood.

Her fingers groped in the dirt as he rammed into her. She felt the knife handle. In his excitement, in his lust, he had dropped his knife. Slowly, she wrapped her hand around it and before she could think about the moment at hand, Kitty brought the blade up and plunged it under his chin, felt the warm gush of blood splashing into her face at the same time as his scream of surprise and pain melted away in the gentle gurgling of his life's blood as it oozed away.

"What the hell . . ." one of the men cried, springing forward. But Kitty was in control of herself. She shoved the dying man to one side, then leaped to her feet, still naked, knife held ominously. He stepped forward, bent over his comrade, and Kitty brought the blade down into his back. He had seen his friend slump forward, heard his melting scream, but had not seen Kitty with a knife. It was a fatal mistake.

Kitty whipped around, ready for the third savage to step forward. When he did, stunned by what was going on, he saw the knife, glinting in spite of the blood upon the blade, and he began backing away. Kitty pulled her arm back, swung, and sent the knife slashing through the air. It caught in his left shoulder and stuck there. Screaming, he kept on running, disappearing into the thick woods beyond.

She stared down at the two bodies—a ghastly sight in the silver moonlight. The blood sparkled like red stars in the night, glistening, gleaming. Blood. The blood of the enemy. The blood of those who would dare to violate her body because she was born a woman. No more. No more would they violate either body or soul—and God pity anyone who tried to defile or control her spirit, her will.

She had been obedient to her vow. Kitty had honestly tried, she felt, to do as Nathan had asked. And what had it gotten her—hiding away in a rotting house with equally decaying people. This was not the place for her. Perhaps

one day . . . but not now. Nathan would have to understand. He would have to if they were to love each other.

And they *would* love each other. Nathan was gentle,
kind, so different from the vicious animals she had known
in the past few years. Travis would become a distant
memory. She would bury him in her mind. When Nathan
returned, all would work out. It had to. But for the present,
Kitty could not cope with the life he had inflicted upon her.

Her torn clothes fell to the ground as Kitty started
walking through the pecan grove, heading back to the
house. Her body gleamed like that of a naked goddess
come to life as she took firm, sure steps. It was over. All
the indecision, the regrets—they were gone. She had tried.
Now it had come to light.

The sound of sobbing made Kitty jerk her head around.
Beneath a pecan tree, perhaps only twenty feet away,
Nancy Warren Stoner crouched, head in hands and sob-
bing convulsively. Turning, Kitty walked to her.

The girl lifted her face. "I'm sorry, Kitty. I just had to
lie. I couldn't let them do *that* to me. I . . . I'm not used
to such things."

"Are you saying I am?" Kitty screamed indignantly.

"You . . . you've been through it"—Nancy spoke cautiously—"I . . . I felt you could withstand it better."

Kitty's hand lashed out like a striking snake, cracking
the girl soundly across her face. Then her hand swept
down again, as Nancy gasped, stunned. Again and again,
the sound of flesh striking flesh, over and over, till Nancy
fell to her knees, covering her head, begging not to be hit
again.

"You *wanted* them to rape me," Kitty whispered raggedly. "Perhaps in the end it would have happened anyway, but damn you, Nancy, you wanted it to happen so
you could make up some vicious lie to tell Nathan. How
could you? How could you hate anyone that much?"

She spun around, head held high, walking naked through
the pecan grove. Nancy's hysterical sobs caught in the wind
and drifted to her ears, but Kitty did not look back. She
had no intention of taking a second glance at that hateful,
traitorous girl nor the bloodied bodies of the two men she
had just killed.

"I'm going to keep right on walking," she whispered out

loud to the swaying tree limbs, the drifting clouds. "I'm going to keep walking straight ahead and never look back again." And it was so easy, she realized, to keep on putting one foot in front of the other . . . and move away from the unpleasantness behind. All those years . . . all those tears and agonies and heartache. Walk away . . . keep going . . . don't look back.

Ahead, Nathan would await her. The war would end. Peace would come. Happiness. Joy. It was all in the future; as surely as the sun would rise again, so it would set, and what transpired in between was gone forever. If it meant heartache, let the memories set with the sun, never to rise again on the same day. But if the time had been joyful, then raise the reflections of all the golden moments with the rising sun. That would be the way she would have to live.

Walking up the steps, Kitty met the astonished eyes of Aunt Sue, who swayed dizzily at the sight and caught the railing to steady herself.

Kitty nodded matter-of-factly, as though it were nothing out of the ordinary for her to walk in the house completely nude. "Don't faint, Aunt Sue," she said calmly. "Someone has to go out there and drag Nancy back here. New mothers should get their rest, you know."

Aunt Sue blinked. "New mothers? I don't think I understand, dear. Are you sure you're all right? I mean . . ." she turned her head away, embarrassed.

"Oh, I'm quite fine. By the way, get one of the other women to go with you and take a shovel. I hope you're strong enough to dig a hole big enough to throw two dead Yankees in. I just killed them."

With a soft moan, Aunt Sue slumped to the floor in a faint.

Kitty kept on walking.

✳ Chapter Forty-three ✷

IN the light flickering from the lantern hanging overhead, the room took on a lonely glow. Kitty stood beside the wounded soldier, holding his hand as he lay prone upon the bloody table. Outside the cold February rain drizzled steadily downward, turning the ground into rivulets and pockets of mud and slush. Roads were impassable. Every available man in Goldsboro was out working to corduroy the road to Smithfield in an effort to get supplies to General Johnston's army. Was Nathan there? She did not know. She had written to tell him of his mother's death weeks ago, and had received no reply. Perhaps he, too, had gone to his grave. Blinking away the tears, she murmured a silent prayer that his life had been spared. God, they had both suffered too hard, for too long, to have death interrupt their future now.

The soldier stirred. Kitty squeezed his hand, hoping, somehow, to reassure him that someone was near, that someone cared. She was tired. Oh, she was so tired her knees ached to buckle. But the wounded kept coming in, and there were not enough doctors and assistants and helpers to staff the hospital. So they were all ready to collapse—and some did—but each tried to carry on, knowing the desperate need to remain and do everything possible to save lives and ease the suffering of these wretched souls who had tasted the battlefields of hell.

The door opened and Doctor Malcolm Jordan stepped inside, moving with great effort. His coat was blood-splotched, his hands dry and chapped from so much scrubbing to rid the skin of blood, tissue, and dirt from the war. He looked at her from beneath bushy brows, nodded, and stepped to the table. He made a quick examination of the soldier's wound, then cursed softly and said: "There's nothing to do but amputate. Can you stand another one tonight, Kitty?"

"If there's no other way, Doctor Jordan, then I'm ready." God, she hated to see limbs taken away.

"I hear you do some of this once in a while when there's a shortage of doctors."

"I do. But I hate each one. I'm afraid I don't have the necessary strength to saw through a bone and I take longer than necessary, prolonging the suffering of the poor soldier I'm attending. I think I can still hear the screams of each and every one when I try to sleep at night."

"I won't say you get used to it because you never do. But remember you probably saved a life."

"Most of them said they would rather have died."

"A usual reaction." He reached for his instrument case. "But let them see a wound turn green with gangrene and they realize they're going to die and they'll beg you to cut that limb off. It isn't pleasant, I know. Have you looked out back lately?"

She shook her head. She had not been out of the hospital in over two weeks.

"There's a pile of arms and legs out there about seven or eight feet high. If it weren't so cold, the smell would run us out of here. We're just so shorthanded we haven't had anyone to dig a hole and bury them. It's a gruesome sight." He shuddered. "I think I'm going to find the time, and strength, somehow, to get out there in the morning, myself, and dig a ditch."

He wielded his scalpel, then the forceps crunched as they gripped the arterial wall. Kitty watched him set the ratchet carefully before he cut the vessel beyond and whipped a ligature in place. "I have the femoral artery tied off now," he said, making a final knot. "The bleeding has stopped. Let's hope he stays asleep. Chloroform is so scarce. We need every drop."

511

"I imagine the pain will awaken him."

"Then prepare the chloroform. We don't want him to suffer. God, I know this must be the agony of the damned."

The doctor took the surgical saw in his hand and began setting steel to bone, whipping down with a low, vicious rasp. The soldier stirred, opened his eyes wildly, at the point of screaming, and Kitty was ready to put him to sleep. He struggled momentarily, then, mercifully, he was out of the horror.

The leg clumped to the floor and Kitty stared at it, in a trancelike state. A leg that had walked, run, kicked a horse into a full run, danced, jumped . . . a living thing, a part of a human being, and now it lay on the floor in a pool of thickening blood—gone forever, severed from the body. Useless. Dead.

When she continued to stare, transfixed, Doctor Jordan, moving quickly, lifted the leg, walked to the window, and pitched it outside. Then he returned to the table, yelling for hot tar a swab. "And send in the next one. . . ."

The next soldier breathed his last as he was placed on the table. Kitty looked at the doctor and snapped sarcastically: "Do we throw him out the window, too?"

He frowned. "Look, Kitty, I think you are due for a rest. You obviously are cracking. Now go to your room and lie down for a few hours. We don't need a hysterical woman around."

"Hysterical?" she cried indignantly. "You call me hysterical because I care? Because it sickens me to see a man's leg tossed out the window so callously, as though it were a bone for a dog? Forgive me, Doctor, but I'm not void of human compassion, and if you are, then I feel only pity."

"Please, just go lie down," he passed a weary hand in front of his face. "I have no time for this."

The door opened and Judith Gibson's dark curly hair bobbed up and down as she looked about before whispering to Kitty, "Can you come with me for a moment, Kitty? It's terribly important."

"No, I can't . . . there's a patient."

"Go!" Doctor Jordan's voice boomed. "Please, Kitty. Go for a little while. You'll feel better and so will I."

Annoyed, she brushed by him, stepping outside into the hall. In the dim glow of the lantern hanging on the wall she saw that Judith was terribly excited about something. "You won't believe it, Kitty, but he's here. I know it's him, from the way you described the way he looks now."

"Him? Who?" She felt icy fingers moving up and down her spine. Nathan? Here?

And Judith's next words made her sway in shock.

"It's your father, Kitty, John Wright. He's outside and he says he has to see you right away."

She stumbled down the hall, past the open doorways of rooms with soldiers stacked almost on top of each other, past the rooms filled with the dead waiting for their graves to be dug when the rains stopped. Judith pointed to a closed door that led outside the building, then smiled, patted her shoulder, and discreetly disappeared.

Kitty stepped into the cold, rainy night. Immediately his arms were around her, his voice cracking as he said, "Kitty, Kitty, my girl, my girl. . . ."

"Poppa, it is you." She returned his caress, tears streaming down her face. "How . . . did you know where to come to find me? Isn't it dangerous?"

"Come with me to the end of the porch, quickly. I haven't much time." He led the way. She noticed he wore an ordinary pair of trousers, shirt, and poncho. With a patch over his eye, he looked like an old retired soldier who had served his country and paid the price. And oh, how she drank in the sight of him!

He told her that he was actually a scout for General Sherman. "I got so close to home, I had to take a chance on findin' you, girl. I figured you'd be here. Leastways, I prayed you would. I wanted to see you one more time."

Forcing a laugh, she echoed, "One more time? Poppa, you talk like this is the last time we'll ever meet. The war will be over soon and you can come home and we'll start a new life, both of us . . ."

He touched her lips with his forefinger, bringing her to silence. "Hush, girl. You're smarter'n that. You know the war news. The South is crumbling fast. They're starving and they're whipped, and it's just a matter of time. Soldiers are so hungry they're eating meat so rotten off of dead mules that it shreds in their fingers before they can even pick it off the bone. Men are without shoes or coats, and they're freezin' to death if they don't starve to death. It's

513

coming to an end, girl, and soon, and General Sherman is headed straight for Goldsboro. I found out what I need to know and I have to go back, but I wanted to see you, tell you how I hope everything works out for the best for you if we don't meet again. I want you to know that I love you . . . I always did."

"Poppa, no." She reached for him, heard a gentle whine, and glanced down, startled. "Killer! Poppa, he's still alive," she said in wonder.

"Sure he is," he laughed in spite of the sadness of the moment. "The Confederates can't kill an old man like me, or an old dog like Killer."

"Say," he cupped her face in his hand, tilting it upward. "Did you marry Nathan Collins? Are you his wife now?"

"No, Poppa. I met up with Nathan and he brought me home just before the battle in Atlanta. He's with General Johnston's army. I was to stay at his house, but I couldn't . . ."

"That's not important," he said, cutting her off. "I don't have much time. This is risky, me being here. If I got spotted, I'd get lynched for sure. Now listen to me. When Sherman marches into town, you stay put here at the hospital. You may have to treat our soldiers, but if you cooperate, you won't be hurt. I'll be close by and I'll keep a watch on you. . . ."

He raised an eyebrow, stared intently out of his one eye as he said: "Me and Travis. We'll watch over you."

The familiar stab of heat and warmth shuddered through her body uncontrollably. "Travis? He's all right?"

"Finer'n a fiddle any day of the week. Still one of the best damned cavalrymen in the whole United States Army, him and Sam Bucher. . . ."

"I don't want to hear about Captain Coltrane," she snapped. "Not after . . ." Her voice trailed off. She didn't want to tell her father all of it, how he'd made a fool of her, how she had been so weak as to let him.

"I know, girl."

She blinked in amazement. "Know what?" How could he possibly know? How could anyone know?

"I know that he loves you and you love him, and the reason you saw him with that woman was because he set it up for you to see him. He figured you'd be so mad you'd do just what you did do, high-tail it to Richmond. Where we went was no place for you, girl. And I think, too, he wanted to give you a chance to get back to Nathan—let you see for yourself how you felt about him."

"Travis told you this?"

"Me and Sam figured it out. Travis ain't one to tell me much what goes on inside him, but I know him pretty good by now. You don't stand up with a man and face death every day and not get to know just about everything inside him."

She didn't speak . . . couldn't speak. Turning away, Kitty went to stand at the railing and looked out at the dark town about her. "You ain't said whether or not you even care," John spoke directly behind her.

"Poppa, I don't know what I feel. Nathan . . . he has me all confused, but then so does Travis. Maybe it's best I forget them both."

He swatted her soundly on her bottom and she jumped. "Maybe it's best you quit actin' so damned stubborn and started figuring a few things out instead o' refusing to see the light. None so blind as those who won't see, I always heard. Now then, I'm going to have to ride out of here. It's a tricky ride back to where I'm goin' and I can't risk being followed."

He kissed both her cheeks, hugged her, and turned away, but Kitty reached out and clutched his shoulder as the tears burned in her eyes. "Poppa . . . the war . . . is it as bad as they say? Are we losing?"

"The South is losing." He spoke sadly in spite of his allegiance. "Sherman is advancing toward Goldsboro, and he's got enough men to take the town if the town doesn't surrender. It's just that simple, girl. It ain't a matter of you and the rest of the citizens running. There's no place to run to now. The war is upon you. At least Sherman stopped the burning and raping and killing once he crossed into North Carolina. Everyone says he's got a soft spot in his heart for North Carolina, but he sure had a hard one everywhere else we've been. He just turned his head to what the soldiers were doing, let them destroy and do whatever they liked. He says we have to teach the South a lesson, but I think the South has learned it already. . . ."

"Halt! Who's there?"

Kitty and John froze as the uniformed Confederate soldier came walking out of the shrubbery with fixed bayonet. "Soldier," his voice cracked with authority, "what the hell you doing out here this time of night? You sick or wounded? You get your butt inside. If you're okay, then you get the hell back to your company. Everyone is standing by. Sherman could get here anytime."

"Yessir, I'll go now. I had to slip out here and see my lady for a few minutes."

"Just git!"

Kitty's heart was racing with tension. Would he be able to just ride away? Would he be able to get back to his own company? There were those who would have said at that moment she should have turned in her own father to the South. Hadn't he just admitted he was practically a spy for General Sherman, that he had the information he had been sent to obtain? She was on one side and he on the other, but where did her allegiance lie?

No. She could never turn him in, no matter what the consequence. "He's just leaving." She spoke to the soldier for the first time. "Please forgive us."

His tone softened somewhat. "Sure. I've got a girl, too, and I wish I could see her, but right now everyone is supposed to be with his company to be ready to fight when the time comes. You, lady, should be inside. The Yankees wouldn't fire on the hospital. At least we hope they wouldn't."

"Yes, yes," she nodded, turning back to her father for one farewell embrace. "God speed," she whispered, choking with dry sobs.

"Any message for Coltrane?" he asked lightly, wanting to stop her crying over his leaving.

She thought for a moment. "Goodbye. You can tell him goodbye. That's what I was doing when I found him that night by the Rapidan."

He laughed. "You take care, girl. We'll meet again. Damn a bear! I didn't know I'd raised such a stubborn little filly!"

And chuckling to himself, he disappeared into the night. The Confederate soldier seemed satisfied and he, too, drifted away. Kitty leaned against the wall, slowly letting herself slide down until she was sitting down in the shadows. She would not be seen unless she chose to be.

Word had just been received that Johnston had assumed command once again on February 23rd. The report was that his army was scattered, dislocated, extending over an area from Kinston to Charlotte. General William J. Hardee, with two divisions totaling seventy-five hundred men, had been in almost daily contact with Sherman's column for several weeks, but everyone said his small force could only delay Sherman's advance momentarily. The feared Yankee General who had left a wave of smoldering destruction behind him on his march to the sea was headed straight for Goldsboro, wanting to capture the valuable railroad center.

And they could do nothing but await his arrival.

And she would have to wait, also.

Travis had wanted her to see him with that woman—the knowledge burned into her being. Was it so? What difference did it make? It was over. All of it. She had been weak, careless. Perhaps she did not even love Nathan. Maybe she was incapable of loving any man. She pressed her fingertips against her temples wearily. God, why wasn't she born a man instead of a woman? She would not have rebelled. She would have accepted her role, her lot in life. That life would have been different.

Closing her eyes she could see that mocking, smirking smile and those steely gray eyes that could be all fire with anger one moment and warm with passion and desire the next. He could hold her gently or shake her into submissiveness—and all the while her blood flowed like rivulets of fire within her veins, leaving her spent and breathless.

Nathan. So boyish and charming. The ideal husband and father. Dreams shared, dreams broken—all because of the war. Was he the man for her? If one existed, then he had to be the one. They were alike in many ways, yet miles apart in others. Marriage would be interesting, perhaps, in bed, but for the most part she saw herself having a baby every year, occupied with womanly things, womanly chatter. The thought was suffocating.

But no man had ever excited her the way Travis Coltrane had been able to do. Even Nathan's kisses, which made her feel warm in a way, were merely the touching of lips compared with the way Travis's seemed to crawl inside the very depths of her soul, making her choke with wanting him to consume all of her. Passion. That was all it could be. What would marriage be like to a man like that? Babies? Yes, he would want sons to carry on his name. But somehow, she knew that he would want a woman to stand beside him all the while they lived. He would not be content to have her at home doing things she despised. No, he would have taken her hunting, fishing, maybe even let her pursue a life of her own in nursing. He believed in freedom—for himself, for everyone. He would not have stood in her way.

But she had to remind herself of one important fact: Travis did not love her. He merely wanted her. Marriage could not be a happy state if based merely on physical needs. But then, as a woman, she was not supposed to care about such things. Her needs were to be filled by a cuddling baby, day-to-day chores. A man took his pleasure and a woman gave it to him. That was the way Nathan viewed it, as did every other man she had ever heard speak of marriage.

Travis would not have shared those views, but it was no longer important how he felt about life because that life would not be shared with her.

And why was marriage so important to a young girl, anyway? Her mother said a girl should marry well, as young as possible, to be assured of security in life. Well, with the war, what security did anyone, male or female, have? And what kind of life if it is spent in total misery?

Bullshit! She did not feel very ladylike as the word entered her brain—the only word that seemed to describe her opinion of the world around her. But then, why did she have to be on guard against her thoughts, to make sure she was always the lady, doing the "acceptable" thing, the "right" thing? Couldn't she even have the precious pleasure of thinking the way she chose privately? Not according to decorum? Should she always be ladylike?"

"Bullshit!" She whispered the word out loud. Maybe it wasn't feminine, but suddenly she felt good saying it, as though the walls were at last torn down. She was free—to say what she pleased, do what she pleased, and most of all, think what she pleased.

"Bullshit!" She said it again, louder this time.

The soldier stepped out of the bushes once again. "You say something?" he snapped. "You get back inside, lady. This is no time for a lady to be outside."

She put both hands on the railing and leaned over as far as she could without toppling over. She stared straight at the soldier in the darkness, searching for his face, and when she found it, she laughed out loud and cried: "Bullshit, soldier!"

And, in spite of the cloud of doom surrounding the South, Kitty lifted her skirts and ran back inside the hospital, laughing, feeling better than she had felt in many, many months.

Praise God, her spirit was free!

☙ Chapter Forty-four ☙

"I'M going!"

Doctor W. A. Holt, Medical Officer of Goldsboro Way Hospital #3, stared at the girl with the blazing eyes. She was a sight to behold, dressed in a dirty, ragged Confederate uniform she admitted taking from a dead soldier's body.

"I'm going and don't try to stop me. I'm not a member of the army. You can't make me stay here."

"Miss Wright." The officer took a deep breath. They were sitting in his office, bare except for a desk and the chair he was sitting in. There was no attempt at frills here.

"Miss Wright, you do not understand. General Sherman is on his way to Goldsboro. There is no way that you could reach the battle at Bentonville without running straight into his lines."

"And you do not understand, Doctor," she snapped, hands on her lips. "I was *born* in that country, grew up in it. I can find my way around in those swamps blindfolded. I can get by his lines without a bit of trouble. All I'm asking is for you to issue me a rifle in case I do need a weapon. And I want as many medical supplies as I can carry. General Johnston is bound to be in desperate need."

He nodded, smiling sadly. "Miss Wright, you could not carry enough supplies to do any good."

Stamping her foot, Kitty cried, "Well, do you give me a rifle or do I walk out of here with no weapon at all? My fiancé is with General Johnston and my father is with General Sherman, and those two armies are going to finish the war right there at Bentonville."

"No, the war will not end at Bentonville. But many will die. It will be a pity to lose a valuable medical assistant."

"I'm not going to stand here and argue any longer. Already they have been in battle for a day. I only heard a short while ago or I would already have left. Goodbye."

She turned and headed for the door. Wearily, he got to his feet and said, "Miss Wright, please . . ."

She turned, eyes blazing defiantly, waiting.

"Here." He walked to the corner of the room and picked up a Sharpes rifle. "You know how to load this?"

"Yes. And I know how to shoot it."

"Then take it and I wish you well."

Kitty snatched the rifle and ran from the room, anxious to be on her way without further argument. Hurrying from the hospital, she brushed by those who called out curiously about her dress. The horse she had stolen was tied at the back of the building and without further hesitation she mounted and rode fast and furiously out of town.

She took to the swamps and the lowlands outside of town, moving cautiously, carefully, lest there be any Yankees about. The little settlement of Bentonville was only a few hours' ride, but she had to be extremely discreet in the path she chose to take.

Within two hours' riding time, she began to hear the explosion of artillery fire. The sky was thick with smoke, the March sun trying to break through the clouds. The air was heavy with the odor of sulphur. Only then did she pause to think of the folly of her decision to go to the battlefield and help the wounded—the wounded that might include Nathan, her father, and, yes, as much as she hated to admit, Travis, as well. The three men in her life were close by—and close to death at any moment—and she could not stay back at that hospital and wait for word of what would eventually happen.

She was forced to abandon her horse as she got closer to the firing. It was easier to be inconspicuous on foot.

521

Perhaps, she thought, it would be best to wait until night —but wait for what? In the darkness, it would be even harder to locate the Confederate army. Everyone was so scattered, it seemed. She would spot a few Confederates only to see them gunned down by Yankees, and she would shrink back into the thick undergrowth and shrubs. Darkness would only make matters worse.

The sun began to sink in a blood-red sky. Bodies were scattered everywhere. Slowly, very slowly, the Confederates began to move from the thick forest to gather their dead and bury them. And Kitty made her move. A soldier in a tattered gray uniform, with gaunt, lost eyes, limped along within a few feet of the clump of foliage where she crouched.

"Please," she whispered. He whipped around, rifle ready, saw her, and jumped in shock.

"Please, take me to the hospital units. I'm Kitty Wright and I'm on your side, soldier."

He all but yanked her to her feet. "Girl, you crazy? I coulda shot you deader'n hell. What do you mean, hidin' like that? You ain't got no business out here. I'm gonna take you to the Colonel and he's gonna be madder'n hell. All we need is a damned woman!"

He jerked her along in the gathering darkness, and from out of nowhere came a burly, grizzly faced officer who viewed her suspiciously. She poured out her story, and he scratched at his beard for only a moment before barking, "All right, git her over to the General's medical wagons. We ain't got time to stand here gawkin'. If she wants to get killed, let her!"

He wasn't a Colonel, Kitty thought spitefully. He was merely a Sergeant. A Colonel wouldn't have been so rude. But what did it matter? She was safe, with her side, and soon, God willing, she would find Nathan.

The doctors put her right to work, and Kitty retched again and again at the sight of the horror about her. She had thought that her resistance to the nightmare of war had become hardened, cold; that she was able to withstand anything. But so many hundreds of bleeding, mangled bodies screaming in pain, emaciated with hunger and disease, fighting a battle that seemed useless in an equally futile war—why? Why did it have to happen? There were no supplies. No chloroform. Men screamed in agony, cursed their country and their God. Hell. It was a living, breathing hell, from which there would never be a return for any of them.

Why am I here? She asked herself that question over and over during the night. So she had made it through the swamps without running into the Yankees. The Yankees were everywhere, anywhere, and soon they would swarm down upon the whole Southland. Why hide from them at all?

A soldier handed her hardtack and coffee, and she took a moment to eat and rest. He watched her silently for a moment, then said, "Lady, what you doin' here?"

"I . . . I had to come," she answered, watching, struck with horror, as they carried a soldier, his body in two pieces, to his grave. "I had to do what I could . . . try to find my fiancé."

"Who might that be?"

"Collins . . . Nathan Collins." Her gaze followed the men carrying the body halves. She gagged on the hardtack, then blinked and whipped around to the soldier. "What did you just say?"

"I said Major Collins is over there in the tent with some of the other officers."

She looked in the direction he pointed to. Her cup went clattering to the ground. With wooden legs, she tried to move, stumbled, fell. The soldier lifted her up. She shoved him aside, forced her legs to move. She reached the tent, bent, stepped inside, and all eyes turned to stare.

"Nathan . . ."

"Katherine . . ."

For a moment they stood there, eyes locked in disbelief, and then Nathan moved first, blinking back tears as he wrapped her in his arms, held her tightly against his chest, murmuring, "Oh, God, Katherine, it is you. But why are you here? I don't want you here in this."

"What difference does it make where I am?" she asked in a voice thick with bitterness. "Sherman marches to Goldsboro. The Yankees surround our homeland. What difference does it make where any of us are?"

Apologizing to the others in the tent, Nathan led her outside. "You didn't write," she babbled. "I never heard a word."

She felt his arms about her stiffen, and his voice was tense as he said, "Nancy wrote me that you deserted my mother and let her die, Katherine."

"That's a lie!" She pulled back to stare at him incredulously. "I left that house because I couldn't stand to be around your people another moment, especially after that night in the pecan grove. I suppose Nancy wrote a pack of lies about *that*, too."

"She . . ."—he hesitated a moment—"she said it wasn't pleasant."

"One day, I'll tell you all about that night, how Nancy lied to turn those foragers on *me*."

He sighed impatiently. "Katherine, Katherine, darling, I don't want to hear about it. I do wish I could lock you away somewhere, as you seem to look for trouble. When this war is over, and you and I can solve our differences and be married, I'm going to chain you to the bed, I swear."

He was attempting humor, Kitty knew, but she noted the strain in his voice.

"Why are you here? Even in Goldsboro you are safer. . . ."

They passed a group of bedraggled soldiers so young-looking that Kitty paused to ask about their youth. "The North Carolina Junior Reserves," Nathan said quietly, "the seed corn of the Confederacy. See how desperate we are? We muster *children*. But I want to know about you, how you got here."

"I know the countryside, remember? I crawled through the swamps on my hands and knees to find the Confederate lines. I came because I knew you were here—and they say Sherman is marching to Goldsboro, and Poppa fights with him."

His arms dropped away from her, and in the glow of an exploding shell in the sky above, she saw that his eyes were narrowed, grim. "John Wright is with Sherman?"

"Yes. Nathan, why do you look like that?"

"Damned traitor! I look around me and see my people dying right and left, and I think how your daddy turned his back on them to help kill them!" He slammed his fist into his open palm. "How can he live with himself? How . . ."

"Nathan, he's my poppa." She grabbed at his arm. Now was not the time to talk about such things. "Please, let's talk of other things. Does it look so terribly bad for us here now?"

"Hell, yes," he said through gritted teeth. "I never thought we'd wind it up right here. We were in Smithfield when General Johnston got the dispatch from Wade Hampton, the Commander of the Confederate cavalry. He was encamped here and sent word he'd just encountered a portion of General Sherman's army that was pushing towards Goldsboro, so the General knew we had to block Sherman's sweep northward. Damn, our troops were so dislocated, we didn't have enough men to counteract Sherman's move."

They reached a ditch, stepped over a body, and Kitty winced painfully. Nathan called out to a burial detail nearby, "Get this soldier buried quick. He's blown to bits." He led Kitty further back to some bushes where they sat down.

"Johnston didn't know which way Sherman was headed for sure," he went on. "We were trying to concentrate our army at Smithfield, where we felt we could threaten the flank of any advance in the direction of either Raleigh or Goldsboro.

"Then, Sherman's left wing turned east at Averasboro, and Hampton, who had his cavalry reporting every move, realized they were advancing in two columns toward Goldsboro. When Johnston heard this, you can bet he didn't hesitate moving us here.

"Hampton moved his cavalry out to meet Sherman's advance, and they held them off till sunset on the 18th, that was two days ago, on Saturday. We got here that night. It's hard to say who's winning, Katherine. We're killing them. They're killing us."

"That's the way it's been for four years," she reflected sadly.

And his next words washed over her in waves of shock. "I wish we would surrender!"

"Surrender? Nathan, you can't mean that." .

"I do!" he said fiercely. "Katherine, we're beaten. We have no uniforms, food, ammunition, supplies. It's gone. All of the Southern cause is gone. It's time to give up and go home and rebuild and try to forget four years of hell."

"No, you can't mean that, Nathan!"

"I do, and it's going to happen sooner or later. I say let it happen now, while *I'm* still alive, while *you're* still alive, before any more good men die! God, I've seen so much killing and bloodshed. I can't stand it." He shook his head from side to side, pressing his hands against his temples.

It was as though she had never really seen him before. Surely, when the war ended, it would take many months, perhaps longer, for her ever to really know him again. But then, she had changed, too. Everyone had. Four years of hell, many more years of the tension and strain of wondering when war would finally come—they had taken their toll on every American, North and South. It would take much longer for the wounds to heal.

Finally, Nathan took her back to the hospital area. "I have to go back to the tent, Katherine. The battle will begin just before dawn. Please take care of yourself. If we retreat, I'll come for you and keep you by my side."

He kissed her long and hard. She wondered if it would be the last kiss he ever gave her, if they would ever meet again, for surely death was raining down.

The drums began beating just before dawn, the trumpets blew, and the color bearers, sweat pouring from every pore in their bodies, stood with chins held high, ready to march forth and meet the enemy. An air of tension hung as heavy as the sulphur clouds. Kitty stood inside the hospital tent, peering out at the gray mist rising from the ground. Garish. Haunting. A scene that would forever be branded in her mind, never to be forgotten.

And then the firing began. In the tents, the hospital staff worked frantically, doing what they could to ease the suffering of the wounded; but without proper supplies and facilities, it was all but hopeless. The bodies began to stack up outside. Someone screamed for burial.

"I can't stand all those bodies stackin' up like firewood out there. Somebody dig."

"You dig, goddamn it! You think I'm gettin' out there

and get kilt myself buryin' the dead? You're full of shit, if you think I am."

"That's right. Bury 'em yourself."

"You want to lie out there and turn black and bloat like a dead mule if you die? You think they like it?"

"You think right now I give a damn? You think I'll give a damn once I'm dead? Go to hell, soldier, and dig them graves yourself!"

The day wore on. Kitty could see blue-clad soldiers falling in the distance, and she wondered if one of them were her father . . . or Travis. And the gray fell, too, and she wondered if Nathan had met his end. But, guiltily, she had to rationalize the fact that Nathan was avoiding open combat. He was staying to the rear. She had spotted him a few times during the day, riding back and forth, searching for deserters, she supposed. She did not like to think he was actually seeking an excuse to stay out of the line of fire.

The sun began to sink. The word came down through the lines, reaching the staff at the hospital. General Johnston was going to wait long enough to pick up the dead and the wounded, and then he was going to fall back across Mill Creek and withdraw. He lacked the number of men necessary for a decisive victory. No substantial reinforcements were expected. To remain meant defeat, and Johnston was entrusted with one of the few Confederate armies still intact.

The movement was quiet but frenzied. The wagons were filled with wounded men, burial details silently dug large trenches and dragged in the dead. Nathan hovered nearby, wanting Kitty to go ahead and leave with him. "Let's get out of here," he urged. "We'll go to Richmond."

"Richmond?" She paused as she wrapped a bandage around an unconscious soldier's head to try to stop the bleeding from the gouging wound. "But General Johnston is withdrawing, not heading for Richmond."

"I tell you, Katherine, I don't give a damn what the Confederacy does now. I'm going to save my life—and *yours*."

She whirled around to face him, eyes glassy with cold fury in the dim glow of the lantern overhead. "Nathan Collins, you *are* a coward! I don't think I ever realized it before now, or maybe I didn't want to accept the fact. But you are a coward! And . . . I think you make me sick!"

She turned back to the wounded soldier, but Nathan was grabbing her shoulder, spinning her around roughly, his hand cracking across her face. "Don't ever say that to me again, you hear? Now you're coming with me, right now. I waited years for you, Katherine, and I've fought a war for you, and the time has come for us to leave together!"

He's gone mad, she thought wildly as he jerked her from the tent. *He's insane*. "Nathan, stop, please," she pleaded, but he jerked her along, reaching two horses and throwing her up on a saddle. When he had mounted, he reached over, snatched her reins, and began to pull her along behind him.

"Nathan, you have to listen to me," she pleaded, but he kept on riding through the trees, past the bodies, the wounded, the soldiers frantically working to bury the dead, preparing to withdraw. In desperation, she called out to the soldiers to help her, but they paid no heed—everyone was hurrying so they, too, could pull back.

Nathan was heading for the swamps he knew so well. Soon, dawn would again streak the sky. The withdrawal would be complete—and Nathan would be a deserter! Kitty slumped in the saddle in defeat. Nathan, Nathan, did I ever really know you? she wondered frantically. Did I ever really love you? Did you ever exist except in my dreams? The boy beneath the weeping willow tree, so kind, so gentle—had it been a myth? A fairy tale? The grim, gaunt-eyed stranger pulling her horse along was the *real* Nathan Collins, and in that moment she hated him as she had never hated another human being!

Suddenly, he stepped out of the swamps, gun pointed straight at Nathan. "Where you takin' my girl, Collins?" John Wright snarled.

Nathan yanked the reins, bringing both horses to a halt. "John!" he gasped in disbelief as Kitty's heart thundered like the guns beginning to explode in the distance. "John, what the hell are you doing here?"

"Scoutin'. I reckon you're runnin' away like the coward you are."

"Retreating is more like it," he said smiling, regaining

some of his confidence. "You can go back to your bastard General and tell him General Johnston has withdrawn."

"Kind of figured he would. Now answer my question. Where you takin' my girl?"

"All the way to Richmond where she'll be safe."

John looked past Nathan to Kitty. "You want to go with him, Kitty? Is this what you want?"

"Poppa, I don't know," she sobbed. Damn, what could she say? If she told him she didn't want to go, he would try to rescue her and there might be a fight. Perhaps it was best to continue, escape later, avoid anyone getting killed. She took a deep breath. "Yes, I . . . think it is. Poppa, the war will be over soon. We'll meet again. I know we will. I love you, Poppa." Tears streamed down her cheeks.

He scratched at his beard thoughtfully. Killer nuzzled his legs, anxious to be on his way. Kitty stared at the faithful old dog who had been through the whole war with his master. "I reckon," he said finally, "you have to make your own way, girl, like I always taught you. I ain't going to try to think for you. Never have. Never will. One day, maybe we'll meet again. If not in this world, then in the better world."

He put his rifle up against his shoulders, which were slumped in defeat, turned and began walking into the thick swamps, the gray mist rising up around him to waist-level. Killer trotted along obediently beside him. Kitty stared with a lump in her throat and a pounding in her ears. Everything within her screamed, "Go with him." She did not want to go to Richmond with Nathan. She wanted to stay here with her poppa—and, yes, search for Travis, too. She had been in love with a dream, because she had been ashamed to admit that what she felt for Travis could be real love. She had disguised her emotions and now she was destroying herself.

But she could not cry out. She had to let him walk away, about to disappear into the gray mist. . . .

Her gaze had been locked on her father. She had not seen Nathan move. The shot rang out, and she stared in horror, first at her father toppling forward in the denseness of the undergrowth, and then at Nathan who smiled triumphantly, the smoking rifle in his hands.

And then Killer gave a snarl as he turned and raced for Nathan, about to leap straight for his throat, and the rifle lowered again. Kitty screamed as the dog exploded into blood and flesh before her horrified eyes.

She was down off the horse, racing through the swamp, with Nathan right behind her, yelling at her to come back. She fell to her knees, gathered her father's head in her arms and held him close, screaming, "Poppa, Poppa, don't die . . . please, don't die . . . I need you, Poppa!"

"Katherine, come with me. He had to die. . . ." Nathan was holding out his hand to her.

"You son of a bitch," she spat at him. "Goddamn you for the cowardly bastard you are, Nathan. Goddamn you, I hate you! I'll kill you!"

And then there was a crashing sound and they both looked about to see Travis Coltrane stepping out of the mist; before Nathan could aim his gun, Travis had kicked it out of his hands and was hurtling him to the ground, pounding into him with his fists, smashing flesh against flesh. And Nathan was no match for a man with the strength or size of Travis. He screamed for mercy.

Travis stood up, mashed his booted foot against his throat, holding him helplessly there in the muck and mire of the swampland. "You son of a bitch, I'll give you the same kind of mercy you gave John Wright when you shot him in the back . . . the same kind you and your bastard Vigilantes gave him when you beat him till you blinded him in one eye."

Kitty cried in horror. "Oh, God, no, Nathan. That was *you?* Why didn't I realize?"

In her arms, John Wright moaned, opened his one eye, which was rapidly glazing over. "Kitty, I love you, girl," he whispered hoarsely.

"Poppa, don't die," she begged, her body convulsing with great, gulping sobs. "Please, Poppa, I need you so. . . ."

His smile was twisted, red rivulets of blood oozed from the corner of his mouth. "Man has to die . . . has to be born . . . can't control nothin' 'cept what's in-between . . ."

"Poppa!"

"Travis . . ." John's eye rolled about as he tried to focus on his friend.

"I'm right here, John," Travis said, voice husky, his foot still planted firmly on Nathan's neck.

"Look after my girl."

"You know you can count on me. . . ." His voice cracked. He looked away.

The world around Kitty was flashing with reds, blues, yellows, with a shadow of black lurking in the background ready to take her under and out of the horror of the present. But she fought to hang on to the present, to her sanity. Her poppa was dying. Every second was precious. Oh, God, she prayed, let him live.

"Pull with him, girl"—his voice rasped out the words. "Two mules can't go nowhere pulling opposite one another."

"Poppa, don't talk anymore, please. . . ."

He coughed, a great ball of blood gushing forth. "Love you . . ." he said in one final gurgle, and then his head slumped sideways, the eye glassed over.

Kitty held him and wept, rocking back and forth.

Travis stared down at the writhing man. Cold, raging fury he never knew he possessed took over. Dimly, he was aware of Sam Bucher catching up with them, heard his exclamation of grief over finding their comrade dead in Kitty's arms. Sam was taking John up in his arms, Kitty stumbling along beside him, sobbing brokenly.

And then everything within him exploded, all the fury and frustrations of the war climaxed by a gun exploding into the back of a man he'd grown to love as a father. It was too much, goddamn it, too much for a man to take. And it was this coward, this squirming, screaming coward —he had killed that man, broken that girl's heart. He deserved to be crushed like the creeping, squirming bug that he was!

"Travis, damnit!" Sam pushed him away, but it was too late.

Travis's body heaved in exhaustion as he stared down at the lifeless body of Nathan Collins, his throat mashed into the ground, blood and flesh hanging from his gaping mouth, eyes bulging out upon his cheeks.

"Travis! Get hold of yourself!" Sam slung his arms around his comrade's shoulder, led him back to where

Kitty waited, sobbing in her grief. "She needs you, Travis. You're all she's got."

Sam quickly put John's body across the back of one of the horses, then mounted the other after lifting what was left of the old hounddog in his arms. Turning into the swamps, he called out to Travis: "You know where to meet me, Coltrane? You know where I'll be?"

Travis did not answer and Sam kept on riding. Travis was staring at Kitty, holding his arms out to her. The war was another world. This was here and this was now, and as she stepped into the circle of his arms and he closed them tightly about her trembling body, that other world and all its grief and heartache and sorrow and sadness disappeared into the gray mist of the shadows.

And out of the shadows a great light swelled and shone and lit the air all about them as a new world was born— the realization of what had always existed between two hearts that would survive the crumbling ashes of a proud Southland.

Together, they walked away—from the past, into the future.

"A rich, stirring novel of the westward
thrust of America, and of a dynamic woman
who went West to tame the wilderness within her."
The Literary Guild

PASTORA

JOANNA BARNES

The passions of two generations, and the rich,
colorful history of 19th-century California, are
woven into this 768-page epic of adventure and
romance! It follows one strong and courageous
woman through tragedy and triumph, public scandal
and private struggle, as she strives to seize a golden
destiny for herself and those she loves!

"Blockbuster historical romance!"
Los Angeles Times

"Readers who like romantic sagas with historical
backgrounds will enjoy this."
Library Journal

AVON Paperback   56184 • $3.50

Bestselling Historical Romance from Patricia Gallagher

**EVERY GENERATION HAS A WOMAN
FOR WHOM THE WORLD IS NOT BIG ENOUGH...**

Emma Harte was that kind of woman. Born to a poverty-stricken Yorkshire family, seduced and left pregnant at age 15, she fled to a grimy manufacturing town to pursue her twin dreams—riches and revenge.

From the moment you meet her, en route by private jet to the Manhattan headquarters of Harte Enterprises, the hub of her vast financial empire, you will be held inescapably in her spell: through two turbulent marriages . . . one great love . . . and the plot by her children that threatens all she has built —and challenges her unshakable faith in herself.

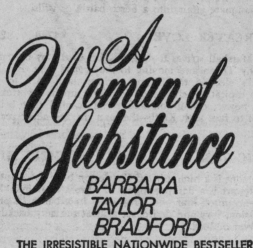

A Woman of Substance

BARBARA TAYLOR BRADFORD

THE IRRESISTIBLE NATIONWIDE BESTSELLER